INTRODUCTION

THE copy of "Scottish Chiefs" which was the companion of my early days had a cover of dark red cloth and when I first caught sight of the last American edition bound in gay tartan I felt a certain bereavement, as if I had lost a friend. The volume of my childhood had been literally "read to death," the common occurrence being that while I was finishing my allotted chapter a younger sister was dancing disturbingly on one foot, awaiting her turn to know what might be happening to Sir William Wallace.

When, however, the belovéd book lay before me for this present re-reading, the magic was still there and my eyes flew to lines that had thrilled me long ago:

"It was the iron head of an arrow which the moon had silvered; and Ker, catching it up exclaimed: 'Wallace is safe! This calls us to Glenfinlass!'"

(Oh, so many years since the arrow had first called me to Glenfinlass; how eagerly I followed, and how ready I was to follow again!)

Then I turned another leaf, haphazard and met the passage:

"And by the ghost of that same Fergus, I swear," exclaimed Murray, "that my honest claymore shall never shroud its head while an invader be left alive in Scotland!"

I might have been a child again, hearing my mother's voice calling me to supper from my nook in the window-seat, while I pleaded: "Oh! only five more minutes, please! Wallace has just rescued Lady Helen and he's bearing her in his arms over the rushing torrent on a bridge of a single tree!"

There was a particular passage that incited us to dangerous acrobatics in those young days. It was one of the miraculous feats of strength and skill daily performed by the gallant Wallace, that acted as a direct inspiration to similar exploits,—exploits most difficult to achieve in the upper chamber of a Maine cottage with beds, chairs and stools to serve for Highland scenery:

"Looking up I beheld a young chieftain with a bow in his hand leaping from cliff to cliff, till, springing from a high projection on the right he alighted at once at the head of a wounded deer."

As I remember, we never arrived precisely at the wounded deer, (impersonated by a sable muff), but oh, the delight of·the attempt, even though bruises were more plentiful than triumphs. So trivial a reminiscence is recounted merely because I feel keenly the value of any work of fiction that can awaken in its readers such ardor of sympathy, such intensity of interest, such a belief in the reality of its characters, such admiration and reverence for their magnificent moments!

You may say that all this means chiefly the enthusiasm of childhood, but when after an interval of more than forty years the book again casts the same spell, what reason for it can there be save that it is not only enchanting, pathetic, romantic, breathless in suspense, but that it is thrilling in its rapidity of movement and its astonishing wealth of incidents? After the lapse of over a century, for readers first wept over its tragedies in 1809, it remains a masterpiece to be enjoyed by each succeeding generation.

If Miss Jane Porter sometimes exaggerated the virtues of the noble Wallace, his achievements never fell upon incredulous ears in the days of youth, nor do they now, when I heartily believe that she is right in acclaiming him as "one of the most complete heroes that ever filled the page of history."

The author's portraits of Wallace, of Robert the Bruce, Edwin Ruthven and Andrew Murray are penned with a high enthusiasm that lifts the reader to her own altitudes. She bathes them in glory and we see them with her eyes; but though "Scottish Chiefs" is a panegyric, rather than a formal history, it has been accepted by critics as genuine in spirit, if not in absolute detail.

In her second preface, written in 1840, the author tells us how the central figures of her novel first appeared before the eyes of her imagination. She was less than six years old when lullabies of "Wallace Wight" were sung to her in her Edinburgh nursery; while in the great hall the old serving-man told wondrous tales of the Battles of Bannockburn and Cambuskenneth.

But her chief instructress in these legends was Luckie Forbes, a pious old dame who lived near by, and who, as she would tell of the times of the brave Sir William Wallace when he fought for Scotland, would narrate his heartrending sacrifices for his country and his tragic death at the hands of a ruthless tyrant.

So the hero of Caledonia was first roughly sketched upon the canvas of the childish mind and the study of after years filled in the details and laid on the colors. The author spared no pains, she tells us, in consulting almost every writing extant which treats of the sister kingdoms during the period of her narrative (1296 to 1305), but to know every word of Speed and Buchanan and Holinshed, of Barbour's "Bruce," of the old epic song of "Thyr Wilham Wallace," of the letters of the royal Edward and Pope Boniface, of the rhymes of Thomas of Ercildowne and the verses of "Blinde Harrie,"—all these would have availed her nothing without the flame of genius with which she fused them into a new and glittering substance.

If, broadly speaking, my particular generation may have been the last to be wholly engrossed in the story, what welcome will it have from the present one?

Neither of the editors believes in abridging the classics; still less in altering, interrupting, or adding to a text that should be sacred; but we hope that we have taken away from the present edition nothing but negligible phrases, paragraphs that are not a part of the main flow of the story; a little of the descriptive matter, retaining the most beautiful where there is little else than sheer beauty; preserving the historic content, and not allowing a single romantic incident to escape us in a world that sometimes threatens to be dull, dreary and lacking in idealism.

It is a thousand pities to let so great a book lose its hold because the readers of the mid-nineteen hundreds are possessed by the demon of haste. I greeted the very "thickness" of "Scottish Chiefs" in my childhood with sighs of ineffable content and blissful anticipation, but one has only to stand nowadays near the public library desks where young people are served, to learn that two thin books are more popular than one thick one.

Happy Jane Porter, carefully-sheltered young English spinster, writing in the green garden of her cottage in Thames-Ditton! Imagine her, unconscious of future glory, penning in 1809 her first preface to a book which was to create a sensation throughout Great Britain, be translated into the languages of the Continent, be read by kings, queens and princes, and finally invoke the censorship of the great Napoleon himself!

There must have been later days of splendid triumph for the modest author, for she was frequently saluted in theaters, concert-rooms and by military bands on parade-grounds, with that true pibroch of Scotland:

> "Scots wha hae wi' Wallace bled,
> Scots wham Bruce hath often led,
> Welcome to your gory bed,
> Or to victory!"

She could never have foreseen that she would write a second fore-word, nineteen years after the first (1828), when many thousands of copies of the book had come from the press; and again a third "Retrospective Preface" in 1840 when an illustrated edition was given to the public.

As to these prefatory essays of Miss Jane Porter, their literary style belongs to the time in which she lived, but "Scottish Chiefs," the book itself, belongs to the ages.

She expresses to her readers in her chaste, pre-Victorian manner, her "grateful sense of the candor with which so adventurous a work from a female pen has been generally received, particularly among the people of her hero's nation—the country in which she first drew the aliments of her intellectual life." She afterwards explains where and when she "first imbibed the impulse which ultimately impelled her to choose a theme of war and bloodshed." These explanations are full of interest though slightly didactic and stilted; but when our dear, modest, delicate Jane forsakes them, turns one page, and be-comes a full-fledged novelist of the romantic school, how amazingly and thoroughly at home she seems in her scenes of "war and blood-shed." She might have been born on a battlefield, baptized from her father's helmet (an ancient Scottish custom), served under arms, and studied military tactics under Julius Cæsar!

When we look at the book as a whole it seems like an ancient tapestry on whose background of soft stitchery the romantic figures still stand out, stirred as when living, by the writer's magic.

What pictures float by as we turn the pages—pictures transcend-ing in interest any to be seen for a dime or for twenty dimes in a theater, with the advantage that each reader makes his own films and apparently they are indestructible.

Can one forget Sir William Wallace blowing his bugle at Corie Lynn, "standing on a cliff like the newly aroused genius of his country, while his long plaid floated afar and his glittering hair streaming on the blast seemed to mingle with the golden fires that shot from the heavens."

Waving his sword, he cries: "I come in the name of all ye hold dear to tell you the poniard of England is unsheathed! With this sword last night did the tyrant Heselrigge break into my home and murder my wife!"

Tumultuous lamentations for Lady Marion, the "sweet Lady of Ellerslie," fill the air, and the slogan, "Death and Lady Marion!" is echoed from mouth to mouth as the peasant-patriots arm themselves for vengeance.

Then there is the heavenly-minded Lady Helen Mar, a heroine to enchant the fancy of any girl or woman, as is her sister Isabella, "beauteous as a ministering seraph." Recall Helen, sitting in her bower, weaving into the silken texture of her father's banner soft threads from the amber locks of the Scottish chief. Wallace had sent to Lord Mar by his faithful harper a lock of his hair stained with the blood of his murdered Marion, with the message that if he fell in battle his friend was to look upon it and read in the memory of his wrongs the future miseries of Scotland, and remember that *God armeth the patriot.*

Is there a boy alive who would not thrill to the many pictures of the young Edwin Ruthven who joined Wallace's standard when he was only fifteen and was adopted by the chieftain as a brother? Never was there a more inspiring friendship in fiction! It glows in almost every chapter of the book, from their memorable first meeting, through the exploit of Edwin's scaling the walls of Dumbarton Rock, his triumphant return to his chief with the information that led to victory, and the knighting of the young hero before his valiant comrades:

"With a bounding heart Edwin bent his knee and Wallace, giving him the hallowed accolade, the young knight rose from his position with all the roses of his springing fame glowing in his countenance."

His honors are not yet ended, for when Lord Mar inquires of Wallace the identity of the wondrous boy who was his pilot over the perilous rocks, that he might give him a soldier's thanks, Wallace beckons Edwin:

"Here," he said, "is my knight of fifteen, for yester-eve he proved himself more worthy of his spurs than many a man who has received them from a king."

"He shall wear those of a king," rejoins Lord Mar, unbuckling from his feet a pair of golden spurs. "These were fastened on my heels by our great King Alexander at the battle of Largs. I had intended them for my only son, but the first knight in the cause of rescued Scotland is the son of my heart and soul."

The towers that Edwin Ruthven so bravely scaled still stand as his noble monument and many a warm-hearted school-boy has shed a tear there over his young mate in years.

The book is so full of arresting pictures that it is hard to select one as more beautiful than another, for Miss Porter was a veritable colorist in words.

Here, for instance, is one of the younger Bruce as he first meets Wallace on the battlefield of Falkirk: "A young and graceful form habited in a white hacqueton wrought in gold, with a helmet of the same costly metal on his head, crested with white feathers. Had the scene been in Palestine he might have been mistaken for a guardian angel in arms."

Miss Porter's constructive imagination and plot-sense are fully equal to her self-imposed task of successfully building a great romantic structure and holding the interest throughout. Thrilling escapes through mysterious underground passages, movable pillars, secret doors, flagstones that lift and lead to friars' cells,—these abound, and with them wardrobes replete with disguises used to evoke suspense, such as that worn by Wallace as a wandering minstrel at the court of Edward, the Usurper.

Of course Margaret of France, Edward's youthful queen, fell in love with him like everybody else, and made him, as well as herself, a deal of trouble by so doing; but no disguise was sufficient to save so heroic a being from that fate!

Then there is the lovely Lady Helen, clad as a page, leaping from her window to the pleasaunce beneath, to travel by land and sea to the side of her adored Wallace, a prisoner in the Tower of London.

As a last example the book holds nothing more breathlessly exciting than the disguise in full armor, of Joanna, the treacherous Countess of Mar, as the "Knight of the Green Plume," with the glowing beauty of her face hidden by a warrior's casque.

Miss Porter had a rare knack at creating villains, and Soulis, De Valence, Heselrigge, Cressingham, and Monteith are certainly an unequalled quintet. It must also be conceded that she did not believe villainy to be a purely masculine attribute, for the above-mentioned Lady Mar, fair Helen's step-mother, seemed to my youthful mind in every way more malignant than Lady Macbeth, whose character often gave me great concern.

The mysterious iron coffer given to Wallace in the first chapter as containing something precious, is an interesting thread in the plot, appearing, disappearing and reappearing on the screen from time to time, passing from hand to hand, continually in danger, but the cover never once lifted, nor its contents disclosed, until the very end of the book, where it is seen on the coffin of Wallace, its preserver, and, being opened by the royal Bruce, is found to contain the regalia of Scotland.

The knight of stainless honor upon whom this regalia had so often been urged, had in the meantime perished on the scaffold in the Tower of London and the pages dealing with his death, and the supreme devotion of Lady Helen, are perhaps the most touching and inspiring in the book.

It ends there, in London Tower, the tragic story filled with lofty sentiment, with splendid deeds, with chivalry to foe and matchless fidelity to friend, with warfare redeemed from bloodshed by the glory of the cause; and from it all there emerges a great and romantic figure in Sir William Wallace. The world has always needed heroes and it needs them sadly now, for the "greatest good a hero does to the race is to be a hero and thereby inspire others to heroic living."

There is a gloom in many literary and dramatic productions that ends nowhere, but diffuses black chaos and a fatalism for which no youthful reader is the better; but the tragedy of the last chapters in "Scottish Chiefs" begets only infinite sadness, shot through by beams of light.

Their trust in God and their passionate love of country make Miss Porter's men and women offer their lives gladly, not grudgingly. Death leaves them with a smile on their lips and the young reader feels a clean wind sweeping across his face, drying the tears in his eyes. A new love of high achievement and brave living has been born in him and as he rises to put the book away he does not forget the phrase: *God armeth the patriot.*

KATE DOUGLAS WIGGIN.

THE SCOTTISH CHIEFS

THE SCOTTISH CHIEFS
By Jane Porter

Edited By KATE DOUGLAS WIGGIN

and

NORA A. SMITH

Illustrated by N.C. WYETH

CHARLES SCRIBNER'S SONS
NEW YORK · LONDON
1956

CONTENTS

CONTENTS

ILLUSTRATIONS

THE SCOTTISH CHIEFS

THE SCOTTISH CHIEFS

CHAPTER I.

SCOTLAND.

BRIGHT was the summer of 1296. The war which had desolated Scotland was then at an end. Ambition seemed satiated; and the vanquished, after having passed under the yoke of their enemy, concluded they might wear their chains in peace. Such were the hopes of those Scottish noblemen who, early in the preceding spring, had signed the bond of submission to a ruthless conqueror, purchasing life at the price of all that makes life estimable,—liberty and honor.

Prior to this act of vassalage, Edward I., king of England, had entered Scotland at the head of an immense army. He seized Berwick by stratagem; laid the country in ashes; and, on the field of Dunbar, forced the Scottish king and his nobles to acknowledge him their liege lord.

But while the courts of Edward, or of his representatives, were crowded by the humbled Scots, the spirit of one brave man remained unsubdued. Disgusted alike at the facility with which the sovereign of a warlike nation could resign his people and his crown into the hands of a treacherous invader, and at the pusillanimity of the nobles who had ratified the sacrifice, William Wallace retired to the glen of Ellerslie. Withdrawn from the world, he hoped to avoid the sight of oppressions he could not redress, and the endurance of injuries beyond his power to avenge.

Thus checked at the opening of life in the career of glory that was his passion, he repressed the eager aspirations of his mind, and strove to acquire that resignation to inevitable evils which alone could reconcile him to forego the promises of his youth, and enable him to view with patience a humiliation of Scotland, which blighted her honor, and consigned her sons to degradation or obscurity. The latter was the choice of Wallace. Too noble to bend his spirit to the usurper, too honest to affect submission, he resigned himself to the only way left of maintaining the independence of a true Scot; and giving up the world at once, all the ambitions of youth became extinguished in his breast. Scotland seemed proud of her chains. Not to share in such debasement appeared all that was now in his power; and within the shades of Ellerslie he found a retreat and a home, whose sweets made him sometimes forget the wrongs of his country in the tranquil enjoyments of wedded love.

During the happy months of the preceding autumn, while Scotland was yet free, and the path of honorable distinction still open before her young nobility, Wallace married Marion Braidfoot, the beautiful heiress of Lammington. Nearly of the same age, and brought up from childhood together, affection had grown with their growth; and sympathy of taste and virtues, and mutual tenderness, had made them entirely one.

Edward's invasion of Scotland broke in upon their innocent joys. Wallace threw aside the wedding garment for the cuirass and the sword. But he was not permitted long to use either: Scotland submitted to her enemies; and he had no alternative but to bow to her oppressors, or to become an exile from man, amid the deep glens of his country.

The tower of Ellerslie was henceforth the lonely abode of himself and his bride. The neighboring nobles avoided him, because the principles he declared were a reproach on their proceedings; and in the course of time, as he forbore to seek them, they even forgot his existence. Indeed, all occasions of mixing with society he now rejected. The hunting-spear with which he had delighted to follow the flying roebuck from glade to glade, the arrows with which he used to bring down the heavy ptarmigan or the towering eagle, all were laid aside. Scottish liberty was no more, and Wallace would have blushed to have shown himself to the free-born deer of his native hills in communion of sports with the spoilers of his country. Had he pursued his once favorite exercises, he must have mingled with the English, now garrisoned in every town, and who passed their hours of leisure in the chase.

Being resigned to bury his youth,—since its strength could no longer be serviceable to his country,—books, his harp, and the sweet converse of his Marion, became the occupations of his days. Ellerslie was his hermitage; and there, closed from the world, with an angel his companion, he might have forgotten Edward was lord in Scotland, had not that which was without his little paradise made a way to its gates, and showed him the slavery of the nobles and the wretchedness of the people. In these cases, his generous hand gave succor, where it could not bring redress. Those whom the lawless plunderer had driven from their houses or stripped of their covering, found shelter, clothing, and food at the house of Sir William Wallace.

Several months of this blissful solitude had elapsed, when Lady Wallace saw a chieftain at her gate. He inquired for his master, requested a private conference, and they remained together for an hour. Wallace then came forth, and ordering his horse, with four followers, said he meant to accompany his guest to Douglas castle. When he embraced his wife at parting, he told her that as Douglas was only a few miles distant, he should be at home again before the moon rose.

She passed the tedious hours of his absence with tranquillity, till the appointed signal of his return appeared from behind the summits of the opposite mountains. So bright were its beams that Marion did not need any other light to show her the stealing sands of her hour-glass, as they numbered the hours of her husband's stay. She dismissed her servants to their rest, all excepting Halbert, the gray-haired harper of Wallace; and he, like herself, was too unaccustomed to the absence of his master to find sleep while Ellerslie was bereft of its joy and its guard.

As the night advanced, Lady Wallace sat in the window of her bed-chamber, which looked towards the west. She watched the winding pathway that led from Lanark down the opposite heights, eager to catch a glimpse of the waving plumes of her husband when he should emerge from behind the hill, and pass under the thicket which overhung the road. How often, as a cloud obscured for an instant the moon's light and threw a shade across the path, did her heart bound with the thought that her watching was at an end! It was he whom she had seen start from the abrupt rock. They were the folds of his tartan that darkened the white cliff. But the moon again rolled through her train of clouds, and threw her light around. Where, then, was her Wallace? Alas! it was only a shadow she had seen; the hill was still lonely, and he whom she sought was yet far away. Overcome with watching and disappointment, unable to say whence arose her fears, she sat down again to look; but her eyes were blinded with tears, and she exclaimed, "Not yet, not yet! Ah, my Wallace, what evil hath betided thee?"

Trembling with a nameless terror, she knew not what to dread. She believed that all hostile encounters had ceased, when Scotland no longer contended with Edward. The nobles, without remonstrance, had surrendered their castles into the hands of the usurper; and the peasantry, following the example of their lords, had allowed their homes to be ravaged without lifting an arm in their defense. Opposi tion being over, nothing could then threaten her husband from the enemy; and was not the person who had taken him from Ellerslie, a friend?

Before Wallace's departure, he had spoken to Marion alone; he told her that the stranger was Sir John Monteith, the youngest son of the brave Walter, Lord Monteith, who had been treacherously put to death by the English in the early part of the foregoing year. This young man was bequeathed by his dying father to the particular charge of his friend William, Lord Douglas, at that time governor of Berwick. After the fall of that place and the captivity of its defender, Sir John Monteith had retired to Douglas castle, in the vicinity of Lanark, and was now the sole master of that princely residence; James Douglas, the only son of its veteran lord, being still at Paris, whither he had been despatched, before the defeat at Dunbar, to negotiate a league between the French monarch and the then King of Scots.

Informed of the privacy in which Wallace wished to live, Monteith had never ventured to disturb it until this day; but knowing the honor of his old school-companion, he came to entreat him, by the respect he entertained for the brave Douglas, and by his love for his country, that he would not refuse to accompany him to the brave exile's castle.

"I have a secret to disclose to you," said he, "which cannot be divulged on any other spot."

Unwilling to deny so small a favor, Wallace, as has been said before, consented, and accordingly was conducted by Monteith towards Douglas.

While descending the heights which led to the castle, Monteith kept a profound silence; and when crossing the drawbridge towards it, he put his finger to his lips, in token to the servants for equal caution. This was explained as they entered the gate and looked around. It was guarded by English soldiers. Wallace would have drawn back, but Monteith laid his hand on his arm and whispered, "For your country!" At these words, a spell to the ear of Wallace, he proceeded, and his attendants followed into the court-yard.

The sun was just setting as Monteith led his friend into the absent earl's room. Its glowing reflection on the distant hills reminded Wallace of the stretch he had to retread to reach his home before midnight; and thinking of his anxious Marion, he awaited with impatience the development of the object of his journey.

Monteith closed the door, looked fearfully around for some time, then, trembling at every step, approached Wallace. When drawn quite near, in a low voice he said, "You must swear upon the cross that you will keep inviolate the secret I am going to reveal."

Wallace put aside the hilt of the sword which Monteith presented to receive his oath: "No," said he, with a smile; "in these times I will not bind my conscience on subjects I do not know. If you dare trust the word of a Scotsman and a friend, speak out; and if the matter be honest, my honor is your pledge."

"You will not swear?"

"No."

"Then I must not trust you."

"Then our business is at an end," returned Wallace, rising, "and I may return home."

"Stop!" cried Monteith. "Forgive me, my old companion, that I have dared to hesitate, but the nature of the confidence reposed in me will, I hope, convince you that I ought not to share it rashly. Of any one but you, I would exact oaths; but your word is given, and on that I rely. Await me here."

Monteith unlocked a door which had been concealed by the tapestry, and after a short absence reentered with a small iron box. He set it on the table near his friend, then went to the great door, tried that the bolts were secure, and returned, with a still more pallid countenance, towards the table. Wallace, surprised at such precaution, and at the apprehension visible in these actions, awaited with wonder the promised explanation. Monteith sat down with his hand on the box, and fixing his eyes on it, began:

"I am going to mention a name which you may hear with patience, since its power is no more. The successful rival of Bruce, and the enemy of your family, is now a prisoner in the Tower of London."

"Baliol?"

"Yes," answered Monteith; "and his present sufferings will, perhaps, avenge to you his vindictive resentment of the injury he received from Sir Ronald Crawford."

"My grandfather never injured him, nor any man," interrupted Wallace. "Sir Ronald Crawford was as incapable of injustice as of flattering the minions of his country's enemy. But Baliol is fallen, and I forgive him."

"Did you witness his degradation," returned Monteith, "you would even pity him."

"I always pity the wicked," continued Wallace; "and as you seem ignorant of the cause of his enmity against Sir Ronald and myself, I will explain it. I first saw Baliol four years ago, when I accompanied my grandfather to witness the arbitration of the King of

England between the two contending claimants for the Scottish crown. Sir Ronald came on the part of Bruce. I was deemed too young to have a voice in the council; but I was old enough to understand what was passing there, and to perceive, in the crouching demeanor with which Baliol received the crown, that it was the price for which he sold his country. However, as Scotland acknowledged him sovereign, and as Bruce submitted, my grandfather silently acquiesced. But Baliol did not forget former opposition. His behavior to Sir Ronald and myself at the beginning of this year, when, according to the privilege of our birth, we appeared in the field against the public enemy, fully demonstrated what was the injury Baliol complains of, and how unjustly he drove us from the standard of Scotland. 'None,' said he, 'shall serve under me who presumed to declare themselves the friends of Bruce.' Edward having made use of him, all these sacrifices of honor and of conscience are insufficient to retain his favor, and Baliol is removed from his kingdom to an English prison. I do indeed pity him. And now that I have cleared my grandfather's name of such calumny, I am ready to hear you further."

Monteith, after remarking on the well-known honor of Sir Ronald Crawford, resumed.

"During the massacre at the capture of Berwick, Lord Douglas, wounded and nearly insensible, was taken by a trusty band of Scots out of the citadel and town. I followed him to Dunbar, and witnessed with him that day's dreadful conflict, which completed the triumph of the English. When the few nobles who survived the battle dispersed, Douglas took the road to Forfar, hoping to meet King Baliol there, and to concert with him new plans of resistance. When we arrived, we found his Majesty in close conversation with the Earl of Athol, who had persuaded him the disaster at Dunbar was decisive, and that if he wished to save his life he must immediately go to the King of England and surrender himself to his mercy.

"Douglas tried to alter Baliol's resolution, but without effect. The king could not return any reasonable answers to the arguments which were offered to induce him to remain, but continued to repeat, with groans and tears, 'It is my fate!' Athol sat knitting his black brows during this conversation; and, at last throwing out some sullen remarks to Lord Douglas, on exhorting the king to defy his liege lord, he abruptly left the room.

"As soon as he was gone, Baliol rose from his seat with an anxious countenance, and taking my patron into an adjoining room, they continued there a few minutes, and then reentered. Douglas brought with him this iron box. 'Monteith,' said he, 'I confide this to your care.' Putting the box under my arm, and concealing it with my cloak —'Carry it,' continued he, 'directly to my castle in Lanarkshire. I will rejoin you there in four and twenty hours after your arrival. Meanwhile, by your fidelity to your king, breathe not a word of what has passed.'

" 'Look on that, and be faithful!' said Baliol, putting this ruby ring on my finger. I withdrew with the haste his look dictated, and as I crossed the outward hall was met by Athol. He eyed me sternly, and inquired whither I was going. I replied, 'To Douglas, to prepare for the coming of its lord.' The hall was full of armed men in Athol's colors. Not one of the remnant who had followed my patron from the bloody field of Dunbar was visible. Athol looked round on his myrmidons: 'Here,' cried he, 'see that you speed this fellow on his journey. We shall provide lodgings for his master.' I foresaw danger to Lord Douglas, but I durst not attempt to warn him; and to secure my charge, which a return to the room might have hazarded, I hastened into the court-yard, and being permitted to mount my horse, set off at full speed.

"On arriving at this place, I remembered that secret closet, and carefully deposited the box within it. A week passed without any tidings of Lord Douglas. At last a pilgrim appeared at the gate, and requested to see me alone; fearing nothing from a man in so sacred a habit, I admitted him. Presenting me with a packet which had been intrusted to him by Lord Douglas, he told me my patron had been forcibly carried on board a vessel at Montrose, to be conveyed with the unhappy Baliol to the Tower of London. Douglas, on this outrage, sent to the monastery at Aberbrothick, and under the pretense of making a religious confession before he sailed, begged a visit from the subprior. 'I am that prior,' continued the pilgrim; 'and having been born on the Douglas lands, he well knew the claim he had on my fidelity. He gave me this packet, and conjured me to lose no time in conveying it to you. The task was difficult; and, as in these calamitous seasons we hardly know whom to trust, I determined to execute it myself.'

"I inquired whether Lord Douglas had actually sailed. 'Yes,' replied the father; 'I stood on the beach till the ship disappeared.' "

A half-stifled groan burst from the indignant breast of Wallace. It interrupted Monteith for an instant, but without noticing it, he proceeded.

"Not only the brave Douglas was then wrested from his country, with our king, but also that holy pillar of Jacob,* which prophets have declared to be the palladium of Scotland."

"What!" inquired Wallace, with a yet darker frown, "has Baliol robbed Scotland of that trophy of one of her best kings? Is the sacred gift of Fergus to be made the spoil of a coward?"

"Baliol is not the robber," rejoined Monteith: "the hallowed pillar was taken from Scone by the command of the King of England, and with the sackings of Iona was carried on board the same vessel with the betrayed Douglas. The archives of the kingdom have also been torn from their sanctuary, and were thrown by Edward's own hands into the fire."

"His depredations," continued Monteith, "the good monk told me, have been wide as destructive. He has not left a parchment, either of public records or of private annals, in any of the monasteries or castles around Montrose; all have been searched and plundered. And, besides, the faithless Earl of March and Lord Soulis have performed the like robberies, in his name, from the eastern shores of the Highlands to the farthest of the Western Isles."

"Do the traitors think," cried Wallace, "that by robbing Scotland of her annals and of that stone they really deprive her of her palladium? Scotland's history is in the memories of her sons; her palladium is in their hearts; and Edward may one day find that she needs not talismans to give her freedom."

"Alas! not in our time," answered Monteith. "The spear is at our breasts, and we must submit. You see this castle is full of Edward's soldiers. Every house is a garrison for England,—but I have yet to tell you the contents of the packet which the monk brought. It contained two others. One directed to Sir James Douglas at Paris, and the other to me. I read as follows:

" 'Athol has persuaded Baliol to his ruin, and betrayed me into the hands of Edward. I shall see Scotland no more. Send the enclosed to my son at Paris; it will inform him what is the last wish of William Douglas for his country. The iron box I confided to you guard as your life, until you can deposit it with my son. But should he remain abroad, and you ever be in extremity, commit the box in strict charge to the worthiest Scot you know; and tell him *that it will be at the peril of his soul, who dares to open it, till Scotland be again free!* When that hour

* The tradition respecting this stone is as follows: Hiber, or Iber, the Phœnician, who came from the Holy Land, to inhabit the coast of Spain, brought this sacred relic along with him. From Spain he transplanted it with the colony he sent to people the south of Ireland; and from Ireland it was brought into Scotland by the great Fergus, the son of Ferchard. He placed it in Argyleshire; but MacAlpine removed it to Scone, and fixed it in the royal chair in which all the succeeding kings of Scotland were inaugurated. Edward I. of England caused it to be carried to Westminster Abbey, where it now stands. The tradition is, that empire abides where it stays.—(1809.)

comes, then let the man by whose valor God restores her rights, receive the box as *his own;* for by him only is it to be opened. DOUGLAS.' "

Monteith finished reading the letter, and remained silent. Wallace, who had listened to it with increasing indignation, spoke first: "Tell me in what I can assist you, or how serve these last wishes of the imprisoned Douglas."

Monteith replied by reading over again this sentence, " 'Should my son remain abroad, and you ever be in extremity, commit the box in strict charge to the worthiest Scot you know.' I am in that extremity now. Edward determined on desolation when he placed English governors throughout our towns; and the rapacious Heselrigge, his representative in Lanark, has just issued an order for the houses of all the absent chiefs to be searched for secret correspondences. Two or three in the neighborhood have already gone through this ordeal; but the event has proved that it was not papers they sought, but plunder, and an excuse for dismantling the castles, or occupying them with English officers.

"The soldiers you saw were sent, by daybreak this morning, to guard this castle until Heselrigge could in person be present at the examination. This ceremony is to take place to-morrow; and as Lord Douglas is considered a traitor to Edward, I am told the place will be sacked to its walls. In such *an extremity,* to you, noble Wallace, as to *the worthiest Scot I know,* I apply to take charge of this box. Within the remote cliffs of Ellerslie it must be safe; and when James Douglas arrives from Paris, to him you will resign it. Meanwhile, as I cannot resist the plunderers, after delivering the keys of the state apartments to Heselrigge to-morrow, I shall submit to necessity, and beg his permission to retire to my lodge on Ben Venu."

Wallace made no difficulty in granting Monteith's request; and, there being two iron rings on each side of his charge, the young chief took off his leathern belt, and putting it through them, swung the box easily under his left arm, while covering it with his plaid.

Monteith's eyes now brightened, the paleness left his cheek, and with a firmer step, as if suddenly relieved of a heavy load, he called a servant to prepare Sir William Wallace's attendants.

While Wallace shook him by the hand, Monteith, in a solemn voice, exhorted him to caution respecting the box. "Remember," added he, "the penalty that hangs over him who looks into it."

"Be not afraid," answered Wallace; "even the outside shall never be seen by other eyes than my own, unless the same circumstance which now induces you, *mortal extremity,* should force me to confide it to safer hands."

"Beware of that!" exclaimed Monteith; "for who is there that would adhere to the prohibition as I have done—as you will do? and besides, as I have no doubt it contains holy relics, who knows what new calamities a sacrilegious look might bring upon our already devoted country?"

"Relics or no relics," replied Wallace, "it would be an equal sin against good faith to invade what is forbidden; but from the weight I am rather inclined to suspect it contains gold, probably a treasure with which the sordid Baliol thinks to compensate the hero who may free his country for all the miseries a traitor king and a treacherous usurper have brought upon it."

"A treasure," repeated Monteith; "I never thought of that; it is indeed heavy; and as we are responsible for the contents of the box, I wish we were certain of what it contains; let us consider that."

"It is no consideration of ours," returned Wallace. "All we have to do is to preserve the contents unviolated; and to that I pledge myself,—farewell!"

"But why this haste?" rejoined Monteith; "indeed, I wish I had thought—stay only a little."

"I thank you," returned Wallace, proceeding to the court-yard; "but it is now dark, and I promised to be at home before the moon rises. If you wish me to serve you further, I shall be happy to see you at Ellerslie to-morrow. My Marion will have pleasure in entertaining the friend of her husband."

While Wallace spoke he advanced to his horse, to which he was lighted by the servants of the castle. A few English soldiers lingered about in idle curiosity. As he put his foot in the stirrup, he held the sword in his hand, which he had unbuckled from his side to leave space for his charge. Monteith, whose dread of detection was ever awake, whispered, "Your loosened weapon may excite suspicion." Fear incurred what it sought to avoid. He hastily pulled aside Wallace's plaid to throw it over the glittering hilt of the sword, and thus exposed the iron box. The light of the torches striking upon the polished rivets, displayed it to all lookers-on, but no remark was made. Wallace, not observing what was done, again shook hands with Monteith, and calling his servants about him galloped away. A murmur was heard, as if of some intention to follow him; but deeming it prudent to leave the open and direct road, because of the English marauders who swarmed there, he was presently lost amid the thick shades of Clydesdale.

CHAPTER II.

LANARK.

THE darkness was almost impenetrable. Musing on what had passed with Monteith, Wallace rode on, till, crossing the bridge at Lanark, he saw the rising moon, and then his meditations embraced a gentler subject. This was the time he had promised Marion he should be returned, and he had yet five long miles to go before he could reach the glen of Ellerslie. He thought of her watching, with an anxious heart, the minutes of his delay. Scotland and its wrongs he now forgot in the idea of her whose happiness was dearer than life. He could not achieve the deliverance of the one, but it was his bliss to preserve the peace of the other; and putting spurs to his horse, he hastened through the town.

Abruptly turning an angle leading to the Mouse river, a cry of murder arrested his ear. He checked his horse and listened. The clashing of arms told him the sound had issued from an alley to the left. He alighted in an instant, and drawing his sword, threw away the scabbard; then, leaving his horse with one of his servants, hastened, with the other three, to the spot whence the noise proceeded.

On arriving, he discovered two men in tartans, with their backs to the opposite wall, furiously assaulted by a throng of Edward's soldiers. At this sight, the Scots who accompanied Wallace were so enraged that, blowing their bugles to encourage the assailed, they joined hand to hand with their gallant leader, and attacking the banditti, each man cut his opponent to the ground.

Such unexpected assistance reanimated the drooping strength of one of the two, from whom the cry had issued. He sprang from the wall with the vigor of a tiger, but at the moment received a wound in his back, which would have thrown him at the feet of his enemies had not Wallace caught him in his left arm, and with his right cleared the way, while he cried to his men who were fighting near him, "To the glen!" As he spoke, he threw the now insensible stranger into their arms. The other man, whose voice had first attracted Wallace, at that instant sunk, covered with blood, on the pavement.

Two of the servants, obeying their master, carried their senseless burden towards the horses; but the third, being hemmed in by the furious soldiers, could not move. Wallace made a passage to his rescue, and effected it; but one base wretch, while the now wounded Scot was retreating, made a stroke which would have severed his head from his body, had not the trusty claymore of Wallace struck down the weapon of the coward, and received his body upon its point. He fell with bitter imprecations, calling aloud for vengeance.

A dreadful cry was now raised by the whole band of assassins: "Murder! treason! Arthur Heselrigge is slain!" The uproar became general. The windows of the adjoining houses were thrown open; people issued from their doors, and pressed forward to inquire the cause of the alarm. Wallace was nearly overpowered; a hundred swords flashed in the torchlight; but at the moment he expected they would be sheathed in his heart, the earth gave way under his feet, and he sank into utter darkness.

He fell upon a quantity of gathered broom; and concluding that the weight of the multitude had burst his way through the arch of a cellar, he sprang on his feet: and though he heard the curses of several wretches, who had fallen with him and fared worse, he made but one step to a half-opened door, pointed out to him by a gleam from an inner passage. The men uttered a shout as they saw him darken the light which glimmered through it, but they were incapable of pursuit; and Wallace, aware of his danger, darting across the adjoining apartment, burst open a window, and leaped out at the foot of the Lanark hills.

He pursued his way over the craigs, through the valley, and across the river, to the cliffs which embattle the garden of Ellerslie. Springing on the projecting point of the nearest, he leaped into a thicket of honeysuckles. This was the favorite bower of his Marion. The soft perfume as it saluted his senses seemed to breathe peace and safety, and he walked with a calmer step towards the house. He approached a door which led into the garden. It was open. He beheld his beloved leaning over a couch, on which was laid the person he had rescued. Halbert was dressing his wounds.

Wallace paused for a moment, to contemplate his lovely wife in this more lovely act of charity. Her beautiful hands held a cup to the lips of the stranger; while her long hair, escaped from its band, fell in jetty ringlets, and mingled with his silver locks.

"Marion!" exclaimed her husband. She looked up at the well-known sound, and with a cry of joy, rushing forward, threw herself into his arms: her tears flowed, she clung to his breast. It was the first time Wallace had been from her; she had feared it would have been the last.

"Art thou indeed here?" exclaimed she. Blood fell from his forehead upon her face and bosom. "O my Wallace!" cried she, in agony.

"Fear not, my love! all is well, since our wounded countryman is safe."

"But you bleed," returned she. No tears now impeded her voice, and she felt as if she expected his life-blood to issue from the wound on which she gazed.

"I hope my preserver is not hurt?" inquired the stranger.

"Oh, no!" replied Wallace, putting back the hair from his forehead; "a mere trifle." That the action had discovered the gash to be wider than he thought, he saw in the countenance of his wife. She turned deadly pale. "Marion," said he, "to convince you how causeless your fears are, you shall cure me yourself, and with no other surgery than your girdle."

When Lady Wallace heard his gay tone, she took courage; and, remembering the deep wounds of the stranger, which she had assisted to dress, she began to hope that she need not now fear for the object dearest to her in existence. Rising from her husband's arms, with a languid smile she unbound the linen fillet from her waist; and Halbert having poured some balsam into the wound, she prepared to apply the bandage; but when she lifted her husband's hair from his temple,— that hair which had so often been the object of her admiration, as it hung in shining masses over his arching brows,—when the clotted blood met her fingers, a mist seemed to pass over her sight: she paused for a moment; but rallying her strength, as the cheerful sound of his voice conversing with his guest assured her, she tied the fillet, and seated herself, yet trembling, by his side.

"Gallant Wallace!" cried the stranger, "it is Donald, Earl of Mar, who owes his life to you."

"Then blest be my arm," exclaimed Wallace, "that has preserved a life so precious to my country!"

"May it indeed be blest!" cried Lord Mar; "for this night it has made the Southrons feel there is yet one man in Scotland who does not fear to resist oppression and to punish treachery."

"What treachery?" inquired Lady Wallace, her spirit still hovering about her soul's far dearer part: "is any meant to my husband?"

"None to Sir William Wallace, more than to any other brave Scot," replied the earl; "but we all see the oppression of our country, we all know the treachery by which it was subjugated, and this night, in my own person, I have felt the effects of both. The English at Lanark despatched a body of men to Bothwell castle on a plea, that as its lord is yet absent, they presume he is adverse to Edward, and therefore they must search his dwelling for documents to settle the point. Considering myself the representative of my brother-in-law, Lord Bothwell, and suspecting that this might be only a marauding party, I refused to admit the soldiers; and saw them depart, swearing to return the next day with a stronger force, and storm the castle. To be ascertained of their commission, and to appeal against such tyranny, should it be true, I followed the detachment to Lanark.

"I saw Heselrigge, the governor. He avowed the transaction, but consented to spare Bothwell while I and my family remain in it. It being nearly dark, I took my leave, and was proceeding towards my servants in the court-yard when a young man accosted me. I recognized him to be the officer who had commanded the party I had driven from the castle. Heselrigge having told me that he was his nephew, I made no hesitation to go back with him, when he informed me his uncle had forgotten something of importance, and begged me to return. I followed his steps; but instead of conducting me to the room in which I had conversed with Heselrigge, he led me into a small apartment, where, telling me his uncle would attend me, he suddenly retreated out of the door, and before I could recollect myself I heard him bolt it after him.

"I now saw myself a prisoner; and alarmed at what might be intended to my family, I made every essay to force the door, but it was in vain. Driven to despair, I remained in a state of mind not to be described, when the bolt was undrawn, and two men entered, with manacles in their hands. They attempted to seize me, telling me I was the prisoner of King Edward. I did not listen further, but wounding one with my dagger, felled the other to the ground, and made my way to a street leading from behind the governor's house. I ran against some one as I rushed from the portal; it was my servant Neil. I hastily told him to draw his sword and follow me. We then hurried forward, he telling me he had stepped out to observe the night, while the rest of my men were wondering at my delay.

"Fearing the worst of consequences from the treachery of Heselrigge, I was hastening onward to the protection of my family, when, at the turning of an angle which leads to the Bothwell road we were suddenly surrounded by armed men. The moon shone full on their faces, and I discovered they were Southrons, and that young Heselrigge was at their head.

"He aimed a blow at my head with his battle-ax, and in a voice of triumph exclaimed to his soldiers, 'The plunder of Bothwell, my lads! Down with its lord! all but the lady Helen shall be yours!'

"In a moment every sword was directed towards me. They

wounded me in several places; but the thought of my daughter gave vigor to my arm, and I defended myself till the cries of my servant brought you to my rescue. But, while I am safe, perhaps my treach-erous pursuer has marched towards Bothwell; there are none to guard my child but a few domestics, the unpractised sword of my stripling nephew, and the feeble arms of my wife."

"Be easy on that head," interrupted Wallace; "I believe the in-famous leader of the banditti fell by my hand, for the soldiers made an outcry that Arthur Heselrigge was killed; and then pressing on me to take revenge, their weight broke a passage into a vault, through which I escaped——"

"Save, save yourself, my master!" cried a man rushing in from the garden. "You are pursued——"

While he spoke he fell insensible at Wallace's feet. It was Dugald, whom he had rescued from the blow of Heselrigge, and who, from the state of his wound, had been thus long in reaching Ellerslie.

Wallace had hardly time to give him to the care of Halbert when the voice of war assailed his ears. The tumult of men demanding admittance, and the sound of spears rattling against the shields of their owners, told the astonished group within that the house was beset by armed foes.

"Blood for blood!" cried a horrid voice, which penetrated the almost palsied senses of Lady Marion. "Vengeance on Wallace for the murder of Heselrigge!"

"Fly, fly!" cried she, looking wildly at her husband.

"Whither?" answered he, supporting her in his arms. "Would this be a moment to leave you and our wounded guest? I must meet them."

"Not now," cried Lord Mar. "Hear you not how numerous they are? Mark that shout; they thirst for blood. If you have pity for your wife, delay not a moment!"

The uproar redoubled, and the room was instantly filled with shrieking women, the attendants of Lady Wallace.

"O my lord!" cried the terrified creatures, wringing their hands, "what will become of us! The Southrons are at the gates, and we shall be lost forever."

"Fear not," replied Wallace; "retire to your chambers. I am the person they seek: none else will meet with injury."

Appeased by this assurance, the women retreated to their apart-ments; and Wallace, turning to the earl, who continued to enforce the necessity of his flight, repeated that he would not consent to leave his wife in such a tumult.

"Leave me," cried she, in an inarticulate voice, "or see me die."

As she spoke, there was a violent crash and a burst of imprecations. Three of Wallace's men ran panting into the room. Two of the assailants had climbed to the hall window, and had just been thrown back upon the cliffs, where one was killed. "Conceal yourself," said the Scots to Wallace, "for in a few minutes more your men will not be able to maintain the gates."

"Yes, my dear lord," cried Halbert, "there is the dry well at the end of the garden; at the bottom of that you will be safe."

"By your love for me, Wallace, harken to him!" cried Lady Marion, falling at his feet. "I kneel for my life in kneeling for yours. Pity the gray hairs of Sir Ronald, whom your untimely death would bring to the grave. Fly, Wallace, if you would have me live!"

"Angel of my life!" exclaimed Wallace, straining her to his heart, "I obey thee. But if the hand of one of these desperate robbers dares to touch thy hallowed person——"

"Think not so, my lord," interrupted Halbert; "it is you they seek. Not finding you, they will be too eager in pursuit to molest your lady."

"I shall be safe," whispered Marion; "only fly—while you are here, their shouts kill me."

"But thou shalt go with me," returned he; "the well will contain us all. But first let our faithful Halbert and these honest fellows lower Lord Mar into the place of refuge. He being the cause of the affray, if discovered, would be immediately sacrificed."

Lord Mar acquiesced; and while the contention was so loud without as to threaten the tearing down of the walls, the earl was carried into the garden. He was followed by Sir William Wallace, to whose arm his wife yet fondly clung.

At the well-side they found the earl bound with the rope that was to lower him to the bottom. By great care it was safely done; and the cord being brought up again, before it was tied round Wallace he recollected that the iron box at his side might hurt the wounded nobleman by striking him in his descent; and, unbuckling it, he said it contained matters of great value, and ordered it to be lowered first.

Lord Mar, beneath, was releasing it from the rope when a shout of triumph pierced their ears. A party of the English, having come round the heights, had leaped the wall of the garden, and were within a few yards of the well. For Wallace to descend now was impossible. "That tree!" whispered Marion, pointing to an oak near which they stood. As she spoke, she slid from his arms, and, along with the venerable Halbert, who had seized her hand, disappeared amid the adjoining thicket. The two servants fled also.

Wallace and Marion

Wallace, finding himself alone, the next instant, like one of his native eagles, was looking down from the towering top of the wood upon his enemies. They passed beneath him, denouncing vengeance upon the assassin of Arthur Heselrigge. One, who by the brightness of his armor seemed to be their leader, stopped under the tree, and complained he had so sprained his ankle in leaping the wall, he must wait a few minutes to recover himself. Several soldiers drew towards him; but he ordered them to pursue their duty, search the house, and bring Wallace, dead or alive, before him.

They obeyed; but others, who had gained admittance to the tower through the now forced gates, soon ran to him with information that the murderer could nowhere be found.

"But here is a *gay ladie*," cried one; "perhaps she can tell of his hiding-place." And at that moment Marion, with Halbert, appeared amongst a band of men. The lighted torches which the soldiers held shone full on her face. Though pale as marble, the beauty of her features and the calm dignity which commanded from her eyes awed the officer into respect and admiration.

"Soldiers, stand back!" cried he, advancing to Lady Wallace. "Fear not, madam." As the words passed his lips a flight of arrows flew into the bosom of the tree. A piercing shriek from Marion was her only answer. "Hah! my lady's falcon!" cried Halbert, alarmed, doubly, for the fate of his master. A sudden agitation of the branches having excited suspicion in a body of archers who stood near, with one impulse they had discharged their arrows to the spot. Halbert's ready excuse, both for the disturbance in the tree and his lady's shriek, was warranted true by the appearance of a large bird, which the rushing of the arrows had frighted from her nest: she rose suddenly from amongst the branches, and soared away with loud screams.

All being again still, Marion hoped that her husband had escaped any serious injury from the arrows; and turning with recovered composure to the officer, heard him reprimand his men for daring to draw their bows without his orders. Then addressing her, "I beg your pardon, madam," said he, "both for the alarm these hot-headed men have occasioned you, and for the violence they have committed in forcing one of your sex and beauty before me. Had I expected to have found a lady here, I should have issued orders to have prevented this outrage; but I am sent hither in quest of Sir William Wallace, who by a mortal attack made on the person of the Governor of Lanark's nephew, has forfeited his life. The scabbard of his sword, found beside the murdered Heselrigge, is an undeniable proof of his guilt.

Direct us to find him, and not only release, but the favor of the English monarch will await your allegiance."

"I am Sir William Wallace's wife," returned the gentle Marion, in a firm tone; "and by what authority you seek him thus, and presume to call him guilty, I cannot understand."

"By the authority of the laws, madam, which he has violated."

"What laws?" rejoined she; "Sir William Wallace acknowledges none but those of God and his country. Neither of these has he transgressed."

The officer replied, "This night he assassinated Arthur Heselrigge in the streets of Lanark, and that condemns him, by the last declaration of King Edward: *Whatever Scot maltreats any one of the English soldiers, or civil officers, garrisoned in the towns of Scotland, shall thereby forfeit his life as the penalty of his crime.*"

"A tyrant's law, sir, to which no freeborn Scot will submit. But even were it allowed by my countrymen, in this case it can have no hold on my husband. That he is a Scot, he glories; and not that he maltreated any Englishman in the streets of Lanark, do I glory, but because, when he saw two defenseless men borne down by a band of armed soldiers, he exposed his unshielded breast in their defense. That the governor's nephew also fell was a retribution for his heading so unequal a contest, and no crime in Sir William Wallace; for he slew him to preserve a feeble old man, who had a hundred English swords leveled at his life."

The officer paused for a moment, and then ordered his soldiers to fall farther back; when they were at a sufficient distance, he offered to take Lady Wallace's hand. She withstood his motion with a reserved air, and said, "Speak, sir, what you would say, or allow me to retire."

"I mean not to offend you, noble lady," continued he; "had I a wife lovely as yourself, and I in like circumstances, I hope in the like manner she would defend my life and honor. I knew not the particulars of the affair in which Arthur Heselrigge fell till I heard them from your lips. I can easily credit them, for I know his unmanly character. Wallace is a Scot, and acted in Scotland as Gilbert Hambledon would have done in England. Wherever you have concealed your husband, let it be a distant asylum. At present no track within the jurisdiction of Lanark will be left unsearched by the governor's revenge."

Lady Wallace, overcome with gratitude at this generous speech of the English officer, uttered some words indicating her grateful feelings. Hambledon continued: "I will use my influence with

Heselrigge to prevent your house being disturbed again; but it being in the course of military operations, I cannot free you from the disagreeable ceremony of a guard being placed to-morrow round the domains. This I know will be done to intercept Sir William Wallace, should he attempt to return."

"Oh that he were indeed far distant!" thought the anxious Marion. The officer then added: "However, you shall be relieved of my detachment directly." And as he spoke he waved his sword to them who had seized the harper. They advanced, still holding their prisoner. He ordered them to commit the man to him, and to sound. The trumpeter obeyed, and in a few seconds the whole detachment were assembled before their commander.

"Soldiers," cried he, "Sir William Wallace has escaped our hands. Mount your horses, that we may return to Lanark, and search the other side of the town. Lead forth, and I will follow."

The troops obeyed, and falling back through the opened gates, left Sir Gilbert Hambledon alone with Lady Wallace and the wondering Halbert. The brave young man took the hand of the grateful Marion, who had stood trembling while so many of her husband's enemies were assembled under the place of his concealment.

"Noble Englishman," said she, as the last body of soldiers passed from her sight, "I cannot enough thank you for this generous conduct; but should you or yours be ever in the like extremity with my beloved Wallace, may the ear which has heard you this night, at that hour repay my gratitude!"

"Sweet lady," answered Hambledon, "I thank you for your prayer. Though I serve my king and obey my commanders, yet it is only to the Lord of battles that I look for a sure reward, and whether he pay me here with victories and honors, or take my soul through a rent in my breast to receive my laurel in paradise, it is all one to Gilbert Hambledon. But the night is cold: I must see you safe within your own doors, and then, lady, farewell!"

Lady Wallace yielded, and with redoubled haste, as she heard another rustling in the tree above her head. Hambledon did not notice it, but desiring Halbert to follow, in a few minutes disappeared with the agitated Marion into the house.

Wallace, whose spirit could ill brook the sight of his domains filled with hostile troops, and his wife brought a prisoner before their commander, would have braved all dangers and have leaped down amongst them; but at the instant he placed his foot on a lower bough to make a spring, the courteous address of Hambledon to his wife had made him hesitate. He listened to the replies of his Marion with exultation;

and when the Englishman ordered his men to withdraw, Wallace could hardly prevent a confidence in such virtue from compelling him to come from his concealment and thank his noble enemy on the spot. But a consideration that this disclosure would put the military duty and the generous nature of the officer at variance, he desisted with such an agitation of spirits that the boughs had again shaken under him, and reawakened the alarm of his trembling wife.

"Sir William! my master!" cried Halbert's voice at this moment, in a suppressed tone. "Speak, my dear lord; are you safe?"

"In heart and body," returned Wallace, sliding from the tree and leaping on the ground. "One only of the arrows touched me, and that merely striking my bugle, fell back amongst the leaves. I must now hasten to the dearest, the noblest of women."

Halbert begged him to stay till they should hear the retreat from the English trumpets. "Till their troops are out of sight," added he, "I cannot believe you safe."

"Hark!" cried Wallace, "the horses are now descending the craig. That must satisfy you, honest Halbert." With these words he flew across the grass, and entering the house, met the returning Marion, who had just bade farewell to Hambledon. She rushed into his arms, and with excess of joy fainted on his neck. What had been the shock of this evening's violence! Her husband pursued as a murderer; herself exposed to the midnight air, and dragged by the hands of merciless soldiers to betray the man she loved. All these scenes were new to her; and though a preternatural strength had supported her through them, yet when the cause of exertion was over, when she fell once more into her husband's arms, she seemed to have found the pillow whereon her soul might repose.

"My life! preserver of thy Wallace! look on him!" exclaimed he; "bless him with a smile from those dear eyes."

His voice soon restored her to sensibility and recollection. She wept on his breast, and thanked Heaven that he had escaped the search and the arrows of his enemies.

"But, my dear lady," interrupted Halbert, "remember my master must not stay here. You know the English commander said he must fly far away. Nay, spies may even now be lurking to betray him."

"You are right," cried she. "My Wallace, you must depart. Should the guard arrive soon, your flight may be prevented. You must go now—but, oh! whither?"

"Not very distant, my love. In going from thee I leave behind all that makes life precious to me; how then can I go far away? No; there are recesses among the Cartlane craigs I discovered while hunting, and which I believe have been visited by no mortal foot but my own. There will I be, my Marion, before sunrise; and before it sets, thither must you send Halbert, to tell me how you fare. Three notes from thine own sweet strains of *Thusa ha measg na reultan mor* ('Thou who art amid the stars, move to thy bed with music'), blown by his pipe, shall be a sign to me that he is there, and I will come forth to hear tidings of thee."

"Ah, my Wallace, let me go with thee!"

"What, dearest!" returned he, "to live amidst rocks and streams! to expose thy tender self to all the accidents of such a lodging!"

"But are not you going to so dangerous a lodging?" asked she. "Oh! would not rocks and streams be paradise to me, when blessed with the presence of my husband? Ah, let me go!"

"Impossible, my lady," cried Halbert, afraid that his master would consent, "you are safe here, and your flight would awaken suspicion in the English that he had not gone far. Your ease and safety are dearer to him than his own life; and most likely by his cares to preserve them he would be traced, and so fall a ready sacrifice to the enemy."

"It is true, my Marion; I could not preserve you in the places to which I go."

"But the hardships you will endure!" cried she; "to sleep on the cold stones, with no covering but the sky or the dripping vault of some dreary cave."

"Cease, my beloved," interrupted he. "Neither rocks nor storms have any threats to me. Before I was thine, my Marion, I have lain whole nights upon the mountain's brow, counting the wintry stars, as I awaited the hunter's horn that was to recall me to the chase in Glenfinlass. Alike to Wallace is the couch of down or the bed of heather; so, best beloved of my heart, grieve not at hardships which were once my sport, and will now be my safety."

"Then farewell! May angels guard thee!" Her voice failed; she put his hand to her lips.

"Courage, my Marion," said he; "remember that Wallace lives but in thee. Revive, be happy for my sake, and God, who putteth down the oppressor, will restore me to thine arms." She spoke not, but rising from his breast clasped her hands together, and looked up with an expression of fervent prayer; then she waved her hand to him to depart, and disappeared into her own chamber.

Wallace gazed at the closed door, with his soul in his eyes. To leave his Marion thus, to quit her who was the best part of his being, was almost too powerful for his resolution. Here indeed his brave spirit gave way; and he would have followed her, had not Halbert, reading his mind, taken him by the arm and drawn him towards the portal.

Wallace soon recovered his reason, and obeying the friendly impulse of his servant, accompanied him through the garden to the quarter which led to the remotest recesses of the Clyde. In their way they approached the well where Lord Mar lay. Finding that the earl had not been inquired for, Wallace deemed his stay to be without peril; and intending to inform him of the necessity which still impelled his own flight, he called to him, but no voice answered. He looked down, and seeing him extended on the bottom, without motion, "I fear," said he, "the earl is dead. As soon as I am gone, and you can collect the servants, send one into the well to bring him forth; and if he be indeed no more, deposit his body in my oratory, till you can receive his widow's commands respecting his remains. The iron box now in the well is of inestimable value: take it to Lady Wallace, and tell her she must guard it as she has done my life; but not to look into it, at the peril of what is yet dearer to her,—my honor."

Halbert promised to adhere to his master's orders; and Wallace, girdling on his sword, and taking his hunting-spear, he pressed the faithful hand that presented it, and again enjoining him to be watchful of his lady, and to send him tidings of her in the evening, to the cave near the Corie Lynn, he climbed the wall, and was out of sight in an instant.

CHAPTER III.

HALBERT returned to the house, and entering the room softly, into which Marion had withdrawn, beheld her on her knees before a crucifix: she was praying for the safety of her husband.

"May he, O gracious Lord!" cried she, "soon return to his home. But if I am to see him here no more, may it please Thee to grant me to meet him within Thy arms in Heaven!"

"Hear her, blessed Son of Mary!" ejaculated the old man. She looked round, and rising from her knees, demanded of him, in an anxious voice, whether he had left her lord in security.

"In the way to it, my lady," answered Halbert. He repeated all that Wallace had said at parting, and then tried to prevail on her to go to rest. "Sleep cannot visit my eyes this night, my faithful creature," replied she; "my spirit will follow Wallace in his mountain flight. Go you to your chamber. After you have had repose, that will be time enough to revisit the remains of the poor earl, and to bring them with the box to the house. I will take a religious charge of both, for the sake of the dear intruster."

Halbert persuaded his lady to lie down, and she, little suspecting that he meant to do otherwise than to sleep also, kindly wished him repose, and retired.

Her maids, during the late terror, had dispersed, and were nowhere to be found; and the men too, after their stout resistance at the gates, had all disappeared—some fled, others were sent away prisoners to Lanark, while the good Hambledon was conversing with their lady. Halbert therefore resigned himself to await with patience the rising of the sun, when he hoped some of the domestics would return; if not, he determined to go to the cotters in the glen and bring some of them to supply the place of the fugitives.

Thus musing, he sat on a stone bench in the hall, watching anxiously the appearance of that orb whose setting beams he hoped would light him back with tidings of Sir William Wallace. The morning was yet gray, and the fresh air blowing in rather chilly, Halbert rose to close the wooden shutter; at that moment his eyes were arrested by a party of armed men in quick march down the opposite declivity. In a few minutes more their heavy steps sounded in his ears, and he saw the platform before the house filled with English. Alarmed at the sight, he was retreating across the apartment, towards his lady's room, when the great hall-door was burst open by a band of soldiers, who rushed forward and seized him.

"Tell me, dotard!" cried their leader, a man of low stature, with gray locks but a fierce countenance, "where is the murderer? Where is Sir William Wallace? Speak, or the torture shall force you!"

Halbert shuddered, but it was for his defenseless lady, not for himself. "My master," said he, "is far from this."

"Where?"

"I know not."

"Thou shalt be made to know, thou hoary-headed villain!" cried the same violent interrogator. "Where is the assassin's wife? I will confront ye. Seek her out."

At that word the soldiers parted right and left, and in a moment afterwards three of them appeared with shouts, bringing in the trembling Marion.

"Alas, my lady!" cried Halbert, struggling to approach her, as with terror she looked around her; but they held her fast, and he saw her led up to the merciless wretch who had given the orders to have her summoned.

"Woman!" cried he, "I am the Governor of Lanark. You now stand before the representative of the great King Edward, and on your allegiance to him, and on the peril of your life, I command you to answer me three questions. Where is Sir William Wallace, the murderer of my nephew? Who is that old Scot for whom my nephew was slain? He and his whole family shall meet my vengeance! And tell me where is that box of treasure which your husband stole from Douglas castle? Answer me these questions on your life."

Lady Wallace remained silent.

"Speak, woman!" demanded the governor. "If fear cannot move you, know that I can reward as well as avenge. I will endow you richly, if you declare the truth. If you persist to refuse, you die."

"Then I die," replied she, scarcely opening her half-closed eyes, as she leaned, fainting, against the soldier who held her.

"What!" cried the governor, stifling his rage, "can so gentle a lady reject the favor of England; large grants in this country, and perhaps a fine English knight for a husband, when you might have all for giving up a traitor, and confessing where his robberies lie concealed? Speak, fair dame; give me this information, and the lands of the wounded chieftain whom Wallace brought here, with the hand of the handsome Sir Gilbert Hambledon, shall be your reward. Lady, can you now refuse to purchase all, by declaring the hiding-place of the traitor Wallace?"

"It is easier to die."

"Fool!" cried Heselrigge, driven from his assumed temper by her steady denial. "What! Is it easier for that beauteous head of thine to decorate my lance? Is this easier than to tell me where to find a murderer and his gold?"

Lady Wallace shuddered: she stretched her hands to heaven.

"Speak once for all!" cried the enraged governor, drawing his sword; "I am no waxen-hearted Hambledon, to be cajoled by your beauty. Declare where Wallace is concealed, or dread my vengeance."

The horrid steel gleamed across the eyes of the unhappy Marion; unable to sustain herself, she sank on the ground.

"Kneel not to me for mercy!" cried the fierce wretch; "I grant none, unless you confess your husband's hiding-place."

Strength darted from the heart of Lady Wallace to her voice. "I kneel to Heaven alone, and may it ever preserve my Wallace from the fangs of Edward and his tyrants!"

"Blasphemous wretch!" cried the infuriated Heselrigge, and in that moment he plunged his sword into her defenseless breast. Halbert, who had all this time been held back by the soldiers, could not believe that the fierce governor would perpetrate the deed he threatened; but seeing it done, with a terrible cry he burst from the hands which held him, and had thrown himself on the bleeding Marion before her murderer could strike his second blow. However, it fell, and pierced the neck of the faithful servant before it reached her heart. She opened her dying eyes, and seeing who it was that would have shielded her life, just articulated, "Halbert! my Wallace—to God—" and with the last unfinished sentence her pure soul took its flight.

The good old man's heart almost burst when he felt her bosom now motionless, and groaning with grief and fainting with loss of blood he lay senseless on her body.

A terrible stillness was now in the hall. Not a man spoke, all stood looking on each other with horror marking each pale countenance. Heselrigge, dropping his blood-stained sword on the ground, perceived by the behavior of his men that he had gone too far, and fearful of arousing them to some act against himself, he addressed the soldiers in an unusual accent of condescension: "My friends," said he, "we will now return to Lanark; to-morrow you may come back, for I reward your services of this night with the plunder of Ellerslie."

"May a curse light on him who carries a stick from its grounds!" exclaimed a veteran, from the further end of the hall. "Amen!" murmured all the soldiers with one consent; and falling back, they disappeared, one by one, out of the great door, leaving Heselrigge alone with the soldier who stood, leaning on his sword, looking on the murdered lady.

"Grimsby, why stand you there?" demanded Heselrigge: "follow me!"

"Never," returned the soldier.

"What!" exclaimed the governor, forgetting his panic; "dare you speak thus to your commander? March on before me this instant, or expect to be treated as a rebel!"

"I march at your command no more," replied the veteran, eying him resolutely; "the moment you perpetrated this bloody deed you became unworthy the name of man, and I should disgrace my own manhood were I ever again to obey the word of such a monster!"

"Villain!" cried the enraged Heselrigge, "you shall die for this!"

"That may be," answered Grimsby, "by the hands of some tyrant like yourself; but no brave man, not the royal Edward, would do otherwise than acquit his soldier for refusing obedience to the murderer of an innocent woman. It was not so he treated the wives and daughters of the slaughtered Saracens when I followed his banners over the fields of Palestine."

"Thou canting miscreant!" cried Heselrigge, springing on him suddenly, and aiming his dagger at his breast. But the soldier arrested the weapon, and at the same instant closing upon the assassin, with a turn of his foot threw him to the ground. Heselrigge, as he lay prostrate, seeing his dagger in his adversary's hand, with the most dastardly promises implored for life.

"Monster!" cried the soldier, "I would not pollute my honest hands with such unnatural blood. Neither, though thy hand has been lifted against my life, would I willingly take thine. I go far from you or your power; but if you forswear your voluntary oath, and attempt to seek me out for vengeance, remember it is a soldier of the cross you pursue, and retribution shall be demanded by Heaven at a moment you cannot avoid."

There was a determination in the voice and manner of the soldier that paralyzed the soul of the governor; he trembled, and repeating his oath of leaving Grimsby unmolested, at last obtained his permission to return to Lanark. The men, in obedience to the orders of their commander, had mounted their horses, and were now far out of sight. Heselrigge's charger was still in the court-yard: he was hurrying towards it, but the soldier, with a prudent suspicion, called out, "Stop, sir! you must walk to Lanark. The cruel are generally false: I cannot trust your word. Leave this horse here—to-morrow you may send for it, I shall then be far away."

Heselrigge saw that remonstrance would be unavailing, and shaking with rage, he turned into the path which, after five weary miles, would lead him once more to his citadel.

From the moment the soldier had dared to deliver his abhorrence of Lady Wallace's murder, he was aware that his life would no longer be safe within reach of Heselrigge; and determined alike by detestation of him and regard for his own preservation, he resolved to take shelter in the mountains, till he could have an opportunity of going beyond sea to join his king's troops in the Guienne wars.

Full of these thoughts he returned into the hall. As he approached the bleeding group on the floor he perceived it move; hoping that perhaps the unhappy lady might not be dead, he drew near; but, alas! as he bent to examine, he touched her hand and found it quite cold. Grimsby shuddered. Again he saw her move; but it was not with her own life—the recovering senses of her faithful servant, as his arms clung around the body, had disturbed the remains of her who would wake no more.

On seeing that existence yet struggled in one of these blameless victims, Grimsby did his utmost to revive the old man. He raised him from the ground, and poured some strong liquor into his mouth. Halbert breathed freer; and his kind surgeon, with the venerable harper's own plaid, bound up the wound in his neck. Halbert opened his eyes. When he fixed them on the rough features and English helmet of the soldier, he closed them again with a deep groan.

"My honest Scot," said Grimsby, "trust in me. I am a man like yourself, and though a Southron, am no enemy to age and helplessness."

The harper took courage at these words; he again looked at the soldier, but suddenly recollecting what had passed, he turned his eyes towards the body of his mistress. He started up, and staggering towards her, would have fallen, had not Grimsby supported him. "Oh what a sight is this!" cried he, wringing his hands. "My lovely lady! see how low she lies, who was once the delight of all eyes, the comforter of all hearts." The old man's sobs suffocated him. The veteran turned away his face; a tear dropped upon his hand. "Accursed Heselrigge," ejaculated he, "thy fate must come!"

"If there be a man's heart in all Scotland, it is not far distant!"

cried Halbert. "My master lives, and will avenge this murder. You weep, soldier; and you will not betray what has escaped me."

"I have fought in Palestine," returned he; "and a soldier of the cross betrays none who trust him. We must both hasten hence. Heselrigge will surely send in pursuit of me. He is too vile to forgive the truth I have spoken to him; and should I fall into his power, death is the best I could expect at his hands. Let me assist you to put this poor lady's remains into some decent place, and then, my honest Scot, we must separate."

Halbert, at these words, threw himself upon the bosom of his mistress, and wept with loud lamentations. In vain he attempted to raise her in his feeble arms. "I have carried thee scores of times in thy blooming infancy," cried he; "and now must I bear thee to thy grave? I had hoped that my eyes would have been closed by this dear hand." As he spoke, he pressed her hand to his lips with such convulsive sobs that the soldier, fearing he would expire in his agony, took him from the dead body, and exhorted him to suppress such grief for the sake of his master. Halbert gradually revived, and listening to him, cast a wistful look on the lifeless Marion.

"There sleeps the pride and hope of Ellerslie! O my master, my widowed master," cried he, "what will comfort thee?"

Fearing the consequence of further delay, the soldier again began his arguments for flight; and Halbert recollecting the oratory in which Wallace had ordered the body of Lord Mar to be deposited, named it for that of his dead lady. Grimsby, immediately wrapping the beauteous corse in the white garments which hung about it, raised it in his arms, and was conducted by Halbert to a little chapel in the heart of a neighboring cliff.

The old man removed the altar; and Grimsby, laying the shrouded Marion upon its rocky platform, covered her with the pall, which he drew from the holy table, and laid the crucifix upon her bosom. Halbert, when his beloved mistress was thus hidden from his sight, threw himself on his knees beside her, and offered up a prayer for her departed soul.

"Hear me, Judge of heaven and earth!" cried he; "as thou didst avenge the blood of innocence shed in Bethlehem, so let the gray hairs of Heselrigge be brought down to the grave, for the murder of this innocent lady!" Halbert kissed the cross, and rising from his knees went weeping out of the chapel, followed by the soldier.

Having closed the door and carefully locked it, Halbert proceeded in silence till he and his companion in passing the well were startled by a groan.

"Here is some one in extremity," cried the soldier. "Is it possible he lives?" exclaimed Halbert, bending down to the edge of the well with the same inquiry. "Yes," feebly answered the earl; "I still exist, but am very faint. If all be safe above, I pray remove me into the upward air." Halbert replied that it was indeed necessary he should ascend immediately, and lowering the rope, told him to tie the iron box to it and then himself. This done, with some difficulty and the assistance of the wondering soldier (who now expected to see the husband of the unfortunate Lady Wallace emerge to the knowledge of his loss), he at last effected the earl's release. For a few seconds the fainting nobleman supported himself on his countryman's shoulder, while the morning breeze gradually revived his exhausted frame. The soldier looked at his gray locks and furrowed brow, and marveled how such proofs of age could belong to the man whose resistless valor had discomfited Arthur Heselrigge and his myrmidons. However, his doubts of the veteran before him being other than the brave Wallace were soon satisfied by the earl himself, who asked for a draught of water; and while Halbert went to bring it, Lord Mar raised his eyes to inquire for Sir William and the Lady Marion. He started when he saw English armor on the man he would have accosted, and rising suddenly from the stone on which he sat, demanded, in a stern voice, "Who art thou?"

"An Englishman," answered the soldier; "one who does not, like the monster Heselrigge, disgrace the name. I would assist you, noble Wallace, to fly this spot. After that, I shall seek refuge abroad, and there, on the fields of Guienne, demonstrate my fidelity to my king."

Mar looked at him steadily. "You mistake; I am not Sir William Wallace."

At that moment Halbert came up with the water. The earl drank it, and turning to the venerable bearer, he asked of him whether his master were safe.

"I trust he is," replied the old man; "but you, my lord, must hasten hence. A foul murder has been committed here since he left it."

"But where is Lady Wallace?" asked the earl; "if there be such danger we must not leave her to meet it."

"She will never meet danger more," cried the old man clasping his hands; "she is in the bosom of the Virgin."

"What!" exclaimed the earl, hardly articulate with horror, "is Lady Wallace murdered?"

"Yes," said the soldier! "and detestation of so unmanly an outrage provoked me to desert his standard. But no time must now be lost in lamentation; Heselrigge will return, and if we also would not be sacrificed to his rage, we must hence immediately."

The earl, struck dumb at this recital, gave the soldier time to recount the particulars. When he had finished, Lord Mar saw the necessity for instant flight, and ordered horses to be brought from the stables. Though he had fainted in the well, the present shock gave such tension to his nerves, that he found, in spite of his wound, he could now ride without difficulty.

Halbert went as commanded, and returned with two horses. Having only amongst rocks and glens to go, he did not bring one for himself; and begging the good soldier might attend the earl to Bothwell, he added, "He will guard you and this box, which Sir William Wallace holds as his life. What it contains I know not, and none, he says, may dare to search into. But you will take care of it for his sake, till more peaceful times allow him to reclaim his own."

"Fatal box!" cried the soldier, "that was the leading cause which brought Heselrigge to Ellerslie."

"How?" inquired the earl. Grimsby then related that immediately after the return to Lanark of the detachment sent to Ellerslie, under the command of Sir Gilbert Hambledon, an officer arrived from the English garrison in Douglas, and told the governor that Sir William Wallace had that evening taken a quantity of treasure from the castle. His report was that the English soldiers who stood near the Scottish knight when he mounted saw a long iron coffer under his arm, but they thought not of it till they overheard Sir John Monteith muttering something about gold and a box. To intercept the robber, the soldiers deemed impracticable, and therefore their captain came immediately to lay the information before the Governor of Lanark. As the scabbard found in the affray with young Arthur had betrayed the victor to have been Wallace, this intimation of his having been also the instrument of wresting from the grasp of Heselrigge, perhaps the most valuable spoil in Douglas, inflamed him with the double furies of revenge and avarice, so he ordered out a new troop, and placing himself at its head took the way to Ellerslie. One of the servants, whom some of Hambledon's men had seized, confessed to Heselrigge that not only Wallace was in the house when it was attacked, but that the person whom he had rescued in the streets of Lanark, and who proved to be a wealthy nobleman, was there also. This whetted the eagerness of the governor to reach Ellerslie; and expecting to get a rich booty, without an idea of the horrors he was going to perpetrate, a large detachment of men followed him.

"To extort money from you, my lord," continued the soldier, "and to obtain that fatal coffer, were his main objects; but disappointed in his passion of avarice, he forgot he was a man, and the blood of innocence glutted his vengeance."

"Hateful gold!" cried Lord Mar, spurning the box with his foot; "it cannot be for itself the noble Wallace so greatly prizes it: it must be a trust."

"I believe it is," returned Halbert, "for he enjoined my lady to preserve it for the sake of his honor. Take care of it then, my lord, for the same sacred reason."

The Englishman made no objection to accompany the earl, and by a suggestion of his own, Halbert brought him a Scottish bonnet and cloak from the house.

"England shall hear more of this outrage!" cried Mar, as he threw himself across the horse. "Give me that fatal box, I will buckle it to my saddle-bow. Inadequate will be my utmost care of it, to repay the sorrows its preservation and mine have brought upon the head of my deliverer."

The soldier in silence mounted his horse, and Halbert opened a gate that led to the hills which lay between Ellerslie and Bothwell castle. Lord Mar took a golden-trophied bugle from his breast. "Give this to your master, and tell him that by whatever hands he sends it, the sight of it shall always command the services of Donald Mar. I go to Bothwell in expectation that he will join me there. In making it his home he will render me happy, for my friendship is now bound to him by bonds which only death can sever."

Halbert took the horn, and promising faithfully to repeat the earl's message, prayed God to bless him and the honest soldier. A rocky promontory soon excluded them from his sight, and in a few minutes more even the sound of the horses' hoofs was lost on the soft herbage of the winding dell.

"Now I am alone in this once happy spot. Not a voice, not a sound. O Wallace!" cried he, throwing up his venerable arms, "thy house is left unto thee desolate, and I am to be the fatal messenger." With the last words he struck into a deep ravine which led to the glen, and pursued his way in silence. He looked to the right and to the left; no smoke curling from behind the intersecting rocks reminded him of the morning hour, or invited him to take a moment's rest from his grievous journey. All was lonely and comfortless; and sighing bitterly over the devastation, he concealed the fatal sword and the horn under his cloak, and with a staff, which he broke from a withered tree, took his way down the winding craigs to the deep caves of Corie Lynn.

CHAPTER IV.

CORIE LYNN.

AFTER having traversed many a weary rood, the venerable minstrel of the house of Wallace, exhausted by fatigue, sat down on the declivity of a steep craig. The burning beams of the midday sun now beat upon the rocks, but a few berries from the brambles, which knit themselves over the path, with a draught of water from a friendly burn, offered themselves to revive his enfeebled limbs. Insufficient as they appeared, he took them, and strengthened by half an hour's rest, again he grasped his staff to pursue his way.

After breaking a passage through the shrubs that grew across the only footing in this wilderness, he went along the side of the expanding stream, which at every turning of the rocks increased in depth and violence. Prodigious craggy heights towered above his head as he ascended; while the rolling clouds which canopied their summits seemed descending to wrap him in their fleecy skirts, and the projecting rocks bending over the waters of the glen left him only a narrow shelf in the cliff, along which he crept till it brought him to the mouth of a cavern.

He must either enter it or return the way he came, or attempt the descent of overhanging precipices, which nothing could surmount but the pinions of their native birds. Above him was the mountain. Retread his footsteps until he had seen his beloved master he was resolved not to do. He therefore entered the cavity, and passing on, soon perceived an aperture, through which emerging on the other side he found himself again on the margin of the river. Having attained a wider bed, it left him a still narrower causeway to perform the remainder of his journey.

But an unlooked-for obstacle baffled his progress. A growing gloom he had not observed in the valley, having entirely overspread the heavens, at this moment suddenly discharged itself, amidst peals of thunder, in heavy floods of rain upon his head.

Fearful of being overwhelmed by the streams which now on all sides crossed his path, he kept upon the edge of the river, to be as far as possible from their violence. And thus he proceeded till the aug-

The pledge

mented storm of a world of waters, dashing from side to side, told him he was indeed not far from the fall of Corie Lynn.

The spray was spread in so thick a mist over the glen he knew not how to advance. A step farther might be on the firm earth, but might dash him into the roaring Lynn, where he would be ingulfed at once in its furious whirlpool. He paused and looked around. The rain had ceased, but the thunder still rolled at a distance. Halbert shook his gray locks, streaming with wet, and looked towards the sun, now gilding with its last rays the vast sheets of falling water.

"This is thine hour, my master," exclaimed the old man, "and surely I am too near the Lynn to be far from thee."

With these words he raised the pipe that hung at his breast, and blew three strains of the appointed air. In former days it used to call from her bower that "fair star of evening," the beauteous Marion, now departed forever into her native heaven. The notes trembled as he breathed them into the instrument; but though the roar of the cataract might have prevented their reaching a less attentive ear than that of Wallace, yet he sprang from the recess under the fall, and dashing through its waters, the next instant was at the side of Halbert.

"Faithful creature!" cried he, catching him in his arms with joy, "how fares my Marion?"

"I am weary," cried the heart-stricken old man; "take me within your sanctuary, and I will tell you all."

Wallace perceived that his time-worn servant was indeed exhausted; and knowing the hazards of the track he must have passed over in his way to this solitude, also remembering how, as he sat in his shelter, he had himself dreaded the effects of the storm upon so aged a traveler, he readily accounted for the pale countenance and tremulous step which at first had excited his alarm.

Giving the old man his hand he led him with caution to the brink of the Lynn, and then folding him in his arms, dashed with him through the tumbling water into the cavern he had chosen for his asylum. Halbert sank against its rocky side, and putting forth his hand to catch some of the water as it fell, drew a few drops to his parched lips and swallowed them. After this he breathed a little and turned his eyes upon his master.

"Are you sufficiently recovered, Halbert, to tell me how you left my dearest Marion?"

Halbert dreaded to see the light which now cheered him from the eyes of his master overclouded with the horrors his story must unfold; he evaded a direct reply. "I saw your guest in safety; I saw him and the iron box on their way to Bothwell."

"What!" inquired Wallace, "were we mistaken? was not the earl dead when we looked into the well?" Halbert replied in the negative, and was proceeding with an account of his recovery and his departure when Wallace interrupted him.

"But what of my wife, Halbert? why tell me of others before of her? She whose safety and remembrance are now my sole comfort."

"Oh, my dear lord!" cried Halbert, throwing himself on his knees in agony; "she remembers you where best her prayers can be heard. She kneels for her beloved Wallace before the throne of God."

"Halbert!" cried Sir William, in a low and fearful voice, "what would you say? My Marion—speak! tell me in one word, she lives!"

"In heaven."

At this confirmation of a sudden terror, imbibed from the ambiguous words of Halbert, Wallace covered his face with his hands and fell with a deep groan against the side of the cavern; a mist seemed passing over his eyes, life was receding, and gladly did he believe his spirit on the eve of joining hers.

In having declared that the idol of his master's heart no longer existed for him in this world, Halbert thought he had revealed the worst, and he went on: "Her latest breath was spent in prayer for you. 'My Wallace' were the last words her angel spirit uttered as it issued from her bleeding wounds."

The cry that burst from the heart of Wallace, as he started on his feet at this horrible disclosure, seemed to pierce through all the recesses of the glen, and was reechoed from rock to rock. Halbert threw his arms round his master's knees. The frantic blaze of his eyes struck him with affright. "Hear me, my lord; for the sake of your wife, now an angel hovering near you, hear what I have to say."

Wallace looked around with a wild countenance. "My Marion near me! Blessed spirit! Oh, my murdered wife! Who made those wounds?" cried he, catching Halbert's arm with a tremendous though unconscious grasp; "tell me who had the heart to aim a blow at that angel's life?"

"The Governor of Lanark," replied Halbert.

"How? for what?" demanded Wallace, with the glare of madness shooting from his eyes. "My wife! my wife! what had she done?"

"He came at the head of a band of ruffians, and seizing my lady, commanded her on the peril of her life to declare where you and the Earl of Mar and the box of treasure were concealed. My lady persisted to refuse him information, and in a deadly rage he plunged his sword into her breast." Wallace clenched his hands over his face, and Halbert went on. "Before he aimed a second blow I had broken from the men who held me and thrown myself on her bosom; but all could not save her: the villain's sword had penetrated her heart."

"Great God!" exclaimed Wallace, "dost thou hear this murder?" His hands were stretched towards heaven; then falling on his knees, with his eyes fixed, "Give me power, Almighty Judge," cried he, "to assert thy justice! Let me avenge this angel's blood, and then take me to thy mercy!"

"What is it you intend, my lord," cried Halbert, viewing with alarm the ferocity which now, blazing from every part of his countenance, seemed to dilate his figure with more than mortal daring. "What can you do? Your single arm——"

"I am not single—God is with me. I am his avenger." At the word he sprang from the cavern's mouth, and had already reached the topmost cliff when the piteous cries of Halbert recalled him to recollection, and returning to his faithful servant, he tried to soothe his fears, and spoke in a composed though determined tone. "I will lead you from this solitude to the mountains, where the shepherds of Ellerslie are tending their flocks. With them you will find a refuge till you have strength to reach Bothwell castle. Lord Mar will protect you for my sake."

Halbert now remembered the bugle, and putting it into his master's hand, with its accompanying message, asked for some testimony in return, that the earl might know he had delivered it safely. "Even a lock of your precious hair, my beloved master, will be sufficient."

"Thou shalt have it, severed from my head by my own dagger," answered Wallace, taking off his bonnet and letting his amber locks fall in tresses on his shoulders. Halbert burst into a fresh flood of tears, for he remembered how often it had been the delight of Marion to twist those bright tresses round her fingers. Wallace looked up as the old man's sobs became audible, and read his thoughts: "It will never be again, Halbert," cried he, and with a firm grasp of his dagger he cut off a handful of his hair.

"Here, Halbert," continued he, knotting it together, "take this to the Earl of Mar: it is all, most likely, he will ever see again of William Wallace. Should I fall, tell him to look on that, and in my wrongs read the miseries of Scotland, and remember that God armeth the patriot's hand. Let him act on that conviction, and Scotland may yet be free."

Halbert placed the lock in his bosom, but again repeated his entreaties that his master would accompany him to Bothwell castle. He urged the consolation he would meet from the good earl's friendship.

"If he indeed regard me," returned Wallace, "for my sake let him cherish you. My consolations must come from a higher hand: I go where it directs. If I live, you shall see me again; but twilight approaches—we must away. The sun must not rise again upon Heselrigge."

Halbert now followed Wallace, who drew him up the precipitous side of the Lynn, and then leaping from rock to rock, awaited with impatience the poor old harper, as he crept round a circuit of over-hanging cliffs, to join him on the summit of the craigs.

Together they struck into the most inaccessible defiles of the mountains, and proceeded till, on discerning smoke whitening the black sides of the impending rocks, Wallace saw himself near the objects of his search. He sprang on a high cliff projecting over this mountain valley, and blowing his bugle with a few notes of the well-known pibroch of Lanarkshire, was answered by the reverberation of a thousand echoes.

At the loved sounds which had not dared to visit their ears since the Scottish standard was lowered to Edward, the hills seemed teeming with life. Men rushed from their fastnesses, and women with their babes eagerly followed, to see whence sprang a summons so dear to every Scottish heart. Wallace stood on the cliff, like the newly aroused genius of his country: his long plaid floated afar, and his glittering hair, streaming on the blast, seemed to mingle with the golden fires which shot from the heavens.

"Scotsmen," cried Wallace, waving his sword, "I come to call you to vengeance. I come in the name of all ye hold dear, of the wives of your bosoms and the children in their arms, to tell you the poniard of England is unsheathed—innocence and age and infancy fall before it. Last night did Heselrigge, the English tyrant of Lanark, break into my house and murder my wife."

The shriek of horror that burst from every mouth interrupted Wallace. "Vengeance! vengeance!" was the cry of the men, while tumultuous lamentations for the sweet Lady of Ellerslie filled the air from the women.

Wallace sprang from the cliff into the midst of his brave countrymen: "Follow me, then, to strike the mortal blow!"

"Lead on!" cried a vigorous old man. "I drew this stout claymore last in the battle of Largs. *Life and Alexander* was then the word of victory: now, ye accursed Southrons, ye shall meet the slogan of *Death and Lady Marion.*"

"Death and Lady Marion!" was echoed with shouts from mouth to mouth. Every sword was drawn; and those hardy peasants who owned none, seizing the instruments of pasturage, armed themselves with wolf-spears, pickaxes, forks, and scythes.

Sixty resolute men now arranged themselves around their chief. Wallace, whose heart turned icy cold at the dreadful slogan of his Marion's name, more fiercely grasped his sword, and murmured to himself, "From this hour may Scotland date her liberty, or Wallace return no more. My faithful friends," cried he, turning to his men and placing his plumed bonnet on his head, "let the spirits of your fathers inspire your souls! ye go to assert that freedom for which they died. Before the moon sets, the tyrant of Lanark must fall in blood."

"Death and Lady Marion!" was the pealing answer that echoed from the hills.

Wallace again sprang on the cliffs. His brave peasants followed him; and taking their rapid march by a cut through the Cartlane craigs, leaping chasms and climbing perpendicular rocks, they suffered no obstacles to impede their steps while thus rushing onward like lions to their prey.

CHAPTER V.

LANARK CASTLE.

WALLACE and his little army now rapidly pursued their march. It was midnight—all was silent as they hurried through the glen, as they ascended the steep acclivities that led to the cliffs which overhung the vale of Ellerslie. Wallace must pass along their brow. Beneath was the tomb of his sacrificed Marion. He rushed forward to snatch one look, even of the roof which shrouded her beloved remains.

But in the moment before he mounted the intervening height, a soldier in English armor crossed the path, and was seized by his men. One of them would have cut him down, but Wallace turned away the weapon. "Hold, Scot!" cried he, "you are not a Southron, to strike the defenseless. This man has no sword."

The rescued man joyfully recognizing the voice of Wallace, exclaimed, "It is my lord! He has saved my life a second time!"

"Who are you?" asked Wallace: "that helmet can cover no friend of mine."

"I am your servant Dugald," returned the man; "he whom your brave arm saved from the battle-ax of Arthur Heselrigge."

"I cannot now ask you how you came by that armor; but if you be yet a Scot, throw it off and follow me."

"Not to Ellerslie, my lord," cried he; "it has been plundered and burnt to the ground by the Governor of Lanark."

"Then," exclaimed Wallace, striking his breast, "are the remains of my beloved Marion forever ravished from my eyes!"

He had now mounted the craig which overlooked Ellerslie. His once happy home had disappeared, and beneath lay a heap of smoking ashes. He hastened from the sight, and directing the point of his sword towards Lanark, reechoed with supernatural strength, "Forward!"

With the rapidity of lightning his little host flew over the hills, reached the cliffs which divided them from the town, and leaped down before the outward trench of the castle of Lanark. In a moment Wallace sprang so feeble a barrier; and with a shout of death, in which the tremendous slogan of his men now joined, he rushed upon the guard that held the northern gate.

Here slept the governor. These opponents being slain by the first sweep of the Scottish swords, Wallace hastened onward, winged with twofold retribution. The noise of battle was behind him, for the shout of his men had aroused the garrison and drawn its soldiers, half naked, to the spot. He reached the door of the governor. The sentinel who stood there flew before the terrible warrior that presented himself. All the mighty vengeance of Wallace blazed in his face and seemed to surround his figure with a terrible splendor. With one stroke of his foot he drove the door from its hinges and rushed into the room.

What a sight for the now awakened and guilty Heselrigge! It was the husband of the defenseless woman he had murdered, come in the power of justice, with vengeance in his eyes. With an outcry for the mercy he dared not expect, he fell back into the bed and sought an unavailing shield beneath its folds.

"Marion! Marion!" cried Wallace, as he threw himself towards the bed and buried his sword through the coverlid deep into the heart of her murderer. Drawing out the sword he took the streaming blade in his hand. "Vengeance is satisfied," cried he; "thus, O God! do I henceforth divide self from my heart!" As he spoke he snapt the sword in twain, and throwing away the pieces, put back with his hand the weapons of his brave companions, who, having cleared the passage of their assailants, had hurried forward to assist in ridding their country of so detestable a tyrant.

" 'Tis done," cried he and turned away; but the men exulting in the sight, with a shout of triumph exclaimed, "So fall the enemies of Sir William Wallace!"

"Rather so fall the enemies of Scotland!" cried he; "from this hour Wallace has neither love nor resentment but for her. Heaven has heard me devote myself to work our country's freedom or to die. Who will follow me in so just a cause?"

"All! with Wallace forever!"

The new clamor which this resolution excited intimidated a fresh band of soldiers, who were hastening across the court-yard to seek the enemy in the governor's apartments. But on the noise they hastily retreated, and no exertions of their officers could prevail on them to advance again when the resolute Scots with Wallace at their head soon afterwards issued from the great gate. The English commanders seeing the panic of their men, which they were less able to surmount on account of the way to the gate being strewn with their slain comrades, fell back into the shadow of the towers, where by the light of the moon, like men paralyzed, they viewed the departure of their enemies over the trenches.

CHAPTER VI.

CARTLANE CRAIGS.

THE sun was rising from the eastern hills when the victorious group reentered the mountain-glen where their families lay. The cheerful sounds of their bugles aroused the sleepers from their caves, and many were the embraces which welcomed the warriors to affection and repose.

Wallace, while he threw himself along a bed of purple heath, gathered for him by many a busy hand, listened with a calmed mind to the inquiries of Halbert, who, awakened by the first blast of the horn, had started from his shelter to hail the return of his master. While his followers retired each to the bosom of his family, the chief of Ellerslie remained alone with the old man, and recounted to him the success of his enterprise, and the double injuries he had avenged. "The assassin," continued he, "has paid with his life for his inexpiable crime. He is slain, and with him several of Edward's garrison. My vengeance may be appeased; but all else is lost to me: I have now nothing to do with this world but as I may be the instrument of good to others. The Scottish sword has now been redrawn against our foes; and with the blessing of Heaven, I swear it shall not be sheathed till Scotland be rid of the tyranny which has slain my happiness. Death or liberty must be the future fate of Wallace and his friends."

At these words tears ran down the cheeks of the venerable harper. "Alas! my master," exclaimed he, "what is it you would do? For the sake of her memory whom you deplore; in pity to the worthy Earl of Mar, who will arraign himself as the cause of all these calamities, and of your death, should you fall, retract this desperate vow."

"No, my good Halbert," returned Wallace, "I am neither desperate nor inefficient; and you, faithful creature, shall have no cause to mourn this night's resolution. Go to Lord Mar and tell him what are my resolves. I have nothing now that binds me to life but my country. Would you, by persuading me to resign my interest in her, devote me to a hermit's seclusion amongst these rocks? for I will never again appear in the tracks of men if it be not as the defender of her rights."

"But where, my master, shall we find you, should the earl choose to join you with his followers?"

"In this wilderness, whence I shall not remove rashly. My purpose is to save my countrymen, not to sacrifice them in needless dangers."

Halbert, oppressed with sorrow, bowed his head with submission, and leaving Wallace to his rest, retired to the mouth of the cavern to weep alone.

It was noon before the chief awaked from the death-like sleep into which nature had plunged his senses. He opened his eyes languidly, and when the sight of his rocky apartment forced on him the recollection of all his miseries, he uttered a deep groan. That sad sound, so different from the jocund voice with which Wallace used to issue from his rest, struck on the heart of Halbert: he drew near his master to receive his last commands for Bothwell. "On my knees," added he, "will I implore the earl to send you succors."

"He needs not prayers for that," returned Wallace; "but depart, dear Halbert; it will comfort me to know you are in safety, and whithersoever you go you carry my blessings with you."

Old age opens the fountain of tears; Halbert's flowed profusely, and bathed his master's hand. Could Wallace have wept, it would have been then; but with a voice of assumed cheerfulness he renewed his efforts to encourage his desponding servant. Persuaded that a superior Being did indeed call his beloved master to exertions for Scotland, Halbert bade him an anxious farewell, and then withdrew to commit him to the companions of his destiny.

After traversing many a weary mile, between Cartlane craigs and Bothwell castle, Halbert reached the valley in which that fortress stands; and calling to the warder at its gates, that he came from Sir William Wallace, was immediately admitted, and conducted into the castle.

Halbert was led by a servant into a spacious chamber, where the earl lay upon a couch. A lady, richly habited, and in the bloom of life, sat at his head. Another, much younger, and of resplendent beauty, knelt at his feet, with a salver of medicinal cordials in her hand. The Lady Marion's loveliness had been that of soft moonlight evening, but the face which now turned upon Halbert as he entered was full of light, and splendor, and joy; and the old man's eyes, even though dimmed in tears, were dazzled. A young man stood near her. On the entrance of Halbert, whom the earl instantly recognized, he raised himself on his arm and welcomed him. The young lady rose and the young man stepped eagerly forward.

The earl inquired anxiously for Sir William Wallace, and asked if he might expect him soon at Bothwell.

"He cannot yet come, my lord," replied Halbert; "hard is the task he has laid upon his valiant head, but he is avenged: he has slain the Governor of Lanark." A faint exclamation broke from the lips of the young lady.

"How?" demanded the earl.

Halbert now gave an account of the anguish of Wallace when he was told of the events which had taken place at Ellerslie. As the honest harper described the zeal with which the shepherds on the heights took up arms to avenge the wrong done to their chief, the countenance of the young lady and of the youth glowed through tears; they looked on each other; and Halbert proceeded:

"When my master and his valiant troop were pursuing their way to Lanark, he was met by Dugal, the wounded man who had rushed into the room to apprise us of the advance of the English forces. During the confusion of that night he crept away, and concealed himself from the soldiers amongst the bushes of the glen. When all was over, he came from his hiding-place; and finding the English soldier's helmet and cloak, and still fearful of falling in with any straggling party of Heselrigge's, he disguised himself in those Southron clothes. He was venturing towards the house in search of food, when he was surprised by seeing flames issue from the windows. Soldiers poured from the doors with shouts of triumph; some carried off the booty, and others watched by the fire till the interior of the building was consumed and the rest sunk a heap of smoking ruins.

"The work completed, these ministers of devastation left the vale to its own solitude. Dugald, after waiting a long time, crawled from the bushes; and ascending the cliffs, he was speeding to the mountains, when, encountering our armed shepherds, they mistook him for an English soldier, and seized him. The chief of ruined Ellerslie recognized his servant, and with redoubled indignation his followers heard the history of the ashes before them."

"Brave, persecuted Wallace!" exclaimed the earl, "how dearly was my life purchased! But proceed, Halbert; tell me that he returned safe from Lanark."

Halbert now recounted the dreadful scenes which took place in that town, and that when the governor fell, Wallace made a vow never to mingle with the world again till Scotland should be free.

"Alas!" cried the earl, "what miracle is to effect that? Surely he will not bury that prime of manhood within the gloom of a cloister."

"No, my lord; he has retired to the fastnesses of Cartlane craigs."

"Why?" resumed Mar; "why did he not rather fly to me? This castle is strong; and while one stone of it remains upon another, not all the hosts of England should take him hence."

"It was not your friendship he doubted," returned the old man; "love for his country compels him to reject all comfort in which she does not share. His last words to me were these: 'I have nothing now to do but to assert the liberties of Scotland and to rid her of her enemies. Go to Lord Mar and take this lock of my hair; it is all, most likely, he will ever again see of William Wallace. Should I fall, tell him to look on that, and in my wrongs read the future miseries of Scotland, and remember that God armeth the patriot.'"

Tears dropped so fast from the young lady's eyes, she was obliged to walk to a window to restrain a more violent burst of grief.

"O my uncle!" cried the youth, "surely the freedom of Scotland is possible. I feel in my soul that the words of the brave Wallace are prophetic."

The earl held the lock of hair in his hands; he regarded it, lost in meditation.

"'God armeth the patriot!'" He paused again; then raising the sacred present to his lips, "Yes," cried he, "thy vow shall be performed; and while Donald Mar has an arm to wield a sword, or a man to follow to the field, thou shalt command both him and them!"

"But not as you are, my lord," cried the elder lady; "your wounds are yet unhealed. Would it not be madness to expose your safety at such a crisis?"

"I shall not take arms myself," answered he, "till I can bear them to effect; meanwhile all of my clan and of my friends that I can raise to guard the life of my deliverer, and to promote the cause, must be summoned. This lock shall be my pennon; and what Scotsman will look on that and shrink from his colors? Here, Helen, my child," cried he, addressing the young lady, "before to-morrow's dawn have this hair wrought into my banner. It will be a patriot's standard; and let his own irresistible words be the motto—*God armeth me!*"

Helen advanced with trepidation. Having been told by the earl of the valor of Wallace and of the cruel death of his lady, she had conceived a gratitude and a pity deeper than language could express for the man who had lost so much by succoring one so dear to her. She took the lock, waving in yellow light upon her hands, and, trembling with emotion, was leaving the room, when she heard her cousin throw himself on his knees.

"I beseech you, my honored uncle," cried he, "if you have love for me, or value for my future fame, allow me to be the bearer of yon banner to Sir William Wallace."

Helen stopped at the threshold to hear the reply.

"You could not, my dear nephew," returned the earl, "have asked me any favor I could grant with so much joy. To-morrow I will collect the peasantry of Bothwell, and with those and my own followers you shall join Wallace the same night."

Ignorant of the horrors of war, Helen sympathized in the ardor of her cousin, and with a thrill of delight hurried to her apartment to commence her task.

Far different were the sentiments of the young countess, her stepmother. As soon as Lord Mar had let this declaration escape his lips, alarmed at the effect so much agitation might have on his enfeebled constitution, and fearful of the cause he ventured thus openly to espouse, she desired his nephew to take the grateful Halbert and see that he was attended with hospitality.

When the room was left to the earl and herself, she ventured to remonstrate with him upon the facility with which he had become a party in so treasonable a matter: "Consider, my lord," continued she, "that Scotland is now entirely in the power of the English monarch. His garrisons occupy our towns, his creatures hold every place of trust in the kingdom."

"And is such a list of oppressions, my dear lady, to be an argument for longer bearing them? Had I and other Scottish nobles dared to resist this overwhelming power after the battle of Dunbar, Scotland might now be free, I should not have been insulted by our English tyrants in the streets of Lanark, and to save my life William Wallace would not now be mourning his murdered wife, and without a home to shelter him!"

Lady Mar paused at this observation, but resumed: "That may be true. But the die is cast; Scotland is lost forever; and, by your attempting to assist your friend, you will only lose yourself also, without preserving him. Now that the contention between the two kings is past, now that Baliol has surrendered his crown to Edward, is not Scotland at peace?"

"A bloody peace, Joanna," answered the earl; "witness these wounds. I have now seen and felt enough of Edward's jurisdiction. It is time I should awake, and, like Wallace, determine to die for Scotland, or avenge her."

Lady Mar wept. "Cruel Donald! is this the reward of all my love and duty? you tear yourself from me, you consign your estates to sequestration, you rob your children of their name; nay, by your example you stimulate our brother Bothwell's son to head the band that is to join this madman, Wallace."

"Hold, Joanna!" cried the earl; "what is it I hear? You call the hero who, in saving your husband's life, reduced himself to these cruel extremities, a madman! Was he mad because he prevented the Countess of Mar from being a widow? Was he mad because he prevented her children from being fatherless?"

The countess, overcome by this reproach, threw herself upon her husband's neck. "Alas, my lord!" cried she, "all is madness to me that would plunge you into danger. Think of your own safety, of my innocent twins now in their cradle. Think of our brother's feelings when you send his only son to join one he, perhaps, will call a rebel."

"If Earl Bothwell considered himself a vassal of Edward's, he would not now be with Lord Loch-awe. From the moment that gallant Highlander retired to Argyleshire, the King of England regarded his adherents with suspicion. Bothwell's present visit to Loch-awe, you see, is sufficient to sanction the plunder of this castle by the peaceful government you approve. You saw the opening of those proceedings. And had they come to their dreadful issue, where, my dear Joanna, would now be your home, your husband, your children? It was the arm of the brave chief of Ellerslie which saved them from destruction."

Lady Mar shuddered. "I admit the truth of what you say. But, oh! is it not hard to put my all to the hazard; to see the bloody field on one side of my beloved Donald, and the mortal scaffold on the other?"

"Hush!" cried the earl; "it is justice that beckons me, and victory will receive me to her arms. Let the victorious field for Scotland be Donald Mar's grave, rather than doom him to live a witness of her miseries!"

"I cannot stay to hear you," answered the countess; "I must invoke the Virgin to give me courage to be a patriot's wife; at present, your words are daggers to me."

In uttering this she hastily withdrew, and left the earl to concert plans for the portentous future.

CHAPTER VII.

BOTHWELL CASTLE.

MEANWHILE the Lady Helen had retired to her own apartments. Lord Mar's banner being brought to her from the armory, she sat down to weave into its silken texture the amber locks of the Scottish chief. Admiring their softness and beauty, while her needle flew she pictured to herself the fine countenance they had once adorned.

"Unhappy Lady Wallace!" sighed she to herself; "what a pang must have rent her heart when the stroke of death tore her from such a husband! and how must he have loved her, when for her sake he thus forswears all future joys but those which camps and victories may yield! Ah, what would I give to be my cousin Murray, to bear this pennon at his side! To be that man's friend would be a higher honor than to be Edward's queen."

Her heart was thus discoursing with itself when a page opened the door, from her cousin, who begged admittance. She had just fastened the flowing charge into its azure field, and while embroidering the motto, gladly assented.

"You know not, my good old man," said the gallant Murray to Halbert, as he conducted him across the galleries, "what a noble mind is contained in that lovely young creature. I was brought up with her, and to her do I owe that love of true glory which carries me to the side of Sir William Wallace. I know she rejoices in my present destination, and to prevent her hearing from your own lips all you have now told me of the virtues of my intended commander, all you have said of the heroism of his wife, would be depriving her of a mournful pleasure, only to be appreciated by a heart such as hers."

The gray-haired bard of Ellerslie, who had ever received the dearest rewards of his songs in the smiles of its mistress, did not require persuasion to appear before the gentle Lady of Mar, or to recite in her ears the story of departed loveliness.

Helen rose as he and her cousin appeared. Murray approved the execution of her work, and Halbert, with a full heart, took the pennon in his hand. "Ah! little did my dear lady think," exclaimed he, "that one of these loved locks would lead men to battle! What changes have a few days made! She, the gentlest of women, laid in a bloody

46

grave; and he, the most benevolent of human beings, wielding an exterminating sword!"

"You speak of her grave, venerable man," inquired Helen; "had you, then, an opportunity of performing the rites of sepulture to her remains?"

"No, madam," replied he; "after the worthy English soldier, now in this castle, assisted me to place her precious body in my lord's oratory, I had no opportunity of returning to give her a more holy grave."

"Alas!" cried Helen; "then her sacred relics have been consumed in the burning house!"

"I hope not," rejoined Halbert; "the chapel I speak of is at some distance from the main building. It was excavated in the rock by Sir Ronald Crawford, who gave the name of Ellerslie to this estate, in compliment to Sir William's place of birth in Renfrewshire, and bestowed it on the bridal pair. Both the parents of my honored master died in the bloom of their lives; and a grievous task will it be to whoever is to tell the good Sir Ronald that the last sweet flower of Ellerslie is now cut down!"

The tears of the venerable harper bore testimony to his resolve that this messenger should not be himself. Lady Helen, who had fallen into a reverie during the latter part of his speech, now spoke, and with something of eagerness.

"Then we may hope," rejoined she, "that the oratory has not only escaped the flames, but perhaps the access of the English soldiers? Would it not comfort your lord to have that sweet victim entombed according to the rites of the Church?"

"Surely, my lady; but how can that be done? He thinks her remains were lost in the conflagration of Ellerslie; and for fear of precipitating him into new dangers, I did not disprove his mistake."

"But her body shall be brought away," rejoined Lady Helen; "it shall have holy burial."

"To effect this, command my services," exclaimed Murray.

Helen thanked him for an assistance which would render the completion of her design easy. The English soldier as guide, and a troop from Bothwell, must accompany him.

"Alas! my young lord," interposed Halbert, "suppose you should meet some of the English still loitering there."

"And what of that, my honest Halbert, would not I and my trusty band make them clear the way? Is it not to give comfort to the deliverer of my uncle that I seek the glen? and shall anything in mortal shape make Andrew Murray turn his back? No, Halbert, I was not born on Saint Andrew's day for naught; and by his bright cross I swear either to lay Lady Wallace in the tomb of my ancestors, or to leave my bones to blanch on the grave of hers."

Helen loved the resolution of her cousin; and believing that Ellerslie had now no attractions to hold marauders amongst its ruins, she dismissed Lord Andrew to make his preparations, and turned herself to prefer her suit accordingly to her father.

Ere Halbert withdrew he respectfully put her hand to his lips. "Good night," continued she; "ere you see me again, I trust the earthly part of the angel now in paradise will be safe within these towers."

On entering her father's apartment, Lady Helen found him alone. She repeated to him the substance of her conversation with Wallace's faithful servant; "and my wish is," continued she, "to have the murdered lady's remains entombed in the cemetery of this castle."

The earl approved her request with expressions of satisfaction at the filial affection which her gratitude to his preserver evinced.

"May I then, my dear father," returned she, "have your permission to pay our debt to Sir William Wallace, to the utmost of our power?"

"You are at liberty, my noble child, to do as you please. My vassals, my coffers, are all at your command."

Helen kissed his hand. "May I have what I please from the Bothwell armory?"

"Command even there," said the earl; "your uncle Bothwell is too true a Scot to grudge a sword in so pious a cause."

Helen threw her arms about her father's neck, thanking him tenderly, and retired to prosecute her plans. Murray, who met her in the anteroom, informed her that fifty men, the sturdiest in the glen, awaited her orders; while she, telling her cousin of the earl's approval, took the sacred banner in her hand, and followed him to the gallery in the hall.

The moment she appeared, a shout of joy bade her welcome. Murray waved his hand in token of silence, while she, smiling upon them, spoke with agitation: "My brave friends," said she, "I thank you for the ardor with which, by this night's enterprise, you assist me to pay, in part, the tribute due to the man who preserved to me the blessing of a father."

"And to us, noble lady," cried they, "the most generous of chiefs."

"With that spirit, then," returned she, "I address ye with greater confidence. Who amongst you will shrink from following this standard to the field for Scotland's honor? Who will refuse to make himself the guardian of the life of Sir William Wallace?"

"None are here," cried a young man, advancing before his fellows, "who would not gladly die in his defense."

"We swear it!" burst from every lip at once.

She bowed her head, and said, "Return from Ellerslie to-morrow with the bier of its sainted mistress. I will then bestow upon every man in this band a war-bonnet plumed with my colors; and this banner shall then lead you to the side of Sir William Wallace. In the shock of battle look at its golden ensign, and remember that God not only *armeth the patriot's hand,* but shieldeth his heart."

"Wallace and Lady Helen! to death or liberty!" was the response to this exhortation; and smiling, in token of thanks to them and to Heaven, she retired in the midst of their acclamations. Murray, ready armed for his expedition, met her at the door. Restored to his usual vivacity by the emotions which the present scene awakened in his heart, he forgot the horrors which had aroused his zeal in the glory of anticipated victory; and giving her a gay salutation, led her back to her apartments, where the English soldier awaited her commands. Lady Helen, with a gentle grace, commended his noble resentment of Heselrigge's violence.

"Lands in Mar shall be yours," added she, "or a post of honor in the little army the earl is now going to raise. Speak but the word, and you shall find, worthy Englishman, that neither a Scotsman nor his daughter knows what it is to be ungrateful."

The blood mounted into the soldier's cheek. "I thank you, lady, for this generous offer; but, as I am an Englishman, I dare not accept it. My arms are due to my own fatherland, and I should be unwarranted in breaking her bonds. I left Heselrigge because he dishonored my country, and for me to forswear her would be to make myself infamous. Hence all I ask is, that after I have this night obeyed your gracious commands in leading your men to Ellerslie, the Earl of Mar will allow me instantly to depart for the nearest port."

Lady Helen replied that she revered his sentiments; and taking a diamond clasp from her bosom, she put it into his hand: "Wear that in remembrance of your virtue and of Helen Mar's gratitude." The man kissed it respectfully, and bowing, swore to preserve the gift to the latest hour of his existence.

Helen retired to her chamber to finish her task, and Murray, bidding her good night, repaired to the earl's apartments to take his final orders before he and his troop set out for the ruins of Ellerslie.

CHAPTER VIII.

BOTHWELL CHAPEL.

Night having passed over the inhabitants of Bothwell castle, the Earl of Mar was carried from his chamber and laid on a couch in the state apartment. His lady had not yet left the room of his daughter, by whose side she had lain the whole night, in hopes of infecting her with the fears which possessed herself.

Helen replied that she could see no reason for such apprehensions, if her father, instead of joining Wallace in person, would, when he had sent him succors, retire with his family into the Highlands, and there await the issue of the contest. "It is too late to retreat, dear madam," continued she; "the first blow against the public enemy was struck in defense of Lord Mar, and would you have my father act so base a part as to abandon his preserver?"

"Alas, my child!" answered the countess, "what great service will he have done to me or to your father if he deliver him from one danger, only to plunge him into another? Edward's power in this country is too great to be resisted now. Have not most of our barons sworn fealty to him? and are not the potent families of the Cummin, the Soulis, and the March all in his interest? You may perhaps say that most of these are my relations, and that I may turn them which way I will; but if I have no influence with a husband, it would be madness to expect it over more distant kindred. How then, with such a host against him, can your father venture, without despair, to support the man who breaks the peace with England?"

"Who can despair, honored lady," returned Helen, "in so just a cause? Let us rather believe with our good King David, that 'Honor must hope always; for no real evil can befall the virtuous, either in this world or in the next.' Were I a man, the justice that leads on the brave Wallace would nerve my arm with the strength of a host!"

Helen's heart panted with a foretaste of the delight she would feel, when all her patriotic wishes should be fulfilled; and pressing the now completed banner to her breast, her lips moved, though her voice did not utter the rapture of her heart.

Lady Mar looked at her. "It is well, romantic girl, that you are of my own powerless sex; had it been otherwise, your disobedience might have made me rue the day I became your father's wife."

"Sex," returned Helen, mildly, "could not have altered my sense of duty. Whether man or woman, I would obey you in all things consistent with my duty to a higher power; but when that commands, then, by the ordinance of Heaven, we must 'leave father and mother, and cleave unto it.' "

"And what, O foolish Helen! do you call a higher duty than that of a child to a parent, or a husband to his wife?"

"Duty of any kind," respectfully answered the young daughter of Mar, "cannot be transgressed with innocence. Nor would it be any relinquishing of duty to you should my father leave you to take up arms in the assertion of his country's rights, for her rights are your safety."

"Who taught you this sophistry, Helen? Not your heart, for it would start at the idea of your father's blood."

Helen turned pale. "Perhaps, madam, had not the preservation of my father's blood occasioned such malignity from the English that nothing but an armed force can deliver his preserver, I too might be content to see Scotland in slavery. But now, to wish my father to shrink behind the excuse of far-strained family duties, and to abandon Sir William Wallace to the bloodhounds who hunt his life, would be to devote the name of Mar to infamy."

"Then it is to preserve Sir William Wallace you are thus anxious. My husband, his vassals, your cousin, and, in short, the sequestration of the estates of Mar and Bothwell, are all to be put to the hazard on account of a frantic outlaw; to whom, since the loss of his wife, I should suppose death would be preferable to any gratitude we can pay him."

Lady Helen, at this ungrateful language, inwardly thanked Heaven that she inherited no part of the blood which animated so unfeeling a heart. "That he is an outlaw, Lady Mar, springs from us. That death would be the comforter of his sorrows, also, he owes to us; for was it not for my father's sake that his wife fell, and that he himself was driven into the wilds? I do not, then, blush for making his preservation my first prayer; and that he may achieve the freedom of Scotland is my second."

"We shall see whose prayers will be answered first," returned Lady Mar. "My saints are perhaps nearer than yours, and before the close of this day you will have reason to repent such extravagant opinions."

"Till now, you never disapproved them."

"I allowed them in your infancy," replied the countess, "because I thought they went no further than a minstrel's song; but since they are become so dangerous, I rue the hour in which I permitted you and your sister to remain at Thirlestane, to imbibe these romantic ideas from the wizard of Ercildown.* Had not Sir Richard been your own mother's father I would not have been so easily prevailed on, and thus am I rewarded for my indulgence."

"I hope, honored madam," said Helen, "you will never be ill-rewarded for that indulgence, either by my grandfather, my sister, or myself. Isabella, in the quiet of Thirlestane, has no chance of giving you the offense that I do; and I am forced to offend you, because I cannot disobey my conscience. Cannot you, dear Lady Mar," continued she, forcing a smile, "pardon the daughter of your early friend, my mother, who loved you as a sister? Cannot you forgive her Helen for revering justice, even more than your favor?"

Influenced by Helen's sweet humility, the countess relaxed the frigid air she had assumed; and kissing her, with many injunctions to bless the hand that might put a stop to so ruinous an enthusiasm in her family, she quitted the room.

As soon as Helen was alone, she called to recollection the generous permission with which her father had endowed her the night before, and wrapping herself in her mantle, and, attended by her page, proceeded to the armory. The armorer was already there, having just given out arms for three hundred men, who, by the earl's orders, were to assemble by noon on Bothwell moor.

Helen told the man she came for the best suit of armor in his custody—"one of the most excellent proof."

He drew from an oaken chest a coat of black mail studded with gold. Helen admired its strength and beauty. "It is the richest in all Scotland," answered he, "and was worn by our great Canmore in all his victories."

"Then it is worthy its destination. Bring it, with its helmet and sword, to my apartment."

The armorer took it up, and, accompanied by the page carrying the lighter parts, followed her into the western tower.

When Helen was again alone, it being yet very early in the morning, she employed herself in pluming the casque, and forming the scarf she meant should adorn her present. Thus time flew, till the sand-glass told her it was the eighth hour. But ere she had finished her task she was roused from the profound stillness in which that part

* Thomas of Ercildown, usually called *The Rhymer*.

of the castle lay, by the doleful lament of the troop returning from Ellerslie.

She dropped the half-formed scarf from her hand, and listened, without daring to draw her breath, to the deep-toned lamentations. She thought that she had never before heard the dirge of her country so thrillingly awful. Her head fell on the armor and scarf. "Sweet lady," sighed she to herself, "who is it that dares thus invade thy duties? But my gratitude to thy once-loved lord will not offend thy pure spirit." Again the mournful wailings on the air; and with a convulsion of feelings she could not restrain, she threw herself on her knees, and leaning her head on the newly adorned helmet, wept profusely.

Murray entered the room unobserved. "Helen, my dear cousin!" cried he. She started, and rising, apologized for her tears by owning the truth. He now told her that the body of Lady Marion was deposited in the chapel of the castle, and that the priests from the adjacent priory only awaited her presence to consign it, with the Church's rites, to its tomb.

Helen retired for a few minutes to recover herself, and then was led by her cousin to the awful scene.

The bier lay before the altar. The prior of St. Fillan stood at its head; a band of monks were ranged on each side. The maids of Lady Helen, in mourning garments, met their mistress at the portal. They had wrapped the beautiful corpse in the shroud prepared for it; and now having laid it, strewed with flowers, upon the bier, they advanced to their trembling lady, expecting her to approve their services. Helen drew near—she bowed to the priests and waving her hand to the prior to begin, the bier was lowered into the tomb beneath. As it descended, Helen sank upon her knees, and the anthem for departed souls was raised. The pealing notes, as they rose and swelled, seemed to bear up the spirit of the sainted Marion to its native heaven; and the tears which now flowed from the eyes of Helen seemed the balm of paradise descending upon her soul.

When all was over, the venerable Halbert, who had concealed his overwhelming sorrow behind a pillar, threw himself on the cold stone which now closed the last chamber of his mistress. With faint cries he gave way to the woe that shook his aged bosom, and called on death to lay him low with her. The women of Lady Helen again chanted forth their melancholy wailings for the dead; and unable longer to bear the scene, she grasped the arm of her cousin, and with difficulty walked from the chapel.

CHAPTER IX.

BOTHWELL DUNGEONS

HAVING rewarded his trusty followers with their promised war-bonnets from the hand of Helen, and despatched them to the foot of Cartlane craigs, to await his arrival with the larger levy, Murray proceeded to the apartment of Lord Mar to inform him how far he had executed his commands, and to learn his future orders. He found the veteran earl surrounded by arms and armed men; fifty brave Scots, who were to lead the three hundred then on Bothwell moor, were receiving their spears and swords and other weapons from the hands of their lord.

"Bear these stoutly, my gallant countrymen," cried he, "and remember, that although the dragon of England has burnt up your harvests and laid your homes in ashes, there is yet a lion in Scotland to wither his power."

The earl had hardly uttered those words when the double-doors of the apartment were abruptly opened, and all eyes were blasted by the sudden sight of Lord Soulis and a man in splendid English armor, with a train of Southron soldiers, following this recreant Scot.

The earl started from his couch "Lord Soulis, what is the occasion of this unapprised visit?"

"The ensign of the liege lord of Scotland is my warrant," replied he: "you are my prisoner, and in the name of King Edward of England I take possession of this castle."

"Never!" cried the earl, "while there is a man's arm within it."

"Man and woman," returned Lord Soulis, "must surrender to Edward. Three thousand English have seized three hundred of your insurgents on Bothwell moor. The castle is surrounded, and resistance impossible. Throw down your arms!" cried he, turning to the clansmen, who thronged round their chief, "or be hanged for rebellion against your lawful sovereign."

"Our lawful sovereign," returned a young man who stood near him, "must be the enemy of Edward; and to none else will we yield our arms."

"Traitor!" cried the English commander, while with a sudden stroke of his battle-axe he laid the body of the generous Scot a headless corpse at his feet. A direful cry proceeded from his enraged comrades. Every sword was drawn; and before the bewildered earl could utter a word, he beheld his brave Scots at one moment victorious, and in the next the floor strewed with their dead bodies. A new succession of bloodhounds had rushed in at every door; and before the sword was allowed to rest, the whole of his faithful troops lay around him, wounded and dying. In vain his voice had called upon his men to surrender—in vain he had implored the iron-hearted Soulis, and his coadjutor Aymer de Valence, to stop the havoc of death.

All now lay in blood; and the heat of the room, thronged by the victors, became so intolerable that De Valence, for his own sake, ordered the earl to be removed into another apartment.

Meanwhile, unconscious of these events, Helen had lain down to seek a few minutes' repose; and having watched the whole of the preceding night, was sunk into a profound sleep.

Murray, who was present at the abrupt entrance of the enemy, no sooner heard them declare that the castle was surrounded by an army, than he foresaw all would be lost. On the instant, and before the dreadful signal of carnage was given in the fall of the young Scot, he slid behind the canopy of his uncle's couch, and lifting the arras, hastily made his way to the chamber of his cousin. As he hurried along, he heard a fearful shout. He paused for a moment, but thinking it best, whatever might have happened, to secure the safety of Helen, he flew onward and entered her room. She lay upon the bed in a deep sleep. "Awake, Helen!" cried he; "for your life awake!"

She opened her eyes; but, without allowing her time to speak, he hastily added, "The castle is full of armed men led hither by the English commander Aymer de Valence and the execrable Soulis. Unless you fly through the vaulted passage you will be their prisoner."

Helen gazed at him in terror. "Where is my father? Leave him, I cannot."

"Fly, in pity to your father! Oh, do not hesitate! What will be his anguish should you fall into the hands of the furious man whose love you have rejected, when it will no longer be in the power of a parent to preserve you! If you had seen Soulis's threatening eyes——" He was interrupted by a clamor in the opposite gallery and the shrieks of women. Helen grasped his arm. "Alas, my poor damsels! I will go with you, whither you will, to be far from him."

As Murray threw his arm about her waist, to impel her failing steps, his eyes fell on the banner and the suit of armor.

"All else must be left," exclaimed he, seizing the banner; and hurrying Helen forward, he hastened with her down the stairs which led from the western watch-tower to the vaults beneath the castle. On entering the first cellar, to which a dim light was admitted through a small grating near the top, he looked round for the archway that contained the avenue of their release. Having descried it, and raised one of the large flags which paved the floor, he assisted his affrighted cousin down a short flight of steps into the secret passage. "This," whispered he, "will carry us in a direct line to the cell of the prior of St. Fillan's."

"But what will become of my father and Lady Mar? This flight, while they are in danger! oh, I fear to complete it!"

"Rather fear the libertine Soulis," returned Murray: "he can only make them prisoners; and even that injury shall be of short duration. I will soon join the brave Wallace, and then, my sweet cousin, liberty, and a happy meeting!"

"Alas! his venerable harper," cried she, suddenly remembering Halbert; "should he be discovered to have belonged to Wallace, he, too, will be massacred by these merciless men."

Murray stopped. "Have you courage to remain in this darkness alone? If so, I will seek him, and he shall accompany us."

Helen had courage for anything but the dangers Murray might encounter by returning into the castle; but the generous youth had entered too fully into her apprehensions concerning the old man to be withheld. "Should I be delayed in coming back," said he, "go forward to the end of this passage; it will lead you to a flight of stairs; ascend them; and by drawing the bolt of a door you will find yourself at once in the prior's cell."

"Talk not of delay," replied Helen; "return quickly, and I will await you at the entrance of the passage." So saying, she swiftly retraced with him her steps to the bottom of the stairs. He raised the flag, sprang out of the aperture, and closing it down, left her in solitude and darkness.

Murray passed through the first cellar, and was proceeding to the second when he saw the great gates open and a large party of English soldiers enter. They were conducted by the butler of the castle, who seemed to perform his office very unwillingly, while they crowded in, thirsty and riotous.

Aware how unequal his single arm would be to contend with such numbers, Murray, at the first glance of these plunderers, retreated behind a heap of casks in a remote corner. While the trembling butler was loading a dozen of the men for the refreshment of their masters above, the rest were helping themselves from the adjacent catacombs. Some left the cellars with their booty, and others remained to drink it on the spot. Glad to escape the insults of the soldiers who lay wallowing in the wine, Bothwell's old servant quitted the cellar with the last company which bore flagons to their comrades above.

Murray listened anxiously in hopes of hearing from his neighbors some intimation of the fate of his uncle and aunt. He hearkened in vain, for nothing was uttered by these intoxicated banditti but loud boastings of the number each had slain in the earl's apartment, execrations against the Scots for their obstinate resistance, and a thousand sanguinary wishes that the nation had but one neck to strike off at a blow.

How often, during this conversation, was Murray tempted to rush out amongst them and seize a desperate revenge! But the thought of his poor cousin now awaiting his return restrained him; and unable to move from his hiding-place without precipitating himself into instant death, he remained nearly an hour in the most painful anxiety, watching the dropping to sleep of this horrid crew.

When all seemed hushed—not a voice, even in a whisper, startling his ear—he ventured forth towards the slumbering groups. He must pass them to reach the private stairs. He paused and listened. Silence still reigned. He took courage, and flew with the lightness of air to the secret door. As he laid his hand on it, it opened from without, and two persons appeared. By the few rays which gleamed from the expiring torches of the sleepers he could see that the first wore English armor. Murray believed himself lost; but determined to sell his life dearly, he made a spring, and caught the man by the throat; when some one seizing his arm, exclaimed, "Stop, my Lord Murray! it is the faithful Grimsby." Murray let go his hold, glad to find that both his English friend and the venerable object of his solicitude were thus brought to meet him; but fearing that the violence of his action and Halbert's exclamation might have alarmed the sleeping soldiers, he laid his finger on the lip of Grimsby, and motioned to the astonished pair to follow him.

As they advanced, they perceived one of the soldiers move as if disturbed. Murray held his sword over the sleeping wretch, ready to plunge it into his heart should he attempt to rise; but he became still again; and the fugitives having approached the flag, Murray drew it up, and eager to haven his double charge he thrust them together down the stairs. At that moment a shriek from Helen (who had discovered, by the gleam of light which burst into the vault, a man descending in English armor) echoed through the cellars. Two of the soldiers jumped upon their feet and rushed upon Murray.

He had let the flag drop behind them; but still remaining by it, in case of an opportunity to escape, he received the strokes of their weapons upon his target, and returned them with equal rapidity. One assailant lay gasping at his feet, but the clashing of arms and the cries of the survivor had already awakened the whole crew. They threw themselves towards the young Scot, and would certainly have cut him to pieces had he not snatched the only remaining torch out of the hand of a staggering soldier, and extinguished it under his foot. Bewildered where to find their prey, they groped in darkness, slashing the air with their swords, and not unfrequently wounding each other in the vain search.

Murray was now far from their pursuit. He had no sooner put out the light than he pulled up the flag, and leaping down, drew it after him, and found himself in safety. Desperate as was the contest, it had been short, for he yet heard the footsteps of the panic-struck Helen flying along the passage. The Englishman and Halbert, on the first falling of the flag, not knowing its spring, had unsuccessfully tried to reraise it that they might assist Murray in the tumult above. On his appearing again so unexpectedly, they declared their joy; but the young lord, impatient to calm the apprehensions of his cousin, returned no other answer than "Follow me!" while he darted forward. Terror had given her wings, and even prevented her hearing the low sounds of Murray's voice, which he durst not raise to a higher pitch, for fear of being overheard by the enemy. Thus, while she lost all presence of mind, he did not come up with her till she fell breathless against the stairs at the extremity of the vault.

CHAPTER X.

ST. FILLAN'S.

As soon as Murray found her, he clasped her insensible form to his breast, and carrying her up the steps, drew the bolt of the door. It opened to his pressure, and discovered a large monastic cell, into which the daylight shone through one long narrow window. A straw pallet, an altar, and a marble basin were the furniture. The cell was solitary, the owner being then at mass in the chapel of the monastery. Murray laid down his death-like burden on the monk's bed. He then ventured to throw some of the holy water upon his cousin's face, and by means of a little chalice which stood upon the altar he poured some into her mouth. At last opening her eyes, she recognized the figure of her young kinsman leaning over her, while Halbert stood at her feet. "Blessed Virgin! I am yet safe, and with my dear Andrew! Oh, I feared you were slain!" cried she, bursting into tears.

"Thank God, we are both safe," answered he; "comfort yourself, beloved cousin! you are now on holy ground; this is the cell of the prior of St. Fillan's. None but the hand of an infidel dare wrest you from this sanctuary."

"But my father, and Lady Mar?" And again her tears flowed.

"The countess, my gracious lady," answered Halbert, "since you could not be found in the castle, is allowed to accompany your father to Dumbarton castle, until De Valence receives further orders from King Edward."

"But for Wallace!" cried she; "ah, where are now the succors that were to be sent to him? And without succors how can he, or you, dearest Andrew, rescue my father from this tyranny?"

"Do not despair," replied Murray; "look but at the banner you held fast, even while insensible; your own hands have engraven my answer—*God armeth the patriot!* Convinced of that, can you still fear for your father? I will join Wallace to-morrow. Your own fifty warriors await me at the bottom of Cartlane craigs; and if any treachery should be meditated against my uncle, that moment we will make the towers of Dumbarton shake to their foundation."

Helen's reply was a deep sigh; she thought it might be Heaven's

will that her father, like the good Lord Douglas, should fall a victim
to royal revenge; and so sad were her forebodings that she hardly
dared to hope what the sanguine disposition of her cousin promised.
Grimsby now came forward, and unloosing an iron box from under
his arm, put it into the hands of Lord Murray.

"This fatal treasure," said he, "was committed to my care by the
earl, your uncle, to deliver to the prior of St. Fillan's."

"What does it contain?" demanded Murray; "I never saw it before."

"I know not its contents," returned the soldier; "it belongs to Sir
William Wallace."

"Indeed!" ejaculated Helen. "If it be treasure, why was it not
rather sent to him?"

"But how, honest soldier," asked Murray, "did you escape with
it, and Halbert, too? I am at a loss to conjecture." He replied
that as soon as the English and their Scottish partizans under Lord
Soulis had surprised the castle, he saw that his only chance of safety
was to throw off the bonnet and plaid, and mix amongst the numerous
soldiers who had taken possession of the gates. His armor and his
language showed he was their countryman, and they easily believed
that he had joined the plunderers as a volunteer from the army,
which at a greater distance beleaguered the castle. He had no difficulty, therefore, after the carnage in the state apartment, to make his
way to the bedchamber where Lord Aymer de Valence had ordered
Lord Mar to be carried. He found the earl alone and lost in grief.
He knew not but that his nephew, and even his daughter and wife,
had fallen beneath the swords of the enemy. Astonished at seeing
the soldier walking at large, he expressed his surprise with some
suspicions. But Grimsby told him the stratagem he had used, and
assured him Lord Andrew had not been seen since the onset. This
information inspired the earl with a hope that his nephew might have
escaped; and when the soldier also said that he had seen the countess
led by Lord Soulis across the hall towards the Lady Helen's apartments, while he overheard him promising them every respect, the
earl seemed comforted. "But how," inquired he of Grimsby, "has
this hard fate befallen us? Have you learnt how De Valence knew
that I meant to take up arms for my country?"

When the soldier was relating this part of the conference, Murray
interrupted him with the same demand.

"On that head I cannot fully satisfy you," replied he; "I could
only gather from the soldiers that a sealed packet had been delivered
to Lord Aymer de Valence late last night at Dumbarton castle.

Soulis was then there, and he immediately set off to Glasgow for the followers he had left in that town. Early this morning he joined De Valence and his legions on Bothwell moor. The consequences there, you know. But they do not end at Bothwell. The gallant Wallace——"

"What of him?" exclaimed Murray.

"No harm has yet happened to him," replied Grimsby; "but at the same moment in which De Valence gave orders for his troops to march to Bothwell, he sent others to intercept that persecuted knight's escape from the Cartlane craigs."

"That accursed sealed packet," cried Murray, "has been the traitor! Some villain in Bothwell castle must have written it. And if so," added he, with tremendous emphasis, "may the blast of slavery ever pursue him and his posterity!"

Helen shuddered as the amen to this malediction was echoed by the voices of Halbert and Grimsby. The latter continued:

"When I informed Lord Mar of these measures against Wallace, he expressed a hope that your first detachment to his assistance might, with yourself at its head, elude their vigilance and join his friend. This discourse reminded him of the iron box. 'It is in that closet,' said his lordship, pointing to an opposite door; 'take it thence, and buckle it to your side.'

"I obeyed; and he then proceeded: 'There are two passages in this house which lead to sanctuary. The one nearest to us is the safest for you. A staircase from the closet you have just left will lead you directly into the chapel. When there, hasten to the image of the Virgin, and slip aside the marble tablet on the back of the pedestal; it will admit you to a flight of steps; descend them, and at the bottom you will find a door that will convey you into a range of cellars. Lift up the largest flagstone in the second, and you will be conducted through a dark vault to an iron door; draw the bolt, and remain in the cell it will open to you, till the owner enters. He is the prior of St. Fillan's, and a Murray. Give him this golden cross, as a mark you come from me, and say it is my request that he assist you to gain the seashore. As for the iron box, tell him to preserve it as he would his life, and never to give it up but to myself, my children, or to Sir William Wallace, its rightful master.' "

"Alas," cried Halbert, "that he had never been its owner! that he had never brought it to Ellerslie, to draw down misery on his head! Wherever it has been deposited, war and murder have followed. I trust my dear master will never see it more."

"He may indeed never see it more," murmured Helen. "Where

are now my proud anticipations of freedom to Scotland? Alas, Andrew," said she, taking his hand and weeping over it, "I have been too presumptuous; my father is a prisoner, and Sir William Wallace is lost!"

"Cease, my dear Helen," cried he; "cease to distress yourself. Such disasters are sent as lessons, to teach us precaution, promptitude, and patience—these are the soldier's graces, my sweet cousin, and depend on it, I will pay them due obedience."

"But why," asked Helen, taking comfort from the spirits of her cousin,—"why, my good soldier, did not my dear father take advantage of this sanctuary?"

"I urged the earl to accompany me," returned Grimsby; "but he said such a proceeding would leave his wife and babes in unprotected captivity. 'No,' added he; 'I will await my fate; for the God of those who trust in him, knows that I do not fear.'

"Having received such orders from the earl, I took my leave; and entering the chapel by the way he directed, was agreeably surprised to find Halbert, whom I supposed had fallen during the carnage in the state-chamber. He was still kneeling by the tomb of his buried mistress. I did not take long to warn him of his danger, and desired him to follow me. We descended together beneath the holy statue, and were just emerging into the cellars when you, sir, met us at the entrance.

"It was while we were yet in the chapel that I heard De Valence and Soulis at high words in the court-yard. The former, in a loud voice, gave orders that as Lady Helen Mar could nowhere be found, the earl and countess, with their two infant children, should not be separated, but be conveyed as his prisoners to Dumbarton castle."

"That is a comfort," cried Helen; "my father will then be consoled by the presence of his wife."

"But very different would have been the case, madam, had you appeared," rejoined the soldier: "one of Lord de Valence's men told me that Lord Soulis intended to have taken you and the countess to Dun-glass castle, near Glasgow, while the sick earl was to have been carried alone to Dumbarton, and detained in solitary confinement. Lord Soulis was in so dreadful a rage when you could not be found, that he accused the English commander of having leagued with Lady Mar to deceive him. In the midst of this contention we descended into the vaults."

Helen shuddered at the thought of how near she was to falling into the hands of so fierce a spirit. In his character he united every quality which could render power formidable, combining prodigious bodily strength with cruelty, dissimulation, and treachery. Helen Mar had twice refused his hand: first, during the contest for the kingdom, when his pretended claim to the crown was disallowed. She was then a mere child, hardly more than fourteen; but she rejected him with abhorrence. Though stung to the quick at being denied the objects both of his love and his ambition at the same moment, he did not hesitate, at another period, to renew his offer to her. At the fall of Dunbar, as soon as he had repeated his oaths of fidelity to Edward, he hastened to Thirlestane, to throw himself a second time at the feet of Lady Helen. Her ripened judgment confirmed her youthful dislike of his ruffian qualities, and again he was rejected.

Helen knew not half the afflictions with which his resentful heart had meditated to subdue her; and therefore, though she shrunk at the sound of a name so infamous, yet, not aware of all the evils she had escaped, she replied with languor, though with gratitude, to the congratulations of her cousin on her timely flight.

At this period the door of the cell opened, and the prior entered from the cloisters; he started on seeing his room filled with strangers. Murray took off his helmet and approached him. On recognizing the son of his patron the prior inquired his commands, and expressed some surprise that such a company, and above all a lady, could have passed the convent-gate without his previous notice.

Murray pointed to the recess behind the altar, and then explained to the good priest the necessity which had compelled them to thus seek the protection of St. Fillan's. "Lady Helen," continued he, "must share your care until Heaven empowers the Earl of Mar to reclaim his daughter, and adequately reward this holy church."

The soldier then presented the cross, with the iron box, repeating the message that confided them also to his keeping.

The prior listened to these recitals with sorrowful attention. He had heard the noise of armed men advancing to the castle, but knowing that the earl was making warlike preparations, he had no suspicion that these were other than the Bothwell soldiers. He took the box, and laying it on the altar, pressed the cross to his lips. "The Earl of Mar shall find that fidelity here which his faith in the Church merits. That mysterious chest, to which you tell me so terrible a denunciation is annexed, shall be preserved sacred as the relics of St. Fillan's."

The father then proceeded: "But for you, virtuous Southron, I will give you a pilgrim's habit. Travel in that privileged garb to Montrose, and there a brother of the Church will, by a letter from me, convey you in a vessel to Normandy: thence you may safely find your way to Guienne."

The soldier bowed his head; and the priest, turning to Lady Helen, told her that a cell should be appointed for her, and some pious woman brought from the adjoining hamlet to pay her due attendance.

"As for this venerable man," continued he, "his silver hairs already proclaim him near his heavenly country. He had best put on the cowl of the holy brotherhood, and in the arms of religion repose securely."

Tears started into the eyes of Halbert. "I thank you, reverend father; I have indeed drawn near the end of my pilgrimage. I accept your invitation thankfully; and, considering it a call from Heaven to give me rest, I welcome the day that marks the poor harper of Ellerslie with the sacred tonsure."

The sound of approaching trumpets, and soon after the clattering of horses and the clang of armor, made an instantaneous silence in the cell. Helen looked fearfully at her cousin and grasped his hand; Murray clasped his sword with a firmer hold. "I will protect you with my life." He spoke in a low tone, but the soldier heard him. "There is no cause of alarm," rejoined he; "Lord de Valence is only marching by on his way to Dumbarton."

"Alas, my poor father!" cried Helen, covering her face with her hands.

The venerable prior, pitying her affliction, knelt down by her. "My daughter, be comforted," said he; "they dare not commit any violence on the earl. King Edward too well understands his own interest to allow even a long imprisonment to so popular a nobleman." This assurance at length raised her head with a meek smile.

The prior, seeing her composed, recommended leaving her to rest and Helen, comforted by holy meditations, allowing her cousin to depart, he led Murray and his companions into the convent library.

CHAPTER XI.

THE CHAPTER-HOUSE.

THE march of De Valence from the castle having proved that no suspicion of any of its late inhabitants being still in the neighborhood remained with its usurpers, Grimsby thought he might depart in safety; and next morning he begged permission of the prior to commence his journey. "I am anxious to quit a land," said he, "where my countrymen are committing violences which make me blush at the name of Englishman."

Murray put a purse of gold into the soldier's hand, while the prior covered his armor with a pilgrim's gown. Grimsby, with a respectful bow, returned the gift. "I cannot take money from you, my lord. But bestow on me the sword at your side, and that I will preserve forever."

Murray took it off and gave it to the soldier. "Let us exchange, my brave friend!" said he; "give me yours, and it shall be a memorial to me of having found virtue in an enemy."

Grimsby unlocked his rude weapon in a moment, and as he put the hilt into the young Scot's hand a tear stood in his eye. "When you raise this sword against my countrymen, think on Grimsby, a humble soldier of the cross, and spare the blood of all who ask for mercy."

Murray looked a gracious assent. Without speaking, he gave the good soldier's hand a parting grasp; and with regret that superior claims called so brave a man from his side, he saw him leave the monastery.

When the poor old harper found himself alone with Murray, he again gave loose to griefs. He wept like an infant; and recounting the afflictions of his master, implored Murray to go without delay to support the now almost friendless Wallace. Murray was consoling him with the assurance that he would set off for the mountains that very evening, when the prior returned to conduct Halbert to a cell appointed for his novitiate.

The sorrowing domestic of Wallace being thus disposed of, the prior and Murray remained together, consulting on the safest means of passing to the Cartlane hills. A lay-brother whom the prior had sent in pursuit of Helen's fifty warriors, to apprise them of the English being in the craigs, at this juncture entered the library. He informed the father that, secure in his religious garb, he had penetrated many of the Cartlane defiles, but could neither see nor hear anything of the party. Every glen or height was occupied by the English; and from a woman, of whom he begged a draught of milk, he had learnt how closely the mountains were invested. The English commander, in his zeal to prevent provisions being conveyed to Wallace and his famishing garrison, had stopped a procession of monks bearing a dead body to the cave of Saint Columba. He would not allow them to ascend the heights until he had examined whether the bier really bore a corpse, or was a vehicle to carry food to the beleaguered Scots.

In the midst of this information the prior and his friends were startled by a shout, and soon after a tumult of voices, in which might be distinguished the cry of "A gallows for the traitor!"

"Our brave Englishman has fallen into their hands," cried Murray, hastening towards the door.

"What would you do?" interrupted the prior, holding him. "Your single arm could not save the soldier. The cross has more power; I will seek these violent men; meanwhile stay here, as you value the lives of all in the convent."

Murray had now recollected himself, and acquiesced. The prior took the crucifix from the altar, and ordering the porter to throw open the great doors, he appeared before a turbulent band of soldiers who were dragging a man along, fast bound with their leathern belts. Blood, trickling from his face, fell on the hands of the ruthless wretches, who, with horrid yells, were threatening him with instant death.

The prior, raising the cross, rushed in amongst them, and in the name of the blessed Son who died on that tree bade them stand. The soldiers trembled before the holy majesty of his figure and at his awful adjuration. The prior looked on the prisoner, but he did not see the dark locks of the Englishman; it was the yellow hair of Scotland that mingled with the blood on his forehead.

"Whither do you hurry that wounded man?"

"To his death," answered a surly fellow.

"What is his offense?"

"He is a traitor."

"How has he proved it?"

"He is a Scot, and he belongs to the disloyal Lord of Mar. This bugle, with its crowned falcon, proves it," added the Southron, holding up the very bugle which the earl had sent by Halbert to Wallace, and which was ornamented with the crest of Mar wrought in gold.

"That this has been Lord Mar's," replied the prior, "there is no doubt; but may not this man have found it? Or may it not have been given to him by the earl before that chief incurred the displeasure of King Edward? Unless you substantiate your charge against this man by a better proof than this bugle his death would be a murder, which the Lord of life will requite, in the perdition of your souls. Release, therefore, that wounded man," continued he. "Before the altar he shall confess himself; and if I find that he is guilty, I promise you, by the holy St. Fillan, to release him to your commanding officer. But if he prove innocent, no monarch on earth shall wrest his children from the protection of the Church."

While he spake, the men who held the prisoner let go their hold; and the prior, stretching out his hand to him, gave him to a party of monks, to conduct into the convent. Then to convince the soldiers that it was the man's life he sought to save, and not the spoil, he returned the golden bugle, and bade them depart in peace.

Awed by the father's address, and satisfied with the money and arms of which they had rifled the stranger, the marauders retreated. Bursting into yeomen's houses and peasants' huts, stripping all of their substance who did or did not swear fealty to Edward, thus robbing the latter and exacting contributions from the former, they sped gaily on, as if murder were pastime and rapine honor.

The prior, on returning into the convent, ordered the gates to be bolted. When he entered the chapter-house, finding the monks had already bound up the wounds of the stranger, he made a sign for the brethren to withdraw; and then approaching the young man, "My son," said he, in a mild tone, "you heard my declaration to the men from whom I took you. Answer me with truth, and you shall find that virtue or repentance have alike a refuge in the arms of the Church. How came you by that bugle?"

The stranger looked steadfastly on his questioner. "You have saved my life, and I should be less than man could I doubt the evidence of that deed. I received the bugle from a brave Scot who dwells amongst the eastern mountains, and who gave it to me to assure the Earl of Mar that I came from him."

The prior apprehended that it was of Wallace he spoke. "You come to request a military aid from the Earl of Mar," rejoined the father, willing to sound him before he committed Murray, by calling him to the conference.

The stranger replied: "If, reverend sir, you are in the confidence of the good earl, pronounce but the Christian name of the man who charged me with the bugle, and allow me then, for his sake, to ask you what has indeed happened to the earl: that I was seized by foes, when I expected to meet with friends only. Reply to this, and I shall speak freely; but at present, though I would confide all of myself to your sacred character, yet the confidence of others is not mine to bestow."

The prior being convinced by this caution that he was indeed speaking with some messenger from Wallace, made no hesitation to answer, "Your master is a knight, and a braver never drew breath since the time of his royal namesake, William the Lion."

The man rose hastily from his seat, and falling on his knees before the prior, put his garment to his lips: "Father, I now know that I am with a friend of my persecuted master. But if, indeed, the situation of Lord Mar precludes assistance from him, all hope is lost. The noble Wallace is penned within the hills, without any hopes of escape. Suffer me, then, to rejoin him immediately, that I may at least die with my friend."

"Hope for a better destiny," returned the prior; "I am a servant, and not to be worshiped: turn to that altar, and kneel to Him who can alone send the succor you need."

The good man, thinking it was now time to call the young lord of Bothwell, entered the library, where Murray was anxiously awaiting his return. On his entrance the impatient youth eagerly exclaimed, "Have you rescued him?"

"Grimsby, I hope, is far and safely on his journey," answered the good priest; "but the man those murderers were dragging to death is in the chapter-house. Follow me, and he will give you news of Wallace."

Murray gladly obeyed.

At sight of a Scottish knight in armor, the messenger of Wallace thought his prayers were answered, and that he saw before him the leader of the host which was to march to the preservation of his commander. Murray told him who he was, and learned from him in return that Wallace now considered himself in a state of siege; that the women, children, and old men with him had nothing to feed on but wild strawberries and bird's eggs, which they found in the hollows of the rocks. "To relieve them from such hard quarters, girded by a barrier of English soldiers," continued the narrator, "is his first wish; but that cannot be effected by our small number. However, he would make the attempt by a stratagem, could we be at all supported by succors from the Earl of Mar."

"My uncle's means," replied Murray, "are for a time cut off, but mine shall be exerted to the utmost. Did you not meet, somewhere, a company of Scots to the number of fifty? I sent them off yesterday to seek your noble chief."

"No," rejoined the young man; "I fear they have been taken by the enemy; for on my way to Sir William Wallace, not knowing the English were so close to his sanctuary, I was nearly seized myself. I had not the good fortune to be with him when he struck the first blow for Scotland in the citadel of Lanark, but as soon as I heard the tale of his wrongs I sought my way to my friend. I found the banks of the Mouse occupied by the English, but exploring the passes, at last gained the bottom of the precipice on the top of which Wallace is encamped; and as I lay among the bushes, watching an opportunity to ascend, I perceived two English soldiers near me. They were in discourse, and I overheard them say that besides Heselrigge himself nearly two hundred of his garrison had fallen by the hand of Wallace's men in the contention at the castle; that the tidings were sent to Sir Richard Arnulff, the deputy-governor of Ayr, and he had despatched a thousand men to surround Cartlane craigs, spies having given notice that they were Sir William's strongholds; and the orders were, that he must be taken dead or alive.

"Such was the information I brought to my gallant friend, when in the dead of night I mounted the rock, and calling to the Scottish sentinel in Gaelic, gave him my name, and was allowed to enter that sacred spot. Wallace welcomed his faithful Ker, and soon unfolded his distress and his hopes. He told me of the famine that threatened his little garrison; of the constant watching, day and night, necessary to prevent a surprise. But in his extremity he observed that one defile was thinly guarded by the enemy; probably because, as it lay at the bottom of a perpendicular angle of the rock, they thought it unattainable by the Scots. To this point, however, my dauntless friend turns his eyes. He would attempt it, could he procure a sufficient number of fresh men to cover the retreat of his exhausted few. For this purpose, as I had so lately explored the most hidden paths of the craigs, I volunteered to visit the Lord Mar, and to conduct, in safety, any succors he might send to our persecuted leader.

"This," continued Ker, "was the errand on which I came to the earl. Think then my horror when in my journey I found redoubled legions hemming in the hills, and on advancing towards Bothwell castle was seized by a party of English, rifled, and declared an accomplice with that nobleman, who, they said, was condemned to lose his head."

"Not so bad as that, my brave Ker," cried Murray, a glow of indignation flushing his cheek; "no true Scottish blood, I trust, will ever stain their scaffolds; for while we have arms to wield a sword, he must be a fool that grounds them on any other terms than freedom or death."

"Noble youth!" exclaimed the prior, "may the innocence which gives animation to your courage continue its moving soul! They only are invincible who are as ready to die as to live."

Murray bowed modestly, and turning to Ker, informed him, that since he must abandon all hope of hearing any more of the fifty brave men his cousin Helen had sent to the craigs, he bethought him of applying to his uncle, Sir John Murray, who dwelt hard by, on his estate at Drumshargard. "It is small," said he, "and cannot afford many men; but still he may spare sufficient to effect the escape of our commander, and that for the present will be a host."

To accomplish his design without delay, and to avoid a surprise from the English lieutenant at Bothwell, Murray determined to take Ker with him; and, disguished as peasants, as soon as darkness should shroud their movements, proceed to Drumshargard.

CHAPTER XII.

DRUMSHARGARD.

WHILE these transactions occupied the morning, Lady Helen slept long and sweetly. Her exhausted frame found renovation, and she awoke with a heavenly calm at her heart. A cheering vision had visited her sleeping thoughts, and a trance of happy feelings absorbed her senses.

She had seen in her dream a young knight enter her cell bearing her father in his arms. He laid the earl down before her; but as she stooped to embrace him, the knight took her by the hand, and leading her to the window of the apartment he smiled, and said, "Look out, and see how I have performed my vow." She obeyed, and saw crowds of rejoicing people, who at sight of the young warrior raised such a shout that Helen awoke. She started, she looked around—she was still in the narrow cell, and alone; but the rapture of beholding her father yet fluttered in her breast, and the touch of the warrior's hand seemed still warm upon hers. "Angels of rest," cried she, "I thank ye for this blessed vision!"

This dream seemed prophetic. "Yes," cried she, "though thousands of Edward's soldiers surrounded my father and his friend, I should not despair. Thy life, O noble Wallace, was not given to be extinguished in an hour! Thy morn has hardly risen, the perfect day must come that is to prove thee the glory of Scotland!"

Owing to the fervor of her apostrophe, she did not observe the door of the cell open till the prior stood before her. After expressing his pleasure at the renovation in her countenance, he informed her of the departure of the English soldier, and of the alarm which he and Murray had sustained for his safety, by the adventure which had thrown a stranger from the craigs into their protection. At the mention of that now momentous spot she blushed, the golden-haired warrior of her dream seemed ready to rise before her, and with a beating heart she prepared to hear some miraculous account of her father's rescue.

Unconscious of what was passing in her eager mind, the prior proceeded to relate all that Ker had told of the extremity to which Wallace was reduced, and then closed his intelligence by mentioning

71

the attempt which her cousin meditated to save him. The color gradually faded from the face of Helen, and sighs were her only responses to the observations the good priest made on the difficulty of the enterprise. But when his pity for the brave men engaged in the cause betrayed him into expressing his fears that the patriotic zeal of Wallace would only make him and them a sacrifice, Helen looked up; there was inspiration in her eyes. "Father," said she, "hast thou not taught me that God shieldeth the patriot as well as armeth him?"

"Daughter of heaven," replied the good prior, "you might teach devotion to age, and cause youth to be enamored of the graces of religion!"

Helen, having replied to this burst from the heart of the holy man, begged to see her cousin before he set off on his expedition. The prior withdrew, and within an hour after, Murray entered the apartment. Their conversation was long, and their parting full of interest. "When I see you again, my brave cousin, tell me that my father is free and his preserver safe. Your own life, dear Andrew," added she, as he pressed his cheek to hers, "must always be precious to me."

Murray hastily withdrew, and Helen was again alone.

The young chieftain and Ker covered their armor with shepherds' plaids; and having received a thousand blessings from the prior and Halbert, proceeded under shelter of the night through the obscurest paths of the wood which divided Bothwell from Drumshargard.

Sir John Murray was gone to rest when his nephew arrived, but Lord Andrew's voice being known by the porter, he was admitted into the house. The old knight was soon aroused, and welcomed his nephew with open arms, for he had feared, from the accounts brought by the fugitive tenants of Bothwell, that he also had been carried away prisoner.

Murray now unfolded his errand: first, to obtain a band of Sir John's trustiest people to assist in rescuing the preserver of the earl's life from destruction; and, secondly, if a commission for Lord Mar's release did not arrive from King Edward, to aid him to free his uncle and the countess from Dumbarton castle.

Sir John listened with growing anxiety to his nephew's details. When he heard of Lady Helen's continuing in the convent, he highly approved it. "That is well," said he; "to bring her to any private protection would only spread calamity. She might be traced, and her protector put in danger; none but the Church, with safety to itself, can grant asylum to the daughter of a state prisoner."

"Then I doubly rejoice she is there," replied Murray; "and there she will remain till your generous assistance empowers me to rescue her father."

"Lord Mar has been very rash, nephew," returned Drumshargard. "What occasion was there for him to volunteer sending men to support Sir William Wallace? and how durst he bring ruin on Bothwell castle, by collecting, unauthorized by my brother, its vassals for so dangerous an experiment?"

Murray started at these unexpected observations. He knew his uncle was timid, but he had never suspected him of meanness; however, he smothered his disgust, and gave him a mild answer. But the old man could not approve of a nobleman of his rank running himself, his fortune, and his friends into peril, to pay any debt of gratitude. "Trust me, Andrew," said he, "nobody profits by these notions but thieves, and desperate fellows ready to become thieves."

"I do not understand you, sir."

"Not understand me?" replied the knight, rather impatiently. "Who suffers in these contests for liberty, as you choose to call them, but such men as Lord Mar and your father? Who gains by rebellion, but a few penniless wretches that embrace these vaunted principles from the urgency of their necessities? They acquire plunder under the mask of disinterestedness; and hazarding nothing of themselves but their worthless lives, they would throw the whole country into flames, that they may catch a few brands from the fire."

Young Murray felt his anger rise with this speech. "I do not come here to dispute the general evil of revolt, sir, but to ask your assistance to snatch two of the bravest men in Scotland from the tyrant who has made you a slave."

"Nephew," cried the knight, starting from his couch and darting a fierce look at him, "if any man but one of my own blood had uttered that word, this hour should have been his last!"

"Every man, sir," continued Murray, "who acts upon your principles must know himself to be a slave; and to resent being called so, is to affront his own conscience. See you not the villages of your country burning around you? the castles of your chieftains razed to the ground? Did not the plains of Dunbar reek with the blood of your kinsmen; and even now, do you not see them led away in chains to the strongholds of the tyrant? And yet you exclaim, 'I see no injury—I spurn at the name of slave!'"

Murray rose from his seat as he ended, and walking the room in agitation, did not perceive the confusion of his uncle, who, at once overcome with conviction and with fear, again ventured to speak: "It is too sure you speak truth, Andrew; but what am I, or any other private individual, that we should make ourselves a forlorn hope for the whole nation? Will Baliol, who was the first to bow to the usurper,—will he thank us for losing our heads in resentment of his indignity? Bruce himself, the rightful heir of the crown, leaves us to our fates, and has become a courtier in England. For whom, then, should I adventure my gray hairs to seek an uncertain liberty, and to meet an almost certain death?"

"For Scotland, uncle," replied he; "just laws are her right. Think not, sir, to preserve your home, or even your gray hairs, by hugging the chains by which you are bound. You are a Scot, and that is sufficient to arm the enemy against your property and life. Remember the fate of Lord Monteith! At the very time he was beset by the parasites of Edward, and persuaded to be altogether as an Englishman, in that very hour, when he had taken a niece of Cressingham's to his arms, by her hands the vengeance of Edward reached him —he fell!"

Murray saw that his uncle was struck, and that he trembled.

"But I am too insignificant, Andrew."

"You are the brother of Lord Bothwell," answered Murray, with all the dignity of his father rising in his countenance. "His possessions made him a traitor in the eyes of the tyrant's representatives. Cressingham, as treasurer for the crew, has already sent his lieutenant to lord it in our paternal castle; and do not deceive yourself in believing that some one of his officers will not require the fertile fields of Drumshargard as a reward for his services. No; cheat not yourself with the idea that the brother of Lord Bothwell will be too insignificant to bear a part in the confiscations of his country. When they need your wealth or your lands, your submission is forgotten, and a prison, or the ax, ready to give them quiet possession."

Sir John Murray, though a narrow-sighted man, now comprehended his nephew's reasoning; and his fears taking a different turn, he hastily declared his determination to set off immediately for the Highlands. "In the morning, by daybreak," said he, "I will commence my journey, and join my brother at Loch-awe; for I cannot believe myself safe a moment while so near the garrisons of the enemy."

Murray approved this plan; and after obtaining his hard-wrung leave to take thirty men from his vassals, he returned to Ker to inform him of the success of his mission. In the course of an hour he brought together the appointed number of the bravest men on the estate and when equipped, he led them into the hall to receive the last command from their feudal lord.

On seeing them armed, with every man his drawn dirk in his hand, Sir John turned pale. Murray, with the unfolded banner of Mar in his grasp, and Ker by his side, stood at their head.

"Young men," said the old knight, striving to speak in a firm tone, "in this expedition you are to consider yourselves the followers of my nephew: he is brave and honorable, therefore I commit you to his command. But as you go on his earnest petition, I am not answerable to any man for the enterprises to which he may lead you."

"Be they all on my own head!" cried Murray, drawing out his sword with an impatience that made the old knight start. "We now have your permission to depart, sir?"

Sir John gave a ready assent: he was anxious to get so hot-headed a youth out of his house, and to collect his gold and servants, that he might commence his own flight by break of day.

It was still dark as midnight when Murray and his little company passed the heights above Drumshargard, and took their rapid march towards the cliffs, which would conduct them to the more dangerous passes of the Cartlane craigs.

CHAPTER XIII.

BANKS OF THE CLYDE.

Two days passed drearily away to Helen. She could not expect tidings from her cousin in so short a time, and anxiety to learn what might be the condition of the earl and countess so possessed her that visions of affright now disturbed both her waking and sleeping senses.

On the morning of the third day, when she was chiding herself for such despondence, her attendant entered to say that a friar was come to conduct her where she should see messengers from Lady Mar. Helen lingered not a moment, but giving her hand to the good father, was led by him into the library, where the prior was standing between two men in military habits. One wore English armor, with his visor closed; the other, a knight, was in tartans. The Scot presented her with a signet set in gold. Helen looked on it, and immediately recognized the same that her stepmother always used.

The Scottish knight was preparing to address her when the prior interrupted him, and taking Lady Helen's hand made her seat herself. "Compose yourself for a few minutes," said he; "this life hourly brings forward events to teach us to be calm, and to resign our wishes and our wills to the Lord."

Helen looked fearfully in his face. "Some evil tidings are to be told me." The blood left her lips; it seemed leaving her heart also. The prior, full of compassion, hesitated to speak. The Scot abruptly answered her:

"Be not alarmed, lady, your parents have fallen into humane hands. I am sent, under the command of this noble Southron knight, to conduct you to them."

"Then my father lives! They are safe!" cried she, in a transport of joy.

"He yet lives," returned the officer; "but his wounds opening afresh and the fatigues of his journey have so exhausted him that Lord Aymer de Valence has granted the prayers of the countess, and we come to take you to receive his last blessing."

A cry of anguish burst from the heart of Lady Helen; and falling into the arms of the prior, she found refuge in a merciful insensibility. The exertions of the venerable father at last recalled her to recollection. She rose from the bench on which he had laid her, and begged permission to retire for a few minutes; tears choked her further utterance; and being led out by the friar, she once more reentered her cell.

Lady Helen passed the moments she had requested in those duties which alone can give comfort to the afflicted, and rising from her knees, she took her mantle and veil, and sent her attendant to the prior to say she was ready to set out on her journey, and wished to receive his benediction. The venerable father, followed by Halbert, obeyed her summons. On seeing the poor old harper, Helen's heart lost some of its newly acquired composure. She held out her hand to him; he pressed it to his lips: "Farewell, sweetest lady! May the prayers of the dear saint to whose remains you gave a holy grave, draw down upon your own head consolation!" The old man sobbed; and the tears of Lady Helen, as he bent upon her hand, dropped upon his silver hair. "May heaven hear you, good Halbert! And cease not, venerable man, to pray for me."

"All that dwell in this house, my daughter," rejoined the prior, "shall put up orisons for your comfort and for the soul of the departing earl." Observing that her grief augmented at these words, he proceeded in a yet more soothing voice: "Regret not that he goes before you, for what is death but entrance into life?"

Helen raised her eyes, and with a divine smile pressing the crucifix to her breast: "You do indeed arm me, my father. This is my strength."

"And one that will never fail thee," exclaimed he. She dropped upon one knee before him. He crossed his hands over her head, he looked up to heaven, his lips moved; then pausing a moment: "Go," said he, "and may the angels which guard innocence, minister to your sorrows."

Helen bowed, and breathing a devout response, rose and followed the prior out of the cell. Before the great gates stood the knights with their attendants. She once more kissed the crucifix held by the prior, and giving her hand to the Scot, was placed by him on a horse richly caparisoned. He sprang on another himself; while the English officer, who was already mounted, drawing up to her, she pulled down her veil; and all bowing to the holy brotherhood at the porch, rode off at a gentle pace.

A long stretch of woods, which spread before the monastery and screened the back of Bothwell castle, lay before them. Through this green labyrinth they pursued their way till they crossed the river.

"Time wears," exclaimed the Scot to his companion; "we must

push on." The English knight nodded, and set his spurs into his steed. The whole troop now fell into a rapid trot.

A sweet breeze played through the valley, and revived Helen's harassed frame. She put aside her veil to enjoy its freshness, and saw that the knights turned their horses' heads into one of the obscurest mountain defiles. She started at its depth, and at the gloom which involved its extremity. "It is our nearest path," said the Scot. Helen made no reply, but turning her steed also, followed him. The Englishman, whose voice she had not yet heard, and his attendants, followed likewise in file; and with difficulty the horses could make their way through the thicket which interlaced the pathway.

When they had been employed for an hour in breaking their way through this glen, they came to a space where broader ravines opened before them. The Scot, taking a pass to the right, raised his bugle, and blew so sudden a blast that the horse on which Lady Helen sat took fright and began to plunge and rear. Some of the dismounted men, seeing her danger, seized the horse by the bridle; while the English knight, extricating her from the saddle, carried her through some clustering bushes, into a cave, and laid her at the feet of an armed man.

Terrified at this extraordinary action, she started up with a shriek, but was at that moment enveloped in the arms of the stranger, while a shout of exultation resounded from the Scot who stood at the entrance. "Blessed Virgin, protect me!" cried she, striving to break from the fierce grasp that held her. "Where am I?" looking wildly at the two men who had brought her. "Why am I not taken to my father?"

She received no answer, and both the Scot and the Englishman left the place. The stranger still held her locked in a grip that seemed of iron. In vain she struggled, in vain she called on earth and heaven for assistance; she was held, and still he kept silence. Exhausted with fruitless attempts for release, she put her hands together, and in a calmer tone exclaimed, "I am an unprotected woman, praying for your mercy; withhold it not, for the sake of heaven and your own soul!"

"Kneel to me then, thou siren," cried the warrior, with fierceness. As he spoke, he threw her upon the rocky floor. His voice echoed terribly in her ears; but obeying him, "Free me," cried she, "for the sake of my dying father!"

"Never, till I have had my revenge!"

At this dreadful denunciation she shuddered to the soul, but yet she spoke: "Surely I am mistaken for some one else! Oh, how can I have offended any man, to incur so cruel an outrage?"

The warrior burst into a satanic laugh, and throwing up his visor, "Behold me, Helen!" cried he, grasping her clasped hands. "My hour is come!"

At the sight of the face of Soulis she comprehended all her danger, and wresting her hands from his hold, she burst through the bushes out of the cave. Her betrayers stood at the entrance, and catching her in their arms, brought her back to their lord. But it was an insensible form they now laid before him: overcome with horror her senses had fled. Short was this suspension from misery; water was thrown on her face, and she awoke to recollection, lying on the bosom of her enemy. Again she struggled, again her cries echoed from side to side of the cavern. "Peace!" cried the monster: "you cannot escape; you are now mine forever! Twice you refused to be my wife; you dare to despise my love and my power; now you shall feel my hatred and my revenge!"

"Kill me!" cried the distracted Helen; "kill me, and I will bless you!" she shrieked; and as he more fiercely held her, her hand struck against the hilt of his dagger. In a moment she drew it; and armed with the strength of outraged innocence, unwitting whether it gave death or not, only hoping it would release her, she struck it into his side. All was the action of an instant; while, as instantaneously he caught her wrist, and exclaiming, "Damnable traitress!" dashed her from him, stunned and motionless to the ground.

The weapon had not penetrated far. But the sight of his blood, drawn by the hand of a woman, incensed the raging Soulis. He called aloud on Macgregor. The two men, who yet stood without the cave, reentered. They started when they saw a dagger in his hand, and Helen, lying apparently lifeless, with blood sprinkled on her garments.

Macgregor, who had personated the Scottish knight, in a tremulous voice asked why he had killed the lady.

Soulis frowned. "Here!" cried he, throwing open his vest; "this wound that beautiful fiend you look upon aimed at my life!"

"My lord," said the other man, who had heard her shrieks, "I expected different treatment for the Earl of Mar's daughter."

"Base Scot!" returned Soulis, "when you brought a woman into these wilds to me, you had no right to expect I should use her otherwise than as I pleased."

"This language, Lord Soulis," rejoined the man much agitated; "but you mistook me—I meant not to reproach."

" 'Tis well you did not"; and turning from him with contempt, he listened to Macgregor, who, stooping towards Helen, observed that her pulse beat. "Fool!" returned Soulis, "did you think I would so rashly throw away what I have been at such pains to gain? Call your wife: she knows how to teach these minions submission to my will."

The man obeyed; and while his companion by the command of Soulis bound a fillet round the bleeding forehead of Helen, cut by the flints, the chief brought two chains, and fastening them to her wrists and ankles, exclaimed with brutal triumph, while he locked them on: "There, my haughty damsel! flatter not thyself that the arms of Soulis shall be thine only fetters."

Macgregor's wife entered, and promised to obey all her lord's injunctions. When she was left alone with the breathless body of Helen, water, and a few cordial drops, which she poured into the unhappy lady's mouth, soon recalled her wretched senses. On opening her eyes, the sight of one of her own sex inspired her with some hope; but attempting to stretch out her hands in supplication, she was horror-struck at finding them fastened, and at the clink of the chains which bound her. "Why am I thus?" demanded she of the woman; but suddenly recollecting having attempted to pierce Soulis with his own dagger, and now supposing she had slain him, she added, "Is Lord Soulis killed?"

"No," replied the woman; "my husband says he is but slightly hurt; and surely your fair face belies your heart, if you could intend the death of so loving a lord."

"You then belong to him?" cried the wretched Helen, wringing her hands. "What will be my unhappy fate! Virgin of heaven, take me to thyself!"

"Heaven forbid," cried the woman, "that you should pray against being the favorite lady of our noble chief! Many around Hermitage castle would come hither on their hands and knees to arrive at that happiness."

"Happiness!" cried Lady Helen, in anguish of spirit; "it can visit me no more till I am restored to my father, till I am released from the power of Soulis. Give me liberty," continued she. "Assist me to escape, and half the wealth of the Earl of Mar shall be your reward."

"Alas!" returned the woman, "my lord would burn me on the spot, and murder my husband, did he think I even listened to such a project. No, lady; you never will see your father more; for none who so enter my lord's Hermitage ever wish to come out again."

"The Hermitage!" cried Helen, in augmented horror. "O Father of mercy, never let me live to enter those accursed walls!"

"They are frightful enough, to be sure," returned the woman; "but you, gentle lady, will be princess there, and in all things commanding the heart of its lord, have rather cause to bless than to curse the castle of Soulis."

"Himself and all that bears his name are accursed to me," returned Helen. "Pity me, kind creature; and if you have a daughter whose honor is dear to you, think you see her in me, and have compassion on me."

"Poor young soul!" cried the woman, looking at her with commiseration; "I would pity you if I durst; but I repeat, my life and my husband's, and my children, who are now near Hermitage, would all be sacrificed to the rage of Lord Soulis." Helen closed her hands over her face in despair, and the woman went on: "And as for the matter of your making such lamentations about your father, if he be as little your friend as your mother is, you have not much cause to grieve on that score."

Helen started. "My mother! what of her!—Speak! tell me! It was indeed her signet that betrayed me into these horrors. She cannot have consented—speak! tell me what you would say of Lady Mar!"

Regardless of the emotion which now shook the frame of her auditor, the woman coolly replied she had heard from her husband, who was the confidential servant of Lord Soulis, that it was to Lady Mar he owed the knowledge of Helen being at Bothwell. The countess had written a letter to her cousin, Lord Buchan, who, being a sworn friend of England. was then with Lord de Valence at Dumbarton. In this epistle she intimated "her wish that Lord Buchan would devise a plan to surprise Bothwell castle the ensuing day, to prevent the departure of its armed vassals then preparing to march to the support of the outlaw, Sir William Wallace, who, with his band of robbers, was lurking about the caverns of the Cartlane craigs."

Lady Mar begged her cousin not to appear in the affair himself, that she might escape the suspicions of her lord; who, she strongly declared, was not arming his vassals for any disloyal disposition towards the King of England, but solely at the instigations of Wallace. And to keep the transaction as close as possible, she proposed that the Lord Soulis, who she understood was then at Dumbarton, should take the command of two or three thousand troops, and, marching to Bothwell next morning, seize the few hundred armed Scots who were there, ready to proceed to the mountains. She ended by saying that her daughter-in-law was in the castle, which she hoped would be an inducement to Soulis to ensure the Earl of Mar's safety for the sake of her hand as his reward.

The greatest part of Lady Mar's injunctions could not be attended to, as Lord de Valence, as well as Soulis, was made privy to the secret. The English nobleman declared that he should not do his duty to his king if he did not head the force that went to quell so dangerous a conspiracy; and Soulis, eager to go at any rate, joyfully accepted the honor of being his companion. Lord Buchan was easily persuaded to the seizure of the earl's person, as De Valence flattered him that the king would endow him with the Mar estates which must now be confiscated. The woman proceeded to relate how, when the party had executed their design at Bothwell castle, she was to have been taken by Soulis to his castle near Glasgow. But on that wily Scot not finding her, he conceived the suspicion that Lord de Valence had prevailed on the countess to give her up to him. He observed that the woman who could be induced to betray her daughter to one man, would easily be bribed to repeat the crime to another, and under this impression he accused the English nobleman of treachery. De Valence denied it vehemently; a quarrel ensued; and Soulis departed with a few of his followers, giving out that he was retiring in indignation to Dun-glass. But the fact was, he lurked about in Bothwell wood; and from its recesses saw Cressingham's lieutenant march by to take possession of the castle in the king's name. At this period, one of the spies who had been left by that chief in quest of news, returned with a tenant of St. Fillan's, who told Lord Soulis all he wanted to know, informing him that a beautiful young lady, who could be no other than Lady Helen Mar, was concealed in that convent.

"In consequence," continued Helen's guardian, "my husband and the stranger, the one habited as a Scottish, and the other as an English knight, set out for St. Fillan's, taking with them the signet which your mother had sent with her letter to the earl her cousin. They hoped such a pledge of their truth would ensure them credit. You know the tale they invented; and its success proves my lord to be no bad contriver."

CHAPTER XIV.

THE PENTLAND HILLS.

HELEN listened with astonishment to this story of her stepmother's ill-judged tenderness or cruel treachery; and remembering the threats which had escaped that lady in their last conversation she saw no reason to doubt what explained the seizure of her father, the betraying of Wallace, and her own present calamity.

"You do not answer me," rejoined the woman; "but if you think I don't say true, Lord Soulis himself will assure you of the fact."

"Alas, no!" returned Helen, profoundly sighing; "I believe it too well. I see the depth of the misery into which I am plunged. And yet," cried she, recollecting the imposition the men had put upon her—"yet I shall not be wholly so if my father lives, and was not in extremity."

"If that thought gives you comfort, retain it," returned the woman; "the whole story of the earl's illness was an invention to bring you at short notice from the protection of the prior."

"I thank thee, gracious Providence, for this comfort!" exclaimed Helen.

Margery shook her head. "Ah, poor victim (thought she), how vain is thy devotion!" But she had not time to say so, for her husband and the deserter from Cressingham reentered the cave. Helen afraid that it was Soulis, started up. The stranger proceeded to lift her in his arms. She struggled, and in the violence of her action struck his beaver; it opened, and discovered a pale and stern countenance with a large scar across his jaw. This mark of contest and the gloomy scowl of his eyes made Helen rush towards the woman for protection. The man hastily closed his helmet, and speaking through the clasped steel, bade her prepare to accompany Lord Soulis in a journey to the south.

Helen looked at her shackled arms, and despairing of effecting her escape by any effort of her own, she thought that gaining time might be some advantage; and allowing the man to take her hand, while Macgregor supported her on the other side, they led her out of the cave. She observed the latter smile significantly at his wife. "Oh!" cried she, "to what am I betrayed? Unhand me—leave me!" Almost fainting with dread she leaned against the arm of the stranger.

83

At that moment Soulis, mounted on his steed, approached and ordered her to be put into the litter. Incapable of contending with the numbers which surrounded her, she allowed them to execute their master's commands. Macgregor's wife was set on a pillion behind him, and Soulis giving the word, they all marched on at a rapid pace.

A dismal hue now overspread the country; the thunder roared in distant peals, and the lightning came down in such sheets that the carriers were often obliged to cover their eyes to regain their sight. A shrill wind pierced the slight covering of the litter, and blowing it aside, discovered at intervals the rough outlines of the distant hills visible through the mist.

The cavalcade with difficulty mounted the steps of a hill, where the storm raged so turbulently that the men who carried the litter stopped and told their lord it would be impossible to proceed in the approaching darkness; they conjured him to look at the perpendicular rocks; to observe the overwhelming gusts of the tempest; and then judge whether they dare venture with the litter on so dangerous a pathway, made slippery by descending rain.

To halt in such a spot seemed to Soulis as unsafe as to proceed. "We shall not be better off," answered he, "should we attempt to return: precipices lie on either side; and to stand still would be equally perilous."

On the remonstrance of their master the men resumed their pace, and after hard contention with the storm they gained the summit of the west side of the mountain, and were descending its eastern brow when the shades of night closed in upon them. Looking down into the black chaos on the brink of which they must pass along, they once more protested they could not advance a foot until the dawn should give them some security.

At this declaration, which Soulis saw could not now be disputed, he ordered the troop to halt under the shelter of a projecting rock. Its huge arch overhung the ledge that formed the road, while the deep gulf at his feet, by the roaring of its waters, proclaimed itself the receptacle of those cataracts which rush tremendous from the Pentland hills.

Soulis dismounted. The men set down the litter, and removed to a distance as he approached. He opened one of the curtains, and throwing himself beside the exhausted but watchful Helen, clasped his arms roughly about her. Ten thousand strengths seemed then to heave him from her heart; and struggling with a power that amazed even herself, she threw him from her, and holding him off with her shackled arms, her shrieks again pierced the heavens.

At that moment her couch was shaken by a sudden shock, and in the next she was covered with the blood of Soulis. A stroke from an unseen arm had reached him, and starting on his feet, a fearful battle of swords took place over the prostrate Helen.

One of the men who hastened to the assistance of their master, fell dead on her body; while the chief himself, sorely wounded, and breathing revenge, was forced off by the survivors. "Where do you carry me, villains?" cried he. "Separate me not from the vengeance I will yet hurl on that demon who has robbed me of my victim." He raved, but more unheeded than the tempest; in spite of his threats the men carried him to a distant hollow in the rock, and laid him down, now insensible from loss of blood. One or two of the most desperate returned to see what was become of Lady Helen, well aware that if they could regain her, their master would be satisfied; but, should she be lost, the whole troop knew their fate would be some merciless punishment.

Macgregor and the deserter of Cressingham were the first who reached the spot where the lady had been left. With horror they found the litter, but not herself. She was gone; but whether carried off by the mysterious arm which had felled their lord or she had thrown herself into the foaming gulf beneath they could not determine. They decided, however, the latter should be their report to Soulis, knowing he would rather believe she had perished than that she had escaped his toils.

Almost stupefied with consternation, they returned to repeat this tale to their furious lord, who, on having his wounds stanched, had recovered from his swoon. On hearing that the beautiful creature he had so lately believed his own was lost to him forever, swallowed up in the whelming wave, he became frantic. He raved, tore up the earth like a wild beast, and, foaming at the mouth, dashed the wife of Macgregor from him, as she approached with a balsam for his wounds. "Off!" cried he. "Where is she whom I intrusted to thy care?"

"My lord," answered the affrighted woman, "you know best. You terrified the poor young creature. You forced yourself into her litter, and can you wonder——"

"That I should force you to perdition, execrable witch," cried he, "that knew no better how to prepare a slave to receive her lord!" As he spoke he struck her again; but it was with his gauntlet hand, and the eyes of the unfortunate woman opened no more. The blow fell on her temple, and a motionless corpse lay before him.

"My wife!" cried the poor Macgregor, putting his trembling arms about her neck.   "Oh, my lord, how have I deserved this?   You have slain her!"

"Suppose I have?" returned the chief with a cold scorn; "she was old and ugly; and could you recover Helen, I would find you a substitute."

Macgregor made no reply, but feeling in his heart that such were the rewards from villainy to its vile instruments, he could not but say to himself, "I deserved it of my God, but not of thee"; and sobbing over the remains of his equally criminal wife, he removed her from the now hated presence of his lord.

CHAPTER XV.

THE HUT.

MEANWHILE the Lady Helen, hardly rational from the horror and hope that agitated her, extricated herself from the dead body, and in her eagerness to escape would certainly have fallen over the precipice had not the same gallant arm which had covered her persecutor with wounds caught her as she sprang from the litter. "Fear not, lady," exclaimed a gentle voice; "you are under the protection of a Scottish knight."

There was a kindness in the sound that seemed to proclaim the speaker to be of her own kindred; she felt as if suddenly rescued by a brother, and dropping her head on his bosom, a shower of grateful tears relieved her heart. Aware that the enemy might soon be on him again, he clasped her in his arms, and with the activity of a mountain deer crossed two rushing streams, leaping from rock to rock, and then treading with a light and steady step a bridge of one single tree which arched the cataract below, he reached the opposite side, where, spreading his plaid upon the rock, he laid the trembling Helen upon it. Then softly breathing his bugle, in a moment he was surrounded by a number of men, whose rough gratulations might have reawakened the alarm of Helen, had she not still heard his voice. There was graciousness in every tone, and she listened in calm expectation.

He directed the men to take their axes and cut away, on their side of the fall, the tree which arched it. It was probable the villain he had just assailed, or his followers, might pursue him, and he thought it prudent to demolish the bridge.

The men obeyed, and the warrior returned to his fair charge. It was raining fast, and he proposed leading her to shelter. "There is a hermit's cell on the northern side of this mountain. I will conduct you thither in the morning, but meanwhile we must seek a nearer refuge."

"Anywhere, sir, with honor my guide," answered Helen, timidly.

"You are safe with me, lady," returned he, "as in the arms of the Virgin. Whoever you are, confide in me, and you shall not be betrayed."

Helen confidently gave him her hand and strove to rise; but at the first attempt, the shackles piercing her ankles, she sank again to the ground. The cold iron on her wrists touched the hand of her preserver. He now recollected his surprise on hearing the clank of chains when carrying her over the bridge. "Who," inquired he, "could have done this unmanly deed?"

"The wretch from whom you rescued me, to prevent my escape from a captivity worse than death."

While she spoke he wrenched open the manacles from her wrists and ankles and threw them over the precipice. As she heard them dash into the torrent, gratitude filled her heart; and again giving her hand to him, she said with earnestness, "Oh, sir, if you have a wife or sister, should they ever fall into the like peril with mine, may Heaven reward you by sending them such a preserver!"

The stranger sighed deeply. "Sweet lady," returned he, "I have no sister, no wife, but I thank thee for thy prayer." He sighed profoundly again, and led her silently down the windings of the declivity whence they descended into a wooded dell, and soon approached the half-standing remains of what had once been a shepherd's hut.

"This," said the knight, as they entered, "was the habitation of a good old man who fed his flock on these mountains; but a band of Southron soldiers forced his only daughter from him, and, plundering his little abode, drove him out upon the waste. He perished the same night, by grief and the inclemencies of the weather. His son, a brave youth, was left for dead; but I found him in this dreary solitude, and he told me the story of his despair. Indeed, lady, when I heard your shrieks from the opposite side of the chasm, I thought they might proceed from this poor boy's sister, and I flew to restore them to each other."

Helen shuddered as he related a tale so nearly resembling her own; and trembling with horror of what might have been her fate had she not been rescued, she sank exhausted upon a turf seat. The chief still held her hand. It was very cold, and he called to his men to seek fuel to make a fire. While his messengers were exploring the crannies of the rocks for dried leaves and sticks, Helen, totally overcome, leaned almost motionless against the wall of the hut. Finding by her shortening breath that she was fainting, the knight took her in his arms, and supporting her on his breast, chafed her hands and her forehead. Alarmed at such signs of death, he spoke to one of his men who remained in the hut.

The man answered his master's inquiry by putting a flask into his hand. The knight poured some of its contents into her mouth.

Her streaming locks wetted his cheek. "Poor lady!" said he; "she will perish in these forlorn regions, where neither warmth nor nourishment can be found."

Several of his men soon after entered with a quantity of boughs, which they had found in the fissures of the rock at some distance. With these a fire was speedily kindled; and its blaze diffusing comfort through the chamber, he had the satisfaction of hearing a sigh from his charge. Her head still leaned on his bosom when she opened her eyes.

"Lady," said he, "I bless God you are revived." Raising herself, she thanked him, and requested a little water which was given to her. She drank some, and would have met the compassionate gaze of the knight had not weakness cast such a film before her eyes that she scarcely saw anything. Being still languid, she leaned her head on the turf seat. Her face was pale as marble, and her long hair, saturated with wet, by its darkness made her look of a more deadly hue.

"Death, how lovely canst thou be!" sighed the knight to himself. Helen started, and looked around her with alarm. "Fear not," said he, "I only dreaded your pale looks; but you revive, and will yet bless all that are dear to you. Suffer me, sweet lady, to drain the dangerous wet from these tresses." He took hold of them as he spoke. She saw the water running from her hair over his hands, and allowing his kind request, he continued wiping her glossy locks with his scarf, till, exhausted by fatigue, she gradually sank into a profound sleep.

Dawn had penetrated the ruined walls of the hut before Lady Helen awoke, and opening her eyes, she turned her head, and fixed them upon the figure of the knight who was seated near her. His noble air and the pensive expression of his fine features struck like a spell upon her gathering recollections; she at once remembered all she had suffered, all that she owed to him. She moved. Her preserver turned his eyes towards her; seeing she was awake, he rose from the side of the embers he had kept alive during her slumber, and expressed his hopes that she felt restored. She returned him a grateful reply; and he quitted her, to rouse his men for their journey to the hermit's cell.

When he reentered, he found Helen braiding up the fine hair which had so lately been scattered by the elements. She would have risen at his approach, but he seated himself on a stone at her feet. "We shall be detained here a few minutes longer," said he; "I have ordered my men to make a litter of crossed branches, to bear you on their shoulders. You would not be equal to the toil of descending these heights to the glen of stones. The venerable man who inhabits there will protect you until he can summon your family, or friends, to receive his charge."

At these words, which Helen thought were meant to reprove her for not having revealed herself, she blushed; but fearful of breathing a name under the interdict of the English governors, fearful of involving her preserver's safety, by making him aware of the persecuted creature he had rescued, she paused for a moment, and then replied: "For your humanity, brave sir, shown this night to a friendless woman, I must be ever grateful, but not even to the hermit may I reveal my name. It is fraught with danger to every honest Scot who should know that he protects one who bears it, and therefore, least of all, noble stranger, would I breathe it to you."

The knight looked at her intensely, profoundly sighed, and tore his eyes from her countenance. "I ask not, madam, to know what you think proper to conceal. But danger has no alarms for me, when, by incurring it, I serve those who need a protector."

A sudden thought flashed across her mind: might it not be possible that this tender guardian of her safety was the noble Wallace? But the vain idea fled. He was pent up amidst the Cartlane craigs, sworn to extricate the helpless families of his followers or to perish with them. This knight was accompanied by none but men, and his eyes shone in too serene a luster to be those of the suffering chief of Ellerslie. "Ah! then," murmured she to herself, "are there two men in Scotland who will speak thus?" She looked up in his face. The plumes of his bonnet shaded his features, but she saw they were paler than on his entrance. His eyes were bent to the ground as he proceeded:

"I am the servant of my fellow-creatures—command me and my few faithful followers; and if it be in the power of such small means to succor you or yours, I am ready to answer for their obedience. If the villain from whom I had the happiness to release you be yet more deeply implicated in your sorrows, tell me how they can be relieved, and I will attempt it. I shall make no new enemies by the deed, for the Southrons and I are at eternal enmity."

Helen could not withdraw her eyes from his countenance. "Alas!" replied she, "ill should I repay such nobleness were I to involve it in the calamities of my house. No, generous stranger, I must remain unknown. Leave me with the hermit, and from his cell I will send to some relation to take me thence."

I urge you no more, gentle lady," replied the knight, rising. "Were I at the head of an army instead of a handful of men, I might then have a better argument for offering my services; but as it is, I feel my weakness and seek to know no further."

Helen trembled with emotion. "Were you at the head of an army I might then dare to reveal the full weight of my anxieties; but Heaven has already been sufficiently gracious to me in redeeming me from my cruelest enemy." At this moment a man entered and told the knight the vehicle was finished, the morning fine, and his men ready to march. He turned towards Helen: "May I conduct you to the rude carriage we have prepared?"

Helen gathered her mantle about her; and the knight throwing his scarf over her head, she gave him her hand, and he led her out of the hut to the side of the bier. It was overlaid with the men's plaids. The knight placed her on it; and the carriers raising it on their shoulders, her deliverer led the way, and they took their course down the mountain.

CHAPTER XVI.

THE GLEN OF STONES.

THEY proceeded in silence through the curvings of the dell till it opened into a path along the top of a cliff, which overhung the western side of a deep loch. As they mounted the wall of this immense amphitheater, Helen watched the sublime uprise of the king of light, issuing from behind the opposite citadel of rocks and borne aloft on a throne of clouds that swam in floating gold. The herbage on the cliffs glittered with liquid emeralds as his beams kissed their summits, and the lake beneath sparkled like a sea of molten diamonds.

As she watched her eyes fell on the noble mien of the knight, who, with his spear in his hand and wrapped in his dark mantle of mingled greens, led the way with a rapid step along the shelving declivity. Turning suddenly to the left, he struck into a defile between two craggy mountains, whose brown cheeks trickling with ten thousand rills seemed to weep over the gloom of the valley beneath.

As they advanced the vale gradually narrowed, and at last shut them within an immense chasm which seemed to have been cleft at its towering summit to admit a few beams of light to the desert below. The men who carried Helen, with some difficulty found a safe footing. However, after frequent rests and unremitted caution they at last were able to follow their chief into a less gloomy part of this chaos of nature. The knight stopped and approaching the bier told Helen they had arrived at the end of their journey.

"In the heart of that cliff," said he, "is the hermit's cell; a desolate shelter, but a safe one. Old age and poverty hold no temptations to the enemies of Scotland."

As he spoke, the venerable man who had heard voices beneath appeared on the rock; and while his tall and majestic figure, clad in gray, moved forward, he seemed the bard of Morven issuing from his cave of shells to bid a hero's welcome to the young and warlike Oscar.

"Bless thee, my son!" cried he, as he descended; "what accident hath returned thee so soon to these solitudes?"

The knight related the circumstances of Helen's rescue, and that he had brought her to share his asylum.

92

The hermit took her by the hand, and promised her every service in his power. He then preceded the knight, whose firmer arm supported her up the rock, to the outer apartment of the cell.

A sacred awe struck her as she entered this place, dedicated wholly to God. She bowed and crossed herself. The hermit, observing her devotion, blessed her and bade her welcome to the abode of peace.

"Here, daughter," said he, "has one son of persecuted Scotland found a refuge. The green herb is all the food these wilds afford, and the limpid water their best beverage."

"Ah!" returned Helen, "would to Heaven that all who love the freedom of Scotland were now within this glen! The herb and the stream would be luxuries when tasted in liberty and hope. My father——" she stopped, recollecting that she had almost betrayed the secrecy she meant to maintain, and looking down, remained in confused silence. The knight gazed at her and wished to penetrate what she concealed, but delicacy forbade him to urge her again. He spoke not; but the hermit, ignorant of her reluctance to reveal her family, resumed:

"I do not wonder, gentle lady, that you speak in terms which tell me even your tender sex feels the tyranny of Edward. Who in Scotland is exempt? Six months ago I was abbot of Scone. Because I refused to betray my trust, and resign the archives of the kingdom lodged there, Edward, the profaner of the sanctuary, sent his emissaries to sack the convent, and to wrest from my grasp the records I refused to deliver. Most of my brethren were slain. Myself and the remainder were turned out upon the waste. We retired to the monastery of Cambus-kenneth; but there oppression found us. Cressingham, having seized on other religious houses, determined to swell his hoards with the plunder of that also. In the dead of night the attack was made. I knew not whither to go, but I took my course over the hills; and finding the valley of stones fit for my purpose, for two months have lived alone in this wilderness."

"Unhappy Scotland!" ejaculated Helen. Her eyes had followed the chief, who, during this narrative, leaned thoughtfully against the entrance of the cave. He turned and approached her. "You hear from the lips of my venerable friend," said he, "a direful story; happy then am I, gentle lady, that you and he have found a refuge, though a rough one. I must now tear myself from this tranquillity to seek scenes more befitting a younger son of the country he deplores."

Helen felt unable to answer. But the abbot spoke: "And am I not to see you again?"

"That is as Heaven wills," replied he; "but as it is unlikely on this side the grave, my best pledge of friendship is this lady. To you she may reveal what she has withheld from me; but in either case, she is secure in your goodness."

"Rely on my faith, my son; and may the Almighty's shield hang on your steps!"

The knight turned to Helen: "Farewell, sweet lady!" said he. She trembled at the words, and held out her hand to him. He took it and drew it towards his lips, but checking himself, he only pressed it, saying, "In your prayer, sometimes remember the most desolate of men."

A mist seemed to pass over the eyes of Lady Helen! "My prayers for my own preserver and for my father's," cried she in an agitated voice, "shall ever be mingled. And if ever it be safe to remember me,—should Heaven indeed *arm the patriot's hand,*—then my father may be proud to know and to thank the brave deliverer of his child."

The knight paused, and looked with animation upon her. "Then your father is in arms, and against the tyrant. Tell me where, and you see before you a man who is ready to join him and to lay down his life in the just cause."

At this declaration Lady Helen's full heart overflowed and she burst into tears. He drew towards her and continued: "My men, though few, are brave. They are devoted to their country, and are willing for her sake to follow me to victory or to death. As I am a knight, I am sworn to defend the cause of right; and where shall I so justly find it as on the side of bleeding Scotland? Speak, gentle lady! trust me with your noble father's name, and he shall not have cause to blame your confidence."

"My father," replied Helen, "is not where your generous service can reach him. Two brave chiefs, one a kinsman of my own and the other his friend, are now colleagued to free him. If they fail, my whole house falls in blood; and to add another victim to the destiny which in that case will overwhelm me—the thought is beyond my strength." She stopped, and then added in a suppressed voice, "Farewell!"

"Not till you hear me further," replied he. "I repeat, I have now a scanty number of followers, but I leave these mountains to gather more. Tell me, then, where I may join these chiefs you speak of; give me a pledge that I come from you; and whoever may be your father, as he is a true Scot, I will compass his release or perish in the attempt."

"Alas! generous stranger," cried she, "to what would you per- suade me? You know not the peril that you ask."

"Nothing is perilous to me," replied he, with a heroic smile, "that is to serve my country. I have no joy but in her. Give me, then, the only happiness of which I am now capable, and send me to serve her by freeing one of her defenders."

Helen hesitated. She looked up with inward agitations painted on her cheeks.

"Fear not, lady," said the hermit, "that you would plunge your deliverer into any danger by involving him in what you might call rebellion against the usurper. He is already a proscribed man."

"Proscribed!" repeated she; "wretched indeed is my country when her noblest spirits are denied the right to live."

"No country is wretched, sweet lady," returned the knight, "till it consents to its own slavery. Bonds and death are the utmost of our enemy's malice: the one is beyond his power to inflict, when a man is determined to die or to live free; and for the other, which of us will think that ruin which leads to the blessed freedom of paradise?"

Helen looked on the chief as she used to look on her cousin when expressions of virtuous enthusiasm burst from his lips. "You would teach confidence to Despair herself," returned she; "again I hope, for God does not create in vain. You shall know my father; but first, let me apprise you of every danger with which that knowledge is surrounded. He is hemmed in by enemies. Not the English only, but the most powerful of his own countrymen, are leagued against him. They sold my father to captivity, and perhaps to death; and I, wretched I, was the price. To free him the noblest of Scottish knights is now engaged; but such hosts impede him, that hope hardly dares hover over his path."

"Then," cried the stranger, "let my arm be second to his in the great achievement. My heart yearns to meet a brother in arms who feels for Scotland what I do; and with such a coadjutor I dare prom- ise your father liberty, and that the power of England shall be shaken."

Helen's heart beat violently at these words. "I would not defer the union of two such minds. Go, then, to the Cartlane craigs. But, alas, how can I direct you?" cried she; "the passes are beset with Eng- lish, and I know not whether at this moment the brave Wallace sur- vives to be again the deliverer of my father."

Helen paused. The recollection of all that Wallace had suffered for the sake of her father, and of the mortal extremity in which Ker had left him, rose like a dreadful train of apparitions before her, and, lost in these remembrances, she did not remark the start and rushing color of the knight as she pronounced the name of Wallace.

"If Wallace ever had the happiness of serving any who belonged to you," returned the knight, "he has at least one source of pleasure in that remembrance. Tell me what he can further do? Only say, where is that father whom you say he once preserved, and I will hasten to yield my feeble aid to repeat the service."

"Alas!" replied Helen, "I cannot but repeat my fears that the bravest of men no longer exists. Two days before I was betrayed into the hands of the traitor from whom you rescued me, a messenger from Cartlane craigs informed my cousin that the gallant Wallace was surrounded, and if my father did not send his forces to relieve him, he must inevitably perish. No forces could my father send; he was then made a prisoner by the English, his retainers shared the same fate, and none but my cousin escaped to accompany the honest Scot back to his master. My cousin set forth with a few followers to join him—a few against thousands."

"They are in arms for their country, lady," returned the knight, "and a thousand angels guard them; fear not for them. But for your father, name to me the place of his confinement, and as I have not the besiegers of Cartlane craigs to encounter, I engage, with God's help and the arms of my men, to set the brave earl free."

"How?" exclaimed Helen, remembering that she had not yet mentioned her father's rank, and gazing at him with astonishment. "Do you know his name? is the misfortune of my father already so far spread?"

"Rather say his virtue, lady," answered the knight; "no man who watches over the destiny of our devoted country can be ignorant of her friends. I know that the Earl of Mar has made himself a generous sacrifice, but I am yet to learn the circumstances from you. Speak without reserve, that I may seek the accomplishment of my vow, and restore to Scotland its best friend."

"Thou brother in heart to the generous Wallace!" exclaimed Lady Helen, "my voice is feeble to thank thee." The hermit, who had listened in silent interest, now presented her with a cup of water and a little fruit to refresh herself before she satisfied the inquiries of the knight. She put the cup to her lips, and turning to the knight she briefly related what had been the design of her father with regard to Sir William Wallace; how he had been seized at Bothwell, and sent with his family a prisoner to Dumbarton castle.

"Proceed, then, thither," continued she. "If Heaven have yet spared the lives of Wallace and my cousin Andrew Murray, you will meet them before its walls. Meanwhile I shall seek the protection of my father's sister, and in her castle near the Forth abide in safety. But, noble stranger, one bond I must lay upon you: should you come up with my cousin, do not discover that you have met with me. His hatred is so hot against Soulis, my betrayer, that should he know the outrage I have sustained, he would, I fear, run himself and the general cause into danger by seeking an immediate revenge."

The stranger readily passed his word to Helen that he would never mention her name until she herself should give him leave. "But when your father is restored to his rights," continued he, "in his presence I hope to claim my acquaintance with his admirable daughter."

Helen blushed at this compliment: it was not more than any man in his situation might have said, but it confused her, and she answered, "His personal freedom may be effected; and God grant such a reward to your prowess! But his other rights, what can recover them? His estates sequestrated, his vassals in bonds; all power of the Earl of Mar will be annihilated, and from some obscure refuge like this must he utter his thanks to his daughter's preserver."

"Not so, lady," replied he; "the sword is now raised in Scotland that cannot be laid down till it be broken or have conquered. All have suffered by Edward, both the powerful and the poor, and when a whole people take up arms to regain their rights, what force can prevent restitution?"

"So I felt," returned Helen, "while I had not yet seen the horrors of the contest. But now, when all whom my father commanded are slain or carried away by the enemy; when he is himself a prisoner, and awaiting the sentence of the tyrant he opposed; when the gallant Wallace, instead of being able to hasten to his rescue, is besieged by a numberless host,—hope almost dies within me."

She turned pale as she spoke, and the stranger resumed: "Lady, if there be that virtue in Scotland which can alone deserve freedom, it will be achieved. Relying on the God of Justice, I promise you your father's liberty; and I now go to rouse a few brave spirits to arms. Remember, the battle is not to the strong, nor victory with a multitude of hosts."

While he yet spoke, the hermit reentered from the inner cell, supporting a youth on his arm. At sight of the knight, who held out his hand to him, he dropped on his knees and burst into tears. "Do you, then, leave me?" cried he. "Am I not to serve my preserver?"

Helen rose in strange surprise; there was something in the feelings of the boy that was infectious; and while her own heart beat violently,

she looked first on his emaciated figure, and then at the noble contour of the knight, "where every god had seemed to set his seal."
Turning from the suppliant boy to Helen, "Rise," said he to the
youth, "and behold in this lady the object of the service to which I
appoint you. You will soon, I hope, be sufficiently recovered to attend upon her wishes. Be her servant and her guard; and when we
meet again, as she will then be under the protection of her father, if
you do not prefer so gentle a service before the rougher one of war,
I will resume you to myself."

The youth, who had obeyed the knight and risen, bowed respectfully; and Helen, uttering some words of thanks to hide her agitation,
turned away. The hermit exclaimed, "Again, my son, I beseech
Heaven to bless thee!"

"And may its guardian care shield all here!" replied the knight.
Helen looked up to bid him a last farewell—but he was gone. The
hermit had left the cell with him, and the youth also had disappeared
into the inner cave. Being left alone, she threw herself down before
the altar, and inwardly implored protection for that brave knight's
life, and by his means to grant safety to Wallace and freedom to
her father.

As she rose, she perceived the hermit, who, on entering, had observed her devout position, and a benediction broke from his lips.
"Daughter," said he, leading her to a seat, "this hero will prevail,
for the Power before whose altar you have just knelt has declared,
'My might is with them who obey my laws and put their trust in me.'
You speak highly of the valiant Sir William Wallace, but I cannot
conceive that he can be better formed for heroic deeds than this chief.
Suppose them, then, to be equal; when they have met, with two such
leaders, what may not a few determined Scots perform?"

Helen sympathized with the hopes of the hermit, and wishing to
learn the name of this rival of a character she had regarded as un-
paralleled, she asked with a blush by what title she must call the
knight who had undertaken so hazardous an enterprise for her.

CHAPTER XVII.

THE HERMIT'S CELL.

"I KNOW not," returned the hermit. "I never saw your gallant deliverer before yesterday morning. Broken from my matins by a sudden noise, I beheld a deer rush down the precipice and fall headlong. As he lay struggling amongst the stones at the entrance of my cave, I had just observed an arrow in his side, when a shout issued from the rocks above, and looking up I beheld a young chieftain, with a bow in his hand, leaping from cliff to cliff, till springing from a high projection on the right he lit at once at the head of the wounded deer.

"I emerged from the recess that concealed me, and addressed him with the benediction of the morning. His plaided followers immediately appeared, and with a stroke of their ready weapons slew the animal. The chief left them to dress it for their own refreshment, and on my invitation entered the cell to share a hermit's fare.

"I told him who I was, and what had driven me to this seclusion. In return, he informed me of a design he had conceived to stimulate the surrounding chiefs to some exertions for their country; but as he never mentioned his name, I concluded he wished it to remain unrevealed, and therefore I forbore to inquire it. The arguments he means to use to arouse the slumbering courage of our country are few and conclusive. They are these: the perfidy of King Edward, who, deemed a prince of high honor, had been chosen umpire in the cause of Bruce and Baliol. He accepted the task in the character of a friend to Scotland; but no sooner was she advanced into the heart of our kingdom, and at the head of the large army he had treacherously introduced, than he declared the act of judgment was his right, as liege lord of the realm. This falsehood, which our records disproved at the outset, was not his only baseness: he bought the conscience of Baliol, and adjudged to him the throne. The recreant prince acknowledged him his master, and in that degrading ceremony of homage he was followed by almost all the lowland Scottish lords. But this vile yielding did not purchase them peace; Edward demanded oppressive services from the king, and the castles of the nobility to be resigned to English governors. These requisitions being remonstrated against by a few of our boldest chiefs, the tyrant repeated them with additional demands, and prepared to resent the appeal on the whole nation.

"Three months have hardly elapsed since the fatal battle of Dunbar, where, indignant at the outrages committed on their passive monarch, our irritated nobles at last rose, but too late, to assert their rights. Alas! one defeat drove them to despair. Baliol was taken, and themselves obliged to swear fealty to their enemy. Then came the seizure of the treasures of our monasteries, the burning of the national records, the sequestration of our property, the banishment of our chiefs, and the slavery or murder of the poor people yoked to the land. The young warrior then informed me that Earl de Warenne (whom Edward had left Lord Warden of Scotland) is taken ill, and retired to London, leaving Aymer de Valence to be his deputy. To this new tyrant De Warenne has lately sent a host of mercenaries, to hold the south of Scotland in subjection.

"With these representations of the conduct of our oppressors, the knight demonstrated the facility with which invaders, drunk with power, could be vanquished by a resolute people. The absence of Edward, who is now abroad, increases the probability of success. The knight's design is to infuse his own spirit into the bosoms of the chiefs in this part of the kingdom, and by their assistance to seize the fortresses in the Lowlands, and so form a chain against the admission of fresh troops from England. For the present he wishes to be furnished with troops enough to take some castle of power sufficient to give confidence to his friends. On his becoming master of such a place it should be the signal for all to declare themselves, and, rising at once, overwhelm Edward's garrisons in every part of Scotland.

"This is the knight's plan; and for your sake, as well as for the cause, I hope the first fortress he gains may be that of Dumbarton; it has always been considered the key of the country."

"May Heaven grant it, holy father!" returned Helen; "and whoever this knight may be, I pray the blessed St. Andrew to guide his arms."

"If I may venture to guess who he is," replied the hermit, "I would say that noble brow was formed to some day wear a crown."

"What!" cried Helen, starting, "you think this knight is the royal Bruce?"

"I am at a loss what to think," replied the hermit; "he has a most princely air."

"But is he not too young?" inquired Helen. "I have heard my father say that Bruce, Lord of Annandale, the opponent of Baliol for the crown, was much his senior; and that his son, the Earl of Carrick, must be now fifty years of age. This knight, if I am to judge of looks, cannot be twenty-five."

"True," answered the hermit; "and yet he may be a Bruce, for it is neither of the two you have mentioned that I mean; but the grandson of the one, and the son of the other. You may see by this silver beard, lady, that the winter of my life is far spent. The elder Bruce, Robert, Lord of Annandale, was my contemporary; we were boys together and educated at the same college. He passed his manhood in visiting different courts; at last, marrying a lady of the princely house of Clare, he took her to France, and confided his only son to be brought up under the renowned Saint Louis; which young Robert took the cross while quite a youth, and carrying the banner of the King of France to the plains of Palestine, covered himself with glory. In storming a Saracen fortress he rescued the person of Prince Edward of England.

"From that hour a strict friendship subsisted between the two young crusaders; and when Edward mounted the throne of England, it being then the ally of Scotland, the old Earl of Annandale, to please his brave son, took up his residence at the English court. When the male issue of our King David failed in the untimely death of Alexander III., then came the contention between Bruce and Baliol for the vacant crown. Our most venerable chiefs, the witnesses of the parliamentary settlement made on the house of Bruce during the reign of the late king, all declared for Lord Annandale. He was not only the male heir in propinquity of blood, but his experienced years and known virtues excited all true Scots to place him on the throne.

"Meanwhile Edward, forgetting friendship to his friend and fidelity to a faithful ally, was undermining the interest of Bruce and the peace of the kingdom, and by covert ways, with bribes and promises, raised such an opposition on the side of Baliol as threatened a civil war. Secure in his right, and averse to plunge his country in blood, Bruce easily fell in with a proposal hinted to him by one of Edward's creatures,—'to require that monarch to be umpire between him and Baliol.' Then it was that Edward, after soliciting the honor, declared it was his right as supreme Lord of Scotland. The Earl of Annandale refused to acknowledge this assumption. Baliol bowed to it; and for such obedience the unrighteous judge gave him the crown. Bruce absolutely refused to acknowledge the justice of this decision; and to avoid the power of the king, who had betrayed his rights, and the jealousy of the other who had usurped them, he immediately left the scene of action, going over seas to join his son, who had been cajoled away to Paris.   But, alas! he died on the road of a broken heart.

"When his son Robert (who was Earl of Carrick in right of his wife) returned to Britain, he, like his father, disdained to acknowledge Baliol as king.   But being more incensed at his successful rival than at the treachery of his false friend, Edward, he believed his glossing speeches, and established his residence at that monarch's court.   This forgetfulness of his royal blood and of the independency of Scotland has nearly obliterated him from every Scottish heart, for when we look at Bruce the courtier we cease to remember Bruce the descendant of St. David,—Bruce the Knight of the Cross, who bled for liberty before the walls of Jerusalem.

"His eldest son may be now about the age of the young knight who has just left us; and when I look on his royal port, and listen to the fervors of his soul, I cannot but think that the spirit of his noble grandsire has revived in his breast, and that, leaving his father to the luxuries of Edward's palace, he is come hither in secret to arouse Scotland and to assert his claim."

"It is very likely," rejoined Helen; "and may Heaven reward his virtue with the crown of his ancestors!"

"Sir William Wallace I never have seen," continued the hermit; "but when he was quite a youth I heard of his victories in the mimic war of the jousts at Berwick, when Edward first marched into this country under the mask of friendship.   From what you have said, I do not doubt his being a worthy supporter of Bruce.   However, dear daughter, as it is only a suspicion of mine that this knight is that young prince, for his safety and for the sake of the cause we must not let that name escape our lips; no, not even to your relations when you rejoin them, nor to the youth whom his humanity put under my protection.   Till he reveals his own secret, for us to divulge it would be folly and dishonor."

As the hermit ended speaking, he rose, and, taking Helen by the hand, led her into an excavation of the rock, where a bed of dried leaves lay on the ground.   "Here, gentle lady," said he, "I leave you to repose.   In the evening I expect a lay brother from St. Oran's monastery, and he will be your messenger to the friends you may wish to rejoin.   At present may gentlest seraphs guard your slumbers!"

Helen, fatigued in spirit and in body, thanked the good hermit for his care, and, bowing to his blessing, he left her to repose.

CHAPTER XVIII.

CARTLANE CRAIGS AND GLENFINLASS.

GUIDED by Ker, Murray led his followers over the Lanark hills by untrodden paths, and hence avoided even the sight of a Southron soldier.

Cheered by so favorable a commencement of their expedition, they even felt no dismay when, at evening, Ker descried a body of armed men at a distance, sitting round a fire at the foot of a rock which guards the western entrance to the Cartlane craigs. Murray ordered his men to proceed under covert of the bushes; and then making a concerted signal, they struck their iron crows into the interstices of the cliff, and catching at the branches which grew out of its precipitous side, with much exertion but in perfect silence at last gained the summit. That effected, they pursued their way with the same caution, till, after a long march and without encountering a human being, they reached the base of the huge rock which Wallace had made his fortress.

Ker, who expected to find it surrounded by an English army, was amazed at the death-like solitude. "The place is deserted," cried he. "My brave friend, compelled by the extremity of his little garrison, has been obliged to surrender."

"We will ascend and see," was Murray's answer.

Ker led round the rock to the most accessible point, and mounting by the projecting stones, with some difficulty gained the top. Silence pervaded every part; and the cavities at the summit, which had formed the temporary quarters of his comrades, were lonely. On entering the recess, where Wallace used to seek a few minutes' slumber, the moon, which shone full into the cave, discovered something bright lying in a distant corner. Ker hastily approached it; recollecting what Wallace had told him, that if during his absence he could find means of escape, he would leave some weapon as a sign: a dagger, if necessity drove him to the south point, where he must fight his way through the valley; and an arrow, if he could effect it without observation, by the north, as he should then seek an asylum for his exhausted followers in the wilds of Glenfinlass.

It was the iron head of an arrow which the moon had silvered;

and Ker catching it up exclaimed, "He is safe! this calls us to Glen-finlass." He then explained to Murray what had been the arrange-ment of Wallace respecting this sign, and without hesitation the young lord decided to follow him up that track.

Turning towards the northern part of the cliff, they came to a spot beneath which had been the strongest guard of the enemy, but now, like the rest, it was abandoned. A narrow path led from this rocky platform to a fall of water, rushing by the mouth of a large cavern. After they had descended the main craig, they clambered over the top of this cave, and entering upon another sweep of rugged hills, commenced a rapid march.

Traversing the lower part of Stirlingshire, and pursuing their course westward, they ascended the Ochil hills, and proceeding along the wooded heights which overhang the banks of Teith, forded that river, and entered at once into the broad valley which opened to them a distant view of Ben Lomond and Ben Ledi.

"There," exclaimed Ker, extending his hand towards the cloud-capped Ledi, "beneath the shadow of that mountain we shall find the light of Scotland, our dear master in arms!"

At this intimation, the wearied Murrays uttered a shout of joy, and hastening forward with renovated strength, met a foaming river in their path. Despising all obstacles, they rushed in, and, buffeting the waves, soon found a firm footing on the opposite shore. The sun shone cheerily above their heads, illuminating the sides of the moun-tains with a dewy splendor, while Ben Ledi, the standard of their hope, seemed to wave them on.

When the little troop halted on the shore of Loch Venachoir, the mists which had lingered on the brow of Ledi slowly descended into the valley, and covering the mouth of the pass, seemed to shut them at once between the mountain and that world of waters. Ker, who had never been in these tracks before, wondered at their sublimity, and became alarmed, lest they should lose their way amid infinite windings. But Murray, who remembered having once explored them with his father, led promptly forward by a steep rough road in the side of the mountain.

The party soon entered a labyrinth of craigs; and passing onward, gradually descended till the roar of waters intimated to Murray they drew near the great fall of Glenfinlass. Here towered a host of stately pines; and there, the lofty beeches, birches, and mountain-oak bending over the flood, formed an arch so impenetrable that while the sun brightened the tops of the mountains, all beneath lay in deepest midnight.

They entered the valley, and with beating hearts pursued their way along the western border of Loch Lubnaig till the forest lost its high trees in the shadows of the surrounding mountains, and told them they were now in the center of Glenfinlass.

Ker put his bugle to his lips and sounded the pibroch of Ellerslie. A thousand echoes returned the notes; and after a pause, which allowed their last response to die away, the air was answered by a horn from the heights of Craignacoheilg. An armed man then appeared on the rock, leaning forwards. Ker drew near, and taking off his bonnet, called aloud: "Stephen, it is William Ker who speaks. I come with the Lord Andrew Murray, of Bothwell, to the support of our commander, Sir William Wallace."

At these words Stephen placed his bugle to his mouth, and in a few minutes the rock was covered with the members of its little garrison. Women and children appeared, shouting with joy; and the men hastened to bid their comrade welcome. One advanced towards Murray, whom he instantly recognized to be Sir Roger Kirkpatrick, of Torthorald. The chiefs saluted each other, and Lord Andrew pointed to his men. "I have brought," said he, "these few brave fellows to the aid of Sir William Wallace. They should have been more but for new events of Southron outrage. Yet I am impatient to lead them to the presence of my uncle's preserver."

Kirkpatrick's answer disappointed the eager spirit of the young warrior. "I am sorry, brave Murray, that you have no better knight to receive you than myself. I and the gallant chief have not yet met; but I am in arms for him, and the hour of retribution for all our injuries, I trust, is at hand."

"But where is Sir William Wallace?" demanded Murray.

"Gone towards the Forth, to rouse that part of sleeping Scotland. If all he meet have my spirit, they will not require a second call. I shall ever give thanks to the accident which brought me the welcome news that an arm is raised to strike it home."

As he spoke he led Murray to the cliffs which crown the summit of Craignacoheilg. In the midst stood a tower which had once been a favorite hunting-lodge of the great King Fergus. There Kirkpatrick joyfully greeted his guest a second time. "This," said he, "is the far-famed Lodge of the Three Kings. Here did our lion, Fergus, attended by his royal allies, Durstus the Pict, and Dionethus the Briton, spread his board during their huntings in Glenfinlass. And here, eight hundred years ago, did the same heroic prince form the plans which saved his kingdom from a foreign yoke. On the same spot we will lay ours, and in their completion rescue Scotland from a tyranny more intolerable than that which menaced him."

"And by the ghost of that same Fergus I swear," exclaimed Murray, "that my honest claymore shall never shroud its head while an invader be left alive in Scotland!"

Kirkpatrick caught him in his arms. "Brave son of the noble Bothwell, thou art after mine own heart! The blow which the dastard Cressingham durst aim at a Scottish chief still smarts upon my cheek and rivers of his countrymen's blood shall wash out the stain. After I had been persuaded by his serpent eloquence to swear fealty to Edward on the defeat at Dunbar, I vainly thought that Scotland had only changed a weak prince for a wise king; but when in the courts of Stirling I heard Cressingham propose to the barons north of the dyke that they should give their castles into English hands; when I opposed the measure with all the indignation of a Scot who saw himself betrayed, he first tried to overturn my arguments, and finding that impossible, he struck me!—Powers of earth and heaven, what was then the tempest of my soul!—I drew my sword—I would have laid him dead at my feet had not my countrymen held my arm and dragged me from the apartment.

"Covered with dishonor by a blow I could not avenge, I fled to my brother-in-law, Sir John Scott, of Loch Doine. With him I buried my injury from the world; but it lived in my heart; it haunted me day and night, calling for revenge.

"In such an hour, how did I receive the tidings that Sir William Wallace was in arms against the tyrant! It was the voice of retribution calling me to peace of mind. Even my bed-ridden kinsman partook my emotions, and with his concurrence I led a band of his hardiest clansmen to reenforce the brave men of Lanark on this rock.

"Two days I have now been here awaiting in impatience the arrival of Wallace. Yes; we will mingle our injured souls together. He has made one offering; I must make another. We shall set forth to Stirling, and there, in the very heart of his den, I will sacrifice the tiger Cressingham to the vengeance of our wrongs."

"But what, my brave friend," asked Murray, "are the forces you deem sufficient for so great an enterprise? How many fighting men may be counted of Wallace's own company, besides your own?"

"We have here about a hundred," replied Kirkpatrick, "including yours."

"How inadequate to storm so formidable a place as Stirling castle!" returned Murray. "Having, indeed, passed the Rubicon, we must go forward; but resolution, not rashness, should be the principle of our actions. And my opinion is, that a few minor advantages obtained, our countrymen would flock to our standard, the enemy would be intimidated, and we should carry thousands, instead of hundreds, before the walls of Stirling. To attempt it now would invite defeat, and pluck upon us the ruin of our entire project."

"You are right, young man," cried Kirkpatrick; "my gray head, rendered impetuous by insult, did not pause on the temerity of my scheme. Oh, I would rather waste all my life in these solitary wilds, and know that at the close of it I should see the blood of Cressingham on these hands, than live a prince and die unrevenged!"

Stephen and Ker now entered; the latter paid his respects to Sir Roger, and the former informed Murray that, having disposed his present followers with those who had arrived before, he was come to lead their lord to some refreshment in the banqueting-room of the tower. "What!" cried Murray, "is it possible that my cousin's faithful band has reached its destination? None other belonging to Bothwell castle had any chance of escaping its jailer's hands."

Kirkpatrick interrupted Stephen's reply by saying that while their guests were at the board he would watch the arrival of certain expresses from two brave Drummonds, each of whom were to send him a hundred men. "So, my good Lord Andrew," cried he, striking him on the shoulder, "shall the snow-launch gather that is to fall on Edward to his destruction."

Murray heartily shared his zeal, and bidding him a short adieu, followed Stephen and Ker into the hall. A haunch of venison of Glenfinlass smoked on the board, and goblets of wine from the bounteous cellars of Sir John Scott brightened the hopes which flowed in every heart.

While the young chieftains were recruiting their exhausted strength, Stephen sat at the table to satisfy the anxiety of Murray to know how the detachment from Bothwell had come to Craignacoheilg, and by what signal act of bravery Wallace could have escaped with his whole train from the foe-surrounded Cartlane craigs.

"Heaven smiled on us," replied Stephen. "The very evening of the day on which Ker left us there was a carousal in the English camp. We heard the sound of the song and riot, and of many an insult cast upon our besieged selves. But about an hour after sunset the noise sank by degrees: a hint that the revelers, overcome by excess, had fallen asleep. At this very time, owing to the heat of the day, so great a vapor had been exhaled from the lake beneath that the whole of the northern side of the fortress cliff was covered with a mist so thick we could not discern each other at a foot's distance. 'Now is the moment!' said our gallant leader; 'the enemy are stupefied with wine; the rock is clothed in a veil; under its shelter let us pass from their hands.'

"He called us together, and making the proper dispositions, commanded the children and women on their lives to keep silence. He then led us to the top of the northern cliff; it overhung an obscure cave which he knew opened at its extremity. By the assistance of a rope held by several men, our resolute chief made his way down the rock, and was the first who descended. He stood at the bottom, enveloped in the cloud which shrouded the mountain, till all the men of the first division had cleared the height; he then marshaled them with their pikes towards the foe, in case of an alarm. But all remained quiet, although the sound of voices, both in song and laughter, intimated that the utmost precaution was still necessary.

"Wallace reascended the rock half-way, and receiving the children, which were lowered into his arms, he handed them to the old men, who carried them safely through the bushes which obscured the cave's mouth. The rest of our little garrison soon followed; then our sentinels, receiving the signal that all were safe, drew silently from their guard, and closed our march through the cavern.

"This effected, we blocked up its mouth, that, should our escape be discovered, the enemy might not find the direct road we had taken.

"We pursued our course without stop till we reached the valleys of Stirlingshire. There some kind shepherds gave the women and children temporary shelter; and Wallace, seeing that if anything were to be done for Scotland, he must swell his host, put the party under my guidance, giving me orders that when they were rested I should march them to Glenfinlass, here to await his return. Selecting ten men, with that small band he turned towards the Forth, hoping to meet some valiant friends in that part of the country ready to embrace her cause.

"He had hardly been an hour departed when Dugald observed a procession of monks descending the opposite mountain. They drew near and halted in the glen. A crowd of women from the neighboring hills had followed the train, and were now gathering round a bier, which the monks set down. I know not by what happy fortune I came close to the leader of the procession, but he saw something in my rough features that declared me an honest Scot. 'Friend,' whispered he, 'for charity conduct us to some place where we may withdraw this bier from the eye of curiosity.'

"I made no hesitation, but desired the train to follow me into a byre belonging to the shepherd who was my host. On this motion the common people went away, and the monks entered the place.

"When the travelers threw up their hoods, which as mourners they had worn over their faces, I could not help exclaiming, 'Alas, for the glory of Scotland, that this goodly group of stout men rather wore the helmet than the cowl!'—'How,' asked their principal, 'do we not pray for the glory of Scotland?'—'True,' replied I; 'but while Moses prayed, Joshua fought. God gives the means of glory, that they should be used.'—'But for what, old veteran,' said the monk, with a penetrating look, 'should we exchange our cowl for the helmet? Knowest thou anything of the Joshua who would lead us to the field?' There was something in the young priest's eyes that seemed to contradict his pacific words; they flashed an impetuous fire. My reply was short. 'Are you a Scot?'—'I am, in soul and in arms.'—'Then knowest thou not the chief of Ellerslie?' As I spoke, for I stood close to the bier, I perceived the pall shake. The monk answered my last question with an exclamation—'You mean Sir William Wallace!'

"'Yes,' I replied. The bier shook more violently at these words, and, with my hair bristling from my head, I saw the pall hastily thrown off, and a beautiful youth, in a shroud, started from it, crying aloud, 'Then is our pilgrimage at an end. Lead us to him.'

"The monk perceived my terror, and hastily exclaimed, 'Fear not; he is alive, and seeks Sir William Wallace. His pretended death was a stratagem to ensure our passage through the English army, for we are soldiers like yourself.' As he spoke he opened his gray habit and showed me the mailed tartans beneath."

"What, then!" interrupted Murray; "those monks were my faithful clansmen?"

"The same," replied Stephen. "I assured them they might now resume their own characters, for all who inhabited the valley were true though aged Scots. The young had long been drafted by Edward's agents to fight his battles abroad.

"'Ah!' interrupted the shrouded youth, 'are we a people that can die for the honor of this usurper, and are we ignorant how to do it for our country? Lead us, soldier of Wallace,' cried he, stepping resolutely on the ground,—'lead us to your brave master, and tell him that a few determined men are come to shed their blood for him and Scotland.'

"This astonishing youth (for he did not appear to be more than fifteen) stood before me in his robes of death, like the spirit of some bright-haired son of Fingal. I looked on him with admiration, and explaining our situation, told him whither Wallace was gone, and of our destination to await him in the forest of Glenfinlass.

"While your clansmen were refreshing themselves, we learnt from Kenneth, their conductor, that the troop left Bothwell under expectation of your soon following them. They had not proceeded far before their scouts perceived the outpost of the English which surrounded Cartlane craigs, and to avoid this danger they took a circuitous path, in hope of finding some unguarded entrance. They reached the convent of St. Columba, at the western side of the craigs. Kenneth knew the abbot, and entering it under cover of the night, obtained permission for his men to rest there. The youth, now their companion, was a student in the church. He had been sent thither by his mother, a pious lady, in the hope that, as he is of a gentle nature, he would attach himself to the sacred tonsure.

"The moment this youth discovered our errand, he tried to prevail on the abbot to permit him to accompany us. But his entreaties were vain, till, wrought up to anger, he threatened that if he were prevented joining Sir William Wallace, he would take the earliest opportunity to escape, and commit himself to the peril of the English pikes.

"Seeing him determined, the abbot granted his wish; 'and then it was,' said Kenneth, 'that the youth seemed inspired. It was no longer an enthusiastic boy we saw before us, but an angel, gifted with wisdom to direct us. It was he proposed disguising ourselves as a funeral procession; and while he painted his blooming countenance of a death-like paleness, and stretched himself on this bier, the abbot sent to the English army to request permission for a party of monks to cross the craigs to the cave of St. Columba, in Stirlingshire, whither they carried a dead brother to be entombed. Our young leader hoped we might thus find an opportunity to apprise Wallace we were friends, and ready to swell the ranks of his little armament.

" 'On our entrance into the passes of the craigs,' continued Kenneth, 'the English captain there mentioned the fate of Bothwell and the captivity of Lord Mar, and with very little courtesy to sons of the church ordered the bier to be opened, to see whether it did really contain a corpse, or provisions for our besieged countrymen. We had expected this investigation, else we might as well have wrapped the trunk of a tree in the shroud we carried as a human being. This ceremony once over, we expected to have passed on without further notice; and in that case the youth would have left his pall and performed the remainder of his journey in disguise with the rest. But the strict watch of an English guard confined him wholly to the bier. In hopes of at last evading this vigilance, on pretense of a vow of the deceased that his bearers should perform a pilgrimage throughout the craigs, we traversed them in every direction; and, I make no doubt, would have finally wearied out our guard and gained our point had not the circumstance transpired of Wallace's escape.

" 'On this disappointment the Southron captains retired to their commander-in-chief, to give as good an account as they could of so disgraceful a termination of their siege and our guard hurried us into Stirlingshire, and left us at the other side of the mountain. Even then we were not free to release our charge, for, attracted by our procession, the country people followed us into the valley, yet had we not met with you, it was our design to throw off our disguises in the first safe place, and, divided into small bands, have severally sought Sir William Wallace.' "

"But where," demanded Murray, who had listened with delighted astonishment to this recital, "where is this admirable youth? Why, if Kenneth have learnt I am arrived, does he not bring him to receive my thanks and friendship?"

"It is my fault," returned Stephen, "that Kenneth will not approach you till your repast is over. I left him to see your followers properly refreshed. And for the youth, he seems timid of appearing before you. Even his name I cannot make known to you till he reveals it himself; none know him here by any other than that of Edwin. He has, however, granted to-morrow morning for the interview."

"I must submit to his determination," replied Murray; "but I am at a loss to guess why so brave a creature should hesitate to meet me. I can only suppose he dislikes the idea of resigning the troop he has so well conducted; and if so, I shall think it my duty to yield its command to him."

"Indeed he richly deserves it," returned Stephen; "for the very soul of Wallace seemed transfused into his breast as he cheered us through our long march from the valley to Glenfinlass. He played with the children, heartened up the women, and when the men were weary, and lagged by the way, he sat him down on the nearest stones and sang to us legends of our ancestors till every nerve was braced with warlike emulation.

"When we arrived at Craignacoheilg, as the women were in great want I suddenly recollected that I had an old friend in the neighborhood. When a boy I had been the playfellow of Sir John Scott, of Loch Doine, and though I understood him to be now an invalid, I went to him. While I told my tale, his brother-in-law, Sir Roger Kirkpatrick, took fire at my relation and declared his determination to accompany me to Craignacoheilg, and you noted that you met him here on your arrival."

While Stephen was still speaking, Kenneth Mackenzie joyfully entered the hall. Murray received him with a warm embrace; and. soon after, the wearied chieftain was led to a bed of freshly gathered heath, prepared for him in an upper chamber.

CHAPTER XIX.

CRAIGNACOHEILG.

THE rest of the youthful Murray was sweet till the shrill notes of a hundred bugles piercing his ear made him start. He listened; they sounded again. The morning had fully broke. He sprang from his couch, hurried on his armor, and snatching up his lance and target, issued from the tower. Several women were flying past the gate. On seeing him they exclaimed, "The Lord Wallace is arrived. His bugles have sounded—our husbands are returned!"

Murray followed their eager footsteps, and reached the edge of the rock just as the brave group were ascending. A stranger was also there, who from his extreme youth and elegance he judged must be the young protector of his clansmen; but he forbore to address him until they should be presented to each other by Wallace himself.

It was indeed the same. On hearing the first blast of the horn the youthful chieftain had hastened from his bed of heath, and buckling on his brigandine, rushed to the rocks; but at sight of the noble figure which first gained the summit the young hero fell back, awe checked his steps, and he stood at a distance while Kirkpatrick welcomed the chief and introduced Lord Andrew Murray. Wallace received the latter with a glad smile, and taking him warmly by the hand, "Gallant Murray," said he, "with such assistance I hope to reinstate your brave uncle in Bothwell castle, and soon to cut a passage to even a mightier rescue. We must carry off Scotland from the tyrant's arms, or," added he in a graver tone, "we shall only rivet her chains the closer."

"I am but a poor auxiliary," returned Murray; "my troop is a scanty one, for it is of my own gathering. It is not my father's nor my uncle's strength that I bring along with me. But there is one here," continued he, "who has preserved a party of men sent by my cousin Lady Helen Mar, almost double my numbers."

At this reference to the youthful warrior, Sir Roger Kirkpatrick discerned him at a distance, and hastened towards him, while Murray briefly related to Wallace the extraordinary conduct of this unknown. On being told that the chief waited to receive him, the youth hastened forward with a trepidation he never had felt before, a confusion so amiable that Wallace, who perceived his youth and emotion, opened

113

his arms and embraced him. "Brave youth," cried he, "I trust that the power which blesses our cause will enable me to return you with many a well-earned glory to the bosom of your family."

Edwin was encouraged by the frank address of a hero whom he expected to have found reserved and wrapped in the deep glooms of his fate; but when he saw a benign countenance hail him with smiles, he made a strong effort to shake off the awe with which the name and the dignity of Wallace had oppressed him, and with a blush he replied: "My family are worthy of your esteem; my father is brave, but my mother, fearing for me, her favorite son, prevailed on him to put me into a monastery. Dreading the power of the English, even there she allowed none but the abbot to know who I was. And as he chose to hide my name, and I have burst from my concealment without her knowledge, till I do something worthy of that name and deserving her pardon, permit me, noble Wallace, to follow your footsteps by the simple appellation of Edwin."

"Noble boy," returned the chief, "your wish shall be respected. We urge you no further to reveal what such bravery must shortly proclaim in the most honorable manner."

The whole of the troop having ascended, while their wives, children, and friends were rejoicing in their embraces, Wallace asked some questions relative to Bothwell, and Murray briefly related the disasters which had happened there.

"My father," added he, "is still with the Lord of Lochawe, and thither I sent to request him to despatch to the Cartlane craigs all the followers he took with him into Argyleshire. But as things are, would it not be well to send a second messenger to say that you have sought refuge in Glenfinlass?"

"Before he could arrive," returned Wallace, "I hope we shall be where Lord Bothwell's reenforcements may reach us by water. Our present object must be the Earl of Mar. He is the first Scottish earl who has hazarded his estates and life for Scotland, and as her best friend, his liberation must be our first enterprise. In my circuit through two or three eastern counties a promising increase has been made to our little army. The Frasers, of Oliver castle, have given me two hundred men, and the brave Sir Alexander Scrymgeour, whom I met in West Lothian, has not only brought fifty Scots to my command, but, as hereditary standard-bearer of the kingdom, has come himself to carry the royal banner of Scotland to glory or oblivion."

"To glory!" cried Murray, waving his sword. "Oh, not while a Scot survives shall that blood-red lion again lick the dust!"

"No," cried Kirkpatrick, his eyes flashing fire; "rather may every

Scot and every Southron fall in the struggle and fill one grave. Let me," cried he, grasping the hilt of his sword and looking upwards,—"let me live but to see the Forth and the Clyde, so often reddened with our blood, dye the eastern and the western oceans with the blood of these our foes; and when none is spared, then let me die in peace."

The eyes of Wallace glanced on the young Edwin, who stood gazing on Kirkpatrick, and turning on the knight with a look of reprehension, "Check that prayer," cried he; "remember, my brave companion, if we would be blessed in the contest we must be merciful."

"To whom?" exclaimed Kirkpatrick; "to the robbers who tear from us our lands, to the ruffians who wrest from us our honors? But you are patient; you never received a blow."

"Yes," cried Wallace, turning paler, "a heavy one,—on my heart."

"True," returned Kirkpatrick, "your wife fell under the steel of a Southron governor, and you slew him for it. You were revenged, your feelings were appeased."

"Not the death of fifty thousand governors," replied Wallace, "could appease my feelings. Revenge were insufficient to satisfy the yearnings of my soul, but I do not denounce the whole nation without reserve. When the sword of war is drawn, all who resist must conquer or fall; but there are some noble English who abhor the tyranny they are obliged to exercise over us, and when they declare such remorse, shall they not find mercy at our hands? I even hope that by our righteous cause and our clemency we shall not only gather our own people to our legions, but turn the hearts of the poor Welsh and the misled Irish, whom the usurper has forced into his armies, and so confront him with troops of his own levying."

"That may be," returned Kirkpatrick; "but surely you would not rank Aymer de Valence, who lords it over Dumbarton, and Cressingham, who acts the tyrant in Stirling,—you would not rank them amongst these conscientious English?"

"No," replied Wallace; "the oppression of the one and the cruelty of the other have given Scotland too many wounds for me to hold a shield before them; meet them, and I leave them to your sword."

"And by heavens," cried Kirkpatrick, gnashing his teeth, "they shall know its point!"

Wallace then informed his friends he purposed marching next morning by daybreak towards Dumbarton castle. "When we make the attack," said he, "it must be in the night, for I propose seizing it by storm."

Murray and Kirkpatrick joyfully acquiesced. Edwin smiled an enraptured assent, and Wallace, with many a gracious look and speech, disengaged himself from the embraces of the weaker part of the garrison, who clung to him as to a presiding deity.

"You, my dear countrywomen," said he, "shall find a home for your aged parents, your children, and yourselves with the venerable Sir John Scott, of Loch Doine. You are to be conducted thither this evening, and there await in comfort the return of your husbands, whom Providence now leads forth to be the champions of your country."

Filled with enthusiasm, the women uttered a shout of triumph, and embracing their husbands, declared they were ready to resign them wholly to Heaven and Sir William Wallace.

Wallace left them with these tender relatives from whom they were so soon to part, and retired with his chieftains to arrange the plan of his proposed attack. Delighted with the glory which seemed to wave him from the pinnacles of Dumbarton rock, Edwin listened in silence to all that was said, and then hastened to his quarters to prepare his armor for the ensuing morning.

CHAPTER XX.

THE CLIFFS OF LOCH LUBNAIG.

In the cool of the evening, while the young chieftain was thus employed, Kenneth entered to tell him that Sir William Wallace had called out his little army to see its strength and numbers. Edwin's soul had become not more enamored of the panoply of war than of his admired leader, and at this intelligence he threw his plaid over his brigandine, and placing a swan-plumed bonnet on his brows, hastened forth to meet his general.

The thirty followers of Murray appeared just as the two hundred Frasers entered from an opening in the rocks. Blood mounted into his face as he compared his inferior numbers and recollected the obligation they were to repay, and the greater one he was now going to incur. However, he threw the standard, worked by Helen, on his shoulder, and turning to Wallace, "Behold," cried he, pointing to his men, "the poor man's mite! It is great, for it is my all."

"Great indeed, brave Murray," returned Wallace, "for it brings me a host in yourself."

"I will not disgrace my standard," said he, lowering the banner-staff to Wallace. He started when he saw the flowing lock which he could not help recognizing. "This is my betrothed," continued Murray in a blither tone; "I have sworn to take her for better for worse, and I pledge you my troth nothing but death shall part us."

Wallace grasped his hand. "And I pledge you mine, that the head whence it grew shall be laid low before I suffer so generous a defender to be separated from this standard." His eyes glanced at the impresse. "Thou art right," continued he, "God doth indeed arm thee; and in the strength of a righteous cause thou goest with the confidence of success to embrace victory as a bride."

"No, I am only the bridegroom's man," replied Murray, gaily moving off. "I shall be content with a kiss or two from the hand-maids, and leave the lady for my general."

"We just muster five hundred men," observed Ker to Wallace; "but they are all stout in heart as condition, and ready, even to-night, if you will it, to commence their march."

"No," replied Wallace; "we must not overstrain the generous

117

spirit. Let them rest to-night, and to-morrow's dawn shall light us through the forest."

Ker, who acted as henchman to Wallace, now returned to the ranks to give the word, and they all marched forward.

Sir Alexander Scrymgeour, with his golden standard, charged with the lion of Scotland, led the van. Wallace raised his bonnet from his head as it drew near. Scrymgeour lowered the staff. Wallace threw up his outstretched hand at this action, but the knight not understanding him, he stepped forward. "Sir Alexander Scrymgeour," cried he, "that standard must not bow to me. It represents the royalty of Scotland, before which we fight for our liberties. If virtue yet dwell in the house of valiant Saint David, some of his offspring will hear of this day, and lead it forward to conquest and to a crown. Till such an hour, let not that standard bend to any man."

Wallace fell back as he spoke, and Scrymgeour, bowing his head in sign of acquiescence, marched on.

Sir Roger Kirkpatrick, at the head of his well-appointed Highlanders, next advanced. His blood-red banner streamed to the air, and as it bent to Wallace, he saw that the indignant knight had adopted the device of the hardy King Archaius, but with a fiercer motto: *"Touch, and I pierce."*

The men of Loch Doine, a strong, tall, and well-armed body, marched on, and gave place to the advancing corps of Bothwell. The eye of Wallace felt as if turning from gloom and horror to the cheerful light of day when it fell on the bright and ingenuous face of Murray. Kenneth, with his troop, followed, and the youthful Edwin, like Cupid in arms, closed the procession.

Being drawn up in line, their chief advanced toward them, and expressing his sentiment of the patriotism which brought them into the field, informed them of his intended march. He then turned to Stephen Ireland: "The sun has now set," said he, "and before dark you must conduct the families of my worthy Lanarkmen to the protection of Sir John Scott. It is time that age, infancy, and female weakness should cease their wanderings with us; to-night we bid them adieu, to meet them again, by the leading of the Lord of Hosts, in freedom and prosperity."

As Wallace ceased, and was retiring from the ground, several old men, and young women with babes in their arms, rushed from behind the ranks, and throwing themselves at his feet, caught hold of his hands and garments. "We go," said the venerable fathers, "to pray for your welfare; and sure we are a crown will bless our country's benefactor, here or in heaven."

"In heaven," replied Wallace, shaking the plumes of his bonnet over his eyes to hide the moisture which suffused them. "I can have no right to any other crown."

"Yes," cried a hoary-headed shepherd; "you free your country from tyrants, and the people's hearts will proclaim their deliverer their sovereign."

"May your rightful monarch, worthy patriarch," said Wallace, "whether a Bruce or a Baliol, meet with equal zeal from Scotland at large!"

The women wept as they clung to his hand, and the daughter of Ireland, holding up her child in her arms, presented it to him. "Look on my son," cried she with energy; "the first word he speaks shall be Wallace; the second, liberty!"

At this speech all the women held up their children towards him. "Here," cried they, "we devote them to Heaven and to our country. Adopt them, noble Wallace, to be thy followers in arms when, perhaps, their fathers are laid low."

Unable to speak, Wallace pressed their little faces to his lips; then returning them to their mothers, laid his hand on his heart and answered in an agitated voice, "They are mine; my weal shall be theirs, my woe my own." As he spoke he hurried from the weeping group, and immerging amid the cliffs, hid himself from their tears and their blessings.

The mists of evening hung on the gigantic tops of Ben Ledi and Ben Vorlich, then sailing forward, by degrees obscured the whole of the mountains, leaving nothing for the eye to dwell on but the long, silent expanse of the waters below.

"So," said he, "did I once believe myself forever shut in from the world by an obscurity that promised me happiness as well as seclusion. But the hours of Ellerslie are gone. No tender wife will now twine her faithful arms around my neck. No child of Marion's will ever be pressed to my fond bosom. Alas, the angel that sank my country's wrongs to a dreamy forgetfulness in her arms, she was to be immolated, that I might awake, and the sacrifice shall not be yielded in vain. No, blessed God!" cried he, stretching his clasped hands towards heaven; "endow me with thine own spirit, and I shall yet lead my countrymen to liberty and happiness!"

The plaintive voice of the Highland pipe at this moment broke upon his ear. It was the farewell of the patriarch Lindsay, as he and his departing company descended the winding paths of Craignacoheilg. Wallace started on his feet. The separation had then taken place between his trusty followers and their families, and guessing the feelings of those brave men from what was passing in his own breast, he dried his tears, and once more resuming the warrior's cheerful look, sought that part of the rock where the Lanarkmen were quartered. As he drew near he saw some standing on the cliff, and others leaning over, to catch another glance of the departing group ere it was lost amid the shades of Glenfinlass.

"Are they quite gone?" asked Dugald. "Quite," answered a young man who seemed to have the most advantageous situation for a view. "Then," cried he, "may St. Andrew keep them till we meet again!"

"May a greater than St. Andrew hear thy prayer!" ejaculated Wallace. At the sound of this response from their chief they all turned round. "My brave companions," said he, "I come to repay this hour's pang by telling you that in the attack of Dumbarton you shall have the honor of first mounting the walls. I shall be at your head to sign each brave soldier with a patriot's seal of honor."

"To follow you, my lord," said Dugald, "is our duty."

"I grant it," replied the chief; "and as I am the leader in that duty, it is mine to dispense to every man his reward."

"Ah, dearest sir!" exclaimed Edwin, who had been assisting the women to carry their infants down the steep, and on reascending heard the latter part of this conversation, "deprive me not of the aim of my life. Oh, my dear commander, let me only carry to the grave the consciousness that, next to yourself, I was the first to mount the rock of Dumbarton, and you will make me noble indeed!"

Wallace looked at him with a smile of such graciousness that the youth threw himself into his arms. "You will grant my boon?"

"I will, noble boy," said he; "act up to your sentiments, and you shall be my brother."

"Call me by that name," cried Edwin, "and I will dare anything."

"Then be the first to follow me on the rock," said he, "and I will lead you to an honor the highest in my gift—you shall unloose the chains of the Earl of Mar. And ye," continued he, turning to his men, "ye shall not find your country slow to commemorate the duty of such sons. Being the first to strike the blow for her freedom, ye shall be the first she will distinguish. I now speak as her minister; and as a badge to times immemorial, I bid you wear the Scottish lion on your shields."

A shout of proud joy issued from every heart. And Wallace, seeing that honor had dried the tears of regret, left them to repose. He sent Edwin to his rest, and himself, avoiding the other chieftains, retired to his own chamber in the tower.

CHAPTER XXI.

LOCH LOMOND.

PROFOUND as was the rest of Wallace, yet the first clarion of the lark awakened him, and a fresh breeze wooed him to rise and meet it. Rising immediately, he put on his glittering hauberk, and issuing from the tower, raised his bugle to his lips and blew so rousing a blast that in an instant the whole rock was covered with soldiers.

Wallace placed his helmet on his head and advanced towards them just as Edwin had joined him and Sir Roger Kirkpatrick appeared from the tower. "Blest be this morn!" cried the old knight. "My sword springs from its scabbard to meet it; and ere its good steel be sheathed again," continued he, shaking it sternly, "what deaths may dye its point!"

Offended at such savageness, but without answering him, Wallace drew towards Murray, and calling to Edwin, ordered him to march at his side. The youth seemed glad of the summons, and Wallace was pleased to observe it, as he thought that a longer stay with one who so grossly overcharged the feelings of patriotism might breed disgust in his innocent mind against a cause which had so furious a defender.

The forces being marshaled according to the preconcerted order, the three commanders, with Wallace at their head, led forward.

They passed through the forest of Glenfinlass, and morning and evening still found them thridding its solitudes in security; night, too, watched their onward march.

The sun had just risen as the little band of patriots emerged upon the eastern bank of Loch Lomond. The bases of the mountains were yet covered with the mist of the morning, and hardly distinguishable from the blue waters of the lake which lashed the shore. The newly awakened sheep bleated from the hills, and the herbage, dropping dew, seemed glittering with a thousand fairy gems.

"Where is the man who would not fight for such a country?" exclaimed Murray as he stepped over a bridge of interwoven trees which crossed one of the mountain-streams; "this land was not made for slaves. Look at these bulwarks of nature. Every mountain-head which forms this chain of hills is a rampart against invasion.

If Baliol had possessed but half a heart, Edward might have returned even worse than Cæsar—without a cockle to decorate his helmet."

"Baliol has found oblivion," returned Wallace; "his son, perhaps, may better deserve the scepter of such a country. Let us cut the way, and he who merits the crown will soon appear to claim it."

"Then it will not be Edward Baliol," rejoined Scrymgeour. "During the reign of his father I once carried a despatch to him from Scotland. He was then banqueting in all the luxuries of the English court; and such a voluptuary I never beheld. I left the scene of folly, only praying that so effeminate a prince might never disgrace the throne of our manly race of kings."

"If such be the tuition of our lords in the court of Edward," observed Ker, "what can we expect from even the Bruce? They were ever a nobler race than the Baliol; but bad education and luxury will debase the most princely minds."

"I saw neither of the Bruce when I visited London," replied Scrymgeour; "the Earl of Carrick was at his house in Cleveland, and Robert Bruce, his eldest son, with the English army in Guienne. But they bore a manly character, particularly young Robert, to whom the troubadours of Aquitaine have given the flattering appellation of Prince of Chivalry."

"It would be more to his honor," interrupted Murray, "if he compelled the English to acknowledge him as Prince of Scotland. With so much bravery how can he allow such a civet-cat as Edward Baliol to bear away the title which is his by the double right of blood and virtue?"

"Perhaps," said Wallace, "the young lion only sleeps. The time may come when both he and his father will rise from their lethargy and throw themselves at once into the arms of Scotland. To stimulate the dormant patriotism of these two princes by showing them a subject leading their people to liberty is one great end of the victories I seek."

"For my part," said Murray, "I have always thought the lady we will not woo, we have no right to pretend to. If the Bruces will not be at the pains to snatch Scotland from drowning, I see no reason for making them a present of what will cost us many a wet jacket before we tug her from the waves."

Wallace did not hear this last sentiment of Murray's, as it was spoken in a lowered voice in the ear of Kirkpatrick. "I agree with you," was that knight's reply, "and in the true Roman style may the death of every Southron now in Scotland, and as many more as fate chooses to yield us, be the preliminary games of his coronation."

Wallace, who heard this, turned to Kirkpatrick with a mild rebuke in his eye. "Balaam blest when he meant to curse," said he; "but some curse when they mean to bless. Such prayers are blasphemy.

"Blood for blood is only justice," returned Murray; "and how can you, noble Wallace, as a Scot and as a man, imply any mercy to the villains who stab us to the heart?"

"I plead not for them," replied Wallace, "but for the poor wretches who follow their leaders, by force, to the field of Scotland. It is not to aggrieve but to redress that we carry arms."

"I do not understand commiserating the wolves who have so long made havoc in our country," cried Kirkpatrick; "methinks such maidenly mercy is rather out of place."

Wallace turned to him with a smile. "I will answer you, my valiant friend, by adopting your own figure. It is that these Southron wolves may not confound us with themselves that I wish to show in our conduct rather the generous ardor of the faithful guardian of the fold, than the rapacious fierceness which equals them with the beasts of the desert. The one is an ambition with which angels may sympathize; the other, a desire which speaks the nature of fiends."

"In some cases this may be," replied Sir Roger, a little reconciled to the argument, "but not in mine. My injury yet burns upon my cheek, and as nothing but the life-blood of Cressingham can quench it, I will listen no more to your doctrine till I am revenged. That done, I shall not forget your lesson."

"Generous Kirkpatrick!" exclaimed Wallace, "nothing that is really cruel can dwell with such manly candor. Say what you will, I can trust your heart after this moment."

They had crossed the river Ennerie, and were issuing from between its ridge of hills, when Wallace, pointing to a stupendous rock which rose in solitary magnificence in the midst of a vast plain, exclaimed, "There is Dumbarton castle; that citadel holds the fetters of Scotland, and if we break them there, every minor link will easily give way."

The men uttered a shout of anticipated triumph at this sight, and proceeding, soon came in view of the fortifications which helmeted the rock. As they approached, they discovered that it had two summits, being in a manner cleft in twain, the one side rising in a pyramidal form, while the other, of a table shape, sustained the ponderous buildings of the fortress.

It was dusk when the little army arrived in the rear of a thicket which skirted the eastern dyke of the castle and reached to a considerable length over the plain. On this spot Wallace rested his men and while they placed themselves under its covert till the appointed time of attack, he perceived through an opening in the wood the gleaming of soldiers' arms on the ramparts, and fires beginning to light on a lonely watch-tower which crowned the pinnacle of the highest rock.

"Poor fools!" exclaimed Murray; "like the rest of their brethren of clay, they look abroad for evils, and prepare not for those which are even at their doors."

"That beacon-fire," cried Scrymgeour, "shall light us to their chambers, and for once we thank them for their providence."

"That beacon-fire," whispered Edwin to Wallace, "shall light me to honor. To-night, by your agreement, I shall call you brother, or lie dead on the summit of those walls."

"Edwin," said Wallace, "act as you say, and deserve not only to be called my brother, but to be the first banneret of freedom in arms."

He then turned towards the lines, and giving his orders to each division, directed them to seek repose on the heather till the moon should have sunk her light in the waves.

CHAPTER XXII.

DUMBARTON ROCK.

ALL obeyed the voice of their commander and retired to rest, but the eyes of Edwin could not close; his eager spirit was already on the walls of Dumbarton, for imagination suggested the difficulties attending so small a force assailing so formidable a garrison without some immediate knowledge of its relative situations. A sudden thought struck him. He would mount that rock alone; he would seek to ascertain the place of Lord Mar's confinement, that not one life in Wallace's faithful band might be lost in a vague search.

"Ah, my general!" exclaimed he, "Edwin shall be the first to spring those ramparts; and when he has thus proved himself not unworthy of thy confidence, he will return to lead thee and thy soldiers to a sure victory, and himself to honor by thy side."

He looked towards the embattled cliff; its summit stood bright in the moonlight, but deep shadows lay beneath. "God be my speed!" cried he, and wrapping himself in his plaid, so mixed its dark hues with the herbage at the base of the rock that he made its circuit without having attracted observation.

The south side seemed the most easy of ascent, and by that he began his daring attempt. Having gained the height, he clambered behind a buttress, the shadow of which cast the wall into such obscurity that he crept safely through one of its crenelles, and dropping gently inwards, alighted on his feet. Still keeping the shadowed side of the battlements, he proceeded cautiously along, and passed undiscovered, even by the sentinels who guarded this quarter of the fortress.

He soon arrived at the open square before the citadel; it was yet occupied by groups of Southron officers, gaily walking to and fro under the light of the moon. In hopes of gaining some information from their discourse, he concealed himself behind a chest of arrows, and as they passed backwards and forwards, distinctly heard them jesting each other about divers fair dames of the country around. The conversation terminated in a debate whether or no the indifference which their governor, De Valence, manifested to the majestic beauties of the Countess of Mar were real or assumed, and Edwin gathered from the discourse that the earl and countess were treated

125

severely, and confined in a large square tower in the cleft of the rock.

Having learned all that he could expect from these officers, he speeded, under the friendly shadow, towards the other side of the citadel, and arrived just as the guard approached to relieve the sentinels of the northern postern. He laid himself close to the ground, and happily overheard the word of the night as it was given to the new watch. This providential circumstance saved his life.

Finding no mode of regress from this place but by the postern at which the sentinel was stationed, or by attempting a passage through a small adjoining tower the door of which stood open, he considered a moment, and then deciding for the tower, stole unobserved into it. Fortunately no person was there; but Edwin found it full of spare arms, with two or three vacant couches in different corners, where, he supposed, the officers on guard occasionally reposed; several watch-cloaks lay on the floor. He readily apprehended the use he might make of this circumstance, and throwing one of them over his own shoulders, climbed to an embrasure in the wall, and forcing himself through it, dropped to a declivity on the other side which shelved down to the cliff, wherein he now saw the square tower.

He had scarcely lit on firm ground when a sentinel, followed by two others with presented pikes, approached him and demanded the word. *"Montjoy!"* was his reply. "Why leap the embrasure?" said one. "Why not enter by the postern?" demanded another. The conversation of the officers had given him a hint on which he formed his answer. "Love, my brave comrades," replied he, "seldom chooses even ways. I go on a message from a young ensign in the keep to one of the Scottish damsels in yonder tower. Delay me, and his vengeance will fall upon us all."—"Good luck to you, my lad!" was their answer, and with a lightened step he hastened towards the tower.

Not deeming it safe to seek an interview with any of the earl's family, he crept along the base of the structure and across the works till he reached the wall that blocks up egress from the north. He found this formidable curtain constructed of fragments of rock, and for the convenience of the guard, a sloping platform from within led to the top of the wall. On the other side it was perpendicular. A solitary sentinel stood there, and how to pass him was Edwin's next device. To attack him would be desperate; being one of a chain of guards around the fortress, his voice need only to be raised to call a regiment to his assistance, and Edwin must be seized on the instant.

Aware of his danger, the adventurous youth bethought him of his former excuse, and remembering a flask of spirits which Ireland had put into his pouch on leaving Glenfinlass, he affected to be intoxicated, and staggering up to the man, accosted him in the character of a servant of the garrison.

The sentinel did not doubt the appearance of the boy, and Edwin holding out the flask, said that a pretty girl in the great tower had not only given him a draught of the same good liquor, but had filled his bottle that he might not lack amusement while her companion, one of Lady Mar's maids-in-waiting, was tying up a true lover's knot to send to his master in the garrison. The man believed Edwin's tale the more readily as he thrust the flask into his hand and bade him drink.

The unsuspecting Southron returned him a merry reply, and putting the flask to his head, soon drained its contents. They had the effect Edwin desired. The soldier became flustered, and impatient of his duty. Edwin perceived it, and yawning, complained of drowsiness. "I would go to the top of that wall and sleep sweetly in the moonbeams," said he, "if any good-natured fellow would meanwhile wait for my pretty Scot."

The half-inebriated Southron liked no better sport; and regardless of duty, he promised to draw nearer the tower, and bring from the fair messenger the expected token.

Having thus far gained his point, with an apparently staggering, but really agile step, Edwin ascended the wall. A leap from this dizzy height was his only way to rejoin Wallace. To retread his steps through the fortress in safety would hardly be possible; and besides, such a mode of retreat would leave him uninformed on the second object of his enterprise: to know the most valuable side of the fortress.

He threw himself along the summit of the wall, as if to sleep. He looked down, and saw nothing but the blackness of space, but hope buoyed him in her arms; and turning his eyes towards the sentinel, he observed him to have arrived within a few paces of the square tower. This was Edwin's moment. Grasping the projecting stone of the embattlement, and commending himself to Heaven, he threw himself from its summit, and fell, a fearful depth, to the cliffs beneath.

Meanwhile, Wallace, having seen his brave followers depart to their repose, reclined himself along a pile of moss-grown stones. He fixed his eyes on the castle, now illumined in every part by the moon's luster, and considered which point would be most assailable by the scaling-ladders he had prepared. Every side seemed a precipice. The Leven surrounded it on the north and the west; the Clyde, broad

as a sea, on the south.   The only place that seemed at all accessible
was the side next the dyke behind which he lay.   Here the ascent to
the castellated part of the rock, because most perpendicular, was
the least guarded with outworks, and by this he determined to make
the attempt, as soon as the setting moon should involve the garrison
in darkness.

While he yet mused on what might be the consequences of the
succeeding hours, he thought he heard a cautious footstep.   He raised
himself, and laying his hand on his sword, saw a figure advancing
towards him.

"Who goes there?" demanded Wallace.

"A faithful Scot," was the reply.

Wallace recognized the voice of Edwin.   "What has disturbed
you?   Why do you not take rest with the others?"

"That we may have the surer, to-morrow," replied the youth.   "I
am just returned from the summit of yonder rock."

"How!" interrupted Wallace; "have you scaled it alone, and are
returned in safety?"

"I wished to learn its most pregnable part," replied Edwin, his
heart beating with triumph; "and particularly where the good earl
is confined, that we might make our attack directly to the point."

"And have you been successful?" demanded Wallace.

"I have," was his answer.   "Lord Mar and his lady are kept in
a square tower which stands in the cleft between the two summits of
the rock.   It is not only surrounded by embattled walls, but the space
on which it stands is bulwarked at each end by a stone curtain of
fifteen feet high, guarded by turrets full of armed men."

"And yet by that side you suppose we must ascend?" said Wallace."

"Certainly; for if you attempt it on the west, we should have to
scale the watch-tower cliff, and the ascent could only be gained in
file.   An auxiliary detachment, to attack in flank, might succeed
there; but the passage being so narrow, would be too tedious for
the whole party to arrive in time.   Should we take the south, we
must cut through the whole garrison before we could reach the earl.
And on this side, the morass lies too near the foot of the rock to
admit an approach without the greatest danger.   But on the north,
where I descended, by wading through part of the Leven, and climbing from cliff to cliff, I have every hope you may succeed."

Edwin recounted his progress through the fortress, and by the
minuteness of his descriptions enforced his arguments for the north
to be the point assailed.   Closing his narrative, he explained how he

Helen descends the Glen of Stones

had escaped accident in a leap of so many feet. The wall was covered with ivy; he caught by its branches in his descent, and at last happily fell amongst a bed of furze. After this, he clambered down the steep, and fording the Leven, there only knee-deep, now appeared before his general, elate in heart and bright in valor.

"The intrepidity of this action," returned Wallace, "merits that every confidence should be placed in the result of your observations. Your safe return is a pledge of our design being approved. This night, when the Lord of battles puts that fortress into our hands, before the whole of our little army you shall receive that knighthood you have so richly deserved. Such, my brother, my noble Edwin, shall be the reward of your toil."

Wallace would now have sent him to repose, but animated by his success, and exulting in the honor which was so soon to stamp a sign of this exploit upon him forever, he told his leader that he felt no want of sleep, and would rather take on him the office of arousing the other captains to their stations, the moon, their preconcerted signal, being then approaching its rest.

CHAPTER XXIII.

THE FORTRESS.

KIRKPATRICK, Murray, and Scrymgeour hastened to their commander, and in a few minutes all were under arms. Wallace explained his altered plan of assault, and marshaling his men, led them in silence through the water, and along the beach which lay between the rock and the Leven. Arriving at the base just as the moon set, they began to ascend. To do this in the dark redoubled the difficulty; but as Wallace had the place of every accessible stone accurately described to him by Edwin, he went confidently forward, followed by his Lanarkmen.

He and they, being the first to mount, fixed and held the tops of the scaling-ladders while Kirkpatrick and Scrymgeour, with their men, gradually ascended and gained the bottom of the wall. Here, planting themselves in the crannies of the rock, under the impenetrable darkness of the night, they awaited the signal for the final ascent.

Meanwhile, Edwin led Lord Andrew with his followers, and the Fraser men, round by the western side to mount the watch-tower rock, and seize the few soldiers who kept the beacon. As a signal of having succeeded, they were to smother the flame on the top of the tower, and thence descend towards the garrison, to meet Wallace before the prison of the Earl of Mar.

While the men of Lanark, with their eyes fixed on the burning beacon, in deadly stillness watched the appointed signal for the attack, Wallace, by the aid of his dagger, which he struck into the firm soil that occupied the cracks in the rock, drew himself up almost parallel with the top of the great wall which clasped the bases of the two hills. He listened; not a voice was to be heard in the garrison of all the legions he had so lately seen glittering on its battlements.

He looked up, and fixing his eyes on the beacon-flame, thought he saw the figures of men pass before it; the next moment all was darkness. He sprang on the wall; and feeling, by the touch of hands about his feet, that his brave followers had already mounted their ladders, he grasped his sword firmly and leaped down on the ground within. In that moment he struck against the sentinel, who was just passing, and by the violence of the shock struck him to the earth; but the man, as he fell, catching Wallace round the waist, dragged him down, and shouted "Treason!"

Several sentinels ran with leveled pikes to the spot, the adjacent turrets emptied themselves of their armed inhabitants, and all assaulted Wallace just as he had extricated himself from the grasp of the prostrate soldier.

"Who are you?" demanded they.

"Your enemy," and the speaker fell at his feet with one stroke of his sword.

"Alarm! Treason!" resounded from the rest, as they aimed their random strokes at the conquering chief. But he was now assisted by the vigorous arm of Ker and of several Lanarkmen, who, having cleared the wall, were dealing about blows in the darkness which filled the air with groans.

One or two Southrons, whose courage was not equal to their caution, fled to arouse the garrison; and just as the whole of Wallace's men leaped the wall and rallied to his support, the inner ballium gate burst open, and a legion of foes, bearing torches, issued to the contest. With horrible threatenings they came on, and by a rapid movement surrounded Wallace and his little company. But his soul brightened in danger, and his men, warmed with the same spirit, stood firm with fixed pikes, receiving without injury the assault. Wallace fought in front, making a dreadful passage through the falling ranks, while the tremendous sweep of his sword, flashing in the intermitting light, warned the survivors where the avenging blade would next descend. The platform was cleared; and the fallen torches, some half-extinguished, and others flaming on the ground by the sides of the dead, showed a few terrified wretches seeking safety in flight. The same lurid rays, casting a transitory light on the iron gratings of the great tower, informed Wallace that the heat of conflict had drawn him to the prison of the earl.

"We are now near the end of this night's work," cried he. "Let us press forward, to give freedom to the Earl of Mar."

"Liberty and Lord Mar!" cried Kirkpatrick, rushing onward. He was immediately followed by his own men, but not quick enough for his daring. The guard in the tower, hearing the outcry, issued from the flanking gates, and, surrounding him, took him prisoner.

"If there be might in your arms," roared he with the voice of a lion, "men of Loch Doine, rescue your leader!"

They hurried forward with yells of defiance, but the strength of the garrison, awakened by the flying wretches from the defeat, turned out all its power, and, with De Valence at their head, pouring on Kirkpatrick's men, would have overpowered them had not Wallace and his sixty heroes, with desperate determination, cut a passage to them through the closing ranks.

Scrymgeour, at the head of the Loch Doine men, in vain attempted to reach this contending party; and fearful of losing the royal standard, he was turning to make a valiant retreat, when Murray and Edwin, having disengaged their followers from the precipices of the beacon rock, rushed into the fray, striking their shields and uttering the inspiring slogan of "Wallace and freedom!" It was re-echoed by every Scot; those that were flying returned; and the terrible thunder of the word pealing from rank to rank struck a terror into De Valence's men which made them pause. The extinction of the beacon made them still more aghast.

On that moment turned the crisis of their fate. Wallace cut his way forward through the dismayed Southrons, who, hearing the shouts of the fresh reenforcement, knew not whether its strength might not be thousands instead of hundreds. Surrounded, mixed with their assailants, they knew not friends from foes; and each individual being bent on flight, they indiscriminately cut to right and left, and finally, after slaughtering half their companions, some few escaped through the small posterns of the garrison, leaving the inner ballia entirely in possession of the foe.

The whole of the field being cleared, Wallace ordered the tower to be forced. A strong guard was still within, and as the assailants drew near, every means were used to render their assaults abortive. As the Scots pressed to the main entrance, stones and heavy metals were thrown upon their heads; but not in the least intimidated, they stood beneath the iron shower till Wallace ordered them to drive a large felled tree, which lay on the ground, against the hinges of the door: it burst open, and the whole party rushed into the hall.

A short, sanguinary, but decisive conflict took place. The hauberk and plaid of Wallace were dyed from head to foot; his own blood and the stream from his enemies mingled in one hue upon his garments.

"Wallace! Wallace!" cried the stentorian lungs of Kirkpatrick. In a moment Wallace was at his side and found him wrestling with two men. The light of a single lamp suspended from the rafters fell direct upon the combatants. A dagger was pointed at the life of the old knight, but Wallace laid the holder of it dead across the body of his intended victim, and catching the other assailant by the throat, threw him prostrate to the ground.

"Spare me, for the honor of knighthood!" cried the conquered.

"For my honor, you shall die!" cried Kirkpatrick. His sword

was already at the heart of the Englishman. Wallace beat it back. "Kirkpatrick, he is my prisoner, and I give him life."

"You know not what you do," cried the old knight, struggling with Wallace to release his sword-arm. "This is De Valence!"

"Quarter!" reiterated the panting and hard-pressed earl. "Noble Wallace, my life, for I am wounded!"

"Sooner take my own," cried the determined Kirkpatrick, fixing his foot on the neck of the prostrate man, and trying to wrench his hand from the grasp of his commander.

"Shame!" cried Wallace; "you must strike through me to kill any wounded man I hear cry for quarter. Release the earl, for your own honor."

"Our safety lies in his destruction," cried Kirkpatrick; and, enraged at opposition, he thrust his commander, little expecting such an action, from off the body of the earl. De Valence seized his advantage, and catching Kirkpatrick by the limb that pressed on him, overthrew him, and by a sudden spring, turning quickly on Wallace, struck his dagger into his side. All this was done in an instant. Wallace did not fall, but, staggering with the weapon sticking in the wound, he could not give the alarm till its perpetrator had disappeared.

The flying earl took his course through a narrow passage between the works, and proceeding swiftly towards the south, issued safely at one of the outer gates, and thence he made his escape in a fisher's boat across the Clyde.

Meanwhile, Wallace, having recovered himself, just as the Scots brought in lighted torches from the lower apartments of the tower, saw Sir Roger Kirkpatrick leaning on his sword, and the young Edwin coming forward in garments too nearly the hue of his own. Andrew Murray stood already by his side. Wallace's hand was upon the hilt of the dagger which the ungrateful De Valence had left in his breast. "You are wounded, you are slain!" cried Murray, in a voice of consternation. Edwin stood motionless with horror.

"That dagger," exclaimed Scrymgeour——

"Has done nothing," replied Wallace, "but let me a little more blood." As he spoke he drew it out, and thrusting the corner of his scarf into his bosom, stanched the wound.

"So is your mercy rewarded," exclaimed Kirkpatrick.

"So I am true to a soldier's duty," returned Wallace, "though De Valence is a traitor to his."

"You treated him as a man," replied Kirkpatrick; "but now you find him a treacherous fiend."

"Your eagerness, my brave friend," returned Wallace, "has lost him as a prisoner. If not for humanity or honor, for policy's sake, we ought to have spared his life, and detained him an hostage for our own countrymen in England."

Kirkpatrick remembered how his violence had released the earl, and he looked down abashed. Wallace, perceiving it, continued, "But let us not abuse our time discoursing on a coward. He is gone, the fortress is ours, and our first measure must be to guard it from surprise."

As he spoke his eyes fell upon Edwin, who, having recovered from the shock of Murray's exclamation, had brought forward the surgeon of their little band. A few minutes bound up the wounds of their chief, even while beckoning the anxious boy towards him. "Brave youth," cried he, "you who at the risk of your own life explored these heights that you might render our ascent more sure, you who have fought like a young lion in this unequal contest, here, in the face of all your valiant comrades, receive that knighthood which derives luster from your virtues."

Edwin bent his knee, and Wallace giving him the hallowed accolate, the young knight rose from his position with all the roses of his springing fame glowing in his countenance. Scrymgeour presented him the knightly girdle, which he unbraced from his own loins; and while the happy boy received the sword to which it was attached he exclaimed, "While I follow the example before my eyes I shall never draw this in an unjust cause, nor ever sheathe it in a just one."

"Go, then," returned Wallace, smiling his approval of this sentiment; "while work is to be done I will keep my knight to the toil; go, and with twenty men of Lanark, guard the wall by which we ascended."

Edwin disappeared, and Wallace, having despatched detachments to occupy other parts of the garrison, took a torch in his hand, and turning to Murray proposed seeking the Earl of Mar. Lord Andrew was soon at the iron door which led from the hall to the principal stairs.

"We must have our friendly battering-ram here," cried he; "a close prisoner do they indeed keep my uncle, when even the inner doors are bolted on him."

The men dragged the tree forward, and striking it against the iron it burst open with the noise of thunder. Shrieks from within followed the sound. The women of Lady Mar, hearing the door forced, expected that some new enemies were advancing, and giving themselves up to despair they flew into the room where the countess sat in equal terror.

At the shouts of the Scots when they began the attack the earl had started from his couch. "That is not peace," said he; "there is some surprise."

"Alas, from whom?" returned Lady Mar; "who would venture to attack a fortress like this garrisoned with thousands?"

The cry was repeated.

"It is the slogan of Sir William Wallace!" cried he; "I shall be free! Oh for a sword!"

As the shouts redoubled and mingled with the various clangors of battle, the impatience of the earl could not be restrained. Hope and eagerness seemed to have dried up his wounds, and unarmed as he was, he hurried down the stairs which led to the iron door. He found it so firmly fastened by bars and padlocks he could not move it. Again he ascended to his terrified wife, who, conscious how little obligation Wallace owed to her, perhaps dreaded even more to see her husband's hopes realized than to find herself yet more rigidly the prisoner of the haughty De Valence.

"Joanna," cried he, "the arm of God is with us! My prayers are heard; Scotland will yet be free! Hear those groans,—those shouts! Victory! Victory!"

As he thus echoed the cry of triumph uttered by the Scots when bursting open the outer gate of the tower, the foundations of the building shook, and Lady Mar, almost insensible with terror, received the exhausted body of her husband into her arms; he fainted from the transport his weakened frame was unable to bear. Soon after this the stair door was forced, and the panic-struck women ran shriek- ing into the room to their mistress.

The countess could not speak, but sat pale and motionless, sup- porting his head on her bosom. Guided by the noise, Lord Andrew flew into the room, and rushing towards his uncle, fell at his feet. "Liberty! Liberty!" was all he could say. His words pierced the ear of the earl like a voice from heaven, and looking up, without a word he threw his arms round the neck of his nephew.

Tears relieved the contending feelings of the countess, and the women, recognizing the young Lord of Bothwell, retired into a distant corner, well assured they had now no cause for fear.

The earl rested but a moment on the breast of his nephew, when, gazing round to seek the mighty leader of the band, he saw Wallace enter with triumph in his eyes.

"Ever my deliverer!" cried the venerable Mar, stretching forth his arms. The next instant he held Wallace to his breast, and remem- bering all that he had lost for his sake since they parted, a soldier's heart melted, and he burst into tears. "Wallace, my preserver, who, by the sacrifice of all thou didst hold dear on earth, art made a blessing to thy country, receive my thanks and my heart!"

Wallace felt all in his soul which the earl meant to imply, but when he raised himself and replied to the acknowledgments of the countess, it was with a serene though glowing countenance.

She, when she had glanced from her nephew to the advancing hero, looked as Venus did when she beheld the god of war rise from a field of blood. She started at the appearance of Wallace; but it was not his garments dropping gore, nor the blood-stained falchion in his hand, that caused the new sensation: it was the figure, breathing youth and manhood; it was the face, where every noble passion of the heart had stamped themselves on his perfect features. All these struck at once upon the sight of Lady Mar and made her exclaim within herself, "This is a wonder of man! This is the hero that is to humble Edward!"

This passed through the mind of the countess in less time than it has been repeated, and she exclaimed to herself, "Helen, thou wert right; thy gratitude was prophetic of a matchless object, while I, wretch that I was, gave information against my husband, that this man, the cause of all, might be secured or slain."

Just as the last idea struck her, Wallace rose from the embrace of his venerable friend and met the eye of the countess. She stammered forth a few expressions of obligation; he attributed her confusion to the surprise of the moment, and replying to her respectfully, turned again to the earl.

The joy of the venerable chief was unbounded when he found that a handful of Scots had put two thousand Southrons to flight, and gained entire possession of the castle. Wallace, having satisfied his questions, gladly perceived the morning light. He rose from his seat. "I shall take a temporary leave of you, my lord," said he to the earl. "I must now visit my brave comrades at their posts, and see the colors of Scotland planted on the citadel."

CHAPTER XXIV.

THE GREAT TOWER.

WHEN Wallace withdrew, Lady Mar, who had detained Murray, whispered to him that she should like to be present at the planting of the standard. Lord Mar declared his willingness to accompany her to the spot, and added, "I can be supported thither by the arm of Andrew." Murray hesitated. "It will be impossible for my aunt to go; the hall below and the ground before the tower are covered with slain."

"Let them be cleared away," cried she, "for I cannot consent to be deprived of a spectacle so honorable to my country."

Murray regarded the indifference with which she gave this order with amazement. "To do that, madam," said he, "is beyond my power; the whole ceremony of the colors would be completed long before I could clear the hearth of half its bleeding load. I will seek a passage for you by some other way."

Before the earl could make a remark, Murray had disappeared, and after exploring the lower part of the tower in unavailing search for a way, he met Sir Roger Kirkpatrick issuing from a small door, which he had hitherto overlooked. It led through the ballium to the platform before the citadel. Lord Andrew returned to his uncle and aunt, and informing them of this discovery, gave his arm to Lord Mar, while Kirkpatrick led forward the agitated countess.

When they approached the citadel, Wallace and Sir Alexander Scrymgeour had just gained its summit. The standard of Edward was yet flying. Wallace looked at it for a moment, then laying his hand on the staff, "Down, thou red dragon," cried he. Even while speaking he rent it from the roof, and casting it over the battlements, planted the Lion of Scotland in its stead.

As it floated on the air, the loud clarion of honest triumph burst from every heart, horn, and trumpet below. It was a shout that pierced the skies and entered the soul of Wallace with a bliss which seemed a promise of immortality.

Feeling as if no eye looked on him but that of Heaven, he dropped on his knee, and rising again, took Sir Alexander by the hand. "My brave friend," said he, "we have here planted the tree of

137

freedom in Scotland. Should I die in its defense, swear to bury me under its branches."

"I swear," cried Scrymgeour, laying his crossed hands upon the arm of Wallace,—"I swear with a double vow: by the blood of my brave ancestors, and by your valiant self, never to sheathe my sword until Scotland be entirely free!"

The colors fixed, Wallace and his brave colleague descended the tower, and perceiving the earl and countess, who sat on a stone bench at the end of a platform, approached them. The countess rose as the chiefs drew near. Lord Mar took his friend by the hand; his lady spoke, hardly conscious of what she said; and Wallace, after a few minutes' discourse, proposed to the earl to retire with Lady Mar into the citadel, where she would be more suitably lodged than in their late prison. Lord Mar was obeying this movement when, suddenly stopping, he exclaimed, "But where is that wondrous boy—your pilot over these perilous rocks? Let me give him a soldier's thanks."

Happy at so grateful a demand, Wallace beckoned Edwin, who, just relieved from his guard, was standing at some distance. "Here," said he, "is my knight of fifteen, for last night he proved himself more worthy of his spurs than many a man who has received them from a king."

"He shall wear those of a king," rejoined the Lord Mar, unbuckling from his feet a pair of golden spurs. "These were fastened on my heels by our great King Alexander, at the battle of Largs. I had intended them for my only son; but the first knight in the cause of rescued Scotland is the son of my heart and soul."

As he spoke he would have pressed the young hero to his breast, but Edwin, trembling with emotion, slid down upon his knees, and clasping the earl's hand, said in a hardly audible voice, "Receive and pardon the truant son of your sister Ruthven."

"What!" exclaimed the veteran, "is it Edwin Ruthven that has brought me this weight of honor? Come to my arms, thou dearest child of my dearest Janet!"

The uncle and nephew were folded in each other's embrace. Edwin murmured a short explanation in the ear of his uncle, and then rising from his arms, with his beautiful face glittering like an April day in tears, allowed his gay cousin Murray to buckle the royal spurs on his feet. The rite over, he kissed Lord Andrew's hand, in token of acknowledgment, and called on Sir William Wallace to bless the new honors conferred on his knight.

Wallace turned towards Edwin with a smile. "Have we not performed our mutual promises?" said he. "I brought you to the spot where you were to reveal your name, and you have declared it to me by the voice of glory. Come, then, my brother, let us leave your uncle awhile to seek his repose."

As he spoke he bowed to the countess, and Edwin joyfully receiving his arm, they walked together towards the eastern postern.

Agitated with the surprise of thus meeting his favorite sister's son, and exhausted by his emotions, the earl readily acquiesced in a proposal for rest, and leaning on Lord Andrew proceeded to the citadel.

Murray led the way into the apartments lately occupied by De Valence. They were furnished with all the luxury of a Southron nobleman. Lady Mar cast her eyes around the splendid chamber, and seated herself on one of its tapestried couches. The earl, not marking whether it were silk or rushes, placed himself beside her.

"My dear Andrew," said the earl, "in the midst of this rejoicing there is yet a canker at my heart. Tell me that when my beloved Helen disappeared in the tumult at Bothwell she was under your protection?"

"She was," replied Murray, "and I thank the holy Saint Fillan she is now in the sanctuary of his church."

Murray then recounted to his uncle every event, from the moment of his withdrawing behind the arras to that of his confiding the English soldier with the iron box to the care of the prior. Lord Mar sighed heavily when he spoke of that mysterious casket. "Whatever it contain," said he, "it has drawn after it much evil and much good. The domestic peace of Wallace was ruined by it, and the spirit which now restores Scotland to herself was raised by his wrongs."

"But tell me," added he, "do you think my daughter safe so near a garrison of the enemy?"

"Surely, my lord," cried the countess, remembering the enthusiasm with which Helen had regarded even the unknown Wallace,— "surely you would not bring that tender child into a scene like this. Rather send a messenger to convey her secretly to Thirlestan; at that distance she will be safe, and under the powerful protection of her grandfather."

The earl acquiesced in her opinion, and saying he would consult with Wallace about the securest mode of travel for his daughter, again turned to Lord Andrew to learn further of their late proceedings. But the countess, still uneasy, once more interrupted him.

"Alas! my lord, what would you do? His generous zeal will offer to go in person for your daughter. If you really feel the weight of the evils into which you have plunged Sir William Wallace, do not increase it by even hinting to him the present subject of your anxiety."

"My aunt is an oracle," resumed Murray. "Allow me to be the happy knight that is to bear the surrender of Dumbarton to my sweet cousin. Prevail on Wallace to remain in this garrison till I return, and then full tilt for the walls of old Stirling and the downfall of Hughie Cressingham!"

Both the countess and the earl were pleased with this arrange· ment. The latter retired to repose, and the former desired Lord Andrew to inform Wallace that she should expect to be honored with his presence at noon to partake of such fare as the garrison afforded.

On Murray's coming from the citadel he learnt that Wallace was gone towards the great tower. He followed him thither, and on issuing from the postern which led to that part of the rock saw the chief standing with his helmet off in the midst of the slain.

"This is a sorry sight," said he to Murray as he approached; "but it shall not long lie thus exposed. I have just ordered that these sad wrecks of human strife may be lowered into the Clyde, its rushing stream will soon carry them to a quiet grave beneath yon peaceful sea." His own dead, amounting to no more than fifteen, were to be buried at the foot of the rock, a prisoner in the castle having described steps in the cliff by which the solemnity could easily be performed.

"But why, my dear commander," cried Lord Andrew, "why do you take any thought about our enemies? Leave them where they are, and the eagles of our mountains will soon find them graves."

"For shame, Murray!" was the reply of Wallace; "they are dead, and our enemies no more. They are men like ourselves, and shall we deny them a place in that earth whence we all sprung?"

"I know," replied Lord Andrew, blushing, "that I am often the assertor of my own folly, and·I do not know how you will forgive my inconsiderate impertinence."

"Because it was inconsiderate," replied Wallace. "Inhumanity is too stern a guest to live in such a breast as yours."

"If I ever give her quarters," replied Murray, "I should most wofully disgrace the companion she would meet there. Next to the honor of fair Scotland, my cousin Helen is the goddess of my idolatry, and she would forswear my kindred could she believe me capable of feeling otherwise than in unison with Sir William Wallace."

Wallace looked towards him with pleasure in his countenance. "Your fair cousin does me honor."

"Ah, my noble friend!" cried Murray, lowering his gay tone to one of softer expression; "if you knew all the goodness that dwells in her gentle heart, you would love her as I do."

The blood fled from the cheek of Wallace. "Not as you do, Murray; I can no more love woman as you love her. Such scenes as these," cried he, turning to the mangled bodies which the men were now carrying away to the precipice of the Clyde, "have divorced woman's love from my heart. I am all my country's, or I am nothing."

"Nothing!" reiterated Murray, laying his hand upon that of Wallace. "Is the friend of mankind, the champion of Scotland, the beloved of a thousand valuable hearts, nothing?"

Wallace looked upon Murray with an expression of mingled feelings. "May I be all this, my friend, and Wallace must yet be happy! But speak not to me of love and woman; tell me not of those endearing qualities I have prized too tenderly, and which are now buried to me forever beneath the ashes of Ellerslie."

"Not under the ashes of Ellerslie," cried Murray, "sleep the remains of your lovely wife." Wallace's penetrating eye turned quick upon him. Murray continued: "My cousin's pitying soul stretched itself towards them; by her directions they were brought from your oratory in the rock and deposited with all holy rites in the cemetery at Bothwell."

The glow that now animated the heart of Wallace overspread his face. His eyes spoke volumes of gratitude, and, fervently pressing the hand of Murray, he turned away and walked towards the cliff.

When all the slain were lowered to their last beds, a young priest, who came in the company of Scrymgeour, gave the funeral benediction, both to the departed in the waves and those whom the shore had received. The rites over, Murray again drew near to Wallace and delivered his aunt's message. "I shall obey her commands," returned he; "but first we must visit our wounded prisoners in the tower."

Murray gladly obeyed the impulse of his leader's arm, and they entered the tower. Ireland welcomed Wallace with the intelligence that he hoped he had succored friends instead of foes; for that most of the prisoners were poor Welsh peasants whom Edward had torn from their mountains to serve in his legions, and a few Irish, who in eagerness for adventure had enlisted in his ranks. "I have shown to them," continued Ireland, "what fools they are to injure themselves in us. They only require your presence, my lord, to forswear their former leaders and to enlist under Scottish banners."

"Thou art an able orator, my good Stephen," returned Wallace; "and whatever promises thou hast made to honest men in the name of Scotland, we are ready to ratify them. Is it not so?" added he, turning to Kirkpatrick and Scrymgeour.

"All as you will," replied they in one voice. "Yes," added Kirkpatrick, "you were the first to rise for Scotland, and who but you has a right to command her?"

Ireland threw open the door which led into the hall, and there, on the ground, on pallets of straw, lay most of the wounded Southrons. Some of their dimmed eyes had discerned their preserver when he discovered them expiring on the rock, and on sight of him now they uttered such a piercing cry of gratitude that, surprised, he stood for a moment. In that moment five or six of the poor wounded wretches crawled to his feet. "Our enemy! our preserver!" burst from their lips as they kissed the edge of his plaid.

"Not to me, not to me!" exclaimed Wallace; "I am a soldier like yourselves. I have only acted a soldier's part: but I am a soldier of freedom; you, of a tyrant who seeks to enslave the world. This lays you at my feet, when I would more willingly receive you to my arms as brothers in one generous cause."

"We are yours," was the answering exclamation of those who knelt and of those who raised their feebler voices from their beds of straw.

"To this we also subjoin," cried several other men, who comprised the whole of the English prisoners.

"Noble people," cried Wallace, "why have you not a king worthy of you!"

"And yet," observed Kirkpatrick, in a surly tone, "Heselrigge was one of these people." Wallace turned upon him with a look of so tremendous a meaning that he fell back a few paces muttering curses, but on whom could not be heard.

"That man would arouse the tiger in our lion-hearted chief," whispered Scrymgeour to Murray.

"Ay," returned Lord Andrew; "but the royal spirit keeps the beast in awe,—see how that bold brow now bows before it."

Wallace marked the impression his glance had made, but where he had struck, being unwilling to pierce also, he dispelled the thunder from his countenance, and once more looking on Sir Roger with a frank serenity, "Come," said he, "my good knight, you must not be more tenacious for William Wallace than he is for himself. While he possesses such a zealous friend as Kirkpatrick, of Torthorald, he need not now fear the arms of a thousand Heselrigges."

"No, nor of Edwards either," cried Kirkpatrick, once more looking boldly up and shaking his claymore. "My thistle has a point to sting all to the death who would pass between this arm and my leader's breast."

"May Heaven long preserve the valiant Wallace!" was the prayer of every feeble voice, as he left the hall to visit his own wounded in an upper chamber. The interview was short and satisfactory. "Ah, sir," cried one of them, "I cannot tell how it is, but when I see you I feel as if I beheld the very soul of my country standing before me."

"You see an honest Scot standing before you, my good Duncan," replied Wallace; "and that is no mean personage, for it is one who knows no use of his life but as it fulfils his duty to his country."

"Oh that the sound of that voice could penetrate to every ear in Scotland!" rejoined the soldier; "it would be more than the call of the trumpet to bring them to the field."

"And from the summit of this rock many have already heard it, and more shall be so aroused," cried Murray, returning from the door, to which one of his men had beckoned him. "Here is a man come to announce that Malcolm, Earl of Lennox, passing by the foot of this rock, saw the Scottish standard flying from its citadel; and overjoyed at the sight, he sends to request the confidence of being admitted."

"Let me bring him hither," interrupted Kirkpatrick; "he is brave as the day, and will be a noble auxiliary."

"Every true Scot must be welcome to these walls," returned Wallace.

Kirkpatrick hastened from the tower to the northern side of the rock, at the foot of which stood the earl and his train. With all the pride of a freeman and a victor Sir Roger descended the height. Lennox advanced to meet him. "What is it I see? Sir Roger Kirkpatrick master of this citadel, and our king's colors flying from its towers! Where is Earl de Valence? Where the English garrison?"

"The English garrison," replied Kirkpatrick, "is now beneath the waters of the Clyde. De Valence is fled; and this fortress, manned with a few hardy Scots, shall sink into yon waves ere it again bear the English dragon on its walls."

"And you, noble knight," cried Lennox, "have achieved all this! You are the dawn to a blessed day for Scotland."

"No," replied Kirkpatrick; "I am but a follower of the man who has struck the blow. Sir William Wallace, of Ellerslie, is our chief; and with the power of his virtues he subdues not only friends but enemies to his command."

He then exultingly narrated the events of the last four and twenty hours. The earl listened with wonder and joy. "What!" cried he, "so noble a plan for Scotland and I ignorant of it? I, that have not waked day nor night for many a month without dreaming of some enterprise to free my country, and behold it is achieved in a moment! Lead me, worthy knight,—lead me to your chief, for he shall be mine too; he shall command Malcolm Lennox and all his clan."

Kirkpatrick gladly turned to obey him, and they mounted the ascent together. Within the barbican gate stood Wallace, with Scrymgeour and Murray. The earl knew Scrymgeour well, having often seen him in the field as hereditary standard-bearer of the kingdom; of the persons of the others he was ignorant.

"There is Wallace!" exclaimed Kirkpatrick.

"Not one of those very young men?" interrogated the earl.

"Even so," was the answer of the knight; "but gray beards are glad to bow before his golden locks, for beneath them is wisdom."

As he spoke they entered the barbican, and Wallace, whom the penetrating eye of Lennox had already singled out for the chief, advanced to meet his guest.

"Earl," said he, "you are welcome to Dumbarton castle."

"Bravest of my countrymen!" returned Lennox, clasping him in his arms, "receive a soldier's embrace; accept my services, my arms, my men; my all I devote to Scotland and the great cause."

Wallace for a moment did not answer, but straining the earl to his breast, said, as he released him, "Such support will give sinews to our power. A few months, and with the blessing of Heaven we shall see Scotland at liberty."

"And may Heaven, brave Wallace," exclaimed Lennox, "grant us thine arm to wield its scythe! But how have you accomplished this? How have your few overthrown this English host?"

"He strikes home when right points his sword," replied Wallace. "We feared nothing, for God was with us, and in his might we conquered."

"And shall yet conquer," cried Lennox, kindling with the enthusiasm that blazed from the eyes of Wallace; "I feel the strength of our cause, and from this hour I devote myself to assert it or to die."

"Not to die, my noble lord," said Murray; "we have yet many an eve to dance over the buried fetters of Scotland. And as a beginning of our jollities, I must remind our leader that my aunt's board awaits him."

Lord Lennox understood from this address it was the brave Murray who spoke to him, for he had heard sufficient from Sir Roger Kirkpatrick to explain how the Countess of Mar and her patriot husband came within those walls.

The countess, having arrayed herself with all her powers to receive her deliverer, awaited the hour of his arrival with emotion at her heart. All others were lost to her impatient eyes, and hastily rising from the window as the chiefs entered the porch she crossed the room to meet them at the door.

The Earl of Lennox stood amazed at sight of so much beauty and splendor in such a scene. Lady Mar had attained her thirty-fifth year, but from the graces of her person and the address with which she set forth all her charms, the enchanted gazer found it impossible to suppose her more than three or four and twenty. Thus happily formed by nature, and habited in a suit of velvet overlaid with cyprus-work of gold, blazing with jewels about her head, and her feet clad in silver-fretted sandals, Lennox thought she looked more like some triumphant queen than a wife who had so lately shared captivity with an outlawed husband. Murray started at such magnificence; but Wallace scarcely observed it was anything unusual, and bowing to her, presented the Earl of Lennox. She smiled, and saying a few words of welcome to the earl, gave her hand to Wallace to lead her back into the chamber.

Lord Mar had risen from his seat, and leaning on his sword, stood up on their entrance. At sight of Lord Lennox he uttered an exclamation of glad surprise. Lennox embraced him. "I too am come to enlist under the banners of this young Leonidas."

"God armeth the patriot," was all the reply that Mar made, and he shook him by the hand.

"I have four hundred stout Lennoxmen," continued the earl, "who by to-morrow's eve shall be ready to follow our leader to the very borders."

"Not so soon," interrupted the countess; "our deliverer needs repose."

"I thank your benevolence, Lady Mar," returned Wallace; "but the issue of last night, and the sight of Lord Lennox this day with the promise of so great a support, are such aliments that—we must go forward."

"Aye, to be sure," joined Kirkpatrick, "Dumbarton was not taken during our sleep; and if we stay loitering here, the devil that holds Stirling castle may follow the scent of De Valence, and so I lose my prey."

"What!" cried the countess, "and is my lord to be left again to his enemies? Sir William Wallace, I should have thought——"

"Everything, madam," rejoined he, "that is demonstrative of my devotion to your venerable lord. But with a brave garrison I hope you will consider him safe here until a wider range of security enable you to retire to Braemar."

As the words to Wallace in the latter part of the countess' speech had been spoken in rather a low voice, his reply was made in a similar tone, so that Lord Mar did not hear any part of the answer except the concluding words. But then he exclaimed, "Nay, my ever-fearful Joanna, art thou making objections to keeping garrison here?"

"I confess," replied Wallace, "that an armed citadel is not the most pleasant abode for a lady; but at present, excepting perhaps the church, it is the safest; and I would not advise your lady to remove hence until the plain be made as free as this mountain."

The sewer now announced the board in the hall, and the countess, leading the way, reluctantly gave her hand to the Earl of Lennox Lord Mar leaned on the arm of Wallace, who was followed by Edwin and the other chieftains.

CHAPTER XXV.

THE CITADEL.

DURING the repast the countess often fixed her gaze on the manly countenance of the heroic Wallace. His plumed helmet was now laid aside, and the heavy corselet unbuckled from his breast, disclosed the symmetry of his fine form, displayed with advantage by the flexible folds of his simple tartan vest. Was it the formidable Wallace she looked on—bathed in the blood of Heselrigge, and breathing vengeance against the adherents of the tyrant Edward? It was, then, the enemy of her kinsmen of the House of Cummin. It was the man for whom her husband had embraced so many dangers. But where now was the rebel, the ruiner of her peace, the outlaw whom she had wished in his grave?

The last idea was distraction. She could have fallen at his feet and, bathing them with her tears, have implored his pity and forgiveness. Even as the wish sprang in her mind, she asked herself, "Did he know all, could he pardon such a weight of injuries?"

Lady Mar found her situation so strange, and her agitation so inexplicable, that feeling it impossible to remain longer without giving way to a burst of tears, she rose from her seat, and forcing a smile with her curtsey to the company, left the room.

On gaining the upper apartment she threw herself along the nearest couch, and striking her breast, exclaimed, "What is this within me? How does my soul seem to pour itself out to this man! Only twelve hours—hardly twelve hours, have I seen this William Wallace, and yet my very being is now lost in his!"

She grew silent; but thoughts not less intense, not less fraught with self-reproach, occupied her mind. Should this god of her idolatry ever discover that it was her information which had sent Earl de Valence's men to surround him in the mountains; should he ever learn that at Bothwell she had betrayed the cause on which he had set his life,—she felt that moment would be her last.

To defer his departure was all her study; and fearful that his valor might urge him to accompany Murray in his intended convoy of Helen to the Tweed, she determined to persuade her nephew to set off without the knowledge of his general. She did not allow that it was the youthful beauty and more lovely mind of her daughter-in-law which she feared. Even to herself she cloaked her alarm under the excuse of care for the chieftain's safety. Composed by this arrangement, her features became smooth, and with a sedate air she received her lord and his brave friends when they soon after entered the chamber.

But the object of her wishes did not appear. Wallace had taken Lord Lennox to view the dispositions of the fortress. Ill satisfied as she was with his prolonged absence, she did not fail to turn it to advantage; and while her lord and his friends were examining a draft of Scotland, which Wallace had sketched after she left the banqueting-room, she took Lord Andrew aside to converse with him on the subject now nearest to her heart.

"It certainly belongs to me alone, her kinsman and friend, to protect Helen to the Tweed, if there she must go," returned Murray; "but, my good lady, I cannot comprehend why I am to lead my fair cousin such a pilgrimage. She is not afraid of heroes; you are safe in Dumbarton, and why not bring her here also?"

"Not for worlds!" exclaimed the countess, thrown off her guard. Murray looked at her with surprise. It recalled her to self-possession, and she resumed. "So lovely a creature in this castle would be a dangerous magnet. You must have known that it was the hope of obtaining her which attracted the Lord Soulis and Earl de Valence to Bothwell. The whole castle rung with the quarrel of these two lords upon her account, when you so fortunately effected her escape. Should it be known that she is here, the same fierce desire of obtaining her would give double excitement to De Valence to recover the place; and the consequences, who can answer for?"

By this argument Murray was persuaded to relinquish the idea of conveying Helen to Dumbarton; but remembering what Wallace had said respecting the safety of a religious sanctuary, he advised that she should be left at St. Fillan's till the cause of Scotland might be more firmly established. "Send a messenger to inform her of the rescue of Dumbarton, and of your and my uncle's health," continued he, "and that will be sufficient to make her happy."

That she was not to be thrown in Wallace's way, satisfied Lady Mar, and she approved Murray's decision. Relieved from apprehension, she rose to welcome the reentrance of Wallace with the Earl of Lennox.

Absorbed in one thought, every charm she possessed was directed to the same point. She played finely on the lute, and sung with all the grace of her country. What gentle heart was not to be affected by

music? She determined it should be one of the spells by which she
meant to attract Wallace. She took up one of the lutes, which with
other musical instruments decorated the apartments of the luxurious
De Valence, and touching it with exquisite delicacy, breathed the most
pathetic air her memory could dictate:

> If on the heath she moved, her breast was whiter than the down of Cana;
> If on the sea-beat shore, than the foam of the rolling ocean.
> Her eyes were two stars of light; her face was heaven's bow in shower;
> Her dark hair flowed around it like the streaming clouds.
> Thou wert the dweller of souls, white-handed Strinadona.

Wallace rose from his chair which had been placed near her. She
had designed that these tender words of the bard of Morven should
suggest to her hearer the observation of her own resembling beauties.
But he saw in them only the lovely dweller of his own soul, and walking towards a window, stood there with his eyes fixed on the descending sun.

The countess vainly believed that some sensibility advantageous
to her new passion had caused the agitation with which she saw him
depart from her side, and, intoxicated with the idea, she ran through
many a melodious descant, till touching on the first strains of *Thusa
ha measg na reultan mor,* she saw Wallace start from his contempla-
tive position and with a pale countenance leave the room. There was
something in his abruptness which excited the alarm of the Earl of
Lennox, who had also been listening to the songs; he rose instantly,
and overtaking the chief at the threshold, inquired what was the matter. "Nothing," answered Wallace, forcing a smile in which the
agony of his mind was too truly imprinted; "but music displeases me,"
and with this reply he disappeared. What was music to him? A
soulless sound or a direful knell, to recall the remembrance of all he
had lost.

Such were his thoughts when the words of *Thusa ha measg* rung
from Lady Mar's voice. Those were the strains which Halbert used
to breathe from his harp to call his Marion to her nightly slumbers;
those were the strains with which that faithful servant had announced
that she slept to wake no more. What wonder, then, that he fled from
the apartment and buried himself amid the distant solitudes of the
beacon-hill.

Edwin had at intervals cast a sidelong glance upon the changing
complexion of his commander; and no sooner did he see him hurry
from the room, than fearful of some disaster having befallen the garri-

son, which Wallace did not choose immediately to mention, he also stole out of the apartment.

After seeking the object of his anxiety for a long time without avail, he was returning on his steps, when, attracted by the splendor of the moon silvering the beacon-hill, he ascended, to tread, once at least, that acclivity in light which he had so miraculously passed in darkness. He moved on till a deep sigh arrested him. He stopped and listened. It was repeated again and again. He gently drew nearer and saw a human figure reclining on the ground. The head of the mourner was unbonneted, and the brightness of the moon shone on his forehead.

A cloud had passed over the moon, but sailing off again, displayed to the anxious boy that he had indeed drawn very near his friend. "Who goes there?" exclaimed Wallace, starting on his feet.

"Your Edwin," returned the youth. "I feared something wrong had happened when I saw you look so sad and leave the room abruptly."

Wallace pressed his hand in silence. "Then some evil has befallen you?" inquired Edwin, in an agitated voice; "you do not speak."

Wallace seated himself on a stone and leaned his head upon the hilt of his sword. "No new evil has befallen me, Edwin; but there is such a thing as remembrance, that stabs deeper than the dagger's point."

"What remembrance can wound you, my general? The Abbot of St. Columba has often told me that memory is a balm to every ill with the good; and have not you been good to all? Surely, if man can be happy, it must be Sir William Wallace."

"And so I am, my Edwin, when I contemplate the end. But in the interval, is it not written here 'that man was made to mourn'?" He put his hand on his heart; and then, after a short pause, resumed: "Doubly I mourn, doubly am I bereaved, for had it not been for mine enemy I might have lived to have gloried in a son like thee. These are the recollections which sometimes draw tears down thy leader's cheeks. And do not believe, brother of my soul," said he, pressing Edwin to his breast, "that they disgrace his manhood."

Edwin sobbed aloud. "No son could love you dearer than I do. I will replace all to you but your Marion, and she the pitying Son of Mary will restore to you in the kingdom of heaven."

Wallace looked steadfastly at the young preacher. " 'Out of the mouths of babes we shall hear wisdom.' Thine, dear Edwin, I will lay to heart. Thou shalt comfort me when my hermit-soul shuts out all the world besides."

"Then I am indeed your brother!" cried the happy youth; "admit me but to your heart, and no tie shall be more strongly linked than mine."

"What affections I can spare from those resplendent regions," answered Wallace, pointing to the skies, "are thine. But thou art too young, my brother," added he, interrupting himself, "to understand all the feelings, all the seeming contradictions, of my heart."

"Not so," answered Edwin, with a modest blush; "what was Lady Marion's you now devote to Scotland. Those affections which were hers would consume your being did you not pour it forth on your country."

"You have read me, Edwin," replied Wallace; "and that you may never love to idolatry, learn this also: Though Scotland lay in ruin, I was happy. Marion absorbed my wishes, my thoughts, my life, and she was wrested from me, that I might feel myself a slave." He struck his hand upon his breast. "Never love as I have loved, and you will be a patriot without needing to taste my bitter cup."

Edwin trembled; "I can love no one better than I do you, my general, and is there any crime in that?"

Wallace in a moment recovered from the transient wildness which had possessed him. "None, my Edwin," replied he; "the affections are never criminal but when by their excess they blind us to other duties. The offense of mine is judged, and I bow to the penalty. When that is paid, then may my ashes sleep in rescued Scotland." As he spoke he took the arm of the silent Edwin, and putting it through his, they descended the hill together.

On the open ground before the great tower they were met by Murray. "I come to seek you," cried he; "we have had woe on woe in the citadel since you left it."

"Nothing very calamitous," returned Wallace, "if we may guess by the merry aspect of the messenger."

"Only a little whirlwind of my aunt's, in which we have had airs and showers enough to wet us through and blow us dry again."

The conduct of the lady had been even more extravagant than her nephew chose to describe. After the knight's departure, when the chiefs entered into conversation respecting his future plans, Lennox mentioned that when his men should arrive, it was Wallace's intention to march immediately for Stirling, whither it could hardly be doubted Aymer de Valence had fled. "I shall be left here," continued the earl, "to assist you, Lord Mar, in the severer duties attendant on being governor of this place."

No sooner did these words reach the ear of the countess than, struck with despair, she hastened toward her husband and earnestly exclaimed, "You will not suffer this?"

"No," returned the earl, mistaking her meaning; "not being able to perform the duties attendant on the station with which Wallace would honor me, I shall relinquish it altogether to Lord Lennox, and be amply satisfied in finding myself under his protection."

"Ah, where is protection without Sir William Wallace?" cried she. "If he go, our enemies will return. Who then will repel them from these walls? Who will defend your wife and only son from falling again into the hands of our foes?"

Mar observed Lord Lennox color at this imputation on his bravery, and, shocked at the affront which his wife seemed to give so gallant a chief, he hastily replied, "Though this wounded arm cannot boast, yet the Earl of Lennox is an able representative of our commander."

"I will die, madam," interrupted Lennox, "before anything hostile approaches you or your children."

She attended slightly to this pledge, and again addressed her lord with arguments for the detention of Wallace. Sir Roger Kirkpatrick, impatient under all this foolery, as he justly deemed it, abruptly said, "Be assured, fair lady, Israel's Samson was not brought into the world to keep guard over women; and I hope our champion will know his duty better than to allow himself to be tied to any nursery girdle in Christendom."

The brave old earl was offended with this roughness; but ere he could so express himself, its object darted her own severe retort on Kirkpatrick, and then turning to her husband, with a hysterical sob, exclaimed, "It is well seen what will be my fate when Wallace is gone! Would he have stood by and beheld me thus insulted?"

Distressed with shame at her conduct, and anxious to remove her fears, Lord Mar whispered her, and threw his arm about her waist. She thrust him from her. "You care not what may become of me, and my heart disdains your blandishments."

Lennox rose in silence and walked to the other end of the chamber. Sir Roger Kirkpatrick followed him, muttering audibly his thanks to St. Andrew that he had never been yoked with a wife. Scrymgeour and Murray tried to allay the storm in her bosom by detailing how the fortress must be equally safe under the care of Lennox as of Wallace. But they discoursed in vain. She was obstinate, and at last left the room in a passion of tears.

On the return of Wallace, Lord Lennox advanced to meet him. "What shall we do?" said he. "Without you have the witchcraft of

Hercules, and can be in two places at once, I fear we must either leave the rest of Scotland to fight for itself, or never restore peace to this castle."

Wallace smiled; but before he could answer, Lady Mar, having heard his voice ascending the stairs, suddenly entered the room. She held her infant in her arms. Her air was composed, but her eyes yet shone with tears. At this sight Lord Lennox, sufficiently disgusted with the lady, taking Murray by the arm withdrew with him out of the apartment.

She approached Wallace. "You are come, my deliverer, to speak comfort to the mother of this poor babe. My cruel lord here, and the Earl of Lennox, say you mean to abandon us in this castle."

"It cannot be abandoned," returned the chief, "while they are in it. But if so warlike a scene alarms you, would not a religious sanctuary——"

"Not for worlds!" cried she, interrupting him; "what altar is held sacred by the enemies of our country? Oh, wonder not, then," added she, putting her face to that of her child, "that I should wish this innocent babe never to be from under the wing of such a protector!"

"But that is impossible, Joanna," rejoined the earl. "Sir William Wallace has duties to perform superior to that of keeping watch over any private family. His presence is wanted in the field, and we should be traitors to the cause did we detain him."

"Unfeeling Mar," cried she, bursting into tears, "thus to echo the words of the barbarian Kirkpatrick, thus to condemn us to die. You will see another tragedy: your own wife and child seized by the returning Southrons and laid bleeding at your feet."

Wallace walked from her much agitated.

"Rather inhuman, Joanna," whispered Lord Mar to her in an angry voice, "to make such a reference in the presence of our protector. I cannot stay to listen to a pertinacity as insulting to the rest of our brave leaders as it is oppressive to Sir William Wallace. Edwin, you will come for me when your aunt consents to be guided by right reason." While yet speaking he entered the passage that led to his own apartment.

Lady Mar sat a few minutes silent. She was not to be warned from her determination by the displeasure of a husband whom she now regarded with the impatience of a bondwoman towards her taskmaster; and, only solicitous to compass the detention of Sir William Wallace, she resolved, if he would not remain at the castle, to persuade him to conduct her himself to her husband's territories in the Isle of Bute. She could contrive to make the journey occupy more than one day, and for holding him longer she would trust to chance and her own inventions. With these resolutions she looked up. Edwin was speaking to Wallace. "What does he tell you," said she; "that my lord has left me in displeasure? Alas! he comprehends not a mother's anxiety for her sole remaining child. One of my sweet twins, my dear daughter, died on my being brought a prisoner to this horrid fortress; and to lose this also would be more than I could bear. Look at this babe," cried she, holding it up to him; "let it plead to you for its life! Guard it, noble Wallace, whatever may become of me."

The appeal of a mother made instant way to Sir William's heart; even her weaknesses, did they point to anxiety respecting her offspring, were sacred to him. "What would you have me do, madam? Tell me where you think you would be safer, and I will be your conductor."

She paused to repress the triumph with which this proposal filled her, and then with downcast eyes replied, "In the seagirt Bute stands Rothsay, a rude but strong castle of my lord's. It possesses nothing to attract the notice of the enemy, and there I might remain in perfect safety. Lord Mar may keep his station here until a general victory sends you, noble Wallace, to restore my child to its father."

Wallace bowed his consent to her proposal, and Edwin, remembering the earl's injunction, inquired if he might inform him of what was decided. When he left the room, Lady Mar rose, and suddenly putting her son into the arms of Wallace, "Let his sweet caresses thank you." Wallace trembled as she pressed the little mouth to his, and, mistranslating this emotion, she dropped her face upon the infant's, and, in affecting to kiss it, rested her head upon the bosom of the chief. There was something in this action more than maternal; it disconcerted Wallace. "Madam," said he, drawing back and relinquishing the child, "I do not require any thanks for serving the wife and son of Lord Mar."

At that moment the earl entered. Lady Mar flattered herself that the repelling action of Wallace and his cold answer had arisen from the expectation of this entrance; yet, blushing with disappointment, she hastily uttered a few agitated words, to inform her husband that Bute was to be her future sanctuary.

Lord Mar approved it, and declared his determination to accompany her. "In my state, I can be of little use here," said he; "my family will require protection even in that seclusion, and therefore, leaving Lord Lennox sole governor of Dumbarton, I shall unquestionably attend them to Rothsay myself."

This arrangement would break in upon the lonely conversations she had meditated to have with Wallace, and therefore the countess objected to the proposal. But none of her arguments being admitted by her lord, and as Wallace did not support them by a word, she was obliged to make a merit of necessity, and consent to her husband being their companion.

Towards evening the next day Ker not only returned with the Earl of Lennox's men, but brought with them Sir Eustace Maxwell, of Carlaveroch. That brave knight happened to be in the neighborhood the very same night in which De Valence fled before the arms of Wallace across the Clyde, and he no sooner saw the Scottish colors on the walls of Dumbarton than his soul took fire, and stung with a generous ambition, he determined to assist, while he emulated the victor.

To this end he traversed the adjoining country, striving to enlighten the stupidly satisfied, and to excite the discontented to revolt. With most he failed. Some took upon them to lecture him on "fishing in troubled waters," and warned him, if he would keep his head on his shoulders, to wear his yoke in peace. Others thought the project too arduous for men of small means; they wished well to the arms of Sir William Wallace, and should he continue successful would watch the moment to aid him with all their little power. Some were too great cowards to fight for the rights they would gladly regain by the exertions of others. And others again who had families shrunk from taking part in a cause which, should it fail, would not only put their lives in danger, but expose their offspring to the revenge of a resentful enemy. The other pleas were so undeserving of anything but scorn that Sir Eustace Maxwell could not forbear expressing it. "When Sir William Wallace is entering full sail, you will send your boats to tow him in; but if a plank could save him now, you would not throw it to him. I understand you, sirs, and shall trouble your patriotism no more."

In short, none but about a hundred poor fellows whom outrages had rendered desperate, and a few brave spirits who would put all to the hazard for so good a cause, could be prevailed on to hold themselves in readiness to obey Sir Eustace when he should see the moment to conduct them to Sir William Wallace. He was trying his eloquence amongst the clan of Lennox, when Ker arriving, stamped his persuasions with truth, and about five hundred men arranged themselves under their lord's standard. Maxwell gladly explained himself to Wallace's lieutenant, and, summoning his little reserve, they marched with flying pennons through the town of Dumbarton.

At sight of so much larger a power than they expected would venture to appear in arms, and sanctioned by the example of the Earl
of Lennox, whose name held a great influence in those parts, several who had before held back now came forward, and nearly eight
hundred well-appointed men marched into the fortress.

So large a reenforcement was gratefully received by Wallace, and
he welcomed Maxwell with a cordiality which inspired that young
knight with an affection equal to his zeal.

A council being held respecting the disposal of the new troops,
it was decided that the Lennox men must remain with their earl in
garrison, while those brought by Maxwell, and under his command,
should follow Wallace in the prosecution of his conquests.

These preliminaries being arranged, the remainder of the day
was dedicated to the unfolding of the plan of warfare which Wallace
had conceived. As he first sketched the general outline of his design, and then proceeded to the particulars of each military movement, he displayed such comprehensiveness of mind, such depth of
penetration, clearness of apprehension, facility in expedients, promptitude in perceiving, and fixing on the most favorable points of at·
tack, that Maxwell gazed on him with admiration and Lennox with
wonder.

Mar had seen the power of his arms, Murray had already drunk
the experience of a veteran from his genius, hence they were not
surprised on hearing that which filled strangers with amazement.

Lennox gazed on his leader's youthful countenance in awe. He
had thought that Wallace might have won Dumbarton by a bold
stroke, ·and that, when his invincible courage should be steered by
graver heads, every success might be expected from his arms; but
now that he had heard him informing veterans on the art of war, he
marveled, and said within himself, "Surely this man is born to be
a sovereign."

Maxwell, though equally astonished, was not so rapt. "You
have made arms the study of your life?" inquired he.

"It was the study of my earliest days," returned Wallace. "But
when Scotland lost her freedom, as the sword was not drawn in hei
defense, I looked not where it lay. I then studied the arts of peace;
that is over, and now the passion of my soul revives. When the mind
is bent on one object only, all becomes clear that leads to it."

Soon after these observations it was admitted that Wallace might
attend Lord Mar and his family on the morrow to the Isle of Bute,

When the dawn broke he arose from his heather-bed, and having
called forth twenty of the Bothwell men to escort their lord, he told

Ireland he should expect to have a cheering account of the wounded on his return.

"But to assure the poor fellows," rejoined the honest soldier, "that something of yourself still keeps watch over them, I pray you leave me the sturdy sword with which you won Dumbarton. It shall be hung up in their sight, and a good soldier's wounds will heal by looking on it."

Wallace smiled. "Were it our holy King David's we might expect such a miracle. But you are welcome to it, and here let it remain till I take it hence. Meanwhile lend me yours, Stephen, for a truer never fought for Scotland."

A glow of conscious valor flushed the cheek of the veteran. "There, my dear lord," said he, presenting it; "it will not dishonor your hand, for it cut down many a proud Norwegian on the field of Largs."

Wallace took the sword and turned to meet Murray with Edwin in the portal. When they reached the citadel, Lennox and all the officers in the garrison were assembled to bid their chief a short adieu. Wallace spoke to each separately, and then approaching the countess, led her down the rock to the horses which were to convey them to the Frith of Clyde. Lord Mar, between Murray and Edwin, followed; and the servants and guard completed the suite.

Being well mounted, they pleasantly pursued their way, avoiding all inhabited places, and resting in the recesses of the hills. Lord Mar had proposed traveling all night; but at the close of the evening his countess complained of fatigue, declaring she could not advance farther than the eastern bank of the river Cart. No shelter appeared in sight excepting a thick wood of hazels; but the air being mild, Lord Mar at last became reconciled to his wife and son passing the night with no other canopy than the trees. Wallace ordered cloaks to be spread on the ground for the countess and her women, and seeing them laid to rest, planted his men to keep guard around the circle.

The moon had sunk before the whole of his little camp were asleep, but when all seemed composed he wandered forth by the light of the stars to view the surrounding country,—a country he had so often traversed in his boyish days. A little onwards in green Renfrewshire lay the lands of his father; but that Ellerslie of his ancestors, like his own Ellerslie of Clydesdale, his country's enemies had leveled with the ground. He turned in anguish of heart towards the south, for there less racking remembrances hovered over the distant hills.

At last the coldness of the hour and the exhaustion of nature putting a seal upon his senses, he sank upon the bank and fell into profound sleep.

When he awoke, the lark was caroling above his head, and to his surprise he found that a plaid was laid over him. He threw it off, and beheld Edwin seated at his feet. "This has been your doing, my kind brother," said he; "but how came you to discover me?"

"I missed you when the dawn broke, and at last found you here, sleeping under the dew."

"And has none else been astir?" inquired Wallace.

"None that I know of. All were fast asleep when I left the party."

Finding everybody ready, Wallace took his station, and setting forth, all proceeded cheerfully, through the delightful valleys of Barochan. By sunset they arrived at the point of embarkation. The journey ought to have been performed in half the time; but the countess petitioned for long rests, a compliance with which the younger part of the cavalcade conceded with reluctance.

CHAPTER XXVI.

THE FIRTH OF CLYDE.

AT Gourock Murray engaged two small vessels, one for the earl and countess, with Wallace as their escort, the other for himself and Edwin, to follow with a few of the men.

It was a fine evening, and they embarked with everything in their favor. The boatmen calculated on reaching Bute in a few hours; but ere they had been half an hour at sea, the wind veering about, obliged them to woo its breezes by a traversing motion, which lengthened their voyage. Sailing under a side wind, they beheld the huge irregular rocks of Dunoon overhanging the ocean, while from their projecting brows hung every shrub which can live in that saline atmosphere.

"There," whispered Lady Mar, gently inclining towards Wallace, "might some beautiful mermaid keep her court. Observe how magnificently those arching cliffs overhang the hollows, and how richly they are studded with shells and sea-flowers."

Wallace assented to the remarks of Lady Mar, who continued to expatiate on the beauties of the shore which they passed; and thus the hours fled, till turning the southern point of the Cowal mountains the scene suddenly changed. The wind blew a violent gale from that part of the coast, and the sea became so boisterous that the boatmen began to think they should be driven upon the rocks of the island. Wallace tore down the sails, and, laying his arm to the oar, assisted to keep the vessel off the breakers against which the waves were driving her.

Lady Mar looked with affright at the gathering tempest, and with difficulty was persuaded to retire under the shelter of a little awning. The earl forgot his debility in the general terror, and tried to reassure the boatmen; but a tremendous sweep of the gale, driving the vessel far across the head of Bute, shot her past the head of Loch Fyne towards the perilous rocks of Arran. "Here our destruction is certain," cried the master of the bark, at the same time confessing his ignorance of this side of the island. Lord Mar, seizing the helm from the stupefied master, called to Wallace, "While you keep the men to their duty," cried he, "I will steer."

The earl being perfectly acquainted with the coast, Wallace gladly saw the helm in his hand; but he had scarcely stepped forward himself to give some necessary directions, when a heavy sea breaking over the deck carried two of the poor mariners overboard. Wallace instantly threw out a couple of ropes. Then, amidst a spray so blinding that the vessel appeared in a cloud, she lay-to for a few minutes to rescue the men from the yawning gulf; one caught a rope and was saved, but the other was seen no more.

Again the bark was set loose to the current. Wallace, now with two rowers only, applied his whole strength to their aid. The master and the third man were employed in the unceasing toil of laving out the accumulating water.

While the anxious chief tugged at the oar, his eye looked for the vessel that contained his friends; but the liquid mountains which rolled around him prevented all view.

All this while Lady Mar lay in a state of stupefaction. Having fainted at the first alarm of danger, she had fallen from swoon to swoon, and now remained almost insensible upon the bosoms of her maids. In a moment the vessel struck with a great shock, and the next instant it seemed to move with a velocity incredible. "The whirlpool! the whirlpool!" resounded from every lip. But again the rapid motion was suddenly checked, and the women, fancying they had struck on some rock, shrieked aloud. The cry, and the terrified words which accompanied it, aroused Lady Mar. She started from her trance, and while the confusion redoubled, rushed toward the dreadful scene.

A little onward, a thousand massy fragments, rent by former tempests from their parent cliffs, lay at the foundations of the immense acclivities which faced the cause of their present alarm—a whirlpool almost as terrific as that of Scarba. The moment the blast drove the vessel within the influence of the first circle of the vortex, Wallace leaped from the deck on the rocks, and with the same rope in his hand with which he had saved the life of the seaman, he called to the two men to follow him, who yet held similar ropes, fastened like his own to the prow of the vessel; and being obeyed, they strove, by towing it along, to stem the suction of the current.

It was at this instant that Lady Mar rushed forward upon deck. "In, for your life, Joanna!" exclaimed the earl. She answered him not, but looked wildly around her. Nowhere could she see Wallace.

"Have I drowned him?" cried she in a voice of frenzy, and striking the women from her who would have held her back. "Let me clasp him, even in the deep waters!"

The storm on the Firth of Clyde

Happily the earl lost the last sentence in the roaring of the storm.

"Wallace! Wallace!" cried she, wringing her hands and still struggling with her women. At that moment a huge wave sinking before her discovered the object of her fears straining along the surface of a rock and followed by the men in the same task, tugging forward the ropes to which the bark was attached. Thus, contending with the vortex and the storm, they at last arrived at the point that was to clear them of the whirlpool. But at that crisis the rope which Wallace held broke, and with the shock he fell backwards into the sea. The foremost man uttered a cry, but ere it could be echoed by his fellows Wallace had risen above the waves, and beating their whelming waters, soon gained the vessel and jumped upon the deck. The point was doubled; but the next moment the vessel struck, and in a manner that left no hope of getting her off. All must take to the water or perish, for the second shock would scatter her piecemeal.

Again Lady Mar appeared. At sight of Wallace she forgot everything but him, and perhaps would have thrown herself into his arms had not the anxious earl caught her in his own.

"Are we to die?" cried she to Wallace, in a voice of horror.

"I trust that God has decreed otherwise," was his reply. "Compose yourself; all may yet be well."

Lord Mar, from his yet unhealed wounds, could not swim; Wallace therefore tore up the benches of the rowers, and binding them into the form of a small raft, made it the vehicle for the earl and countess, with her two maids and the child. While the men were towing it and buffeting with it through the breakers, he, too, threw himself into the sea to swim by its side, and be in readiness in case of accident.

Having gained the shore, Wallace and his sturdy assistants conveyed the countess and her terrified women up the rocky acclivities. Fortunately, though the wind raged, its violence was of some advantage, for it nearly cleared the heavens of clouds, and allowed the moon to send forth her light to the mouth of a cavern, where Wallace gladly sheltered his dripping charges.

The child, whom he had guarded in his own arms during the difficult ascent, he now laid on the bosom of its mother. Lady Mar kissed the hand that relinquished it, and gave way to a flood of grateful tears.

The earl, as he sank almost powerless against the side of the cave, yet had strength enough to press Wallace to his heart. "Ever preserver of me and mine!" cried he, "how must I bless thee? My wife, my child——"

"Have been saved to you, my friend," interrupted Wallace, "by the presiding care of Him who walked the waves: therefore let our thanksgivings be directed to Him alone."

"So be it!" returned the earl; and dropping on his knees he breathed forth so pathetic a prayer of thanks that the countess trembled and bent her head upon the bosom of her child. She could not utter the solemn *Amen* that was repeated by every voice in the cave for her unhappy infatuation saw no higher power in this great preservation than the hand of the man she adored.

Sleep soon sealed every eye excepting those of Wallace. Anxiety respecting the fate of the other vessel, in which were the brave men of Bothwell, and his two dear friends, filled his mind with forebodings. Sometimes, when wearied nature for a few minutes sank into slumber, he would start, grief-struck, from the body of Edwin floating on the briny flood, and as he awoke a cold despondence would tell him that his dream was perhaps too true. "Oh, I love thee, Edwin!" exclaimed he to himself. "Must thou, too, die, that Scotland may have no rival, that Wallace may feel himself quite alone?"

At last morning began to dawn, and spreading upon the mountains of the opposite shore, shed a soft light over their misty sides. All was tranquil and full of beauty. That element, which so lately in its rage had threatened to engulf them all, now flowed by the rocks at the foot of the cave in gentle undulations; and where the cliffs gave resistance the rays of the rising sun, striking on the bursting waves, turned their showers into dropping gems.

While his companions were still wrapped in sleep, Wallace stole away to seek some knowledge respecting the part of the Isle of Arran on which they were cast. Close by the mouth of the cave he discovered a cleft in the rock, into which he turned, and finding the upward footing sufficiently secure, clambered to the summit. The morning vapors were fast rolling their snowy wreaths down the opposite mountains, whose heads, shining in resplendent purple, seemed to view themselves in the reflections of the now smooth sea. Nature, like a conqueror, appeared to have put on a triumphal garb in exultation of the devastation she had committed the night before. Wallace shuddered as the parallel occurred to his mind, and turned from the scene.

On reentering the cave he despatched the seamen, and disposed himself to watch by the sides of his still sleeping friends. An hour hardly had elapsed before the men returned, bringing with them a large boat and its proprietor, but alas! no tidings of Murray and

Edwin. In bringing the boat round to the creek under the cliff, the men discovered that the sea had driven their wreck between two projecting rocks, where it now lay wedged. Though ruined as a vessel, sufficient held together to warrant their exertions to save the property. Accordingly they entered it, and drew thence most of the valuables which belonged to Lord Mar.

While this was doing, Wallace reascended to the cave, and finding the earl awake, told him a boat was ready for their reembarkation. "But where, my friend, are my nephews?" inquired he. "Alas! has this fatal expedition robbed me of them?"

Wallace tried to inspire him with a hope he scarcely dared credit himself, that they had been saved on some more distant shore. The voices of the chiefs awakened the women, but the countess still slept. Aware that she would resist trusting herself to the waves again, Lord Mar desired that she might be moved on board without disturbing her. This was readily done, the men having only to take up the extremities of the plaid on which she lay, and so carry her, with an imperceptible motion, to the boat. The earl received her head on his bosom. All were then on board; the rowers struck their oars, and once more the little party found themselves launched upon the sea.

While they were yet midway between the isles, with a bright sun playing its sparkling beams upon the waves, the countess, heaving a deep sigh, slowly opened her eyes. All around glared with the light of day; she felt the motion of the boat, and raising her head, saw that she was again embarked on the treacherous element on which she had lately experienced so many terrors. She grew deadly pale, and grasped her husband's hand. "My dear Joanna," cried he, "be not alarmed, we are all safe."

"And Sir William Wallace has left us?" demanded she.

"No, madam," answered a voice from the steerage; "not till this party be safe at Bute do I quit it."

She looked round with a grateful smile. "Ever generous! How could I for a moment doubt our preserver?"

Wallace bowed, but remained silent, and they passed calmly along till the vessel came in sight of a small boat, which, bounding over the waves, was presently so near the earl's that the figures in each could be distinctly seen. In it, the chiefs, to their rapturous surprise, beheld Murray and Edwin. The latter, with a cry of joy, leaped into the sea; the next instant he was over the boat's side and clasped in the arms of Wallace. "Thank God! thank God!" was all that Edwin could say, while at every effort to tear himself from Wallace, he clung the closer to his breast.

While this was passing, the boat had drawn closer, and Murray, shaking hands with his uncle and aunt, exclaimed to Wallace, "That urchin is such a monopolizer, I see you have not a greeting for any one else." On this Edwin raised his face and turned to the welcomes of Lord Mar. Wallace stretched out his hand to the ever-gay Lord Andrew, and, inviting him into the boat, soon learnt that on the beginning of the storm Murray's company made direct to the nearest creek in Bute, being better seamen than Wallace's helmsman. By this prudence, without having been in much peril, Murray's party had landed safely. The night came on dark and tremendous, but not doubting that the earl's rowers had carried him into a similar haven, the young chief and his companion kept themselves easy in a fisher's hut till morning. At an early hour they then put themselves at the head of the Bothwell men, and, expecting they should come up with Wallace and his party at Rothsay, walked over to the castle. Their consternation was unutterable when they found that Lord Mar was not there, neither had he been heard of. Full of terror, Murray and Edwin threw themselves into a boat to seek their friends upon the seas, and when they did espy them, the joy of Edwin was so great that not even the unfathomable gulf could stop him from flying to the embrace of his friend.

While mutual felicitations passed, the boats, now nearly side by side, reached the shore, and the seamen jumping on the rocks, moored their vessels under the projecting towers of Rothsay. The old steward hastened to receive a master who had not blessed his aged eyes for many a year, and when he took the infant in his arms that was to be the future representative of the house of Mar, he wept aloud. The earl spoke to him affectionately, and then walked on with Edwin, whom he called to support him up the bank. Murray led the countess out of the boat, while the Bothwell men so thronged about Wallace, congratulating themselves on his safety, that she saw there was no hope of his arm being then offered to her.

Having entered the castle, the steward led them into a room in which he had spread a plentiful repast. Here Murray, having recounted the adventures of his voyage, called for a history of what had befallen his friends. The earl gladly took up the tale, and, with many a glance of gratitude to Wallace, narrated the perilous events of their shipwreck and providential preservation on the Isle of Arran.

Happiness now seemed to have shed her heavenly influence over every bosom. The complacency with which Wallace regarded every one, the pouring out of his beneficent spirit, which seemed to embrace all, turned every eye and heart towards him, as to a being who seemed made to love and be beloved by every one. Lady Mar looked at him, listened to him, with her rapt soul seated in her eye.

But when he withdrew for the night, what was then the state of her feelings? The overflowing of heart he felt for all, she appropriated solely to herself. The sweetness of his voice, the expression of his countenance, while, as he spoke, he veiled his eyes under their long, brown lashes, had raised such vague hopes in her bosom, that, he being gone, she hastened her adieus to the rest, eager to retire to bed, and there muse on the happiness of having at last touched the heart of a man for whom she would resign the world.

CHAPTER XXVII.

ISLE OF BUTE.

THE morning would have brought annihilation to the countess's new-fledged hopes had not Murray been the first to meet her as she came from her chamber.

While walking on the cliffs near the castle, he met Wallace and Edwin. They had already been across the valley to the haven and ordered a boat round to convey them back to Gourock. "Postpone your flight, for pity's sake!" cried Murray, "if you would not by discourtesy destroy what your gallantry has preserved." He then told them that Lady Mar was preparing a feast in the glen behind the castle; "and if we do not stay to partake it," added he, "we may expect all the witches in the isle will be bribed to sink us before we reach the shore."

After this the meeting of the morning was not less cordial than the separation of the night before; and when Lady Mar withdrew to give orders for her rural banquet, that time was seized by the earl for the arrangement of matters of more consequence. In a private conversation with Murray the preceding evening he had learned that just before the party left Dumbarton a letter had been sent to Helen at St. Fillan's, informing her of the taking of the castle and of the safety of her friends. This having satisfied the earl, he did not advert to her at all in his present discourse with Wallace, but rather avoided encumbering his mind with anything but the one great theme.

While the earl and his friends were marshaling armies, taking towns and storming castles, the countess, intent on other conquests, was meaning to beguile and destroy that manly spirit by the soft delights of love.

When her lord and his guests were summoned to the feast she met them at the mouth of the glen. Having tried the effect of splendor, she now left all to the power of her natural charms, and appeared simply clad in her favorite green. Moraig, the pretty grandchild of the steward, walked beside her like the fairy queen of the scene, so gaily was she decorated in all the flowers of spring. "Here is the lady of my elfin revels, holding her little king in her arms." As the countess spoke Moraig held up the infant of Lady

166

Mar, dressed like herself in a tissue gathered from the field. The sweet babe laughed and crowed and made a spring to leap into Wallace's arms. The chief took him, and with an affectionate smile pressed his little cheek to his.

Though he had felt an abhorrence of the countess when she allowed her head to drop on his breast in the citadel; and though, while he remained at Dumbarton, he had certainly avoided her: yet, since the wreck, the danger she had escaped, the general joy of all meeting again, had wiped away even the remembrance of his former cause of dislike, and he now sat by her as by a sister, fondling her child.

The repast over, the piper of the adjacent cottages appeared, and placing himself on a projecting rock, at the carol of his merry instrument the young peasants of both sexes came forward and began to dance. At this sight Edwin seized the little hand of Moraig, while Lord Andrew called a pretty lass from amongst the rustics and joined the group.

Lady Mar watched the countenance of Wallace as he looked upon the joyous company. It was placid, and a soft complacency illumined his eye. How different was the expression in hers, had he marked it! All within her was in tumult, and the characters were but too legibly imprinted on her face. But he did not look on her, for the child, whom the perfume of the flowers overpowered, began to cry. He rose, and having resigned it to the nurse, turned into a narrow vista of trees, where he walked slowly on, unconscious whither he went.

Lady Mar, with eager haste, followed him till she saw him turn out of the vista, and then she lost sight of him. To walk with him undisturbed in so deep a seclusion; to improve the impression which she was sure she had made upon his heart; all these thoughts ran in this vain woman's head; and inwardly rejoicing that the shattered health of her husband promised her a ready freedom to become the wife of the man to whom she would gladly belong, she hastened forward, as if the accomplishment of her wishes depended on this meeting. Peeping through the trees she saw him standing with folded arms, looking intently into the bosom of a large lake.

Having stood for some time, he walked on. Several times she essayed to emerge and join him, but a sudden awe of him, a conviction of that saintly purity which would shrink from the vows she was meditating to pour into his ear—these thoughts made her pause.

She had no sooner returned to the scene of festivity than she repented having allowed what she deemed an idle alarm of delicacy to drive her from the lake. She would have hastened back, had not two or three aged peasants almost instantly engaged her, to listen to long stories respecting her lord's youth. She remained thus an unwilling auditor, and by the side of the dancers, for nearly an hour before Wallace reappeared. But then she sprang towards him as if a spell were broken: "Where, truant, have you been?"

"In a beautiful solitude," returned he, "amongst a luxuriant grove of willows."

"Aye," cried she, "it is called Glenshealeach; and a sad scene was acted there. About ten years ago a lady of this island drowned herself in the lake they hang over, because the man she loved—despised her."

"Unhappy woman!" observed Wallace.

"Then you would have pitied her?" rejoined Lady Mar.

"He cannot be a man that would not pity a woman under such circumstances."

"Then you would not have consigned her to such a fate?"

Wallace was startled by the peculiar tone in which this simple question was asked. It recalled the action in the citadel, and unconsciously turning a penetrating look on her, his eyes met hers. He need not have heard further to have learnt more. She looked down and colored, and he, wishing to misunderstand a language so dishonoring to her husband, gave some trifling answer; then, making a slight observation about the earl, he advanced to him. Lord Mar was become tired with so gala a scene, and taking the arm of Wallace they returned together into the house.

Edwin soon followed with Murray, arriving time enough to see their little pinnace draw up under the castle and throw out her moorings. The countess, too, descried its streamers, and hastening into the room where she knew the chiefs were yet assembled, though the wearied earl had retired to repose, inquired the reason of that boat having drawn so near the castle.

"That it may take us from it, fair aunt," replied Murray.

The countess fixed her eyes with an unequivocal expression upon Wallace. "My gratitude is ever due to your kindness, noble lady," said he, still wishing to be blind to what he could not but perceive, "and that we may ever deserve it, we go to keep the enemy from your doors."

"Yes," added Murray, "and to keep a more insidious foe from our own. Edwin and I feel it rather dangerous to bask too long in these sunny bowers."

"But surely your chief is not afraid?" said she, casting a soft glance at Wallace.

"Yet, nevertheless, I must fly," returned he, bowing to her.

"That you positively shall not," added she, with a fluttering joy at her heart, thinking she was about to succeed; "you stir not this night, else I shall brand you all as a band of cowards."

"Call us by every name in the poltroon's calendar," cried Murray, seeing by the countenance of Wallace that his resolution was not to be moved; "yet we must gallop off."

"So, dear aunt," rejoined Edwin, smiling, "if you do not mean to play Circe to our Ulysses, give us leave to go."

Lady Mar started, confused, she knew not how, as he innocently uttered these words. The animated boy snatched a kiss from her hand when he ceased speaking, and darted after Murray, who had disappeared to give some directions respecting the boat.

Left thus alone with the object of her every wish, in the moment when she thought she was going to lose him perhaps forever, she forgot all prudence, and laying her hand on his arm, as with a respectful bow he was also moving away, she arrested his steps. She held him fast; but agitation preventing her speaking, she trembled violently, and, weeping, dropped her head upon his shoulder. He was motionless. Her tears redoubled. He felt the embarrassment of his situation; and at last, extricating his tongue, which shame for her had chained, in a gentle voice he inquired the cause of her uneasiness. "If for the safeties of your nephews——"

"No, no," cried she, interrupting him; "read my fate in that of the Lady of Glenshealeach."

Again he was silent; fearful of too promptly understanding so disgraceful a truth, he found no words in which to answer her, and her emotions became so uncontrolled that he expected she would swoon in his arms.

"Cruel, cruel Wallace!" at last cried she, clinging to him, for he had once or twice attempted to disengage himself and reseat her on the bench, "your heart is steeled, or it would understand mine. But I am despised,—and I can yet find the watery grave from which you rescued me."

To dissemble longer would have been folly. Wallace, now resolutely seating her, though with gentleness, addressed her: "Your husband, Lady Mar, is my friend; had I a heart to give to woman, not one sigh should arise in it to his dishonor. But I am lost to all warmer affections than that of friendship."

"But were it otherwise," cried she, "only tell me that had I not been bound with chains which my kinsmen forced upon me; had I not been made the property of a man who, however estimable, was of too paternal years for me to love; ah! tell me if these tears should now flow in vain?"

Wallace seemed to hesitate what to answer.

Wrought up to agony, she threw herself on his breast, exclaiming, "Answer! but drive me not to despair. I never loved man before— and now to be scorned! Oh, kill me, Wallace, but tell me not that you never could have loved me!"

Wallace was alarmed at her vehemence. "Lady Mar," returned he, "I am incapable of saying anything to you that is inimical to your duty to the best of men. I will even forget this conversation, and continue through life to revere the wife of my friend."

The countess, awed by his solemnity, but not put from her suit, exclaimed, "What thy Marion was I would be to thee—thy consoler, thine adorer. Time may set me free. Oh! till then, only give me leave to love thee, and I shall be happy."

"You dishonor yourself, lady," returned he, "by these petitions; and for what? I repeat, I am dead to woman; and the voice of love sounds like the funeral knell of her who will never breathe it to me again." He rose as he spoke, and the countess, pierced to the heart and almost despairing of now retaining any part in his esteem, was devising what next to say when Murray came into the room.

Wallace instantly observed that his countenance was troubled. "What has happened?" inquired he.

"A messenger from the mainlano with bad news from Ayr."

"Of private or public import?" rejoined Wallace.

"Of both. There has been a horrid massacre, in which the heads of many noble families have fallen." As he spoke, the paleness of his countenance revealed to his friend that part of the information he had found himself unable to communicate.

"I comprehend my loss," cried Wallace. "Sir Ronald Crawford is sacrificed! Bring the messenger in."

Murray withdrew, and Wallace, seating himself, remained, with a fixed countenance, gazing on the ground.

Lord Andrew reentered with a stranger. Wallace rose to meet him, and seeing Lady Mar, "Countess," said he, "these bloody recitals are not for your ears"; and waving her to withdraw, she left the room.

"This gallant stranger," said Murray, "is Sir John Graham. He has just left that new theater of Southron perfidy."

"I have hastened hither," cried the knight, "to call your victorious arm to take a signal vengeance on the murderers of your grandfather. He and eighteen other Scottish chiefs have been treacherously put to death in the Barns of Ayr."

Graham then gave a brief narration of the direful circumstance. He and his father, Lord Dundaff, having crossed the south coast of Scotland on their way homeward, stopped to rest at Ayr. They arrived there the very day that Lord Aymer de Valence had entered it a fugitive from Dumbarton castle. Much as that earl wished to keep the success of Wallace a secret from the inhabitants of Ayr, he found it impossible, and in half an hour after the arrival of the English earl, every soul knew that the recovery of Scotland was begun. Elated with this intelligence, the Scots went, under night, from house to house, congratulating each other on so miraculous an interference in their favor; and many stole to Sir Ronald Crawford to felicitate the venerable knight on his glorious grandson. The good old man listened with joy to their eulogiums on Wallace; and when Lord Dundaff, in offering his congratulations with the rest, said, "But while all Scotland lay in vassalage, where did he imbibe this spirit to tread down tyrants?" the venerable patriarch replied, "He was always a noble boy. From infancy to manhood he has been a benefactor, and, though the cruelty of our enemies have widowed his youthful years, the brightness of his virtues will spread more glories round the name of Wallace than a thousand posterities." Other ears than those of Dundaff heard this honest exultation.

The next morning this venerable man and other chiefs of similar consequence were summoned by Sir Richard Arnulf, the governor, to his palace, there to deliver in a schedule of their estates; "that quiet possession," the governor said, "might be granted to them under the great seal of Lord Aymer de Valence, the deputy-warden of Scotland."

The gray-headed knight, not being so active as his compeers of more juvenile years, happened to be the last who went to this tiger's den. Wrapped in his plaid, his silver hair covered with a blue bonnet, and leaning on his staff, he was walking along, attended by two domestics, when Sir John Graham met him at the gate of the palace. He smiled on him as he passed, and whispered, "It will not be long before my Wallace makes even the forms of vassalage unnecessary; and then these failing limbs may sit undisturbed at home."

"God grant it!" returned Graham; and he saw Sir Ronald admitted within the interior gate. The servants were ordered to remain without. Sir John walked there some time, expecting the reappearance of the knight; but after an hour, finding no signs of regress from the palace, and thinking his father might be wondering at his delay, he turned his steps towards his own lodgings. While passing along, he met several Southron detachments hurrying across the

streets. In the midst of some of these companies he saw one or two
Scottish men of rank, strangers to him, but who, by certain indications,
seemed to be prisoners. He did not go far before he met a chieftain
in these painful circumstances whom he knew; but as he was hastening
towards him, the noble Scot raised his manacled hand, and turned
away his head. This was a warning to the young knight, who darted
into an alley which led to the gardens of his father's lodgings, and
was hurrying forward when he met one of his own servants running
in quest of him.

Panting with haste, he informed his master that a party of armed
men had come, under De Valence's warrant, to seize Lord Dundaff
and bear him to prison, to lie there with others who were charged
with having taken part in a conspiracy with the grandfather of the
insurgent Wallace.

The officer of the band who took Lord Dundaff told him in the
most insulting language that "Sir Ronald, his ringleader, with
eighteen nobles, his accomplices, had already suffered the punishment
of their crime, and were lying, headless trunks, in the judgment-hall."

"Haste, therefore," repeated the man; "my lord bids you haste
to Sir William Wallace and require his hand to avenge his kinsman's
blood and to free his countrymen from prison. These are your
father's commands; he directed me to seek you and give them to you."

Alarmed for the life of his father, Graham hesitated how to act
on the moment. To leave him, seemed to abandon him to the death
the others had received; and yet, only by obeying him could he have
any hopes of averting his threatened fate. Once seeing the path he
ought to pursue, he struck immediately into it, and giving his signet
to the servant, to assure Lord Dundaff of his obedience, he mounted
a horse which had been brought to the town end for that purpose, and
setting off full speed, allowed nothing to stay him till he reached
Dumbarton castle. There, hearing that Wallace was gone to Bute,
he threw himself into a boat, and plying every oar, reached that island
in a shorter space of time than the voyage had ever before been
completed.

Being now conducted into the presence of the chief, he narrated
his tale with a simplicity which would have instantly drawn the
retributive sword of Wallace had he had no kinsman to avenge, no
friend to release from the Southron dungeons. But as the case stood,
his bleeding grandfather lay before his eyes, and the ax hung over
the heads of the most virtuous nobles of his country.

He heard the chieftain to an end without speaking or altering the
stern attention of his countenance. But at the close, with his brows

denouncing some tremendous fate, he rose. "Sir John Graham," said he, "I attend you."

"Whither?" demanded Murray.

"To Ayr," answered Wallace. "This moment I will set out for Dumbarton, to bring away the sinews of my strength. God will be our speed! and then this arm shall show how I loved that good old man."

"Your men," interrupted Graham, "are already awaiting you on the opposite shore. I presumed to command for you. For on entering Dumbarton, and finding you were absent, I dared to interpret your mind, and to order Sir Alexander Scrymgeour and Sir Roger Kirkpatrick, with all your own force, to follow me to the coast of Renfrew."

"Thank you, my friend," cried Wallace, grasping his hand; "may I ever have such interpreters. I cannot stay to bid your uncle farewell," said he to Lord Andrew. "Remain to tell him to bless me with his prayers, and then, dear Murray, follow me to Ayr."

Ignorant of what the stranger had imparted, at the sight of the chiefs approaching from the castle gate Edwin hastened with the news that all was ready for embarkation. He was hurrying out his information when the altered countenance of his general checked him. He looked at the stranger. His face was agitated and severe. He turned towards his cousin. All there was grave and distressed. Again he glanced at Wallace. No word was spoken, but every look threatened; and Edwin saw him leap into the boat followed by the stranger. The astonished boy, though unnoticed, would not be left behind, and stepping in also, sat down beside his chief.

"I shall follow you in an hour," exclaimed Murray. The seamen pushed off; then giving loose to their swelling sail, in less than ten minutes the light vessel was wafted out of the little harbor, and turning a point, those in the castle saw it no more.

CHAPTER XXVIII.

THE BARNS OF AYR.

WHILE the little bark bounded over the waves towards the mainland, its passengers bent towards each other, intent on the further information they were to receive.

"Here is the list of the murdered chiefs, and of those who are in the dungeons expecting the like treatment," continued Graham, holding out a parchment; "it was given to me by my faithful servant." Wallace took it, but seeing his grandfather's name at the top he could look no farther. "Gallant Graham," said he, "if the sword of Heaven be with us, not one perpetrator of this horrid massacre shall be alive to-morrow to repeat the deed."

"What massacre?" Edwin ventured to inquire. Wallace put the parchment into his hand. Edwin opened the roll, and on seeing the words, "A list of the Scottish chiefs murdered on the 18th of June, 1297, in the judgment-hall of the English barons at Ayr," his cheek reddened with the hue of indignation; but when the name of his general's grandfather met his sight, his horror-struck eye sought the face of Wallace, who was now in earnest discourse with Graham.

Forbearing to interrupt him, Edwin continued to read over the blood-registered names. In turning the page his eye glanced to the opposite side, and he saw at the head of "A list of prisoners in the dungeons of Ayr," the name of Lord Dundaff, and immediately after it that of Lord Ruthven. He uttered a piercing cry, and extending his arms to Wallace, the terror-struck boy exclaimed, "My father is in their hands! Oh! if you are indeed my brother, fly to Ayr and save him!"

Wallace took up the open list which Edwin had dropped. He saw the name of Lord Ruthven amongst the prisoners, and folding his arms round this affectionate son, "Compose yourself," said he, "it is to Ayr I am going, and if the God of justice be our speed, your father and Lord Dundaff shall not see another day in prison."

"Who is this youth?" inquired Graham. "To which of the noble companions of my captive father is he son?"

"To William Ruthven," answered Wallace, "the valiant Lord of the Carse of Gowrie. And it is a noble scion from that glorious root. He it was that enabled me to win Dumbarton. Look up, my brother!" cried Wallace, "look up, and hear me recount the first-fruits of your maiden arms to our gallant friend."

Covered with blushes arising from emotion, as well as from a consciousness of having won the praises of his general, Edwin rose, and bowing to Sir John, still leaned his head upon the shoulder of Wallace, who began the recital of his first acquaintance with young Sir Edwin. He enumerated every particular: his bringing the detachment from Bothwell to Glenfinlass, his scaling the walls of Dumbarton to make the way smooth to the Scots to ascend, and his after prowess in that well-defended fortress. As Wallace proceeded, the wonder of Graham was raised to a pitch only to be equaled by his admiration; and taking the hand of Edwin, "Receive me, brave youth," said he, "as your second brother; Sir William Wallace is your first; but this night we shall fight side by side for our fathers, and let that be our bond of kindred."

Edwin pressed the young chief's cheek with his innocent lips. "Let us together free them," cried he, "and then we shall be born twins in happiness."

"So be it," cried Graham, "and Sir William Wallace be the sponsor of that hour."

Wallace smiled on them, and turning his head towards the shore when the vessel doubled a certain point, he saw the beach covered with armed men. To be sure they were his own, he drew his sword and waved it in the air. At that moment a hundred falchions flashed in the sunbeams, and the shouts of "Wallace!" came loudly on the breeze.

Graham and Edwin started on their feet; the seamen plied their oars; the boat dashed into the breakers, and Wallace, leaping on shore, was received with acclamations by his eager soldiers.

He no sooner landed than he commenced his march. Murray joined him on the banks of the Irwin, and as Ayr was no great distance from that river, at two hours before midnight the little army entered Laglane wood, where they halted, while Wallace with his chieftains proceeded to reconnoiter the town. He had already declared his plan of destruction, and Graham, as a first measure, went to the spot he had fixed on with Macdougal, his servant, as a place of rendezvous. He returned with the man, who informed Wallace that in honor of the lands of the murdered chiefs having been that day partitioned by De Valence amongst certain lords, a grand feast was going on in the governor's palace. Under the very roof where they had shed the blood of the trusting Scots, they were now keeping this carousal.

"*Now,* then, is our time to strike!" cried Wallace; and ordering detachments of his men to take possession of the avenues to the town, he set forth with others to reach the front of the castle gates. The darkness being so great that no object could be distinctly seen, they had not gone far before Macdougal, who had undertaken to be their guide, discovered by the projection of a hill on the right that he had lost the road.

"Our swords will find one!" exclaimed Kirkpatrick.

Unwilling to miss any advantage, in a situation where so much was at stake, Wallace gladly hailed a twinkling light, which gleamed from what he supposed the window of a distant cottage. Kirkpatrick, with Macdougal, offered to go forward and explore what it might be. In a few minutes they arrived at a thatched building, from which, to their surprise, issued the wailing strains of the coronach. Kirkpatrick paused. Its melancholy notes were sung by female voices. Hence, there being no danger in applying to such harmless inhabitants to learn the way to the citadel, he proceeded to the door, when, intending to knock, the weight of his mailed arm burst open its slender latch, and discovered two poor women, in an inner apartment, wringing their hands over a shrouded corse. While the chief entered his friend came up. Murray and Graham, struck with sounds never breathed over the vulgar dead, lingered at the porch, wondering what noble Scot could be the subject of lamentation in so lowly an abode. The stopping of these two chieftains impeded the steps of Wallace, who was pressing forward, without eye or ear for anything but the object of his march. Kirkpatrick at that moment appeared on the threshold, and without a word, putting forth his hand, seized the arm of his commander and pulled him into the cottage. Before Wallace could ask the reason of this, he saw a woman run forward with a light in her hand, the beams of which falling on the face of the knight of Ellerslie, with a shriek of joy she rushed towards him and threw herself upon his neck.

He instantly recognized Elspa, his nurse, the faithful attendant of his grandfather, and with an anguish of recollections that almost unmanned him, he returned her embrace.

"Here he lies!" cried the old woman, drawing him towards the rushy bier; and before he had time to demand "Who?" she pulled down the shroud and disclosed the body of Sir Ronald Crawford. Wallace gazed on it with a look of such dreadful import that Edwin, whose anxious eyes sought his countenance, trembled with horror.

"Sorry, sorry bier for the good Lord Ronald!" cried the old woman; "a poor wake to mourn the loss of him who was the benefactor of all the country round. But had I not brought him here the salt sea must have been his grave." Here sobs prevented her utterance, but after a short pause, she related that as soon as the woful tidings were brought, she and the clan's-folk who would not swear fidelity to the new lord were driven from the house. She hastened to the theater of massacre, and there beheld the bodies of the murdered chiefs drawn on sledges to the seashore. Elspa knew that of her master by a scar on his breast which he had received in the battle of Largs. When she saw corpse after corpse thrown with a careless hand into the waves, and the man approached who was to cast the honored chief of Monktown to the same unhallowed burial, she threw herself frantically on the body, and so moved the man's compassion, that, taking advantage of the time when his comrades were out of sight, he permitted her to wrap the dead Sir Ronald in her plaid and so carry him away between her sister and herself. But ere she had raised her sacred burden the man directed her to seek the venerable head from amongst the others which lay mingled in a sack. Drawing it forth she placed it beside the body, and then hastily retired with both to the hovel where Wallace had found her. She had hoped that in so lonely an obscurity she might have performed without notice a chieftain's rites to the remains of the murdered lord of the very lands on which she wept him. These over, she meant he should be interred in secret by the fathers of a neighboring church which he had once richly endowed. With these intentions she and her sister were chanting over him the sad dirge of their country when Sir Roger Kirkpatrick burst open the door.

Wallace looked upon his grandfather's body with a countenance whose deadly hue gave fire to the denunciation of his eyes. "Was it necessary," said he, "to turn my heart to iron that I was brought to see this sight?" All the tremendous purpose of his soul was read in his face while he bent above the bier. His lips again moved, but none heard what he said. He rushed from the hut, and with rapid strides proceeded in profound silence towards the palace.

He well knew that no honest Scot could be under that roof. The building, though magnificent, was altogether a structure of wood; to fire it, then, was his determination. To destroy all at once in the theater of their cruelty was his resolution; for they were not soldiers he was seeking, but assassins, and to pitch his brave Scots in the open field against such unmanly wretches would be to dishonor his men.

All being quiet in the streets through which he passed, and having set men at the mouth of every sally-port of the citadel, he made a bold attack upon the guard at the barbican-gate, and ere they could give the alarm, all being slain, he and his chosen troop entered the portal and made direct to the palace. The lights which blazed through the windows of the banqueting-hall showed him the spot; and having detached Graham and Edwin to storm the keep where their fathers were confined, he took the half-intoxicated sentinels at the palace-gates by surprise, and striking them into a sleep from which they would wake no more, he fastened the doors upon the assassins. His men surrounded the building with hurdles filled with combustibles which they had prepared according to his directions; and, when all was ready, Wallace, with a spirit of retribution nerving every limb, mounted to the roof, and tearing off the shingles, with a flaming brand in his hand, showed himself to the affrighted revelers beneath, and as he threw it blazing amongst them he cried aloud, "The blood of the murdered calls for vengeance, and it comes!"

At that instant the matches were put to the fagots which surrounded the building, and the party within springing from their seats hastened towards the doors. All were fastened on them, and retreating into the midst of the room they fearfully looked towards the tremendous figure above, which, like a supernatural being, seemed indeed come to rain fire upon their guilty heads. Some shook with superstitious dread; others, driven to despair, with horrible execrations again strove to force a passage through the doors. A second glance told De Valence whose was the hand which had launched the thunderbolt at his feet, and, turning to Sir Richard Arnulf, he cried in a voice of horror, "My arch-enemy is there!"

Thick smoke rising from within and without the building now obscured his terrific form. The shouts of the Scots, as the fire covered its walls, and the streaming flames poured into every opening of the building, raised such a terror in the breasts of the wretches within, that, with the most horrible cries, they again and again flew to the doors to escape. Not an avenue appeared; almost suffocated with smoke and scorched by the blazing rafters which fell from the burning roof, they at last made a desperate attempt to break a passage through the great portal. Arnulf was at their head, and, sunk to abjectness by his despair, in a voice which terror rendered piercing he called for mercy. The words reached the ear of Sir Roger Kirkpatrick, who stood nearest to the door. In a voice of thunder he replied, "That ye gave, ye shall receive. Where was mercy when our fathers and our brothers fell beneath your murderous axes?"

Aymer de Valence came up at this moment with a wooden pillar which he and the strongest men in the company had torn from under the gallery that surrounded the room, and, with all their strength dashing it against the great door, they at last drove it from its bolts. But now a wall of men opposed them. Desperate at the sight, and with a burning furnace in their rear, it was not the might of man that could prevent their escape; and with the determination of despair, rushing forward the foremost rank of the Scots fell. But ere the exulting Southrons could press out into the open space, Wallace himself had closed upon them, and Arnulf, the merciless Arnulf, whose voice had pronounced the sentence of death upon Sir Ronald Crawford, died beneath his hand.

Wallace was not aware that he had killed the Governor of Ayr till the exclamations of his enemies informed him that the instigator of the massacre was slain. This even was welcome news to the Scots, and hoping that the next death would be that of De Valence, they pressed on with redoubled energy.

Meanwhile the men who guarded the prisoners in the keep, having their commanders with them, made a stout resistance there, and one of the officers, seeing a possible advantage, stole out, and gathering a company of the scattered garrison, suddenly taking Graham in flank, made no inconsiderable havoc amongst that part of his division. Edwin blew the signal for assistance. Wallace heard the blast, and seeing the day was won at the palace, he left the finishing of the affair to Kirkpatrick and Murray, and, drawing off a small party to reenforce Graham, he took the Southron officer by surprise. The enemy's ranks fell around him like corn beneath the sickle; and grasping a huge battering-ram, which his men had found, he burst open the door of the keep. Graham and Edwin rushed in; and Wallace, sounding his own bugle with the notes of victory, his reserves, whom he had placed at the ends of the streets, entered in every direction and received the flying soldiers of De Valence upon their pikes.

Dreadful was now the carnage, but the relenting heart of Wallace pleaded for bleeding humanity, and he ordered the trumpet to sound a parley. He was obeyed; and, standing on an adjacent mound, he proclaimed that "whoever had not been accomplices in the horrible massacre of the Scottish chiefs, if they would ground their arms, and take an oath never to serve again against Scotland, their lives should be spared."

Hundreds of swords fell to the ground, and their late holders, kneeling at his feet, took the oath prescribed. At the head of those who surrendered appeared the captain who had commanded at the prison. He was the only officer of all the late garrison who survived;

and when he saw that not one of his companions existed to go through the same humiliating ceremony, with an aghast countenance he said to Wallace, as he presented his sword, "Then I must believe that, with this weapon, I am surrendering to Sir William Wallace the possession of this castle and the government of Ayr. I see not one of my late commanders—all must be slain; and for me to hold out longer would be to sacrifice my men. But I serve severe exactors; and I hope that your testimony, my conqueror, will assure my king I fought as became his standard."

Wallace gave him a gracious answer, and committing him to the generous care of Murray, he turned to give orders to Ker respecting the surrendered and the slain. During these momentous events Graham had deemed it prudent that, exhausted by anxiety and privations, the noble captives should not come forth to join in the battle, and not until the sound of victory echoed through the arches of their dungeons would he suffer the eager Dundaff to see and thank his deliverer. Meanwhile the young Edwin appeared before the eyes of his father like the angel who opened the prison gates to Peter; after embracing him with all a son's fondness; after recounting in a few hasty sentences the events which had brought him to be a companion of Sir William Wallace, and to avenge the injuries of Scotland in Ayr, he knocked off the chains of his amazed father. Eager to perform the like service to all who had suffered in the like manner, and accompanied by the happy Lord Ruthven, he hastened around to the other dungeons and gladly proclaimed to the astonished inmates freedom and safety. Having rid them of their shackles, he had just entered with his noble company into the vaulted chamber which contained the released Lord Dundaff when the peaceful clarion sounded. At the joyful tidings Graham started on his feet. "Now, my father, you shall see the bravest of men!"

Morning was spreading in pale light over the heavens when Wallace, turning round at the glad voice of Edwin, beheld the released nobles. This was the first time he had ever seen the Lords Dundaff and Ruthven, and, while welcoming to his friendship those to whom his valor had given freedom, how great was his surprise to see in the person of a prisoner suddenly brought before him Sir John Monteith, the young chieftain whom he had parted with a few months ago at Douglas, and from whose fatal invitation to that castle he might date the ruin of his happiness.

"We found Sir John Monteith amongst the slain before the palace," said Ker; "he, of the whole party, alone breathed. How he came there I know not; but I have brought him hither to explain it himself." Ker withdrew to finish the interment of the dead. Monteith, still leaning on the arm of a soldier, grasped Wallace's hand: "My brave friend," cried he, "to owe my liberty to you is a twofold pleasure; for," added he, in a lowered voice, "I see before me the man who is to verify the words of Baliol, and be not only the guardian, but the possessor of the treasure he committed to our care."

Wallace, who had never thought on the coffer since he knew it was under the protection of St. Fillan, shook his head. "A far different meed do I seek, my friend," said he; "to behold these happy countenances of my liberated countrymen is greater reward to me than would be the development of all the mysteries which the head of Baliol could devise."

"Aye!" cried Dundaff, who overheard this part of the conversation, "had we rejected Baliol, we had never been ridden by Edward. But the rowel has gored the flanks of us all, and who amongst us will not lay himself and fortune at the foot of him who plucks away the tyrant's heel?"

"If all held our cause in the light that you do," returned Wallace, "the blood which these Southrons have sown would rise up to overwhelm the murderers. But how," inquired he, turning to Monteith, "did you happen to be in Ayr at this period? and how, above all, amongst the slaughtered Southrons at the palace?"

Sir John Monteith readily replied: "My adverse fate accounts for all." He then proceeded to inform Wallace that on the very night in which they parted at Douglas, Sir Arthur Hesselrigge was told the story of the box, and accordingly sent to have Monteith brought prisoner to Lanark. He lay in the dungeons of its citadel at the time Wallace entered that town and destroyed the governor. Though the Scots did not pursue the advantage offered by the panic into which this retribution threw their enemies, care was immediately taken by the English lieutenant to prevent a repetition of the same disaster; and, in consequence, every suspected person was seized, and those already in confinement loaded with chains. Monteith being known as a friend of Wallace, was sent under a strong guard towards Stirling, there to stand his trial before Cressingham. "By a lucky chance," said he, "I made my escape; but I was soon retaken by another party and conveyed to Ayr, where the Lieutenant-Governor Arnulf, discovering my talents for music, compelled me to sing at his entertainments. For this purpose he last night confined me in the banqueting-room at the palace, and thus, when the flames surrounded that building, I found myself exposed to die the death of a traitor. Snatching up a sword, and striving to join my brave countrymen, the Southrons impeded my passage, and I fell under their arms."

Happy to have rescued his old acquaintance from further indignities, Wallace committed him to Edwin to lead into the citadel. Then taking the colors of Edward from the ground, where the Southron officer had laid them, he gave them to Sir Alexander Scrymgeour, with orders to fill their former station on the citadel with the standard of Scotland, which action he considered as the seal of each victory.

The standard was no sooner raised than the clarion of triumph was blown from every warlike instrument in the garrison; and the Southron captain, placing himself at the head of his disarmed troops, under the escort of Murray, marched out of the castle. He announced his design to proceed immediately to Newcastle, and thence embark with his men to join their king in Flanders. Not more than two hundred followed their officer in this expedition; the rest, to nearly double that number, being like the garrison of Dumbarton, Irish and Welsh, were glad to escape enforced servitude.

Some other necessary regulations being then made, Wallace dismissed his gallant Scots to find refreshment in the well-stored barracks of the dispersed Southrons, and retired himself to join his friends in the citadel.

CHAPTER XXIX.

BERWICK AND THE TWEED.

In the course of an hour Murray returned from having seen the departing Southrons beyond the barriers of the township. But he did not come alone: he was accompanied by Lord Auchinleck, the son of one of the betrayed barons who had fallen in the palace of Ayr. This young chieftain, at the head of his vassals, hastened to support the man whose hand had thus satisfied his revenge; and when he met Murray at the north gate of the town, and recognized in his flying banners a friend of Scotland, he was happy to make himself known to an officer of Wallace, and to be conducted to that chief.

While Lord Andrew and his new colleague were making the range of the suburbs, the glad progress of the victor Scots had turned the whole aspect of that lately gloomy city. Doors and windows, so recently closed in mourning for the sanguinary deeds done in the palace, now opened teeming with smiling inhabitants.

Sons who in secret had lamented the treacherous death of their fathers now opened their gates and joined the valiant troops in the streets. Widowed wives and fatherless daughters almost forgot they had been bereaved of their natural protectors when they saw Scotland rescued from their enemies.

Thus, then, with every heart rejoicing, every house teeming with numbers to swell the ranks of Wallace, did he, the day after he had entered Ayr, see all arranged for its peaceful establishment. But ere he bade that town adieu in which he had been educated, and where almost every man, remembering its preserver's boyish years, thronged round him with recollections of former days, one duty yet demanded his stay,—to pay funeral honors to the remains of his beloved grandfather.

Accordingly the time was fixed, and with every solemnity due to his virtues and his rank Sir Ronald Crawford was buried in the chapel of the citadel. The mourning families of the chiefs who had fallen in the same bloody theater with himself closed the sad retinue, and while the holy rites committed his body to the ground, the sacred mass was extended to those who had been plunged into the weltering element.

While Wallace confided the aged Elspa and her sister to the care of Sir Reginald Crawford, to whom he also resigned the lands of his grandfather, "Cousin," said he, "I leave you to be the representative of your venerable uncle, to cherish these poor women whom he loved, to be the protector of his people and the defender of the town. The citadel is under the command of the Baron of Auchinleck, he, with his brave followers, being the first to hail the burning of the Barns of Ayr."

After these dispositions Wallace called a review of his troops, and found that he could leave five hundred men at Ayr and march an army of at least two thousand out of it.

His present design was to take his course to Berwick, and, by seizing every castle of strength in his way, form a chain of works across the country which would not only bulwark Scotland against any further inroads from its enemies, but render the subjugation of the interior Southron garrisons more certain.

On the third morning after the conflagration of the palace, Wallace quitted Ayr, and marching over its hills, manned every watch-tower on their summits, for now, whithersoever he moved, he found his victories had preceded him, and all, from hall to hovel, turned out to greet and offer him their services. Thus, heralded by fame, the panic-struck Southron governors fled at the distant view of his standards; the flames of Ayr seemed to menace them all, and castle and fortalice opened their gates before him.

Arrived under those blood-stained towers, which had so often been the objects of dispute between the powers of England and of Scotland, he prepared for their immediate attack. Berwick being a valuable fortress to the enemy, not only as a key to the invaded kingdom, but a point whence, by their ships, they commanded the whole of the eastern coast of Scotland, Wallace expected that a desperate stand would be made here to stop the progress of his arms; but being aware that the most expeditious mode of warfare was the best adapted to promote his cause, he first took the town by assault, and then, having driven the garrison into the citadel, assailed it by a vigorous siege.

After ten days' hard duty before the walls, Wallace devised a plan to obtain possession of the English ships which commanded the harbor. He found among his own troops many men who had been used to a seafaring life; these he disguised as fugitive Southrons from the late defeats, and sent in boats to the enemy's vessels which lay in the roads. By these means getting possession of those nearest to the town, he manned them with his own people, and going out with them himself, in three days made himself master of every ship on the coast.

By this maneuver the situation of the besieged was rendered so hopeless that no mode of escape was left but by desperate sallies. They made them, but without other effect than weakening their strength and increasing their miseries.

Foiled in every attempt, as their opponent, guessing their intentions, was prepared to meet their different essays, their governor stood without resource. Without provisions, without aid of any kind for his wounded men, and hourly annoyed by the victorious Scots, who continued day and night to throw showers of arrows and other missile weapons from the towers with which they had overtopped the walls, the unhappy Earl of Gloucester seemed ready to rush on death, to avoid the disgrace of surrendering the fortress. Wallace even found means to dam up the spring which had supplied the citadel with water. The men, famished with hunger, smarting with wounds, and now perishing with thirst, threw themselves at the feet of their officers, imploring them to represent to their royal governor that if he held out longer he must defend the place alone, for they could not exist another day under their present sufferings.

The earl, indeed, repented the rashness with which he had thrown himself unprovisioned into the citadel. When his first division had been overpowered in the assault on the town, his evil genius then suggested that it was best to take the second, unbroken, into the citadel, and there await the arrival of a reenforcement by sea. But he thence beheld the ships which had defended the harbor seized by Wallace before his eyes. Hope was then crushed, and nothing but death or dishonor seemed to be his alternatives. To fall under the ruins of Berwick castle was his resolution. Such was the state of his mind when his officers appeared with the petition from his men; and in a wild despair he told them "they might do as they would, but for his part, the moment they opened the gates to the enemy, that should be the last of his life. He, that was the son-in-law of King Edward, would never yield his sword to a Scottish rebel."

Terrified at these threats, the soldiers, who loved their general, declared themselves willing to die with him, and, as a last effort, proposed making a mine under the principal tower of the Scots, and, by setting fire to it, at least destroy the means by which they feared their enemies might storm the citadel.

As Wallace gave his orders from this commanding station he observed the besieged passing in numbers behind a mound in a direction to the tower where he stood; he concluded what was their design, and ordering a countermine to be made, what he anticipated happened, and Murray, at the head of his miners, encountered those of the castle at the very moment they would have set fire to the combustibles laid to consume the tower. The instant struggle was violent but short, for the impetuous Scots drove their enfeebled adversaries through the aperture back into the citadel. At this crisis, Wallace, with a band of resolute men, sprang from the tower upon the wall, leaped into the midst of the conflict, and the battle became general. It was decisive, for beholding the undaunted resolution with which the weakened and dying were supporting the cause their governor was determined to defend to the last, Wallace found his admiration and his pity alike excited, and resolved to stop the carnage. At the moment when a gallant officer, who, having assaulted him with the vehemence of despair, now lay disarmed under him; at that moment, when the discomfited knight exclaimed, "In mercy strike and redeem the honor of Ralph de Monthermer" (Earl of Gloucester), Wallace raised his bugle and sounded the note of peace. Every sword was arrested, and the universal clangor of battle was hushed in expecting silence.

"Rise, brave earl!" cried Wallace to the governor; "I revere virtue too sincerely to take an unworthy advantage of my fortune. The valor of this garrison commands my respect, and, as a proof of my sincerity, I grant to it what I have never yet done to any: that yourself and these dauntless men march out with the honors of war and without any bonds on your future conduct towards us."

While he was speaking, De Monthermer leaned gloomily on the sword he had returned to him, with his eyes fixed on his men. They answered his glance with looks that said they understood him, and passing a few words in whispers to each other, one at last spoke aloud: "Decide for us, earl; we are as ready to die as to live, so that in neither we may be divided from you."

At this generous declaration the despair of De Monthermer gave way to nobler feelings, and he turned to Wallace, and stretching out his hand to him, "Noble Scot," said he, "your generosity and the fidelity of these heroic men have compelled me to accept the life I had resolved to lose under these walls rather than resign them. When I became the husband of King Edward's daughter, I believed myself pledged to victories or to death; but there is a conquest greater than over hosts in the field; and the husband of the Princess of England, the proud Earl of Gloucester, consents to live, to be a monument of Scottish nobleness, and of the fidelity of English soldiers."

"You live, illustrious Englishman," returned Wallace, "to redeem that honor of which too many sons of England have robbed their country. Go forth, therefore, as my conqueror, for you have extinguished that antipathy with which William Wallace had vowed to extirpate every Southron from off this ravaged land. Honor, brave earl, makes all men brethren, and as a brother I open these gates for you to pass into your country. When there, if you ever remember William Wallace, let it be as a man who fights not for conquest, but to restore Scotland to her rights, and then resign his sword to peace."

"I shall remember you, Sir William Wallace," returned De Monthermer; "and as a pledge of it, you shall never see me again in this country till I come an ambassador of that peace for which you fight. Had I not believed that Scotland was unworthy of freedom, I should never have appeared upon her borders; but now that I see she has brave hearts within her, who resist oppression, I detest the zeal with which I volunteered to rivet her chains. And I repeat, that never again shall my hostile foot impress this land."

These sentiments were answered in the same spirit by his soldiers, and the Scots, following the example of their leader, treated them with every kindness. After dispensing amongst them provisions, and appointing means to convey the wounded in comfort, Wallace bade a cordial farewell to the Earl of Gloucester, and his men conducted their reconciled enemies over the Tweed. There they parted. The English bent their course toward London, and the Scots returned to their victorious general.

CHAPTER XXX.

STIRLING.

THE happy effects of these rapid conquests were soon apparent. The fall of Berwick excited such a confidence in the minds of the neighboring chieftains that every hour brought fresh recruits to Wallace. Every mouth was full of the praises of the young conqueror; and while the men were emulous to share his glory, the women in their secret bowers put up prayers for the preservation of one so handsome and so brave.

Amongst the many of every rank and age who hastened to pay their respects to the deliverer of Berwick was Sir Richard Maitland, of Thirlestane, the *Stalwarth Knight of Lauderdale.*

Wallace was no sooner told of the approach of the venerable chief than he set forth to bid him welcome. At sight of the champion of Scotland, Sir Richard threw himself off his horse with a military grace that might have become even youthful years, and hastening toward Wallace, clasped him in his arms.

"Let me look on thee!" cried the old knight; "let me feast my eyes on a true Scot!" While he spoke he viewed Wallace from head to foot. "I knew Sir Ronald Crawford and thy valiant father," continued he. "Oh, had they lived to see this day! But the base murder of the one thou hast nobly avenged, and the honorable grave of the other on Loudon hill, thou wilt cover with a monument of thine own glories."

While he thus discoursed, Wallace drew him towards the castle, and there presented to him the two nephews of the Earl of Mar. He paid some warm compliments to Edwin on his early success in the career of glory; and then turning to Murray, "Aye," said he, "it is joy to me to see the valiant house of Bothwell in the third generation. Thy grandfather and myself were boys together at the coronation of Alexander the Second, and that is eighty years ago. Since then what have I not seen! the death of two noble Scottish kings; our blooming princes ravished from us by untimely fates; the throne sold to a coward, and at last seized by a foreign power. Then, in my own person, I have been the father of as brave and beauteous a family as ever blessed a parent's eye; but they are all torn from me. Two of my sons sleep on the plains of Dunbar; my third, my dauntless William, since that fatal day has been kept a prisoner in England. And my daughters, the tender blossoms of my aged years, they grew around me, the fairest lilies of the land; but they too are passed away. My last and only daughter married the Lord Mar; and in giving birth to my dear Isabella she, too, died. Ah, my good young knight, were it not for that living image of her mother, I should be alone; my hoary head would descend to the grave unwept, unregretted."

The joy of the old man having recalled such melancholy remembrances, he wept upon the shoulder of Edwin, who had drawn so near that the story which was begun to Murray was ended to him. To give the mourning father time to recover himself, Wallace was moving away, when he was met by Ker, bringing information that a youth had just arrived in breathless haste from Stirling with a sealed packet which he would not deliver into any hands but those of Sir William Wallace. Wallace requested his friends to show every attention to the Lord of Thirlestane, and then withdrew to meet the messenger.

On his entering the anteroom, the youth sprang forwards; but suddenly checking himself, he stood, as if irresolute whom to address.

"This is Sir William Wallace, young man," said Ker; "deliver your embassy."

At these words the youth pulled a packet from his bosom, and, putting it into the chief's hand, retired in confusion. Wallace gave orders to Ker to take care of him, and then turned to inspect its contents. He wondered from whom it could come, aware of no Scot in Stirling who would dare to write to him while that town was possessed by the enemy; but not losing a moment in conjecture, he broke the seal.

How was he startled at the first words! and how was every energy of his heart roused to redoubled action when he turned to the signature! The first words in the letter were these:

"A daughter, trembling for the life of her father, presumes to address Sir William Wallace." The signature was "Helen Mar." He began the letter again:

"A daughter, trembling for the life of her father, presumes to address Sir William Wallace. You have been his deliverer from the sword, from chains, and from the waves. Refuse not to save him again to whom you have so often given life, and hasten, brave Wallace, to preserve the Earl of Mar from the scaffold.

"A cruel deception brought him from the Isle of Bute, where you imagined you had left him in security. Lord Aymer de Valence, escaping a second time from your sword, fled, under covert of the night, from Ayr to Stirling. Cressingham, the rapacious robber of all our castles, found in him an apt coadjutor. They concerted how to avenge your late successes; and Cressingham suggested that you would most easily be made to feel through the bosoms of your friends. These cruel men have therefore determined, by a mock trial, to condemn my father to death, and thus put themselves in possession of his lands.

"Having learned from some spy that Lord Mar had retired to Bute, these enemies to our country sent a body of men disguised as Scots to Gourock. There they despatched a messenger into the island to inform Lord Mar that Sir William Wallace was on the banks of the frith waiting to converse with him. My noble father, unsuspicious of treachery, hurried to the summons. Lady Mar accompanied him, and so both fell into the snare.

"They were brought prisoners to Stirling, where another affliction awaited him,—he was to see his daughter and his sister in captivity.

"After I had been betrayed from St. Fillan's monastery by the falsehoods of one Scottish knight, and rescued from his power by the gallantry of another, I sought the protection of my aunt, Lady Ruthven, who then dwelt at Alloa, on the banks of the Forth. Her husband had been invited to Ayr, by Governor Arnulf, and with many other lords was thrown into prison. Report says, bravest of men, that you have given freedom to my betrayed uncle.

"The moment Lord Ruthven's person was secured, his estates were seized, and my aunt and myself being found at Alloa, we were carried prisoners to this city. Lady Ruthven's first-born son was slain in the fatal day of Dunbar, and in terror of the like fate, she has placed her eldest surviving boy in a convent.

"Some days after our arrival, my dear father was brought to Stirling. While he was yet passing through the streets rumor told my aunt that the Scottish lord then leading to prison was her beloved brother. She flew to tell me the dreadful tidings. I heard no more, till having rushed into the streets, and bursting through every obstacle of crowd and soldiers, I found myself clasped in my father's shackled arms!

"The next day a packet was put into my aunt's hands containing a few precious lines from my father to me; also a letter from the countess to Lady Ruthven, full of your goodness to her and to my father, and narrating the cruel manner in which they had been rav-

ished from the asylum in which you had placed them. She then
said, that could she finds means of apprising you of the danger in
which she and her husband are now involved, she would be sure of
a second rescue. Whether she· has found these means I know not,
for all communication between us has been rendered impracticable.
The messenger that brought the packet was a good Southron who
had been won by Lady Mar's entreaties, but on his quitting our
apartments he was seized by a servant of De Valence, and on the
same day put publicly to death, to intimidate all others from the like
compassion to unhappy Scotland.

"Earl de Valence compelled my aunt to yield the packet to him.
We had already read it, but feared the information it might give
relative to you. In consequence of this circumstance I was made a
closer prisoner. But captivity could have no terrors for me did it
not divide me from my father. And, grief on grief! what words
have I to write it? they have CONDEMNED HIM TO DIE! That fatal
letter of my stepmother's was brought out against him, and as your
adherent, they have sentenced him to lose his head.

"I have knelt to Earl de Valence, I have implored my father's
life at his hands, but to no purpose. He tells me that Cressingham
at his side, and Ormsby by letters from Scone, declare it necessary
that an execution of consequence should be made, to appal the discontented Scots, and that as no lord is more esteemed in Scotland
than the Earl of Mar, he must be the sacrifice.

"Hasten, then, my father's preserver, to save him, for the sake of
the country he loves, for the sake of the hapless beings dependent
on his protection! I shall be on my knees till I hear your trumpet
before the walls, for in you and Heaven now rest all the hopes of
Helen Mar."

A cold dew stood on the limbs of Wallace as he closed the letter.
It might be too late. The sentence was passed on the earl, and his
executioners were prompt as cruel; the ax might already have fallen.

He called to Ker for the messenger to be brought in. He entered. Wallace inquired how long he had been from Stirling.
"Only thirty-four hours," replied the youth, adding that he had traveled night and day for fear the news of the risings in Annandale
and the taking of Berwick should precipitate the earl's death.

"I accompany you this instant," cried Wallace. "Ker, see that
the troops get under arms." As he spoke he turned into the room
where he had left the Knight of Thirlestan.

"Sir Richard Maitland," said he, willing to avoid exciting his
alarm, "there is more work for us at Stirling. Lord Aymer de

Valence has again escaped the death we thought had overtaken him, and is now in that citadel. I have just received a summons thither which I must obey." At these words Sir Roger Kirkpatrick gave a shout and rushed from the apartment. Wallace looked after him for a moment and then continued: "Follow us with your prayers, Sir Richard, and I shall not despair of sending blessed tidings to the banks of the Lauder."

"What has happened?" inquired Murray, who saw that something more than the escape of De Valence had been imparted to his general.

"We must spare this good old man," returned he, "and have him conducted to his home before I declare it publicly; but the Earl of Mar is again a prisoner, and in Stirling."

Murray, who instantly comprehended his uncle's danger, speeded the departure of Sir Richard, and as Wallace held his stirrup, the chief laid his hand on his head and blessed him. Wallace bowed his head in silence, and the bridle being in the hand of Lord Andrew he led the horse out of the eastern gate of the town, where, taking leave of the veteran knight, he soon rejoined his commander.

Wallace had informed them of the Earl of Mar's danger, and the policy, as well as justice, of rescuing so powerful a nobleman from the threatened execution. Lord Ruthven needed no arguments to precipitate him to the assistance of his brother and his wife, and the anxieties of Edwin were all awake when he knew that his mother was a prisoner. Lord Andrew smiled proudly when he returned his cousin's letter to Wallace. "We shall have the rogue on the nail yet," cried he; "my uncle's brave head is not ordained to fall by the stroke of such a coward."

"So I believe," replied Wallace; and then turning to Lord Dundaff, "My lord," said he, "I leave you governor of Berwick."

The veteran warrior grasped Wallace's hand. "To be your representative in this fortress is the proudest station I have ever filled. My son must be my representative with you in the field." He waved Sir John Graham towards him; the young knight advanced, and Lord Dundaff placing his son's hands upon his target, continued: "Swear, that as this defends the body, you will ever strive to cover Scotland from her enemies, and that from this hour you will be the faithful follower of Sir William Wallace."

"I swear," returned Graham, kissing the shield. Wallace pressed his hand. "I have brothers around me, rather than what the world calls friends. And with such fidelity to aid me, can I be otherwise than a victor?"

Edwin, who stood near, whispered to Wallace as he turned towards

The battle of Stirling Castle

his troops: "But amongst all these brothers, cease not to remember Edwin, the youngest and the least. Ah, my beloved general, what Jonathan was to David I would be to thee; only love me as David did Jonathan, and I shall be the happiest of the happy."

At that moment Sir John Graham rejoined them, and some other captains coming up, Wallace made the proper dispositions, and every man took his station at the head of his division.

Until the men had marched far beyond the chance of rumors reaching Thirlestane, they were not informed of the Earl of Mar's danger. They conceived their present errand was the recapture of De Valence. "But at a proper moment," said Wallace, "they shall know the whole truth; for," added he, "the people who follow our standards, not as hirelings, but with willing spirits, ought to know our reasons for requiring their services."

"They who follow you," said Graham, "have too much confidence in their leader to require any reasons for his movements."

"It is to place that confidence on a sure foundation, my brave friends," returned Wallace, "that I explain what there is no just reason to conceal."

Sir Roger Kirkpatrick had been the first to fly to arms on the march to Stirling being mentioned, and when Wallace stood forward to declare that rest should be dispensed with till Stirling fell, the ardent knight darted over every obstacle to reach his aim; he flew to the van of his troops, and hailing them forward, "Come on!" cried he, "and in the blood of Cressingham let us forever sink King Edward's Scottish crown."

The shouts of the men, who seemed to drink in the spirit that blazed from Kirkpatrick's eyes, made the echoes of Lammermuir ring. It was the voice of liberty; leaping every bound, the eager van led the way and dragging their war-machines in the rear, the rest pressed on till they reached the Carron side. At the moment the foaming steed of Wallace was plunging into the stream to take the ford, Ker snatched the bridle of the horse. "My lord," cried he, "a man on full speed from Douglas castle has brought this packet."

In his march from Ayr Wallace had left Sir Eustace Maxwell governor of that castle and Monteith as his lieutenant.

Wallace opened the packet and read as follows:

The patriots in Annandale have been beaten by Lord de Warenne. Sir John Monteith, who volunteered to head them, is taken prisoner with twelve hundred men.

Earl de Warenne comes to resume his arrogant title of Lord Warden of Scotland, and thereby to relieve his deputy, Aymer de Valence, who is recalled to take possession of the lordship of Pembroke. In pursuance of his commission, the earl is now marching towards the Lothians, in the hope of intercepting your progress.

Thanks to the information you send us of your movements, for being enabled to apprise you of this danger. I should have attempted to have checked the Southron by annoying his flanks had not his numbers rendered such an enterprise hopeless. But his aim being to come up with you, if you meet him in the van we shall have him in the rear; and, so surrounded, he must be cut to pieces.

Ever my general's and Scotland's true servant,

EUSTACE MAXWELL.

"What answer?" inquired Ker.

Wallace hastily engraved with his dagger's point upon his gauntlet, "Reviresco! (*I bud again!*) Our sun is above!" and desiring it might be given to the messenger to carry to Sir Eustace Maxwell, he refixed himself in his saddle and spurred over the Carron.

The moon was near her meridian as the wearied troops halted on the deep shadows of the Carse of Stirling. An hour's rest was sufficient to restore the followers of Wallace, and as the morning dawned, the sentinels on the ramparts of the town were not only surprised to see a host below, but that part, by the most indefatigable labor and a silence like death, had not merely passed the ditch, but having gained the counterscarp, had fixed their movable towers, and were at that instant overlooking the highest bastions.

At a sight so unexpected, which seemed to have arisen out of the earth like an exhalation, the Southrons, struck with dread, fled a moment from the walls, but immediately discovering their presence of mind they returned and discharged a cloud of arrows upon their assailants. A messenger meanwhile was sent into the citadel to apprise De Valence and Cressingham of the assault. The interior gates now sent forth thousands to the walls, but in proportion to the numbers which approached, the greater was the harvest of death prepared for the terrible arm of Wallace, whose tremendous warwolfs throwing prodigious stones, and lighter springalls casting forth brazen darts, swept away file after file of the reenforcements. It grieved the heart of the Scottish commander to see so many valiant men urged to destruction; but still they advanced, and that his own might be preserved they must fall. To shorten the contest his direful weapons were worked with redoubled energy, and so mortal a shower fell that the heavens seemed to rain iron. The crushed and stricken enemy, shrinking under the mighty tempest, forsook their ground.

The ramparts deserted, Wallace sprang from his tower upon the walls. At that moment De Valence opened one of the gates, and, at the head of a formidable body, charged the nearest Scots. A good soldier is never taken unawares, and Murray and Graham were prepared to receive him. Furiously driving him to a retrograde motion, they forced him back into the town. But there all was confusion; Wallace had already put Cressingham and his legions to flight, and closely pursued by Kirkpatrick they threw themselves into the castle. Meanwhile the victorious Wallace surrounded the amazed De Valence, who, caught in double toils, called to his men to fight for their king, and neither give nor take quarter.

The brave fellows obeyed, and while they fell on all sides he supported them with a courage which horror of Wallace's vengeance for his grandfather's death, and the attempt on his own life in the hall at Dumbarton, rendered desperate. At last he encountered the conquering chief arm to arm. Great was the dismay of De Valence at this meeting; but he resolved, if he must die, that the soul of his enemy should attend him to the other world.

He fought, not with the steady valor of a warrior determined to vanquish or to die, but with the fury of despair. Drunk with rage, he made a desperate plunge at the heart of Wallace,—a plunge armed with all his strength; but his sword missed its aim and entered the side of a youth who at that moment had thrown himself before his general. Wallace saw where the deadly blow fell, and instantly closing on the earl, with one grasp of his arm the chief hurled him to the ground, and, setting his foot upon his breast, would have buried his dagger there had not De Valence dropped his uplifted sword, and, with horror in every feature, raised his clasped hands in supplication.

Wallace suspended the blow, and De Valence exclaimed, "My life, this once again, gallant Wallace! by your hopes of heaven, grant me mercy!"

Wallace looked on the recreant with a glance which, had he possessed the soul of a man, would have made him grasp at death rather than deserve a second. "And hast thou escaped me again?" cried Wallace; then turning his indignant eyes from the abject earl to his bleeding friend, "I yield him his life, Edwin, and you, perhaps, are slain?"

"Forget not your own principles to avenge me," said Edwin; "he has only wounded me. But you are safe, and I hardly feel a smart."

Wallace replaced his dagger in his girdle. "Rise, Lord de Valence, it is my honor, not my will that grants your life. You threw away your arms. I cannot strike even a murderer who bares his breast. I give you that mercy you denied to nineteen defenseless old men, whose hoary heads your ax brought with blood to the ground. Let memory be the sword I have withheld."

The whole of the survivors in De Valence's train having surrendered themselves when their leader fell, in a few minutes Wallace was surrounded by his chieftains bringing in the colors and the swords of their prisoners.

"Sir Alexander Ramsay," said he to a brave knight who, with his kinsman, William Blair, had joined him in the Lothians, "I confide Earl de Valence to your care. See that he is strongly guarded and has every respect, according to the honor of him to whom I commit this charge."

The town was now in possession of the Scots, and Wallace having set off the rest of his prisoners to safe quarters, reiterated his persuasions to Edwin to leave the ground and submit his wounds to the surgeon. "No, no," replied he; "the same hand that gave me this inflicted a worse on my general at Dumbarton; he kept the field then, and shall I retire now, and disgrace my example?"

"Do as you will," answered Wallace, with a grateful smile, "so that you preserve a life that must never again be risked to save mine. While it is necessary for me to live, my Almighty Captain will shield me; but when His word goes forth that I shall be recalled, it will not be in the power of friendship nor of hosts to turn the steel from my breast."

Edwin bowed his modest head, and having suffered a balsam to be poured into his wound, braced his brigandine over his breast, and was again at the side of his friend, just as he had joined Kirkpatrick before the citadel. The gates were firmly closed, and the dismayed Cressingham was panting behind its walls as Wallace commanded the parley to be sounded. Afraid of trusting himself within arrow-shot of an enemy who he believed conquered by witchcraft, the terrified governor sent his lieutenant upon the walls to answer the summons.

The herald of the Scots demanded the immediate surrender of the place. Cressingham was at that instant informed by a messenger that De Warenne was approaching with an immense army. Inflated with new confidence, he mounted the wall himself, and in haughty language returned for answer, "that he would fall under the towers of the citadel before he would surrender to a Scottish rebel. And as an example of the fate which such a delinquent merits," continued he, "I will change the milder sentence passed on Lord Mar, and immediately hang him and all his family on these ramparts in sight of your insurgent army."

"Then," cried the herald, "thus says Sir William Wallace: If even one hair on the heads of the Earl of Mar and his family fall with violence to the ground, every Southron soul who has this day surrendered to the Scottish arms shall lose his head by the ax."

"We are used to the blood of traitors," cried Cressingham, "but the army of Earl de Warenne is at hand; and it is at the peril of all your necks for the rebel, your master, to put his threat in execution. Withdraw, or you shall see the dead bodies of Donald Mar and his family fringing these battlements; for no terms do we keep with man, woman, or child who is linked with treason."

At these words an arrow winged from a hand behind Cressingham flew directly to the unvisored face of Wallace; but it struck too high, and ringing against his helmet fell to the ground.

"Treachery!" resounded from every Scottish lip, while indignant at so villainous a rupture of the parley, every bow was drawn to the head, and a flight of arrows flew towards the battlements. All hands were now at work to bring the towers to the wall, and mounting on them, while the archers by their rapid showers drove the men from the ramparts, soldiers below, with pickaxes, dug into the wall to make a breach.

Cressingham began to fear that his auxiliaries might arrive too late, but determining to gain time at least, he shot flights of darts and large stones from a thousand engines; also discharged burning combustibles over the ramparts, in hopes of setting fire to the enemy's machines.

But all his promptitude proved of no effect. The walls were giving way in parts, and Wallace was mounting by scaling-ladders and clasping the parapets with bridges from his towers. Driven to extremity, Cressingham resolved to try the attachment of the Scots for Lord Mar, ordered the imprisoned earl to be brought out upon the wall of the inner ballia. A rope was round his neck, which was instantly run through a groove that projected from the nearest tower.

At this sight horror froze the blood of Wallace. But the earl, descrying his friend on the ladder which might soon carry him to the summit of the battlement, exclaimed, "Forward! Let not my span of life stand between my country and this glorious day for Scotland's freedom!"

"Execute the sentence!" cried Cressingham.

At these words Murray and Edwin precipitated themselves upon the ramparts and mowed down all before them in a direction towards their uncle. The lieutenant who held the cord, aware of the impolicy of the cruel mandate, hesitated to fulfil it; and now fearing a rescue from the impetuous Scots, hurried his victim off the works back to his prison. Meanwhile Cressingham, perceiving that all would be lost should he suffer the enemy to gain this wall also, sent such numbers upon the brave Scots, who had followed the cousins, that, overcoming some and repelling others, they threw Murray with a sudden shock over the ramparts. Edwin was surrounded, and his successful adversaries were bearing him off, struggling and bleeding, when Wallace, springing like a lioness on hunters carrying away her young, rushed in singly amongst them. He seized Edwin, and with a backward step he fought his passage to one of the wooden towers he had fastened to the wall.

Cressingham, being wounded in the head, commanded a parley to be sounded.

"We have already taken Lord de Valence and his host prisoners," returned Wallace, "and we grant you no cessation of hostilities till you deliver up the Earl of Mar and his family and surrender the castle into our hands."

"Think not, proud boaster," cried the herald of Cressingham, "that we ask a parley to conciliate. It was to tell you, that if you do not draw off directly, not only the Earl of Mar and his family, but every Scottish prisoner within these walls, shall perish in your sight."

While he yet spoke the Southrons uttered a great shout, and the Scots, looking up, beheld several high poles erected on the roof of the keep, and the Earl of Mar, as before, was led forward; but he seemed no longer the tranquil patriot. He was surrounded by female forms clinging to his knees, and his trembling hands were lifted to heaven.

"Stop!" cried Wallace in a voice whose thundering mandate rang from tower to tower; "the instant he dies, Lord Aymer de Valence shall perish!"

He had only to make the sign, and in a few minutes that nobleman appeared between Ramsay and Kirkpatrick. "Earl," exclaimed Wallace, "though I granted your life in the field with reluctance, yet here I am ashamed to put it in danger; but your own people compel me. Look on that spectacle! A father in the midst of his family; he and they doomed to an ignominious death, unless I betray my country and abandon these walls. Were I weak enough to purchase their lives at such an expense, they could not survive that disgrace; but that they shall not die while I have power to preserve them. Life, then, for life; yours for this family."

Wallace, directing his voice towards the keep: "The moment," cried he, "in which that vile cord presses too closely on the neck of the Earl of Mar, or on any of his blood, the ax shall sever the head of Lord de Valence from his body."

De Valence was now seen on the top of one of the besieging towers. He was pale as death. He trembled, but not with dismay only: ten thousand varying emotions tore his breast

Cressingham became alarmed on seeing the menace of Wallace brought so directly before his view, and dreading the vengeance of De Valence's powerful family, he ordered a herald to say that if Wallace would draw off his troops to the outer ballium, and the English chief along with them, the Lord Mar and his family should be taken from their perilous situation, and he would consider terms of surrender.

Aware that Cressingham only wanted to gain time until De Warenne should arrive, Wallace determined to foil him with his own weapons, and make the gaining of the castle the consequence of vanquishing the earl. He told the now perplexed governor that he should consider Lord de Valence as the hostage of safety for Lord Mar and his family, and therefore he consented to withdraw his men from the inner ballium till the setting of the sun, at which hour he should expect a herald with the surrender of the fortress.

Thinking that he had caught the Scottish chief in a snare, and that the lord warden's army would be upon him long before the expiration of the armistice, Cressingham congratulated himself upon this maneuver, and, resolving that the moment Earl de Warenne should appear Lord Mar should be secretly destroyed in the dungeons, he ordered him to their security again.

Wallace fully comprehended what were his enemy's views, and what ought to be his own measures, as soon as he saw the unhappy group disappear from the battlements of the keep. He then recalled his men from the inner ballium wall, and stationing several detachments along the ramparts and in the towers of the outer wall, committed De Valence to the stronghold of the barbican, under the especial charge of Lord Ruthven.

CHAPTER XXXI.

HAVING secured the advantages he had gained in the town and on the works of the castle, by manning all the strong places, Wallace set forward with his chosen troops to intercept De Warenne.

He took his position on a commanding ground about half a mile from Stirling. The Forth lay before him, crossed by a wooden bridge, over which the enemy must pass to reach him, the river not being fordable in that part.

He ordered the timbers which supported the bridge to be sawed at the bottom, but not displaced in the least, that they might stand perfectly firm for as long as he should deem it necessary. To these timbers were fastened strong cords, all of which he intrusted to the sturdiest of his Lanark men, who were to lie concealed amongst the flags. These preparations being made, he drew up his troops in order of battle. Kirkpatrick and Murray commanded the flanks In the center stood Wallace himself, with Ramsay on one side of him, and Edwin, with Scrymgeour, on the other.

Cressingham was not less well informed of the advance of De Warenne, and burning with revenge against Wallace, he first gave secret orders to his lieutenant, then set forth alone to seek an avenue of escape never divulged to any but the commanders of the fortress. He soon discovered it, and by the light of a torch, making his way through a passage bored in the rock, emerged at its western base, screened from sight by the surrounding bushes. He had disguised himself in a shepherd's bonnet and plaid, in case of being observed by the enemy; but fortune favored him, and unseen he crept along through the thickets till he descried the advance of De Warenne's army.

De Warenne divided his army into three divisions, to enter Stirlingshire by different routes, and so, he hoped, certainly to intercept Wallace in one of them. The Earl of Montgomery led the first, of twenty thousand men; the Barons Hilton and Blenkinsopp, the second, of ten thousand; and De Warenne himself, the third, of thirty thousand.

It was the first of these divisions that Cressingham encountered

in Tor wood, and revealing himself to Montgomery, he recounted
how rapidly Wallace had gained the town, and in what jeopardy
the citadel would be if he were not instantly attacked. The earl advised waiting for a junction with Hilton or the lord warden, "which,"
said he, "must happen in the course of a few hours."

"In the course of a few hours," returned Cressingham, "you will
have no Stirling castle to defend. The enemy will seize it at sunset,
in pursuance of agreement. Therefore, no hesitation, if we would
not see him lock the gates of the north of Scotland upon us."

By arguments such as these the young earl was induced to give
up his judgment, and, accompanied by Cressingham, whose courage
revived amid such a host, he proceeded to the southern bank of the
Forth.

The bands of Wallace were drawn up on the opposite shore,
hardly five thousand strong, but so disposed the enemy could not calculate their numbers, though the narrowness of their front suggested
to Cressingham that they could not be numerous. "It will be easy
to surround the rebel," cried he; "and that we may effect our enterprise before the arrival of the warden robs us of the honor, let us about
it directly and cross the bridge."

Montgomery proposed a herald being sent to inform Wallace, that
besides the troops he saw, De Warenne was advancing with double
hosts; and if he would now surrender, a pardon should be granted to
him and his, in the king's name, for all their late rebellions. Cressingham was vehement against this measure; but Montgomery being
resolute, the messenger was despatched.

In a few minutes he returned and repeated to the Southron commanders the words of Wallace: "Go," said he, "tell your masters we
came not here to treat for pardon; we came to set Scotland free. All
negotiation is vain. Let them advance, they will find us prepared."

"Then onward!" cried Montgomery; and, spurring his steed, he
led the way to the bridge; his eager soldiers followed, and the whole
of his center ranks passed over. The flanks advanced; and the
bridge, from end to end, was filled with archers, cavalry, men-at-arms,
and war-carriages. Cressingham, in the midst, was hallooing in
triumph to those who occupied the rear of the straining beams, when
the blast of a trumpet sounded from the till now silent and immovable
Scottish phalanx. It was reechoed by shouts from behind the passing enemy; and in that moment the supporting piers of the bridge
were pulled away, and the whole of its mailed throng was precipitated
into the stream.

The cries of the maimed and the drowning were joined by the

terrific slogan of two bands of Scots. The one, with Wallace, towards the head of the river; while the other, under the command of Sir John Graham, rushed from its ambuscade on the opposite bank upon the rear of the dismayed troops; and both divisions sweeping all before them, drove those who fought on land into the flood.

In the midst of this conflict, Kirkpatrick, having heard the shouts of Cressingham on the bridge, now sought him amidst its shattered timbers. With the ferocity of a tiger, he ran from man to man; and as the struggling wretches emerged from the water, he plucked them from the surge; but even while he looked on them with imprecations of disappointment, he rushed forward on his chase. Almost in despair that the waves had cheated his revenge, he was hurrying on in another direction when he perceived a body moving through a hollow on his right. He turned, and saw the object of his search crawling amongst the sedges.

"Ha!" cried Kirkpatrick, "art thou yet mine? Villain!" cried he, springing upon his breast; "behold the hot cheek your dastard hand defiled! Thy blood shall obliterate the stain!"

"Mercy! mercy!" cried Cressingham, struggling with preternatural strength to extricate himself.

"No mercy for thee!" cried Kirkpatrick, and with one stroke he severed the head from its body. "I am a man again!" shouted he; "I go to show my general how proudly I am avenged!" As he spoke he dashed amongst the victorious ranks and reached Wallace at the very moment he was freeing himself from his fallen horse, which a random arrow had shot under him. Murray, at the same instant, was bringing up the wounded Montgomery, who came to surrender his sword and to beg quarter for his men. The earl turned deadly pale, for the first object that struck his sight was the fierce Knight of Torthorald walking with the head of Cressingham, as he held it exultantly in air.

"If that be your chief," cried Montgomery, "I have mistaken him much; I cannot yield my sword to him."

Murray understood him. "If cruelty be an evil spirit," returned he, "it has fled every breast in this army, to shelter with Sir Roger Kirkpatrick, and its name is Legion. *That* is my chief," added he, pointing to Wallace with an evident consciousness of deriving honor from his command. The chief rose from the ground, dyed in the same hue which had excited the abhorrence of Montgomery, though it had been drawn from his own veins and those of his horse. His eye momentarily fell on the approaching figure of Kirkpatrick, who blew from his bugle triumphal notes and cried to his chief, "I have slain the wolf! So perish all the enemies of Scotland!"

"And with the extinction of that breath, Kirkpatrick," cried Wallace, looking sternly from the head to him, "let your revenge perish also. For your own honor commit no indignities on the body you have slain."

" 'Tis for you to conquer like a god," cried Kirkpatrick. "I have felt as a man, and like a man I revenge." While speaking he disappeared amongst the ranks, and as the victorious Scots hailed him in passing, Montgomery, thinking of his perishing men, suffered Murray to lead him to the scene of his humility.

The ever-comprehensive eye of Wallace perceived him as he advanced, and guessing by his armor and dignified demeanor who he was, with a noble grace he raised his helmed bonnet from his head when the earl approached him. Montgomery looked on him; he felt his soul, even more than his arms, subdued; the blood mounted into his cheeks, and he held out his sword in silence to the victor, for he could not bring his tongue to pronounce the word "surrender."

Wallace understood the sign, and holding up his hand to a herald, the trumpet of peace was raised. It sounded; and where the moment before were the clash of arms, the yell of conquest, and cries for mercy, all was hushed as death.

The voice of Wallace rose from this awful pause. "Soldiers!" cried he, "God has given victory, let us show our gratitude by moderation and mercy. Gather the wounded into quarters and bury the dead."

Wallace then turned to the extended sword of the earl; he put it gently back with his hand. "Ever wear what you honor," said he; "but, gallant Montgomery, when you draw it next, let it be in a better cause. Learn, brave earl, to discriminate between the defender of his country and the unprovoked ravager of other lands."

Montgomery blushed scarlet at these words, but it was not with resentment. Then raising his eyes to Wallace, he said, "Were you not the enemy of my king, who, though a conqueror, sanctions none of the cruelties that have been committed in his name, I would give you my hand before the remnant of his brave troops whose lives you grant. But you have my heart,—a heart that knows no difference between friend or foe when the bonds of virtue unite them."

"Had your king possessed the virtues you believe he does," replied Wallace, "my sword might have now been a pruning-hook. But that is past. We are in arms for injuries received, and to drive out a tyrant. To connive at cruelty is to practise it. And has Edward ever frowned on one of those despots who in his name have for these two years past laid Scotland in blood and ashes?"

The appeal was too strong for Montgomery to answer; he felt its truth, and bowed, with an expression in his face that told more than as a subject of England he dared declare.

The late silence was turned into the activity of eager obedience. The prisoners were conducted to the rear of Stirling; while the major part of the Scots, leaving a detachment to unburden the earth of its bleeding load, returned in front of the gates just as De Warenne's division appeared on the horizon. At this sight Wallace sent Edwin into the town with Lord Montgomery, and, marshaling his line, prepared to bear down upon the approaching earl.

But the lord warden had received information which fought better for the Scots than a host of swords. When advanced a very little onward on the Carse of Stirling, one of his scouts brought intelligence that having approached the south side of the Forth, he had seen that river floating with dead bodies, and soon after met Southron soldiers in full flight, while he heard from afar the Scottish horns blowing the notes of victory. From what he learned from the fugitives, he also informed his lord that not only the town and citadel of Stirling were in the possession of Sir William Wallace, but the two detachments under Montgomery and Hilton had both been discomfited and their leaders slain or taken.

At this intelligence Earl de Warenne stood aghast; and while he was still doubting that such disgrace to King Edward's arms could be possible, two or three fugitives came up and witnessed to its truth, adding that the Scots army was so disposed by Sir William Wallace as to appear inconsiderable, that he might ensnare his enemies by filling them with hopes of an easy conquest.

These accounts persuaded De Warenne to make a retreat, and, intimidated by the representations of them who had fled, his men, with precipitation, turned to obey.

Wallace perceived the retrograde motion of his enemy's lines; and while a stream of arrows from his archers poured upon them like hail, he bore down upon the rear-guard with his cavalry and men-at-arms, and sent Graham round by the wood to surprise the flanks.

All was executed with promptitude; and the tremendous slogan sounding from side to side, the terrified Southrons now threw away their arms, to lighten themselves for escape. Sensible that it is not the number of the dead but the terror of the living which gives the finishing stroke to conquest, De Warenne saw the effects of this panic in the disregard of his orders, and dreadful would have been the carnage of his troops had he not sounded a parley.

The bugle of Wallace instantly answered it. De Warenne sent forward his herald. He offered to lay down his arms provided he might be exempted from relinquishing the royal standard, and that he and his men might be permitted to return without delay into England.

Wallace accepted the first article, granted the second, but with regard to the third, it must be on condition that he, the Lord de Warenne, and the officers taken in his army, or in other engagements lately fought in Scotland, should be immediately exchanged for the like number of noble Scots Wallace should name who were prisoners in England; and that the common men of the army, now about to surrender their arms, should take an oath never to serve again against Scotland.

These preliminaries being agreed to, the Lord Warden advanced at the head of his thirty thousand troops, and first laying down his sword, which Wallace immediately returned to him, the officers and soldiers marched by with their heads uncovered, throwning down their weapons as they approached their conqueror. Wallace extended his line while the procession moved, for he had too much policy to show his enemies that thirty thousand men had yielded almost without a blow to scarce five thousand. The privates thus disposed of, to release himself from the commanders also, Wallace told De Warenne that duty called him away, but every respect would be paid to them by the Scottish officers.

He then gave directions to Sir Alexander Ramsay to escort De Warenne and the rest of the noble prisoners to Stirling. Wallace himself turned with his veteran band to give a conqueror's greeting to the Baron of Hilton; and so ended the famous battles of Cambus-Kenneth and the Carse of Stirling.

CHAPTER XXXII.

STIRLING CASTLE.

THE prisoners which had been taken with Montgomery were lodged behind the town and the wounded carried into the abbey of Cambus-Kenneth; but when Edwin came to move that earl himself, he found him too faint with loss of blood to sit a horse to Snawdoun. He therefore ordered a litter, and so conveyed his brave prisoner to that palace of the kings of Scotland in Stirling.

Messengers meanwhile had arrived from Wallace acquainting his chieftains in Stirling with the surrender of De Warenne's army, hence no surprise was created in the breast of Montgomery when he saw his commander enter the palace as a prisoner.

Montgomery held out his hand to the lord warden in silence and with a flushed cheek.

"Blush not, my noble friend," cried De Warenne; "these wounds speak more eloquently than a thousand tongues the gallantry with which you maintained the sword that fate compelled you to surrender. But I, without a scratch, how can I meet the unconquered Edward? And yet it was not for myself I feared; my brave and confiding soldiers were in all my thoughts."

While the English generals thus conversed, Edwin's impatient heart yearned to be again at the side of Wallace; and as soon as he observed a cessation in the conversation of the two earls, he drew near Montgomery to take his leave.

"Farewell till we meet again," said the young earl, pressing his hand. "You have been a brother rather than an enemy to me."

"Because," returned Edwin, "I follow the example of my general, who would willingly be the friend of all mankind."

Warenne looked at him with surprise. "And who are you who in that stripling form utters gallant sentiments which might grace the maturest years?"

With a sweet dignity Edwin replied: "I am Edwin Ruthven, the adopted brother of Sir William Wallace."

"And the son of him," asked De Warenne, "who, with Sir William Wallace, was the first to mount Dumbarton walls?"

At these words the cheeks of Edwin were suffused with a more animated bloom. This question of De Warenne conveyed to him that he had found fame himself; that he was publicly acknowledged to be an object not unworthy of being called the brother of Sir William Wallace; and, casting down his eyes, he answered, "I am that happy Ruthven who had the honor to mount Dumbarton rock by the side of my general; and from his hand there received the stroke of knighthood."

De Warenne rose much agitated. "If such be the boys of Scotland, need we wonder, when the spirit of resistance is roused in the nation, that our strength should wither before its men."

"At least," said Montgomery, "it deprives defeat of its sting, when we are conscious we yielded to a power that was irresistible. But, my lord," added he, "if the courage of this youth amazes you, what will you say ought to be the crown of Sir William Wallace's career when you know the chain of brave hearts by which he is surrounded! Even tender woman loses the weakness of her sex when she belongs to him." Earl de Warenne, surprised at the energy with which he spoke, looked at him with an expression that told him so. "Yes," continued he, "I witnessed the heroism of Lady Wallace when she defended the character of her husband in the midst of an armed host, and preserved the secret of his retreat inviolate. I saw that loveliest of women whom the dastard Heselrigge slew."

"Disgrace to knighthood!" cried Edwin, with indignant vehemence. "If you were spectator of that bloody deed, blast not his eyes with a second sight of one who could have beheld his wife murdered."

Lord Montgomery held out his hand to Edwin. "By this right arm I swear, noble youth, that had I been on the spot when Heselrigge lifted his sword against the breast of Lady Wallace, I would have sheathed my sword in his. It was before then that I saw that matchless woman, and, offended with my want of severity in the scrutiny I had made at Ellerslie, Heselrigge sent me back to Ayr. Arnulf quarreled with me there on the same subject, and I immediately retired in disgust to England."

"Then how? you ought to be Sir Gilbert Hambledon?" replied Edwin; "but whoever you are, as you were kind to Lady Marion, I cannot but regret my late hasty charge."

Montgomery took his hand and pressed it. "Generous Ruthven, your warmth is too honorable to need forgiveness. I am that Sir Gilbert Hambledon, and had I remained so, I should not now be in Scotland. But in my first interview with the Prince of Wales, after my accession to the earldom of Montgomery, his highness told me it had been rumored from Scotland that I was disloyal in my heart to my king. 'And, to prove the falsehood of such calumniators,' continued the prince, 'I appoint you second in command there to the Earl de Warenne.' To have refused to fight against Sir William Wallace would have been to have accused myself of treason, and with the same spirit you follow him to the field, I obeyed the commands of my sovereign."

"Lord Montgomery," returned Edwin, "I am rejoiced to see one who proves to me what my general always inculcates, that all the Southrons are not base and cruel. When he knows who is indeed his prisoner, what recollections will it awaken!"

The brave youth then telling Ramsay in what parts of the palace the rest of the lords were to be lodged, descended to the court-yard, to take horse for Tor wood. He was galloping along under the bright light of the moon when he heard a squadron on full speed approaching, and presently Murray appeared at its head. "Hurrah, Edwin!" cried he, "well met! We come to demand the instant surrender of the citadel. Hilton's division has surrendered."

The two barons had indeed come up about half an hour after Earl de Warenne's division was discomfited. Sir William Wallace had sent forward to the advancing enemy two heralds, bearing the colors of De Valence and Montgomery, with the captive banner of De Warenne, and requiring the present division to lay down its arms also. The nature of Hilton's position precluded retreat, and not seeing any reason for ten thousand men disputing the day with a power to whom fifty thousand had just surrendered, he and his compeer embraced the terms of surrender.

The instant Hilton put his banner into the victor's hand, Wallace knew the castle must now be his, and impatient to apprise Lord Mar and his family of their safety, he despatched Murray to demand its surrender.

Murray gladly obeyed, and now, accompanied by Edwin, with the standards of Cressingham and De Warenne trailing in the dust, he arrived before the castle and summoned the lieutenant to the walls. But that officer, well aware of what was going to happen, feared to appear. From the battlements of the keep he had seen the dreadful conflict on the banks of the Forth; he had seen the thousands of De Warenne pass before the conqueror. To punish his treachery, in not only having suffered Cressingham to steal out under the armistice, but upholding also the breaking of his word to surrender at sunset, the terrified officer believed that Wallace was now come to put the whole garrison to the sword.

At the first sight of Murray's approaching squadron the lieutenant hurried to Lord Mar, to offer him immediate liberty if he would go forth to Wallace and treat with him to spare the lives of the garrison. Closed up in a solitary dungeon, the earl knew nought of what was occurring without, and when the Southron entered, he expected it was to lead him again to the death which had been twice averted. But the trembling lieutenant had no sooner spoken the first word than Mar discerned it was a suppliant, not an executioner, he saw before him, and he was even promising clemency from Wallace when Murray's trumpet sounded.

The lieutenant started, horror-struck. "It is now too late! There sounds the death-bell of this garrison. I saved your life, earl," cried he, imploringly, to Lord Mar. "When the enraged Cressingham commanded me to pull the cord which would have launched you into eternity, I disobeyed him. For my sake, then, preserve this garrison, and accompany me to the ramparts."

The chains were immediately knocked off the limbs of Mar, and the lieutenant presenting him with a sword, they appeared together on the battlements. As the declining moon shone on their backs, Murray did not discern that it was his uncle who mounted the wall, but calling to him in a voice which declared there was no appeal, he pointed to the colors of Edward, and demanded the surrender of the citadel.

"Let it be, then, with the pledge of Sir William Wallace's mercy?" cried the venerable earl.

"With every pledge, Lord Mar," returned Murray, now joyfully recognizing his uncle, "which you think safe to give."

"Then the keys of the citadel are yours," cried the lieutenant; "I only ask the lives of my garrison."

This was granted, and immediate preparations were made for the admission of the Scots. As the enraptured Edwin heard the heavy chains of the portcullis drawing up, and the massy bolts of the huge doors grating in their guards, he thought of his mother's liberty, of his father's joy in pressing her again in his arms, and hastening to the tower where Lord Ruthven held watch over the now sleeping De Valence, he told him all that had happened. "Go, my father," added he; "enter with Murray, and be the first to open the prison doors of my mother."

Lord Ruthven embraced his son. "My dear Edwin, I have a duty to perform superior even to the tenderest private ones. I am planted here by my commander and shall I quit my station? No, my son: be you my representative to your mother."

Edwin no longer urged his father, and flew to the gate of the inner ballium. It was open, and Murray already stood on the platform before the keep, receiving the keys of the garrison.

"Blessed sight!" cried Lord Mar to his nephew. "When I put our banner into your unpractised hand, little could I expect that in the course of four months I should see you receive the keys of proud Stirling from its commander."

Murray smiled in gratitude to his uncle, and, turning to the lieutenant, "Now," said he, "lead me to the Ladies Mar and Ruthven, that I may assure them they are free."

The gates of the keep were now unclosed, and the lieutenant conducted his victors along a gloomy passage to a low door studded with knobs of iron. As he drew the bolt, he whispered to Lord Mar, "These severities are the hard policy of Governor Cressingham."

He pushed the door slowly open and discovered a small, miserable cell, its walls of rugged stone. On the ground on a pallet of straw lay a female figure in a profound sleep. But the light which the lieutenant held, streaming full upon the slumberer, she started, and with a shriek of terror at sight of so many armed men, discovered the pallid features of the Countess of Mar. With anguish the earl rushed forward, and, throwing himself beside her, caught her in his arms.

"Are we, then, to die?" cried she, in a voice of horror. "Has Wallace abandoned us? Are we to perish?"

Overcome by his emotions, the earl could only strain her to his breast. Edwin saw a picture of his mother's sufferings in the present distraction of the countess, and he felt his powers of utterance locked up; but Lord Andrew, whose heart was ever gay, jocosely answered, "My fair aunt, there are many hearts to die by your eyes before that day, and, meanwhile, I come from Sir William Wallace—to set you free."

The name of Wallace drove every thought of death and misery from her mind; she saw not her prison walls; she felt herself again in his presence, and in a blissful trance endured the congratulations of her husband on their mutual safety.

Edwin and Murray turned to follow the lieutenant, who, preceding them, stopped at the end of the gallery. "Here," said he, "is Lady Ruthven's habitation, and, alas! not better than the countess's." While he spoke he threw open the door and discovered its sad inmate, also asleep. But when the glad voice of her son pierced her ear, when his fond embraces clung to her bosom, her surprise and emotions were almost insupportable. Hardly crediting her senses, that he whom she had believed was safe in the cloisters of St. Columba could be within the dangerous walls of Stirling; that it was his voice she heard exclaiming, "Mother, we come to give you freedom!" all appeared to her like a dream.

She listened, she found her cheek wet with his tears. "Am I in my right mind?" cried she, looking at him with a fearful, yet overjoyed countenance. "Am I not mad? Oh! tell me," cried she, turning to Murray and the lieutenant, "is this my son that I see, or has terror turned my brain?"

"It is indeed your son, your Edwin," returned he, alarmed at the expression of her countenance. Murray advanced, and, kneeling down by her, respectfully took her hand. "He speaks truth, my dear madam. It is your son Edwin. He left his convent to be a volunteer with Sir William Wallace. He covered himself with honor on the walls of Dumbarton, and here, also, a sharer in his leader's victories, he is come to set you free."

At this explanation Lady Ruthven gave way to the happiness of her soul, and falling on the neck of her son, embraced him. "And thy father, Edwin, where is he? Did not the noble Wallace rescue him from Ayr?"

"He did, and he is here." Edwin then repeated to his mother the message of his father and the particulars of his release. Perceiving how happily they were engaged, Murray, now with a flutter in his own bosom, rose from his knees and requested the lieutenant to conduct him to Lady Helen Mar.

His guide led the way by a winding staircase into a stone gallery, where, letting Lord Andrew into a spacious apartment, divided in the midst by a vast screen of carved cedarwood, he pointed to a curtained entrance. "In that chamber," said he, "lodges the Lady Helen."

While he spoke the lieutenant bowed in silence, and Murray entered alone. The chamber was magnificent, and illumined by a lamp which hung from the ceiling. He cautiously approached the bed, and gently pulling aside the curtain, beheld vacancy. An exclamation of alarm had almost escaped him, when, observing a half-open door at the other side of the apartment, he there beheld his cousin, with her back to him, kneeling before a crucifix. She spoke not, but the fervor of her action manifested how earnestly she prayed.

"Thou blessed angel!" cried Murray, throwing himself towards her. She started from her knees, and with a cry Helen threw herself on the bosom of her cousin. "My father? All are safe?" demanded she. "All, my best beloved!" answered Murray, forgetting, in the powerful emotions of his heart, that what he felt, and what he uttered, were beyond even a cousin's limits; "my uncle, the countess, Lord and Lady Ruthven; all are safe."

"And Sir William Wallace?" cried she; "you do not mention him. I hope no ill——"

"He is conqueror here," interrupted Murray. "He has subdued every obstacle between Berwick and Stirling, and he has sent me hither to set you and the rest of the dear prisoners free."

Helen's heart throbbed with a new tumult as he spoke. She longed to ask whether the unknown knight from whom she had parted in the hermit's cell had ever joined Sir William Wallace. She yearned to know that he yet lived: and with a hope she dared hardly whisper to herself of seeing him in the gallant train of the conqueror, she falteringly said, "Now, Andrew, lead me to my father."

Murray would, perhaps, have required a second bidding had not Lord Mar, impatient to see his daughter, appeared with the countess at the door of the apartment. Hastening towards them, Helen fell on the bosom of her father.

Lady Mar gazed with a frown on her lovely form. "Wallace will behold these charms!" cried her distracted spirit to herself, "and then where am I?"

While her thoughts thus followed each other, she darted looks on Helen, which, if an evil eye had any witching power, would have withered all her beauties. At one of these moments the eyes of Helen met her glance; she started with horror. It made her remember how she had been betrayed, and all that she had suffered from Soulis. But she could not forget that she had also been rescued, and with that blessed recollection, the image of her preserver rose before her. At this gentle idea, her countenance took a softer expression, and, she turned to her father's question of "How she came to be with Lady Ruthven, when he had been taught by Lord Andrew to believe her safe at St. Fillan's?"

"Yes," cried Murray, throwing himself on a seat beside her, "I found in your letter to Sir William Wallace that you had been betrayed from your asylum by some traitor Scot, and but for my joy at our present meeting, I should have inquired the name of the villain."

Lady Mar felt a deadly sickness at her heart on hearing that Wallace was already so far acquainted with her daughter as to have received a letter from her; and in despair, she prepared to listen to what she expected would bring a death-stroke to her hopes. They had met—but how? where? They wrote to each other! Then far indeed had proceeded that communication of hearts which was now the aim of her life—and she was undone. Helen glanced at the face of Lady Mar, and observing its changes, regarded them as corroborations of her having been the betrayer. "If conscience disturbs you thus," thought Helen, "let it rend your heart, and perhaps remorse may follow."

Helen no longer feared that her cousin would seek vengeance on the traitor Soulis, when he might soon have an opportunity of making it certain at the head of an army; she therefore commenced her narrative from the time of Murray's leaving her at the priory, and continued it to the hour in which she had met her father a prisoner in the streets of Stirling. As she proceeded, the indignation of the earl and of Murray against Soulis became vehement. The nephew was full of immediate personal revenge, but the father, with arguments similar to those which had suggested themselves to his daughter, calmed the lover's rage.

The conscience of Lady Mar did indeed vary her cheeks with a thousand dyes, when, as Helen repeated part of her conversation with Macgregor's wife, Murray abruptly said, "Surely that woman could name the traitor who betrayed us to our enemies. Did she not hint it?"

Helen cast down her eyes, that even a glance might not overwhelm with shame the already trembling countess. Lady Mar saw that she was acquainted with her guilt; and expecting no more mercy than she knew she would show to Helen in the like circumstances, she hastily rose from her chair, internally vowing vengeance against her triumphant daughter.

While all the furies raged in the breast of the guilty woman Helen simply answered, "Lord Soulis would be weak, as he is vile, to trust a secret of that kind with a servant"; then hurried on to the relation of subsequent events. The countess breathed again; and, almost deceiving herself with the idea that Helen was ignorant of her treachery, listened with emotions of another kind when she heard of the rescue of her daughter-in-law. She saw Wallace in that brave act. But as Helen never named the graces of his person, Lady Mar thought that to have viewed Wallace with so little notice would have been impossible, and therefore was glad of such a double conviction that he and her daughter had never met, which seemed verified when Helen said that the unknown chief had promised to join his arms with those of Wallace.

Murray had observed Helen while she spoke with an impression at his heart that made it pause. Something in this interview had whispered to him what he had never dreamt before, that she was dearer to him than fifty thousand cousins. And while the blood flushed and retreated in the complexion of Helen, and she hastily ran over the circumstances of her acquaintance with the stranger knight, Murray's own emotions declared the secret of hers, and with a lip as pale as her own, he said, "But where is this brave man? He cannot have yet joined us; for surely he would have told Wallace or myself that he came from you?"

"I warned him not to do so," replied she, "for fear that your indignation against my enemies, my dear cousin, might have precipitated you into dangers to be incurred for our country only."

"Then if he have joined us," replied Murray, rising from his seat, "you will probably soon know who he is. To-morrow morning Sir William Wallace will enter the citadel, attended by his principal knights; and in that gallant company you must doubtless discover the man who has laid such obligations on us all."

In reciting the narrative of her late sufferings to her father, when Helen came to the mentioning of the stranger's conduct to her, she felt her growing emotions as she drew near the subject, and could only excuse herself for such perturbation by supposing that the treason of Lady Mar now excited her alarm with fear she should fix it on a new object. She hastily passed from the theme to speak of De Valence, and the respect with which he had treated her during her imprisonment. His courtesy had professed to deny nothing to her wishes except her personal liberty and any conference with her parents or aunt. Her father's life, he declared, was altogether out of his power to grant. He might suspend the sentence, but he could not abrogate it.

"Yes," cried the earl, "though false and inflexible, I must not accuse him of having been so barbarous in his tyranny as Cressingham. For it was not until De Valence was taken prisoner that Joanna and I were divided. Till then we were lodged in decent apartments, but on that event Cressingham tore us from each other and threw us into different dungeons."

During part of this conversation Murray withdrew, to bring Lady Ruthven and her son to share the joy of full domestic reunion. The happy Edwin and his mother having embraced these dear relatives, accompanied Murray to the door of the barbican which contained Lord Ruthven. They entered on the wings of love, but the for once pensive Lord Andrew, with a musing step, returned into the castle to see that all was safely disposed for the remainder of the night.

CHAPTER XXXIII.

STIRLING CITADEL.

At noon next day Murray received a message from Wallace desiring him to acquaint the Earl of Mar that he was coming to the citadel.

Each member of the family hastened to prepare for the interview: Lady Mar, well satisfied that Helen and Wallace had never met, and clinging to the vague words of Murray, that he had sent to give her liberty, called forth every art of the tiring-room to embellish her still fine person. Lady Ruthven, eager to see the man who had so often been the preserver of her brother, and who had so lately delivered her husband, was the first who joined the earl in the gallery. Lady Mar soon after entered like Juno in all her plumage of majesty and beauty.

But the trumpet of Wallace had sounded in the gates before the trembling Helen could leave her apartment. It was the herald of his approach, and she sank breathless into a seat. He whom she had mourned as one stricken in sorrow, and feared for as an outlaw doomed to suffering and to death, was now to appear before her. Awful as this picture was to the timidity of her gentle nature, it alone did not occasion that inexpressible sensation which seemed to check the pulses of her heart. Was she, or was she not, to recognize in his train the young and noble Bruce? Or by seeking him everywhere in vain, ascertain that he had perished lonely and unknown?

While these ideas thronged her mind, the platform below was filling with the triumphant Scots, and her door suddenly opening, Edwin entered in delighted haste. "Come, cousin," cried he; "Sir William Wallace has almost finished his business in the great hall. He has made my uncle governor of this place, and has committed nearly a thousand prisoners of rank to his care. If you be not expeditious, you will allow him to enter the gallery before you."

Hardly observing her face from the emotions which dazzled his own eyes, he seized her hand and hurried her to the gallery.

Only her aunt and stepmother were as yet there. Lady Ruthven sat composedly on a tapestried bench, awaiting the arrival of the company, but Lady Mar was near the door, listening impatiently to the voices beneath. At sight of Helen she drew back, but she

215

smiled exultingly when she saw that all the beauty she had so lately beheld was flown. Her unadorned garments gave no particular attraction to the simple lines of her form, the effulgence of her complexion was gone, her cheek was pale, and the tremulous motion of her step deprived her of the grace which was usually the charm of her figure.

Triumph now sat in the eyes of the countess, and with an air of authority she waved Helen to take a seat beside Lady Ruthven. But Helen, fearful of what might be her emotion when the train should enter, had just placed herself behind her aunt when the steps of many a mailed foot sounded upon the oaken floor of the outward gallery. The next moment the great doors of the huge screen opened, and a crowd of knights in armor flashed upon her eyes. A strange dimness overspread her faculties, and nothing appeared to her but an indistinct throng approaching. She would have given worlds to have been removed from the spot, but was unable to stir; and on recovering her senses she beheld Lady Mar leaning on the bosom of one of the chiefs whose head was bent as if answering her in a low voice. By the golden locks which hung down upon the jeweled tresses of the countess and obscured his face, she judged it must indeed be the deliverer of her father, the knight of her dream. But where was he who had delivered herself from a worse fate than death?

Helen with a timid and anxious gaze glanced from face to face of the chieftains around; but all were strange. Then withdrawing her eyes with a conviction that their search was in vain, in the very moment of that despair they were arrested by a glimpse of the features of Wallace. He had raised his head, he shook back his clustering hair, and her secret was revealed. In that god-like countenance she recognized the object of her devoted wishes, and with a gasp of surprise she must have fallen from her seat had not Lady Ruthven, hearing a sound like the sigh of death, turned round and caught her in her arms. The cry of her aunt drew every eye to the spot. Wallace immediately relinquished the countess to her husband, and moved towards the senseless form that lay on the bosom of Lady Ruthven. The earl and his agitated wife followed.

"What ails my Helen?" asked the affectionate father.

"I know not," replied his sister; "she sat behind me, and I knew nothing of her disorder till she fell as you see."

Murray instantly supposed that she had discovered the unknown knight; and looking from countenance to countenance amongst the train, to try if he could discern the envied cause of such emotions, he read in no face an answering feeling with that of Helen's. Wallace, who, in the form before him, saw not only the woman whom he had preserved with a brother's care, but the saint who had given a hallowed grave to the remains of an angel pure as herself, now hung over her with an anxiety so eloquent in every feature, that the countess would willingly at that moment have stabbed her in every vein.

Lady Ruthven had sprinkled her niece with water, and so she began to revive; Wallace motioned to his chieftains to withdraw. Her eyes opened slowly; but recollection returning, and fearful of again encountering that face which declared the Bruce of her meditations and the Wallace of her veneration were one, she buried her blushes in the bosom of her father.

Trembling at what might be the consequences of this scene, Lady Mar determined to hint to Wallace that Helen loved some unknown knight; and bending to her daughter, said in a low voice, yet loud enough for him to hear, "Retire, my child; you will be better in your own room, whether pleasure or disappointment about the person you wished to discover in Sir William's train have occasioned these emotions."

Helen recovered herself at this remark, and raising her head with that dignity which only belongs to the purest mind, gently said, "I obey you, madam; and he whom I have seen will be too generous not to pardon the effects of so unexpected a weight of gratitude." As she spoke her eye met the fixed gaze of Wallace. His countenance became agitated, and dropping on his knee beside her, "Gracious lady," cried he, "mine is the weight of gratitude; but it is dear and precious to me; a debt that my life will not be able to repay." He pressed her hand fervently between his, and, rising, left the room.

Lady Mar gazed on Helen without understanding the meaning of her looks. Judging from her own impassioned feelings, she could only resolve the resplendent beauty which shone from the now animated face and form of Helen into the rapture of finding herself beloved. Had she not heard Wallace declare himself to be the unknown knight who had rescued her? She had heard him devote his life to her, and was not his heart included in that dedication?

Murray, too, was confounded, but his reflections were far different from those of Lady Mar. He saw his newly-discerned passion smothered in its first breath. At the moment in which he found that he loved his cousin above all women, a voice in his bosom bade him crush every fond desire. That heart, which had throbbed so entrancingly against his, was become the captive of Wallace's virtues —of the only man who his judgment would have said deserved Helen Mar. "Loveliest of created beings," thought he, looking on Helen with an expression which, had she met it, would have told her all that was passing in his soul, "if I am not to be thy love, I will be thy friend, and live for thee and Wallace!"

Believing that she had read her sentence in what she thought the glances of a happy passion, Lady Mar turned from her daughter-in-law with such a hatred kindling in her heart she durst not trust her eyes to the inspection of the bystanders. But her tongue could not be restrained beyond the moment in which the object of her jealousy left the room. As the door closed upon Helen, who retired leaning on the arms of her aunt and Edwin, the countess turned to her lord and with a bitter smile, she said, "So, my lord, you find the icy bosom of your Helen can be thawed!"

"How do you mean, Joanna?" returned the earl, doubting her words and looks; "you surely cannot blame our daughter for being sensible of gratitude."

"I blame all young women," replied she, "who give themselves airs of unnatural coldness, and then, when the proof comes, behave in a manner so extraordinary."

"My Lady Mar!" ejaculated the earl with an amazed look, "what am I to think of you from this? How has my daughter behaved indelicately? Have a care, madam, that I do not see more in this spleen than would be honorable to you!"

Fearing nothing so much as that her husband should really suspect her passion, she presently recalled her former duplicity, and with a surprised air, replied, "I do not understand what you mean, Donald." Then turning to Lord Ruthven, who stood uneasily viewing this scene, "How," cried she, "can my lord discover spleen in my anxiety respecting the daughter of the husband I honor above all the earth? Any woman would say with me that to faint at the sight of Sir William Wallace was declaring an emotion not to be revealed before so large a company."

"It only declared surprise, madam," cried Murray,—"the surprise of an ingenuous mind that did not expect to recognize its mountain friend in the person of the protector of Scotland."

Lady Mar put up her lip, and turning to the still silent Lord Ruthven, again addressed him. "Stepmothers, my lord," said she, "have hard duties to perform; and when we think we fulfil them best, our suspicious husband turns all our good to evil."

"Array your good in a less equivocal garb, my dear Joanna," answered the Earl of Mar; "judge my child by her usual conduct, and I shall ever be grateful for your solicitude. But in this instance, though she might betray the weakness of an enfeebled constitution, it was certainly not the frailty of a love-sick heart."

"Judge me by your own rule, dear Donald," cried his wife, kissing his forehead, "and you will not again wither the mother of your boy with such a look as I just now received."

Glad to see this reconciliation, Lord Ruthven made a sign to Murray, and they withdrew together.

Meanwhile the honest earl, surrendering his whole heart to the wiles of his wife, poured into her ear all his wishes for Helen; all the hopes to which her late meeting with Wallace, and their present recognition, had given birth. "I had rather have that man my son," said he, "than see my beloved daughter placed on an imperial throne."

"I do not doubt it," thought Lady Mar; "for there are many emperors, but only one William Wallace." However, her sentiments she confined to herself, neither assenting nor dissenting, but answering so as to secure his confidence.

According to the inconsistency of the passion that possessed her, one moment she saw nothing but despair before her, and in the next it seemed impossible that Wallace should in heart be proof against her charms. She remembered Murray's words, that he was sent to set her free, and that recollection reawakened every hope. Sir William had placed Lord Mar in a post as dangerous as honorable. Should the Southrons return in any force into Scotland, Stirling must be one of the first places they would attack. The earl was brave, but his wounds had robbed him of much of his martial vigor; might she not then be indeed set free? and might not Wallace, on such an event, mean to seek her hand?

These wicked meditations passed even at the side of her husband, and she determined to spare no exertion to secure the support of her own family, which was the most powerful of any in the kingdom. Her father, the Earl of Strathearn, was now a recluse in the Orkneys, she therefore did not calculate on his assistance; but she resolved on requesting Wallace to put the names of her cousins, Athol and Badenoch, into the exchange of prisoners, for by their means she expected to accomplish all she hoped.

She recollected that Wallace had not this time thrown her from his bosom, when she cast herself upon it; he only whispered, "Beware, lady! there are those present who may think my services too richly paid." With these words he had relinquished her to her husband, but in them she saw nothing inimical to her wishes.

Eager, therefore, to break away from Lord Mar's projects relating to his daughter, at the first decent opportunity she said, "We will consider more of this, Donald. I now resign you to the duties of your office, and shall pay mine to her whose interest is our own."

Lord Mar pressed her hand to his lips, and they parted.

Prior to Wallace's visit to the citadel, which was to be at an early hour the same morning, a list of the noble prisoners was put into his hand. Edwin pointed to the name of Lord Montgomery. "That," said he, "is the name of a person you already esteem; but how will you regard him when I tell you who he was?"

Wallace turned on him an inquiring look.

"You have often spoken to me of Sir Gilbert Hambledon——"

"And this is he!" interrupted Wallace.

Edwin recounted the manner of the earl discovering himself, and how he came to bear that title. Wallace listened in silence, and when his young friend ended, sighed heavily. "I will thank him," was all he said, and rising, he proceeded to the chamber of Montgomery. Even at that early hour it was filled with his officers, come to inquire after their late commander's health. Wallace advanced to the couch, and the Southrons drew back. The expression in his countenance told the earl that he now knew him.

"Noblest of Englishmen!" cried Wallace in a low voice, "I come to express a gratitude to you as lasting as the memory of the action which gave it birth. Your generous conduct to all that was dearest to me on earth was that night in the garden of Ellerslie witnessed by myself. I was in the tree above your head, and nothing but a conviction that I should embarrass the honor of my wife's protector could at that moment have prevented my springing from my covert and declaring my gratitude on the spot.

"Receive my thanks now, inadequate as they are to express what I feel. But you offered me your heart on the field of Cambus-Kenneth. I will take that as a generous intimation how I may best acknowledge my debt."

The answer of Montgomery could not but refer to the same subject, and by presenting the tender form of his wife almost visibly again before her widowed husband, nearly forced open the fountain of tears which he had buried deep in his heart, and rising suddenly for fear his emotions might betray themselves, he warmly pressed the hand of his English friend and left the room.

In the course of the same day the Southron nobles were transported into the citadel, and the family of Mar removed from the fortress, to take up their residence in the palace of Snawdoun.

CHAPTER XXXIV.

THE CARSE OF STIRLING.

THE fame of these victories, the seizure of Stirling, the conquest of above sixty thousand men, and the lord warden with his late deputy taken prisoners,—all spread through the country on the wings of the wind.

Messengers were despatched by Wallace, not only to the nobles who had already declared for the cause by sending him their armed followers, but to the clans who yet stood irresolute. To the chiefs who had taken the side of Edward he sent no exhortation. And when Lord Ruthven advised him to do so, "No, my lord," said he; "we must not spread a snare under our feet. If these men could be affected by the interest of their country, they would not have colleagued with her enemies. All honest minds will come to us of themselves; and those who are not so had better be avoided than shown the way by which treachery may affect what open violence cannot accomplish."

This reasoning, drawn from the experience of nature, was evident to every honest understanding, and decided the question.

Lady Mar, unknown to any one, again applied to her fatal pen, but with other views than for the ruin of the cause or the destruction of Wallace. It was to strengthen his hands with the power of all her kinsmen; and finally, by the crown which they should place on his head, exalt her to the dignity of a queen. She wrote first to John Cummin, Earl of Buchan, enforcing a thousand reasons why he should now leave a sinking cause and join the rising fortunes of his country.

"You see," said she, "that the happy star of Edward is setting. The proud barons of England are ready to revolt; and the Lords Hereford and Norfolk are now conducting themselves with such domineering consequence, that even the Prince of Wales submits to their directions; and the throne of the absent tyrant is shaken to its center.

"Sir William Wallace has rescued Scotland from his yoke. The country now calls for her ancient lords, those who made her kings and supported them. Come, then, my cousin! espouse the cause that may aggrandize the House of Cummin with still higher dignities than any with which it has hitherto been blazoned."

221

With these arguments she tried to bring him to her purpose and to awaken what ambition he possessed. She despatched her letter by a messenger whom she bribed to secrecy, and added in her post-script that the "answer she should hope to receive would be an offer of his services to Sir William Wallace."

While the Countess of Mar was devising her plans the despatches of Wallace had taken effect. Their simple details, and the voice of fame, had roused a general spirit throughout the land, and in the course of a short time after the different messengers had left Stirling the plain around the city was covered with a mixed multitude. All Scotland seemed pressing to throw itself at the feet of its preserver.

Neil Campbell, the brave Lord of Loch-awe, and Lord Bothwell, the father of Lord Andrew Murray, with a strong reenforcement, arrived from Argyleshire. The chiefs of Ross, Dundas, Gordon, Lockhart, Logan, Elphinstone, Scott, Erskine, Lindsay, Cameron, and of almost every noble family in Scotland, sent their sons at the head of detachments from their clans to swell the victorious ranks of Sir William Wallace.

When this host assembled on the Carse of Stirling, every inmate of the city turned out to view the glorious sight. Mounted on a rising ground, they saw each little army, and the emblazoned banners of all the chivalry of Scotland floating afar over the lengthened ranks.

At this moment the lines which guarded the outworks of Stirling opened from right to left and discovered Wallace advancing on a white charger. When the conqueror of Edward's hosts appeared, the deliverer of Scotland, a mighty shout from the thousands around rent the skies and shook the earth on which they stood.

Wallace raised his helmet from his brow as by an instinctive motion every hand bent the sword or banner it contained.

"He comes in the strength of David," cried the venerable Bishop of Dunkeld, who appeared at the head of his church's tenantry. "Scots, behold the Lord's anointed!"

The exclamation which burst like inspiration from the lips of the bishop struck to every heart. "Long live our *William the Lion!* our *Scottish King!*" was echoed with transport by every follower on the ground, and the lords themselves joined in the glorious cry. Galloping up from the front of their ranks they threw themselves from their steeds, and before Wallace could recover from the surprise into which this unexpected salutation had thrown him, Lord Bothwell and Lord Loch-awe, followed by the rest, had bent their knees and acknowledged him to be their sovereign. The Bishop of Dunkeld, at the same moment drawing from his breast a silver dove of sacred oil, poured it upon the unbonneted head of Wallace. "Thus, O king!" cried he, "do I consecrate on earth what has already received the unction of Heaven."

Wallace at this action was awestruck and looking on the bishop, "Holy Father," said he, "this unction may have prepared my brows for a crown; but it is not of this world, and Divine Mercy must bestow it. Rise, lords!" and as he spoke he flung himself off his horse, and, taking Lord Bothwell by the hand, as the eldest of the band, "kneel not to me," cried he. "I cannot assume the scepter you would bestow, for He who rules us all has yet preserved to you a lawful monarch. Bruce lives. And were he extinct the blood-royal flows in too many noble veins in Scotland for me to usurp its rights."

"The rights of the crown lie with the only man in Scotland who knows how to defend them. Baliol has abdicated our throne; the Bruce desert it; all our nobles slept till you awoke; and shall we bow to men who may follow, but will not lead? No, bravest Wallace, from the moment you drew the first sword for Scotland you made yourself her lawful king."

Wallace turned to the veteran Lord of Loch-awe, who uttered these words with a blunt determination that meant to say, the election which had passed should not be recalled. "I made myself her champion, to fight for her freedom, not my own aggrandizement. Were I to accept the honor with which this grateful nation would repay my service, I should not bring it that peace for which I contend. The circumstance of a man from the private stations of life being elevated to such dignity would be felt as an insult by every royal house, and foes and friends would arm against us. As your general I may serve you gloriously; as your monarch, in spite of myself, I should incur your ultimate destruction."

"From whom, noblest of Scots?" asked the Lord of Bothwell.

"From yourselves, my friends," answered Wallace, with a gentle smile. "Could I take advantage of the generous enthusiasm of a grateful nation; could I forget the duty I owe to the blood of our Alexanders, and leap into the throne,—there are many who would soon revolt against their own election. Jealousies and rebellions would mark my reign, till even my closest adherents, seeing the miseries of civil war, would fall from my side and leave the country again open to the inroads of her enemies.

"These, my friends and countrymen, would be my reasons for rejecting the crown did my ambition point that way. But as I have no joys in titles, let my reign be in your hearts; and with the appellation of your fellow-soldier, your friend, I will fight for you, I will conquer for you—I will live or die!"

"This man," whispered Lord Buchan, who, having arrived in the rear of the troops on the appearance of Wallace, advanced within hearing,—"this man shows more cunning in repulsing a crown than most are capable of exerting to obtain one."

"Aye, but let us see," returned the Earl of March, who accompanied him, "whether it be not Cæsar's coyness; he thrice refused the purple, and yet he died Emperor of the Romans."

"He that offers me a crown." returned Buchan, "shall never catch me playing the coquet with its charms." A shout rent the air. "What is that?" cried he, interrupting himself.

"He has followed your advice," answered March, with a satirical smile; "it is the preliminary trumpet to 'Long live King William the Great!' Onward, my gallant Cospatrick, to make our bow to royalty in masquerade."

When these scorners approached they found Wallace standing uncovered in the midst of his happy nobles. There was not a man present to whom he had not given proofs of his divine commission; each individual was snatched from a state of oppression and placed in security and honor. With overflowing gratitude, they all thronged around him, and the young, the isolated Wallace, found a nation waiting on his nod; the hearts of half a million of people offered to his hand. No crown sat on his brows; but the halo of true glory beamed from his countenance. It even checked the arrogant smiles with which the haughty March and the voluptuous Buchan came forward to mock him with their homage.

As the near relations of Lady Mar, he received them with courtesy; but one glance of his eye penetrated to the hollowness of both, and then remounting his steed, the stirrups of which were held by Edwin and Ker, he touched the head of the former with his hand. "Follow me, my friend; I now go to pay my duty to your mother. For you, my lords," said he, turning to the nobles around, "I shall hope to meet you at noon in the citadel, where we must consult together on further prompt movements. Nothing with us can be considered as won till all is gained."

The chieftains, with bows, acquiesced in his mandate, and fell back towards their troops. But the foremost ranks of those brave fellows, having heard much of what had passed, were so inflamed with admiration of their Commander, who had sworn to be their Regent that they rushed forward, and collecting in crowds around his horse and in his path, some pressed to kiss his hand, and others his garments, while the rest ran in his way, calling down blessings upon him, till he stopped at the gate of Snawdoun.

The wounded Helen

CHAPTER XXXV.

OWING to the multiplicity of affairs which engaged Wallace's attention after the capture of Stirling, the ladies of Mar had not seen him since his first visit to the citadel. The countess passed this time in writing her despatches to the numerous lords of her house, both in Scotland and in England, and by her arguments she completely persuaded her husband to put the names of Lord Athol and Lord Badenoch into the list of noble prisoners he should request.

When this was proposed to Wallace he recollected the conduct of Athol at Montrose; and made some objections against inviting him back into the country. But the earl, who was prepared by his wife to overcome every obstacle in the way of her kinsman's return, answered that he believed that their treason was more against Baliol than the kingdom, and that he understood they would now be glad to take a part in its recovery.

"That may be the case with the Earl of Badenoch," replied Wallace, "but something less friendly to Scotland must be in the breast of the man who could betray Lord Douglas into the hands of his enemies."

"So I should have thought," replied the earl, "had not the earnestness with which my wife pleads his cause convinced me she knows more of his mind than she chooses to intrust me with."

Though these explanations did not at all raise the absent lords in his esteem, yet to appear hostile to the return of Lady Mar's relations would be a violence to her. He was therefore not displeased to have this opportunity of obliging her; and as he hoped that amongst so many warm friends a few cool ones could not do much injury, he gave in the names of Badenoch and Athol, with those of Lord Douglas, Sir William Maitland (the only son of the venerable Knight of Thirlestane), Sir John Monteith, and many other brave Scots.

For these, the Earls de Warenne, de Valence, and Montgomery, the Barons Hilton and Blenkinsopp, and others of note, were to be exchanged. Those of lesser consequence, man for man, were to be returned for Scots of the same degree.

In arranging preliminaries to effect the speedy return of the Scots from England and on other subjects of equal moment had passed the time between the surrender of Stirling and the hour when Wallace was called to the plain to receive the homage of his grateful country.

Impatient to behold him again, Lady Mar hastened to the window of her apartment when the shouts in the streets informed her of the approach of Wallace. The loud huzzas, accompanied by the acclamations of "Our Protector and Prince!" seemed already to bind her brows with her anticipated diadem. Her ambitious vision was disturbed by the crowd rushing forward; the gates were thronged with people of every age and sex, and Wallace himself appeared on his white charger, with his helmet off, bowing and smiling upon the populace.

Another eye besides Lady Mar's had witnessed the triumphant entry of Wallace. Helen was this witness. She had passed the long interval since she had seen Wallace in the state of one in a dream. The glance had been so transient, that every succeeding hour seemed to lessen the evidence of her senses that she had really seen him.

In the moment of her beholding the chief of Ellerslie in the citadel she recognized in his form the resplendent countenance of him whom she supposed the Prince of Scotland. That two images so opposite should at once unite, that in one bosom should be mingled all the virtues she had believed peculiar to each, struck her with amazement; but when she recovered from her short swoon and found Wallace at her feet, when she felt that all the devotion her heart had hitherto paid to the simple idea of virtue alone would now be attracted to that glorious mortal in whom all human excellence appeared summed up, she trembled under an emotion that seemed to rob her of herself.

All was so extraordinary, so bewildering, that from the moment in which she had retired from her first interview in the gallery with him, she became altogether like a person in a trance; and hardly answering her aunt, only complained she was ill, and threw herself upon a couch.

At the very time that her heart told her, in a language she could not misunderstand, that she irrevocably loved this glorious Wallace, it as powerfully denounced to her that she had devoted herself to one who must ever be to her as a being of air.

"Were this a canonized saint," cried she as she laid her throbbing head upon her pillow, "how gladly should I feel these emotions! For could I not fall down and worship him? Ah, could I be in Edwin's place, and wait upon his smiles! But that may not be; I am a woman, and formed to suffer in silence and seclusion. But even at a distance, brave Wallace, my spirit shall watch over you and my prayers shall follow you, so that when we meet in heaven the blessed Virgin shall say with what hosts of angels my vigils have surrounded thee!"

Thus did Helen commune with her own heart. She seldom appeared from her own rooms and such retirement was not questioned, her father being altogether engaged at the citadel, the countess absorbed in her own speculations, and Lady Ruthven alone interrupting the solitude of her niece. Little suspecting the cause of Helen's indisposition, she generally selected Wallace for the subject of conversation. She descanted with enthusiasm on the perfection of his character; told her all that Edwin had related of his actions, from the taking of Dumbarton to the present moment; and then bade Helen remark the miracle of such wisdom, valor, and goodness being found in one so young and handsome.

"So, my child," added she, "depend on it, before he was Lady Marion's husband he must have heard sighs enough from the fairest in our land to have turned the wits of half the male world. There is something in his very look, did you meet him on the heath, without better garb than a shepherd's plaid, sufficient to declare him the noblest of men."

With these words she turned the subject to the confidential hours he passed with the young adopted brother of his heart. When Lady Ruthven repeated his pathetic words concerning Lady Marion, she wept, while silent tears flowed from the heart to the eyes of Lady Helen.

"Alas!" cried Lady Ruthven, "that a man so formed to grace every relation in life should be deprived of the wife on whom he doted; that he should be cut off from all hope of posterity; that, when he shall die, nothing will be left of William Wallace,—breaks my heart."

While Lady Ruthven was uttering these words, shouts in the streets made her pause, and soon recognizing the name of Wallace sounding from the lips of the rejoicing multitude, she turned to Helen. "Here comes our deliverer!" cried she; "we have not seen him since the first day of our liberty. It will do you good to look on his beneficent face."

She obeyed the impulse of her aunt's arm, and reached the window just as he passed into the court-yard. Helen's soul seemed rushing from her eyes. "Ah! it is indeed he!" thought she; "no dream, no illusion, but his very self."

He looked up, but not on her side of the building: it was to the window of Lady Mar, and as he bowed he smiled. All the charms of that smile struck upon the soul of Helen, and hastily retreating, she sank breathless into a seat.

"Oh, no! that man cannot be born for the isolated state I have just lamented!" Lady Ruthven ejaculated this with fervor, her cheeks flushing with a sudden and more forcible admiration of the person of Wallace. "There was something in that smile, Helen, which tells me all is not chilled within. And, indeed, how should it be otherwise? That generous interest in the happiness of all cannot spring from a source incapable of dispensing the softer streams of it again."

Helen, whose well-poised soul was not affected by the agitations of her body, calmly answered, "Such a hope little agrees with all you have been telling me of his conversations with Edwin. Sir William Wallace will never love woman more, and even to name the idea seems an offense against the sacredness of his sorrow."

"Blame me not, Helen," returned Lady Ruthven, "that I forgot probability in grasping at a possibility which might give me such a nephew as Sir William Wallace, and you a husband worthy of your merits."

"No more of this, if you love me, my dear aunt!" returned Helen; "it neither can nor ought to be. I revere the memory of Lady Marion too much not to be agitated by the subject; so, no more."

At that instant Edwin, throwing open the door, put an end to the conversation. He came to apprise his mother that Sir William Wallace was in the state apartments, come purposely to pay his respects to her.

"I will not interrupt his introduction now," said Helen, with a faint smile; "a few days' retirement will strengthen me, and then I shall see our protector as I ought."

"I will stay with you," cried Edwin; "and I dare say Sir William Wallace will have no objection to be speedily joined by my mother, for as I came along I met my Aunt Mar hastening through the gallery; and between ourselves, my sweet coz, I do not think my noble friend quite likes a private conference with your fair stepmother."

Lady Ruthven had withdrawn before he made this observation.

"Why, Edwin! surely she would not do anything ungracious to one to whom she owes so great a weight of obligations?"

"Ungracious! oh, no! but her gratitude is full of absurdity. I will not repeat the fooleries with which she sought to detain him at Bute. And that some new fancy respecting him is now about to menace his patience, I am convinced, for on my way hither I met her hurrying along, and as she passed me she exclaimed, 'Is Lord Buchan arrived?' I answered, 'Yes.'—'Ah, then he proclaimed him king!' cried she, and into the great gallery she darted."

"You do not mean to say," demanded Helen, turning her eyes with an expression which seemed confident of his answer, "that Sir William Wallace has accepted the crown of Scotland?"

"Certainly not," replied Edwin; "but as certainly it has been offered to him, and he has refused it."

"I could have sworn it," returned Helen, rising from her chair; "all is loyal, all is great and consistent there, Edwin."

"He is indeed the perfect exemplar of all nobleness," rejoined the youth, "and I believe I shall even love you better, my dear cousin, because you seem to have so clear an apprehension of his real character." He then proceeded, with the most zealous affection, to narrate to Helen the particulars of the late scene on the Carse of Stirling. And while he deepened still more the profound impression the virtues of Wallace had made on her heart, he reopened its more tender sympathies by repeating, with even minuter accuracy than he had done to his mother, details of those hours which he passed with him in retirement.

"When," said Edwin, "after a conversation on his beloved Marion, a few natural regrets pass his lips, and my tears tell how deep is my sympathy, then he turns to comfort me; then he shows me the world beyond this—that world which is the aim of all his deeds, the end of all his travails. It is this belief that bathes his lips in the smiles of paradise, that throws a divine luster over his eyes, and makes all dream of love and happiness that look upon him."

Edwin paused. "Is it not so, my cousin?"

Helen raised her thoughtful face. "He is not a being of this earth, Edwin. We must learn to imitate him, as well as to——" She hesitated, and then added, "as well as to revere him. I do revere him with such a sentiment as fills my heart when I bend before the altars of the saints, and this sentiment, my dear Edwin, you partake."

"It possesses me wholly," cried the youth. "I have no thought, no wish, nor ever move or speak, but with the intent to be like him. He calls me his brother, and I will be so in soul, though I cannot in blood; and then, my dear Helen, you shall have two Sir William Wallaces to love."

"Sweetest boy!" cried Helen, putting her quivering lips to his forehead; "you will then always remember that Helen so dearly loves Scotland as to be jealous, above all earthly things, for the lord regent's safety. Beware of treason, in man and woman, friend and kindred. It lurks, my cousin, under the most specious forms; and, as one, mark Lord Buchan; in short, have a care of all whom any of the House of Cummin may introduce. Watch over your general's life in the private hour. It is not the public field I fear for him; his valiant arm will there be his own guard. But, in the day of confidence, envy will point its dagger; and then be as eyes to his trusting soul, as a shield to his breast."

"I will be all this," cried Edwin, who saw nothing in her solicitude but the affection which glowed in his own heart; "and I will be your eyes, too, my cousin; for when I am absent with Sir William Wallace I shall consider myself your representative, and so will send you regular despatches of all that happens to him."

Thanks would have been a poor means of imparting what she felt at this assurance, and rising from her seat, she pressed Edwin's hand to her heart; then withdrew into an inner apartment.

CHAPTER XXXVI.

THE countess's greeting from the window gave Wallace reason to anticipate her company in his visit to Lady Ruthven, and on finding the room vacant, he despatched Edwin for his mother, that he might not be distressed by the advances of a woman whom, as the wife of Lord Mar, he was obliged to see. Respect the countess he could not, nor, indeed, could he feel any gratitude for a preference which seemed to him to have no foundations in the only true basis of love— the virtues of the object.

In the midst of thoughts so little to her advantage Lady Mar entered the room. Wallace turned to meet her, while she, hastening towards him and dropping on one knee, exclaimed, "Let me be the first woman in Scotland to acknowledge its king!"

Wallace put forth both his hands to raise her, and smiling replied, "Lady Mar, you would do me an honor I can never claim."

"How?" cried she, starting up. "What then was that cry I heard? Did they not call you 'prince,' and 'sovereign'? Did not my Lord Buchan——"

Confused, disappointed, she left the sentence unfinished, sank on a seat and burst into tears. At that moment she saw her anticipated crown fall from her head, and having united the gaining of Wallace with his acquisition of this dignity, all her hopes seemed again the sport of winds. She felt as if Wallace had eluded her power, and now all was rejected, and she wept in despair. He gazed at her with amazement. What these emotions and his elevation had to do with each other he could not guess; but recollecting her manner of mentioning Lord Buchan's name, he answered, "Lord Buchan I have just seen. He and Lord March came upon the carse at the time I went thither to meet my gallant countrymen, and these two noblemen united with the rest in proclaiming me regent."

This word dried the tears of Lady Mar. She saw the shadow of royalty behind it, and calmly said, "Do not condemn this weakness; it is not that of vain wishes for your aggrandizement. You are the same to Joanna Mar whether as a monarch or a private man; it is for Scotland's sake alone that I wish you to be her king. You

231

have taught me to forget all selfish desires," cried she, "and from this hour I conjure you to wipe from your memory all my folly, all my love——"

With the last word her bosom heaved, and she rose in agitation. Wallace now gazed on her with redoubled wonder. She saw it, and hearing a foot in the passage, turned, and grasping his hand, said in hurried tone, "Forgive that what is entwined with my heart should cost me some pangs to wrest thence again! Only respect me and I am comforted." Wallace in silence pressed her hand, and the door opened.

Lady Ruthven entered. The countess, whose present aim was to throw the virtue of Wallace off its guard, and to take that by sap which she found resisted open attack, disappeared by another passage. Lord Ruthven with others soon entered, and at the appointed hour they attended their chief to the citadel.

The council-hall was already filled with the lords who had brought their clans to the Scottish standard. On the entrance of Wallace they rose, and Mar, coming forward, followed by the heralds and other officers of ceremony, saluted him with the due forms of regent, and led him to the throne. Wallace ascended, but it was only to take thence a packet which had been deposited for him on its cushion, and coming down again he laid the parchment on the council-table.

"I can do all things best," said he, "when I am upon a level with my friends." He then broke the seal of the packet. It was from the Prince of Wales, agreeing to Wallace's proposed exchange of prisoners, but denouncing him as the instigator of the rebellion, and threatening him with a future judgment from his incensed king. The letter was finished with a demand that the town and citadel of Berwick should be surrendered to England as a gage for the quiet of the borders till Edward should return.

Kirkpatrick scoffed at the menace of the young prince. "He should come amongst us like a man," cried he, "and we would soon show him who it is that works mischief in Scotland."

"Be not angry with him, my friend," returned Wallace; "these threats are words, of course, from the son of Edward. Did he not fear both our rights and our arms he would not so readily accord with our propositions. You see, every Scottish prisoner is to be on the borders by a certain day, and to satisfy your impatient valor you will retake your castles in Annandale."

"Give me but the means to recover those stout gates of our country," cried Kirkpatrick, "and I will warrant you to keep the keys in my hand till doomsday."

Wallace resumed: "Three thousand men are at your command. When the prisoners pass each other on the Cheviots, the armistice will terminate. You may then fall back upon Annandale, and that night light your own fires in Torthorald. Send the expelled garrisons into Northumberland, and show this haughty prince that we know how to replenish his depopulated towns."

"But first I will set my mark on them," cried Kirkpatrick, with one of those laughs which ever precluded some savage proposal.

"I can guess it would be no gentle one," returned Wallace. "Why, brave knight, will you ever sully the fair field of your fame with an ensanguined tide?"

"It is the fashion of the times," replied Kirkpatrick, roughly. "You only, my victorious general, who, perhaps, had most cause to go with the stream, have chosen a path of your own. Sir William Wallace, you would make women of us!"

"Shame, shame! Kirkpatrick," resounded from every voice; "you insult the regent."

Kirkpatrick stood proudly frowning, with his left hand on the hilt of his sword. Wallace, by a motion, hushed the tumult, and spoke. "No true chief of Scotland can offer me greater respect than frankly to trust me with his sentiments."

"Though we disagree in some points," cried Kirkpatrick, "I am ready to die for him at any time, for I believe a trustier Scot treads not the earth; but I repeat, why seek to turn our soldiers into women?"

"I seek to make them men," replied Wallace; "to be aware that they fight with fellow-creatures with whom they may one day be friends; and not like the furious savages of old Scandinavia, drink the blood of eternal enmity."

"Then I am not to cut off the ears of the freebooters in Annandale?" cried Kirkpatrick, with a good-humored smile. "Have it as you will, my general; only you must new christen me, to wash the war-stain from my hand."

While he spoke, Ker entered to ask permission to introduce a messenger from Earl de Warenne. Wallace gave consent. It was Sir Hugh le de Spencer, a near kinsman of the Earl of Hereford. He was the envoy who had brought the Prince of Wales's despatches to Stirling. Wallace was standing when he entered, and so were the chieftains, but at his appearance they sat down. Wallace retained his position.

"I come," cried the Southron knight, "from the lord warden of Scotland, who, like my prince, too greatly condescends to do otherwise than command where now he treats. I come to the leader of this rebellion, William Wallace, to receive an answer to the terms granted by the clemency of my master, the son of his liege lord, to this misled kingdom."

"Sir Knight," replied Sir William Wallace, "when the Southron lords delegate a messenger to me who knows how to respect the representative of the nation to which he is sent, and the agents of his own country, I shall give them my reply. You may withdraw."

The Southron stood, resolute to remain where he was. "Do you know, proud Scot," cried he, "to whom you dare address this language? I am the nephew of the lord high constable of England."

"It is pity," cried Murray, looking coolly up from the table, "that he is not here to take his kinsman into custody."

Le de Spencer fiercely half drew his sword. "Sir, this insult——"

"Must be put up with," cried Wallace, interrupting him and motioning Edwin to lay his hand on the sword. "You have insulted the nation to which you were sent on a peaceful errand, but in consideration of your youth, and probable ignorance of what becomes the character of an ambassador, I grant you the protection your behavior has forfeited. Sir Alexander Scrymgeour," said he, turning to him, "you will guard Sir Hugh le de Spencer to the Earl de Warenne, and tell that nobleman I am ready to answer any proper messenger."

The young Southron, frowning, followed Scrymgeour from the hall, and Wallace, turning to Murray: "My friend," said he, "it is not well to stimulate insolence by repartee. This young man's speech, though an insult to the nation, was directed to me, and by me only it ought to have been answered. The haughty spirit of this man should have been quelled, not incensed; and had you proceeded further, you would have given him an apparently just cause of complaint against you."

"I know," returned Murray, blushing, "that my wits are too many for me, ever throwing me, like Phaëthon's horses, into the midst of some very fiery mischief. But pardon me now, and I promise to rein them close when next I see this prancing knight."

Wallace then engaged himself in discourse with the elder nobles. In half an hour Scrymgeour returned and with him Baron Hilton. He brought an apology from De Warenne for the behavior of his ambassador, and added his persuasions to the demands of England, that the Regent would surrender Berwick, not only as a pledge for the Scots keeping the truce on the borders, but as a proof of his confidence in Prince Edward.

Wallace answered that he had no reason to show confidence in one who manifested by such a requisition that he had no faith in Scotland, and therefore, Scotland, a victorious power, should not surrender the eastern door of her kingdom to the vanquished. Wallace declared himself ready to dismiss the English prisoners to the frontiers, and to maintain the armistice till they had reached the south side of the Cheviots. "But," added he, "my word must be my bond, for, by the honor of Scotland, I will give no other."

"Then," answered Baron Hilton, with an honest flush passing over his cheek, as if ashamed of what he had next to say, "I am constrained to lay before you the last instructions of the Prince of Wales to Earl de Warenne."

He took a royally sealed roll of vellum from his breast and read aloud:

Thus saith Edward, Prince of Wales, to Earl de Warenne, lord warden of Scotland: If that arch-rebel, William Wallace, who now assumeth to himself the rule of all our royal father's hereditary dominions north of the Cheviots, refuseth to give unto us the whole possession of the town and citadel of Berwick-upon-Tweed, as a pledge of his faith to keep the armistice on the borders from sea to sea, we command you to tell him, that we shall detain, in the Tower in London, the person of William, the Lord Douglas, as a close captive until our prisoners now in Scotland arrive safely at Newcastle-upon-Tyne. This mark of supremacy over a rebellious people we owe as a pledge of their homage to our royal father, and as a tribute of our gratitude to him for having allowed us to treat at all with so undutiful a part of his dominions.

(Signed)
EDWARD, P.W.

"Baron," cried Wallace, "it would be beneath the dignity of Scotland to retaliate this act with the like conduct. The exchange of prisoners shall yet be made, and the armistice held sacred on the borders. But, as I hold the door of war open in the interior of the country, before the Earl de Warenne leaves this citadel, the Southron usurpers of all our castles on the eastern coast shall be our hostages for the safety of Lord Douglas!"

"And this is my answer, noble Wallace?"

"It is; and you see no more of me till that which I have said is done."

Baron Hilton withdrew, and Wallace, turning to his peers, rapidly made dispositions for a sweeping march from frith to frith; and having sent those who were to accompany him to prepare for departure, he retired with the Lords Mar and Bothwell to arrange affairs relative to the prisoners.

CHAPTER XXXVII.

THE GOVERNOR'S APARTMENTS.

THE sun rose on Wallace and his brave legions as they traversed the once romantic glades of Strathmore. Sheep, without a shepherd, fled wild from the approach of man, and wolves issued howling from the cloisters of depopulated monasteries. The army approached Dumblane; but it was without inhabitant; grass grew in the streets, and the birds flew scared from the windows as the trumpet of Wallace sounded through the town. Loud echoes repeated the summons from its hollow walls; but no other voice was heard, no human face appeared, for the ravening hand of Cressingham had been there.

They proceeded over many a hill and plain, and found that the same touch of desolation had burnt up and overwhelmed the country. Wallace saw that his troops were faint for want of food; cheering them, he promised that Ormsby should provide them a feast in Perth; and, with reawakened spirits, they took the river Tay at its fords, and were soon before the walls of that city. But it was governed by a coward; and Ormsby fled to Dundee at the first sight of the Scottish army. His flight might have warranted the garrison to surrender without a blow; but a braver man being his lieutenant, sharp was the conflict before Wallace could compel that officer to abandon the ramparts.

This enterprise achieved, Wallace, with a host of prisoners, turned his steps towards the Forth; but ere he left the banks of the Tay and Dee he detached three thousand men, under the command of Lord Ruthven, giving him a commission to range the country from the Carse of Gowrie to remotest Sutherland, and in all that tract reduce every town and castle which had admitted a Southron garrison. Wallace took leave of Lord Ruthven at Huntingtower; and that nobleman, when he assumed this extensive command, said, as he grasped the regent's hand, "I say not, bravest of Scots, what is my gratitude for thus making me an arm of my country, but deeds will show."

A rapid march round by Fifeshire brought the conqueror and his troops again within sight of the towers of Stirling. It was on the eve of the day which he had promised Earl de Warenne should see the English prisoners depart for the borders. No doubt of his arriving at the appointed time was entertained by the Scots or by the Southrons in the castle, for they knew the sacredness of his word.

De Warenne, as he stood on the battlements of the keep, beheld from afar the long line of Scottish soldiers as they descended the Ochil hills. When he pointed it out to De Valence, that nobleman, against the evidence of his eyesight, contradicted the observation of the veteran earl.

"Your sight deceives you," said he; "it is only the sunbeams playing on the cliffs."

"Then those cliffs are moving ones," cried De Warenne. "We shall find Wallace here before sunset, to show us how he has resented the affront our prince cast on his honor."

"His honor," returned De Valence, "is like that of his countrymen's—an enemy alike to his own interest and to that of others. Had it allowed him to accept the crown of Scotland, and so have fought Edward with the arm of a king, all might go well; but as the honor you speak of prevents his using these means of ending the contest, destruction must close his career."

"And what quarrel," demanded De Warenne, "can you, my Lord de Valence, have against this nice honor of Sir William Wallace, since you allow it secures the final success of our cause?"

"His honor and himself are hateful to me," impatiently answered De Valence; "he crosses me in my wishes, public and private." He turned pale as he spoke and met the penetrating glance of De Warenne.

"Which man of us all, from the general to the meanest follower in our camps, has he injured?" asked De Warenne.

Lord Aymer frowned. "Did he not expose me, threaten me with an ignominious death, on the walls of Stirling?"

"But was it before he saw the Earl of Mar, with his hapless family, brought with halters on their necks to be suspended from this very tower? Ah! what a tale has the lovely countess told me of that direful scene!"

"I care not," cried De Valence, "what are the offenses of this Wallace, but I hate him, and my respect for his advocates cannot but correspond with that feeling." As he spoke he abruptly turned away and left the battlements.

Pride would not allow the enraged earl to confess his private reasons for this enmity against the Scottish chief. A conference which he had held the preceding evening with Lord Mar was the cause of this hatred, and from that moment the haughty Southron vowed the destruction of Wallace, by open attack or secret treachery. The instant in which he knew that the young creature, whom he discerned clinging around the Earl of Mar's neck in the streets of Stirling, was the same Lady Helen on whose account Lord Soulis had poured on him such invectives in Bothwell Castle, he ordered her to be immediately conveyed to his apartments in the citadel.

On their first interview he was more struck by her personal charms than he had ever been with any woman's, although few were so noted for gallantry in the English court as himself. To all others of her sex he had declared his wishes with ease, but when he looked on Helen the admiration her loveliness inspired was checked by an indescribable awe. No word of passion escaped his lips; he sought to win her by a deportment consonant with her own dignity, and obeyed all her wishes excepting when they pointed to any communication with her parents. Seeing the anguish of her fears for her father, and hearing the fervor with which she implored for his life, De Valence adopted the plan of granting the earl reprieves from day to day; and in spite of the remonstrances of Cressingham he intended to grant to her her father's release on condition of her accepting his advances.

Ambition, as well as love, impelled him to this resolution, for he aspired to the dignity of lord warden of Scotland, and he foresaw that the vast influence which his marriage with the daughter of Mar must give him in the country would be a decisive argument with the King of England.

To this purpose, not doubting the Scottish earl's acceptance of such a son-in-law, on the very day that Wallace marched towards the coast De Valence sent to request an hour's private audience of Lord Mar. He could not then grant it; but at noon next day they met in the governor's apartments.

The Southron, without much preface, opened his wishes, and proffered his hand for the Lady Helen. "I will make her the proudest lady in Great Britain," continued he, "for she shall have a court in my Welsh province little inferior to that of Edward's queen."

"Pomp would have no sway with my daughter," replied the earl; "it is the princely mind she values, not its pageantry. I shall repeat to her what you have said, and to-morrow deliver her answer."

Not deeming it possible that it should be otherwise than favorable, De Valence allowed his imagination to roam over every anticipated delight. He exulted in the pride with which he would show this perfection of northern beauty to the fair of England; how would the simple graces of her seraphic form, which looked more like a being of air than of earth, put to shame the labored beauties of the court.

Full of these anticipations, he attended the Governor of Stirling the next day, to hear his daughter's answer. But unwilling to give the earl that advantage over him which a knowledge of his views in the marriage might occasion, he affected a composure he did not feel, and with a lofty air entered the room, as if he were come rather to confer than to beg a favor. This deportment did not lessen the satisfaction with which the brave Scot opened his mission.

"My lord, I have just seen my daughter. She duly appreciates the honor you would confer on her; she is grateful for all your courtesies whilst she was your prisoner; but beyond that sentiment, her heart, attached to her native land, cannot sympathize with your wishes."

De Valence started. He did not expect anything in the shape of a denial; but supposing that perhaps a little of his own art was tried by the father to enhance the value of his daughter's yielding, he threw himself into a chair, and affecting chagrin at a disappointment which he did not believe was seriously intended, exclaimed with vehemence, "Surely, Lord Mar, this is not meant as a refusal? I cannot receive it as such, for I know Lady Helen's gentleness. Her marriage with me may facilitate that peace with England which must be the wish of us all, and perhaps the lord wardenship, which De Warenne now holds, may be transferred to me. I have reasons for expecting that it will be so; and then she, as a queen in Scotland, and you as her father, may claim every distinction from her fond husband, every indulgence for the Scots, which your patriot heart can dictate."

The silence of the Earl of Mar, who, willing to hear all that was in the mind of De Valence, had let him proceed uninterrupted, encouraged the Southron lord to say more than he had at first intended to reveal; but when he made a pause, and seemed to expect an answer, the earl spoke:

"I am fully sensible of the honor you would bestow upon my daughter and myself by your alliance; but, as I have said before, her heart is too devoted to Scotland to marry any man who does not make it his duty to prefer the liberty of her native land, even before his love for her. That hope, to see our country freed from a yoke unjustly laid upon her, is the only passion, I believe, that lives in the bosom of my Helen, and therefore, noble earl, not even your offers can equal the measures of her wishes."

At this speech De Valence bit his lip with real disappointment. "I am not to be deceived, Lord Mar," cried he. "I am not to be cajoled by the pretended patriotism of your daughter; I know the sex too well to be cheated with these excuses. What leads your daughter from my arms is not the freedom of Scotland, but the handsome rebel who conquers in its name, but he will fall, Lord Mar, and then what will be the fate of his adherents?"

"Earl de Valence," replied the veteran, "sixty winters have checked the tides of passion in my veins; but the indignation of my soul against any insult offered to my daughter, or to the name of the lord regent of Scotland, is not less powerful in my breast. You are my prisoner, and I pardon what I could so easily avenge. I will even answer you, and say, that I do not know of any exclusive affection subsisting between my daughter and Sir William Wallace; but this I am assured of, that were it the case, she would be more ennobled in being the wife of so true a patriot, and so virtuous a man, than were she advanced to the bosom of an emperor."

"It is well that is your opinion," replied De Valence, stopping in his wrathful strides: "cherish these heroics, for you will assuredly see him exalted on a scaffold. Start not, old man,—for by all the powers of hell I swear that some eyes which now look proudly on the Southron host shall close in blood! Were you wise enough to embrace the advantage I offer, you might be a prophet of good to your nation, for all that you could promise I would take care should be fulfilled. But you cast from you your safety; my vengeance shall, therefore, take its course. Though you now see me a prisoner, tremble, haughty Scot, at the resentment which lies in this head and heart!"

He left the room as he spoke, and Lord Mar, shaking his venerable head as he disappeared, said to himself, "Impotent rage of passion and of youth, I pity and forgive you!"

It was not, therefore, so extraordinary that De Valence, when he saw Wallace descending the Ochil hills with the flying banners of new victories, should break into curses and swear inwardly the most determined revenge.

Fuel was added to this fire at sunset when the almost measureless defiles of prisoners marshaled before the ramparts of Stirling, and taking the usual oath to Wallace, met his view.

"To-morrow we quit these dishonoring walls," cried he to himself; "but ere I leave them, if there be power in gold or strength in my arm, he shall die!"

CHAPTER XXXVIII.

THE regent's reentrance into the citadel of Stirling being on the eve of the day he had promised should see the English lords depart for their country, De Warenne, as a mark of respect to a man whom he could not but regard with admiration, went to the barbican-gate to bid him welcome.

Wallace appeared, and as the cavalcade of noble Southrons who had lately commanded beyond the Tay followed him, Murray glanced his eye around and said with a smile to De Warenne, "You see, Sir Earl, how we Scots keep our word!" and then he added, "You leave Stirling to-morrow, but these remain till Lord Douglas opens their prison-doors."

"I cannot but acquiesce in the justice of your commander's determination," returned De Warenne; "and to comfort these gentlemen under their captivity, I can only tell them, that if anything can reconcile them to the loss of liberty, it is being the prisoners of Sir William Wallace."

After having transferred his captives to the charge of Lord Mar, Wallace went alone to the chamber of Montgomery to see whether the state of his wounds would allow him to march on the morrow. While he was yet there an invitation arrived from the Countess of Mar, requesting his presence at an entertainment which, by her husband's consent, she meant to give that night at Snawdoun to the Southron lords, before their departure for England.

At this moment a messenger entered from Lord Mar to request the regent's presence in his closet. He found him with Lord de Warenne. The latter presented him with another despatch from the Prince of Wales. It was to say that news had reached him of Wallace's design to attack the castles garrisoned by England on the eastern coast. Should this information prove true, he (the Prince) declared that as a punishment for such audacity he would put Lord Douglas into closer confinement, and while the Southron fleets would inevitably baffle Wallace's attempts, the moment the exchange of prisoners was completed on the borders an army from England should enter Scotland and ravage it with fire and sword.

241

When Wallace had heard this despatch, he smiled and said, "The deed is done, my Lord de Warenne. Both the castles and the fleets are taken; and what punishment must we now expect from this terrible threatener?"

"Little from him or his headlong counselors," replied De Warenne; "but Thomas, Earl of Lancaster, the king's nephew, is come from abroad with a numerous army. He is to conduct the Scottish prisoners to the borders, and then to fall upon Scotland with all his strength, unless you previously surrender not only Berwick, but Stirling, and the whole of the district between the Forth and the Tweed."

"My Lord de Warenne," replied Wallace, "you can expect but one return to these absurd demands. I shall accompany you myself to the Scottish borders, and there make my reply."

De Warenne replied: "I anticipated that such would be your determination, and I have to regret that the wild counsels which surround my prince precipitate him into conduct which must draw much blood on both sides, before his royal father's presence can regain what he has lost."

"Ah, my lord!" replied Wallace, "is it to be nothing but war? Have you now a stronghold of any force in all the Highlands? Is not the greater part of the Lowlands free? and before this day month not a rood of land in Scotland is likely to hold a Southron soldier. Not a blade of grass would I disturb on the other side of Cheviot if we might have peace. Let Edward yield us that, and though he has pierced us with many wounds, we will yet forgive him."

De Warenne shook his head. "I know my king too well to expect pacific measures. He may die with the sword in his hand, but he will never grant an hour's repose to this country till it submits to his scepter."

"Then," replied Wallace, "the sword must be the portion of him and his!—ruthless tyrant!"

A flush overspread the face of De Warenne at this term, and forcing a smile, "This strict notion of right," said he, "is very well in declamation, but how would it crop the wings of conquerors and shorten the warrior's arm did they measure by this rule!"

"How would it, indeed!" replied Wallace; "and that they should is most devoutly to be wished. All warfare that is not defensive is criminal. This is the plain truth, Lord de Warenne."

"I have never considered it in that light," returned the earl, "nor shall I turn philosopher now. I revere your principle, Sir William Wallace, but it is too sublime to be mine. By the sword my ancestors gained their estates, and with the sword I have no objection to extend my territories."

Wallace did not answer his remark, and the conference soon closed.

Though burning with stifled passions, Earl de Valence accepted the invitation of Lady Mar. He hoped to see Helen, and, above all, to find some opportunity, during the entertainment, of taking his meditated revenge on Wallace. The dagger seemed the surest way, for, could he render the blow effectual, he should not only destroy the rival of his wishes, but by ridding his monarch of a powerful foe deserve every honor at the royal hands. Love and ambition again swelled his breast, and with a glow on his countenance, which reawakened hope had planted there, he accompanied De Warenne to the palace.

The hall for the feast was arrayed with feudal grandeur. The seats at the table spread for the knights of both countries were covered with highly wrought stuffs, while the emblazoned banners and other armorial trophies of the nobles being hung aloft, according to the degree of the owner, each knight saw his precedence and where to take his place. The most costly meats, with the royally attired peacock, served up in silver and gold dishes, and wine of the rarest quality sparkled on the board. During the repast two choice minstrels were seated in the gallery above, to sing the friendship of King Alfred, of England, with Gregory the Great, of Caledonia. The squires and other military attendants of the nobles present were placed at tables in the lower part of the hall, and served with courteous hospitality.

Resentful alike at his captivity and thwarted passion, De Valence had hitherto refused to show himself beyond the ramparts of the citadel; he was therefore surprised on entering the hall at Snawdoun with De Warenne to see such regal pomp, and at the command of the woman who had so lately been his prisoner at Dumbarton. Forgetting these indignities in the pride of displaying her present consequence, Lady Mar came forward to receive her illustrious guests. Her dress corresponded with the magnificence of the banquet; a robe of cloth of gold enriched, while it displayed the beauties of her person, her wimple blazed with jewels, and a superb necklet emitted its rays from her bosom.

De Warenne followed her with his eyes as she moved from him. With an unconscious sigh he whispered to De Valence, "What a land is this, where all the women are fair, and the men all brave!"

"I wish that it and all its men and women were in perdition!" returned De Valence in a fierce tone. Lady Ruthven, entering with the wives and daughters of the neighboring chieftains, checked the further expression of his wrath, and his eyes sought amongst them, but in vain, for Helen.

The chieftains of the Scottish army, with the Lords Buchan and March, were assembled around the countess at the moment a shout from the populace without announced the arrival of the regent. His noble figure was now disencumbered of armor, and with no more sumptuous garb than the simple plaid of his country, he appeared in the glory of his recent deeds. De Valence frowned heavily as he looked on him, and thanked his stars that Helen was absent. The eyes of Lady Mar at once told the impassioned De Valence what were her sentiments toward the young regent, and the eager civilities of the ladies around displayed how much they were struck with the now fully discerned and unequaled graces of his person.

The entertainment was conducted with every regard to that courtesy which a noble conqueror always pays to the vanquished. Indeed, from the wit and pleasantry which passed from the opposite sides of the tables, and in which the ever gay Murray was the leader, it rather appeared a convivial meeting of friends than an assemblage of foes. During the banquet the bards sung legends of the Scottish worthies, and as the board was cleared they struck at once into a full chorus. Wallace caught the sound of his own name accompanied with epithets of extravagant praise and with his hand motioned them to cease. They obeyed; but Lady Mar remonstrating with him, he smilingly said it was an ill omen to sing a warrior's actions till he were incapable of performing more.

As the hours moved on, the spirits of Wallace subsided from their usual cheering tone into a sadness which he thought might be noticed, and whispering to Mar that he would go for an hour to visit Montgomery, he withdrew, unnoticed by all but his watchful enemy.

De Valence, who hovered about his steps, had heard him inquire of Lady Ruthven why Helen was not present. He was within hearing of this whisper also, and with a satanic joy the dagger shook in his hand. He knew that Wallace had many a solitary place to pass between Snawdoun and the citadel; and the company being too absorbed to mark who entered or disappeared, he took an opportunity and stole out after him.

But for once the fury of hatred met a temporary disappointment. While De Valence was cowering like a thief under the eaves of the houses, and prowling along the lonely paths to the citadel, Wallace had taken a different track.

As he walked through the illuminated archways which led from the hall he perceived a darkened passage. Hoping by that avenue to quit the palace unobserved, he immediately struck into it. He followed the passage for a considerable time, and at last was stopped by a door, which yielded to his hand, and he found himself at the entrance of a large building. He advanced, and passing a high screen of carved oak, by a dim light which gleamed from waxen tapers on the altar, he perceived it to be the chapel.

"A happy transition," said he to himself, "from the jubilant scene I have now left. Here, gracious God, may I, unseen by any other eye, pour out my heart to thee. And here, before thy footstool, will I with my tears wash from my soul the blood I have been compelled to shed."

While advancing towards the altar he was startled by a voice with gently breathed fervor uttering these words: "Defend him, Heavenly Father, day and night, from the devices of this wicked man, and, above all, during these hours of revelry and confidence guide his unshielded breast from treachery and death." A figure, which had been hidden by the rails of the altar, with these words rose, and stretching forth her clasped hands, exclaimed, "But thou who knowest I had no blame in this, will not afflict me by his danger! Thou wilt deliver thy Wallace, O God, out of the hand of this cruel foe!"

Wallace was not more astonished at hearing that some one in whom he reposed was his secret enemy, than at seeing Lady Helen in that place at that hour, and addressing Heaven for him. There was something so celestial in the maid as she stood in her white robes, before the divine footstool, that although her prayers were delivered with a pathos which told they sprang from a heart more than commonly interested in their object, yet every word and look breathed so eloquently the hallowed purpose of her petitions that Wallace did not hesitate to discover himself. He stepped from the shadow which involved him. The pale light of the tapers shone upon his advancing figure. Helen's eyes fell upon him as she turned round. He moved forward. "Lady Helen," said he, in a respectful and even tender voice. At the sound, shame seemed to overwhelm her faculties, for she knew not but that he had heard her beseech Heaven to make him less the object of her thoughts. She sank on her knees beside the altar and covered her face with her hands.

The action might have betrayed her secret to Wallace. But he only remembered that it was she who had given a holy grave to the only woman he could ever love, and full of gratitude, as a pilgrim would approach a saint he drew near to her. "Holiest of earthly maids," said he, kneeling down beside her, "in the sacred presence of Almighty Purity, receive my soul's thanks for the prayers I have this moment heard you breathe for me! They are a greater reward to me than would have been the crown with which Scotland sought to endow me, for do they not give me what all the world cannot,— the protection of Heaven!"

"I would pray for it," softly answered Helen, but not venturing to look up.

"Continue, then, to offer up that incense for me," added he, "and I shall march forth to-morrow with redoubled strength, for I shall think that I have yet a Marion to pray for me on earth as well as one in heaven."

Lady Helen's heart beat at these words; she withdraw her hands from her face, and clasping them, looked up. "Marion will indeed echo all my prayers, and He who reads my heart will grant them. They are for your life, Sir William Wallace," added she, turning to him with agitation, "for it is menaced."

"I will inquire by whom," answered he, "when I have first paid my duty at this altar for guarding it so long. I would beseech Heaven for pardon on my own transgressions; I would ask its mercy to establish the liberty of Scotland. Pray with me, Lady Helen, and we shall meet the promise of Him who said, 'Where two or three are joined together in prayer, there am I in the midst of them.'"

Helen looked on him with a holy smile, and pressing the crucifix which she held to her lips, bowed her head on it in mute assent. Wallace threw himself prostrate on the steps of the altar, and the fervor of his sighs alone breathed the deep devotion of his soul. But the bell of the palace striking the matin hour, reminded him he was yet on earth, and looking up his eyes met those of Helen. His devotional rosary hung on his arm; he kissed it. "Wear this, holy maid," said he, "in remembrance of this hour." She bowed her fair neck, and he put the consecrated chain over it. "Let it bear witness to a friendship," added he, clasping her hands in his, "which will be cemented by eternal ties in heaven."

At that moment Helen raised her head and with a terrible shriek, threw her arms around the body of Wallace. She saw an assassin's steel directed toward his back, and she fell senseless on his breast. He started on his feet; a dagger fell from his wound to the ground, but the hand which had struck the blow he could nowhere see. To search further was then impossible, for Helen lay on his bosom like one dead. Not doubting that she had seen his assailant and fainted from alarm, he was laying her on the steps of the altar, that he might bring some water from the basin of the chapel to recover her, when he saw that her arm was not only stained with his blood, but streaming with her own. The dagger had gashed it in reaching him.

"Execrable villain!" cried he, turning cold at the sight, and comprehending that it was to defend him she had thrown her arms around him, he exclaimed in a voice of agony, "Are two of the most matchless women the earth ever saw to die for me!" Trembling with alarm, for the terrible scene of Ellerslie was now brought in all its horror before him, he tore off her veil to stanch the blood; but the cut was too wide for his surgery, and losing every other consideration in fears for her life, he again took her in his arms and bore her out of the chapel. He hastened through the dark passage, and almost flying along the lighted galleries entered the hall. The fright of the servants as he broke through their ranks at the door alarmed the revelers, and turning round, what was their astonishment to behold the regent, pale, and streaming with blood, bearing in his arms a lady apparently lifeless and covered with the same dreadful hue.

Mar instantly recognized his daughter, and rushed towards her with a cry of horror. Wallace sank with his breathless load upon the nearest bench, and while her head rested upon his bosom, ordered surgery to be brought. Lady Mar gazed on the specter with dismay. None present durst ask a question, till a priest drawing near unwrapped the arm of Helen and discovered its deep wound.

"Who has done this?" cried her father to Wallace, with all the anguish of a parent in his countenance.

"I know not," replied he; "but I believe some villain who aimed at my life."

"Where is Lord de Valence?" exclaimed Mar, suddenly recollecting his menaces against Wallace.

"I am here," replied he, in a composed voice. "Would you have me seek the assassin?"

"No, no," replied the earl, ashamed of his suspicion; "but there has been some foul work, and my daughter is slain!"

"Oh, not so!" cried Murray, who had hurried towards the dreadful group and knelt at her side; "so much excellence cannot die!" A stifled groan from Wallace, accompanied by a look, told Murray that he had known the death of similar excellence. With this unanswerable appeal the young chieftain dropped his head on the other hand of Helen, and could any one have seen his face, buried as it was in her robes, they would have beheld tears of agony drawn from that ever-gay heart.

The wound was closed by the aid of another surgical priest, who had followed the former into the hall, and Helen sighed convulsively. At this intimation of recovery the priest made all stand back. But, as Lady Mar lingered near Wallace, she saw the paleness of his countenance turn to a ghastly hue, and his eyes closing, he sank back on the bench.

At the instant Wallace fell, De Valence, losing all self-command, caught hold of De Warenne's arm, and whispering, "I thought it was sure,—Long live King Edward!" rushed out of the hall. These words revealed to De Warenne who was the assassin; and though struck to the soul with the turpitude of the deed, he thought the honor of England would not allow him to accuse the perpetrator, and he remained silent.

The body of Wallace was now drawn from under that of Helen, and in the act discovered the tapestry seat clotted with blood, and the regent's back bathed in the same vital stream. Having found his wound, the priests laid him on the ground, and were administering their balsams when Helen opened her eyes. Her mind was too strongly possessed with the horror which had entered it before she became insensible to lose the consciousness of her fears; and immediately looking around her, her sight met the outstretched body of Wallace. "Oh! is it so!" cried she, throwing herself on the bosom of her father. He understood what she meant. "He lives, my child! but he is wounded like yourself. Have courage; revive, for his sake and for mine."

"Helen! dear Helen!" cried Murray, clinging to her hand; "while you live, what that loves you can die!"

While these acclamations surrounded her couch, Edwin, in speechless apprehension, supported the head of Wallace; and De Warenne, inwardly execrating the perfidy of De Valence, knelt down to assist the good friars in their office.

A few minutes longer, and the stanched blood refluxing to the chieftain's heart, he too opened his eyes, and instantly turning on his arm, "What has happened to me? Where is Lady Helen?" demanded he.

At his voice, which aroused Helen, she burst into a shower of relieving tears, and breathed out her rapturous thanks to God.

The dimness having left the eyes of Wallace and the blood being stopped by an embalmed bandage, he seemed to feel no impediment from his wound, and rising, hastened to the side of Helen. Lord Mar softly whispered his daughter, "Sir William Wallace is at your feet, my dearest child; look on him and tell him that you live."

"I am well, my father," returned she, in a faltering voice.

"I, too, am alive and well," answered Wallace; "but thanks to God and to you, blessed lady, that I am so! Had not that lovely arm received the greater part of the dagger, it must have reached my heart."

"Thanks to the Protector of the just," cried Helen, "for your preservation! who raised my eyes to see the assassin! His cloak was held before his face and I could not discern it, but I saw a dagger aimed at the back of Sir William Wallace. How I caught it I cannot tell, for I seemed to die on the instant."

Lady Mar reentered the hall just as Wallace had knelt down beside Helen. Maddened with the sight of the man on whom her soul doted in such a position before her rival, she advanced hastily, and in a voice which she vainly attempted to render composed, sternly addressed her daughter-in-law. "Alarmed as I have been by your apparent danger, I cannot but be uneasy at the attendant circumstances; tell me, therefore, and satisfy this anxious company, how it happened that you should be with the regent when we supposed you an invalid in your room, and were told he was gone to the citadel?"

A blush overspread the cheeks of Helen at this question, but as innocence dictated she answered, "I was in the chapel at prayers. Sir William Wallace entered with the same design, and at the moment he desired me to mingle mine with his, this assassin appeared, and," she repeated, "I saw his dagger raised against our protector, and I saw no more."

There was not a heart present that did not give credence to this account but that of Lady Mar. She smiled incredulously, and turning to the company, "Our noble friends will accept my apology, if in so delicate an investigation I should beg that my family alone may be present."

Wallace perceived the tendency of her words, and not doubting the impression they might make, he instantly rose. "For once," cried he, "I must counteract a lady's orders. It is my wish, lords, that you will not leave this place till I explain how I came to disturb the devotions of Lady Helen. Wearied with festivities in which my heart cannot share, I thought to pass an hour with Lord Montgomery in the citadel, and in seeking to avoid the crowded avenues of the palace I entered the chapel. To my surprise I found Lady Helen there. I heard her pray for the happiness of Scotland, for the safety of her defenders, and my mind being in a frame to join in such petitions, I apologized for my intrusion, and begged permission to mingle my devotions with hers. It was at this moment that the assassin appeared. I heard Lady Helen scream, I felt her head on my breast, and at that instant the dagger entered my back.

"This is the history of our meeting; and the assassin, whosoever he may be, and how long soever he was in the church before he sought to perpetrate the deed, were he to speak, and capable of uttering truth, could declare no other."

"But where is he to be found?" suspiciously demanded Lady Mar.

"If his testimony be necessary to validate mine," returned Wallace, with dignity. "I believe Lady Helen can point to his name."

"Name him, my dear cousin!" cried Murray; "oh, let me avenge this deed, and so yield me all that thou canst now bestow on Andrew Murray!"

There was something in the tone of Murray's voice that penetrated to the heart of Helen. "I cannot name him whom I suspect to any but Sir William Wallace, and I would not do it to him," replied she, "were it not to warn him against future danger."

"If he be a Southron," cried Baron Hilton, coming forward, "name him, gracious lady, and I will answer for it that were he the son of a king he would meet death from our monarch for this unknightly outrage."

"I thank your zeal, brave chief," replied she, "but I would not abandon to certain death even a wicked man. I will name him to Sir William Wallace alone; and when he knows his secret enemy, the vigilance of his own honor, I trust, will be his guard. Meanwhile, my father, I would withdraw." Then whispering him, she was lifted in his arms and Murray's, and carried from the hall.

As she moved away, her eyes met those of Wallace. He rose; but she waved her hand to him, with an expression in her countenance of an adieu so firm, yet so tender, that, feeling as if he were parting with a beloved sister who had just risked her life for him, and whom he might never see again, he uttered not a word to any that were present, but leaning on Edwin, left the hall by an opposite door.

CHAPTER XXXIX.

THE CARSE OF STIRLING.

DAYBREAK gleamed over the sky before the spectators of the late scene had dispersed to their quarters. De Warenne was so well convinced by what had dropped from De Valence of his having been the assassin, that when they met at sunrise to take horse for the borders, he made him no other salutation than an exclamation of surprise, "not to find him under an arrest for the last night's work."

"The wily Scot knew better," replied De Valence, "than so to expose the reputation of the lady. He knew that she received the wound in his arms, and he durst not seize me, for fear I should proclaim it."

"He cannot fear that," replied De Warenne, "for he has proclaimed it himself. He has told every particular of his meeting with Lady Helen in the chapel, so there is nothing for you to declare but your own infamy. For infamous I must call it, Lord Aymer; and nothing but the respect I owe my country prevents me pointing the eyes of the indignant Scots to you."

De Valence laughed at this speech of De Warenne's. "Why, my lord warden," said he, "have you been taking lessons of this doughty Scot, that you talk thus? It was not with such sentiments you overthrew the princes of Wales, and made the kings of Ireland fly before you! You would tell another story were your own interest in question; and I can tell you that my vengeance is not satisfied. I will yet see the brightness of those eyes, on which the proud daughter of Mar hangs so fondly, extinguished in death."

"Shame, De Valence! I should blush to owe my courage to rivalry, or my perseverance in the field to a guilty passion."

"Every man according to his nature," returned De Valence; and shrugging his shoulders he mounted his horse.

The cavalcade of Southrons now appeared. They were met on the carse by the regent, who advanced at the head of ten thousand men to see his prisoners over the borders. By Helen's desire, Lord Mar had informed Wallace what had been the threats of De Valence, and that she suspected him to be the assassin. But this suspicion was put beyond a doubt by the evidence of the dagger, which Edwin

251

had found in the chapel; its hilt was enameled with the martlets of De Valence.

At sight of it a general indignation filled the Scottish chiefs, and assembling round their regent, with one breath they demanded that the false earl should be detained, and punished as became the honor of nations. Wallace replied that he believed the attack to have been instigated by a personal motive, and, therefore, as he was the object, not the state of Scotland, he should merely acquaint the earl that his villany was known, and let disgrace be his punishment.

"Ah!" observed Lord Bothwell, "men who trample on conscience soon get over shame."

"True," replied Wallace; "but I suit my actions to my own mind, not to my enemy's; and if he cannot feel dishonor, I will not so far disparage myself as to think one so base worthy my resentment."

While he was quieting the reawakened indignation of his nobles, the Southron lords, conducted by Lord Mar, approached. When that nobleman drew near, Wallace's first inquiry was for Lady Helen. The earl informed him he had received intelligence of her having slept without fever, and that she was not awake when the messenger came off with his good tidings. That all was likely to be well with her was comfort to Wallace; and, with an unruffled brow, riding up to the squadron of Southrons, which was headed by De Warenne and De Valence, he immediately approached the latter, and drawing out the dagger held it towards him. "The next time, Sir Earl," said he, "that you draw this dagger, let it be with a more knightly aim than assassination."

De Valence, surprised, took it in confusion, and without answer; but his countenance told the state of his mind. Having taken the dagger, he wreaked his malice upon the senseless steel, and breaking it asunder, threw the pieces into the air, while turning from Wallace with an affected disdain, he exclaimed to the shivered weapon, "You shall not betray me again!"

"Nor you betray our honors, Lord de Valence," exclaimed Earl de Warenne; "and therefore, though the nobleness of Sir William Wallace leaves you at large after this outrage on his person, we will assert our innocence of the deed; and, as lord warden of this realm, I order you under an arrest till we pass the Scottish lines."

De Valence, with an ironical smile, looked towards the squadron which approached to obey De Warenne, and haughtily answered, "Though it be dishonor to you to march with me out of Scotland, the proudest of you all will deem it an honor to be allowed to return with me hither. And for you, Sir William Wallace," added he, turning to him, "I hold no terms with a rebel, and deem all honor that would rid my sovereign and the earth of such low-born arrogance."

Before Wallace could answer he saw De Valence struck from his horse by the Lochaber-ax of Edwin. Indignant at the insult offered to his beloved commander he had suddenly raised his arm, and aiming a blow with all his strength, the earl was immediately precipitated to the ground.

At sight of the fall of the Southron chief the Scottish troops, aware of there being some misunderstanding between their regent and the English lords, uttered a shout. Wallace, to prevent accidents, sent instantly to the lines to appease the tumult, and throwing himself off his horse hastened to the prostrate earl. A fearful pause reigned throughout the Southron ranks. They did not know but that the enraged Scots would now fall on them, and, in spite of their regent, exterminate them on the spot. The troops were running forward when Wallace's messengers arrived and checked them, and himself, calling to Edwin, stopped his further chastisement of the recovering earl.

"Edwin, you have done wrong," cried he; "give me that weapon which you have sullied by raising it against a prisoner totally in our power."

With a vivid blush the boy resigned the weapon to his general, yet he exclaimed, "But have you not granted life twice to this prisoner? and has he not, in return, raised his hand against your life and Lady Helen? You pardon him again, and in the moment of your clemency he insults the lord regent of Scotland in the face of both nations! I could not hear this, and live, without making him feel that you have those about you who will not forgive such crimes."

"Edwin," returned Wallace, "had not the lord regent power to punish? And if he see right to hold his hand, those who strike for him invade his dignity. I should be unworthy the honor of protecting a brave nation did I stoop to tread on every reptile that stings me in my path. Leave Lord de Valence to the sentence his commander has pronounced; and, as an expiation for your having offended both military and moral law, this day you must remain at Stirling till I return into Scotland."

De Valence, hardly awake from the stupor which the blow of the battle-ax had occasioned, was raised from the ground, and soon after coming to himself, he was taken, foaming with rage and mortification, into the center of the Southron lines.

Alarmed at the confusion he saw at a distance, Lord Montgomery ordered his litter round from the rear to the front, and hearing all that had passed joined with De Warenne in pleading for the abashed Edwin.

"His youth and zeal," cried Montgomery, "are sufficient to excuse the intemperance of the deed."

"No," interrupted Edwin; "I have offended, and I will expiate. Only, my honored lord," said he, approaching Wallace, "when I am absent, sometimes remember that it was Edwin's love which hurried him to this disgrace."

"My dear Edwin," returned Wallace, "there are many impetuous spirits in Scotland who need the lesson I now enforce upon you; and they will be brought to maintain the law of honor when they see that their regent spares not its violation, even when committed by his best beloved friend. Farewell, till we meet again!"

Edwin kissed Wallace's hand in silence, and drawing his bonnet hastily over his eyes he retired into the rear of Lord Mar's party. That nobleman soon after took leave of the regent, whose trumpets blew the signal of march. Edwin, at the sound, which a few minutes before he would have greeted with so much joy, felt his heart give way, and, striking his heel on the side of his horse, galloped to a distance to hide from all eyes the violence of his regrets. The trampling of the departing troops rolled over the ground like receding thunder. Edwin at last stole a look towards the plain; he beheld a vast cloud of dust, but no more the squadrons of his friend.

CHAPTER XL.

THE CHEVIOTS.

As Wallace pursued his march along the once fertile valleys of Clydesdale, their present appearance affected him like the sight of a friend whom he had seen depart in all the graces of prosperity, but met again overcome with wretchedness.

The pastures of Carstairs on the east of the river, which used at this season to be whitened with sheep and sending forth the lowings of abundant cattle, and the vales, which had teemed with reapers rejoicing in the harvest, were now laid waste and silent. The remains of villages were visible, but the blackness of ashes marked the walls of the ruined dwellings.

Wallace felt that he was passing through the country in which his Marion had been rifled of her life; and as he moved along, nature all around seemed to have partaken her death. As he rode over the moors which led towards the district of Crawford Lammington, he became totally silent. Time rolled back; he was no longer the regent of Scotland, but the fond lover of Marion Braidfoot.

One shattered tower alone remained of the house of Lammington. Fire had embrowned its sides, and the uprooted garden marked where the ravager had been. While his army marched before him, Wallace slowly moved forward, musing on the scene. In turning the angle of a wall his horse started, and the next moment he perceived an aged figure with a beard white as snow and wrapped in a dark plaid emerging from the ground. At sight of the apparition, Murray, who accompanied his friend, and had hitherto kept silent, suddenly exclaimed, "I conjure you, honest Scot, ghost or man, pray tell me to whom this ruined tower belonged?"

The sight of two warriors in the Scottish garb encouraged the old man, and stepping out on the ground he drew near to Murray. "Ruined indeed, sir," replied he, "and its story is very sad. When the Southrons who hold Annandale heard of the brave acts of Sir William Wallace, they sent an army to destroy this castle and domains, which are his in right of the Lady Marion of Lammington. Sweet creature! I hear they foully murdered her in Lanark."

"And did you know the Lady Marion, old man?" inquired Wallace, in a voice so descriptive of what was passing in his heart that the man turned towards him, pulled off his bonnet and bowing, answered, "Did I know her? She was nursed on these knees. And my wife, who cherished her sweet infancy, is now within yon brae. It is our only home, for the Southrons burnt us out of the castle, where our young lady left us when she went to be married to the brave young Wallace. He was as handsome a youth as ever the sun shone upon; and he loved my lady from a boy. I never shall forget the day when she stood on the top of that rock and let a garland he had made for her fall into the Clyde. Without more ado, he jumps in after it, and I after him; and well I did, for when I caught him by his golden locks he was insensible. His head had struck against a stone in the plunge, and a great cut was over his forehead. God bless him! a sorry scar it left; but many, I warrant, hath the Southrons now made on his comely countenance."

Gregory, the honest steward of Lammington, was now recognized in this old man's narration; but time and hardship had so altered his appearance that Wallace could not have otherwise recollected his well-remembered companion. When he ended, the chief threw himself from his horse. He approached the old man; with one hand he took off his helmet, and with the other putting back the same golden locks, he said, "Was the scar you speak of anything like this?" His face was now close to the eye of Gregory, who in the action, the words, and the mark immediately recognizing the young playmate of his happiest days, threw himself on his neck and wept; then looking up, he exclaimed, "O Power of Mercy, take me to thyself, since my eyes have seen the deliverer of Scotland!"

"Not so, my venerable friend," returned Wallace; "you must make these desolated regions bloom anew. Decorate them, Gregory, as you would do the tomb of your mistress. I give them to you and yours. Let Marion's foster-brother, if he still live, be now the laird of Lammington."

"He does live," replied the old man, "but the shadow of what he was. In attempting, with a few resolute lads, to defend these domains, he was severely wounded. We fled with him to the woods, and there remained till all about here was laid in ashes. Fearful of fresh incursions, we dug us subterraneous dwellings, and ever since have lived like fairies in the green hillside. Alas! the Southrons, in conquering Scotland, have not gained a kingdom, but made a desert."

"And there is a God who marks!" returned Wallace; "I go to reap the harvests of Northumberland; a few days, and your granaries shall overflow. Meanwhile I leave with you my friend," said he, pointing

Wallace and the children

to Murray, "at the head of five hundred men. To-morrow he may commence the reduction of every English fortress that yet casts a shade on the stream of our native Clyde; for, when the sun next rises, the truce expires."

He then spoke apart to Murray, who cheerfully acquiesced in a commission that promised him not only the glory of being a conqueror, but the private satisfaction, he hoped, of driving the Southron garrison out of his own paternal castle. It was arranged between the young chief and his commander that watch-towers should be thrown up on every eminence throughout the country, whence signals of victories, or other information, might be interchanged. The regent's bugle then brought Ker and Sir John Graham to his side. The appointed number of men were left with Murray; and Wallace, joining his other chieftains, bade his friend and honest servant adieu.

He now speeded his legions over hill and dale till they entered on the once luxuriant banks of the Annan,—this territory of some of the noblest in Scotland till Bruce, their chief, deserted them. It lay in more terrific ruin than even the tracts he had left, and in the midst of a barren waste a few houseless wretches rushed forward at sight of the regent, threw themselves before his horse, and begged a morsel of food for their famishing selves and dying infants.

Wallace turned to his troops. "Fast for a day, my brave friends," cried he; "lay the provisions you have brought with you before these hapless people. To-morrow you shall feast largely on Southron tables."

He was instantly obeyed. As his men marched on they threw their loaded wallets among the famishing groups, and, followed by their blessings, descended with augmented speed the hills of Annandale. Dawn was brightening the dark head of Brunswark as they advanced towards the Scottish boundary. At a distance, like a wreath of white vapors, lay the English camp along the Southern bank of the Esk. At this sight Wallace ordered his bugles to sound. They were immediately answered by those of the opposite host. The heralds of both armies advanced; and the sun, rising from behind the eastern hills, shone full upon the legions of Scotland.

Two hours arranged every preliminary to the exchange of prisoners, and when the trumpet announced that each party was to pass over the river to the side of its respective country, Wallace stood in the midst of his chieftains to receive the adieus of his illustrious captives. When De Warenne approached the regent took off his helmet. The Southron had already his in his hand. "Farewell, gallant Scot," said he; "if aught could embitter this moment of recovered freedom, it is that I leave a man I so revere still confident in a hopeless cause!"

"It would not be the less just were it indeed desperate," replied Wallace; "but had not Heaven shown on which side it fought, I should not now have the honor of thus bidding the brave De Warenne farewell."

The earl passed on, and the other lords, with grateful and respectful looks, paid their obeisance.

The escort which guarded De Valence advanced, and the proud earl, seeing where his enemy stood, took off his gauntlet, and throwing it fiercely towards him, exclaimed, "Carry that to your minion Ruthven, and tell him the hand that wore it will yet be revenged."

As the Southron ranks filed off towards Carlisle, those of the returning Scottish prisoners approached their deliverer. Now it was that the echoes rang with loud huzzas of "Long live the valiant Wallace, who brings our nobles out of captivity! Long live our matchless regent!" The captive Scots, to the number of several hundreds, were ready to kiss the feet of the man who thus restored them to their country, and their friends, and Wallace bowed his happy head under a shower of blessings which poured on him from a thousand grateful hearts.

CHAPTER XLI.

LOCHMABEN CASTLE.

THIS being the season of harvest in the northern counties of England, Wallace carried his reapers, not to lay their sickles to the field, but, with their swords, to open a way into the Southron granaries.

The careful victor, meanwhile, provided for the wants of his friends on the other side of the Esk. The plunder of Percy's camp was despatched to them, which, being abundant in all kinds of provisions, was more than sufficient to keep them in ample store till they could reach Stirling. From that point the released chiefs had promised their regent they would disperse to their separate estates, collect recruits, and reduce the distracted state of the country into some composed order. Wallace had disclosed his wish, and mode of effecting this renovation of public happiness before he left Stirling. It contained a plan of military organization, by which each youth able to bear arms should not only be instructed in the use of the weapons of war, but in the duties of subordination, and above all, have the nature of the rights for which he was to contend explained to him.

There was an expansive providence in all this, which few of the nobles had ever even glanced at, as a design conceivable for Scotland. There were many of these warrior chiefs who could not even understand it.

"Ah! my lords," replied he to their objections, "deceive not yourselves with the belief that by the mere force of arms a nation can render itself great and secure. Industry, temperance, and discipline amongst the people, with moderation and justice in the higher orders, are the only aliments of independence."

The graver council at Stirling had received his plan with enthusiasm. And when, on the day of his parting with the released chiefs on the banks of the Esk, with all the modesty of his nature he submitted his design to them, rather to obtain their approbation as friends than to enforce it with the authority of a regent; when they saw him thus coming down from the dictatorship to which his unrivaled talents had raised him to equal himself still with them, all were struck with admiration.

When the messenger from Wallace arrived on the banks of the

Esk with so large a booty, and the news of his complete victory over the gallant Percy, the exultation of the Scottish nobles knew no bounds.

On Lord Badenoch opening the regent's despatches he found they repeated his wish for his coadjutors to proceed to the execution of the plan they had sanctioned; they were to march directly for Stirling, and in their way dispense the plunder amongst the perishing inhabitants of the land. At the close of this account Wallace added, that himself, with his brave band, were going to traverse the English counties to the Tee's mouth, and, should Heaven bless his arms, he would send the produce round by the Berwick fleet to replenish the exhausted stores of the Highlands. "Next year," continued he, "I trust they will have ample harvests of their own."

Wallace's commission was not to destroy, but to save; and though he carried his victorious army to feed on the Southron plains, and sent the harvests of England to restore the wasted fields of Scotland, yet he did no more. No fire blasted his path; no innocent blood cried against him from the ground. When the impetuous zeal of his soldiers, flushed with victory, and in the heat of vengeance, would have laid several hamlets in ashes, he seized the brand from the destroying party, and, throwing it into an adjoining brook, "Show yourselves worthy the advantages you have gained," cried he, "by the moderation with which you use them. Consider yourselves as the soldiers of God, who alone has conducted you to victory.

"I wish you to distinguish between a spirit of reprisal in what I do, and that of retaliation, which actuates your present violence. What our enemies have robbed us of, as far as they can restore, I can take again. Their bread shall feed our famishing country; their wool clothe its nakedness. But blood for blood is a doctrine abhorrent to God and to humanity.

"Thus I reason with you, and I hope many are convinced. But they who are insensible to argument must fear authority, and I declare that every man who inflicts injury on the houses or on the persons of the quiet peasantry of this land, shall be punished as a traitor to the state."

According to the different dispositions of men, this reasoning prevailed. And from the end of September to the month of November, when, having scoured the counties of England, even to the gates of York, he returned to Scotland, not an offense was committed which could occasion his merciful spirit regret. It was on All-Saints' day when he again approached the Esk, and so great was his spoil that his return seemed more like some vast caravan moving the merchandise of half the world, than the march of an army which had so lately passed that river a famishing though valorous host.

The outposts of Carlaveroch soon informed Maxwell that the lord regent was in sight. At the joyful intelligence a double smoke streamed from every watch-hill in Annandale; and Sir Eustace had hardly appeared on the Solway bank to meet his triumphant chief when the eager speed of the rough knight of Torthorald brought him there also. Wallace, as his proud charger plunged into the ford and the heavy wagons groaned after him, was welcomed to the shore by the shouts not only of the soldiers which had followed Maxwell and Kirkpatrick, but by the people, who came in crowds to hail their preserver and each smiling countenance, beaming with health, security, and gratitude, told Wallace, more emphatically than a thousand tongues, the wisdom of the means he had used to regenerate his country.

Maxwell had prepared the fortress of Lochmaben, once the residence of Bruce, for the reception of the regent. And thither Wallace was conducted, in prouder triumph than ever followed the chariot wheels of Cæsar.

When he arrived in sight of the two lochs which spread like wings on each side of the castle, he turned to Graham. "What pity," said he, "that the rightful owner of this regal dwelling does not act as becomes his blood! He might now be entering its gates as a king, and Scotland find rest under its lawful monarch."

"But he prefers being a parasite in the court of a tyrant," replied Sir John, "and from such a school Scotland would reject its king."

"But he has a son," replied Wallace; "a brave and generous son. I am told by Lord Montgomery, who knew him in Guienne, that a nobler spirit does not exist. On his brows, my dear Graham, we must hope one day to see the crown."

"Then only as your heir, my lord regent," interrupted Maxwell; "for while you live, I can answer for it that no Scot will acknowledge any other ruler."

"I will first eat my own sword," cried Kirkpatrick.

At this moment the portcullis of the gate was raised, and Maxwell falling back to make way for the regent, Wallace had no time to answer a sentiment, now familiar to him, by hearing it from every grateful heart.

CHAPTER XLII.

LAMMINGTON.

DAY succeeded day in the execution of these beneficial designs. When fulfilled, the royal halls of Lochmaben did not long detain him who knew no satisfaction but when going about doing good. While he was then employed, raising with the quickness of magic, by the hands of his soldiers, the lately ruined hamlets into well-built villages; while the gray smoke curled from a thousand russet cottages, which now spotted the sides of the snow-clad hills; while all the lowlands, whithersoever he directed his steps, breathed of comfort and abundance, he felt like the father of a large family in the midst of a happy home, where every eye turned on him with reverence.

He had hardly gone the circuit of these now cheerful valleys when an embassy from England, which had first touched at Lochmaben, overtook him at the tower of Lammington. The ambassadors were Edmund, Earl of Arundel (a nobleman who had married the only sister of De Warenne), and Anthony Beck, Bishop of Durham.

At the moment their splendid cavalcade, escorted by a party from Sir Eustace Maxwell, entered the gate of Lammington, Wallace was in hourly expectation of Edwin, and hearing the trampling of horses he hastened into the court-yard, attended by Gregory's grandchildren. One was in his arms, two others held by his plaid, and a fourth played with the sword he had unbuckled from his side. It was a clear frosty day, and the keenness of the air brightened the complexion of Wallace, while it deepened the roses of his infant companions. The leader of the Scottish escort immediately proclaimed to the ambassadors that this was the regent. At sight of so uncourtly a scene, the haughty prelate of Durham drew back.

"This man will not understand his own interest," said he, in a disdainful whisper to Lord Arundel.

"I am inclined to think his estimation of it will be beyond ours." As the earl made this reply, the officer of Maxwell informed Wallace of the names and errand of the illustrious strangers. At the mention of a Southron, the elder children ran screaming into the house, leaving the youngest, who continued on the breast of Wallace.

The bishop drew near.

"We come, Sir William Wallace," cried the prelate, in a lordly tone, "from the King of England with a message for your private ear."

"And I hope, gallant chief," joined Lord Arundel, "what we have to impart will give peace to both nations, and establish in honor the most generous, as well as the bravest, of enemies."

Wallace bowed to the earl's compliment, and, resigning the child into the arms of Graham, with a graceful welcome he conducted the Southron lords into the hall.

Lord Arundel looking around, said, "Are we alone, Sir William?"

"Perfectly," he replied; "and I am ready to receive any proposals for peace which the rights of Scotland will allow her to accept."

The earl drew from his bosom a gold casket, and laying it on a table before him, addressed the regent: "Sir William Wallace, I come to you not with the denunciations of a lord whom a vassal has offended, but in the grace of the most generous of monarchs, anxious to convert a brave insurgent into a loyal friend. My lord the king, having heard, by letters from my brother-in-law, the Earl de Warenne, of the honorable manner with which you treated the English whom the fate of battle threw into your power, instead of sending over from Flanders a mighty army to overwhelm this rebellious kingdom, has deputed me to reason with the rashness he is ready to pardon. Also, with this diadem," continued the earl, drawing a circlet of jewels from the casket, "which my brave sovereign tore from the brows of a Saracen prince, he sends the assurance of his regard for the heroic virtues of his enemy. And to these jewels, he commands me to say, he will add a more efficient crown, if Sir William Wallace will acknowledge, as he is in duty bound to do, the supremacy of England over this country. Speak but the word, noblest of Scots," added the earl, "and the Bishop of Durham has orders from the generous Edward immediately to anoint you King of Scotland; that done, my royal master will support you in your throne against every man who may dare to dispute your authority."

At these words Wallace rose from his seat. "My lord," said he, "since I took up arms for injured Scotland I have been used to look into the hearts of men; I therefore estimate with every due respect the compliment which this message of your king pays to my virtues. Take back the Saracen's diadem; it shall never dishonor the brows of him who has sworn by the Cross to maintain the independence of Scotland, or to lay down his life in the struggle."

"Weigh well, brave sir,' resumed the earl, "the consequences of this answer. Edward will soon be in England; he will march hither himself, not at the head of such armies as you have discomfited, but with countless legions, and when he falls upon any country in indignation the places of its cities are known no more."

"Better for a brave people so to perish," replied Wallace, "than to exist in dishonor."

"What dishonor, noble Scot, can accrue from acknowledging the supremacy of your liege lord? or to what can the proudest ambition in Scotland extend beyond that of possessing its throne?"

"I am not such a slave," cried Wallace, "as to prefer what men might call aggrandizement before the higher destiny of preserving to my country its independence. To be the guardian of her laws, and of the individual rights of every man born on Scottish ground, is my ambition."

"Put from you all the prejudices," interrupted Lord Arundel, "which the ill conduct of Edward's officers have excited, and you must perceive that in accepting his terms you will best repay your country's confidence by giving it peace."

"So great would be my sin in such an acceptance," cried Wallace, "that I should be abhorred by God and man. You talk of noble minds, earl; look into your own, and will it not tell you that in the moment a people bring themselves to put the command of their actions and their consciences into the hands of a usurper, they sell their birthright and become unworthy the name of men? Neither the threats nor the blandishments of Edward have power to shake the resolves of them who 'draw the sword of the Lord and of Gideon.' "

"Rebellious man!" exclaimed Beck, who listened impatiently, "since you dare quote Scripture to sanction crime hear my embassage: To meet the possibility of this obstinacy, I came armed with the thunder of the church and the indignation of a justly incensed monarch. Accept his most gracious offers delivered to you by the Earl of Arundel. Here is the cross to receive your oath of fealty," cried he, stretching it forth as if he thought his commands were irresistible; "but beware! keep it with a truer faith than did the traitor Baliol, or expect the vengeance of your liege lord!"

Wallace was not discomposed by this attack from the stormy prelate. "My Lord of Durham," replied he with his usual tranquil air, "had your sovereign sent me such proposals as became a just king, and were possible for an honest Scot to admit, he should have found me ready to have treated him with the respect due to his rank and honor. But I ask you, priest of Heaven, is he a god greater than Jehovah, that I should fear him?"

"And durst thou presume, audacious rebel!" exclaimed Beck, "that the light of Israel deigns to shine on a barbarian nation in arms against a hero of the Cross? Does not the church declare the claims of Edward to be just? and who dares gainsay her decrees?"

"The voice of Him you pretend to serve. Bishop, I know in whom I trust. Is the minister greater than his Lord that I should believe the word of a synod against the will of God? Neither anathema nor armed thousands shall make me acknowledge the supremacy of Edward."

"Then," cried Beck, suddenly rising, black with choler, and stretching his crosier over the head of Wallace, "as the rod of Moses shed plagues, miseries, and death over the land of Egypt, I invoke the like judgments to fall on this rebellious land, on its blasphemous leader. And thus I leave it my curse."

Wallace smiled as the terrific words fell from the lips of this demon in sacred guise. Lord Arundel observed him. "You despise this malediction, Sir William Wallace. I thought more piety had dwelt with so much military nobleness."

"I should not regard the curses of a world," replied Wallace, "when my conscience as loudly proclaims that God is on my side. Did the clouds rain fire, and the earth open beneath me, I would not stir; for I know who planted me here; and as long as he wills me to stand, neither men nor devils can move me hence."

"Thou art incorrigible!" cried Beck.

"I would say firm," rejoined Arundel, overawed by the majesty of virtue, "could I regard, as he does, the cause he has espoused. But, as it is, noble Wallace," continued he, "I must regret your infatuation; and instead of the peace I thought to leave with you, hurl war upon the head of this devoted nation." As he spoke he threw his lance against the opposite wall, in which it stuck and stood shivering; then taking up the casket with its splendid contents, he replaced it in his bosom.

Beck had turned away in wrath from the table, and, advancing to the door, he threw it open, as if he thought that longer to breathe the same air with the person he had excommunicated would infect him with his own curses. On opening the door, a group of Scots, who waited in the antechamber, hastened forward. At sight of the prelate they raised their bonnets and hesitated to pass. He stood on the threshold, proudly neglectful of their respect. In the next minute Wallace appeared with Lord Arundel.

"Brave knight," said the earl, "the adieus of a man as sensible of your private worth as he regrets the errors of your public opinions, abide with you."

"Were Edward sensible to virtue, like his brave subjects," replied the chief, "I should not fear that another drop of blood need be shed in Scotland to convince him of his present injustice. Farewell, noble earl; the generous candor of yourself and of your brother-in-law will ever live in the remembrance of William Wallace."

While he yet spoke a youth broke from the group before them, and, rushing towards the regent, threw himself with a cry of joy at his feet. "My Edwin, my brother!" exclaimed Wallace, and, immediately raising him, clasped him in his arms. The throng of Scots who had accompanied their young leader from Stirling now crowded about the chief, some kneeling and kissing his garments, others ejaculating with uplifted hands their thanks at seeing their protector in safety and with redoubled glory.

"You forgive me, my master and friend?" cried Edwin, forgetting, in the agitation of his mind, the presence of the English ambassadors.

"It was only as a master I condemned you, my brother," returned Wallace. "Every proof of your affection must render you dearer to me, and had it been exerted against an offender not so totally in our power you would not have met my reprimand."

Lord Arundel, who had lingered to observe this scene, now ventured to interrupt it. "May I ask, noble Wallace," said he, "if this youth be the brave young Ruthven who distinguished himself at Dumbarton, and who, De Warenne told me, incurred a severe, though just, sentence from you, in consequence of his attack upon one whom, as a soldier, I blush to name?"

"It is the same," replied Wallace; "the valor and fidelity of such as he are as sinews to my arms."

"I have often seen the homage of the body," said the earl, "but here I see that of the soul, and were I a king I should envy Sir William Wallace."

"This speech is that of a courtier or a traitor!" suddenly exclaimed Beck, turning with a threatening brow on Lord Arundel. "Beware, earl! for what has now been said must be repeated to the royal Edward, and he will judge whether flattery to this proud rebel be consistent with your allegiance."

"Every word that has been uttered in this conference I will myself deliver to King Edward," replied Lord Arundel; "he shall know the man on whom he may be forced by justice to denounce the sentence of rebellion, and when his royal arm lays this kingdom at his feet, the virtues of Sir William Wallace may then find the clemency he now contemns."

Beck did not condescend to listen to the latter part of this explanation, but proceeding to the court-yard, had mounted his horse before his worthier colleague appeared from the hall. Taking a gracious leave of Sir John Graham, who attended him to the door, the earl exclaimed, "What miracle is before me! Not the mighty mover only of this wide insurrection is in the bloom of manhood, but all his generals that I have seen appear in the very morning of youth. And you conquer our veterans; you make yourselves names which, with us, are only purchased by hairs grown gray in camps and battles."

"Then by our morning judge what our day may be," replied Graham, "and show your monarch that as surely as the night of death will in some hour close upon prince and peasant, this land shall never again be overshadowed by his darkness."

Arundel made some courteous reply to Graham, then bowing to the rest of the Scottish officers who stood around, turned his steed, and, followed by his escort, pursued the steps of the bishop along the snow-covered banks of the Clyde.

When Wallace was left alone with Edwin, the happy youth took from his bosom two packets, one from Lord Mar and the other from the countess. "My dear cousin," said he, "has sent you many blessings; but I could not persuade her to register even one on paper, while my aunt wrote all this. Almost ever since her own recovery, Helen has confined herself to my uncle's sick chamber, now totally deserted by the fair countess."

Wallace remarked on the indisposition of Mar and the attention of his daughter with tenderness, and Edwin proceeded sportively to describe the regal style which the countess had affected, and the absurd pomp with which she had welcomed the Earls Badenoch and Athol to their native country. "Indeed," continued he, "I cannot guess what vain idea has taken possession of her; but when I went to Snawdoun to receive her commands for you, I found her seated on a kind of throne, with ladies standing in her presence, and our younger chieftains thronging the gallery, as if she were the regent herself. Helen entered for a moment, but amazed, started back, never before having witnessed the morning courts of her step-mother."

But Edwin did not relate to his friend all that had passed in the succeeding conference between him and his gentle cousin. Blushing for her father's wife Helen would have retired immediately to her own apartments, but Edwin drew her into one of Lady Mar's rooms, and seating her beside him, began to speak of his anticipated meeting with Wallace. He held her hand in his. "My dearest cousin," said he, "will not this tender hand, which has suffered so much for our brave friend, write him one word of kind remembrance? Our queen here will send him volumes."

"Then he would hardly have time to attend to one of mine," replied Helen, with a smile; "besides, he requires no assurances to convince him that Helen Mar can never cease to remember her benefactor with the most grateful thoughts."

"And is this all I am to say to him, Helen?"

"All, my Edwin."

"What! not one word of the life you have led since he quitted Stirling? Shall I not tell him of the sweet maid who lives here the life of a nun for him? Or must I entertain him with the pomps and vanities of my most unsaintly aunt?"

Helen had in vain attempted to stop him, while with an arch glance at her blushes he whispered these insidious questions. "Ah, my sweet cousin, there is something more at the bottom of that beating heart than you will allow your faithful Edwin to peep into!"

Helen's heart did beat violently, both before and after this remark; but conscious of the determined purpose of her soul, she turned on him a steady look. "Edwin," said she, "there is nothing in my heart that you may not see. That it reveres Sir William Wallace beyond all other men, I do not deny. Is not he a brighter object than I can anywhere look upon? I am happy with my thoughts, and thrice happy at the side of my father's couch, for there I meet the image of the most exemplary of human beings, and there I perform the duties of a child to a parent deserving all my love and honor."

"Ah, Helen! Helen!" cried Edwin, "dare I speak the wish of my heart! But you and Sir William Wallace would frown on me, and I may not."

"Then never utter it," exclaimed Helen, too well guessing, by the generous glow in his countenance, what would have been that wish.

At this instant the door opened and Lady Mar appeared. Both rose at her entrance. She bowed her head coldly to Helen. To Edwin she graciously extended her hand. "Why, my dear nephew, did you not come into the audience-hall?"

Edwin answered, smiling, that as he did not know the Governor of Stirling's lady lived in the state of a queen, he had retired, till he could bid her adieu in a less public scene.

Lady Mar, with much stateliness replied, "Perhaps it is necessary to remind you, Edwin, that I am more than Lord Mar's wife. I am not only heiress to the sovereignty of the northern isles, but, like Lord Badenoch, am of the blood of the Scottish kings."

To conceal a laugh at this folly in a woman otherwise of shrewd understanding, Edwin turned towards the window, but not before the countess had observed the ridicule which played on his lips. Vexed, but afraid to reprimand one who might so soon resent it by speaking of her disparagingly to Wallace, she unburdened her anger upon the unoffending Helen. Not doubting that she felt as Edwin did, and fancying that she saw the same expression in her countenance, "Lady Helen," cried she, "I request an explanation of that look of derision which I now see on your face. I wish to know whether your vanity dare impel you to despise claims which may one day be established to your confusion."

This attack surprised Helen, who, absorbed in other meditations, had scarcely heard her mother's words to Edwin. "I neither deride you, Lady Mar, nor despise the claims of your kinsman Badenoch. But since you have condescended to speak to me on the subject, I must, out of respect to yourself and duty to my father, frankly say that the assumption of honors not legally in your possession may excite ridicule on him and even trouble to our cause."

Provoked at the just reasoning of this reply, Lady Mar answered rather inconsiderately, "Your father is an old man, and has outlived every noble emulation. He neither understands my actions nor shall he control them." Struck dumb by this unexpected declaration, Helen suffered her to proceed. "And as to Lord Badenoch giving me the rank to which my birth entitles me, that is a foolish dream— I look to a greater hand."

"What!" inquired Edwin, with a playful bow, "does my highness aunt expect my uncle to die, and that Bruce will come hither to lay the crown of Scotland at her feet?"

"I expect nothing of Bruce nor of your uncle," returned she, with a haughty rearing of her head, "but I look for respect from the daughter of Lord Mar and from the friend of Sir William Wallace."

She rose from her chair, and presenting Edwin with a packet for Wallace, told Helen coldly that she might retire to her own room.

The substance of the latter part of this scene Edwin did relate to Wallace. He smiled at the follies of the countess and broke the seal of her letter. It was in the same style with her conversations; at one moment declaring herself his disinterested friend, in the next, uttering wild professions of never-ending attachment. She deplored the sacrifice which had been made of her when quite a child to the doting passion of Lord Mar, and complained of his want of sympathy with any of her feelings.   The conclusion of this strange epistle told him that the devoted gratitude of all her relations of the house of Cummin was ready at any moment to relinquish their claims on the crown, to place it on brows so worthy to wear it.

The words of this letter were artfully and persuasively penned, but Wallace felt that the writer would always be, were she even free, not merely the last object in his thoughts, but the first in his aversion. Therefore, hastily running over her letter, he recurred to a second perusal of Lord Mar's, in which he found satisfactory details of the success of his dispositions.   Lord Loch-awe had possessed himself of the western coast of Scotland; Lord Ruthven had met him there, having completed the recovery of the Highlands, by a range of conquests; Lord Bothwell, also, as his colleague, had brought from the shore of Ross and the hills of Caithness every Southron banner which had disgraced their embattled towers.

Graham was sent for by Wallace to hear these pleasant tidings.

"Ah!" cried Edwin in triumph, "not a spot north of the Forth now remains that does not acknowledge the supremacy of the Scottish lion."

"Nor south of it, either," returned Graham; "from the Mull of Galloway to my gallant father's government on the Tweed; from the Cheviots to the northern ocean, all now is our own."

The private accounts were not less gratifying to Wallace, for he found that his plans for disciplining and bringing the people into order were everywhere adopted, and that in consequence alarm and penury had given way to peace and abundance.   To witness the success of his designs, and to settle a dispute between Lord Ruthven and the Earl of Athol, relative to the government of Perth, Lord Mar strongly urged him to repair immediately to the scene of controversy. "Go," added the earl, "through the Lothians and across the Queensferry, directly into Perthshire.   I would not have you come to Stirling, lest it should be supposed that you are influenced in your judgment either by myself or my wife.   But I think there cannot be a question that Lord Ruthven's services to the great cause invest him with a claim which his opponent does not possess.   Lord Athol has none beyond that of superior rank; but being the near relation of my wife, I believe she is anxious for his elevation.   Therefore, come not near us if you would avoid female importunity, and spare me the pain of hearing what I must condemn."

Wallace now recollected a passage in Lady Mar's letter which, though not speaking out, insinuated how she expected he would decide. She said, "As your interest is mine, my noble friend, all that belongs to me is yours. My kindred are not withheld in the gift my devoted heart bestows on you. Use them as your own; make them bulwarks around your power, the defenders of your rights."

Well pleased to avoid another rencontre with this lady's love and ambition, Wallace sent off the substance of these despatches to Murray; and next morning, taking a tender leave of the venerable Gregory and his family, with Edwin and Sir John Graham he set off for the Frith of Forth.

CHAPTER XLIII.

It was on the eve of St. Nicholas that the boat which contained Wallace drew near to the coast of Fife. A little to the right towered the tremendous precipice of Kinghorn.

"Behold, Edwin," said he, "the cause of all our woe! From those horrible cliffs fell the best of kings, the good Alexander. My father accompanied him in that fatal ride, and was one of the unhappy group to find his mangled body amongst the rocks below."

"I have heard," observed Graham, "that the sage of Ercildown prophesied this calamity to Scotland."

"He did prognosticate," replied Wallace, "that on the eighteenth of April a storm should burst over this land which would lay the country in ruins. Fear seized the farmers, but his prophecy regarded a nobler object than their harvests. The day came, rose unclouded, and continued perfectly serene. Lord March, to whom the seer had presaged the event, at noon reproached him with the unlikeliness of its completion. But even at the moment he was ridiculing the sage, a man on a foaming steed arrived at the gate with tidings that the king had accidentally fallen from the precipice of Kinghorn, and was killed. 'This,' said the Lord of Ercildown, 'is the dreadful tempest which shall long blow calamity and trouble on the realm of Scotland.' And surely his words have been verified; for still the storm rages around our borders."

The regent's arrival soon spread throughout the province, and the hall of the castle was speedily crowded with chieftains come to pay their respects to their benefactor, while grateful peasantry from the hills filled the suburbs of the town, begging for one glance only of their beloved lord. To oblige them, Wallace mounted his horse, and between the Lords Ruthven and Athol, with his bonnet off, rode from the castle to the populace-covered plain which lay to the west of the city. He gratified their affectionate eagerness by this condescension, and received in return the sincere homage of a thousand grateful hearts.

Ruthven beheld this eloquence of nature with sympathetic feelings. Wallace had proved himself not only a warrior but a legislator. In the midst of war he had planted the fruits of peace, and now the olive and the vine waved abundant on every hill.

Different were the thoughts of the gloomy Athol, as he rode by the side of the regent. Could he by a look have blasted those valiant arms, have palsied that youthful head, whose judgment shamed the hoariest temples, gladly would he have made Scotland the sacrifice. Thus did he muse, and thus did envy open a way into his soul for demons to enter.

The issue of Ruthven's claims did not lessen Lord Athol's hatred of the regent. Wallace simply stated the cause to him, only changing the situations of the opponents; he supposed Athol to be in the place of Ruthven, and then asked the frowning earl—if Ruthven had demanded a government which Athol had bravely won, and nobly secured, whether he should deem it just to be sentenced to relinquish it into the hands of his rival? By this question he was forced to decide against himself. He, however, affected to be reconciled to the issue of the affair, and taking a friendly leave of the regent retired to Blair; and there amongst the numerous fortresses which owned his power, he determined to pass his days and nights in devising the sure fall of this proud usurper. For so the bitterness of envy impelled him internally to designate the unpretending Wallace.

Meanwhile the unconscious object of this hatred bade adieu to the warm hospitalities of Hunting-tower, and accompanied by Graham and his young friend Edwin, with a small but faithful train, commenced a journey which he intended should comprehend the circuit of the Highlands.

With the chieftain of almost every castle in his progress he passed a day, and according to the interest which the situation of the surrounding peasantry created in his mind, he lengthened his sojourn. Everywhere he was welcomed with enthusiasm, and he beheld the festivities of Christmas with a delight which recalled past emotions till they wrung his heart.

The hospitable rites of the season being over, the earl accompanied his illustrious guest to make the circuit of Argyleshire. At Castle-Urquhardt they parted, and Wallace, proceeding with his two friends, performed his visits from sea to sea. Having traversed with perfect satisfaction the whole of the northern parts of the kingdom, he returned to Hunting-tower on the very morning that a messenger had reached it from Murray. That vigilant chieftain informed the regent of King Edward's arrival from Flanders, and that he was preparing a large army to march into Scotland.

"We must meet him," cried Wallace, "on his own shores, and so let the horrors attending the seat of war fall on the country whose king would bring desolation to ours."

The word was despatched from chief to chief to call the clans of the Highlands to meet their regent by a certain day in Clydesdale. Wallace himself set forward to summon the strength of the Lowlands, but at Kinclavin castle, on the coast of Fife, he was surprised with another embassy from Edward, a herald, accompanied by that Sir Hugh le de Spencer who had conducted himself so insolently on his first embassage.

On his entering the chamber where the regent sat, the two Englishmen walked forward, but before the herald could pay the customary respects, Le de Spencer advanced to Wallace and, elated at being empowered to insult with impunity, he broke forth: "Sir William Wallace, the contumely with which the ambassadors of Prince Edward were treated is so resented by the King of England that he——"

"Stop, Sir Hugh le de Spencer," cried the herald, touching him with his scepter; "whatever may be the denunciations with which our sovereign has intrusted you, you must allow me to perform my duty before you declare them."

He then addressed Wallace, and in the king's name accusing him of rebellion, promised him pardon for all if he would immediately disband his followers and acknowledge his offense.

Wallace motioned with his hand for his friends to keep silence, for he perceived that the most violent were ready to break forth in defiance of King Edward; and calmly replied to the herald: "When we were desolate your king came to us as a comforter, and he put us in chains. While he was absent I invaded his country as an open enemy. I rifled your barns, but it was to feed a people whom his robberies had left to perish. I leave the people of Northumberland to judge between me and your monarch. And that he never shall be mine, or Scotland's, our deeds shall further prove."

"Vain determination!" exclaimed Le de Spencer. "King Edward comes against you with an army that will reach from sea to sea. The sword and the fire shall make a desert of this land; and your head, proud Scot, shall bleed upon the scaffold."

"He shall first see my fires and meet my sword in his own fields," returned Wallace; "and if God continue my life, I will keep my Easter in England in despite of King Edward and of all who bear armor in his country."

As he spoke he rose from his chair, and bowing his head to the herald, the Scottish marshals conducted the ambassadors from his presence.

Wallace foresaw the heavy tempest to Scotland threatened by these repeated embassies. He perceived that Edward, by sending overtures which he knew could not be accepted, meant to throw the blame of the continuation of hostilities upon the Scots. The same policy was likewise meant to change the aspect of the Scottish cause in the eyes of Philip of France, who had lately sent congratulations to the regent on the victory of Cambus-Kenneth.

To prevent this last inquiry, Wallace despatched a quick-sailing vessel with Sir Alexander Ramsay, to inform King Philip of the particulars of Edward's proposals, and of the consequent continued warfare.

On the twenty-eighth of February Sir William Wallace joined Lord Andrew Murray on Bothwell moor, where he had the happiness of seeing his brave friend again lord of the domains he had so lately lost in the Scottish cause.

A strong force from the Highlands joined the troops from Stirling, and Wallace had the satisfaction of seeing before him thirty thousand well-appointed men eager for the fight. Hardly had he set forth when he was met by a courier from Sir Roger Kirkpatrick with information that the Northumbrians, being apprised of King Edward's approach, were assembling in immense bodies, and had driven Sir Eustace Maxwell with great loss into Carlaveroch; and, though harassed by Kirkpatrick himself, were ravaging the country. The letter of the brave knight added, "These Southron thieves blow the name of Edward before them, and with its sound have spellbound the courage of every soul I meet. Come, then, valiant Wallace, and conjure it down again!"

Wallace made no reply to this message, but proclaiming to his men that the enemy were in Dumfriesshire, every foot was put to the speed, and in a short time they arrived on the summits of the eastern mountains of Clydesdale. His troops halted for rest near the village of Biggar, and it being night, he ascended to the top of the highest craig and lit a fire, whose far-streaming light he hoped would send the news of his approach to Annandale. The air being calm, the signal rose in such a long pyramid of flame that distant shouts of rejoicing were heard breaking the deep silence of the hour. A moment after a hundred answering beacons burnt along the horizon. Torthorald saw the propitious blaze; he showed it to his terrified followers." "Behold that *hill of fire!*" cried he, "and cease to despair."

"Wallace comes!" was their response; "and *we will do or die!*"

Day broke upon Wallace as he crossed the heights of Drumlanrig, and like a torrent he swept the invaders back upon their steps. He took young Percy (leader of this inroad) prisoner, and leaving him shut up in Lochmaben, drove his flying vassals far beyond the borders.

Annandale again free, he went into its various quarters, and summoning the people (who now crept from their caves and woods to shelter under his shield) he reproved them for their cowardice, and showed them that unless every man possess a courage equal to his general he must expect to fall under the yoke of the enemy.

Some looked manfully up at this exhortation, but most hung their heads in shame, while he continued: "Dishonor not your fathers and your trust in God by relying on any one human arm, or doubting that from heaven. Partake my spirit, brethren of Annandale, fight as stoutly over my grave as by my side, or before the year expires you will again be the slaves of Edward."

Such language, while it covered the fugitives with confusion, awoke emulation in all to efface the memory of their disgrace. With augmented forces he therefore marched into Cumberland, and having drawn up his array between a river and a high ground which he covered with archers, he stood prepared to meet the approach of King Edward.

But Edward did not appear till late the next day, and then the Scots descried his legions advancing from the horizon to pitch their vanguard on the plain of Stanmore. Wallace knew that for the first time he was now going to pit his soldiership against that of the greatest general in Christendom.

His present aim was to draw the English towards the Scottish lines, where at certain distances he had dug deep pits, and having covered them lightly with twigs and loose grass, left them as traps for the Southron cavalry, for in cavalry, he was told by his spies, would consist the chief strength of Edward's army. Delay was an advantage to the Scottish regent, and observing that his enemy held back, as if he wished to draw him from his position, he determined not to stir, although he might seem to be struck with awe of so great an adversary. To this end he offered him peace, hoping either to obtain what he asked, or by filling Edward with an idea of his fear, urge him to precipitate himself forward to avoid the dangers of a prolonged sojourn in so barren a country. Instructing his heralds what to say, he sent them on to Roycross, near which the tent of the King of England was pitched. Supposing that his enemy was now at his feet, and ready to beg the terms he had before rejected, Edward admitted the ambassadors, and bade them deliver their message. Without further parley the herald spoke.

"Thus saith Sir William Wallace: 'Were it not that the kings and nobles of the realm of Scotland have ever asked redress of injuries before they sought revenge, you, King of England, and invader of our country, should not now behold orators in your camp persuading concord, but an army in battle array advancing to the onset. Our lord regent being of the ancient opinion of his renowned predecessors, that the greatest victories are never of such advantage to a conqueror as an honorable and bloodless peace, sends to offer this peace to you at the price of restitution. The lives you have rifled from us you cannot restore, but the noble Lord Douglas, whom you now unjustly detain a prisoner, we demand, and that you retract those claims on our monarchy which never had existence till ambition begot them. Grant these just requisitions, and we lay down our arms; but continue to deny them, and our nation is ready to rise to a man, and avenge the injuries we have sustained. For these William Wallace is in arms; but yield us the peace we ask, withdraw from our quarters, relinquish your unjust pretensions, and we shall once more consider Edward of England as the kinsman of Alexander the Third, and his subjects the friends and allies of our realm.'"

Not in the least moved by this address, Edward contemptuously answered, "Intoxicated by success, your leader is vain enough to suppose that he can discomfit the King of England, as he has done his officers, by insolent words; but we are not so weak as to bear argument from a rebel. I come to claim my own; to assert my supremacy over Scotland; and it shall acknowledge its liege lord, or be left a desert, without a living creature to say, 'This was a kingdom.' Depart; this is my answer to you; your leader shall receive his at the point of my lance."

Wallace, who did not expect a more favorable reply, ere his ambassadors returned had marshaled his lines for the onset. Lord Bothwell, with Murray, his valiant son, took the lead on the left wing; Sir Eustace Maxwell and Kirkpatrick commanded on the right. Graham, in whose quick observation and promptitude Wallace placed the first confidence, held the reserve behind the woods; and the regent himself, with Edwin and his brave standard-bearer, occupied the center. Having heard the report of his messengers, he repeated to his troops the answer they had brought, and while he stood at the head of the lines he exhorted them to remember that on that day the eyes of all Scotland would be upon them. They were the first of their country who had gone forth to meet the tyrant in a pitched battle, and in proportion to the danger they confronted would be their meed of glory.

Though affecting to despise his young opponent, Edward was too good a general to contemn an enemy who had so often proved himself worthy of respect; and therefore, by declaring his determination to put all the Scottish chieftains to death and to transfer their estates to his conquering officers, he stimulated their avarice as well as love of fame, and with every passion in arms they rushed to the combat.

Wallace stood unmoved. Not a bow was drawn till the impetuous squadrons, in full charge towards the flanks of the Scots, fell into the pits; then it was that the Highland archers on the hill launched their arrows; the plunging horses were instantly overwhelmed by others, who could not be checked in their career. A confusion ensued so perilous that the king thought it necessary to precipitate himself forward, and in person attack the main body of his adversary, which yet stood inactive. Giving the spur to his charger, he ordered his troops to press on over the struggling heaps before them; and being obeyed, with much difficulty and great loss he passed the first range of pits, but a second and a wider awaited him; and there seeing his men sink into them by squadrons, he beheld the whole army of Wallace close in upon them. Terrific was now the havoc. The very numbers of the Southrons, and the mixed discipline of their army, proved its bane. In the tumult they hardly understood the orders which were given; and some mistaking them, acted so contrary to the intended movements, that Edward, galloping from one end of the field to the other, appeared, regardless of every personal danger, so that he could but fix others to front death with himself. His officers trembled at every step he took, for fear that some of the secret pits should ingulf him. However, the courage of their monarch rallied a part of the distracted army, which, with all the force of desperation, he drove against the center of the Scots. But at this juncture the reserve under Graham, having turned the royal position, charged him in the rear; and the archers redoubling their discharge of artillery, the Flanderkins, who were in the van of Edward, suddenly giving way, the amazed king found himself obliged to retreat or run the risk of being taken. He gave a signal, the first of the kind he had ever sounded in his life, and drawing his English troops around him after much hard fighting fell back in tolerable order beyond the confines of his camp.

The Scots were eager to pursue him, but Wallace checked the motion. "Let us not hunt the lion till he stand at bay," cried he.

"He will retire far enough from the Scottish borders without our leaving this vantage-ground to drive him."

What Wallace said came to pass. Soon no vestige of a Southron soldier but the dead which strewed the road was to be seen from side to side of the wide horizon. The royal camp was immediately seized by the triumphant Scots, and the tent of King Edward, with its costly furniture, was sent to Stirling as a trophy of the victory.

CHAPTER XLIV.

MANY chieftains from the north had drawn to Stirling to be near intelligence from the borders. They were aware that this meeting between Wallace and Edward must be the crisis of their fate. They had seen the prowess of their leader, they had shared the glory of his destiny, and they feared not that Edward would deprive him of one ray. But they who at the utmost wilds of the Highlands had only heard his fame, doubted how his fortunes might stand the shock of Edward's happy star. The lords whom he had released from the Southron prisons were all of the same opinion, for they knew what numbers Edward could bring against the Scottish power, and how hitherto unrivaled was his skill in the field. "Now," thought Lord Badenoch, "will this brave Scot find the difference between fighting with the officers of a king and a king himself!" Full of this idea, and resolving never to fall into the hands of Edward again, he kept a vessel in readiness at the mouth of the Forth to take him, as soon as the news of the regent's defeat should arrive, to a quiet asylum in France.

The meditations of Athol, Buchan, and March were of a different tendency. It was their design on the earliest intimation of such intelligence to set forth and be the first to throw themselves at the feet of Edward, and acknowledge him their sovereign. Thus, with various projects in their heads, which none but the three last breathed to each other, were several hundred expecting chiefs assembled round the Earl of Mar, when Edwin Ruthven, glowing with his general's glory and his own, rushed into the hall, and throwing the royal standard of England on the ground, exclaimed, "There lies the supremacy of King Edward!"

Every man started on his feet. "You do not mean," cried Athol, "that King Edward has been beaten?"—"He has been beaten, and driven off the field," returned Edwin. "These despatches," added he, laying them on the table before his uncle, "will relate every particular. A hard battle our regent fought, for our enemies were numberless; but a thousand good angels were his allies; and Edward himself fled. I saw the king after he had thrice rallied his troops, and brought them to the charge, at last turn and fly. It was at that moment I wounded his standard-bearer and seized this dragon."

Lord Mar, who had stood in speechless gratitude, opened the despatches, and finding a narrative of the battle, with accounts of the previous embassies, he read them aloud. Their contents excited a variety of emotions. When the nobles heard Edward had offered Wallace the crown, and when in the same breath they read that their regent had refused royalty, and was now, as a servant of the people, preparing to strengthen their borders, the most extravagant suspicions awoke in almost every breast. A dead silence reigned, while the demon of hatred was taking possession of the chiefs; and none but the Lords Mar, Badenoch, and Loch-awe escaped the black contagion.

When the meeting broke up, Lord Mar placed himself at the head of the officers of the garrison, and with a herald holding the banner of Edward beneath the colors of Scotland, rode forth to proclaim to the country the decisive victory of its regent. Badenoch and Loch-awe left the hall to hasten with the tidings to Snawdoun. The rest of the chiefs dispersed, but as if actuated by one spirit, they were seen wandering about the outskirts of the town, where they soon drew together in groups and whispered among themselves: "He refused the crown offered to him in the field by the people; he rejected it from Edward because he would reign uncontrolled. If we are to be slaves, let us have a tyrant of our own choosing."

As the trumpets before Lord Mar blew the acclaim of triumph, Athol said to Buchan, "Cousin, that is but the forerunner of what we shall hear to announce the usurpation of this Wallace, and shall we sit tamely by and have our birthright wrested from us by a man of yesterday? No; if the race of Alexander be not to occupy the throne, let us not hesitate between the monarch of a mighty nation and a low-born tyrant!"

Murmurings such as these passing from chief to chief, descended to the minor chieftains. Petty interests extinguished gratitude, and by secret meetings, at the heads of which were Athol, Buchan, and March, a conspiracy was formed to overset the power of Wallace. They were to invite Edward once more to take possession of the kingdom, and meanwhile, to accomplish this with certainty, each chief was to assume a zeal for the regent.

Such suggestions met with full approval from these dark incendiaries, and as their meetings were usually held at night, they walked forth in the day with cheerful countenances and joined the general rejoicing.

They feared to hint even a word of their intentions to Lord Bade-noch, for on Buchan having expressed some discontent to him at the homage that was paid to a man so much their inferior, his answer was, "Had we acted worthy of our birth, Sir William Wallace never could have had the opportunity to rise upon our disgrace; but as it is, we must submit, or bow to treachery instead of virtue." This reply determined them to keep their proceedings secret from him, and also from Lady Mar, for both Lord Buchan and Lord Athol had, at different times, listened to the fond dreams of her love and ambition.

Thus were they situated when the news of Wallace's decisive vic-tory, placing him at the pinnacle of power, determined the dubious to become at once his mortal enemies. Lord Badenoch had listened with a different temper to the first breathings of Lady Mar on her favorite subject, but now he made no hesitation to be the first who should go to Snawdoun to communicate to her the brilliant despatches of the regent, and to declare the freedom of Scotland to be now almost secured. He and Lord Loch-awe set forth, but they had been some time preceded by Edwin.

The moment the countess heard the name of her nephew an-nounced she made a sign for her ladies to withdraw, and starting forward at his entrance, "Speak!" cried she; "tell me, Edwin, is the regent still a conqueror?"—"Where are my mother and Helen," re-plied he, "to share my tidings?"—"Then they are good!" exclaimed Lady Mar, with one of her bewitching smiles. "Ah! you sly one, like your chief you know your power."—"And like him I exercise it," replied he, gaily; "therefore, to keep your ladyship no longer in suspense, here is a letter from the regent himself." He presented it as he spoke, and she, catching it from him, and pressing it rapturously to her lips, eagerly ran over its brief contents. While reperusing it, Lady Ruthven and Helen entered the room. The former hastened forward; the latter trembled as she moved, for she did not yet know the information which her cousin brought. But the first glance of his face told her all was safe, and as he broke from his mother's em-brace to clasp Helen in his arms, she fell upon his neck, and whispered, "Wallace lives? Is well?"—"As you would wish him," answered he; "and with Edward at his feet."—"Thank God, thank God!" While she spoke, Lady Ruthven exclaimed, "But how is our regent? Speak, Edwin!"—"Still the lord of Scotland," answered he; "the puissant Edward has acknowledged the power of Sir William Wallace, and after being beaten on the plain of Stanmore, is now making the best of his way towards his own capital."

"The regent does not mention these matters in his letter to me,"

said Lady Mar, casting an exulting glance over the glowing face of
Helen. But Helen did not notice it, she was listening to Edwin, who
related every particular that had befallen Wallace, from the time of
his rejoining him to that very moment. The countess heard all with
complacency till he mentioned the issue of the conference with
Edward's first ambassadors. "Fool!" exclaimed she to herself, "to
throw away the golden opportunity that may never return." Not observing her disturbance, Edwin went on with his narrative, every word
of which spread the countenance of Helen with admiration.

In such a frame of mind did she listen to the relation of Edwin,
did she welcome the entrance of Badenoch and Loch-awe, and their
encomiums on the lord of her heart. Then sounded the trumpet, and
the herald's voice in the streets proclaimed the victory of the regent.
Lady Mar rushed to the window, as if there she would see himself.
Lady Ruthven followed; and, as the acclamations of the people echoed
through the air, Helen pressed the precious cross of Wallace to her
bosom, and hastily left the room to enjoy the rapture of her thoughts.

In the course of a few days it was announced that the regent was
on his return to Stirling. Lady Mar was not so inebriated with her
hopes as to forget that Helen might traverse the dearest of them
should she again present herself to its object. She therefore hastened
to her when the time of his expected arrival drew near, and putting
on all the matron, affected to give her the counsel of a mother, saying
that she came to advise her, in consideration of what had passed in
the chapel before the regent's departure, not to submit herself to the
observation of so many eyes. Not suspecting the devices which worked
in her stepmother's heart, Helen meekly acquiesced, with the reply,
"I shall obey." But she inwardly thought, "I, who know the heroism
of his soul, need not pageants nor acclamations of the multitude to
tell me what he is."

The "obey" was sufficient for Lady Mar; she had gained her point.
For though she did not seriously think that anything more had passed
between Wallace and Helen than what they had openly declared,
yet she could not but discern the harmony of their minds. Lady Mar
had understanding to perceive his virtues, but they found no answering qualities in her breast. The matchless beauty of his person, the
splendor of his fame, the magnitude of his power,—all united to set
her impassioned and ambitious soul in a blaze. Education had not
given her any principle by which she might have checked the impulse
of her now aroused passions. Brought up as a worshiped object in
the little court of her parents at Kirkwall, in the Orkneys (her father,
the Earl of Strathern, in Scotland, and her mother being a princess

of Norway, whose dowry brought him the sovereignty of those isles), their daughter never knew any law but her own will; and on the loss of that mother, the bereaved daughter fell into such a despair that her father (whose little dominions happened then to be menaced by a descent of the Danes) sought a safe home for his only child by sending her over sea to the protecting care of his friend, the Earl of Mar, and to his lovely countess, then an only three years' wife, with one infant daughter. Though fond of admiration, the young Joanna of Orkney had held herself at too high a price to bestow a thought on the crowd of rough sons of the surge that surrounded her. But when she crossed to the mainland, and found herself by the side of a woman almost as young as herself, and equally beautiful and that the husband of that woman, though of veteran years, was handsomer than any man she had ever seen,—she felt, what she had never done before, that she had met a rival and an object worthy to subdue.

What Joanna began in mere excited vanity, ended in a fatal attachment to the husband of her innocent protectress. And he, alas! betrayed by her overpowering demonstrations of devoted love, was so far won from the propriety of his noble heart as to regard with admiration the beautiful victim of a passion he had so unwittingly raised. In the midst of these scenes, too often acted for his peace, his beloved Isabella, the wife of his bosom, died breathing her last sigh in the birth of a daughter. Scarcely was the countess consigned to her bed of earth, when the desperate Joanna rushed into the weeping husband's presence, fearful of being now reclaimed by her father, who had, only a short while before, intimated his intention to send a vessel for his daughter to bring her back to Kirkwall, there to be united in marriage to the brave native chieftain whose prowess had preserved the island from a Danish yoke. Dreading this event, even while her tears mingled with those of the widowed Mar, she wrought on him by protestations of a devoted love for his two infant orphans (Helen, then a child of hardly two years, and the poor babe whose existence had just cost its mother her life) to rescue her from her now-threatened fate, even to give her his vow to wed her himself. In a sudden agony of self-blame Lord Mar assented to her supplication, that, as soon as propriety would permit, she should become his wife.

The Earl of Strathern arrived himself within the week, to condole with his friend and to take back his daughter, but the scene he met changed his ultimate purpose. Joanna declared that were she to be carried away to marry any man save that friend whose protection during the last six months had been everything to her, she should expire on the threshold of Castle Braemer, for she never would cross it alive!

And as the melancholy widower, but grateful lover, verified his vow to her by repeating it to her father,—within four months from that day the Earl of Mar rejoined the Lady Joanna at Kirkwall, and brought her away as his bride. Soon after her marriage she took the Lady Helen, the supplanted Isabella's first-born daughter, from her grandfather, at Thirlestane, where both children had been left on the departure of their father and his bride for France. Though hardly past the period of absolute childhood, the Lord Soulis at this time offered the young heiress of Mar his hand. The countess had then no interest in wishing the union; having not yet any children of her own to make her jealous for their father's love, she permitted her daughter-in-law to decide as she pleased. A second time he presented himself, and Lady Mar, still indifferent, allowed Helen a second time to refuse him.

Years flew over the heads of the ill-joined pair; but while they whitened the raven locks of the earl, the beauty of his countess blew into fuller luxuriance. Such was her state when she first heard of the rise of Sir William Wallace, and when she thought that her husband might not only lose his life, but risk the forfeiture of his family honors by joining him, for her own sake and for her children, she had then determined, if it were necessary, to make the outlawed chief a sacrifice. To this end she became willing to bribe Soulis's participation by the hand of Helen. She had never felt what real love was, and her vanity being no longer agitated, she now lived tranquilly with Lord Mar. What, then, was her astonishment when she first beheld Sir William Wallace, and found in her breast for him all which she had ever felt for her lord, with the addition of sentiments the existence of which she had never believed! The prolonged life of Lord Mar cost her many tears, for the passions of her nature, which she had laid asleep on her marriage with the earl, broke out with redoubled violence at the sight of Wallace. His was the most perfect of manly forms—and she loved; he was great—and her ambition blazed into an inextinguishable flame. Her husband was abhorred, her infant son forgotten, and nothing but Wallace and a crown could find a place in her thoughts.

The few chieftains who had remained on their estates before the battle of Stanmore from a belief that if the issue proved unfavorable they should be safest amongst their native glens, now came to greet the return of their victorious regent. The ladies brought forth their most splendid apparel; and the houses of Stirling were hung with tapestry, to hail with due respect the benefactor of the land.

At last the hour arrived when a messenger, whom Lord Mar had sent out for the purpose, returned on full speed with information that the regent was passing the Carron. At these tidings the old earl called out his retinue, mounted his coal-black steed, and ordered a sumptuous charger to be caparisoned with housings wrought in gold by the hands of Lady Mar and her ladies. The horse was intended to meet Wallace and to bring him into the city. Edwin led it forward. In the rear of the Earls Mar and Badenoch came all the chieftains of the country in gallant array. Their ladies, on splendid palfreys, followed the superb car of the Countess of Mar, and preceding the multitudes of Stirling left the town a desert. Not a living being seemed now within its walls excepting the Southron prisoners, who had assembled on the top of the citadel to view the return of their conqueror.

Helen remained in Snawdoun, believing that she was the only soul left in that vast palace. The distant murmur of the populace thronging out of the streets towards the carse gradually subsided, and at last she was left in profound silence. "He must be near," thought she; "he whose smile is more precious to me than the adulation of all the world besides now smiles upon every one. All look upon him, all hear him, but I—and I—— Ah, Wallace, did Marion love thee dearer?" As her heart demanded this question, she hid her face in her hands. A pause of a few minutes, and a sound as if the skies were rent tore the air; a noise like the distant roar of the sea succeeded, and soon after the shouts of an approaching multitude shook the palace to its foundations. At this instant every bell in the city began its peals, and the door of Helen's room opened. Lady Ruthven hurried in. "Helen," cried she, "I would not disturb you before, but as you were to be absent, I would not make one in Lady Mar's train, and I come to enjoy with you the return of our beloved regent."

Helen did not speak, but her countenance told her aunt what were the emotions of her heart; and Lady Ruthven, taking her hand, attempted to draw her towards a window which opened on the High street, but Helen begged to be excused. "I hear enough," said she, "my dear aunt. Sights like these overcome me; let me remain where I am."

Lady Ruthven was going to remonstrate when the loud huzzas of the people and soldiers, accompanied by acclamations of "Long live victorious Wallace, our prince and king!" struck Helen back into her seat, and Lady Ruthven, darting towards the window, cried aloud, "He comes, Helen, he comes! His bonnet off his noble brow. Oh, how princely does he look!—and now he bows. Ah, they shower flowers upon him from the houses on each side of the street! Come, Helen, come!"

Helen did not move, but Lady Ruthven, stretching out her arm, in a moment had drawn her within view of Wallace. She saw him attended as a conqueror and a king, but with the eyes of a benefactor and a brother. She drew a quick sigh, and, closing her eyes, dropped against the arras: she distinguished nothing, her senses were in tumult; and had not Lady Ruthven seen her disorder she would have fallen motionless to the floor. The matron was not so forgetful of the feelings of a youthful heart not to have discovered something of what was passing in that of her niece. From the moment in which she had suspected that Wallace had made a serious impression there, she dropped all trifling with his name. And now that she saw the distressing effects of that impression, she took the fainting Helen in her arms, and laying her on a couch, restored her to recollection. When the noise of the populace died away Helen raised her head, and said, with a forced smile, "My more than mother, fear me not! I am grateful to Sir William Wallace; I venerate him as the Southrons do their St. George, but I need not your tender pity." As she spoke her beautiful lip quivered, but her voice was steady. "My sweetest Helen," replied Lady Ruthven, "how can I pity her for whom I hope everything!"—"Hope nothing for me," returned Helen, understanding by her looks what her tongue had left unsaid, "but to see me a vestal here and a saint in heaven."

The holy composure which spread over the countenance of Helen as she uttered this seemed to extend itself to the mind of Lady Ruthven; she pressed her tenderly in her arms, and kissing her, "Gentlest of human beings!" cried she, "whatever be thy lot it must be happy."

Far different were the emotions which agitated the bosoms of every person present at the entry of Sir William Wallace. All but himself regarded it as the triumph of the king of Scotland. And while some of the nobles exulted in their future monarch, the major part felt the demon of envy so possess their souls that they who, before his arrival, were ready to worship his name, now looked on the empire to which he seemed borne on the hearts of the people with a jealousy which from that moment vowed his humiliation or the fall of Scotland.

Those ladies who had not retired from the cavalcade to hail their regent a second time from their windows, preceded him in Lady Mar's train to the hall, where she had caused a sumptuous feast to be spread to greet his arrival. Two seats were placed under a canopy of cloth of gold at the head of the board. The countess stood there in all the splendor of her ideal rank, and would have seated Wallace in the royal chair on her right hand, but he drew back. "I am only a guest in this citadel," returned he, "and it would ill become me to take the place of the master of the banquet." As he spoke he looked on Lord Mar, who without a word took the kingly seat, and so disappointed the countess. By this refusal she still found herself as no more than the governor of Stirling's wife, when she had hoped a compliance with her arrangement would have hinted to all that she was to be the future queen of their acknowledged sovereign.

As the ladies took their seats at the board, Edwin, who stood by the chair of his beloved lord, whispered, "Our Helen is not here."

Lady Mar overheard the name of Helen, but she could not distinguish Wallace's reply, and fearing that some second assignation of more happy termination than that of the chapel might be designed, she determined that if Edwin were to be the bearer of a secret correspondence between the man she loved and the daughter she hated, to deprive them speedily of so ready an assistant.

King Edward

CHAPTER XLV.

BANKS OF THE FORTH.

In collected council the following day the Earl of March made his treacherous request, and Wallace, trusting his vehement oaths of fidelity, granted him charge of the Lothians. The Lords Athol and Buchan were not backward in offering their services to the regent, and the rest of the discontented nobles, with equal deceit, bade him command their lives and fortunes. While asseverations of loyalty filled the walls of the council-hall, and the rejoicings of the people still sounded from without, all spoke of security and confidence to Wallace; and never, perhaps, did he think himself so absolute in the heart of Scotland as at the very moment when three-fourths of its nobility were plotting his destruction.

Lord Loch-awe knew his own influence in the minds of the bravest chieftains, and previous to the regent's appearance in the council-hall he opened his intentions to the assembled lords. Some assented with satisfaction, the rest acquiesced in what they had laid so sure a plan to circumvent.

Wallace soon after entered. Loch-awe rising, stood forth before him, and in a persuasive speech once more declared the wishes of the nation, that he would strike the decisive blow on the pretensions of Edward by himself accepting the crown. The Bishop of Dunkeld, with the most animated devotion to the interest of Scotland, seconded the petition. Mar and Bothwell enforced it. The disaffected lords thought proper to throw in their conjurations also, and every voice but that of Badenoch poured forth entreaties that he, their liberator, would grant the supplication of the nation.

Wallace rose, and every tongue was mute. "My gratitude to Scotland increases with my life, but my answer must still be the same —I cannot be its king."

At these words the venerable Loch-awe threw himself on his knees before him. "In my person," cried he, "see Scotland at your feet! still bleeding with the effects of former struggles. She has no more arguments to utter; these are her prayers, and thus I offer them."

"Kneel not to me, brave Loch-awe!" cried Wallace. "Were I to comply with your wishes I should disobey Him who has hitherto made me His agent. Your rightful king lives; he is an alien from his country, but Heaven may return him to your prayers. My ancestors were ever faithful to the blood of Alexander, and in the same fidelity I will die."

The firmness with which he spoke convinced Loch-awe that he was not to be shaken, and rising from his knee he bowed in silence. March whispered to Buchan, "Behold the hypocrite! But we shall unmask him!"

When the council broke up, these sentiments were disseminated amongst the disaffected throng, and each recess in the woods murmured with seditious meetings. But every lip in the country at large breathed the name of Wallace, while the land that he had blessed bloomed on every hill and valley like a garden.

Stirling now exhibited a constant carnival; peace was in every heart, and joy its companion. As Wallace had commanded in the field he decided in the judgment-hall; and while all his behests were obeyed with a promptitude which kept the machine of state constantly moving in order, his bitterest enemies could not but secretly acknowledge the perfection they were determined to destroy.

The good abbot of Scone was invited from his hermitage, and when he heard from the ambassadors sent to him that the young warrior whom he had entertained was Wallace, he no longer thought of the distant Bruce, but centered every wish for his country in the authority of her deliverer. A few days brought him to Stirling, and wishing to remain near his noble friend, he requested that instead of being restored to Scone he might be installed in the vacant monastery of Cambus-Kenneth. Wallace gladly acquiesced; and the venerable abbot, being told that his late charge, the Lady Helen, was in the palace, went to visit her, and as he communicated his happiness, she rejoiced in the benedictions which he invoked on the head of her almost worshiped sovereign.

During the performance of these things the Countess of Mar was absorbed in the one great object of her passion. Eager to be rid of so dangerous a spy as she deemed Edwin to be, she was laboring day and night to effect his banishment, when an unforeseen circumstance carried him far away. Lord Ruthven, while on an embassy to the Hebrides, fell ill. As his disorder was attended with extreme danger, he sent for his wife; and Edwin, impelled by love for his father and anxiety for his mother, readily left the side of his friend to accompany her to the isles. Lady Mar had now no scrutinizing eye to fear; her nephew Murray was still on duty in Clydesdale; the earl

her husband trusted her implicitly, and Helen, she contrived, should
be as little in her presence as possible.

Busy, then, as this lady was, the enemies of the regent were not
less active in the prosecution of their plans. The Earl of March
had arrived at Dunbar, and having despatched his treasonable proposals to Edward, had received letters from that monarch by sea,
accepting his services, and promising every reward that could satisfy
his ambition. The wary king then told the earl that if he would send
his wife and family to London as hostages for his faith, he was ready
to bring a mighty army to Dunbar, and by that gate once more enter
Scotland. These negotiations from London to Dunbar, and from
Dunbar to the treacherous lords at Stirling, occupied much time, and
the more as great precaution was necessary to escape the vigilant eyes
of Wallace.

From the time that Edward had again entered into terms with
the Scottish chiefs, Lord March sent regular tidings to Lord Soulis
of the progress of their negotiation. He knew that nobleman would
gladly welcome the recall of the King of England. Chagrin at having
lost Helen was not the least of his mortifications, and the wounds he
had received from the hand which had released her were not even
now healed, thus their smart made his vengeance burn the fiercer
against Wallace, who he now learnt was the mysterious agent of her
rescue.

While treason secretly prepared to spring its mine beneath the
feet of the regent, he, unsuspicious that any could be discontented
where all were free and prosperous, thought of no enemy to the fulfilment of his duties but the persecutions of Lady Mar. No day escaped
without bringing him letters either to invite him to Snawdoun, or
to lead her to the citadel where he resided. In every one of these
epistles she declared that it was no longer the wildness of passion which
impelled her to seek his society, but the moderated regard of a friend.
And though aware of all that was behind these asseverations, he
found himself forced at times out of the civility due to her sex to
comply with her invitations.

Things were in this situation when Wallace, one night, received
a hasty summons by a page of Lord Mar's, requesting him to immediately repair to his chamber. Concluding that something alarming
must have happened, he threw on his plaid and entered the apartments
of the governor. Mar met him with a countenance the herald of a
dreadful matter. "What has happened?" inquired Wallace.—"Treason," answered Mar, "but from what point I cannot guess. My
daughter has braved a dark and lonely walk from Snawdoun to bring

the proofs." While speaking he led the chief into the room where Helen sat like some fair specter of the night, her long hair, mingling with the gray folds of the mantle which enveloped her. Wallace hastened forward. She now no longer flitted away, scared from his approach by the frowning glances of her stepmother. Now he beheld her in a presence where he could declare all his gratitude without subjecting her to one harsh word in consequence, and almost forgetting the tidings he had just heard, he remembered only the manner in which she had shielded his life with her arms, and he bent his knee respectfully before her as she rose to his approach. Blushing and silent she extended her hand to him to rise. He pressed it warmly. "Sweet excellence!" said he, "I am happy in this opportunity again to pour out my acknowledgments to you."

"It is my happiness as well as my duty, Sir William Wallace," replied she, "to regard you and my country as one, and that, I hope, will excuse the perhaps rash action of this night." As she spoke, he rose and looked at Lord Mar for explanation.

The earl held a roll of vellum towards him. "This writing," said he, "was found this evening by my daughter. She was enjoying with my wife and other ladies a moonlight walk on the shores of the Forth behind the palace, when, having strayed at some distance from her friends, she saw this packet lying in the path before her as if it had been just dropped. It bore no direction; she therefore opened it, and part of the contents soon told her she must conceal the whole till she could reveal them to me. Not even to my wife did she intrust the dangerous secret, nor would she run any risk by sending it by a messenger. As soon as the family were gone to rest she wrapped herself in her plaid and made her way to me. She gave me the packet. Read it, my friend, and judge if we have not made a critical discovery."

Wallace took the scroll and read it as follows:

"Our trusty fellows will bring you this, and deliver copies of the same to the rest. We shall be with you in four-and-twenty hours after it arrives. The army of our liege lord is now in the Lothians, passing through them under the appellation of succors for the regent from the Hebrides. Keep all safe, and neither himself nor any of his adherents shall have a head on their shoulders by this day week."

Neither superscription, name, nor date was to this letter, but Wallace immediately knew the handwriting to be that of Lord March. "Then we must have traitors even within these walls!" exclaimed Mar; "none but the most powerful chiefs would the proud Cospatrick admit into his conspiracies. And what are we to do? for by to-morrow's evening the army this traitor has let into the heart of the country will be at our gates."

"No!" cried Wallace; "thanks to God and this guardian angel," fervently clasping Helen's hand as he spoke, "we must not be intimidated by treachery! Let us but be faithful to ourselves and all will go well. Sound your bugles, my lord, to summon the heads of our council."

At this command Helen arose, but replaced herself in her chair on Wallace exclaiming, "Stay, Lady Helen; let the sight of such delicacy, braving the terrors of the night to warn betrayed Scotland, nerve every heart with redoubled courage!" Wallace often turned to look on her, while her eyes, unconscious of the admiration which spoke in their beams, followed his god-like figure as it moved through the room.

The Lords Bothwell, Loch-awe, and Badenoch were the first that obeyed the call. They started at sight of Helen, but Wallace in a few words related the cause of her appearance, and the letter was laid before them. All were acquainted with the handwriting of Lord March, and all agreed in attributing to its real motive his solicitude to obtain the command of the Lothians. "What," cried Bothwell, "but to open his castle-gates to the enemy!"

"And to repel him before he reaches ours, my brave chiefs," replied Wallace. "Edward will not make this attempt without tremendous powers. Lose not, then, a moment; even to-night, go out and bring in your followers. I will call up mine from the banks of the Clyde, and be ready to meet him ere he crosses the Carron."

While he gave these orders other nobles thronged in; and Helen, being severally thanked by them all, became so agitated, that, stretching out her hands to Wallace, who was nearest to her, she softly whispered, "Take me hence." He read in her face the oppression her modesty sustained in such a scene, and with faltering steps she leaned upon his arm as he conducted her to an interior chamber. Overcome by the emotions of the last hour, she sank into a chair and burst into tears. Wallace stood near her, and as he looked on her he thought, "If aught on earth ever resembled the beloved of my soul, it is Helen Mar!" She raised her head, she felt that look; it thrilled to her soul. Was she then beloved?

The impression was evanescent. "No, no!" said she to herself; and waving her hand gently, "Leave me, Sir William Wallace. Forgive me, but my frame is weaker than my mind." She spoke this at intervals, and Wallace respectfully touching the hand she extended, pressed it to his breast. "I obey you, dear Lady Helen, and when next we meet, it will, I hope, be to dispel every fear in that gentle bosom." She bowed her head without looking up, and Wallace left the room.

CHAPTER XLVI.

FALKIRK.

BEFORE the sun rose every brave Scot within a few hours' march of Stirling was on the carse, and Lord Andrew Murray, with his Clydesdale men, were already resting on their arms in view of the city walls. The messengers of Wallace had hastened with the speed of the winds east and west, and the noon of the day saw him at the head of thirty thousand men, determined to fight or to die for their country.

The surrounding landscape shone in the brightness of midsummer, for sky and earth bore witness to the luxuriant month of July. The heavens were clear, the waters of the Forth danced in the sunbeams, and the green of the extended plain stretched its borders to the deepening woods. All nature smiled; all seemed in harmony and peace but the breast of man.

When the conspiring lords appeared on the carse, and Mar communicated to them the lately discovered treason, they so well affected surprise at the contents of the scroll that Wallace might not have suspected their connection with it had not Lord Athol declared it altogether a forgery and then added with bitterness, "To gather an army on such authority is ridiculous." While he spoke Wallace regarded him with a look which pierced him to the center, and the blood rushing into his guilty heart, for once in his life he trembled before the eye of man. "Whoever be the degenerate Scot to whom this writing is addressed," said Wallace, "his baseness cannot betray us further. The troops of Scotland are ready to meet the enemy; and woe to the man who that day deserts his country!"—"Amen!" cried Lord Mar, and "Amen!" sounded from every lip.

Badenoch's eye followed that of Wallace, and his suspicions fixed where the regent's fell. For the honor of his blood he forbore to accuse the earl, but he determined to watch his proceedings. However, the hypocrisy of Athol baffled even the penetration of his brother; and on his retiring from the ground to call forth his men for the expedition, he complained to Badenoch of the stigma cast upon their house by the regent's implied charge. "But," said he, "he shall see the honor of the Cummin emblazoned in blood. His pride heeds not where it strikes, and this comes of raising men of low estate to rule over princes."—"His birth is noble, if not royal," replied Baden-och; "and before this the posterity of kings have not disdained to recover their rights by the sword of a brave subject."—"True," an-swered Athol, "but is it customary for princes to allow that subject to sit on their throne? It is nonsense to talk of Wallace having re-fused a coronation. He laughs at the name, but he is absolute and there is no voice in Scotland but his own. Can you behold this, Lord Badenoch, and not find the royal blood of your descent boil in your veins? Humble him, my brother; be faithful to Scotland, but humble its proud dictator!"

Lord Badenoch replied to this exhortation with the tranquillity belonging to his nature. "I see not the least foundation for any of your charges against Sir William Wallace. The nation with one voice made him their regent, and he fulfils the duties of his office with modesty, which I never saw equaled. I dissent from you in all that you have said, and I fear the blandishing arguments of the faithless Cospatrick have persuaded you to embrace his treason. You deny it; that is well. Prove your innocence in the field against Scotland's enemies, and John of Badenoch will then see no cloud to darken the honor of the name of Cummin."

The brothers immediately separated; and Athol, calling his cousin Buchan, arranged a new device to counteract the vigilance of the regent. One of their means was to baffle his measures by stimulating the discontented chiefs to thwart him in every motion. At the head of this last class was John Stewart, Earl of Bute. Aware of the con-sequence Stewart's name would attach to any cause, Athol had gained his ear before he was introduced to the regent; and then poisoned his mind against Wallace.

While Athol marshaled his rebellious ranks, some to follow his treason in the face of day, and others to lurk behind and delude the council left in Stirling, Wallace led forth his royal chiefs to take their stations at the heads of their different clans. Sir Alexander Scrymgeour, with the proudest expectations for Scotland, unfurled his golden standard to the sun. The Lords Loch-awe and Bothwell, with others, rode on to the right of the regent. Lord Andrew Murray, with the brave Sir John Graham, and a bevy of young knights, kept the ground on his left. Wallace looked around; Edwin was far away, and he felt but half-appointed when wanting his youthful sword-bearer.

As the regent moved forward, his heralds blew the trumpets of his approach, and a hundred embattled clans appeared in the midst of the plain awaiting their leaders. Each chief advanced to the head of his line and stood to hear the charge of Wallace.

"Brave Scots!" cried he, "Treachery has admitted the enemy whom Patriotism had driven from our borders. Be steady in your fidelity to Scotland, and you will lay invasion again in the dust!"

The cheers of anticipated victory burst from the soldiers, mingled with the clangor of their striking shields at the voice of their leader. Wallace waved his truncheon to the chiefs to fall back towards their legions, and while some appeared to linger, Athol, armed cap-a-pie, and spurring his roan into the area before the regent, demanded in a haughty tone, "Which of the chiefs now in the field is to lead the vanguard?"

"The regent of Scotland," replied Wallace, for once asserting the majesty of his station; "and you, Lord Athol, with the Lord Buchan, are to defend your country, under the command of the brave head of your house, the Prince Badenoch."

"I stir not from this spot," returned Athol, fiercely striking his lance into its rest, "till I see the honor of my country established by a leader worthy of her rank being placed in her vanguard."

"What he says," cried Buchan, "I second." "And in the same spirit, chieftain of Ellerslie," exclaimed Lord Bute, "do I offer to Scotland myself and my people. Another must lead the van, or I retire from her standard."

"Speak on!" cried Wallace, surprised by this extraordinary attack.

"What these illustrious chiefs have uttered is the voice of us all!" was the general exclamation from a band of warriors who now thronged around the incendiary nobles.

"Your reign is over, proud chieftain!" rejoined Athol. To be thus ridden by a man of vulgar blood, to present him as the head of our nation to the King of England, is beneath the dignity of our country, and I again demand of you to yield the vanguard to one more worthy of the station. Before God and St. Magdalen I swear," added he, holding up his sword to the heavens, "I will not stir an inch this day towards the enemy unless a Cummin or a Stewart leads our army!"

"And is this your resolution also, Lord Bute?" said Wallace, looking on Stewart.

"It is," was the reply; "a foe like Edward ought to be met as becomes a great and independent kingdom. I therefore demand to follow a more illustrious leader to the field."

"The eagles have long enough followed their owl in peacock's feathers," cried Buchan.

"Resign that baton!" cried Athol. "Give place to a more honorable leader," repeated he, supposing that he had intimidated Wallace; but Wallace, raising the visor of his helmet, looked on Athol with all the majesty of his royal soul in his eyes. "Earl," said he, "the voices cf the three estates of Scotland declared me their regent, and God ratified the election by the victories with which he crowned me. If in aught I have betrayed my trust, let the powers which raised me be my accusers. Four pitched battles have I fought, and gained, for this country. Twice I beat the representatives of King Edward on the plains of Scotland, and a few months ago I made him fly before me over the fields of Northumberland. I neither tremble at the name of Edward, nor will I so disgrace my own as to abandon at such a crisis the power with which Scotland has invested me. Whoever chooses to leave the cause of their country, let them go; I remain, and I lead the vanguard. Scotsmen, to your duty!"

As he spoke with a voice of command, several chiefs fell back into their ranks. But some made a retrograde motion towards the town. Lord Bute hardly knew what to think, so was he startled by the appeal of the accused regent and the noble frankness with which he maintained his rights. He stood frowning as Wallace turned to him and said, "Do you, my lord, adhere to these violent men? or am I to consider you a chief still faithful to Scotland? Will you fight her battles?"

"I shall never desert them," replied Stewart; "'tis truth I seek; therefore be it to you, Wallace, this day according to your conscience." Wallace bowed his head and presented him the truncheon, round which his line of battle was wrapped. On opening it, he found that he was appointed to command the third division, Badenoch and Bothwell to the first and second, and Wallace himself to the vanguard.

When the scouts arrived they informed the regent that the English army had advanced near to the boundary of Linlithgow, and, from the rapidity of their march, must be on the Carron the same evening. On this intelligence Wallace put his troops to their speed, and before the sun had declined he was within view of Falkirk. But just as he had crossed the Carron, and the Southron banners appeared in sight, Lord Athol, at the head of his rebellious colleagues, rode up to him. Stewart kept his appointed station, and Badenoch, doing the same, ashamed of his brother's disorder, called after him to keep his line. Regardless of all check, the obstinate chief galloped on, and, extending his bold accomplices across the path of the regent, demanded of him, on the penalty of his life, that moment to relinquish his pretensions to the vanguard.

"I am not come here," replied Wallace, indignantly, "to betray my country. I know you, Lord Athol, and your conduct and mine will this day prove who is most worthy the confidence of Scotland."—"This day," cried Athol, "shall see you lay down the power you have usurped."—"It shall see me maintain it to your confusion," replied Wallace; "and were you not surrounded by Scots of tried worth, I would this moment make you feel the arm of justice. But the foe is in sight; do your duty now, sir earl, and for the sake of the house to which you belong, even this intemperate conduct shall be forgotten." At this instant Sir John Graham, hastening forward, exclaimed, "The Southrons are bearing down upon us!" Athol glanced at their distant host, and turning to Wallace with a sarcastic smile, "My actions," cried he, "shall indeed decide the day," and striking his spurs furiously into his horse he rejoined Lord Badenoch's legion.

Edward did indeed advance in terrible array. Above a hundred thousand men swelled his ranks, and with these were united all whom the influence of the faithless March and the vindictive Soulis could bring into the field.

Wallace had drawn himself up on the ascent of the hill of Falkirk, and planted his archers on an eminence flanked by the legions of Badenoch. Lord Athol, who knew the integrity of his brother, and who cared not in such a cause how he removed an adversary from Edward and a censor from himself, gave an order to one of his emissaries. Accordingly, in the moment when the trumpet of Wallace sounded the charge and the arrows from the hill darkened the air, the virtuous Badenoch was stabbed through the back to the very heart. Athol had placed himself near to watch his purpose; but in the instant the deed was done he threw himself on the perpetrator, and, wounding him in the same vital part, exclaimed, holding up his dagger, "Behold the weapon that has slain the assassin hired by Sir William Wallace! Let us fly from his steel to the shield of a king!"

The men had seen their leader fall; they doubted not the words of his brother, and with a shout, exclaiming, "Whither you lead, we follow!" all at once turned towards him. "Seize the traitor's artillery!" At this command they mounted the hill, and the archers, little expecting an assault from their countrymen, were either instantly cut down or hurried away prisoners by Athol and Buchan, who, now at the head of the whole division of the Cummins, galloped towards the Southrons, and with loud cries of "Long live King Edward!" threw themselves *en masse* into their arms. The firm battalion of the vanguard alone remaining unbroken, stood before the pressing and now victorious thousands of Edward without receding a step. The archers being lost by the treachery of the Cummins, all hope lay on the strength of the spear and sword; and Wallace, standing immovable as the rock of Stirling, saw rank after rank of his infantry mowed down by the Southron arrows, while fast as they fell their comrades closed over them, and still presented the same front of steady valor against the heavy charges of the enemy's horse. The King of England, indignant at this pause in his conquering onset, accompanied by a squadron of resolute knights, in fury threw themselves towards the Scottish pikemen. Wallace descried the jeweled crest of Edward amidst the cloud of battle there, and rushing forward hand to hand engaged the king. Edward knew his adversary, not so much by his snow-white plume as by the prowess of his arm. Twice did the claymore of Wallace strike fire from the steely helmet of the monarch, but at the third stroke the glittering diadem fell in shivers to the ground, and the royal blood of Edward followed the blow. The cry that issued from the Southron troops at this sight again nerved the vengeful Edward, and ordering the signal for his reserve to advance, he renewed the attack, and assaulting Wallace with all the fury of his heart he tore the earth with the trampling of vengeance when he found the phalanx still stood firm. "I will reach him yet!" cried he, and turning to De Valence, he commanded that the new artillery should be called into action. On this order a blast of trumpets in the Southron army blew, and the answering war-wolves it had summoned sent forth showers of red-hot stones into the midst of the Scottish battalions. The field was heaped with dead; the brooks which flowed down the heights ran with blood; but no confusion was there, though, with amazement and horror, Wallace beheld the saltire of Annandale, the banner of Bruce, leading onward the last exterminating division. Scot now contended with Scot, brother with brother. Those valiant spirits, who had left their country twenty years before to accompany their chief to the Holy Land, now reentered Scotland, to wrest from her her liberties. A horrid mingling of tartans with tartans, a tremendous rushing of the flaming artillery, which swept the Scottish ranks like blasting lightning, for a moment seemed to make the reason of their leader stagger. Arrows winged with fire flashed through the air, and, sticking in men and beasts, drove them against each other in maddening pain. Twice was the horse of Wallace shot under him, and on every side were his closest friends wounded and dispersed. But his horror at the scene passed away in the moment of its perception, and though the Southron and the Bruce pressed on him in overwhelming numbers, his few remaining ranks obeyed his call, and with military skill that was exhaustless, he maintained the fight till darkness parted the combatants. When Edward gave command for his troops to rest till morning, Wallace, with the remnant of his faithful band, slowly recrossed the Carron, that they also might repose till dawn should renew the conflict.

Lonely was the sound of his bugle, as he blew its melancholy blast to summon his chiefs around him. Its penetrating voice pierced the hills; but no answering note came upon his ear. A direful conviction seized upon his heart; but they might have fled far distant; he blushed as the thought crossed him, and hopeless again, dropped the horn, which he had raised to blow a second summons. At this instant he saw a shadow darken the moonlight ruins, and Scrymgeour, who had gladly heard his commander's bugle, hastened forward.

"What has been the fate of this dismal day?" asked Wallace, looking onward, as if he expected others to come up. "Where are my friends? Where Graham, Badenoch, and Bothwell? Where all, brave Scrymgeour, that I do not now see?" He rose from his seat at sight of an advancing group. It approached near, and laid the dead body of a warrior down before him. "Thus," cried one of the supporters in stifled sounds, "has my father proved his love for Scotland!" It was Murray who spoke; it was the Earl of Bothwell that lay a breathless corpse at his feet.

"Grievous has been the havoc of Scot on Scot!" cried the intrepid Graham, who had seconded the arm of Murray in the contest for his father's body. "Your steadiness, Sir William Wallace, would have retrieved the day but for the murderer of his country; that Bruce, for whom you refused to be our king, thus destroys her bravest sons. Their blood be on his head!" continued the young chief, extending his martial arms towards heaven!

"My brave friend!" replied Wallace, "his deeds will avenge themselves; he needs no further malediction. Let us rather bless the remains of him who is gone before us to his heavenly rest. Murray, my friend!" cried he to Lord Andrew, "we must not let the brave dead perish in vain. Their monument shall yet be Scotland's liberties. Fear not that we are forsaken because of these traitors; but remember, our time is in the hand of the God of justice!"

Tears were coursing each other down the cheeks of the affectionate son. He could not for some time answer Wallace, but he grasped his hand, and at last rapidly articulated: "Others may have fallen, but not mortally like him. Life may yet be preserved in some of our brave companions. Leave me, then, to mourn my dead alone, and seek ye them."

Wallace saw that filial tenderness yearned to unburden its grief unchecked by observation. He arose, and making a sign to his friends, withdrew towards his men. Then sending Scrymgeour, with a resolute band, across the Carron, to bring in the wounded, he took his lonely course along the northern bank towards a shallow ford, near which he supposed the squadrons of Lord Loch-awe must have fought, and where he hoped to gain accounts of him from some straggling survivor of his clan. When he arrived at a point where the river winds its dark stream beneath impending heights, he blew the Campbell pibroch. The notes reverberated from rock to rock; but, unanswered, died away in distant echoes. Still he would not relinquish hope, and pursuing the path emerged on an open glade. The unobstructed rays of the moon illumined every object. Across the river, at some distance from the bank, a division of the Southron tents whitened the shadows of the woods, and before them, on the blood-stained plain, he thought he descried a solitary warrior. Wallace stopped. The man approached the margin of the stream and looked towards the Scottish chief. The visor of Wallace being up, discovered his heroic countenance bright in the moonbeams, and the majesty of his mien seemed to declare him to the Southron knight to be no other than the regent of Scotland.

"Who art thou?" cried the warrior, with a voice of command that better became his lips than it was adapted to the man whom he addressed.

"The enemy of England!" cried the chief.

"Thou art Wallace," was the immediate reply; "none else dare answer the Lord of Carrick and of Annandale with such haughty boldness."

"Every Scot in this land," returned Wallace, inflamed with indignation, "would thus answer Bruce, not only in reference to England, but to himself! to that Bruce who, not satisfied with having abandoned his people to their enemies, has come to slay his brethren in their home. I come from gazing on the murdered body of the Earl of Bothwell. The Lords Bute and Fyfe, and perhaps Loch-awe, have fallen, and yet do you demand what Scot would dare to tell you that he holds the Earl of Carrick and his coadjutors as his most mortal foes?"

"Ambitious man! I know the motive of all this pretended patriotism, and I came, not to fight the battles of King Edward, but to punish the usurper of the rights of Bruce. I have gained my point. My brave followers slew the Lord of Bothwell; my brave followers made the hitherto invincible Sir William Wallace retreat. I came in the power of my birthright, and, as your lawful king, I command you this hour to lay your sword at my feet. Obey, proud knight, or to-morrow puts you into Edward's hand, and you die the death of a traitor."

"Unhappy prince!" cried Wallace, now suspecting that Bruce had been deceived; "is it over the necks of your most loyal subjects that you would mount your throne? How have you been mistaken! The cause is now, probably, lost forever; and from whom are we to date its ruin but from him to whom the nation looked as to its appointed deliverer?"

"Burden not my name, young man," replied Bruce, "with the charges belonging to your own ambition. Who disturbed the peace in which Scotland reposed after the battle of Dunbar but William Wallace? Who raised the country in arms but William Wallace? Who affected to repel a crown that he might the more certainly fix it on his head, but William Wallace?"

"Shall I answer thee, Lord of Carrick," replied Wallace, "with a similar appeal? Who, when the Southron tyrant preferred a false claim to this realm, subscribed to the falsehood, and by that action did all in his power to make a free people slaves? Who, when cruelty swept this kingdom, lay indolent in the usurper's court and heard of these oppressions without a sigh? Who brought an army into his own inheritance to slay his brethren? Thy heart will tell thee, Bruce, who is this man; and, if honor yet remain in that iron region, thou wilt not disbelieve the asseverations of an honest Scot who proclaims that it was to supply the place of thy desertion that he assumed the rule with which a grateful people invested him."

"Bold chieftain!" exclaimed Bruce, "is it thus you continue to brave your offended prince? But in pity to your youth, in admiration of your prowess I would deign to tell you that in granting the suprem-acy of Edward, the royal Bruce submits not to the dish of a despot, but to the necessity of the times. This is not an era of so great loyalty that any sovereign may venture to contend against such an imperial arm as Edward's. If the love of your country be indeed your motive, your obstinacy tends only to lengthen her misery. But if you carry your views to private aggrandizement, reflect on their probable issue. Should Edward withdraw his armies, and an intoxicated people ele-vate their minion to the throne, the lords of Scotland would reject the bold invasion, and hurl from his height the proud usurper of their rights and mine."

"To usurp any man's rights, and least of all my king's," replied Wallace, "never came within the range of my thoughts. I saw my country made a garrison of Edward's; I beheld its people outraged in every relation that is dear to man. Who heard their cry? Where was Bruce? Where the nobles of Scotland, that none arose to extinguish her burning villages, to shelter the mother and the child, to rescue purity from violation, to defend the bleeding father and his son? The hand of violence fell on my own house—the wife of my bosom was stabbed to the heart by a magistrate of the usurper. I then drew the sword—I took pity on those who suffered, as I had suffered. I espoused their cause; and never will I forsake it till life forsake me. Therefore, that I became the champion of Scotland, Lord of Carrick, blame not my ambition, but chiefly yourself—you, who, uniting personal merit to dignity of descent, had deserted the post which both nature and circumstance called upon you to occupy. If you now start from your delusion, it may not be too late to rescue Scotland from the perils which surround her. Listen, then, to my voice, prince of the blood of Alexander; forswear the tyrant who has cajoled you to this abandonment of your country, and resolve to be her deliverer. Awake to yourself, noble Bruce, and behold what it is that I propose. Heaven itself cannot set a more glorious prize before the eyes of virtue or ambition than to join in one object, the acquisition of royalty with the maintenance of national independence. Such is my last appeal to you."

The truth and gallantry of these sentiments struck the awakened mind of Bruce with the force of conviction. Another auditor was nigh who also lost not a syllable; and the flame was conveyed from the breast of one hero to that of the other.

Lord Carrick secretly repented of all that he had done, but being too proud to acknowledge so much, he briefly answered: "Wallace, your words have made an impression on me that may one day still more brighten the glory of your fame. Be silent respecting this conference; be faithful to the principles you have declared, and ere long you shall hear royally of Bruce." As he spoke he turned away and was lost among the trees.

Wallace stood for some minutes musing on what had passed, when, hearing a footstep behind him, he turned round and beheld approaching him a young and graceful form habited in a white hacqueton wrought in gold, with golden spurs on his feet, and a helmet of the same costly metal on his head crested with white feathers. Had the scene been in Palestine he might have mistaken him for the army's guardian angel. But the moment the eyes of Wallace fell on him, the stranger hastened forward and threw himself on one knee before him with so noble a grace that the chief was lost in wonder what this beautiful apparition could mean. The youth, after an agitated pause, bowing his head, exclaimed: "Pardon this intrusion, bravest of men! I come to offer you my heart, my life! To wash out, by your side, in the blood of the enemies of Scotland, the stigma which now dishonors the name of Bruce!"—"And who are you, noble youth?" cried Wallace, raising him from the ground. "Surely my prayers are at last answered, and I hear these sentiments from one of Alexander's race."

"I am indeed of his blood," replied he; "and it must now be my study to prove my descent by deeds worthy of my ancestor. I am Robert Bruce, the eldest son of the Earl of Carrick and Annandale. Grieving over the slaughter that his valiant arm has made of his own people, he walked out in melancholy. I followed at a distance, and I heard, unseen, all that has passed between you and him. He has retired to his tent, and, unknown to him, I hastened across the Carron, to declare my determination to live for Scotland or to die for her, and to follow the arms of Sir William Wallace till he plants my father in the throne of his ancestors."

"I take you at your word, brave prince," replied the regent, "and this night shall give you an opportunity to redeem to Scotland what your father's sword has this day wrested from her. What I mean to do must be effected in the course of a few hours. That done, it will be prudent for you to return to the Carrick camp, and there take the most effectual means to persuade your father to throw himself at once into the arms of Scotland. The whole nation will then rally round their king, and as his weapon of war, I shall rejoice to fulfil the commission with which God has intrusted me." He then briefly unfolded to the eagerly listening Bruce an attack which he meant to make on the camp of Edward while his victorious troops slept in fancied security.

He had sent Sir John Graham to Stirling to call out its garrison; Ker he had despatched on a similar errand; and expecting that by this time some of the troops would be arrived on the southern extremity of the carse, he threw his plaid over the prince's splendid garb to conceal him from notice; then returning to the few who lay on the northern bank of the river, he asked one of the young Gordons to lend him his armor, saying he had use for it, and to seek another suit in the heap that had been collected from the buried dead. The brave Scot cheerfully acquiesced, and Wallace, retiring amongst the trees with his royal companion, Bruce soon covered his gay hacqueton with this rough mail, and placing the Scottish bonnet on his head, put a large stone into the golden helmet and sunk it in the waters of the Carron. Being thus armed like one of the youthful clansmen in the ranks, Wallace put the trusty claymore of his country into its prince's hand, and clasping him with a hero's warmth to his heart—"Now it is," cried he, "that William Wallace lives anew, since he has seen this hour."

On reemerging from the wood, they met Sir John Graham, who had just arrived with five hundred fugitives from Lord Bute's slaughtered division. He informed his friend that the Earl of Mar was within half a mile of the Carron with three thousand more, and that he would soon be joined by other reenforcements to a similar amount. While Graham yet spoke a squadron of armed men approached from the Forth side. Wallace, advancing towards them, beheld the Bishop of Dunkeld at their head, but with a corselet on his breast, and instead of his crosier he carried a drawn sword. "We come to you, champion of Scotland," cried the prelate, "with the prayers and the arms of the church. In the faith that the God of Justice will go before us this night, we come to fight for Scotland's liberties."

His followers were the younger brethren of the monastery of Cambus-Kenneth, and others from the neighboring convents; altogether making a stout and well-appointed legion.

"With this handful," cried Wallace, "Heaven may find a David who shall yet strike yon Goliath on the forehead."

Lord Mar and Lord Lennox now came up, and Wallace, marshaling his train, found that he had nearly ten thousand men. He gave to each leader his plan of attack, and having placed Bruce with Graham in the van, before he took his station at its head, he retired to visit the mourning solitude of Murray. He found the pious son sitting silent by the side of his dead parent. Without arousing the violence of grief by any reference to the sight before him, Wallace briefly communicated his project. Lord Andrew started on his feet. "I shall again grapple with the foe that has thus bereaved me. This dark mantle," cried he, turning towards the breathless corse and throwing his plaid over it, "will shroud thy hallowed remains till I return. I go where thou wouldst direct me. Oh, my father!" exclaimed he in a burst of grief, "the trumpet shall sound, and thou wilt not hear! But I go to take vengeance for thy blood." So saying he sprang from the place, and accompanying Wallace to the plain, took his station in the silent but swiftly moving army.

CHAPTER XLVII.

CARRON BANKS.

THE troops of King Edward lay overpowered with wine. Elated with victory, they had drunk largely, and the banquet over, a deep sleep lay upon every man. The king himself, whose many thoughts had long kept waking, now fell into a slumber.

Guards had been placed around the camp, more from military ceremony than an idea of their necessity. The strength of Wallace they believed broken, and that they should have nothing to do next morning but to chase him into Stirling and take him there. But the spirit of the regent was not so easily subdued, and now, leading his determined followers, he detached half his force under Mar, to take the Southron camp in the rear, while he should pierce his way to the royal pavilion.

With caution the battalion of Mar wound round the banks of the Forth to reach the point of its destination, and Wallace, proceeding with as noiseless a step, gained the hill which overlooked his sleeping enemies. His front ranks, shrouded by branches they had torn from the trees in Torwood, now stood still. Without this precaution, had any eye looked from the Southron line they must have been perceived; but now, should a hundred gaze on them, their figures were so blended with the adjoining thickets they might easily be mistaken for a part of them. As the moon sank in the horizon they moved gently down the hill, and scarcely drawing breath, were within a few paces of the first outpost when one of the sentinels, starting from his reclining position, exclaimed, "What sound is that?"—"Only the wind amongst the trees," returned his comrade; "I see their branches waving. Let me sleep; for Wallace yet lives, and we may have hot work to-morrow." Wallace did live, and the man slept— to wake no more, for the next instant a Scottish brand was through every Southron heart on the outpost. That done, Wallace threw away his bough, leaped the narrow dyke which lay in front of the camp, and with Bruce and Graham at the head of a chosen band of brave men cautiously proceeded onward to reach the pavilion. At the moment he should blow his bugle, the divisions he had left with

Lennox and Murray and the Lord Mar were to press forward to the same point.

Still all lay in profound repose; and guided by the lamps which burnt around the royal quarters, the dauntless Scots reached the tent. Wallace had already laid his hand upon the curtain that was its entrance, when an armed man demanded, "Who comes here?" The regent's answer laid the man at his feet; but the voice had awakened the ever-watchful king. Perceiving his own danger in the fall of the sentinel, he snatched his sword, and, calling aloud on his sleeping train, sprang from his couch. He was immediately surrounded by half a score knights, who started on their feet before Wallace could reach the spot. Short, however, would have been their protection; they fell before his arm and that of Graham, and left a vacant place, for Edward had disappeared. Foreseeing, from the first prowess of these midnight invaders, the fate of his guards, he had made a timely escape by cutting a passage for himself through the canvas of his tent. Wallace perceived that his prize had eluded his grasp; but hoping to at least drive him from the field, he blew the appointed signal to Mar and Lennox, caught one of the lamps from the monarch's table, and setting fire to the adjoining drapery, rushed from its blazing volumes to meet his brave colleagues. Graham and his followers, with firebrands in their hands, threw conflagration into all parts of the camp, and with the war-cries of their country assailed the terrified enemy from every direction. Men half dressed and unarmed rushed from their tents upon the pikes of their enemies; hundreds fell without striking a blow; and they who were stationed nearest the outposts betook themselves to flight, scattering themselves in throngs over the plains of Linlithgow.

The king in vain sought to rally his men, to remind them of their late victory, but his English alone hearkened to his call. Opposition seemed everywhere abandoned excepting on the spot still maintained by the king and his brave countrymen. The faithless Scots who had followed the Cummins to the field also stood there and fought with desperation. Wallace opposed the despair of his adversaries with the steadiness of his men, and Graham, having seized some of the war-engines, discharged a shower of blazing arrows upon the Southron phalanx.

The camp was now on fire in every direction, and putting all to the hazard of one blow, Edward ordered his men to make at once to the point where, by the light of the flaming tents, he could perceive the waving plumes of Wallace. With his ponderous mace held terribly in the air the king himself bore down to the shock, and, breaking through the intervening combatants, assaulted the chief. The might of ten thousand souls was then in the arm of the regent of Scotland; Edward trembled; his mace was struck from his hand, but immediately a glittering falchion supplied its place, and with recovering presence of mind he renewed the combat.

Meanwhile the young Bruce, who, in his humble armor, might have been passed by as an enemy for meaner swords, checking the onward speed of March, pierced him at once through the heart. "Die, thou disgrace to the name of Scot," cried he, "and with thy blood expunge my stains!" His sword now laid all opposition at his feet; and the outcries of those who were perishing in the flames drove the king's ranks to distraction, and raised so great a fear in the minds of the Cummin clan that they fled in all directions.

Edward saw the Earl of March fall, and finding himself wounded in many places, with a backward step he received the blows of Wallace; but that determined chief, following his advantage, made a stroke at the king which threw him, astounded, into the arms of his followers. The Southron ranks closed immediately before their insensible monarch, and a contest more desperate than any which had preceded it took place. At last the Southrons, having stood their ground till Edward was carried from further danger, suddenly wheeled about and fled precipitately towards the east. Wallace pursued them on full charge, driving them across the lowlands of Linlithgow, where he learned that the Earl of Carrick was in the Lothians, having retreated thither on the first tidings that the Scots had attacked the English camp.

"Now is your time," said Wallace to Bruce, "to rejoin your father. Bring him to Scotland, where a free crown awaits him. Your actions of this night must be a pledge to your country of the virtues which will support his throne."

The younger warrior, throwing off his rugged hauberk in a retired glen, appeared again as a prince, and embracing the regent, "A messenger from myself or from my father," said he, "shall meet you at Stirling. Meanwhile, farewell!"

Bruce mounted the horse Wallace had prepared, and, spurring along the banks of the Almond, was soon lost amidst its luxuriant shades.

Wallace still led the pursuit of Edward, and meeting those auxiliaries from the adjoining counties which his orders had prepared, he drove the flying host of England far into Northumberland. There, checking his triumphant squadrons, he recalled his stragglers, and returned into his own country. At Peebles he was agreeably surprised by the sight of Edwin who, as they continued their route together, inquired the events of the past time, and heard them with wonder, horror, and gratitude. The death of his uncle Bothwell made his heart tremble within him at the thought of how much severer might have been his deprivation. At last he said, "But if my uncle Mar and our brave Graham were in the last conflict, where are they that I do not see them share your victory?"—"I hope," returned Wallace, "that we shall rejoin them in safety at Stirling. Our troops parted in the pursuit, and you see I have none with me now but my own particular followers."

The regent's expectations that he should soon fall in with some of the chasing squadrons were the next morning gratified. Crossing the Bathgate hills, he met the returning battalions of Lennox, with Lord Mar's, and also Sir John Graham's. Lord Lennox was thanked by Wallace for his good services, and immediately despatched to reoccupy his station in Dumbarton. But the captains of Mar and of Graham could give no other account of their leaders than that they saw them last fighting valiantly in the Southron camp, and had since supposed that during the pursuit they must have joined the regent's squadron. A cold dew fell over the limbs of Wallace at these tidings; he looked on Murray and on Edwin. The expression of the former's face told him what were his fears; but Edwin, ever sanguine, strove to encourage the hope that all might yet be well.

These comfortings were soon dispelled by the appearance of Lord Ruthven, who, having been apprised of the regent's approach, came forth to meet him. The pleasure of seeing the earl so far recovered was checked by the first glance of his face, on which was characterized some tale of grief. Edwin, with a cheering voice, exclaimed: "Courage, my father! our regent comes again a conqueror. Edward has once more recrossed the plains of Northumberland."

"Thanks be to God for that!" replied Ruthven; "but what have not these last conflicts cost our country? Lord Mar is wounded unto death, and lies in a chamber next to the yet unburied corses of Lord Bute and the dauntless Graham." Wallace turned pale; a mist passed over his eyes, and staggering, he breathlessly supported himself on the arm of Edwin.

"Lead me to their chambers," cried Wallace. "Show me where my friends lie; let me hear the last prayer for Scotland from the lips of the bravest of her veterans."

Ruthven turned the head of his horse, and as he rode along he informed the regent that Edwin had not left Hunting-tower for the Forth half an hour when an express arrived there from Falkirk.

By it he learned that as soon as the inhabitants of Stirling saw the fire of the Southron camp, they had hastened thither to enjoy the spectacle. Some, bolder than the rest, entered its deserted confines, and amidst the slaughtered near the royal tent one of these visitors thought he distinguished groans. Whether friend or foe, he stooped to render assistance to the sufferer, and soon found it to be Lord Mar. The earl begged to be carried to some shelter, that he might see his wife and daughter before he died. The people drew him out from under his horse, and wrapping him in their plaids, conveyed him to Falkirk, where they lodged him in the convent. "A messenger was instantly despatched to me," continued Ruthven, "and I set out immediately. Many of our fallen nobles, amongst whom was the princely Badenoch, have been conveyed to the cemetery of their ancestors; others are entombed in the church of Falkirk; but the bodies of Sir John Graham and my brother Bothwell," said he in a lower tone, "I have retained till your return."—"You have done right," replied Wallace; and ascending the hills of Falkirk, the venerable walls of its monastery soon presented themselves to his view. He threw himself off his horse and entered, preceded by Lord Ruthven.

He stopped before the cell which contained the dying chief, and desired the abbot to apprise the earl of his arrival. The sound of that voice, whose tones could be matched by none on earth, penetrated to the ear of his almost insensible friend. Mar started from his pillow, and Wallace, through the half-open door, heard him say, "Let him come in, Joanna. All my mortal hopes now hang on him."

Wallace instantly stepped forward, and beheld the veteran stretched on a couch, the image of that death to which he was so rapidly approaching. He hastened towards him, and the dying man, stretching forth his arms, exclaimed, "Come to me, Wallace, my son; the only hope of Scotland, the only human trust of this anxious heart!"

Wallace threw himself on his knees beside him, and taking his hand pressed it in anguish to his lips. Lady Mar sat by her husband, but she bore no marks of the sorrow which convulsed Wallace. She looked serious, but her cheek wore its freshest bloom. She spoke not; and the veteran allowed tears to fall on the bent head of his friend. "Mourn not for me," cried he, "I die, as I have wished, in the field, for Scotland. But, dearest of friends! still the tears will flow; for I leave my children fatherless. And my Helen!—Oh, Wallace! the angel who exposed her precious self, through the dangers of that midnight walk, to save Scotland, her father, and his friends is—lost to us!—Joanna, tell the rest," said he, gasping, "for I cannot."

Wallace turned to Lady Mar with a look of such horror that she found her tongue cleave to the roof of her mouth. "Surely," exclaimed he, "the Lady Helen is not dead?" "No," rejoined the earl; "but——" He could proceed no further, and Lady Mar forced herself to speak. "She has fallen into the hands of the enemy. On my lord's being brought to this place, he sent for myself and Lady Helen, but in passing by Dunipacis an armed squadron issued from behind the mound, and, putting our attendants to flight, carried her off. I escaped hither. The reason of this attack was explained afterwards by one of the Southrons, who said that Lord Aymer de Valence, learning that Lady Helen Mar was to be brought to Falkirk, stationed himself behind Dunipacis, and springing out as soon as our cavalcade was in view, seized her. But as Lord de Valence loves Helen, I cannot doubt he will have sufficient honor not to insult the fame of her family, and so will make her his wife."

"God forbid!" ejaculated Mar, holding up his trembling hands; "God forbid that my blood should ever mingle with that of any one of the people who have wrought such woe to Scotland! Swear to me, valiant Wallace, that you will move heaven and earth to rescue my Helen from the power of this Southron lord!"

"So help me Heaven!" answered Wallace, looking steadfastly upwards. A groan burst from the lips of Lady Mar, and her head sank on the side of the couch. "What? Who is that?" exclaimed Mar, raising his head in alarm from his pillow. "Think of your country, Donald," replied she. "To what do you bind its only defender? Are you not throwing him into the very center of his enemies by making him swear to rescue Helen? Oh, my lord, release Sir William Wallace from a vow that must destroy him!" "Wallace!" cried the now soul-struck earl, "has a father's anxiety asked of you amiss? If so, I dare not accept your vow."—"But I will fulfil it," cried Wallace. "Let thy paternal heart rest in peace and Lady Helen shall again be free in her own country. Edward's legions are far beyond the borders; but wherever this earl may be, yet I will reach him."

Lord Ruthven, followed by Edwin and Murray, entered the room, and the two nephews were holding each a hand of their dying uncle in theirs when Lady Ruthven, who, exhausted with fatigue, had retired an hour before, reappeared at the door of the apartment. She had been informed of the arrival of the regent and her son, and now hastened to give them a sorrowful welcome. "Ah, my lord!"

cried she, as Wallace pressed her matron cheek to his; "this is not as your triumphs are wont to be greeted! You are still a conqueror, and yet death lies all around us. And our Helen, too——" "Shall be restored to you by the blessed aid of Heaven," returned he. "What is yet left for me to do must be done, and then——" He paused, and added, "The time is not far distant, Lady Ruthven, when we shall all meet in the realms to which so many of our dearest have just hastened."

With swimming eyes Edwin drew towards his master. "My uncle would sleep," he said; "he is exhausted, and will recall us when he awakes from rest." The eyes of the veteran were at that moment closed with heavy slumber. Lady Ruthven remained with the countess to watch by him, and Wallace, withdrawing, was followed by Ruthven and the two young men out of the apartment.

Lord Loch-awe, with the Bishop of Dunkeld and other chiefs, lay in different chambers pierced with many wounds, but none so grievous as those of Lord Mar. Wallace visited them all; and having made quarters for his wounded men, at the gloom of evening he returned to Falkirk. He sent Edwin forward to inquire after the repose of his uncle, but on himself reentering the monastery, he requested the abbot to conduct him to the apartment in which the remains of Sir John Graham were deposited. The father obeyed; leading him along a dark passage, he opened a door and discovered the slain hero lying on a bier. Two monks sat at its head, with tapers in their hands. Wallace waved them to withdraw; they set down the lights and departed and he was then alone.

Edwin, having learned from his father that Lord Mar still slept, and being told by the abbot where the regent was, followed him to the consecrated chamber. On entering he perceived him kneeling by the body of his friend. The youth drew near. He loved the brave Graham, and he almost adored Wallace. The scene, therefore, smote upon his heart. He dropped down by the side of the regent and in a convulsive voice exclaimed, "Our friend is gone; but I yet live, and only in your smiles, my brother!" Wallace strained him to his breast; he was silent for some minutes, and then said, "To every dispensation of God I am resigned, my Edwin. While I bow to this stroke, I acknowledge the blessing I still hold in you and Murray." He rose as he spoke, and opening the door, the monks reentered, and placing themselves at the head of the bier, chanted the vesper requiem. When it was ended, Wallace kissed the crucifix they laid on his friend's breast, and left the cell.

CHAPTER XLVIII.

CHURCH OF FALKIRK.

No eye closed that night in the monastery of Falkirk. The Earl of Mar awaked about the twelfth hour, and sent to call Lord Ruth-ven, Sir William Wallace, and his nephews to attend him. As they approached, the priests, who had just anointed his dying head with the sacred unction, drew back. The countess and Lady Ruthven supported his pillow. He smiled as he heard the advancing steps of those so dear to him. "I send for you," said he, "to give you the blessing of a true Scot and a Christian. May all who are here in thy blessed presence, Redeemer of mankind," cried he, looking up with a supernatural brightness in his eye, "die as I do, rather than survive to see Scotland enslaved!" His eyes closed as the conclud-ing word died upon his tongue. Lady Ruthven looked intently on him; she bent her face to his, but he breathed no more; and, with a feeble cry, she fell back in a swoon.

The soul of the veteran earl was indeed fled, and Wallace, Edwin, and Murray remained kneeling around the corse. Anthems for the departed were raised over the body, and when they concluded, the mourners withdrew and separated to their chambers.

By daybreak Wallace met Murray by appointment in the clois-ters. The remains of his beloved father had been brought from Dunipacis to the convent, and Murray now prepared to take them to Bothwell castle, there to be interred in the cemetery of his an-cestors. Wallace entered with him into the solitary court-yard, where the war-carriage stood which was to convey the deceased earl to Clydesdale. Four soldiers of his clan brought the corse of their lord from a cell and laid him on his martial bier. His bed was the sweet heather of Falkirk, spread by the hands of his son. As Wal-lace laid the venerable chief's sword and helmet on his bier, he cov-ered the whole with the flag he had torn from the standard of Eng-land in the last victory. "None other shroud is worthy of thy vir-tues!" cried he; "dying for Scotland, thus let the memorial of her glory be the witness of thine!"

"Oh, my friend!" answered Murray, looking on his chief, "thy gracious spirit can divest even death of its gloom! My father yet lives in his fame!"

"And in a better existence, too," gently replied Wallace, "else the earth's fame were an empty sound."

The solemn procession, with Murray at its head, departed towards the valleys of Clydesdale, and Wallace returned to his chamber. Two hours before noon he was summoned by the tolling of the chapel bell. The Earl of Bute and his dearer friend were to be laid in their last bed. With a spirit that did not murmur he saw the earth closed over both graves; and while he yet lingered beside them, a monk approached him, attended by a shepherd boy. At the sound of steps Wallace looked up. "This young man," said the father, "brings despatches to the lord regent." Wallace rose, and the youth presented his packet. Withdrawing to a little distance, he broke the seal and read to this effect:

"My father and myself are in the castle of Durham, and both under arrest. We are to remain so till our arrival in London renders its sovereign, in his own opinion, more secure. Meanwhile be on your guard: the gold of Edward has found its way into your councils. Beware of them who, with patriotism in their mouths, are purchased to betray you and their country into the hands of your enemy. Truest, noblest of Scots, farewell!

"P.S.—The messenger who takes this is a simple border shepherd; he knows not whence comes the packet; hence he cannot bring an answer."

Wallace closed the letter, and putting gold into the shepherd's hand, left the chapel. In passing through the cloisters he met Ruthven just returned from Stirling, whither he had gone to inform the chiefs of the regent's arrival. "When I summoned them to the council-hall," continued Lord Ruthven, "and told them you had defeated Edward on the Carron, instead of the usual gratulations on such a communication, a low whisper murmured through the hall, and the young Badenoch, unworthy of his patriotic father, rising from his seat, gave utterance to so many invectives against you that I should deem it treason even to repeat them. Suffice it to say, that out of five hundred chiefs and chieftains who were present, not one of them now breathes one word for Sir William Wallace. But this ingratitude I bore with patience, till Badenoch declared that late last night despatches had arrived from the King of France to the regent; and that he (in right of his birth), had put their bearer, Sir Alexander Ramsay, under confinement for having persisted to dispute his authority to withhold them from you."

Wallace, who had listened in silence, drew a deep sigh as Ruthven concluded, and exclaimed, "God must be our fortress still,

Ramsay shall be released, but I must first meet these violent men. And it must be alone, my lord," continued he; "you and our coadjutors may wait my return at the city gates; but the sword of Edward, if need be, shall defend me against his gold." As he spoke he laid his hand on the jeweled weapon which hung at his side, and which he had wrested from that monarch in the last conflict.

Aware that this treason aimed at him would strike his country unless warded off, he took his resolution, and requesting Ruthven not to communicate to any one what had passed, he mounted his horse and struck into the road to Stirling. He took the plume from his crest, and closing his visor, enveloped himself in his plaid, that the people might not know him as he went along, but casting away his cloak, and unclasping his helmet at the door of the keep, he entered the council-hall, openly and abruptly. He bowed to the assembly, and walked with a composed, but severe, air up to his station at the head of the room. Young Badenoch stood there; and as Wallace approached, he fiercely grasped his sword. "Proud upstart!" cried he; "set a foot farther towards this chair, and every man in this council shall fall on you for your presumption!"

"It is not in the arms of thousands to put me from my right," replied Wallace, calmly drawing the regent's chair towards him.

"Will ye bear this?" cried Badenoch, plucking forth his sword. "Is the man to exist who thus braves the assembled lords of Scotland?" While speaking he made a desperate lunge at the regent's breast. Wallace caught the blade in his hand, and wrenching it from his intemperate adversary, broke it into shivers and cast the pieces at his feet; then turning resolutely towards the chiefs, who stood appalled, he said, "I, your duly elected regent, left you only a few days ago to repel the enemy whom the treason of Lord March would have introduced into these very walls. Many brave chiefs followed me to that field, and more, whom I see now, loaded me as I passed, with benedictions. The late Lord Badenoch stood his ground like a true Scot; but Athol and Buchan deserted to Edward." While speaking he turned towards the furious son of Badenoch. "Young chief," cried he, "from their treachery date the fate of your brave father and the whole of our grievous loss of that day. But the wide destruction has been avenged; Edward himself fell wounded by my arm, and was borne by his flying squadrons over the wastes of Northumberland. Thus have I returned to you with my duties achieved in a manner worthy of your regent. What, then, means the arrest of my ambassador? what this silence, when the representative of your power is insulted to your face?"

"They mean," cried Badenoch, "that my words are the utterance of their sentiments."

"Mean they what they will," returned Wallace, "they cannot dispossess me of the rights with which assembled Scotland invested me on the plain of Stirling. And again I demand by what authority do you and they presume to imprison my officer, and withhold from me the papers sent by the king of France to the regent of Scotland?"

"By an authority that we will maintain," replied Badenoch; "by the right of my royal blood, and by the sword of every Scot who spurns the name of Wallace!"—"And as a proof that we speak not more than we act," cried Macdougal of Lorn, making a sign to the chiefs, "you are our prisoner!" Many weapons were instantly unsheathed, and their bearers attempted to lay hands on Wallace; but he, drawing the sword of Edward, with a sweep of his arm that made the glittering blade seem a brand of fire, set his back against the wall and exclaimed, "He that first makes a stroke at me shall find his death on this Southron steel! This sword I made the arm of the usurper yield to me; and this sword shall defend the regent of Scotland."

The chieftains who pressed on him recoiled at these words; but their leaders, Badenoch and Lorn, waved them forward with vehement exhortations. "Desist, young men," continued he; "provoke me not beyond my bearing. With a single blast of my bugle I could surround this building with a band of warriors who at sight of their chief being thus assaulted would lay this tumult in blood. Let me pass, or abide the consequence!"

"Through my breast, then!" exclaimed Badenoch; "for with my consent you pass not here but on your bier. What is in the arm of a single man," cried he to the lords, "that ye cannot fall on him at once and cut him down?"

"I would not hurt a son of the virtuous Badenoch," returned Wallace; "but his life be on your heads," said he, turning to the chiefs, "if one of you point a sword to impede my passage."—"And wilt thou dare it, usurper of my power and honors?" cried Badenoch. "Lorn, stand by your friend! All here who are true to the Cummin and Macdougal hem in the tyrant."

Many a hand now drew forth its dagger, and Badenoch, snatching a sword from one of his accomplices, made another violent plunge at Wallace; but its metal flew in splinters on the guard-stroke of the regent, and left Badenoch at his mercy. "Defend me, chieftains, or I am slain!" cried he. But Wallace did not follow his advantage; with dignity he turned from the vanquished, and casting the enraged Lorn from him, who had thrown himself in his way, he exclaimed, "Scots! that arm will wither which dares to point its steel at me." The crowd, struck in astonishment, parted before him as they would have done in the path of a thunderbolt, and, unimpeded, he passed to the door.

That their regent had entered the keep was soon rumored through the city; and when he appeared from the gate he was hailed by the acclamations of the people. Now it was, when surrounded by the grateful citizens of Stirling, that he blew the summons for his captains. Every man in the keep flew to arms, expecting that Wallace was returning upon them with the host he had threatened. In a few minutes the Lord Ruthven with his brave followers entered the inner ballium gate. Wallace smiled proudly as they drew near. "My lords," said he, "you come to witness the last act of my delegated power. Sir Alexander Scrymgeour, enter into that hall, which was once the seat of council, and tell the violent men who fill it that for the peace of Scotland, which I value more than my life, I allow them to stand unpunished of their offense against me. But the outrage they have committed on the freedom of one of her bravest sons I will not pardon, unless he be immediately set at liberty. Let them deliver to you Sir Alexander Ramsay, and then I permit them to hear my final decision. If they refuse obedience they are all my prisoners."

Eager to open the prison door for his friend Ramsay, and little suspecting to what he was calling the insurgents, Scrymgeour hastened to obey. Lorn and Badenoch gave him a rough reception, uttering such defiance of the regent that the standard-bearer lost all patience, and denounced the immediate deaths of the whole refractory assembly. "The court-yard," cried he, "is armed with thousands of the regent's followers; his foot is on your necks; obey, or this will be a more grievous day for Scotland than even that of Falkirk, for the castle of Stirling will run with Scottish blood." At this menace Badenoch became more enraged, and Scrymgeour, seeing no chance of prevailing by argument, sent a messenger to tell Wallace the result. The regent immediately placed himself at the head of twenty men, and, reentering the keep, went directly to the warder, whom he ordered on his allegiance to the laws to deliver Sir Alexander Ramsay into his hands. He was obeyed, and returned with his recovered chieftain to the platform.

When Wallace looked around him and saw the space before the keep filled with armed men and citizens, he ascended an elevated piece of ground which rose a little to the left, and waving his hand in token that he intended to speak, a profound silence took the place of the buzz of admiration, gratitude, and discontent. He then addressed the people: "Brother soldiers, Friends, and—am I so to distinguish Scots?—Enemies!" At this word a loud cry of "Perish all who are the enemies of our glorious regent!" penetrated to the inmost chambers of the citadel.

Believing that the few of his partizans who had ventured out were falling under the vengeance of Wallace, Badenoch, with a brandished weapon, sallied towards the door; but there he stopped, for he saw his friends standing unmolested.

Wallace proceeded, and with dignity announced the hatred that was now poured upon him by a large part of that nobility who had been so eager to invest him with the high office he then held. "Though they have broken their oaths," cried he, "I have fulfilled mine. They vowed to me all lawful obedience. I swore to free Scotland or to die. Every castle in this realm is restored to its ancient lord; every fortress is filled with a native garrison; the sea is covered with our ships; and the kingdom sits secure behind her well-defended bulwarks. Such have I, through the strength of the Almighty arm, made Scotland. To-day I deliver up my commission, since its design is accomplished. I resign the regency." As he spoke he took off his helmet and stood uncovered before the people.

"No, no!" seemed the voice from every lip; "we will acknowledge no other power, we will obey no other leader."

Wallace expressed his sense of their attachment; but repeating that he had fulfilled the end of his office by setting them free, he explained that his retaining it was no longer necessary. "Should I remain your regent," continued he, "the country would be involved in ruinous dissensions. So I bequeath your liberty to the care of your chiefs. But, should it be again in danger, remember that while life breathes in this heart, the spirit of William Wallace will be with you still."

With these words he descended the mound and mounted his horse, amidst the cries and tears of the populace. They clung to his garments as he rode along; and the women, with their children, throwing themselves on their knees in his path, implored him not to leave them to the inroads of a ravager. Wallace answered their entreaties with encouragement, adding that he was not their prince, to lawfully maintain a disputed power over the legitimate chiefs of the land. "But," he said, "a rightful sovereign may yet be yielded to your prayers; and to procure that blessing, daughters of Scotland, night and day invoke the Giver of every good gift."

When Wallace and his weeping train separated at the foot of

Falkirk hill he was met by his veterans of Lanark, who, having heard of what had passed in the citadel, advanced to him with one voice to declare that they never would fight under any other commander. "Wherever you are, my faithful friends," returned he, "you shall still obey my word." When he entered the monastery, the opposition that was made to his resignation of the regency by the Bishop of Dunkeld, Lord Loch-awe, and others, was so vehement, so persuasive, that had not Wallace been steadily principled not to involve his country in domestic war, he must have yielded to their pleading. But showing to them the public danger attendant on his provoking the wild ambition of the Cummins and their multitudinous adherents, his arguments, which the sober judgments of his friends saw conclusive, at last ended the debate. He then rose, saying, "I have yet to perform my vow to our lamented Mar. I shall seek his daughter, and then, my brave companions, you shall hear of me, and, I trust see me again."

Wallace draws the King's sword

CHAPTER XLIX.

THE MONASTERY.

IT being Lady Ruthven's wish that the remains of her brother should be entombed with his ancestors, preparations were made for the mournful cavalcade to set forth towards Braemar castle. The countess, hoping that Wallace might be induced to accompany them, did not long object to this proposal. At the moment of her husband's death, Lady Mar had felt a shock; but it was not that of sorrow for her loss. Every obstacle between her and Wallace she now believed removed. Her husband was dead; Helen was carried away by a man devotedly enamored of her, and most probably was at that time his wife. She no longer thought of death and judgment, and, under a pretense that her feelings could not bear the sight of her husband's bier, she determined to seclude herself in her own chamber till Wallace's grief for his friend should have passed away. But when she heard from the indignant Edwin of the rebellious conduct of the young Lord Badenoch, and that the regent had abdicated, her consternation superseded all caution. "I will soon humble that proud boy," exclaimed she, "and let him know that in opposing the elevation of Sir William Wallace he treads down his own interest. You are beloved by the regent, Edwin," cried she, clasping his hand with earnestness; "teach his heart the true interests of his country. I am the first woman of the house of Cummin, and is not that family the most powerful in the kingdom? By the adherence of one branch to Edward, the battle of Falkirk was lost; by the rebellion of another, the regent of Scotland is obliged to relinquish that dignity. If Wallace would mingle his blood with theirs, would espouse me, every nerve would then be strained to promote the elevation of their kinswoman. Wallace would reign in Scotland, and the whole land lie at peace."

Edwin eyed her with astonishment while she spoke. All her late conduct to his cousin Helen, to his uncle, and to Wallace was now explained, and he saw in her flushed cheek that it was not the patriot who desired this match, but the enamored woman.

"You do not answer me?" said she; "have you any apprehension that Sir William Wallace would reject the hand which would dispense happiness to many thousand people?"

"No," replied he; "I believe that much as he is devoted to the memory of her whom alone he can ever love, could he purchase happiness to Scotland by the sacrifice, he would espouse any virtuous woman who could bring him so blest a dowry. But in your case, my honored aunt, I can see no probability of such a consequence. In the first place, I know, that, now the Earl of Badenoch is no more, he neither respects nor fears the Cummins, and that he would scorn to purchase even the people's happiness by baseness in himself. Therefore I am sure, if you wish to marry Sir William Wallace, you must not urge the use he may make of the Cummins as an argument. He need not stoop to cajole the men he may command. So, honored lady, believe it no longer necessary to wound your delicacy by offering him a hand which cannot produce the good you meditate."

The complexion of the countess varied a thousand times during this answer. Her reason assented to many parts of it, but the passion she could not acknowledge to her nephew urged her to persist. "You may be right," she replied, "but still, as there is nothing very repugnant in me, the project is surely worth trying. And, sweet Edwin, I must whisper you that your friend will never be happy till he again live in domestic affection."

"Ah! but where is he to find it?" cried Edwin. "What will ever restore his Marion to his arms?"

"I," cried she; "I will be more than ever Marion was to him; she knew not the boundless love that fills my heart for him!" Edwin's blushes at this wild declaration told her how far she had betrayed herself, and covering her face, she exclaimed, "You, who love Sir William Wallace, cannot be surprised that all who adore human excellence should participate in the sentiment. How could I see him, the benefactor of my family, the blessing to all Scotland, and not love him?"

"True," replied Edwin, "but not as a wife would love her husband. And was it possible you could feel thus when my uncle lived, for surely love should not enter a widow's heart at the side of an unburied husband."

"Edwin," replied she, "when you love and struggle with a passion that drinks your very life, you will pity Joanna of Mar, and forgive her."

"I pity you now, aunt," replied he; "but you bewilder me. I cannot understand the possibility of a noble lady suffering any passion of this kind to get such domination over her. If it be virtue that you love in Sir William Wallace, had you not virtue in your husband?"

The countess perceived by the remarks of Edwin that he was deeper read in the human heart than she had suspected; and, therefore, with a blush she replied: "Think for a moment before you condemn me. I acknowledge every good quality that your uncle possessed; but, oh, Edwin! he had frailties that you know not of,—frailties that reduced me to be what the world never saw—the most unhappy of women." Edwin turned pale at this charge against his uncle, but little did he think that the artful woman meant a frailty in which she had equally shared. She proceeded: "I married your uncle when I was a girl, and knew not that I had a heart. I saw Wallace and his virtues stole me from myself. He was reserved during Mar's life, but he did not repulse me with unkindness; I therefore hope, and do you, my Edwin, influence him in my favor, and I will forever bless you."

"Aunt," answered he, looking at her attentively, "can you without displeasure hear me speak a few perhaps ungrateful truths?"

"Say what you will," said she, trembling, "only be my advocate with the noblest of human beings, and I can take naught amiss."

"Lady Mar," resumed he, "I answer you with sincerity, because I love you, and venerate the memory of my uncle, and because I would spare you much future pain, and Sir William Wallace a task that would pierce him to the soul. You confess that he already knows you love him; that he has received such demonstrations with coldness. Recollect what it is you love him for, and then judge if he could do otherwise. Could he approve affections which a wife transferred to him from her husband, and that husband his friend?" —"Ah! but he is now dead!" interrupted she; "that obstacle is removed." "No," replied Edwin, "Wallace never could pledge his faith to one whose passions had so far silenced her sense of duty; and did he even love you, he would not for the empire of the world repose his honor in such keeping."

"Edwin," cried she, at last summoning power to speak, for during this address she had sat gasping from rage; "are you not afraid to breathe all this to me? I have given you my confidence, and do you abuse it?"—"No, my dear aunt," replied he; "I speak the truth to you to prevent you hearing it in perhaps a more painful form from Wallace himself."—"Oh, no!" cried she with haughtiness; "he is a man, and he knows how to pardon the excesses of love! What is there in me, a princess of the crowns of Scotland and of Norway, a woman who has had the nobles of both kingdoms at her feet, that I should now be contemned? You mistake, Edwin; you know not the heart of man."—"Not of the common race of men, perhaps," replied he; "but certainly that of Sir William Wallace. Purity and he are too sincerely one for personal vanity to blind his eyes to the deformity of the passion you describe."

He rose. Lady Mar wrung her hands in conviction that what he said was true. "Then, Edwin, I must despair!" "Penitence," said he, "appeases God, and shall it not find grace with man?"

"Blessed Edwin!" cried she, falling on his neck; "whisper but my penitence to Wallace. Oh! make me that in his eyes which you would wish, and I will adore you on my knees!"

The door opened at this moment and Lord Ruthven entered. The tears she was shedding he attributed to some conversation she might be holding respecting her deceased lord, and taking her hand, he told her he came to propose her removal from the scene of so many horrors. "My dear sister," said he, "I will attend you as far as Perth. After that, Edwin shall be your guard to Braemar, and my Janet will stay with you there till time has softened your griefs." Lady Mar looked at him. "And where will be Sir William Wallace?"— "Here," answered Ruthven. "Some considerations, consequent to his receiving the French despatches, will hold him some time longer south of the Forth." Lady Mar shook her head doubtfully, and reminded him that the chiefs in the citadel had withheld the despatches.

Lord Ruthven then informed her that unknown to Wallace Lord Loch-awe had summoned the most powerful of his friends then near Stirling, and attended by them was carried on a litter into the citadel. It entered the council-hall, and from that bed of honorable wounds he threatened the assembly with instant vengeance from his troops without, unless they would immediately swear fealty to Wallace, and compel Badenoch to give up the French despatches. Violent tumults were the consequence, but Loch-awe's litter being guarded by a double rank of armed chieftains, and the keep being hemmed round by his men, the insurgents at last complied, and forced Badenoch to relinquish the royal packet. This effected, Loch-awe and his train returned to the monastery. Wallace, however, refused to resume the dignity he had resigned. "No," said he to Loch-awe; "it is indeed time that I should sink into the shades, since I am become a word of contention amongst my countrymen."

"He was not to be shaken," continued Ruthven; "but seeing matter in the French despatches that ought to be answered without delay, he yet remains a few days at Falkirk."

"Then we will await him here," cried the countess.

"That cannot be," answered Ruthven; "it would be against ecclesiastical law to detain the sacred dead so long from the grave. Wallace will doubtless visit Braemar; therefore I advise that to-morrow you leave Falkirk."

Edwin seconded this counsel, and fearing to make further opposition, she silently acquiesced, but at night, when she went to her cell, her wakeful fancy aroused a thousand images of alarm. She remembered the vow that Wallace had made—to seek Helen. He had already given up the regency, an office which might have detained him from such a pursuit; and might not a passion softer than indignation against the ungrateful chieftains have dictated this act? Racked by jealousy, she rose from her bed and paced the room in wild disorder. All Edwin's admonitions were forgotten; and forgetful of her rank and sex, she determined to see Wallace, and appeal to his heart for the last time. She knew that he slept in an apartment at the other end of the monastery; and that she might pass thither unobserved, she glided into an opposite cell belonging to a sick monk, and stealing away his cloak, threw it over her and hurried along the cloisters.

The chapel doors were open. In passing, she saw the bier of her lord awaiting the hour of its removal, surrounded by priests singing anthems for the repose of his soul, but no tender recollections knocked at the heart of Lady Mar as she sped along.

His door was fastened with a latch; she gently opened it, and found herself in his chamber. She trembled, she looked around, but he was not there. Disappointment palsied her, and she sank upon a chair. "Am I betrayed?" said she to herself. "Has that youthful hypocrite warned him hence?" And then again she thought, "But how should Edwin guess that I should venture here?"

She now determined to await his return, and nearly three hours she passed there, but he appeared not. At last, hearing the matin-bell, she started up, fearful that her maids might discover her absence, and once more crossed the cloisters. While again drawing towards the chapel, she saw Wallace himself issue from the door, supporting on his bosom the fainting head of Lady Ruthven. Edwin followed them. Lady Mar pulled the monk's cowl over her face and withdrew behind a pillar. "Ah!" thought she, "absenting myself from my duty, I fled from thee!" She listened with breathless attention to what might be said.

Lord Ruthven met them at that instant. "This night's watching by the bier of her brother," said Wallace, "has worn out your lady; we strove to support her through these vigils, but at last she sank." What Ruthven said in reply when he took his wife in his arms, the countess could not hear; but Wallace answered, "I have not seen her."—"I left her late in the evening drowned in tears," replied Ruthven; "I therefore suppose that in secret she offers those prayers for her husband which my tender Janet pours over his grave."

"Such tears," replied Wallace, "are Heaven's own balm. I know they purify the heart whence they flow."

Lady Mar heard, and while she contemplated the matchless form before her she exclaimed to herself, "Why is it animated by as fault-less a soul? O Wallace! wert thou less excellent, I might hope!" She tore her eyes from a view which blasted while it charmed her, and rushed from the cloisters.

CHAPTER L.

DURHAM.

THE sun rose as the funeral procession of the Earl of Mar left the monastery at Falkirk. Lord Ruthven and Edwin mounted their horses. The maids of the two ladies led them forth towards the litters which were to convey them on so long a journey. Lady Ruthven came first, and Wallace placed her tenderly in her carriage. The countess next appeared, clad in the weeds of widowhood. Lord Ruthven then rode up to bid adieu to his friend, and the litters moved on, Wallace promising that both he and Edwin should hear of him in the course of a few days.

Hear of him they should, but not see him; for it was his determination to set off that night for Durham, where, he was informed, Edward now lay, and, joined by his young queen, meant to sojourn till his wounds were healed. Believing that his presence in Scotland could be no longer serviceable, Wallace did not hesitate in fixing his course. His first object was to fulfil his vow to Lord Mar. He thought it probable that Helen might have been carried to the English court, and that in seeking her he might also attempt an interview with young Bruce, hoping to learn how far he had succeeded in persuading his father to resume the scepter of his ancestors.

To effect his plan without hindrance, Wallace retired to his apartment to address a letter to Lord Ruthven. In this epistle he told the chief that he was going on an expedition which he hoped would prove beneficial to his country; but as it was an enterprise of rashness he would not make any one his companion; all the brother was in his letter to Edwin, conjuring him to prove his affection for his friend by abiding at home till they should meet again in Scotland.

He wrote to Andrew Murray (now Lord Bothwell), addressing him as the first of his compatriots who had struck a blow for Scotland and confiding to his care the valiant troop which had followed him from Lanark. "Tell them," said he, "that in obeying you they still serve with me; they perform their duty to Scotland at home— I abroad."

These letters he enclosed in one to Scrymgeour, with orders to despatch two of them according to their directions; but that to Murray, Scrymgeour was himself to deliver at the head of the **Lanark** veterans.

At the approach of twilight Wallace quitted the monastery, leaving his packet with the porter to present to Scrymgeour when he should arrive at his usual hour. As the chief meant to assume a border-minstrel's garb, that he might travel the country unrecognized, he took his way towards a large hollow oak in Torwood, where he had deposited his means of disguise. When arrived there, he disarmed himself of all but his sword, dirk, and breastplate; he covered his tartan with a minstrel's cassock, and staining his bright complexion with the juice of a nut, concealed his brighter locks beneath a close bonnet. Being thus equipped he threw his harp over his shoulder, and having first in that deep solitude invoked a blessing on his enterprise, he pursued his way along the broom-clad hills of Muiravenside.

Not a human creature crossed his path till the carol of the lark summoned the husbandman to his toil, and spread the thymy hills and daisied pastures with herds and flocks. He stopped at a little moss-covered cabin, on a burnside, and was hospitably entertained by its simple inhabitants. Wallace repaid their kindness with a few ballads, which he sang, accompanied by his harp. As he gave the last notes of "King Arthur's Death in Glory," the worthy cotter raised his head from the spade on which he leaned, and asked whether he could not sing of Wallace, the glory of Scotland. The wife and the children, who clung around their visitant, joined in this request. Wallace rose with a saddened smile and replied, "I cannot do what you require, but I can yield you an opportunity to oblige your hero. Will you take a letter from him, of which I am the bearer, to Lord Dundaff, at Berwick? It is to reveal to a father's heart the death of a son for whom Scotland must mourn to her latest generations."

The honest shepherd respectfully accepted this mission, and his wife, loading their guest's scrip with her choicest fruits and cakes, accompanied him, followed by the children, to the bottom of the hill.

In this manner, sitting at the board of the lowly, and sleeping beneath the thatched roof, did Wallace pursue his way through Tweedale and Ettrick forest, till he reached the Cheviots. From every lip he heard his own praises; heard them with redoubled satisfaction, for he could have no suspicion of their sincerity.

Late one evening he arrived on the banks of the river that surrounds the city of Durham. His minstrel garb prevented his being stopped by the guard at the gate; but as he entered its porch, a horse that was going through started at his abrupt appearance. Its rider suddenly exclaimed, "Fool, thou dost not see Sir William Wallace!" Then turning to the disguised knight, "Harper," cried he, "you frighten my steed, draw back till I pass." Not displeased to find the terror of him so great amongst the enemies of Scotland that they even addressed their animals as sharers in the dread, Wallace stood out of the way, and saw the speaker to be a young Southron knight, who with difficulty kept his seat on the restive horse. Rearing and plunging, it would have thrown its rider had not Wallace put forth his hand and seized the bridle. By his assistance the animal was soothed, and the young lord, thanking him for his service, told him that as a reward he would introduce him to play before the queen, who that day held a feast at the bishop's palace. Wallace thought it probable he might see or hear of Lady Helen in this assembly, or find access to Bruce, and he gladly accepted the offer. The knight, who was Sir Piers Gaveston, ordering him to follow, turned his horse towards the city, and conducted Wallace through the gates of the citadel to the palace within its walls.

On entering the banqueting-hall he was placed by the knight in the musicians' gallery, there to await his summons to her majesty. The entertainment being spread, and the room full of guests, the queen was led in by the haughty bishop of the see, the king being too ill of his wounds to allow his joining so large a company. The beauty of the lovely sister of Philip le Bel seemed to fill the gaze of all the bystanders, and none appeared to remember that Edward was absent. Wallace hardly glanced on her youthful charms; his eyes roamed from side to side in quest of a dearer object,—the captive daughter of his dead friend. She was not there, neither was De Valence; but Buchan, Athol, and Soulis were near the royal Margaret, in all the pomp of feudal grandeur.

Immediately on the royal band ceasing to play, Gaveston pressed towards the queen, and told her he had presumed to introduce a traveling minstrel into the gallery, hoping that she would order him to perform for her, as he could sing legends from the descent of the Romans to the victories of her royal Edward. With all her age's eagerness in quest of novelties, she commanded him to be brought to her.

Gaveston having presented him, Wallace bowed with the respect due to her sex and dignity, and to the esteem in which he held the character of her royal brother. Margaret desired him to place his harp before her, and begin to sing. As he knelt on one knee, and struck its sounding chords, she stopped him by the inquiry of whence

he came. "From the north country," was his reply. "Were you ever
in Scotland?" asked she. "Many times."

The young lords crowded round to hear this dialogue between
majesty and lowliness. She smiled and turned towards them. "Do
not accuse me of disloyalty, but I have a curiosity to ask another
question.—Tell me," cried she, "for you wandering minstrels see all
great people, good or bad, did you ever see Sir William Wallace in
your travels?"—"Often, madam."—"Pray tell me what he is like;
you probably will be unprejudiced, and that is what I can hardly
expect in this case from any of these brave lords." Wishing to avoid
further questioning, Wallace replied, "I have never seen him so distinctly as to be enabled to give any opinion."—"Cannot you sing me
some ballad about him?" inquired she, laughing; "and if you are a
little poetical in your praise, I can excuse you, for my royal brother
thinks this bold Scot would have shone brightly in a fairer cause."—
"My songs are dedicated to glory set in the grave," returned Wallace: "therefore Sir William Wallace's faults or virtues will not be
sung by me."—"Then he is a very young man, I suppose, for you
are not old, and yet you speak of not surviving him? I was in hopes,"
cried she, addressing Bishop Beck, "that the king would have brought
this Wallace to have supped with me here; but for once rebellion
overcame its master."

Beck made some reply which Wallace did not hear, and the queen,
again turning to him, resumed, "Minstrel, we French ladies are very
fond of a good mien, and I shall be a little reconciled to your northern
realms if you tell me this Sir William Wallace is anything like
as handsome as some of the gay knights by whom you see me surrounded." Wallace smiled, and replied, "The comeliness of Sir
William Wallace lies in a strong arm and a feeling heart; and if these
be charms in the eyes of female goodness, he may hope not to be
an object of abhorrence to the sister of Philip le Bel." The minstrel
bowed as he spoke, and the young queen, laughing again, said, "I
wish not to come within the influence of either. But sing me some
Scottish legend, and I will promise wherever I see the knight to treat
him with all courtesy."

Wallace again struck the chords of his harp, and sang the triumphs
of Reuther, the Scottish prince. The queen fixed her eyes upon him,
and when he ended she turned and whispered to Gaveston, "If the
voice of this man had been Wallace's trumpet, I should not now
wonder at the discomfiture of England." Speaking, she rose, and
presenting a jeweled ring to the minstrel, left the apartment.

The lords crowded out after her, and the musicians coming down from the gallery, seated themselves with much rude jollity to regale on the remnants of the feast. Wallace, who had discovered the bard of Bruce by the escutcheon of Annandale suspended at his neck, gladly saw him approach. He came to invite the stranger minstrel to partake of their fare. Wallace did not appear to decline it, and as the court bard seemed rather devoted to the pleasures of wine, he found it not difficult to draw from him what he wanted to know. He learnt that young Bruce was still in the castle under arrest; "and," added the bard, "I shall be obliged, in the course of half an hour, to relinquish these festivities for the gloomy duties of his apartment."

This was precisely the point to which Wallace had wished to lead him, and pleading disrelish of wine, he offered to supply his place in the earl's chamber. The half-intoxicated bard accepted the proposition with eagerness, and as the shades of night had long closed in, he conducted his illustrious substitute to the large round tower of the castle, informing him that he must continue playing in a recess adjoining to Bruce's room till the last vesper bell from the abbey in the neighborhood should give the signal for his laying aside the harp. By that time the earl would be fallen asleep, and he might then lie down on a pallet he would find in the recess.

All this Wallace promised punctually to obey, and being conducted up a spiral staircase was left in a little anteroom. The chief drew the cowl of his minstrel cloak over his face and set his harp before him in order to play. He could see through its strings that a group of knights were in earnest conversation at the further end of the apartment, but they spoke so low he could not distinguish what was said. One of the party turned round, and the light of a suspended lamp discovered him to be the brave Earl of Gloucester, whom Wallace had taken and released at Berwick. The same ray showed another to be Percy, Earl of Northumberland. Wallace found the strangeness of his situation. He, the conqueror of Edward, had been singing as a mendicant in his halls; and having given laws to the two great men before him, he now sat in their view unobserved and unfeared. Their figures concealed that of Bruce; but at last, when all rose together, he heard Gloucester say in rather an elevated voice, "Keep up your spirits. It cannot be long before King Edward discovers the motives of their accusation, and his noble nature will acquit you accordingly."

"My acquittal," replied Bruce, in a firm tone, "cannot restore what Edward's injustice has rifled from me. Your king may depend upon it," added he, with a sarcastic smile, "that I am not a man to be influenced against the right. Where I owe duty I will pay it to the utmost farthing."

Not apprehending the true meaning of this speech, Percy immediately answered, "I believe you, and so must all the world, for did you not give proofs of it that night on the Carron in bearing arms against the triumphant Wallace?"—"I did indeed give proofs of it," returned Bruce, "which I hope the world will one day know, by bearing arms against the usurper of my country's rights; and before men and angels I swear," cried he, "to perform my duty to the end, to retrieve the insulted name of Bruce!"

The two earls fell back before this burst from the soul of Bruce, and Wallace caught a glimpse of his youthful form, which stood preeminent between the Southron lords.

Gloucester, as little as Northumberland, comprehending Bruce's ambiguous declaration, replied, "Let not your heart, my brave friend, burn too hotly against the king for this arrest. He will be the more urgent to obliterate by kindness this injustice when he understands the aim of the Cummins. Good-night, Bruce. May propitious dreams repeat the augury of your true friends!" Percy shook hands with the young earl, and the two English lords left the room.

Wallace could now take a more leisurely survey of Bruce. He no longer wore the gay embroidered hacqueton; his tunic was black velvet, and all the rest of his garments accorded with the same mourning hue. Soon after the lords had quitted him the elasticity of his figure, which before seemed ready to rise from the earth, gave way to melancholy retrospections, and he threw himself into a chair with his eyes fixed in musing gaze upon the floor. It was now that Wallace touched the strings of his harp. The "Death of Cuthullin" wailed from the sounding notes, but Bruce heard as though he heard them not. His posture remained the same, and sigh after sigh gave the only response to the strains of the bard.

Wallace grew impatient for the chimes of that vesper-bell which, by assuring Bruce's attendants that he was gone to rest, would secure from interruption the conference he meditated. Two servants entered. Bruce scarcely looking up bade them withdraw; he did not know when he should go to bed, and he desired to be no further disturbed. The men obeyed, and Wallace changing the melancholy strain of his harp, struck the chords to the proud triumph he had played in the hall. Not one note of either ballad had he yet sung to Bruce, but when he came to the passage in the latter appropriated to these lines,—

"Arise, glory of Albin, from thy cloud,
And shine upon thy own!"

he could not forbear giving the words voice. Bruce started from his
seat. He looked towards the minstrel—he walked the room in great
disorder. Wallace slowly advanced from the recess. The agitated
Bruce, accidentally raising his head, beheld a man in a minstrel's
garb, much too tall to be his bard, approaching him with a caution
which he thought portended treachery. He sprang on his feet and
caught his sword from the table, but in that moment Wallace threw
off his cowl. Bruce stood gazing on him, stiffened with astonishment. Wallace, in a low voice, exclaimed, "My prince! do you not
know me?" Bruce, without speaking, threw his arms about his neck.
As Wallace returned the fond embrace he gently said, "How is it that
I not only see you a close prisoner, but in these weeds?" Bruce at
last forced himself to articulate: "I have known misery in all its
forms since we parted, but I have not power to name my griefs,
while trembling at the peril to which you have exposed yourself by
seeking me. I am surrounded by spies, and should you be discovered,
Robert Bruce will then have the curses of his country added to the
judgments which already have fallen on his head." As he spoke they
sat down together, and he continued: "Before I answer your questions, tell me what cause could bring you to seek the alien Bruce in
prison, and by what stratagem you came in this disguise into my
apartment."

Wallace briefly related the events which had sent him from Scotland, his rencounter with Piers Gaveston, and his arrangement with
the bard. To the first part of the narrative Bruce listened with indignation. "I knew," exclaimed he, "that Athol and Buchan had
left in Scotland some dregs of their own refractory spirits; but I could
not have guessed that envy had so obliterated gratitude in the hearts
of my countrymen. The wolves have now driven the shepherd from
the fold," cried he, "and the flock will soon be devoured."

Wallace recapitulated his reasons for having refrained from
forcing the obedience of the young Lord Badenoch and his adherents.
Bruce acknowledged the wisdom of this conduct, but could not restrain his animadversions on the characters of the Cummins. He told
Wallace that he had met the two sons of the late Lord Badenoch in
Guienne; that James, who now pretended such resentment of his
father's death, had ever been a rebellious son. John, who yet remained in France, appeared of a less violent temper; "but," added
the prince, "I have been taught by one who will never counsel me
more, that all the Cummins, male and female, would be ready at any

time to sacrifice earth and heaven to their ambition. It is to Buchan and Athol that I owe my prolonged confinement, and to them I may date the premature death of my father."

The start of Wallace declared his shock at this information. "How!" exclaimed he, "the Earl of Carrick dead?" The emotions of his soul would not allow him to proceed, and Bruce resumed: "It is for him I wear these sable garments,—poor emblems of the mournings of my soul; mournings not so much for his loss, but because he lived not to let the world know what he really was. There, Wallace, is the bitterness of this cup to me!"

"But can you not sweeten it, my dear prince," cried Wallace, "by retrieving all that he was cut off from redeeming? To open the way to you I come."—"And I will enter where you point," returned Bruce; "but heavy is my woe, that, knowing the same spirit was in my father's bosom, he should be torn from the opportunity to make it manifest."

Bruce now proceeded to narrate to Wallace the particulars of his father's meeting with the king at Durham. Instead of that monarch receiving the Earl of Carrick with his wonted welcome, he turned coldly from him when he approached, and suffered him to take his usual seat at the royal table without deigning him the slightest notice. Young Bruce was absent from the banquet, having determined never to mingle again in social communion with the man whom he now regarded as the usurper of his father's rights. The insolent Buchan seized a pause in the conversation that he might draw the attention of all present to the disgrace of the chief, and said with affected carelessness, "My Lord of Carrick, to-day you dine with clean hands; the last time I saw you at meat they were garnished with your own blood." The earl turned on him a look which asked him to explain. Lord Buchan laughed and continued, "When we last met at table was it not in his majesty's tent after the victory at Falkirk? You were then red from the slaughter of those people to whom I understand you now give the appellation of sons. Having recognized the relationship, it was not probable we should again see your hands in their former brave livery, and their present pallid hue convinces more than myself of the truth of our information."

"And me," cried Edward, rising on the couch to which his wounds confined him, "that I have discovered a traitor! You fled, Lord Carrick, at the first attack which the Scots made on my camp, and you drew thousands after you. I know you too well to believe that cowardice impelled the motion. It was treachery to your friend and king, and you shall feel the weight of his resentment!"—"To this hour, King Edward," replied the earl, starting from his chair, "I have been more faithful to you than my country or my God. How often have you pledged yourself that you fought in Scotland only for my advantage! I gave my faith and my power to you; and how often have you promised, after the next successful battle, to restore me to the crown of my ancestors! I still believed you, and engaged all who yet acknowledged the influence of Bruce to support your name in Scotland. Was not such the promise by which you allured me to the field of Falkirk? And when I had covered myself, as the Lord Buchan too truly says, with the blood of my children; when I asked my friend for the crown I had served for, what was his answer? 'Have I naught to do but to win kingdoms to make gifts of?' Thus, then, did a king, a friend, break his often-repeated word!"

Edward, who had been prepared by the Cummins to discredit all that Carrick might say in his defense, turned with a look of contempt towards him, and said, "You speak like a madman; and as maniacs both yourself and your son shall be guarded till I have leisure to consider any evidence you may offer in your vindication."—"And is this the manner, King Edward, that you treat your friend, once your preserver?"—"The vassal," replied Edward, "who presumes upon the condescension of his prince, and acts as if he were his equal, ought to meet the punishment due to such arrogance. You saved my life on the walls of Acre, but you owed that duty to the son of your liege lord. In the fervor of youth I rewarded you with my friendship, and the return is treason." As he concluded he turned from Lord Carrick, and the marshals immediately seizing the earl took him to the keep of the castle.*

His son, who had been sought in the Carrick quarters and laid under an arrest, met his father in the guard-chamber. Carrick could not speak, but motioning to be conducted to the place appointed for his prison, the men, with equal silence, led him through a range of apartments, and stopping in the farthest left him there with his son. Bruce was not surprised at his own arrest, but at that of his father he stood in speechless astonishment until the guards withdrew; then seeing Lord Carrick, with a changing countenance, throw himself on the bed, he exclaimed, "What is the meaning of this, my father? Has any charge against me brought suspicion on you?"—"No, Robert," replied the earl; "it is I who have brought you into this prison, and into disgrace with all the world, for having surrendered my inheritance to the invader of my country. You are implicated in my crime, and

---

* These speeches are historically true, as is also Edward's after-treatment of the Earl of Carrick.

for not joining the Southrons to repel the Scots from the royal camp we are both prisoners."

"Then," replied Bruce, "Edward shall feel that you have a son who has virtue to be what he suspects, and from this hour I proclaim eternal enmity to the betrayer of my father."

Carrick gazed on him with pride, and, sighing heavily, called him to approach him. "Come to me, my Robert," said he, "and abide by the last injunctions of your father, for from this bed I may never rise. A too late sense of the injuries my sanction has doubled on the people I was born to protect, and the ingratitude of him for whom I have offended my God and wronged my country, have broken my heart. I shall die, Robert, but you will avenge me."—"May God so prosper me!" cried Bruce, raising his arms to heaven. Carrick resumed: "Attend to me, my dear son, and do not mistake the nature of my last wish. Do not allow the words I have used to hurry you into any personal revenge on Edward. Pierce him on the side of his ambition; there he is vulnerable, and there you will heal while you wound. This would be my revenge, dear Robert: that you should one day have his life in your power; and in memory of what I now say, spare it. Let your aim be the recovery of the kingdom which Edward rifled from your fathers. Join the triumphant Wallace. Tell him of my remorse, of my fate, and be guided wholly by his counsels; then by his arm and your own, seat yourself firmly on the throne of your fathers. That moment will avenge me on Edward, and in that moment, Robert, let the English ground which will then hold my body give up its dead. Remove me to a Scottish grave, and, standing over my ashes, proclaim to them who might have been my people, that dying I beg their forgiveness, and bequeath them my best blessing, my virtuous son to reign in my stead."

Such injunctions at last prevailed with Bruce, and next day, writing the hasty lines which Wallace received at Falkirk, he intrusted them to his bard, who conveyed them to Scotland by means of the shepherd youth.

Shortly after the dispatch of this letter, the presage of Lord Carrick was verified: he was seized in the night with spasms and died in the arms of his son.

When Bruce related these particulars his grief became so violent that Wallace was obliged to enforce the dying words of the father he thus deplored. "Ah!" exclaimed the young earl, "I have indeed needed some friend to save me from myself, some one to reconcile me to the Robert Bruce who has so long slept in the fatal delusions which poisoned his father. Oh, Wallace! at times I am mad. I doubt

whether my father meant what he spoke; that he did not yet seek to
preserve the life of his son at the expense of his honor, and I have
been ready to precipitate myself on the steel of Edward so that he
should but meet the point of mine."

Bruce then added that in his more rational meditations he had
resolved to attempt an escape in the course of a few days. He understood that a deputation of English barons seeking a ratification of
their charter were soon to arrive in Durham; the bustle attendant
on their business would, he hoped, draw attention from him and afford
him the opportunity he sought. "In that case," continued he, "I
should have made directly to Stirling; and had not Providence conducted you to me I might have unconsciously thrown myself into
the midst of enemies. James Cummin is too ambitious to have allowed
my life to pass unattempted."

Bruce's two attendants entered at this moment; a couch was laid
for Wallace in an interior apartment, and with a grateful pressure
of the hands, in which their hearts silently embraced, the chiefs separated to repose.

CHAPTER LI.

THE BISHOP'S PALACE.

THE second matin-bell sounded from the abbey before the eyes of Wallace opened from the sleep which had sealed them. A bath refreshed him, then renewing the stain on his face and hands with the juice of a nut which he carried about him, and once more covering his martial figure and golden hair with the minstrel's cassock and cowl, he rejoined his friend.

Bruce had previously affected to consider the bard as still disordered by his last night's excess, and ordering him from his presence for at least a day, commanded that the traveling minstrel should be summoned to supply his place.

The table was spread when Wallace entered, and several servants were in attendance. Bruce hastily rose and would have embraced him, but before these people it would have been more than imprudent, so he made a sign to him to take his place at a board near his own.

The meal finished, Wallace, to maintain his assumed character while the servants were removing the table, was tuning his harp, when the Earl of Gloucester entered the room. The earl told Bruce the king had required the attendance of the border minstrel, and that after searching over the castle, the royal seneschal had at last discovered he was in the keep with him. On this being intimated to Gloucester, he chose rather to come himself to demand the harper from his friend than to subject him to the insolence of the royal servants. The king desired to hear "The Triumph" with which the minstrel had so much pleased the queen. Bruce turned pale at this message, and was opening his mouth to utter a denial, when Wallace immediately spoke. "If my Lord Bruce will grant permission, I should wish to comply with the King of England's request."—"Minstrel," replied Bruce, "you know not, perhaps, that the King of England is at an enmity with me, and cannot mean well to any one who has been my guest or servant. The Earl of Gloucester will excuse your attendance in the presence."

"Not for my life or the minstrel's," replied the earl. "The king would suspect some mystery; but as it is, his majesty merely wishes to hear him play and sing, and I pledge myself he shall return in safety."

Further opposition would only have courted danger, and with as good a grace as he could assume Bruce gave his consent. A page, who followed Gloucester, took up the harp, and, with a glance at his friend which spoke the fearless mind with which he ventured into the power of his enemy, Wallace accompanied Gloucester out of the room.

The earl moved swiftly forward, and leading him through a double line of guards, the folding-doors of the royal apartment were thrown open by two knights-in-waiting, and Wallace found himself in the presence. Perforated with the wounds which the chief's own hand had given him, the king lay upon a couch overhung with a crimson-velvet canopy with long golden fringes which swept the floor. His crown stood on a cushion at his head, and his queen, the blooming Margaret of France, sat full of smiles at his feet. The young Countess of Gloucester occupied a seat by her side.

The countess, who had not been at court the preceding day, fixed her eyes on the minstrel as he advanced into the middle of the room, where the page, by Gloucester's orders, planted the harp. She observed the manner of his obeisance to the king and queen and to herself; and the queen, whispering to her with a smile, said, "Have your British troubadours usually such an air as that? Am I right or am I wrong?"—"Quite right," replied the countess in as low a voice.

During this short dialogue, Edward was speaking with Gloucester, and Wallace leaned upon his harp.

"That is enough," said the king to his son-in-law; "now let me hear him play."

The earl gave the word, and Wallace, striking the chords with the hand of genius, called forth such strains and uttered such tones from his richly modulated voice that the king listened with wonder and the queen and countess scarcely allowed themselves to breathe. As the last sweep of the harp rolled on the ear of the king, the monarch deigned to pronounce him unequaled in his art. The queen approached him, laid her hand upon the harp, and touching the strings with a light finger said with a smile, "You must remain with the king's musicians and teach me how to charm as you do." Wallace replied to this innocent speech with a smile sweet as her own and bowed.

The countess drew near. Though not much older than the youthful queen she had been married twice, and being therefore more acquainted with the proprieties of life, her compliments were uttered in a form more befitting her rank.

Edward desired Gloucester to bring the minstrel closer to him.

Wallace approached the royal couch. Edward looked at him from head to foot before he spoke, but Wallace bore this eagle gaze with an undisturbed countenance.

"Who are you?" at length demanded Edward, who, surprised at the noble mien of the minstrel, conceived some suspicions of his quality. Wallace saw what was passing in the king's mind, and, determining by a frank reply to uproot his doubts, fearlessly answered, "A Scot."—"Indeed!" said the king, satisfied that no incendiary would dare thus to proclaim himself. "And how durst you, being of that outlawed nation, venture into my court?"—"I fear nothing on earth," replied Wallace. "This garb is privileged. None who respect that sacred law dare commit violence on a minstrel." "You are a bold man and an honest man, I believe," replied the king, "and as my queen desires it I order your enrolment in my traveling train of musicians. You may leave the presence."

"Then follow me to my apartment," cried the queen. "Countess, you will accompany me to see me take my first lesson."

A page took up the harp, and Wallace, bowing to the king, was conducted by Gloucester to the queen's apartments.

The royal Margaret herself opened the door, so eager was she to admit her teacher, and placing herself at the harp, she attempted a passage of "The Triumph" which had particularly struck her, but she played wrong. Wallace was asked to set her right; he obeyed. She was quick, he clear in his explanations, and in less than half an hour he made her execute the whole movement in a manner that delighted her. "Why, minstrel," cried she, "you are a magician. I have studied three long years to play the lute, and could never bring forth any tone that did not make me ready to stop my own ears. And now, countess," cried she, "did you ever hear anything so entrancing?"

"I suppose," returned the countess, "all your former instructors have been novices, and this Scot alone knows the art to which they pretended."—"Do you hear what the countess says?" exclaimed the queen, affecting to whisper to him; "she will not allow of any spiritual agency in my awakened talent. If you can contradict her, do, for I want very much to believe in fairies and magicians."

Wallace, with a respectful smile, answered, "I know of no spirit that has interposed in your majesty's favor but that of your own genius, and it is more efficient than the agency of all fairyland." The queen looked at him very gravely, and said, "If you really think there are no such things as fairies and enchantments, for so your words would imply, then everybody in your country must have genius, for they seem to be excellent in everything." "I have yet to ask you," resumed she, "the warriors of Scotland being so resistless, and their minstrels so perfect in their art, whether all the ladies can be so beautiful as the Lady Helen Mar?"

The eagerness with which Wallace grasped at any tidings of Helen disturbed the composure of his air at once. "But perhaps you have never seen her?" added the queen. Wallace replied, "I have heard many praise her beauty, but more her virtues."—"Well, I am sorry," continued her majesty, "since you sing so sweetly of female charms, that you have not seen this wonder of Scottish ladies. You have now little chance of that good fortune, for Earl De Valence has taken her abroad, intending to marry her amidst all the state with which my lord has invested him."—"Is it to Guienne he has taken her?" inquired Wallace.—"Yes," replied the queen, rather pleased than offended at the minstrel's ignorance of court ceremony in thus familiarly presuming to put a question to her; she continued to answer. "While so near Scotland he could not win her to forget her native country and her father, who it seems was dying when De Valence carried her away, and to prevent bloodshed between the earl and Soulis, who is also madly in love with her, my ever-gracious Edward gave the English lord a high post in Guienne, and thither they are gone."

Before Wallace could reply to some remark which the queen laughingly added to her information, the countess thought it proper to give her gay mother-in-law a more decisive reminder of decorum, and, rising, she whispered something which covered the youthful Margaret with blushes. Her majesty rose directly, and pushing away the harp, said, "You may leave the room," and turning her back to Wallace, walked away through an opposite door.

Wallace was yet recounting the particulars of his royal visit to Bruce (who had anxiously watched his return) when one of the queen's attendants appeared, and presenting him a silk handkerchief curiously coiled up, said that he brought it from her majesty, who supposed it must be his, as she found it in the room where he had been playing the harp. Wallace was going to say that it did not belong to him, when Bruce gave him a look that directed him to take the handkerchief. He obeyed without a word, and the boy withdrew.

Bruce smiled. "There is more in that handkerchief than silk, my friend. Queens send not these embassies on trifling errands." While Bruce spoke, Wallace unwrapped it. "I told you so," cried the prince, pointing to a slip of emblazoned vellum, which became unfolded. "Shall I look aside while you peruse it?"—"Look on it, my dear prince," replied Wallace; "for in trifles, as well as in things of moment, I would hold no reserves with you." The vellum was then opened, and these words presented themselves:

"Presume not on condescension. This injunction may be necessary, for the noble lady who was present at our interview tells me the men of this island are very presuming. I did not leave you this morning so abruptly out of unkindness and I write this because, having the countess ever with me, I shall not even dare to whisper it in her presence. Be always faithful and respectful, minstrel, and you shall ever find an indulgent mistress.

"A page will call for you when your attendance is desired."

Wallace and Bruce looked on each other. Bruce spoke first. "Had you vanity, my friend, this letter, from so lovely and innocent a creature, might be a gratification; but in our case, the sentiment it breathes is full of danger and I fear it will point an attention to you which may prove ruinous to our projects."—"Then," answered Wallace, "our alternative is to escape it by getting away this very night. And, as you persevere in your resolution not to enter Scotland unaccompanied by me, and will share my attempt to rescue Lady Helen Mar, we must direct our course immediately to the Continent."

"Yes, instantly, and securely too, under the disguise of priests," returned Bruce. "I have in my possession the wardrobe of the confessor who followed my father's fortunes, and who, on his death, retired into the abbey which contains his remains."

It was then settled between the friends that when it became dark they should dress themselves in the confessor's robes, and by means of the queen's signet, which she had given to Wallace at the banquet, pass the guard as priests who had entered by some other gate, and were returned from shriving her majesty. Once without the city they could make a swift progress southward to the nearest seaport, and there safely embark for France.

In these arrangements, and in planning their future movements relative to the rescue of Lady Helen, they passed several hours, and were only interrupted by the arrival of a lute from the queen for her minstrel to tune. Wallace obeyed, and returning it by the page who brought it congratulated himself that it was not accompanied by any new summons. Then continuing his discourse with Bruce, time moved on till the shadow deepened into night.

"Now is our hour," cried Bruce, starting on his feet; "go you into that room and array yourself in the confessor's robes, while I call my servants to dispense with their usual nightly attendance." With determination and hope, Wallace gladly obeyed. In that very same instant the Earl of Gloucester suddenly entered, and looking around the room with a disturbed countenance, abruptly said, "Where is the minstrel?"—"Why?" answered Bruce, alarm appearing in his face. Gloucester advanced close to him. "Is any one within hearing?"—"No one."—"Then," replied the earl, "his life is in danger. He is suspected to be not what he seems, and, I am sorry to add, to stand in a favor with the queen, of a nature to incur his mortal punishment."

Bruce was so confounded with this stoppage of all their plans that he could not speak. Gloucester proceeded: "My dear Bruce, from the circumstance of his being with you, I cannot but suppose that you know more of him than you think proper to disclose. Whoever he may be, whether he came from France, or really from Scotland, as he says, his life is now forfeited. And that by attempting to screen him you may not seem to share his imputed guilt, I come to warn you of this discovery. A double guard is set around the keep, so no visible means are left for his escape."

"Then what will become of him?" exclaimed Bruce, forgetting all caution in dismay for his friend. "Am I to see the savior of my country butchered before my eyes by a tyrant? I may die, Gloucester, in his defense, but I will never surrender him to his enemy."

Gloucester stood aghast at this disclosure. He came to accuse the friend of Bruce; but now that he found this friend to be Wallace, the preserver of his own life, he immediately resolved to give him freedom. "Bruce," cried he, "when I recollect the deportment of this minstrel, I am surprised that, in spite of his disguise, I did not recognize the regent of Scotland; but now I know him, he shall find that generosity is not confined to his own breast. Give me your word that you will not stimulate suspicion by remonstrating with Edward against your own arrest, till the court leaves Durham, and I will instantly find a way to conduct your friend in safety from the castle." —"I pledge you my word of honor," cried Bruce; "release but him, and if you do demand it of me, I would die in chains."—"He saved me at Berwick," replied Gloucester, "and I am anxious to repay the debt. If he be near, explain what has happened in as few words as possible, for we must not delay a moment. I left a council with the enraged king, settling what horrible death was to be his punishment." —"When he is safe," answered Bruce, "I will attest his innocence to you; meanwhile rely on my faith that you are giving liberty to a guiltless man."

Bruce hastened to Wallace, who had just completed his disguise. He briefly related what had passed, and received for answer that he would not leave his prince to the revenge of the tyrant. But Bruce, urging that the escape of the one could alone secure that of the other, implored him not to persist in refusing his offered safety, but to make direct for Normandy. "I will join you at Rouen, and thence we can proceed to Guienne," added he. "The hour the court leaves Durham is that of my escape, and when free, what shall divide me from you and our enterprise?"

Wallace had hardly assented when a tumultuous noise broke the silence of the court-yard, the great iron doors of the keep were thrown back on their hinges, and the clangor of arms, with many voices, resounded in the hall. Thinking all was lost, with a cry of despair Bruce drew his sword and threw himself before his friend. At that instant Gloucester entered the room. "They are quicker than I thought," cried he; "but follow me. Bruce, remain where you are; sheathe your sword; be bold; deny you know anything of the minstrel, and all will be well." As he spoke, Gloucester grasped the Scottish hero by the hand, turned into a short gallery, and plucking the broad shaft of a cedar pilaster from under its capital, let himself and his companion into a passage within the wall of the building. The ponderous beam closed after them into its former situation, and the silent pair descended, by a flight of stone steps, to a dungeon without any visible outlet, but the earl found one by raising a flat stone marked with a cross, and again they penetrated lower into the bosom of the earth by a gradually declining path, till they stopped on a level ground. "This vaulted passage," said Gloucester, "reaches in a direct line to Fincklay abbey. My uncle, the then abbot of that monastery, discovered it to me ten years ago. Since my coming hither this time I took it into my head to revisit this recess one day and happily for the gratitude I owe to you, I found all as I had left it in my uncle's lifetime. But for the sake of my honor with Edward, I must enjoin you to secrecy. You were my benefactor, noble Wallace, and I should deserve the rack could I suffer one hair of your head to fall with violence to the ground."

Wallace declared his sense of the earl's generosity, and commended the young Bruce to his friendship. "The impetuosity of his mind," continued he, "at times may overthrow his prudence and leave him exposed to dangers which a little caution might avoid. When the flood of indignation swells his bosom, then tell him that I conjure him on the life of his dearest wishes to be silent."

Gloucester replied, "What you say I will repeat to Bruce. I am too sensible my royal father-in-law has trampled on his rights, and should I ever see him restored to the throne of his ancestors, I could not but acknowledge the hand of Heaven in the event. Far would it have been from me to have bound him to remain a prisoner during Edward's sojourn at Durham, had I not been certain that your escape and his together would give birth to suspicion in the minds of my enemies. The result would be my disgrace, and a broken heart to her who has raised me by her generous love to the rank of a prince and her husband."

Gloucester then informed Wallace that about two hours before he came to alarm Bruce for his safety, he was summoned by Edward to attend him immediately. When he obeyed he found Soulis standing by the royal couch and his majesty talking with violence. At sight of Gloucester he beckoned him to advance, and striking his hand fiercely on a letter he held, he exclaimed, "Here, my son, behold the record of your father's shame!—of a King of England dishonored by a slave!" As he spoke he dashed it from him. Soulis answered, smiling, "Not a slave, my lord and king. Can you not see, through the disguise, the figure of nobility?" "Enough!" interrupted the king. "I know I am dishonored, but the villain shall die. Read the letter, Gloucester, and say what tortures shall stamp my vengeance."

Gloucester opened the vellum and read, in the queen's hand:

"Gentle minstrel! My lady countess tells me I must not see you again. Were you old or ugly, as most bards are, I might, she says; but being young it is not for a queen to smile upon one of your calling. I used to smile as I liked when I was in France. Oh, if it were not for those I love best, who are now in England, I wish I were there again! and you would go with me, gentle minstrel, would you not? And you would teach me to sing so sweetly. I will see you this evening, and your harp shall sing all my heartaches to sleep. My French lady of honor will conduct you secretly to my apartments. I am sure you are too honest even to guess at what the countess thinks you might fancy when I smile on you. But, gentle minstrel, presume not, and you shall ever find an indulgent mistress in M——.

"P.S.—At the last vespers to-night my page shall come for you."

Gloucester knew the queen's handwriting, and not being able to contradict that this letter was hers, he inquired how it came into his majesty's hands. "I found it," replied Soulis, "in crossing the courtyard; it lay on the ground, where, doubtless, it had been accidentally dropped by the queen's messenger."

Gloucester, wishing to extenuate for the queen's sake, affirmed that from the simplicity with which the note was written and from her innocent references to the minstrel's profession, he could not suppose that she addressed him in any other character.

"If he be only an itinerant harper," replied the king, "the deeper is my disgrace; for if a passion of another kind than music be not portrayed in every word of this artful letter, I never read a woman's heart." Gloucester inwardly thanked Heaven that none other than Soulis and himself were present to hear Edward fasten such dishonor on his queen, but remaining silent, Edward believed him convinced of the queen's crime, and being too wrathful to think of caution, he sent for the bishop and others of his lords, and when they entered, vented to them also his indignation. Many were not of the same opinion with their sovereign; some thought with Gloucester; others deemed the letter a forgery; but all united in recommending an immediate apprehension and private execution of the minstrel. "It is not fit," cried Soulis, "that a man who has even been suspected of invading our monarch's honor should live another hour."

This sanguinary sentence was acceded to, and with as little remorse, by the whole assembly, as if they had merely condemned a tree to the ax. Earl Percy proposed—as he believed the queen innocent—that to clear her, the Countess of Gloucester and the French lady of honor should be examined relative to the letter.

The king immediately ordered their attendance.

The royal Jane of Acre appeared at the first summons, and spoke with an air of truth which convinced every candid ear of the innocence of the queen. Her testimony was that she believed the minstrel to be other than he seemed; but she was certain, from the conversation which the queen had held with her that she was ignorant of his real rank. On being questioned by the bishop, the countess acknowledged that her majesty had praised his figure, as well as his singing; "yet no more," added she, "than she afterwards did to the king, when she awakened his curiosity to send for him." Her highness said that she herself thought his demeanor much above his situation; but when he accompanied the queen and herself into her majesty's apartments, she had an opportunity to observe him in conversation; and by his easy, yet respectful, deportment, she became convinced he was not what he appeared.

"And why, Jane," asked the king, "did you not impart these suspicions to your husband or to me?"

"Because," replied she, "the countenance of this stranger was so ingenuous, I could not suspect he came on any disloyal errand."

"Lady," observed one of the elder lords, "if you thought so well of the queen and of this man, why did you caution her against his smiles, and deem it necessary to persuade her not to see him again?"

The countess blushed, but replied, "Because I saw the minstrel was a gentleman. He possessed a noble figure and a handsome face, in spite of his Egyptian skin. Like most young gentlemen, he might be conscious of these advantages, and attribute the innocent smiles of my gracious queen to a source more flattering to his vanity. I have known many lords to make similar mistakes on as little grounds," added she, looking towards some of the younger nobles, "and therefore, to prevent such insolence, I desired his final dismission."

"Thank you, my dear Jane," replied the king; "you almost persuade me of Margaret's innocence."

"Believe it, sire," cried she with animation; "whatever thoughtlessness her youth may have led her into, I pledge my life on her purity."

"First, let us hear what that French woman has to say to the assignation," exclaimed Soulis, whose cruel disposition exulted in torturing and death. "Question her, and then her majesty may have full acquittal."

Again the brow of Edward was overcast, and ordering the Countess of Gloucester to withdraw, he commanded the Baroness de Pontoise to be brought into the presence.

When she saw the king's threatening looks, she shrank with terror. Though she knew nothing really bad of her unhappy mistress, yet fancying that she did, she stood before the royal tribunal with the air of a culprit.

"Repeat to me," demanded the king, "or answer it with your head, all that you know of Queen Margaret's intimacy with the man who calls himself a minstrel."

At these words, which were delivered in a tone that seemed the sentence of death, the French woman fell on her knees, and in a burst of terror exclaimed, "Sire, I will reveal all, if your majesty will grant me a pardon for having too faithfully served my mistress."

"Speak! speak!" cried the king with desperate impatience. "I swear to pardon you even if you have joined in a conspiracy against my life; but speak the truth, and all the truth!"

"I obey," answered the baroness and raised from her kneeling position by Soulis, she began:

"The only time I ever saw this man to my knowledge was when he was brought to play before my lady at the bishop's banquet, and when I attended her majesty's disrobing after the feast she put to me so many questions about what I thought of the minstrel that I began to think her admiration too great to have been awakened by a mere song. And then she asked me if a king could have a nobler air than he had, and she laughed and said she would send your majesty to school to learn of him."

"Vile traitress!" exclaimed the king. The baroness paused, and retreated from before the fury which flashed from his eyes. "Go on!" cried he; "hide neither word nor circumstance, that my vengeance may lose nothing of its aim."

She proceeded: "Her majesty then talked of his beautiful eyes; so blue, she said, yet proud in their looks. 'De Pontoise,' added she, 'can you explain that?' I, being rather, perhaps, too well learned in the idle tales of our troubadours, heedlessly answered, 'Perhaps he is some king in disguise, just come to look at your charms, and go away again.' 'The Countess of Gloucester,' my lady continued, 'with persuasions too much like commands, will not allow me to see the minstrel any more.' She then declared her determination that she would see him, and he should come and sing to her when she was alone, and that she was sure he was too modest to presume on her condescension. I said something to dissuade her, but she overruled me, and I consented to assist her. She gave me a letter to convey to him, which I did by slipping it beneath the handle of her lute, which I sent as an excuse for the minstrel to tune. It was to acquaint him with her intentions, and this night he was to have visited her apartment."

During this recital, the king sat with compressed lips, listening. On mentioning the letter he clenched his hand as if then he grasped the thunderbolt. The lords immediately apprehended that this was the letter which Soulis found.

"Take the woman hence," cried the king, in a burst of wrath, "and never let me see her traitor face again!" The baroness withdrew in terror, and Edward, calling Sir Piers Gaveston, commanded him to place himself at the head of a double guard and go in person to bring the object of his introduction to meet the punishment due to his crime. "For," cried the king, "be he prince or peasant, I will see him hanged before my eyes."

Soulis now suggested that as the delinquent was to be found with Bruce, most likely that young nobleman was privy to his designs. "We shall see to him hereafter," replied the king; "meanwhile look that I am obeyed."

The moment this order passed the king's lips Gloucester, now not doubting the queen's guilt, hastened to warn Bruce of what had occurred, that he might separate himself from the crime of a man who appeared to have been under his protection. But when he found that the accused was no other than the beloved and generous Wallace, all other considerations were lost in the desire of delivering him from danger. He knew the means, and he did not hesitate to employ them.

During the recital of this narrative Gloucester narrowly observed his auditor, and by the horror he evinced at the crime he was suspected of having committed, the earl, while convinced of his innocence, easily conceived how the queen's sentiments for him might have gone no farther than a childish admiration, pardonable in a guileless creature hardly more than sixteen.

"See," cried Wallace, "the power which lies with the describer of actions! The chaste mind of your countess saw nothing in the conduct of the queen but thoughtless simplicity. The contaminated heart of the Baroness de Pontoise descried passion in every word, and, judging of her mistress by herself, she has wrought this mighty ruin. Were it not for endangering the safety of Bruce, I myself would return and stake my life on proving the innocence of the Queen of England. But, if a letter, with my word of honor, could convince the king——"

"I accept the offer," interrupted Gloucester. "I am too warmly the friend of Bruce, too grateful to you, to betray either into danger; but from Sunderland, whither I recommend you to go and there embark for France, write the declaration you mention and enclose it to me. I can contrive that the king shall have your letter without suspecting by what channel, and then I trust all will be well."

During this discourse they passed on through the vaulted passage, till, arriving at a wooden crucifix which marked the boundary of the domain of Durham, Gloucester stopped. "I must not go farther. Should I prolong my stay from the castle during the search for you, suspicion may be awakened. You must, therefore, proceed alone. Go straight forward, and at the extremity of the vault you will find a flagstone surmounted like the one by which we descended; raise it, and it will let you into the cemetery of the abbey of Fincklay. One end of that burying-place is always open to the east. Thence you will emerge to the open world, and may it in future, noble Wallace, ever treat you according to your unequaled merits. Farewell!"

The earl turned to retrace his steps, and Wallace pursued his way through the darkness towards the Fincklay extremity of the vault.

CHAPTER LII.

GALLIC SEAS.

WALLACE, having issued from his subterranean journey, made direct to Sunderland, where he arrived about sunrise. A vessel belonging to France rode there, waiting a favorable wind. Wallace secured a passage in her, and going on board, wrote his promised letter to Edward. It ran thus:

"This testament is to assure Edward, King of England, upon the word of a knight, that Queen Margaret, his wife, is in every respect guiltless of the crimes alleged against her by the Lord Soulis and sworn to by the Baroness de Pontoise. I came to the court of Durham on an errand connected with my country, and that I might be unknown I assumed the disguise of a minstrel. By accident I encountered Sir Piers Gaveston; and, ignorant that I was other than I seemed, he introduced me at the royal banquet. It was there I first saw her majesty. And I never had that honor but three times: one I have named, the second was in your royal presence, and the third and last in her apartments, to which your majesty's self saw me withdraw. The Countess of Gloucester was present the whole time, and to her highness I appeal. The queen saw in me only a minstrel; on my art alone as a musician was her favor bestowed, and by expressing it with a warmth which none other than an innocent heart would have dared to display, she has thus exposed herself to the false representations of a worthless friend.

"I have escaped the snare which the queen's enemies laid for me, and for her sake, for the sake of truth and your own peace, King Edward, I declare before the Searcher of all hearts, and before the world, that your wife is innocent. And should I ever meet the man who, after this declaration, dares to unite her name with mine in a tale of infamy, by the power of truth I swear that I will make him write a recantation with his blood. Pure is, and shall ever be, the honor of William Wallace."

This letter was enclosed in one to the Earl of Gloucester, and having despatched his packet to Durham, the Scottish chief gladly saw a brisk wind blow up from the northwest. The ship weighed anchor, cleared the harbor, and, under a fair sky, swiftly cut the waves

towards the Gallic shores. But ere she reached them the warlike star
of Wallace directed to his little bark the terrific sails of the Red
Reaver, a formidable pirate who then infested the Gallic seas, swept
their commerce, and insulted their navy. He attacked the French
vessel, but it carried a greater than Cæsar and his fortunes: Wallace
and his destiny were there, and the enemy struck to the Scottish chief.
The Red Reaver (so surnamed because of his red sails and sanguinary
deeds) was killed in the action, but his younger brother, Thomas de
Longueville, was found alive within the captive ship, and a yet greater
prize, Prince Louis of France, who, having been out the day before
on a sailing-party, had been descried and seized as an invaluable
booty by the Red Reaver.

Adverse winds for some time prevented Wallace from reaching
port with his capture; but on the fourth day after the victory he cast
anchor in the harbor of Havre. The indisposition of the prince from
a wound he had received in his own conflict with the Reaver made it
necessary to apprise King Philip of the accident. In answer to
Wallace's despatches on this subject, the grateful monarch added
to the proffers of friendship, which had been the substance of his
majesty's embassy to Scotland, a pressing invitation that the Scottish
chief would accompany the prince to Paris, and there receive a public
mark of royal gratitude, which, with due honor, should record this
service done to France to future ages. Meanwhile Philip sent the
chief a suit of armor, with a request that he would wear it in remembrance of France and his own heroism. But nothing could tempt
Wallace to turn aside from his duty. Impatient to pursue his journey
towards the spot where he hoped to meet Bruce, he wrote a respectful
excuse to the king, but arraying himself in the monarch's martial
present, he went to the prince to bid him farewell. Louis was preparing for their departure, all three together, with young De Longueville (whose pardon Wallace had obtained from the king) ; and the
two young men expressed their disappointment when they found that
their benefactor was going to leave them. Wallace gave his highness
a packet for the king, containing a brief statement of his vow to
Lord Mar, and a promise that when he had fulfilled it, Philip should
see him at Paris. The royal cavalcade then separated from the deliverer of its prince, and Wallace, mounting a richly barbed Arabian,
which had accompanied his splendid armor, took the road to Rouen.

Meanwhile events not less momentous took place at Durham. The
instant Wallace had followed the Earl of Gloucester from the apartment in the castle, it was entered by Sir Piers Gaveston. He demanded the minstrel. Bruce replied he knew not where he was.

Gaveston, eager to convince the king that he was no accomplice with the suspected person, put the question a second time, and in a tone which he meant should intimidate the Scottish prince. "Where is the minstrel?"—"I know not," replied Bruce.—"And will you dare to tell me, earl," asked his interrogator, "that within this quarter of an hour he has not been in this tower, nay, in this very room? The guards in your ante-chamber have told me that he was, and can Lord Carrick stoop to utter a falsehood?"

While he was speaking Bruce stood eying him with increasing scorn. Gaveston paused. "You expect me to answer you?" said the prince. "Out of respect to myself, I will. The man you seek may have been in this tower, in this room, as you at present are, and as little am I bound to know where he now is as whither you go when you relieve me from an inquisition which I hold myself accountable to no man to answer."—"'Tis well," cried Gaveston; "and I am to carry this haughty message to the king?"—"If you deliver it as a message," answered Bruce, "you will prove that they who are ready to suspect falsehood find its utterance easy. My reply is to you. When King Edward speaks to me, I shall find the answer that is due to him."—"These attempts to provoke me into a private quarrel," cried Gaveston, "will not succeed. I must seek the man through your apartments."—"By whose authority?" demanded Bruce.—"By my own as the loyal subject of my outraged monarch. He bade me bring the traitor before him, and thus I obey." While speaking Gaveston beckoned to his attendants to follow him to the door whence Wallace had disappeared. Bruce threw himself before it. "I must forget the duty I owe to myself before I allow you to invade my privacy. I have already given you the answer that becomes Robert Bruce, and in respect to your knighthood, instead of compelling I request you to withdraw." Gaveston hesitated; but he knew the character of his opponent, and therefore, with no very good grace, muttering that he should hear of it from a more powerful quarter he left the room. And certainly his threats were not in this instance vain, for prompt was the arrival of a marshal and his officers to force Bruce before the king.

"Robert Bruce, Earl of Cleveland, Carrick, and Annandale, I come to summon you into the presence of your liege lord, Edward of England."

"The Earl of Cleveland obeys," replied Bruce, and with a fearless step he walked out before the marshal.

When he entered the presence chamber, Sir Piers Gaveston stood beside the royal couch as if prepared to be his accuser. The king

Wallace rescues Helen

sat supported by pillows, paler with jealousy and baffled authority than from the effects of his wounds. "Robert Bruce!" cried he, "are you not afraid that I shall make that audacious head answer for the man whom you thus dare to screen from my just revenge?" Bruce felt all the injuries he had suffered from this proud king rush upon his memory, and without lowering the lofty expression of his looks he firmly answered: "The judgment of a just king I cannot fear; the sentence of an unjust one I despise." Edward noted his reply and with a sensation of shame he would gladly have repressed, he said that in consideration of his youth he would pardon him what had passed, and reinstate him in all the late Earl of Carrick's honors, if he would declare where he had hidden the offending minstrel. "I have not hidden him," cried Bruce, "nor do I know where he is; but had that been confided to me, as I know him to be an innocent man, no power on earth should have wrenched him from me."

"Robert Bruce," cried the king, "before I came this northern journey I ever found you one of the most devoted of my servants, and how do I see you at this moment? Braving me to my face. How is it that until now this spirit never broke forth?"—"Because," answered the prince, "until now I had never seen the virtuous friend whom you call upon me to betray."—"Then you confess," cried the king, "that he was an instigator to rebellion?"—"I avow," answered Bruce, "that I never knew what true loyalty was till he taught it me, nor what virtue might be till he allowed me to see in himself incorruptible fidelity, and a purity of heart not to be contaminated."

"Your vindication," cried the king, "confirms his guilt. You admit that he is not a minstrel in reality. Wherefore then did he steal into my palace, but to betray either my honor or my life?"— "His errand here was to see me."—"Rash boy!" cried Edward, "then you acknowledge yourself a conspirator against me!"

The Earl of Gloucester at that moment entered from seeing Wallace through the cavern. At sight of him, Bruce knew that his friend was safe, and fearless for himself, he suddenly exclaimed, "By one word, King Edward, I will confirm what I have said. Listen to me, not as a monarch and an enemy, but with the unbiased judgment of man with man,—and then ask your own brave heart if it would be possible for Sir William Wallace to be a traitor and conspirator."

Every mouth was dumb at the enunciation of that name, and the king himself, thunderstruck, alike with the boldness of his conqueror venturing within the grasp of his revenge, and at the daring of

Bruce in thus declaring his connection with him, for a few minutes knew not what to answer, for he was too well acquainted with the history and uniform conduct of Wallace to doubt his honor. "Bruce," said he, "though Wallace is my enemy, I know him to be of an integrity which neither man nor woman can shake. And whoever, after this, mentions one word of what has passed in these investigations, shall be punished as guilty of high treason."

Bruce was then ordered to be reconducted to the round tower, and the rest of the lords withdrew by command.

Bruce was now more closely immured than ever. Not even his bard was allowed to approach him, and double guards were kept constantly around his prison. On the fourth day of his seclusion an extra row of iron bars was put across his windows. He asked the captain of the party the reason for this new rivet on his captivity, but he received no answer. His own recollection, however, solved the doubt; for he could not but see that his declaration respecting his friendship with Wallace had increased the alarm of Edward. One of the warders, on having the same inquiry put to him which Bruce had addressed to his superior, in a rough tone replied, "He had best not ask questions, lest he should hear that his majesty had determined to keep him under Bishop Beck's padlock for life." Bruce was not to be deprived of hope by a single evidence, and, smiling, said, "There are more ways of getting out of a tyrant's prison than by the doors and windows."—"Why, you would not eat through the walls," cried the man.—"Certainly," replied Bruce, "if I have no other way, and through the guards, too."—"We'll see to that," answered the man.—"And feel it too, my sturdy jailer," returned the prince; "so look to yourself." Bruce threw himself recklessly into a chair as he spoke, while the man, eying him askance, and remembering how strangely the minstrel had disappeared, began to think that some people born in Scotland held a magic power of executing whatever they determined.

Though careless in his manner of treating the warder's information, Bruce thought of it with anxiety, and he remained immovable on the spot where the man had left him, till another sentinel brought in a lamp. He set it down in silence and withdrew. Bruce then heard the bolts on the outside of his chamber pushed into their guards. "There they go," said he to himself, "and those are to be the morning and evening sounds to which I am to listen all my days. Well, Edward, kindness might bind generous minds even to forget their rights; but, thanks to you, neither in my own person nor for any of my name do I owe you aught but to behold me King of Scotland,

and, please God, that you shall, if the prayers of faith may set me free."

While resolutions respecting the consequences of his hoped-for liberty occupied his mind, he heard the tread of a foot in the adjoining passage. He listened breathless, for no living creature, he thought, could be in that quarter of the building, as he had suffered none to enter it since Wallace had disappeared by that way. He half rose from his couch as the door at which he had seen him last gently opened. He started up, and Gloucester, with a lantern in his hand, stood before him. The earl put his finger on his lip, and, taking Bruce by the hand, led him, as he had done Wallace, down into the vault which leads to Fincklay abbey.

Having led him in safety through the vaulted passage, they parted in the cemetery of Fincklay, Gloucester to walk back to Durham by the banks of the Wear, and Bruce to mount the horse the good earl had left tied to a tree to convey him to Hartlepool. There he embarked for Normandy.

When he arrived at Caen he made no delay, but taking a rapid course across the country towards Rouen, on the second evening of his traveling, having pursued his route without sleep, he felt himself so overcome with fatigue that in the midst of a dreary plain he found it necessary to stop for rest at the first habitation he might find. It happened to be the abode of one of those poor but pious matrons who, attaching themselves to some neighboring order of charity, live alone in desert places for the purpose of succoring distressed travelers. Here Bruce found the widow's cruse and a pallet to repose his wearied limbs.

CHAPTER LIII.

NORMANDY.

WALLACE, having separated from the prince royal of France, pursued his solitary way towards the capital of Normandy, till night overtook him ere he was aware. Clouds so obscured the sky that not a star was visible, and his horse, terrified at the darkness and the difficulties of the path, suddenly stopped. This aroused Wallace from a fit of musing to look around him, but on which side lay the road to Rouen he could form no guess. To pass the night in so exposed a spot might be dangerous, and spurring the animal he determined to push onward.

He had ridden nearly another hour when the dead silence of the scene was broken by the roll of distant thunder. Then forked lightning shooting from the horizon showed a line of country unmarked by any vestige of human habitation. The storm approached till, breaking in peals over his head, it discharged such sheets of fire at his feet that the horse reared, and, plunging amidst the blaze, flashed the light of his rider's armor on the eyes of a troop of horsemen, who also stood under the tempest, gazing with affright at the scene. Wallace, by the same illumination, saw the travelers as they seemed to start back at his appearance, and mistaking their apprehension, he called to them that his steed would do theirs no harm. One of them advanced and respectfully inquired of him the way to Rouen. Wallace replied that he was a stranger in this part of the country, and was also seeking that city. While he was yet speaking, the thunder became more tremendous, the horses of the troop became restive, and one of them threw its rider. Cries of lamentation, mingling with the groans of the fallen person, excited the compassion of Wallace. He rode towards the spot whence the latter proceeded, and asked the nearest bystander whether the unfortunate man were much hurt. The answer returned was full of alarm for the sufferer, and anxiety to obtain some place of shelter, for rain began to fall. Wallace cheered them by saying he would seek a shelter for their friend and blow his bugle when he had found one, and with the word he turned his horse, and as he galloped along called aloud on any Christian man who might live near to open his doors to a dying traveler. After riding about in all directions he saw a glimmering light for a moment, and then all was darkness; but again he cried aloud, and a shrill female voice answered, "I am a lone woman with already one poor traveler in my house, but, for the Virgin's sake, I will open my door to you, whatever you may be." The good woman relit her lamp, which the rain had extinguished, and on her unlatching her door, Wallace entreated her permission to bring the unfortunate person into the cottage. She readily consented, and giving him a lantern to guide his way, he blew his bugle, which was instantly answered by so loud a shout that it assured him his companions could not be far distant.

The men directed him through the darkness by their voices, for the lantern threw its beams but a very little way, and arriving at their side, by his assistance the bruised traveler was brought to the cottage. It was a poor hovel, but the good woman had spread a clean woolen coverlet over her own bed, and thither Wallace carried the invalid. He seemed in great pain; but his kind conductor answered their hostess' inquiries respecting him with a belief that no bones were broken. "But yet," cried she, "sad may be the effects of internal bruises on so emaciated a frame. I will venture to disturb my other guest, who sleeps in the loft, and bring down a decoction that I keep there. It is made from simple herbs, and I am sure will be of service."

The old woman, having showed to the attendants where they might shelter their horses, ascended a few steps to the chamber above. Meanwhile the Scottish chief disengaged the sufferer from his wet garments and covered him with the blankets. Recovered to recollection by the comfort of his bodily feelings, the stranger opened his eyes. He fixed them on Wallace, then looked around and turned to Wallace again. "Generous knight!" cried he, "I have nothing but thanks to offer for this kindness. You seem to be of the highest rank, and yet have succored one whom the world abjures." The knight returned a courteous answer, and the invalid, in a paroxysm of emotion, added, "Can it be possible that a prince of France has dared to act thus contrary to his peers?"

Wallace, not apprehending what had given rise to this question, supposed the stranger's wits were disordered, and looked with inquiry towards the attendant. Just at that moment a step, more active than that of their aged hostess, sounded above, and an exclamation of surprise followed it in a voice that startled Wallace. He turned hastily round, and a young man sprang from the cottage stairs into the apartment; joy danced in every feature, and the ejaculation, "Wallace!" "Bruce!" burst at once from the hearts of the two friends as they rushed into each other's arms. While the chiefs freely spoke in their native tongue before a people who could not be supposed to understand them, the aged stranger on the bed reiterated his moans. Wallace, in a few words telling Bruce the manner of his rencounter with the sick man and his belief that he was disordered in his mind, drew towards the bed and offered him some of the decoction which the woman now brought. The invalid drank it and gazed earnestly first on Wallace and then on Bruce. "Pierre, withdraw," cried he to his personal attendant. The man obeyed. "Sit down by me, noble friends," said he to the Scottish chiefs, "and read a lesson which I pray ye lay to your hearts." Wallace drew a stool, while his friend seated himself on the bed. The old woman, perceiving something extraordinary in the countenance of the stranger, thought he was going to reveal some secret heavy on his mind, and also withdrew.

"You think my intellects are injured," resumed he, turning to Wallace, "because I addressed you as one of the house of Philip. Those jeweled lilies round your helmet led me into the error. I never before saw them granted to other than a prince of the blood. But think not, brave man, I respect you less since I have discovered that you are other than a prince. Look at this emaciated form, and behold the reverses of all earthly grandeur. He that used to be followed as the source of honor, with suppliants at his feet, would now be left to solitude were it not for these few faithful servants who have preserved their allegiance to the end. Look on me, chiefs, and behold him who was the king of Scots."

At this declaration both Wallace and Bruce, struck with compassion at meeting their ancient enemy reduced to such misery, with one impulse bowed their heads to him with an air of reverence. The action penetrated the heart of Baliol, for when at the meeting and exclamation of the two friends he recognized in whose presence he lay, he remembered that, by his base submissions turning the scale of judgment in his favor, he had defrauded the grandsire of the very Bruce now before him of his rights to the crown, and when he looked on the man who had brought him to a shelter from the raging terrors of the night, his conscience doubly smote him, for from the hour of his elevation to that of his downfall he had ever persecuted the family of Wallace. He, her king, had resigned her into the hands of an usurper, but the injured Wallace had arisen like a star of light on the darkness of her captivity, and Scotland was once more free. To these young men, so strangely brought before him, and both of whom he had wronged, he determined immediately to reveal himself, and see whether they were as resentful of injuries as those he had served had proved ungrateful for benefits received. He spoke, and when, instead of seeing the pair rise in indignation on his pronouncing his name, they bowed their heads and sat in respectful silence, his desolate heart expanded at once, and he burst into tears. He caught the hand of Bruce, who sat nearest to him, and stretching out the other to Wallace, exclaimed, "I have not deserved this goodness from either of you. Perhaps you two are the only men now living whom I ever greatly injured, and you, excepting my four poor attendants, are perhaps the only men living who would compassionate my misfortunes?"

"These are lessons, king," returned Wallace with reverence, "to fit you for a better crown. And never in my eyes did the descendant of Alexander seem so worthy of his blood." The grateful monarch pressed his hand. Bruce continued to gaze on him with a thousand awful thoughts occupying his mind. Baliol read in his countenance the reflections which chained his tongue. "Behold how low is laid the proud rival of your grandfather!" exclaimed he, turning to Bruce. "I bartered the liberties of my country for a crown I knew not how to wear, and was repaid with a prison. There I expiated my crime against the upright Bruce. Not one of all the Scottish lords who crowded Edward's court came to beguile a moment of sorrow from their captive monarch. Lonely I lived, for the tyrant even deprived me of the comfort of seeing my fellow-prisoner, Lord Douglas, he whom attachment to my true interests had betrayed to an English prison. I never saw him after the day of his being put into the tower until that of his death." Wallace interrupted Baliol with an exclamation of surprise. "Yes," added he, "I myself closed his eyes. At that awful hour he had petitioned to see me, and the boon was granted. I went to him, and then with his dying breath he spoke truths to me which were indeed messengers from heaven; they taught me what I was and what I might be. Edward was then in Flanders, and you, brave Wallace, being triumphant in Scotland, and laying such a stress in your negotiations for the return of Douglas, the Southron cabinet agreed to conceal his death, and by making his name an instrument to excite your hopes and fears, turn your anxiety for him to their own advantage."

A deep scarlet kindled over the face of Bruce. "With what a race have I been so long connected! what mean subterfuges, what dastardly deceits, for the leaders of a great nation to adopt!" He rose in agitation. Baliol followed him with his eyes. "Amiable

Bruce! you too severely arraign a fault that was venial in you. Your father gave himself to Edward, and his son accompanied the tribute." Bruce vehemently answered, "If King Edward ever said that, he uttered a falsehood. My father loved him, confided in him, and the ingrate betrayed him. His fidelity was no gift of himself, in acknowledgement of inferiority; it was the pledge of a friendship exchanged on equal terms on the fields of Palestine. But my father found liberty in the grave, and I am ready to take a sure revenge in"—he would have added "Scotland," but he forebore to give the last blow to the unhappy Baliol by showing him that his kingdom had indeed passed from him, and that the man was before him who might be destined to wield his scepter.

"Hesitate not," said Baliol, "to say where you will take your revenge. I know that the brave Wallace has laid open the way. Had I possessed such a leader of my troops, I should not now be a mendicant in this hovel. Wear him, Bruce, wear him in your heart's core. He gives the throne he might have filled."—"Make not that a subject of praise," cried Wallace, "which if I had left undone would have stamped me a traitor. I have only performed my duty, and may God guide Bruce to his kingdom, and keep him there in peace and honor!"

Baliol rose in his bed at these words. "Bruce," said he, "approach me near." He obeyed. The feeble monarch turned to Wallace. "You have supported what was my kingdom through its last struggles for liberty. Put forth your hand and support its exiled sovereign in his last regal act." Wallace raised the king so as to enable him to assume a kneeling posture. Dizzy with the exertion, for a moment he rested on the shoulder of the chief, and then, looking up, he met the eye of Bruce gazing on him with compassionate interest. The unhappy monarch stretched out his arms to heaven. "May God pardon the injuries which my fatal ambition did to you and yours, the miseries I brought upon my country, and let your reign redeem my errors. May the spirit of wisdom bless you, my son!" His hands were now laid with pious fervor on the head of Bruce, who sank on his knees before him. "Whatever rights I had to the crown of Scotland, by the worthlessness of my reign they are forfeited, and I resign all unto you, even to the participation of the mere title of king." * Exhausted by his feelings, he sank back into the arms of Wallace.

Memory was now busy with the thoughts of Bruce. He remembered his father's weak devotion at that time to the interests of

* This renunciation of Baliol's in favor of Bruce is an historical fact, and it was made in France.

Edward. He remembered his heartwrung death, and looking at the desolate old age of another of Edward's victims, his brave soul melted to pity and regret, and he retired into a distant part of the room to shed, unobserved, the tears he could not restrain. Wallace soon after saw the eyes of the exhausted king close in sleep, and cautious of awakening him he did not stir, but leaning against the thick oaken frame of the bed, was soon lost in as deep a repose.

CHAPTER LIV.

CHÂTEAU GALLIARD.

THE entrance of the old woman about an hour after sunrise awakened Wallace, but Baliol continued to sleep. On the chief's opening his eyes, Bruce, with a smile, stretched out his hand to him. Wallace rose, and, whispering the widow to abide by her guest till they should return, the twain went forth to enjoy the confidence of friendship. A wood opened its arms at a little distance, and thither, over the dew-bespangled grass, they bent their way. The birds sang from tree to tree, and Wallace, seating himself under a beech which canopied a narrow winding of the river Seine, listened with mingled pain and satisfaction to the communications which Bruce had to impart relative to the recent scenes at Durham.

"So rapid have been the events," observed the Scottish prince when he concluded his narrative, "that all appears to me a troubled vision; and blest indeed was the awakening of last night when your voice, sounding from the room below that in which I slept, called me to embrace my best friend."

The discourse next turned on their future plans. Wallace, narrating his adventure with the Red Reaver and the acknowledgments of Philip for the rescue of his son, proposed that the favor he should ask in return (the King of France being earnest to bestow on him some mark of gratitude) should be his interference with Edward to grant the Scots a peaceable retention of their rights. "In that case, my prince," said he, "you will take possession of your kingdom with the olive-branch in your hand." Bruce smiled, but shook his head. "And what, then, will Robert Bruce be? A king, to be sure, but a king without a name. Who won me my kingdom? Who accomplished this peace? Was it not William Wallace? I am not jealous of your fame, Wallace; but I would prove my right to the crown by deeds worthy of a sovereign. Till I have shown myself in the field against Scotland's enemies, I cannot consent to be restored to my inheritance, even by you."

They discoursed until morning was advanced, and then turned towards the cottage, intending to see Baliol safe, and afterward proceed together to Guienne to the rescue of Lady Helen. That accomplished, they would visit Paris and learn whether King Philip would further their designs.

On entering the humble mansion, they found Baliol awake and anxiously inquiring of the widow what was become of the two knights. At sight of them he stretched out his hands to both, and said he should be able to travel in a few hours. Wallace proposed sending to Rouen for a litter to carry him the more easily thither. "No," cried Baliol with a frown, "Rouen shall never see me again within its walls. It was coming from thence that I lost my way last night, and though my poor servants would gladly have returned with me sooner than see me perish in the storm, yet rather would I have been found dead on the road, a reproach to the kings who have betrayed me, than have taken an hour's shelter in that inhospitable city."

While the friends took the simple breakfast prepared for them by the widow, Baliol related that in consequence of the interference of Philip le Bel with Edward he had been released from the Tower of London and sent to France, but under an oath never to leave that country. Philip gave the exiled king the castle of Galliard for a residence, where for some time he enjoyed the shadow of royalty, having still a sort of court composed of his own noble followers. Philip allowed him guards and a splendid table, but on the peace being signed between France and England, the French monarch consented to relinquish the cause of Baliol, and though he should continue to grant him a shelter in his dominions, he removed from him all the appendages of a king.

"Accordingly," continued Baliol, "the guard was taken from my gates, my establishment reduced to that of a private nobleman, and no longer having it in my power to gratify the avidity of those who came about me, I was soon left nearly alone. In vain I remonstrated with Philip; either my letters never reached him or he disdained to answer me. Things were in this state when the other day an English lord found it convenient to bring his suite to my castle. I received him with hospitality, but soon found that what I gave in courtesy he seized as a right. And on my attempting to plead with him for a Scottish lady, whom his passions have forced from her country, he derided my arguments, telling me that had I taken care of my kingdom, the door would not have been left open for him to steal its fairest prize——"

Wallace interrupted him—"Heaven grant you may be speaking of Lord de Valence and Lady Helen Mar!"—"I am," replied Baliol; "they are now at Galliard, and as her illness seems a lingering one, De Valence declared to me his intentions of continuing there. He seized upon the best apartments and carried himself with so much haughtiness that, provoked beyond endurance, I ordered my horse, and accompanied by my honest courtiers rode to Rouen to obtain redress from the governor. But the unworthy Frenchman advised me to go back, and by flattering De Valence, try to regain the favor of Edward. I retired in indignation, determining to assert my rights in my own castle; but the storm overtook me, and being forsaken by false friends, I am saved by generous enemies."

Wallace explained his errand respecting Lady Helen, and anxiously inquired of Baliol whether he meant to return to Galliard. "Immediately," replied he; "go with me, and if the lady consent, which I do not doubt, for she scorns his prayers for her hand and passes night and day in tears, I engage to assist in her escape."

Baliol then advised they should not all return to the castle together, the sight of two knights of their appearance accompanying his host being likely to alarm De Valence. "The quietest way," continue the deposed king, "is the surest. Follow me at a short distance, and towards evening knock at the gates and request a night's entertainment. I will grant it, and then your happy destiny, Wallace, must do the rest."

This scheme being approved a litter of hurdles was formed for the invalid monarch, and the old woman's pallet spread upon it. "I will return it to you, my good widow," said Baliol, "and with proofs of my gratitude." The two friends assisted the king to rise. When he set his foot to the floor he felt so surprisingly better that he thought he could ride the journey. Wallace overruled this wish, and, with Bruce, supported his emaciated figure towards the door. The widow stood to see her guests depart. As Baliol mounted he slid a piece of gold into her hand. Wallace saw not what the king had given and gave a purse as his reward. Bruce had naught to bestow. He had left Durham with little, and that little was expended. "My good widow," said he, "I am poor in everything but gratitude. In lieu of gold, you must accept my prayers."—"May they, sweet youth," replied she, "return on your own head, giving you bread from the barren land and water out of the sterile rock!" Wallace pressed the old woman's withered hand, Bruce did the same. She saw them mount their horses, and when they disappeared from her eyes she returned into her cottage and wept.

When Baliol arrived within a few miles of Château Galliard he pointed to the forest, and told the friends that they had best shelter themselves there till the sun set, soon after which he should expect them at the castle.

Long indeed seemed the interval. In all Wallace's warlike exploits each achievement had immediately followed the moment of resolve; but here he was delayed, as he contemplated an essay in which every generous principle of man was summoned into action. He was going to rescue a helpless woman from the hands of a man of violence and she was also the daughter of his first ally in the great struggle for Scotland. Glad was he then to see the sun sink behind the distant hills. At that moment he and his friend closed their visors, mounted their horses, and set off on full speed towards the château.

When they came in view of the antique towers of Galliard they slackened their pace and leisurely advanced to the gates. The bugle of Wallace demanded admittance; a courteous assent was brought by the warder, the gates unfolded, the friends entered, and in the next instant they were conducted into a room where Baliol sat. De Valence was walking to and fro in a great chafe. He started at sight of the princely armor of Wallace, for he, as Baliol had done, now conceived from the lilied diadem that the stranger must be of the royal house of France; and composing his spirit, he bowed respectfully to the supposed prince. Wallace returned the salutation, and Baliol, rising, accosted him with a dignified welcome. He saw the mistake of De Valence, and perceived how it might facilitate the execution of their project.

On his host's return to the château De Valence had received him with more than his former insolence, for the governor of Rouen had sent him information of the despised monarch's discontent, and when the despotic lord heard a bugle at the gate, and learned that it was answered by the admission of two traveling knights, he flew to Baliol in displeasure, commanding him to recall his granted leave. At the moment of his wrath Wallace entered and covered him with confusion. Struck at seeing a French prince in one of the persons he was going to treat with such indignity, he shrank into himself, and bowed before him with all the meanness of a base soul. Wallace bent his head in acknowledgment, with a majesty which convinced the earl that he was not mistaken. Baliol welcomed his guest in a manner not to dispel the illusion.

"Happy am I," cried he, "that the hospitality which John Baliol intended to show to a mere traveler confers on him the distinction of serving one of a race whose favor confers protection, and its friendship, honor." Wallace returned a gracious reply to this speech, and turning to Bruce, said, "This knight is my friend, and though neither of us chooses to disclose our names during our journey, yet, whatever they may be, I trust you will confide in the word of one whom you have honored by the address you have now made, and believe that his friend is not unworthy the hospitalities of him who was once King of Scots."

De Valence now approached, and announcing who he was, assured the knights in the name of the King of England, whom he was going to represent in Guienne, of every respect from himself and assistance from his retinue to bring them properly on their way. "I return you the thanks due to your courtesy," replied Wallace, "and shall certainly remain to-night a burden on King Baliol; but in the morning we must depart as we came, having a vow to perform which excludes the service of attendants."

A splendid supper was served, at the board of which De Valence sat as well as Baliol. From the moment that the strangers entered the English earl never withdrew, so cautious was he to prevent Baliol informing his illustrious guests of the captivity of Lady Helen Mar. Wallace ate nothing; he sat with his visor still closed, and almost in profound silence, never speaking but when spoken to, and then only answering in as few words as possible. De Valence supposed that this taciturnity was connected with his vow, and did not further remark it; but Bruce (who at Caen had furnished himself with a complete suit of black armor) appeared, though equally invisible under his visor, infinitely more accessible. The humbler fashion of his accouterment did not announce the prince, but his carriage was so noble, his conversation so accomplished, that De Valence did not doubt that both the men before him were of the royal family. He had never seen Charles de Valois, and believing that he now saw him in Wallace, he directed all that discourse to Bruce which he meant should reach the ear of De Valois, and from him pass to that of the King of France. Bruce guessed what was passing in his mind, and with as much amusement as design, led forward the earl's mistake.

Notwithstanding Baliol's resolution to keep awake and assist his friends in their enterprise, he was so overcome by fatigue that he fell asleep soon after supper, and so gave de Valence opportunity to unveil his mind to the Scottish chiefs. Wallace now saw that the execution of his project must depend wholly upon himself, and how to inform Helen that he was in the castle, and of his plan to get her out of it, hardly occupied him more than what to devise to detain De Valence in the banqueting-room while he went forth to prosecute his design. As these thoughts absorbed him, by an unconscious movement he turned towards the English earl. De Valence paused and looked at him, supposing he was going to speak, but finding him still silent the earl addressed him, though with some hesitation. "I seek not, illustrious stranger," said he, "to inquire the name you have intimated must be concealed, but I have sufficient faith in that brilliant circlet around your brows to be convinced (as none other than the royal hand of Philip could bestow it) that it distinguishes a man of the first honor. You now know my sentiments, prince, and for the advantage of both kings I confide them to your services." Wallace rose. "Whether I am prince or vassal," replied he, "my services shall ever be given in the cause of justice, and of that, Earl de Valence, you will be convinced when next you hear of me. My friend," cried he, turning to Bruce, "you will remain with our host; I go to perform the vigils of my vow."

Bruce understood him. It was not merely with their host he was to remain, but to detain De Valence, and opening at once the powers of his mind, the magnificence of his views in policy corroborated to De Valence the idea that he was conversing with one whose birth had placed him beyond ambition. Bruce, in his turn, listened with interest to all De Valence's dreams of aggrandizement, and recollecting his reputation for a love of wine, he replenished the earl's goblet so often that the fumes made him forget all reserves; and after pouring forth the whole history of his attachment to Helen, and his resolution to subdue her abhorrence, he at last fell fast asleep.

Meanwhile, Wallace wrapped himself in Baliol's blue cloak which lay in the ante-room, and enveloping even his helmet in the friendly mantle, he moved swiftly along the gallery towards the chamber of Helen. To be prepared for obstacles, he had obtained from Baliol a particular description of the situation of every apartment leading to it. It was now within an hour of midnight. He passed through several large vacant rooms, and at last arrived at the important door. It opened into a small chamber, in which two female attendants lay asleep. He gently raised the latch, and, with caution, taking the lamp which burned on the table, glided softly through the curtains which filled the cedar arch that led into the apartment of Helen. He approached the bed, covering the light with his hand while he observed her. She was in a profound sleep, but pale as the sheet which enveloped her; her countenance seemed troubled, her brows frequently knit themselves, and she started as she dreamed, as if in apprehension. Suddenly she awoke; she looked up; she believed her dream realized: De Valence leaning over her bed, and herself wholly in his power! A shriek of horror was bursting from her lips when Wallace hastily raised his visor. At the moment when despair was in her heart, she met the eyes dearest to her on earth—those of her father's friend. Stretching forth her arms, for an instant she seemed flying to the protection of him to whose honor she had been bequeathed; but falling back again on her bed, the surprise shook her with such emotion that Wallace feared to see her sink into some deadly swoon. Alarmed for the accomplishment of her deliverance, he threw himself on his knees beside her and whispered, "Be composed, for the love of Heaven and your own safety. Be firm, and you shall fly this place with me to-night." Hardly conscious of the action Helen grasped the hand that held hers, and would have replied, but her voice failing, she fainted on his arm. Wallace now saw no alternative but to remove her hence, even in this insensible state, and raising her gently in his arms, enveloped in the silk coverlid, with cautious steps he bore her through the curtained entrance, and past the sleeping damsels, into the ante-rooms. To meet any of De Valence's men, while in this situation, would betray all. To avoid this he hastened through the passages, and turning into the apartment appointed for himself, laid the now reviving Helen upon a couch. "Water," said she, "and I shall soon be myself again." He gave her some; and at the same time laying a page's suit of clothes (which Baliol had provided) beside her, "Dress yourself in these, Lady Helen," said he; "I shall withdraw, meanwhile, into the passage; but your safety depends on expedition."

Before Helen could answer he had disappeared and, obeying Wallace, the moment she was equipped she laid her hand upon the latch; but the watchful ear of her friend heard her, and he immediately opened the door. The lamps of the gallery shone full upon the light grace of her figure, as shrinking with modesty, and yet eager to be with her preserver, she stood hesitating before him. He threw his cloak over her, and putting her arm through his, in the unobscured blaze of his princely armor he descended to the lower hall of the castle. One man only was there. Wallace ordered him to open the great door. "It is a fine night," said he, "and I shall ride some miles before I sleep." The man asked if he were to saddle the horses; he answered in the affirmative; and the gate being immediately unbarred Wallace led his precious charge into the freedom of the open air. As soon as she saw the outside of those towers, which she had entered as the worst of all prisoners, her heart so overflowed with gratitude to her deliverer that, sinking by his side upon her knees, she could only grasp his hand and bathe it with the tears of innocence.

The man now brought the horses from the stable. He knew that two strangers had arrived at the castle, and not noticing Helen's

stature, supposed they were both before him. He had been informed
by the servants that the taller of the two was the Count de Valois,
and he held the stirrup for him to mount. But Wallace placed Helen
on Bruce's horse, and then vaulting on his own put a piece of gold
into the attendant's hand. "You will return, noble prince?" inquired
the man. "Why should you doubt it?" answered Wallace. "Because," replied the servant, "I wish the brother of the King of France
to know the foul deeds which are doing in his dominions."—"By
whom?" asked Wallace, surprised at this address. "By the Earl de
Valence, prince," answered he; "he has now in this castle a beautiful
lady whom he brought from a foreign land and treats in a manner
unbecoming a knight or a man."—"And what would you have me
do?" said Wallace. "Come in the power of your royal brother," answered he, "and demand the Lady Helen Mar of Lord de Valence."

Helen, who had listened with trepidation to this dialogue, drew
nearer Wallace, and whispered, "Ah, let us hasten away." The man
was close enough to hear her. "Hah!" cried he, in a burst of doubtful
joy, "is she here? Say so, noble knight, and Joppa Grimsby will
serve ye both forever!"—"Grimsby!" cried Helen, recollecting his
voice the moment he had declared his name. "What! the honest English soldier? I and my preserver will indeed value so trusty a follower."

The name of Grimsby was too familiar to the memory of Wallace
for him not to recognize it with melancholy pleasure. He had never
seen Grimsby, but he knew him well worthy of his confidence, and
ordered him to bring two more horses from the stables. When they
were brought Wallace made the joyful signal concerted with Bruce
and Baliol—to sound the Scottish pryse as soon as he and his fair
charge were out of the castle.

The sound met the ear of the prince while anxiously watching
the sleep of De Valence, for fear he should awake and interrupt Wallace in his enterprise. What then was his transport when the first
note of the horn burst upon the silence around him! He sprang on
his feet. The impetuosity of the action roused Baliol, who had been
lying all the while sound asleep in his chair. Bruce made a sign to
him to be silent, and, pressing his hand with energy, forgot the former Baliol in the present, and for a moment bending his knee kissed
the hand he held, then rising, disappeared in an instant.

He flew through the open gates. Wallace perceiving him, rode
out from under the shadow of the trees. The bright light of the
moon shone on his sparkling crest; that was sufficient for Bruce, and
Wallace, falling back again into the shade, was joined the next mo-

ment by his friend. Who this friend was for whom her deliverer had told Helen he waited she did not ask, for she dreaded while so near danger to breathe a word, but she guessed that it must be either Murray or Edwin. De Valence had barbarously told her that not only her father was no more, but that her uncles the Lords Bothwell and Ruthven had both been killed in the last battle. As Bruce approached, his black mantle so wrapped him she could not distinguish his figure. Wallace stretched forth his hand to him in silence, he grasped it with the warm congratulation of friendship, and throwing himself on his horse triumphantly exclaimed, "Now for Paris!" Helen recognized none she knew in that voice, and drawing close to the white courser of Wallace, with something like disappointment mingling with her happier thoughts, she made her horse keep pace with the fleetness of her companions.

CHAPTER LV.

FOREST OF VINCENNES.

AVOIDING the frequented track to Paris, Wallace took a sequestered path by the banks of the Marne, and entered the forest of Vin-cennes just as the moon set. Having ridden far and without cessa-tion, Grimsby proposed their alighting, to allow the lady an oppor-tunity of reposing awhile under the trees. Helen was indeed nearly exhausted; though the idea of her happy flight for a long time had kept her insensible to fatigue.

"I want no rest," she replied to Grimsby. "I could feel none till we are beyond the possibility of being overtaken." "You are safe in this wood, lady," returned the soldier. "It is many miles from the château, and lies in so remote a direction that were the earl to pursue us, I am sure he would never choose this path."—"And did he even come up with us, dear Lady Helen," said Wallace, "could you fear when with your father's friend?"—"It is for my father's friend I fear," gently answered she; "I can have no dread for myself while under such protection."

A very little more persuaded Helen, and Grimsby having spread his cloak on the grass, Wallace lifted her from the horse. As soon as she put her foot to the ground, her head grew giddy, and she must have fallen but for the supporting arm of her watchful friend. He carried her to the couch prepared by the good soldier, and laid her on it. Grimsby had been more provident than they could have ex-pected; for after saddling the second pair of horses, he had returned into the hall for his cloak, and taking an undrawn flask of wine from the supper-table, put it into his vest. This he now produced, and Wallace made Helen drink some of it. The cordial revived her, and sinking on her pillow of leaves, she soon found the repose her wearied frame demanded. For fear of disturbing her, not a word was spoken. Wallace watched at her head and Bruce at her feet, while Grimsby remained with the horse, as a kind of outpost.

Sweet was her sleep, for the thoughts with which she sank into slumber occupied her dreams, but some wild animal, in its nightly prowl, crossing before the horses, they began to snort and plunge, and it was with difficulty the management of Grimsby could quiet

371

them. The noise suddenly awoke Helen, and her scattered faculties not immediately recollecting themselves, she felt an instant impression that all had indeed been but a dream, and exclaimed, "Wallace, where art thou?"—"Here," cried he, pressing her hand, "I am here; you are safe with your friend and brother." Her heart beat with a terror which this assurance could hardly subdue. At last she said in an agitated voice, "Forgive me if my senses are a little strayed. This release seems so miraculous that at moments I hardly believe it real."

"What you feel, lady, is only natural," observed Bruce. "I experienced the same when I first regained my liberty and found myself on the road to join Sir William Wallace."—"Who speaks to me?" said Helen, in a low voice to Wallace. "One," answered Wallace, in the same tone, "who is not to be publicly known until occasion demands it,—one who I trust in God will one day seal the happiness of Scotland,—Robert Bruce."

The answer which she made to the reply of Wallace was spontaneous, and it struck upon the heart of Bruce. "How long," said she, "have you promised Scotland it should see that day!"

"Long, to my grief, Lady Helen," rejoined Bruce; "I would say to my shame, had I ever intentionally erred towards my country; but ignorance of her state and of the depth of Edward's treachery was my crime. I only required to be shown the right path to pursue it, and Sir William Wallace came to point the way." The words were sufficient to impress Helen with that respect he deserved, and which her answer showed. "My father taught me to consider the Bruce the rightful heirs of Scotland, and now that I see the day which he so often wished to hail, I cannot but regard it as the termination of Scotland's woes. If my country be to rest under the happy reign of Robert Bruce, then envy cannot again assail Sir William Wallace, and my father has not shed his blood in vain. His spirit, with those of my uncles Bothwell and Ruthven, will rejoice in such a peace." Surprised at her associating the name of Lord Ruthven with those who had fallen, Wallace interrupted her with the assurance of her uncle's safety. The Scottish chiefs easily understood that De Valence had given her the opposite intelligence, to impress her with an idea that she was friendless, and so precipitate her into the determination of becoming his wife; but she did not repeat to her brave auditors all the arguments he had used to shake her heart. He had told her that the very day in which she would give him her hand, King Edward would send him viceroy into Scotland, where she should reign with all the power and magnificence of a queen. He was handsome, accomplished, and adored her; but Helen

could not love him whom she could not esteem. She had seen and
known the virtues of Sir William Wallace, and from that hour all
that was excellent in man seemed to her to be in him summed up.

Every word which this adored friend now said to comfort her
with regard to her own losses, to assure her of the peace of Scotland, took root in her soul and sprang up into resignation and happiness. She listened to the plans of Wallace and of Bruce, and
the hours of the night passed to her not only in repose, but in enjoyment. Wallace, though pleased with the interest she took in
even the minutest details of their design, became fearful of over-
tasking her weakened frame; he whispered Bruce gradually to drop
the conversation, and slumber again stole over her eyelids.

The dawn had spread far over the sky while she yet slept. Wallace sat contemplating her and the now sleeping Bruce, who had
also imperceptibly sunk to rest. He had hardly seen seven-and-
twenty years, yet so had he been tried in the vicissitudes of life that he
felt as if he had lived a century, and instead of looking on the lovely
Helen as on one whose charms might claim a lover's wishes, he regarded her with sentiments more like parental tenderness. That,
indeed, seemed the affection which now reigned in his bosom, for he
felt as a father towards Scotland.

The shades of night vanished before the uprise of the king of day,
and with them Helen's slumbers. She stirred, she awoke. The lark
was then soaring with shrill cadence over her head; its notes pierced
the ear of Bruce, and he started on his feet. "You have allowed
me to sleep, Wallace?"—"And why not?" replied he. "Here it was
safe for all to have slept. Yet had there been danger I was at my
post to have called you."

The morning vapors having dispersed and Helen refreshed by
her long repose, Wallace seated her on horseback and they recommenced their journey. The helmets of both chiefs were now open.
Grimsby looked at one and the other: the countenance of both assured him that he should find a protector in either. He drew towards
Helen; she noticed his manner, and observing to Wallace that she believed the soldier wished to speak with her, checked her horse. At
this action Grimsby presumed to ride up, and, bowing respectfully,
said that before he followed her to Paris it would be right for the
Count de Valois to know whom he had taken into his train; "one,
madam, who has been degraded by King Edward—degraded," added
he, "but not debased. That last disgrace depends on myself, and
I should shrink from your protection rather than court it, were I
indeed vile."—"I have too well proved your integrity, Grimsby,"

replied Helen, "to doubt it now; but what has the Count de Valois to do with your being under my protection? It is not to him we go, but to the French king."—"And is not that knight with the diadem," inquired Grimsby, "the Count de Valois? The servants at Château Galliard told me he was so." Surprised at this, Helen said the knight should answer for himself, and, quickening the steps of her horse, followed by Grimsby, rejoined his side.

When she informed Wallace of what had passed, he called the soldier to approach. "Grimsby," said he, "you have claims upon me which should ensure you my protection, were I not already your friend. You have only to speak, and all in my power to serve you shall be done."—"Then, sir," returned he, "as mine is a melancholy story, and parts of it have already drawn tears from Lady Helen, if you will honor me with your attention apart from her I would relate how I fell into disgrace with my sovereign."

Wallace fell a little back with Grimsby, and while Bruce and Helen rode briskly forward, he, at a slower pace, prepared to listen to the recapitulation of scenes in which he was only too deeply interested. The soldier began by narrating the fatal events at Ellerslie which had compelled him to leave the army in Scotland and related that after quitting the priory of St. Fillan he reached Guienne, and there served under the Earl of Lincoln until the marriage of Edward with King Philip's sister gave the English monarch quiet possession of that province. Grimsby went on to recount his recognition by one of Heselrigge's captains who accused him of mutiny and treason and his sentence to death for these alleged crimes. He related his escape from prison and the manner in which he had been enabled to take refuge at Château Galliard.

"This," added Grimsby, "is my story, and whoever you are, noble lord, if you think me not unworthy your protection, grant it, and you shall find me faithful unto death."

"I owe you that and more," replied the chief. "I am that Wallace on whose account you fled your country, and if you be willing to share the fortunes of one who may live and die in camps, I pledge you that my destiny shall be yours." Could Grimsby have thrown himself at the feet of Wallace, he would have done so; but taking hold of the end of his scarf, he pressed it to his lips and exclaimed, "This is beyond my prayers, to meet here the triumphant lord of Scotland. I fell innocently into disgrace; ah, how am I now exalted unto honor! My country would have deprived me of life; I am therefore dead to it, and live only to gratitude and you."—"Then," replied Wallace, "as the first proof of the confidence I repose in you, know that the young chief who is riding forward with Lady Helen is Robert Bruce, the Prince of Scotland. Our next enterprise is to place him upon the throne of his ancestors. Meanwhile keep our names a secret and call us by those we may hereafter think fit to assume."

Grimsby, once more reinstated in the station he deserved, no longer hung his head, but looking erect as one born again from disgrace, he became the active and faithful servant of Wallace.

During Wallace's conversation with the soldier, Helen was listening with delight to the encomiums which Bruce passed upon his friend and champion. Before, she had scarcely remarked that he was more than young and handsome; but now, while she contemplated the noble confidence which breathed in every feature, she said to herself, "This man is worthy to be the friend of Wallace."

Bruce remarked the unusual expression of her eyes as she looked on him. "You feel all I say of Wallace," said he. And it was not a charge at which she had need to blush.

At this moment Wallace joined them. He saw the animation of each countenance, and looked at Bruce with a glance of inquiry which carried the wish of a friend to share what had impressed them with such happiness.

"We have been talking of you," returned the prince, "and if to be beloved is a source of joy, you must be peculiarly blest. The affections of Lady Helen and myself made your heart the altar on which we have pledged our fraternal love." Wallace regarded each with a look of tenderness. "It is my joy to love you both like a brother, but Lady Helen must consider me as even more than that to her. I am her father's representative; I am the voice of Scotland thanking her for the preservation her exertions yielded. And to you, my prince, I am your friend, your subject, all that is devoted and true." Thus did these three friends journey towards the gates of Paris, and every hour seemed an age of blessedness to Helen. Wallace animated the scene, and she moved as if on enchanted ground. Hardly did she know what it was to draw any but sighs of bliss till she saw the towers of Paris. They reminded her that she was now to be occasionally divided from him, that when entered within those walls it would no longer be deemed decorous for her to pass days and nights in listening to his voice. She would hardly have acknowledged to herself that what she felt was love, had not the anticipation of even an hour's separation from him whispered the secret to her heart.

CHAPTER LVI.

PARIS.

WHEN they were arrived within a short distance from Paris Wallace wrote a few lines to King Philip, informing him who were the companions of his journey, and that he would rest near the abbey of St. Genevieve until he should receive his majesty's greetings to Bruce, also the queen's granted protection for the daughter of the Earl of Mar. Grimsby was the bearer of this letter. He soon returned with an escort of honor, accompanied by Prince Louis himself. At sight of Wallace he flew into his arms, and after embracing him with all the ardor of youthful gratitude, he presented to him a packet from the king.

It expressed the satisfaction of Philip at the prospect of seeing the man whose valor had wrought him such service as the preservation of his son. He then added that he had other matters to thank him for, and subjects to discuss which would be more elucidated by the presence of Bruce. "According to your request," continued he, "the name of neither shall be made public at my court. My own family only know who are to be my illustrious guests. The queen is impatient to bid them welcome, and no less eager to greet the Lady Helen Mar with her friendship and protection."

A beautiful palfrey, superbly caparisoned, was led forward by a page. Two ladies also, bearing rich apparel for Helen, appeared in the train. When their errand was made known to Wallace he communicated it to Helen. Her delicacy indeed wished to lay aside her page's apparel before she was presented to the queen—but she had been so happy while she wore it! "Days have passed with me, in these garments," said she to herself, "which may never occur again." The ladies were conducted to her. They delivered a gracious message from their royal mistress, and opened the caskets. Helen sighed; she could urge nothing in opposition to their embassy, and assented to the change they were to make in her appearance. She stood mute while they disarrayed her of her humble guise and clothed her in the robes of France. During their attendance, they broke out in encomiums on the graces of her person; but to all this she turned an inattentive ear.

One of the women was throwing the page's clothes carelessly into a bag, when Helen perceiving her, cried, "Take care of that suit; it is more precious to me than gold or jewels."—"Indeed!" answered the attendant, more respectfully folding it; "it does not seem of very rich silk."—"Probably not," returned Helen; "but it is valuable to me, and wherever I lodge I will thank you to put it into my apartment." A mirror was now presented, that she might see herself. She started at the load of jewels with which they had adorned her; and while tears filled her eyes, she mildly said, "I am a mourner; these ornaments must not be worn by me." The ladies obeyed her wish to have them taken off, and she was conducted towards the palfrey. Wallace approached her, and Bruce flew forward with his usual haste to assist her; but it was no longer the beautiful little page that met his view; it was a lovely woman arrayed in all the charms of female apparel, trembling and blushing as she again appeared before the eyes of the man she loved. Bruce looked at her with delighted wonder and held out his hand to her with a cordial smile. "Lady Helen, we are still to be the same. Robes of no kind must ever separate the affections born in our pilgrimage." She put her hand into his with a glow of delight. "While Sir William Wallace allows me to call him brother," answered she, "that will ever sanction our friendship; but courts are formal places, and I now go to one."—"And I will soon remove you to another," replied he, "where"—he hesitated, and then resumed—"where every wish of my sister Helen's heart shall be gratified, or I be no king." Helen blushed deeply and hastened towards the palfrey. Wallace placed her on the embroidered saddle, and Prince Louis preceding the cavalcade, it moved on.

As Bruce vaulted into his seat he said something to his friend of the beauty of Helen. "But her soul is fairer," returned Wallace. The Prince of Scotland, with a gay smile, softly whispered, "Fair. doubly fair, to you." Wallace drew a deep sigh. "I never knew but one woman who resembled her, and she did indeed excel all others. But those hours are past. My heart will never throb as it has throbbed, for she who doubled all my joys is gone. Oh, my prince! though blest with friendship, there are times when I feel that I am solitary." Bruce looked at him with some surprise. "Solitary, Wallace! can you ever be solitary and near Helen Mar?"—"Perhaps more so then than at any other time, for her excellencies remind me of what were once mine, and recall every regret. Oh, Bruce! thou canst not comprehend my loss. I live, but still my heart will mourn."

"And is love so tenacious?" exclaimed Bruce. "Is it to consume your youth, Wallace? Ah! am I not to hope that the throne of my children may be upheld by a race of thine?" Wallace shook his head, but replied, "Your throne and your children's, if they follow your example, will be upheld by Heaven."

In discourse like this the youthful Prince caught a clearer view of the inmost thoughts of his friend than he had been able to discern before; for war, or Bruce's own interests, having engaged them in all their former conversations, Wallace had never been induced to glance at the private circumstances of his history. While Bruce sighed in pity for Helen, he the more deeply revered his suffering and heroic friend.

A few hours brought the royal escort to the Louvre, and, through a train of nobles, Lady Helen was led by Prince Louis into the regal saloon. The Scottish chiefs followed. The queen and the Count D'Evereux received Bruce and Helen, while De Valois conducted Wallace to the king, who had retired, for the purpose of this conference, to his closet.

At sight of the armor which he had sent to the preserver of his son, Philip instantly recognized the Scottish hero, and, rising from his seat, hastened forward and clasped him in his arms. "Wonder not, august chief," exclaimed he, "at the weakness exhibited in these eyes! It is the tribute of nature to a virtue which loads even kings with benefits. You have saved my son's life, you have preserved from taint the honor of my sister." Philip then proceeded to inform his auditor that he had heard from a confessor of Queen Margaret's, just arrived from England, all that had lately happened at Edward's court, and of Wallace's letter to clear the innocence of that injured princess. "She is perfectly reinstated in the king's confidence," added Philip, "but I can never pardon the infamy with which he would have overwhelmed her. I yield to the prayers of my gentle sister not to resent this wrong openly, but in private he shall feel a brother's indignation. I do not declare war against him, but ask what you will, bravest of men, and were it to place the crown of Scotland on your head, demand it of me and it shall be effected." The reply of Wallace was simple. He claimed no merit in the justice he had done the Queen of England, neither in his rescue of Prince Louis; but as a proof of King Philip's friendship he gladly embraced his offered services with regard to Scotland. "Not," added he, "to send troops into that country against England. Scotland is now free of its Southron invaders; all I require is that you will use your royal influence with Edward to allow it to remain so. Pledge your faith, most gracious monarch, with my master, the royally descended Bruce, who is now in your palace. He will soon assume the crown that is his right, and with such an ally as France to hold the ambition of Edward in check, we may certainly hope that the bloody feuds between Scotland and England may at last be laid at rest."

Wallace explained to Philip the dispositions of the Scots, the nature of Bruce's claims, and the virtues of his youthful character. The monarch took fire at the speaker's enthusiasm, and giving him his hand, exclaimed, "Wallace, I know not what manner of man you are! You seem born to dictate to kings, while you put aside as things of no moment the crowns offered to yourself. You are young, and I would say, without ambition, did I not know that your deeds have set you above all earthly titles. But to convince me that you do not disdain gratitude, at least accept a name in my country, and know that the armor you wear, the coronet around your helmet, invested you with the rank of a prince of France, and the title of Count of Gascony." To have refused this mark of the monarch's esteem would have been an act of churlish pride. He graciously accepted the offered distinction, and bowing his head, allowed the king to throw the brilliant collar of Gascony over his neck.

To attach his new count to France was now all the wish of Philip, and he closed the conference with every expression of friendship which man could deliver to man. Wallace lost not the opportunity of pleading for the abdicated King of Scots, and Philip, eager as well to evince his resentment to Edward as to oblige Wallace, promised to send immediate orders to Normandy that De Valence should leave Château Galliard, and Baliol be attended with his former state.

The king then led his guest into the royal saloon, where they found the queen seated between Bruce and Helen. At sight of the Scottish chief her majesty rose. Philip led him up to her, and Wallace, bending his knee, put the fair hand she extended to his lips. "Welcome," said she, "bravest of knights, receive a mother's thanks." She clasped the hand of her son and his together, and added, "Louis, wherever our Count of Gascony advises you to pledge this hand, give it."— "Then it will follow mine," cried the king, putting his into that of Bruce. "You are Wallace's acknowledged sovereign, young prince, and you shall ever find brothers in me and my son. Sweet lady," added he, turning to the glowing Helen, "thanks to your charms for having drawn this friend of mankind to bless our shores."

The court knew Wallace merely as Count of Gascony, and to preserve an equal concealment, Bruce assumed the name of the young De Longueville, whom Prince Louis had, in fact, allowed to retire to Chartres, there to pass a year of mourning within its penitential monastery. Only two persons ever came to the Louvre who could recognize Bruce to be other than he seemed, and they were John Cummin, the elder twin brother of the present regent of Scotland, and James, Lord Douglas. The former had remained in France out of dislike to his brother's proceedings, and as Bruce knew him in Guienne, and believed him to be a blunt, well-meaning young man, he saw no danger in trusting him. The brave son of William Douglas was altogether of a nobler mettle, and both Wallace and his prince rejoiced at the prospect of receiving him to their friendship.

Philip opened the affair to the two lords, and having declared his designs in favor of Bruce, conducted them into the queen's room, and pointing where he stood, "There," cried he, "is the King of Scotland." Douglas and Cummin would have bent their knees to their young monarch, but Bruce hastily caught their hands and prevented them. "My friends," said he, "regard me as your fellow-soldier only till you see me on the throne of my fathers. Till then that is our prince," added he, looking on Wallace; "he is my leader, my counselor, my example; and if you love me, he must be yours." Douglas and Cummin turned towards Wallace at these words. Royalty did indeed sit on his brow, but with a majesty which spoke only in love and honor.

Helen had eyes for none but Wallace. Nobles, princes, kings, were all involved in one uninteresting mass to her when he was present. Yet she smiled on Douglas when she heard him express his gratitude to the champion of Scotland for the services he had done a country for which his own father had died. Cummin, when he paid his respects to Wallace, told him that he did so with double pleasure, since he had two unquestionable evidences of his unequaled merit: the confidence of his father, the Lord Badenoch, and the hatred of his brother, the present usurper of that title.

The king soon after led his guests to the council-room, where a secret cabinet was held to settle the future bonds between the two kingdoms, and Helen, looking long after the departing figure of Wallace, with a pensive step followed the queen to her apartment.

CHAPTER LVII.

THE LOUVRE.

THESE preliminaries of lasting friendship being arranged and sworn to by Philip, Wallace despatched a messenger to Scotland to Lord Ruthven at Hunting-tower, informing him of the present dispositions with regard to their native land. He made inquiries respecting the state of the public mind, and declared his intentions not to introduce Bruce amongst his chieftains until he knew exactly how they were all disposed. Some weeks passed before a reply to this letter arrived. During the time, the health of Helen, which had been much impaired by the sufferings inflicted on her by De Valence, gradually recovered, and her beauty became the admiration of the French nobles. A new scene of royalty presented itself in this gay court to Wallace, for all was pageant and chivalric gallantry; but it had no other effect on him than that of exciting those affections which rejoiced in the innocent gaieties of his fellow-beings.

With a natural superiority which looked over these court pastimes to objects of greater moment, Bruce merely endured them, but it was with an urbanity congenial with his friend's; and while the princes of France were treading the giddy mazes of the dance or tilting at each other in the mimic war of the tournament, the Prince of Scotland, who excelled in all these exercises, left the field of gallantry undisputed, and talked with Wallace or Helen on events which yet lay in fate. So accustomed had the friends now been to share their thoughts with Lady Helen that they imparted to her their plans, and listened with pleasure to her timid, yet judicious, remarks. Her soul was inspired with the same zeal for Scotland which animated their own breasts; like Bruce's, it was ardent, but like Wallace's, it was tempered with moderation.

The winds of this season of the year being often adverse, Wallace's messenger did not arrive at his destined port in Scotland till the middle of November, and the January of 1299 had commenced before his returning bark entered the mouth of the Seine.

Wallace was alone, when Grimsby, opening the door, announced Sir Edwin Ruthven. In a moment the friends were locked in each other's arms. Edwin, straining Wallace to his heart, reproached him in affectionate terms for having left him behind, and again and again he kissed his friend's hand. Wallace answered him with similar affection, and learnt from Edwin that he had left the messenger at some distance on the road, so impatient was he to embrace his friend again and to congratulate his dear cousin on her escape.

Edwin answered the anxious inquiries of Wallace respecting his country by informing him that Badenoch, having arrogated to himself the supreme power in Scotland, had determined to take every advantage of the last victory gained over King Edward. In this resolution he was supported by the Lords Athol, Buchan, and Soulis, who were returned full of indignation from the court of Durham. Edward removed to London, and Badenoch, hearing that he was preparing other armies for the subjugation of Scotland, sent ambassadors to the Vatican to solicit the Pope's interference. Flattered by this appeal, Boniface wrote a letter to Edward exhorting him to refrain from further oppressing a country over which he had no lawful power. Edward's answer was full of artifice, maintaining his pretensions to Scotland, and declaring his determination to consolidate Great Britain into one kingdom, or to make the northern part one universal grave.

"The speedy consequence of this correspondence," Edwin continued, "was a renewal of hostilities against Scotland. Many places fell, and battles were fought in which the English were everywhere victorious; for," added Edwin, "none of your generals would draw a sword under the command of Badenoch, and, alarmed at these disasters, the Bishop of Dunkeld is gone to Rome to entreat the Pope to order your return. The Southrons are advancing into Scotland in every direction. They have landed again on the eastern coast, they have possessed themselves of all the border counties, and without your arm to avert the blow our country must be irretrievably lost.

Edwin had brought letters from Ruthven and the young Earl of Bothwell, which more particularly narrated these ruinous events, to enforce every argument to Wallace for his return. They gave it as their opinion, however, that he must revisit Scotland under an assumed name. Did he come openly the jealousy of the Scottish lords would be reawakened and the worst of them might put a finishing stroke to their country by taking him off by assassination. Ruthven and Bothwell, therefore, entreated that, as it was his wisdom as well as his valor their country required, he would hasten to Scotland and condescend to serve her unrecognized till Bruce should be established on the throne.

While Edwin was conducted to the apartments of Lady Helen, Wallace took these letters to his prince. On Bruce being informed of the circumstances in which his country lay, and of the wishes of its most virtuous chiefs for his accession to the crown, he assented to the prudence of their advice with regard to Wallace. "But," added he, "our fortunes must be in every respect, as far as we can mold them, the same. While you are to serve Scotland under a cloud, so will I. At the moment Bruce is proclaimed King of Scotland, Wallace shall be declared its bravest friend. We will go together, as brothers, if you will," continued he. "I am already considered by the French nobility as Thomas de Longueville; you may personate the Red Reaver. Scotland does not yet know that he was slain, and the reputation of his valor having placed him in the estimation of our shores rather in the light of one of their own island *Sea-kings* than in that of his real character, the aid of his name would bring no evil odor to our joint appearance. But were you to wear the title you bear here, a quarrel might ensue between Philip and Edward, which I perceive the former is not willing should occur openly. Edward must deem it a breach of their amity, did his brother-in-law permit a French prince to appear in arms against him in Scotland. But the Reaver being considered in England as outlawed by France, no surprise can be excited that he and his brother should fight against Philip's ally. We will then assume their characters, and I shall have the satisfaction of serving for Scotland before I claim her as my own. When we again drive Edward over the borders, on that day we will throw off our visors, and Sir William Wallace shall place the crown on my head."

Bruce received Edwin with a welcome which convinced the youth that he met a friend, rather than a rival, in the heart of Wallace, and every preliminary being settled by the three friends respecting their return to Scotland, they repaired to Philip to inform him of Lord Ruthven's despatches, and their consequent resolutions.

The king liked all they said, but urged them to wait the return of a second ambassador he had sent to England. Immediately on Wallace's arrival, Philip had despatched a request to the English king that he would grant the Scots the peace which was their right. Not receiving any answer he sent another messenger with a more categorical demand. The persevered hostilities of Edward against Scotland explained the delay. But the king yet hoped for a favorable reply, and made such entreaties to Bruce and his friend to remain in Paris till it should arrive that they at last granted a reluctant consent.

At the end of a week the ambassador returned with a conciliatory letter to Philip, but affirming Edward's right to Scotland, declared his determination never to lay down his arms till he had again brought the whole realm under his scepter.

Wallace and his royal friend now saw no reason for lingering in France, and having visited the young De Longueville at Chartres, they apprised him of their intention still further to borrow his name. "We will not disgrace it," cried Bruce. "I promise to return it to you, a theme for your country's minstrels." When the friends rose to depart, the brave and youthful penitent grasped their hands. "You go, valiant Scots, to cover with a double glory in the field of honor a name which my unhappy brother dyed deep in his own country's blood. The tears I weep before this cross for his and my transgressions have obtained me mercy, and I believe that my brother also is forgiven."

At an early hour next day Wallace and Bruce took leave of the French king. The queen kissed Helen affectionately, and whispered, while she tied a jeweled collar round her neck, that when she returned she hoped to add to it the coronet of Gascony. Helen's only reply was a sigh, and her eye turned unconsciously on Wallace. He was clad in a plain chain suit of black armor, with a red plume in his helmet, the ensign of the Reaver whose name he had assumed. All of his former habit that he now wore about him was the sword which he had taken from Edward. At the moment Helen looked towards Wallace, Prince Louis was placing a cross-hilted dagger in his girdle. "My deliverer," said he, "wear this for the sake of the descendant of St. Louis. It accompanied that holy king through all his wars in Palestine. It twice saved him from the assassin's steel, and I pray Heaven it may prove as faithful to you."

Soon after this, Douglas and Cummin entered to pay their parting respects to the king; and that over, Wallace, taking Helen by the hand, led her forth, followed by Bruce and his friends.

At Havre they embarked for the frith of Tay, and a favorable gale driving them through the straits of Calais, they launched out into the wide ocean.

Bruce on the beach

CHAPTER LVIII.

SCOTLAND.

THE eighth morning from the day in which the Red Reaver's ship was relaunched from the Norman harbor, Wallace, now the representative of that pirate, bearing the white flag of good faith, entered between the castled shores of the frith of Tay and cast anchor under the towers of Dundee.

When Bruce leaped upon the beach, he turned to Wallace and said with exultation, though in a low voice, "Scotland now receives her king. This earth shall cover me, or support my throne."—"It shall support your throne and bless it too," replied Wallace; "you are come in the power of justice, and that is the power of God."

The chiefs did not stay long at Dundee where Ruthven still bore sway. When they arrived he was at Hunting-tower, and thither they went. The meeting was fraught with many mingled feelings. Helen had not seen her uncle since the death of her father, and as soon as the first gratulations were over she retired to an apartment to weep alone.

On Cummin's being presented to Lord Ruthven, the earl told him he must now salute him as Lord of Badenoch, his brother having been killed a few days before in a skirmish. Ruthven then turned to welcome the entrance of Bruce, who, raising his visor, received from the loyal chief the homage due to his sovereign dignity. Wallace and the prince soon learned that Scotland did indeed require the royal arm and the counsel of its best, and lately almost banished, friends for much of the eastern part of the country was again in the possession of Edward's generals. They had seized on every castle in the lowlands; nor could the quiet of reposing age elude the general devastation; and after a dauntless defense of his castle, the veteran Knight of Thirlestane had fallen and with him his only son. On hearing this disaster, the sage of Ercildown, having meanwhile protected Lady Isabella Mar at Learmont, conveyed her northward, but falling sick at Roslyn he had stopped there. And the messenger he despatched to Hunting-tower with these calamitous tidings bore also information that an immense army was approaching from Northumberland. Ercildown said he understood Sir Simon Fraser was hastening forward with a small body to attempt cutting off these advanced squadrons. But he added, while the contentions continued between Athol and Soulis for the vacant regency, no man could have hope of any steady stand against England.

At this communication, Cummin bluntly proposed himself as the terminator of this dispute. "If the regency were allowed to my brother, as head of the House of Cummin, that dignity now rests with me; give the word, my sovereign," said he, addressing Bruce, "and none there shall dare oppose my rights." Ruthven approved this proposal, and Wallace seconded the advice of Ruthven. Thus John Cummin, Lord Badenoch, was invested with the regency, and immediately despatched to the army, to assume it as if in right of his being the next heir to the throne, in default of the Bruce.

Meanwhile, as Hunting-tower would be an insecure asylum for Helen, Wallace proposed to Edwin that he should escort his cousin to Braemer and place her there under the care of his mother and the widowed countess. "Thither," continued he, "we will send Lady Isabella also, should Heaven bless our arms at Roslyn." Edwin acquiesced, and Helen, aware that fields of blood were no scenes for her, yielded a reluctant assent—not merely to go, but to take that look of Wallace which might be the last.

The sight of her uncle and the objects around had so recalled the image of her father that ever since her arrival sadness had hung over her spirits. She remembered that a few months ago she had seen that beloved parent go out to a battle, whence he never returned. Should the same doom await her with regard to Wallace! The idea shook her frame with an agitation that overcame her, in spite of herself, when Edwin approached to lead her to her horse. "My gentle sister," said Wallace, "do not despair of our final success—of the safety of all whom you regard."—"Ah! Wallace," faltered she, "but did I not lose my father?"—"Sweet Helen!" returned he, tenderly grasping her hand; "you lost him, but he gained by the exchange. Were I to fall, my sister, my sorrows would be over, and from the region of universal blessedness I should enjoy the sight of Scotland's happiness."

"Were we all to enter those regions at one time," faintly replied Helen, "there would be a comfort in such thoughts, but as it is"— here she paused, tears stopped her utterance. "A few years is a short separation," returned Wallace, "when we are hereafter to be united to all eternity. This is my consolation when I think of Marion, and whatever may be the fate of those who now survive, call to remembrance my words, dear Helen, and God will send you comfort."

"Then farewell, my friend, my brother!" cried she, tearing herself away and throwing herself into the arms of Edwin; "leave me now, and the angel of the just will bring you in glory here or hereafter to your sister Helen." Wallace fervently kissed the hand she again extended to him, and with an emotion which he had thought he should never feel again for mortal woman, left the apartment.

The day after the departure of Helen, Bruce became impatient to take the field, and to indulge this eagerness, Wallace set forth with him to meet the returning steps of Ruthven and his gathered legions.

Having passed along the romantic borders of Invermay, the friends descended towards the precipitous banks of the Earn, at the foot of the Grampians. In these green labyrinths they wound their way till Bruce, who had never before been in such mountain wilds, expressed a fear that Wallace had mistaken the track, for this seemed far from any human footstep.

Wallace replied with a smile, "The path is familiar to me as the garden of Hunting-tower."

The day, which had been cloudy, suddenly turned to wind and rain, which spread an air of desolation over the scene very dreary to an eye accustomed to the fertile plains and azure skies of the south. The whole of the road was rough, dangerous, and dreadful. The steep and black rocks, towering above their heads, seemed to threaten the precipitation of their masses into the path below, but Wallace had told Bruce they were in the right track, and he gaily breasted both the storm and the perils of the road.

Enveloped in a sea of vapors, with torrents of water pouring down the sides of their armor, the friends descended the western brow of this part of the Grampians, until they approached Loch Earn. They had hardly arrived there before the rain ceased, and the clouds disappearing from the side of the mountains, discovered the vast and precipitous Ben Vorlich.

The gray mantle, with which the tops of the mountains had been obscured, rolled away towards the west, and discovered to the eye of Wallace that a line of light which he had discerned through the mist was the host of Ruthven descending Ben Vorlich in defiles. From the nature of the path they were obliged to move in a winding direction, and as the sun now shone full upon their arms, and their lengthened lines gradually extended from the summit of the mountain to its base, no sight could contain more of the sublime and Bruce forgot his horror of the wastes he had passed over in the joy of beholding so noble an army of his countrymen, thus approaching to place him upon the throne of his ancestors.

Lord Ruthven no sooner reached the banks of **Loch Earn** than he espied the prince and Wallace. He joined them; then marshaling his men at the head of that vast body of water, placed himself with the two supposed De Longuevilles in the van, and in this array marched into Stirlingshire. The young Earl of Fife held the government of the castle and town of Stirling, and as he had been a zealous supporter of Lord Badenoch, Bruce negatived Ruthven's proposal to send in a messenger for the earl's division of troops. "No, my lord," said he, "like my friend Wallace, I will have no divided spirits near me; all must be earnest in my cause!"

After rapid marches, they arrived safe at Linlithgow, where Wallace proposed staying a night to refresh the troops, who were now joined by Sir Alexander Ramsay, at the head of a thousand of his clan. While the men took rest, their chiefs waked to think for them, and Wallace, with Bruce and Ruthven, and the brave Ramsay (to whom Wallace had revealed himself, but still kept Bruce unknown), were in deep consultation, when Grimsby entered to inform his master that a young knight desired to speak with Sir Guy de Longueville. "His name?" demanded Wallace. "He refused to tell it," replied Grimsby, "and wears his beaver shut." Wallace looked around with a glance that inquired whether the stranger should be admitted. "Certainly," said Bruce; "but first put on your mask." Wallace closed his visor, and the moment after Grimsby reentered with a knight of elegant mien, habited in a suit of green armor linked with gold. He wore a close helmet, from which streamed a long feather of the same hue. Wallace rose at his entrance; the stranger advanced to him. "You are he whom I seek. I am a Scot, and a man of few words; accept my services; allow me to attend you in this war and I will serve you faithfully." Wallace replied, "And who is the brave knight to whom Sir Guy de Longueville must owe so great an obligation?"—"My name," answered the stranger, "shall not be revealed till he who now wears that of the Reaver proclaims his own in the day of victory. I know you, sir, but your secret is safe with me. Place me to fight by your side and I am yours forever."

Wallace was surprised by this speech. "I have only one question to ask you, noble stranger," replied he, "before I confide a cause dearer to me than life in your integrity. How did you become master of a secret which I believed out of the power of treachery to betray?" —"No one betrayed your secret to me. I came by my information in an honorable manner, but the means I shall not reveal till I see the time to declare my name, and that, perhaps, may be in the moment when the assumed brother of yon young Frenchman," added the stranger, turning to Bruce and lowering his voice, "again appears publicly in Scotland as Sir William Wallace."

"I am satisfied," replied he, well pleased that, whoever this knight might be, Bruce yet remained undiscovered. "I grant your request. Yon brave youth, whose name I share, forgives me the success of my sword. I slew the Red Reaver, and, therefore, would restore a brother to Thomas de Longueville, in myself. He fights on my right hand; you shall be stationed at my left."—"On the side next your heart!" exclaimed the stranger; "let that ever be my post!"

This enthusiasm did not surprise any present; it was the usual language of all who approached Sir William Wallace; and Bruce, pleased with the energy with which it was uttered, forgot his disguise, and half arose to welcome him to his cause; but a look from Wallace arrested his intention, and the prince sat down, thankful for so timely a check on his precipitancy.

In passing the Pentland Hills into Mid-Lothian, the chiefs were met by Edwin, who had crossed from the north, and having heard no tidings of the Scottish army in the neighborhood of Edinburgh, had turned to meet it on the most probable road. Wallace introduced him to the Knight of the Green Plume, for that was the appellation by which the stranger desired to be known, and then made inquiries how Lady Helen had borne the fatigues of her journey to Braemar. "Pretty well there," replied he, "but much better back again." He then explained that on his arrival with her, neither Lady Mar nor his mother would consent to remain so far from the spot where Wallace was to contend again for the safety of their country. Helen did not say anything in opposition to their wishes, and at last Edwin yielded to the entreaties of his mother and aunt, to bring them to where they might at least not long endure the misery of suspense. Having consented, without an hour's delay he set forth with the ladies to retrace his steps to Hunting-tower, and there he left them under a guard of three hundred men, whom he brought from Braemar for that purpose.

Bruce, whose real name had not been revealed to the other ladies of Ruthven's family, in a lowered voice asked Edwin some questions relative to the spirits in which Helen had parted with him. "In losing her," added he, "my friend and I feel but as part of what we were. Her presence ever reminded me of the angelic guard by whom Heaven points our way."—"I left her with looks like the angel you speak of," answered Edwin; "she bade me farewell upon the platform of the eastern tower of the castle. When I gave her the parting embrace she raised herself from my breast, and stretching her arms to heaven, she exclaimed, 'Bless him, gracious God! bless him and his noble commander!'" In such discourses the Scottish leaders marched along, till, passing before the lofty ridge of the Corstophine Hills, they were met by groups of flying peasantry. At sight of the Scottish banners they stopped, and informed their armed countrymen that the new regent, John of Badenoch, having rashly attacked the Southron army, had suffered defeat, and was in full retreat towards Edinburgh, while the country people fled on all sides before the victors.

Wallace was at no loss in comprehending how much to believe in this panic; but determining, whether great or small the power of his adversary, to intercept him at Roslyn, he sent to Cummin and to Fraser, the two commanders in the beaten and dispersed armies, to rendezvous on the banks of the Esk. The brave troops which he led, though ignorant of their real leader, obeyed his directions, under an idea they were Lord Ruthven's, who was their ostensible general, and steadily pursued their march. Every village and solitary cot seemed recently deserted; and through an awful solitude they took their rapid way, till the towers of Roslyn castle hailed them as a beacon. "There," cried Ramsay, pointing to the embattled rock, "stands the fortress of my forefathers! It must this day be made famous by the actions performed before its walls."

Wallace, whose knowledge of this part of the country was not quite so familiar as that of Ramsay, learnt sufficient from him to decide at once which would be the most favorable position for a small band to assume against a large army, and, accordingly disposing his troops, which did not amount to more than eight thousand men, he despatched one thousand, under the command of Ramsay, to occupy the numerous caves in the southern banks of the Esk, whence they were to issue in various divisions, and with shouts, on the first appearance of advantage either on his side or on the enemy's.

Ruthven, meanwhile, went for a few minutes into the castle to embrace his niece, and to assure the venerable Lord of Roslyn that assistance approached his beleaguered walls.

Edwin, who with Grimsby had volunteered the dangerous service of reconnoitering the enemy, returned within an hour bringing a straggler from the English camp, whose life was promised him on condition of his revealing the strength of the advancing army. The terrified wretch did not hesitate, and from him they learnt that it was commanded by Sir John Segrave and Ralph Confrey, who were preparing for a general plundering. And, to sweep the land at once, Segrave had divided his army into three divisions, to scatter themselves over the country, and everywhere gather in the spoil. To be assured of this being the truth, while Grimsby remained to guard the prisoner, Edwin went alone into the track he was told the Southrons would take, and from a height he discerned about ten thousand of them winding along the valley. With this confirmation of the man's account he brought him to the Scottish lines, and Wallace, who well knew how to reap advantage from the errors of his enemies, being joined by Fraser and the discomfited regent, made the concerted signal to Ruthven. That nobleman immediately pointed out to his men the waving colors of the Southron host, as it approached beneath the overhanging woods of Hawthorndean. He exhorted them by their fathers, wives, and children to breast the enemy at this spot, to grapple with him till he fell. "Scotland," cried he, "is lost or won this day. Fight stoutly, and God will yield you an invisible support."

The Scots answered their general by a shout, and calling on him to lead them forward, Ruthven placed himself with the regent and Fraser in the van, and led the charge. Little expecting an assault from an adversary they had so lately driven off the field, the Southrons were taken by surprise. But they fought well, and resolutely stood their ground till Wallace and Bruce, who commanded the flanking divisions, closed in upon them with an impetuosity that drove Confrey's division into the river. Then the ambuscade of Ramsay poured from his caves; the earth seemed teeming with mailed warriors; and the Southrons, seeing the surrounding heights and the deep defiles filled with the same terrific appearances, fled with precipitation towards their second division, which lay a few miles southward. In several points the Southrons gained so greatly the advantage that Wallace and Bruce threw themselves successfully into those parts where the enemy most prevailed, and by example, and prowess, they a thousand times turned the fate of the day. Segrave was taken and forty English knights besides. The green borders of the Esk were dyed red with Southron blood, and the enemy on all sides were calling for quarter, when of a sudden the cry of "Havoc and St. George!" issued from the adjoining hill. Terror struck to many a Scottish heart. The Southrons, who were just giving up their arms, leaped upon their feet. The fight recommenced with redoubled fury. Sir Robert Neville, at the head of the new reenforcement, charged into the center of the Scottish legions. Bruce and Edwin threw themselves into the breach, and fighting man to man, would have taken Neville had not a follower of that nobleman, wielding a ponderous mace, struck Bruce so terrible a blow as to fracture his helmet and cast him from his horse to the ground. The fall of so active a leader excited as much dismay in the surrounding Scots as it encouraged the reviving spirits of the enemy. Edwin exerted himself to preserve his prince from being trampled on, and while he fought for that purpose, and afterwards sent his senseless body off the field, Neville rescued Segrave and his knights. Lord Ruthven now contended with a feeble arm. Fatigued with the two preceding conflicts, covered with wounds, and perceiving indeed a host pouring upon them on all sides, the Scots, in despair, gave ground; some threw away their arms to fly the faster, and by thus exposing themselves, panic-struck, redoubled the confusion. Indeed, so great was the havoc that the day must have ended in the universal destruction of every Scot in the field had not Wallace felt the crisis, and that, as Guy de Longueville, he shed his blood in vain. In vain his terrified countrymen saw him rush into the thickest of the carnage; in vain he called to them by all that was sacred to man, to stand to the last. He was a foreigner, and they had not confidence in his exhortations; death was before them, and they turned to fly. The fate of his country hung on an instant. The last rays of the setting sun shone full on the rocky promontory of the hill which projected over the field of combat. He took his resolution, and spurring his steed up the steep ascent, stood on the summit, where he could be seen by the whole army; then, taking off his helmet, he waved it in the air with a shout; and having drawn all eyes upon him, suddenly exclaimed, "Scots! you have this day vanquished the Southrons twice! If you be men, remember Cambus-Kenneth and follow William Wallace to a third victory!" The cry which issued from the amazed troops was that of a people who beheld the angel of their deliverance. "Wallace!" was the charge-word of every heart. The hero's courage seemed diffused through every breast, and with braced arms and determined spirits forming at once into the phalanx his thundering voice dictated, the Southrons again felt the weight of the Scottish steel, and a battle ensued which covered the glades of Hawthorndean with the bodies of its invaders.

Sir John Segrave and Neville were both taken. And ere night closed in upon the carnage, Wallace granted quarter to those who sued for it, and receiving their arms, left them to repose in their depopulated camp.

CHAPTER LIX.

ROSLYN CASTLE.

WALLACE having planted an adequate force in charge of the prisoners, went to the two Southron commanders to pay them the courtesy he thought due to their bravery and rank, before he retired with his followers towards Roslyn castle. He entered their tent alone. At sight of the warrior who had given them so signal a defeat, the generals rose. Neville, who had received a slight wound in one of his arms, stretched out the other to Wallace. "Sir William Wallace," said he, "that you were obliged to declare a name so renowned before the troops I led could be made to relinquish their advantage was an acknowledgment in their favor almost equivalent to a victory."

Sir John Segrave, who stood leaning on his sword with a disturbed countenance, interrupted him: "The fate of this day cannot be attributed to any earthly name or hand. I believe my sovereign will allow the zeal with which I have ever served him; and yet thirty thousand as brave men as ever crossed the marshes have fallen before a handful of Scots. Three victories won over Edward's troops in one day are not events of a common nature. God alone has been our vanquisher."—"I acknowledge it," cried Wallace; "and believe that he is on the side of justice."

Edwin, with the Knight of the Green Plume, awaited Wallace's return from his prisoners' tent. Ruthven came up with Wallace before he joined them, and told him that Bruce was safe under the care of the sage of Ercildown; and that the regent, who had been wounded in the beginning of the day, was also in Roslyn castle. Wallace then called Edwin to him, giving him orders that all of the survivors who had suffered in these three desperate battles should be collected from amongst the slain and carried into the neighboring castles. The rest of the soldiers were commanded to take their refreshment still under arms. These duties performed, Wallace turned with the eagerness of friendship to see how Bruce fared.

At the gate of Roslyn castle, its aged master, the Lord Sinclair, met Wallace to bid him welcome. "Blessed be the saint of this day," exclaimed he, "for thus bringing our best defender. My gates, like my heart, open to receive the true regent of Scotland."—"I have only done a Scotsman's duty, venerable Sinclair," replied Wallace, "and must not arrogate a title which Scotland has transferred to other hands."—"Not Scotland, but rebellion," replied the old chief. "It was rebellion against the gratitude of the nation that invested the Black Cummin with the regency, and only some similar infatuation has bestowed the same title on his brother."—"The present Lord Badenoch is an honest and a brave man," replied Wallace, "and, as I obey the power which gave him his authority, I am ready, by fidelity to him, to serve Scotland with as vigorous a zeal as ever."

Wallace then asked to be conducted to his wounded friend, Sir Thomas de Longueville; for Sinclair was ignorant of the real rank of his guest. Eager to oblige him, his noble host immediately led the way through a gallery, and, opening the door of an apartment, discovered to him Bruce lying on a couch, and a venerable figure, whose silver beard and sweeping robes announced him to be the sage of Ercildown, was bathing the wounded chief's temples with balsams. A young creature, beautiful as a ministering seraph, also hung over the prostrate chief. She held a golden casket in hand, out of which the sage drew the unctions he applied. At the sound of Wallace's voice, the wounded prince started on his arm, to greet his friend; but he as instantly fell back. Wallace hastened forward. When Bruce recovered from the swoon into which the suddenness of his attempt to rise had thrown him, he felt a hand grasping his, and gently pressing it, smiled; a moment afterwards he opened his eyes, and in a low voice articulated, "My dear Wallace! you are victorious?"—"Completely so, my prince and king," returned he, in the same tone. "All is now plain before you; speak but the word, and render Scotland happy!"—"Not yet, oh, not yet," whispered he. "My more than brother, allow Bruce to be himself again before he is known in the land of his fathers. This cruel wound in my head must heal first, and then I may again share your dangers and your glory."

Wallace saw that his prince was not in a state to bear argument, and he turned towards the other inmates of the chamber. The sage advanced to him, and recognizing in Wallace's now manly form the fine youth he had seen with Sir Ronald Crawford at the claiming of the crown, he saluted him with a paternal affection, and then beckoning the beautiful girl who had so compassionately hung over the couch of Bruce, she drew near the sage. He took her hand. "Sir William Wallace," said he, "this sweet child is the youngest daughter of the brave Mar, who died in the field of glory on the Carron. Her grandfather, the stalworth Knight of Thirlstane, fell a few weeks ago defending his castle, and I am almost all that is left to her, though she has, or had, a sister, of whom we can learn no tidings." Isabella, for it was she, covered her face to conceal her emotions. "Dear lady," said Wallace, "these heroes were both known to and beloved by me, and now that Heaven has resumed them to itself, as a last act of friendship, I shall convey you to that sister whose heart yearns to receive you."

To disengage Isabella's thoughts, Ercildown put a cup of the mingled juice of herbs into her hand, and commissioned her to give it to their invalid. Wallace now learned that his friend's wound was not only in the head, accompanied by a severe concussion, but that it must be many days before he could remove from his bed without danger. Anxious to release him from even the whispers of his companions, Wallace immediately proposed leaving him to rest, and, beckoning the chiefs, they followed him out of the apartment.

On the following morning he was aroused at daybreak by the abrupt entrance of Andrew, Lord Bothwell, into his tent. "Murray! my brave Murray!" cried he; "thou art welcome once more to the side of thy brother in arms!" The young Lord Bothwell returned his embrace in silence, but sitting down by Wallace's couch, he grasped his hand, and said, "I feel a happiness here which I have never known since the day of Falkirk. You quitted us, Wallace, and all seemed gone with you. But you return, bringing conquest and peace; you restore our Helen to her family; you bless us with yourself! And shall you not see again the gay Andrew Murray? Melancholy is not my climate, and I shall now live in your beams." —"Dear Murray," returned Wallace, "this enthusiasm can only be equaled by my joy in all that makes you and Scotland happy." He then proceeded to confide to him all that related to Bruce, and to describe the minutiæ of those plans for his establishment which had only been hinted in his letters from France. Bothwell entered with ardor into these designs, and regretted that the difficulty he found in persuading the veterans of Lanark to follow him to any field where they did not expect to find their beloved Wallace had deprived him of the participation of the late danger and new glory of his friend. "To compensate for that privation," replied Wallace, "while our prince is disabled from pursuing victory in his own person, we must not allow our present advantages to lose their expected effects. You shall accompany me through the Lowlands, where we must recover the places which the ill-fortune of James Cummin has lost."

Murray gladly embraced this opportunity of again sharing the field with Wallace, and the chiefs joined Bruce. Bothwell was presented to his young sovereign, and Douglas entering, the discourse turned on their different posts of duty. Wallace suggested to his royal friend that as his restoration to health could not be speedy, it would be necessary not to await that event, but begin the recovery of the border counties before Edward could reenforce their garrisons. Bruce sighed, but with a glow suffusing his pale face said, "Go, my friend! Bless Scotland which way you will, and let my acquiescence convince future ages that I love my country beyond my own fame. Men may say that I have lain on a couch while you fought for me; but I will bear all obloquy rather than withhold you an hour from the work of Scotland's peace."—"It is not for the breath of men, my dear prince," returned Wallace, "that either you or I act. Our deeds and intentions have one great Judge, and he will award the only true glory."

Though the wounded John Cummin remained possessed of the title of regent, Wallace was virtually endowed with the authority. Whatever he suggested was acted upon as by a decree; the jealousies which had driven him from his former supreme seat seemed to have died with their instigator, the late regent, and no chief of any consequence, excepting Soulis and Athol, breathed a word in opposition to the general gratitude.

Wallace, having dictated his terms and sent his prisoners to England, commenced the march that was to clear the Lowlands of the foe. His own valiant band, headed by Scrymgeour and Lockhart of Lee, rushed towards his standard with a zeal that rendered each individual a host in himself. The fame of his new victories, seconded by the enthusiasm of the people and the determination of the troops, soon made him master of all the lately lost fortresses.

Hardly four weeks were consumed in these conquests, and not a rood of land remained south of the Tay in the possession of England, excepting Berwick. Before that often-disputed stronghold, Wallace drew up his forces to commence a regular siege. The governor, intimidated by the powerful works which he saw the Scottish chief forming against the town, despatched a messenger to Edward with the tidings, not only praying for succors, but to inform him that if he continued to refuse the peace for which the Scots fought, he would find it necessary to begin the conquest of the kingdom anew.

CHAPTER LX.

BERWICK.

WHILE Wallace was thus carrying all before him from the Grampian to the Cheviot Hills, Bruce was rapidly recovering. His eager wishes seemed to heal his wounds, and on the tenth day after the departure of Wallace, he left that couch which had been cheered by the tender Isabella. The ensuing Sabbath beheld him still more restored, and having imparted his intentions to the Lords Ruthven and Douglas, who were with him, the next morning he joyfully buckled on his armor. Isabella, when she saw him thus clad, started, and the roses left her cheek. "I am armed to be your guide to Hunting-tower," said he, with a look that showed her he read her thoughts. He then called for pen and ink to write to Wallace. The reassured Isabella, rejoicing in the glad beams of his eyes, held the standish. As he dipped his pen, he looked at her with a tenderness that thrilled her soul, and made her bend her blushing face to hide emotions which whispered bliss. Thus, with a spirit wrapped in felicity, for victory hailed him from without, and love seemed to woo him within, he wrote the following letter to Wallace:

"I am now well, my best friend. This day I attend my lovely nurse with her venerable guardian to Hunting-tower. Eastward of Perth almost every castle of consequence is yet filled by the Southrons, whom the folly of James Cummin allowed to reoccupy the places whence you had so lately driven them. I go to root them out, to emulate in the north what you are now doing in the south. You shall see me again when the banks of the Spey are as free as you have made the Forth. In all this I am yet Thomas de Longueville. Isabella knows me as no other, for would she not despise the unfamed Bruce? To deserve and win her love as De Longueville, and to marry her as King of Scotland, is the fond hope of your friend and brother, Robert ——. God speed me! I shall send you despatches of my proceedings."

Wallace had just made a successful attack upon the outworks of Berwick when this letter was put into his hand. He was surrounded by his chieftains, and having read it, he informed them that Sir Thomas de Longueville was going to the Spey to rid its castles of the enemy. "I doubt not that what he promises, God, and the justice of our cause, will perform," said Wallace, "and we may soon expect to hear Scotland has no enemies in her Highlands."

But in this hope Wallace was disappointed. Day after day passed and no tidings from the north. He became anxious; Bothwell, and Edwin too, began to share his uneasiness. Continued successes against Berwick had assured them of a speedy surrender, when unexpected succors being thrown in by sea, the confidence of the garrison became reexcited, and the ramparts appearing doubly manned, Wallace saw the only alternative was to surprise—take possession of the ships and turn the siege into a blockade. By a masterly stroke, he effected his design on the shipping, and having closed the Southrons within their walls he despatched Lord Bothwell to Hunting-tower, to learn the state of military operations there, and above all, to bring back tidings of the prince's health.

On the evening of the very day in which Murray left Berwick, a desperate sally was made by the garrison, but they were beaten back with such effect that Wallace gained possession of one of their most commanding towers. The contest did not end till night, and after passing a brief while in the council-tent, listening to the suggestions of his friends relative to the use that might be made of the new acquisition, he retired to his own quarters at a late hour. At these momentous periods he never seemed to need sleep, and seated at his table, settling the dispositions for the succeeding day, he marked not the time, till the flame of his exhausted lamp expired in the socket. He replenished it, and had again resumed his labors when the curtain which covered the door of his tent was drawn aside and an armed man entered. Wallace looked up, and seeing that it was the Knight of the Green Plume, asked if anything had occurred from the town.

"Nothing," replied the knight, in an agitated voice, and seating himself beside Wallace. "Any evil tidings from Perthshire?" demanded Wallace, who now hardly doubted that ill news had arrived of Bruce. "None," was the knight's reply, "but I am come to unite myself forever to your destiny, or you behold me this night for the last time." Surprised at this address, and the emotion which shook the frame of the unknown warrior, Wallace answered him with expressions of esteem, and added, "If it depend on me to unite so brave a man to my friendship forever, only speak the word, declare your name, and I am ready to seal the compact."—"My name," returned the knight, "will indeed put these protestations to the proof. I have fought by your side, Sir William Wallace. I would have died at any moment to have spared that breast a wound, and yet I dread to raise this visor to show you who I am. A look will make me live, or blast me."—"Your language confounds me, noble knight," replied Wallace; "I know of no man living, saving the violators of Lady Helen Mar's liberty, who need tremble before my eyes. It is not possible that either of these men is before me, and whoever you are, brave chief, your deeds have proved you worthy of a soldier's friend-ship."

The knight was silent. He took Wallace's hand—he grasped it; the arms that held it did indeed tremble. Wallace again spoke: "What is the meaning of this? I have a power to benefit, but none to injure."—"To benefit and to injure!" cried the knight in a trans-port of emotion; "you have my life in your hands. Look on me, and say whether I am to live or die." As the warrior spoke he cast him-self on his knees and threw open his visor. Wallace saw a fine but flushed face. It was much overshadowed by the helmet. "My friend," said he, attempting to raise him, "so little right can I have to the power you ascribe to me that, although it seems to me as if I had seen your features before, yet——"—"You forget me," cried the knight, starting on his feet and throwing off his helmet to the ground; "again look on this face, and stab me at once by a second declaration that I am remembered no more."

The countenance of Wallace now showed that he too well remem-bered it. He was pale and aghast. "Lady Mar," cried he, "not ex-pecting to see you under a warrior's casque, you will pardon me that I should not immediately recognize the widow of my friend." She gasped for articulation. "And is it thus," cried she, "you answer the sacrifices I have made for you? I have put on me this abhorrent steel; I have braved the dangers of many a hard-fought day, to con-vince you of a love unexampled in woman, and thus you recognize her who has risked honor and life for you."—"With neither, Lady Mar," returned he. "I am grateful for the generous motives of your conduct, but in respect to the memory of him whose name you bear, I cannot but wish that so hazardous an instance of interest in me had been left undone."—"If that is all," returned she, drawing towards him, "it is in your power to ward from me every stigma. Who will asperse the name of Mar, when you displace it with that of Wal-lace? Make me yours, dearest of men," cried she, "and you will receive one who will be to you what woman never yet was, and who will endow you with territories nearly equal to those of the King of Scotland. My father is no more, and now, as Countess of Strat-hearn and Princess of the Orkneys, I have it in my power to bring

a sovereignty to your head and the fondest of wives to your bosom."
In vain Wallace attempted to raise her with gentleness from her
indecorous situation.   She had no perception but for the idea which
had now take possession of her heart, and whispering him softly, said,
"Be but my husband, Wallace, and all rights shall perish before my
love.   In these arms you shall bless the day you first saw Joanna
of Strathearn."

She saw not that every look and movement on her part filled
Wallace with aversion, and not until he forcibly broke from her did
she doubt the success of her fond caresses.

"Lady Mar," said he, "I must repeat that I am not ungrateful
for the regard you have bestowed on me; but such excess of attachment is lavished upon a man that is a bankrupt in love."   Wallace
said even more than this.   He remonstrated with her on the shipwreck she was making of her own happiness, in adhering thus tena-
ciously to a man who could only regard her with esteem.   Lady Mar
threw herself upon her knees, she implored his pity, but still he continued to urge her by every argument to relinquish her ill-directed
love; to return to her domains, before her absence could be generally
known.   She looked up to read his countenance.   A friend's anxiety, nay, authority, was there, but no glow of passion.   Her beauty,
then, had been shown to a man without eyes; her eloquence poured
on an ear that was deaf.   In a paroxysm of despair she dashed the
hand she held far from her, and standing proudly on her feet—"Hear
me, thou man of stone!" cried she, "and answer me on your life and
honor, for both depend on your reply: Is Joanna of Strathearn to
be your wife?"

"Cease to urge me," returned Wallace; "you already know the
decision of this ever-widowed heart."   Lady Mar looked steadfastly
at him.   "Then receive my last determination," and drawing near
him, with a desperate countenance, she suddenly plucked St. Louis'
dagger from his girdle and struck it into his breast.   He caught the
hand which grasped the hilt.   Her eyes glared with fury, and she exclaimed, "I have slain thee, insolent triumpher in my love and agonies!   I know that it is not for the dead Marion you have trampled
on my heart, but for the living Helen."   As she spoke, he moved her
hold from the dagger and drew the weapon from the wound.   A
torrent of blood flowed over his vest and stained the hand that grasped
hers.   She turned of a deadly paleness, but a demoniac joy still
gleamed in her eyes.   "Lady Mar," cried he, while he thrust the
thickness of his scarf into the wound, "I pardon this outrage.   Go
in peace; and I shall never breathe to man nor woman the occurrences

of this night. Only remember that with regard to Lady Helen, my wishes are as pure as her own innocence."—"So they may be now, immaculate Wallace!" answered she, with bitter derision. "Think not to impose on her who knows how this vestal Helen followed you in page's attire. Did you not follow her to France? Did you not tear her from the arms of Lord Aymer de Valence? Wallace, I now know you; and as I have been fool enough to love you beyond all woman's love, I swear by all the powers to make you feel the weight of woman's hatred!"

Her denunciations had no effect on Wallace, but her slander against her step-daughter agitated him with an indignation that almost dispossessed him of himself. In vehement words he denied all that she had alleged against Helen, and appealed to the whole court of France to witness her spotless innocence. Lady Mar exulted in this emotion, though every sentence, by the interest it displayed in its object, seemed to establish the truth of a suspicion which she had at first only uttered from the vague workings of her revenge. Maddened that another should have been preferred before her, her jealous pride blazed into redoubled flame. "I go," cried she, "not to proclaim Helen's dishonor to the world, but to deprive her of her lover—to yield the rebel Wallace into the hands of justice! When on the scaffold, remember that it was Joanna of Strathearn who laid thy matchless head upon the block! Remember that my curse pursues you here and hereafter!" Fire seemed to dart from her scornful eyes, and with the last malediction thundering from her tongue, she darted from his sight.

CHAPTER LXI.

THE CAMP.

NEXT morning Wallace was recalled from the confusion into which his visitor had thrown his mind, by the entrance of Ker, who came with the reports of the night. In the course of the communication he mentioned that about three hours before sunrise the Knight of the Green Plume had left the camp with his despatches for Stirling. Wallace was scarcely surprised at this ready falsehood of Lady Mar's, and not intending to betray her, he merely said, "Long ere he appears again, I hope we shall have good tidings from our friends in the north."

But day succeeded day, and notwithstanding Bothwell's embassy, no accounts arrived. The countess had left an emissary in the Scottish camp who did as she had done before, intercept all messengers from Perthshire.

Indeed, from the first of her flight to Wallace, to the hour of her quitting him, she had never halted in her purpose from any regard to honor. Previous to her stealing from Hunting-tower she had bribed the seneschal to say that on the morning of her disappearance he had met a knight near St. Concal's well, coming to the castle, who told him that the Countess of Mar was gone on a secret mission to Norway, and she therefore had commanded him, by that knight, to enjoin her sister-in-law, for the sake of the cause most dear to them all, not to acquaint Lord Ruthven, or any of their friends, with her departure, till she should return with happy news for Scotland. Fearful that Helen might communicate her flight to Wallace, from the moment of her joining him at Linlithgow she intercepted every letter from Hunting-tower, and when Bruce went to that castle, she continued the practice, being jealous of what might be said of Helen by this Sir Thomas de Longueville. To this end, even after she left the camp, all packets from Perthshire were conveyed to her by the spy she had stationed near Wallace, while all which were sent from him to Hunting-tower were stopped by the treacherous seneschal and thrown into the flames. No letters, however, ever came from Helen; a few bore Lord Ruthven's superscription, and all the rest were addressed by Sir Thomas de Longueville to Wallace. She broke the seals of this correspondence, but she looked in vain on their contents. Bruce and his friend, as well as Ruthven, wrote in a cipher, and only one passage, which the former had by chance written in the common character, could she ever make out. It ran thus:

"I have just returned to Hunting-tower, after the capture of Kinfouns. Lady Helen sits by me on one side, Isabella on the other. Isabella smiles on me like the spirit of happiness. Helen's look is not less gracious; for I tell her I am writing to Sir William Wallace. She smiles, but it is with such a smile as that with which a saint would relinquish to heaven the dearest object of its love. Her manner checks me, dear Wallace, but I would give worlds that you could bring your heart to make her smile, as I do her sister."

Lady Mar crushed the wish in her hand, and though she was never able to decipher a word more of Bruce's numerous letters, she destroyed them all.

She had ever shunned the eyes of young Lord Bothwell, and to have him on the spot when she should discover herself to Wallace, she thought would only invite discomfiture. Affecting to share the general anxiety respecting the failure of communications from the north, she it was who had suggested the propriety of sending some one to make inquiries. By covert insinuations, she easily induced Ker to propose Bothwell to Wallace, and, on the very night that she had prevailed to despatch him on this embassy, she went to declare herself to the man for whom she had thus sunk herself in falsehood.

Though Wallace heard the denunciation with which she left his presence, yet he did not conceive it was more than the rage of passion, and, anticipating persecutions rather from her love than her revenge, he was relieved by the intelligence that the Knight of the Green Plume had really taken his departure.

Wallace now hourly anticipated the surrender of the enemy. Reduced for want of provisions, and seeing all succors cut off by the seizure of the fleet, the inhabitants, detesting their new rulers, collected in bands, and lying in wait for the soldiers of the garrison, murdered them in great numbers. But here the evil did not end; for by the punishments which the governor thought proper to inflict by lots on the guilty or the guiltless the distress of the town was augmented to a horrible degree. Such a state of things could not be long maintained. Aware that should he continue in the fortress his troops must perish either by insurrection within or from the enemy without, the Southron commander determined no longer to wait the appearance of relief, and to stop the internal confusion he sent a flag of truce to Wallace, accepting and signing his offered terms of capitulation. By this deed he engaged to open the gates at sunset, but begged the interval between noon and that hour to allow him time to settle the animosity between his men and the people, before he should surrender his followers entirely into the hands of the Scots.

Having despatched his assent to this request of the governor's, Wallace retired to his own tent. That he had effected his purpose without the carnage which must have ensued had he again stormed the place gratified his humanity, and congratulating himself on such a termination of the siege, he turned with more than usual cheerfulness towards a herald who brought him a packet from the north. The man withdrew and Wallace broke the seal; but what was his astonishment to find it a citation for himself to repair immediately to Stirling, "to answer," it said, "certain charges brought against him by an authority too illustrious to be set aside without examination." He had hardly read this extraordinary mandate, when Sir Simon Fraser, his second in command, entered, and with consternation in his looks, put an open letter into his hand. It ran as follows:

SIR SIMON FRASER: Allegations of treason against the liberties of Scotland having been preferred against Sir William Wallace, until he clears himself of these charges to the lords of Scotland here assembled, you, Sir Simon Fraser, are directed to assume in his stead command of the forces; and as the first act of your duty, you are ordered to send the accused towards Stirling under a strong guard, within an hour after you receive this despatch.

(Signed)   JOHN CUMMIN,
Earl of Badenoch, Lord Regent of Scotland.

STIRLING CASTLE.

Wallace returned the letter to Fraser, with an undisturbed countenance. "I have received a similar order from the regent," said he, "and though I cannot guess the source whence these accusations spring, I shall require no guard to speed me to the scene of my defense. I am ready to go, my friend, and happy to resign the brave garrison that has just surrendered, to your honor." Fraser answered that he should be emulous to follow his example in all things, and to abide by his agreements with the Southron governor. He then retired to prepare the army for the departure of their commander, and much against his feelings to call out the escort that was to attend the calumniated chief to Stirling.

When the marshal of the army read to the officers and men the orders of the regent, consternation seized on one part of the troops, and violent indignation agitated the other. The veterans who had followed the chief of Ellerslie, from the first hour of his appearing as a patriot in arms, could not brook this aspersion upon their leader's honor, and had it not been for the exhortations of Scrymgeour and Lockhart, they would have risen in instant revolt. Though persuaded to sheathe their swords, they could not be withheld from quitting the field and marching to Wallace's tent. He was conversing with Edwin when they arrived, and, in some measure, he had broken the shock to him of so dishonoring a charge by his being the first to communicate it. While Edwin strove to guess who could be the inventor of so dire a falsehood, he awakened an alarm in Wallace for Bruce, which could not be excited for himself, by suggesting that perhaps some intimation had been given to the most ambitious of the lords respecting the arrival of their rightful prince. "And yet," returned Wallace, "I cannot altogether suppose that, for even they could not torture my share in Bruce's restoration to his country into anything like treason. But," added he with a smile, "we need not disturb ourselves with such thoughts; the regent is in our prince's confidence, and did this accusation relate to him, he would not, on such a plea, have arraigned me as a traitor."

Edwin again revolved in his mind the nature of the charge, and, at last, suddenly recollecting the Knight of the Green Plume, he asked if it were not possible that he might be the traitor. "I must confess to you," continued Edwin, "that this knight, who ever appeared to dislike your closest friends, seems to me the probable instigator of this mischief, and is, perhaps, the author of the strange failure of communication between you and Bruce. Accounts have not arrived even since Bothwell went, and that is more than natural. Though brave in his deeds, this unknown may prove only the more subtle agent of our enemies."

Wallace changed color at these suggestions, but merely replied, "A few hours will decide your suspicion, for I shall lose no time in confronting my accuser."—"I go with you," said Edwin; "never while I live will I consent to lose sight of you again."

It was at this moment that the approach of the Lanark veterans was heard from without. The whole band rushed into the tent, and Stephen Ireland, who was foremost, raising his voice above the rest, exclaimed, "They are the traitors, my lord, who accuse you! It is determined by our corrupted thanes that Scotland shall be sacrificed, and you are to be made the first victim. Lead us on, and we will hurl these usurpers from their thrones."

This demand was reiterated by every man present. The Bothwellmen and Ramsay's followers joined the men of Lanark, and the mutiny against the orders of the regent became general. Wallace walked out into the open field, and mounting his horse rode forth amongst them. At sight of him the air resounded with acclamations, proclaiming him their only leader, but stretching out his arm to them in token of silence they became profoundly still. "My friends and brother soldiers," cried he, "as you value the honor of William Wallace, yield him implicit obedience."—"Forever!" shouted the Bothwell-men. "We never will obey any other," rejoined his faithful Lanark followers, and with an increased uproar they demanded to be led to Stirling. His extended hand again stilled the storm, and he resumed: "You shall go with me to Stirling, but as my friends only; never as the enemies of the regent of Scotland. I am charged with treason; it is his duty to try me by the laws of my country; it is mine to submit to the inquisition. I invite you to accompany me, not to avenge an iniquitous sentence denounced on a guiltless man, but to witness my acquittal."

At this mild persuasive every upraised sword dropped before him, and Wallace, turning his horse into the path which led towards Stirling, his men, with a silent determination to share the fate of their master, fell into regular marching order and followed him. Edwin rode by his side, equally wondering at the composure with which he sustained such a weight of insult.

At the west of the camp, the detachment appointed to guard Wallace in his arrest came up with him. It was with difficulty that Fraser could find an officer who would command it, and he who did at last consent, appeared before his prisoner with downcast eyes, seeming rather the culprit than the guard. Wallace observing his confusion said a few gracious words to him, and the officer more overcome by this than he could have been with reproaches, with downcast eyes retired into the rear of his men.

CHAPTER LXII.

STIRLING CASTLE.

WALLACE entered on the Carse of Stirling, that scene of his many victories, and beheld its northern horizon white with tents. An armed cavalcade met him near the Carron, to conduct him without opposition to Stirling. In case it should be insufficient to intimidate him who had never yet been made to fear, the regent had summoned all the vassals of the various seigniories of Cummin, and planted them in battle array before the walls of Stirling. But whether they were friends or foes was equally indifferent to Wallace, for strong in integrity, he went securely forward to his trial; and he met the heralds of the regent with as much ease as if they had been coming to congratulate him on the capitulation of Berwick, the ratification of which he brought in his hand.

It was then night. In the morning, at an early hour, Wallace was summoned before the council in the citadel.

On his reentrance into that room which he had left the dictator of the kingdom, when every knee bent and every head bowed to his supreme mandate, he found not one who even greeted his appearance with the commonest ceremony of courtesy. Badenoch, the regent, sat upon the throne with evident symptoms of being yet an invalid. The Lords Athol and Buchan, and the numerous chiefs of the clans of Cummin, were seated on his right; on his left were arranged the Earls of Fife and Lorn, Lord Soulis, and every Scottish baron of power who at any time had shown himself hostile to Wallace. A very few who still respected Wallace were present, not because they were sent for, but in consequence of a rumor of the charge having reached them; and these were the Lords Lennox and Loch-awe, with Kirkpatrick and two or three chieftains from the western Highlands. None of them had arrived till within a few minutes of the council being opened, and Wallace was entering at one door as they appeared at the other.

At sight of him a low whisper buzzed through the hall, and a marshal took the plumed bonnet from his hand, which out of respect to the nobility of Scotland he had raised from his head at his entrance. A herald meanwhile proclaimed in a loud voice, "Sir William Wallace, you are charged with treason, and by an ordinance of Fergus the First, you must stand uncovered before the representative of the majesty of Scotland until that loyalty be proved which would again restore you to a seat amongst her faithful barons."

Wallace bowed his head to the marshal in token of acquiescence; but Edwin, whose indignation was reawakened at this exclusion of his friend from the privilege of his birth, said something so warm to the marshal that Wallace, in a low voice, was obliged to check his vehemence by a declaration that it was his determination to submit himself in every respect to whatever was exacted of him by the laws of his country.

On Loch-awe and Lennox observing him stand thus before the bonneted and seated chiefs, they took off their caps, and, bowing to Wallace, refused to occupy their places on the benches while the defender of Scotland stood. Kirkpatrick drew eagerly towards him, and throwing down his casque and sword at his feet, cried in a loud voice, "Lie there till the only true man in all this land commands me to take ye up in his defense." Wallace regarded this ebullition from the heart of the honest veteran with a look that was eloquent to all.

"Is it thus, presumptuous Knight of Ellerslie," cried Soulis, "that by your looks you dare encourage contumely to the lord regent and his peers?" Wallace did not deign him an answer, but turning calmly towards the throne, "Representative of my king," said he, "in duty to the power whose authority you wear, I have obeyed your summons, and I here await the appearance of the accuser who has had the hardihood to brand the name of William Wallace with disloyalty to prince or people."

The regent was embarrassed. He did not suffer his eyes to meet those of Wallace, but looked down in manifest confusion during this address; and then, without reply, turned to Lord Athol and called on him to open the charge. Athol required not a second summons; he rose immediately, and, in a bold manner, accused Wallace of having been won over by Philip of France to sell those rights of supremacy to him which, with a feigned patriotism, his sword had wrested from the grasp of England. For this treachery, Philip was to endow him with the sovereignty of Scotland; and, as a pledge of the compact, he had invested him with the principality of Gascony, in France. "This is the ground-work of his treason," continued Athol; "but the superstructure is to be cemented with our blood. I have seen a list in his own handwriting of those chiefs whose lives are to pave his way to the throne."

At this point of the charge Edwin sprang forward; but Wallace, perceiving the intent of his movement, caught him by the arm and, by a look, reminded him of his engagement to keep silent.

"Produce the list," cried Lord Lennox. "No evidence that does not bring proof to our eyes ought to have any weight with us against the man who has bled in every vein for Scotland."—"It shall be brought to your eyes," returned Athol; "that, and other damning proofs, shall convince this credulous country of its abused confidence." —"I see these damning proofs now," cried Kirkpatrick, who had frowningly listened to Athol; "the abusers of my country's confidence betray themselves at this moment by their eagerness to impeach her friends."—"We all know," cried Athol, turning on Kirkpatrick, "to whom you belong. For the right to kill Cressingham did you sell yourself to William Wallace; and a bloody champion you are, always ready for your murderous master."

"Hear you this and bear it?" cried Kirkpatrick and Edwin in one breath, and grasping their daggers, Edwin's flashed in his hand. "Seize them!" cried Athol; "my life is threatened." Marshals instantly approached; but Wallace, who had hitherto stood in silent dignity, turned to them, with that tone of justice which had ever commanded from his lips, and bade them forbear. "Touch these knights at your peril, marshals!" said he. "No man in this chamber is above the laws, and they protect every Scot who resents unjust aspersions upon his own character, or attacks on that of an arraigned friend. It is before the majesty of the law that I now stand; but were injury to usurp its place, not all the lords in Scotland should detain me a moment in a scene so unworthy of my country." The marshals retreated, for they had been accustomed to regard with deference the opinion of Sir William Wallace; and though he now stood in the light of their violator, yet to this hour he had ever appeared to make them the guide of his actions.

Athol saw that none in the assembly had courage to enforce this act of violence, and, blazing with fury, he poured his whole wrath upon Wallace. "Imperious traitor!" cried he; "this presumption only deepens our impression of your guilt! Demean yourself with more reverence to this august court, or expect to be sentenced on the proof which such insolence gives. We require no other to proclaim your domineering spirit, and at once to condemn you as the tyrant of our land."—"Lord Athol," replied Wallace, "what is just I would say in the face of all the courts in Christendom. It is not in the power of man to make me silent when I see the laws of my country outraged and my countrymen oppressed. I have answered you, earl, to this point, and am ready to hear you to the end."

Athol resumed: "I am not your only accuser, confident man; you shall see one whose truth cannot be doubted, and whose first glance will cover that bold front with shame. My lord," cried he, turning to the regent, "I shall bring a most illustrious witness before you, one who will prove on oath that it was the intention of this arch-hypocrite, before another moon, to bury deep in blood the very people whom he now affects to protect. But to open your and the nation's eyes at once, I now call forth the evidence."

The marshals opened a door in the side of the hall and led a lady forward, habited in regal splendor, and covered from head to foot with a veil of so transparent a texture that her costly apparel and majestic contour were distinctly seen through it. She was conducted to a chair on an elevated platform, a few paces from where Wallace stood. On her being seated, the regent rose, and in a tremulous voice addressed her:

"Joanna, Countess of Strathearn and Mar, Princess of the Orkneys, we adjure thee by thy princely dignity, and in the name of the King of kings, to bear a just witness to the truth or falsehood of the charges of treason and conspiracy now brought against Sir William Wallace."

The name of his accuser made Wallace start, and the sight of her unblushing face—for she threw aside her veil the moment she was addressed,—overspread his cheek with a tinge of that shame for her which she was now too hardened to feel herself.* Edwin gazed at her in horror, while she, casting a glance on Wallace, in which the purpose of her soul was declared, turned to the regent, and spoke:

"My lord," said she, "you see before you a woman who never knew what it was to feel a self-reproachful pang till an evil hour brought her that treacherous man. But as my first passion has ever been the love of my country, I will prove it to this assembly, by making a confession of what was once my heart's weakness, and by that candor I trust they will fully honor the rest of my narrative."

Lennox and Loch-awe looked on each other with amazement. Kirkpatrick, recollecting the scenes at Dumbarton, exclaimed, "Jezebel!" but the ejaculation was lost in the general burst of applause; and the countess, opening a folded paper which she held in her hand, in a calm voice, but with a flushing cheek, resumed:

"I have written my deposition that my memory might not err,

---

* The treasonable crimes of this wicked woman are truly verified in history.

and that my country may be satisfied of the accuracy of every syllable I utter."

She drew a quick breath, and proceeded reading from the paper, thus:

"I am not to tell you, my lord, that Sir William Wallace twice released the late Earl of Mar and myself from Southron captivity. Our deliverer was what you see him, fraught with attractions which he directed against the peace of a young woman married to a man of paternal years. I revered my nuptial vow too sincerely to listen to him, but I blush to own that his agonies of love, and the virtues I believed he possessed, cooperating with my gratitude, at last wrought such a change that I became wretched. No guilty wish was there, but a pity for him which undermined my health. I tried to wrest him from my memory, and nearly had succeeded when I was informed by my late husband's nephew (the youth who now stands beside Sir William Wallace) that he was returned under an assumed name from France. Edwin Ruthven left me at Hunting-tower, and that very evening, while walking alone in the garden, I was surprised by the sudden approach of an armed man. He threw a scarf over my head to prevent my screams; took me from the garden by the way he had entered, and placing me on a horse before him, carried me whither I know not; but on my recovery I found myself in a chamber with a woman standing beside me and the same warrior. His visor was so closed that I could not see his face. On my expressing alarm, he addressed me in French, telling me he had provided a man to carry an excuse to Hunting-tower to prevent pursuit, and then he gave me a letter which he said he brought from Sir William Wallace. Believing that a man who had sworn to me devoted love could not premeditate a more serious outrage, I broke the seal and, nearly as I can recollect, read to this effect:

"He told me that as he had often read in my blushes the sympathy which my virtue made me conceal, he would now wrest me from my cheerless widowhood, and having nothing to reproach myself with, compel me to be happy. His friend, the only confidant of his love, had brought me to a spot whence I could not fly; there I should remain till he, Wallace, could leave the army for a few days, and, throwing himself on my compassion, be received as the most faithful of lovers, the fondest of husbands.

"This letter," continued the countess, "was followed by others, and suffice it to say that the latent affection in my heart, and his subduing love, were too powerful in his cause. At last the knight who had brought me to the place, and who wore green armor and a green plume, reappeared."—"Prodigious villain!" broke from the lips of Edwin. The countess turned her eye on him for a moment, and then resumed: "He was the warrior who had borne me from Hunting-tower, and from that hour until the period I now speak of I had never seen him. He put another packet into my hand, desiring me to peruse it with attention, and return Sir William Wallace a verbal answer by him. 'Yes' was all he required. I retired to open it, and what was my horror when I read a development of the treasons for which he is now brought to account. He wrote, that until he saw me he had no other end in his exertions for Scotland than her rescue from a foreign yoke; 'but,' added he, 'from the moment in which I first beheld my adored Joanna, I aspired to place a crown on her brows.' He then told me that he did not deem the time of its presentation to him on the Carse of Stirling a safe juncture for its acceptance; neither was he tempted to run the risk of maintaining an unsteady throne when I was not free to partake it; but since the death of Lord Mar every hope was reawakened, and then he determined to become a king. Philip of France had made secret articles with him to that end. He was to hold Scotland of him, while to make the surrender of his country's independence sure to Philip, and its scepter to himself and his posterity, he attempted to persuade me there would be no crime in destroying the chiefs whose names he enrolled in this list. On our bridal day he proposed the deed should be done; he would invite all these lords to a feast, and poison or the dagger should lay them at his feet.

"So impious a proposal restored me to myself. My love at once turned to abhorrence, and hastening to the Knight of the Green Plume I told him to carry my resolution to his master: that I would never see him more till I should appear as his accuser before the tribunal of his country. The knight tried to dissuade me, but at last becoming alarmed at the punishment which might overtake himself, he confessed to me that the scene of his first appearance was devised by Wallace, who had brought him from France to assist him in his scheme. If I would guarantee his life, he offered to convey me safe to Stirling. All else that he asked was that I would allow him to be the bearer of the casket which contained Sir William Wallace's letters, and suffer my eyes to be blindfolded during the first part of our journey. This I consented to, but the murderous list I had undesignedly put into my bosom. It was very dark, and we traveled swiftly till we came to a wood, and, being overcome with fatigue, my conductor persuaded me to take rest. I slept beneath the trees. In the morning when I awoke I looked round for the knight; he was gone, and I saw him no more. I then explored my way to Stirling to unmask to the world the direst hypocrite that ever prostituted the name of virtue."

The countess ceased, and a hundred voices broke out at once, pouring invectives on the traitorous ambition of Sir William Wallace, and invoking the regent to pass some condemnation on so monstrous a crime.

"And will you not speak?" cried Edwin, in agony, clasping Wallace's arm,—"will you not speak, before these ungrateful men shall dare to brand your name with infamy? Make yourself heard, my noblest friend! Confute that wicked woman, who surely has proved what I suspected,—that this self-concealing knight came to be a traitor."—"I will speak, my Edwin," returned Wallace, "at the proper moment, but not in this tumult of my enemies. Rely on it, your friend will submit to no unjust decree."

"Where is this Knight of the Green Plume?" cried Lennox, almost startled in his opinion of Wallace by the consistency of the countess's narrative. "No mark of dishonor shall be passed on Sir William Wallace without the strictest scrutiny. Let the mysterious stranger be found and confronted with Lady Strathearn." Notwithstanding the earl's insisting on impartial justice, she perceived the doubt in his countenance, and, eager to maintain her advantage, replied: "The knight, I fear, has fled beyond our search; but that I may not want a witness to corroborate the love I once bore this hypocrite, and, consequently, the sacrifice I make to loyalty in thus unveiling him to the world, I call upon you, Lord Lennox, to say whether you did not observe, at Dumbarton Castle, the state of my too grateful heart."

Lennox, who well remembered her conduct in the citadel of that fortress, hesitated, aware that his reply might substantiate a guilt which he now feared would be but too strongly made manifest. Wallace determining to allow all men to show what was in their hearts towards him and justice, looked towards the earl and said, "Do not hesitate, my lord; speak all that you know, or think, of me. Could my breast be laid open for men to scan, I should be content; for then Scotland would know me, as my Creator knows me."

Lord Lennox, stung with remorse for having for a moment credited anything against the frank spirit which gave him this permission, replied: "To Lady Strathearn's question I must answer that at Dumbarton I did perceive her preference of Sir William Wallace, but I never saw anything in him to warrant the idea that it was reciprocal. And yet, were it even so. as true Scots we cannot relinquish to a single witness our faith in a man who has so eminently served his country."

"No," cried Loch-awe; "if the Knight of the Green Plume be above ground he shall be brought before this tribunal. He alone can be the traitor, and to destroy us by exciting suspicions against our best defender, he has wrought with his own false pen this device to deceive the patriotic widow of the Earl of Mar."—"No, no!" interrupted she; "I read the whole in his own handwriting and this list of the chiefs condemned by him to die shall fully evince his guilt. Even your name, generous earl, is in the catalogue."

"Let me speak or stab me to the heart," hastily whispered Edwin to his friend. Wallace did not withhold him, for he guessed what would be the remark of his ardent soul. "Hear that woman," cried the vehement youth to the regent, "and say whether she now speaks the language of one who had ever loved the virtues of Sir William Wallace? Were she innocent of malice towards the deliverer of Scotland, would she not have rejoiced in Loch-awe's suggestion that the Green Knight is the traitor? Would she not have shown some sorrow at being obliged to maintain the guilt of one she professes once to have loved?—or one who saved herself, her husband, and her child from perishing! Even a beardless boy can now discern that however vile the Green Knight may be she shares his wickedness."

While Edwin spoke Lady Strathearn twice attempted to rise and interrupt him, but Sir Roger Kirkpatrick having fixed his eyes on her with a determination to prevent her, she found herself obliged to remain quiescent. Full of fear that Wallace had confided to her nephew the last scene in his tent, she started up, and again addressing the regent, said that before this apparently ingenuous defense could mislead impartial minds, she thought it just to inform the council of the infatuated attachment of Edwin Ruthven to the accused; for she had cause to assert that the boy was so bewitched by his commander that he was ready at any time to sacrifice every consideration of truth.

"Such may be in a boy," observed Lord Loch-awe, interrupting her, "but as I know no occasion in which it is possible for Sir William Wallace to falsify the truth, I call upon him, in justice to himself and to his country, to reply to three questions." Wallace bowed to the venerable earl, and he proceeded: "Sir William Wallace, are you guilty of the charge brought against you of a design to mount the throne of Scotland by means of the King of France?"

Wallace replied, "I never designed to mount the throne of Scotland, either by my own means, or by any other man's."

Loch-awe proceeded: "Was this scroll, containing the names of certain Scottish chiefs noted down for assassination, written by you or under your connivance?"

"I never saw nor heard of the scroll until this hour. And harder than death is the pang at my heart when a Scottish chief finds it necessary to ask me such a question regarding a people to save, even the least of whom, he has so often seen me risk my life."

"Another question," replied Loch-awe, "and then, bravest of men, if your country acquits you not in thought and deed, Campbell, of Loch-awe, sits no more amongst its judges. What is your knowledge of the Knight of the Green Plume, that, in preference to any Scottish friend, you should intrust him with your wishes respecting the Countess of Strathearn?"

Wallace's answer was brief. "I never had any wishes respecting the wife or the widow of my friend the Earl of Mar that I did not impart to every chief in the camp, and those wishes went no further than for her safety. As to love, that is a passion I shall know no more, and Lady Strathearn alone can say what is the end she aims at by attributing feelings to me which I never conceived. Like this passion with which she says she inspired me," added he, turning his eyes steadfastly on her face, "was the Knight of the Green Plume. You are all acquainted with the manner of his introduction to me at Linlithgow. By the account that he then gave of himself, you all know as much of him as I did, till on the night that he left me at Berwick, and then I found him, like the story of Lady Strathearn, all a fable."

"What is his proper title? Name him on your knighthood," exclaimed Buchan, "for he shall yet be dragged forth to support the veracity of my illustrious kinswoman."

"Your kinswoman, Earl Buchan," replied Wallace, "can best answer your question."

Lord Athol approached the regent and whispered something in his ear. This unworthy representative of the generous Bruce immediately rose from his seat. "Sir William Wallace," said he, "you have replied to the questions of Lord Loch-awe, but where are your witnesses to prove that what you have spoken is the truth?"

Wallace was struck with surprise at this address from a man who, whatever might be demanded of him in the fulfilment of his office, he believed could not be otherwise than his friend, because, from the confidence reposed in him by Bruce and himself, he must be fully aware of the impossibility of these allegations being true. But Wallace's astonishment was only for a moment; he now saw, with an eye that pierced through the souls of the whole assembly, and with firmness he replied, "My witnesses are in the bosom of every Scotsman."

"I cannot find them in mine," interrupted Athol.—"Nor in mine," was echoed from various parts of the hall.

"Invalidate the facts brought against you by legal evidence, Sir William Wallace," added the regent, "else the sentence of the law must be passed on so tacit an acknowledgment of guilt."

"Acknowledgment of guilt!" cried Wallace, indignation suffusing his noble brow. "If any one of the chiefs who have just spoken knew the beat of an honest heart they would not have declared that they heard no voice proclaim the integrity of William Wallace. Let them look out on yon carse, where they saw me refuse that crown offered by themselves which my accuser alleges I would yet obtain by their blood. Let them remember the banks of the Clyde, where I rejected the Scottish throne offered me by Edward. Let these facts bear witness for me; and, if they be insufficient, look on Scotland, now, for the third time, rescued by my arm from the grasp of a usurper. That scroll locks the door of the kingdom upon her enemies." As he spoke he threw the capitulation of Berwick upon the table. It struck a pause into the minds of the lords; they gazed with pallid countenances, on the parchment where it lay, while he proceeded: "If my actions do not convince you of my integrity, then believe the unsupported evidence of words, the tale of a woman whose mystery, were it not for the memory of the honorable man whose name she once bore, I would publicly unravel;—believe her, and leave Wallace naught of his country to remember but that he had served it, and that it is unjust."

"Noblest of Scots!" cried Loch-awe, coming towards him, "did your accuser come in the shape of an angel of light, still we should believe your life in preference to her testimony, for God himself speaks on your side. 'My servants,' He declares, 'shall be known by their fruits.' And have not yours been peace to Scotland and good-will to men?"—"They are the serpent folds of his hypocrisy," cried Athol, alarmed at the awe-struck looks of the assembly.—"They are the baits by which he cheats fools," reechoed Soulis.—"They are snares which shall catch us no more," was now the general exclamation. And in proportion to the transitory respect which had made them bow, though but for a moment, to virtue, they now vociferated their contempt both of Wallace and this his last achievement. Inflamed with rage at the manifest determination to misjudge his commander, Kirkpatrick threw off all restraint, and with the bitterness of his reproaches still more incensed the nobles and augmented the tumult. Lennox, vainly attempting to make himself heard, drew towards Wallace, hoping

Wallace's vision

to show on whose side he thought justice lay. At this moment, while the uproar raged with redoubled clamor—the one party denouncing the Cummins as the source of this conspiracy against Wallace, the other demanding that sentence should be instantly passed upon him as a traitor—the door burst open, and Bothwell, covered with dust, and followed by a throng of armed knights, rushed into the center of the hall.

"Who is it ye arraign?" cried the young chief, looking indignantly around him. "Is it not your deliverer you would destroy? Has he not plucked you, this third time, out of the furnace that would have consumed you? And yet, in this hour, you would sacrifice him to the disappointed passions of a woman. Wallace!" cried he, "speak! Would not this woman have persuaded you to disgrace the name of Mar? When my uncle died, did she not urge you to intrigue for that crown which she knew you had so loyally declined?"—"My errand here," answered Wallace, "is to defend myself, not to accuse others. I have shown that I am innocent, and my judges will not look on the proofs. They obey not the laws in their judgment, and whatever may be the decree, I shall not acknowledge its authority." As he spoke he turned away and walked with a firm step out of the hall.

His disappearance gave the signal for a tumult more threatening to the welfare of the state than if the armies of Edward had been in the midst of them. The Lords Lennox, Bothwell, and Loch-awe were vehement against the unfairness with which Wallace had been treated. Kirkpatrick declared that no arguments could be used with men so devoid of reason; and words of reviling passing on all sides, swords were fiercely drawn. The Countess of Strathearn, fearful that the party of Wallace might at last gain the ascendency, and that herself might meet their hasty vengeance, rose abruptly, and giving her hand to a herald, hurried out of the assembly.

The marshals with difficulty interrupted the attack which the enemies and friends of Wallace made on each other. With horrid menaces the two parties separated, the one to the regent's apartments, the other to the camp of Wallace.

Lord Bothwell found him encircled by his veterans, in whose breasts he was trying to allay the storm raging there against the injustice of the regent and the ingratitude of the Scottish lords. At sight of the ardent Bothwell, their clamor to be led instantly to revenge the indignity offered to their general redoubled, and Murray, not less incensed, turning to them, exclaimed, "Yes, my friends, keep quiet for a few hours, and then what honor commands we will do."

At this assurance they retired to their quarters, and Bothwell turned with Wallace into his tent.

"Before you utter a word concerning the present scenes," cried Wallace, "tell me how is the hope of Scotland?"—"Alas!" replied Bothwell, "after regaining by a valor worthy of his destiny every fortress north of the Forth, his last achievement was making himself master of Scone; but in storming its walls, a fragment of stone falling heavily, rent the muscles of his breast, and he now lies at Hunting-tower reduced to infant weakness. All this you would have known had you received his letters; but villany must have been widely at work, for none of yours have reached his hands." This intelligence respecting Bruce was a more mortal blow to Wallace than all he had just sustained in his own person. Was Scotland to be indeed lost? And should he behold her again made a sacrifice to the rivalry of her selfish and contending nobles?

Bothwell continued to speak of the prince, and added that it was with reluctance he had left him, even to share the anticipated success at Berwick. But Bruce, impatient to learn the issue of the siege, had despatched him back to the borders. At Dunfermline he was stricken with horror by the information that treason had been alleged against Wallace, and turning his steps westward, he flew to give that support to his friend which his enemies might render needful.

"The moment I heard how you were beset," continued Bothwell, "I despatched a messenger to Lord Ruthven, warning him not to alarm Bruce with such tidings, but to send hither all the spare forces in Perthshire to maintain you in your rights."—"No force, my dear Bothwell, must be used to hold me in a power which now would only keep alive a spirit of discord in my country. If they are weary of me, let me go. Bruce will recover; they will rally round his standard, and all will be well."—"Oh, Wallace, Wallace!" cried Bothwell; "the scene I have this day witnessed is enough to make a traitor of me. I could forswear my country!" "Cousin, you declare my sentiments," rejoined Edwin; "I cannot recognize a countryman in any one of these men and should Sir William Wallace quit a land so unworthy of his virtues, where he goes, I will go; his asylum shall be my country, and Edwin Ruthven will forget that he ever was a Scot."—"Never!" cried Wallace, turning on him one of those looks which struck conviction into the heart. "Though a thousand of your countrymen offend you by their crimes, yet while there remains one honest Scot, for his sake and his posterity, it is your duty to be a patriot. I would not leave the helm of my country did she not thrust me from it, but though cast by her into the waves, would you not blush for your friend should he wish her other than a peaceful haven?" Edwin spoke not, but putting the hand of Wallace to his lips, left the tent. "Oh," cried Bothwell, looking after him, "that the breast of woman had but half that boy's tenderness! And yet, all of that dangerous sex are not like this hyena-hearted Lady Strathearn. Tell me, my friend, did she not, when she disappeared so strangely from Hunting-tower, fly to you? I now suspect, from certain remembrances, that she and the Green Knight are one and the same person. Acknowledge it, and I will unmask her at once to the court she has deceived."—"She has deceived no one," replied Wallace. "Before she spoke, the members of that court were determined to brand me with guilt, and her charge merely supplied the place of others which they would have devised against me. Whatever she may be, my dear Bothwell, for the sake of him whose name she once bore let us not expose her to open shame. I have done my duty to Scotland, and that conviction must live in every honest heart. Heaven shield our prince! I dread that Badenoch's next shaft may be at him."—"No," cried Bothwell, "all is leveled at his best friend. I taxed the regent with disloyalty, for permitting this outrage on you, and his basely envious answer was: *Wallace's removal is Bruce's security. Who will acknowledge him when they know that this man is his dictator?*" Wallace sighed at this reply, and told Bothwell that he saw no alternative, if he wished to still the agitations of his country and preserve its prince from premature discovery, but to remove the subject of all these contentions from their sight. "Attempt it not!" exclaimed Bothwell. "Propose but a step towards that end, and you will determine me to avenge my country, at the peril of my own life, on all in that accursed assembly who have menaced yours!" In short, the young earl's denunciations were so earnest against the lords in Stirling that Wallace, thinking it dangerous to exasperate him further, consented to remain in his camp till the arrival of Ruthven should bring him the advantage of his counsel.

The issue showed that Bothwell was not mistaken. The majority of the Scottish nobles envied Wallace his glory, and hated him for that virtue which drew the eyes of the people to compare him with their selfish courses. The regent, hoping to become the first in Bruce's favor, was not less urgent to ruin the man who so deservedly stood the highest in that prince's esteem. He had therefore entered warmly into the project of Lady Strathearn. But when, during a secret conference between them, previous to her open charge of Wallace, she named Sir Thomas de Longueville as one of his foreign emissaries, Cummin observed, "If you would have your ac-

cusation succeed, do not mention that knight at all. He is my friend.
He is now ill near Perth, and must know nothing of this affair till
it be over. Should he live, he will nobly thank you for your forbearance; should he die, I will repay you, as becomes your nearest kinsman." All were thus united in one determined effort to hurl Wallace
from his station in the state.

In the midst of these feuds, Sir Simon Fraser abruptly appeared
in the council-hall. His countenance proclaimed his tidings. Lennox
and Loch-awe listened, with something like exultation, to his disastrous information. When the English governor at Berwick learnt
the removal of Wallace from his command, and the consequent consternation of the Scottish troops, instead of surrendering at sunset,
as was expected, he sallied out at the head of the whole garrison, and,
attacking the Scots by surprise, gave them a total defeat. Every
outpost around the town was retaken by the Southrons, the army of
Fraser was cut to pieces or put to flight, and himself, now arriving
in Stirling, smarting with many a wound, but more under his dishonor, to show to the regent of Scotland the evil of having superseded
the only man whom the enemy feared. The council stood in silence,
staring on each other, and, to add to their dismay, Fraser had hardly
completed his narration before a messenger from Tiviotdale arrived
to inform the regent that King Edward was himself within a few
miles of the Cheviots, and from the recovered position of Berwick
must have even now poured his thousands over those hills upon the
plains beneath. While all in the citadel was indecision, tumult, and
alarm, Lennox hastened to Wallace's camp with the news.

Lord Ruthven and the Perthshire chiefs were already there. They
had arrived early in the morning, but with unpromising tidings of
Bruce. The state of his wound had induced a constant delirium, but
still Wallace clung to the hope that his prince's recovery was only
protracted. In the midst of this anxiety, Lennox entered, and relating what he had just heard, turned the whole current of his auditor's ideas. Wallace started from his seat. His hand mechanically,
caught up his sword, which lay upon the table. Lennox gazed at
him with animated veneration. "There is not a man in the citadel,"
cried he, "who does not appear at his wit's end and incapable of fac-
ing this often-beaten foe. Will you, Wallace, again condescend to
save a country that has treated you so ungratefully?"—"I would die
in its trenches!" cried the chief, with a generous forgiveness of all
his injuries.

CHAPTER LXIII.

ARTHUR'S SEAT.

FOR a day or two the terrors of the people and the tumults in the citadel seemed portentous of immediate ruin. A large detachment from the royal army had entered Scotland by the marine gate of Berwick, and, headed by De Warenne, was rapidly advancing towards Edinburgh. Not a soldier belonging to the regent remained on the Carse, and the distant chiefs, to whom he sent for aid, refused it, alleging that the discovery of Wallace's patriotism having been a delusion, had made them suspect all men, and now, locking themselves within their own castles, each true Scot would there securely view a struggle in which they could feel no personal interest.

Seeing the danger of the realm, and hearing from the Lords Ruthven and Bothwell that their troops would follow no other leader than Sir William Wallace, Badenoch yielded a stern assent to the only apparent means of saving his sinking country. He turned ashy pale, while his silence granted to Lord Loch-awe the necessity of imploring Sir William Wallace again to stretch out his arm in their behalf. With this embassy the venerable chief had returned exultingly, and Wallace, so lately branded as the intended betrayer of Scotland—was solicited by his accusers to assume the trust of their defense.

"Such is the triumph of virtue," whispered Edwin to his friend as he vaulted on his horse. A smile from Wallace acknowledged that he felt the tribute, and, looking up to heaven ere he placed his helmet on his head, he said, "Thence comes my power! and the satisfaction it brings, whether attended by man's applause or his blame, he cannot take from me."

While Wallace pursued his march, the regent was at a stand, hardly knowing whether to make another essay to collect forces for the support of their former leader, or to follow the counsels of his lords, and await in inactivity the issue of the expected battle. He knew not how to act, but a letter from Lady Strathearn decided him.

Though partly triumphant in her charges, yet the accusations of Bothwell had disconcerted her; and though the restoration of Wallace to his authority in the state seemed to her next to impossible, still she resolved to take another step and ensure the vengeance she panted to bring upon her victim's head. To this end, on the very evening that she retreated in terror from the council-hall, she set forward to the borders, and easily passing thence to the English camp, was soon admitted to the castle, where De Warenne lodged. She had remarked the admiration with which that earl had regarded her while he was a prisoner in Stirling, and hoping that he might not be able to withstand her charms, she opened her mission with no less art than effect. De Warenne was made to believe that on the strength of a passion Wallace had conceived for her, he had repented of his former refusal of the crown of Scotland, and, misled by a hope that she would not reject his hand could it present her a scepter, he was now attempting to compass that dignity by intrigues. She then related how, at her instigation, the regent had deposed him from his military command; and she ended with saying that, impelled by loyalty to Edward (whom she now recognized as the lawful sovereign of her country), she had come to exhort him to renew his invasion of the kingdom. Intoxicated with her beauty, De Warenne drank in all her words, and ere he allowed this romantic conference to break up, he had thrown himself at her feet, and implored her to grant him the privilege of presenting her to Edward as his intended bride. De Warenne was in the meridian of life, and being fraught with a power at court beyond most of his peers, she determined to accept his hand and wield its influence to the destruction of Wallace. De Warenne drew from her a half-reluctant consent; and while he poured forth the transports of a happy lover, he was not so much enamored of Lady Strathearn as to be altogether insensible to the advantages which his alliance with her would give to Edward in his Scottish pretensions. And as it would consequently increase his own importance with that monarch, he lost no time in communicating the circumstance to him. Edward suspected something in this sudden attachment of the countess, which, should it transpire, might cool the ardor of his officer for uniting so useful an agent to his cause; therefore, having highly approved De Warenne's conduct in the affair, to hasten the nuptials, he proposed being present at their solemnization that very evening. The solemn vows which Lady Strathearn then pledged at the altar to De Warenne were pronounced by her as a means of completing her revenge on Wallace, and by depriving him of life, prevent the climax to her misery of seeing him the future husband of Helen Mar. The day after she became De Warenne's wife she accompanied him by sea to Berwick, and from that place she despatched messengers to the regent and to her kinsmen, fraught with promises which Edward, in the event of success, had solemnly pledged himself to ratify. Her ambassador arrived at Stirling the day succeeding that in which Wallace and his troops had marched from Ballochgeich. The letters he brought were eagerly opened by Badenoch and his chieftains, and they found their contents to this effect. She announced to them her marriage with the lord warden, who was returned into Scotland with every power for the subjugation of the country; and therefore she besought the regent and his council not to raise a hostile arm against him, if they would not merely escape the indignation of a great king, but ensure his favor.

Meanwhile, Wallace, taking his course along the banks of the Forth, when the night drew near encamped his little army at the base of the craigs, east of Edinburgh castle. His march having been long and rapid, the men were much fatigued, and hardly were laid upon their heather beds before they fell asleep. Wallace had learned from his scouts that the main body of the Southrons were approached within a few miles of Dalkeith. Thither he hoped to go next morning, and there, he trusted, strike the conclusive blow for Scotland, by the destruction of a division which he understood comprised the flower of the English army. With these expectations he gladly saw his troops lying in that repose which would rebrace their strength for the combat; and as the hours of night stole on, while his mind waked for all around, he was pleased to see Edwin sink down in a profound sleep.

It was Wallace's custom, once, at least, in the night, to go himself the round of his posts to see that all was safe. He passed from line to line, from station to station, and all was in order. One post alone remained to be visited, and that was a point of observation on the craigs near Arthur's Seat. As he proceeded along a lonely defile between the rocks which overhang the ascent of the mountain, he was startled by the indistinct sight of a figure seated on a towering cliff directly in the way he was to go. The light of the moon shone full upon the spot, and discovered a majestic form in gray robes leaning on a harp, while his face, mournfully gazing upward, was rendered venerable by a long white beard. Wallace paused, and stopping at some distance from this apparition, looked on it in silence. The strings of the harp seemed softly touched, but it was only the sighing of a breeze passing over them. The vibration ceased; but in the next moment the hand of the master indeed struck the chords, and with so melancholy a sound that Wallace for a few minutes was riveted to the ground; then moving forward with breathless caution not to disturb the bard, he gently approached. He was, however, descried. The venerable figure clasped his hands, and in a voice of mournful solemnity exclaimed, "Art thou come, doomed of Heaven, to hear thy sad coronach?" Wallace started at this salutation. The bard, with the same emotion, continued: "No hymns hallow thy corse—wolves howl thy requiem—eagles scream over thy desolate grave! Fly, chieftain, fly!"—"What venerable father of the harp," cried Wallace, "thus addresses one whom he must mistake for some other warrior?"—"Can the spirit of inspiration mistake its object?" demanded the bard. "Can he whose eyes have been opened be blind to Sir William Wallace?"—"And what, or who, am I to understand art thou?" replied Wallace.—"Who I am," resumed the bard, "will be shown to thee when thou hast passed yon starry firmament. The hoofs of opposing squadrons charge! Scotland falls! Look not on me, champion of thy country! Sold by thine enemies, betrayed by thy friends! Fly, bravest of the brave, and live! Stay, and perish!" With a shriek of horror, and throwing his aged arms towards the heavens, while his gray beard mingled in the rising blast, the seer rushed from sight. Wallace saw the misty rocks alone, and was left in awful solitude.

For a few minutes he stood in profound silence. He had heard the destruction of Scotland declared, and himself sentenced to perish, if he did not escape the general ruin by flying from her side. This decree of fate, so corroborated by the extremity of Bruce and the divisions in the kingdom, had been pronounced by one of those sages of his country on whom the spirit of prophecy yet descended. Could he then doubt its truth? He did not; he believed the midnight voice he had heard. But recovering from the first shock of such a doom, and remembering that it still left the choice to himself between dishonored life or glorious death, he resolved to show his respect to the oracle by obedience to the eternal voice which gave those agents utterance; and while he bowed to the warning, he vowed to be the last who should fall from the side of his devoted country. "If devoted," cried he, "then our fates shall be the same. My fall from thee shall be into my grave. Scotland may have struck the breast that shielded her, yet, Father of Mercies, forgive her blindness, and grant me permission a little longer to oppose my heart between her and this fearful doom!"

CHAPTER LXIV.

DALKEITH.

AWED, but not intimidated, by the prophecy of the seer, Wallace, next day, drew up his army in order for the new battle, near Dalkeith. The two rivers Esk flowing on each side of the little phalanx, formed a temporary barrier between it and the pressing legions of De Warenne. The earl's troops seemed countless, while the Southron lords who led them on, being elated by the representations which the Countess of Strathearn had given to them of the disunited state of the Scottish army, bore down upon the Scots with an impetuosity which threatened their universal destruction. Deceived by the falsehoods of his bride, De Warenne had changed his former opinion of his brave opponent, and, having brought his mind to adopt stratagems unworthy of his nobleness, he placed himself on an adjoining height, intending from that commanding post to dispense his orders and behold his victory. "Soldiers!" cried he, "the rebel's hour is come. The sentence of Heaven is gone forth against him. Charge resolutely, and he and his host are yours."

The sky was obscured; an awful stillness reigned through the air, and the spirits of the mighty dead seemed leaning from their clouds to witness this last struggle of their sons. Fate did indeed hover over the opposing armies. She descended on the head of Wallace, and dictated from amidst his waving plumes. She pointed his spear; she wielded his flaming sword; she charged with him in the dreadful shock of battle. De Warenne saw his foremost thousands fall. He heard the shout of the Scots, the cries of his men, and the plains of Stirling rose to his remembrance. He hastily ordered the knights around him to bear his wife from the field, and descending the hill to lead forward himself, was met and almost overwhelmed by his flying troops. He called to them; he waved the royal standard; he rallied, and led them back again. The fight recommenced. Long and bloody was the conflict. De Warenne fought for conquest, and to recover a lost reputation. Wallace contended for his country, and to show himself worthy of her latest blessing, "before he should go hence and be no more seen."

The issue declared for Scotland. But the **ground was covered**

425

with the slain, and Wallace chased a wounded foe with troops whicn dropped as they pursued. At sight of the melancholy state of his intrepid soldiers, he tried to check their ardor, but in vain. "It is for Wallace that we conquer!" cried they; "and we die, or prove him the only captain in this ungrateful country."

Night compelled them to halt, and while they rested on their arms Wallace was satisfied that he had destroyed the power of De Warenne. As he leaned on his sword, and stood with Edwin near the watch-fire over which that youthful hero kept a guard, he contemplated, with generous forbearance, the terrified Southrons as they fled precipitately by the foot of the hill towards the Tweed.

The splendor of this victory struck to the souls of the council at Stirling, but with no touch of remorse. Scotland being again rescued from the vengeance of her foe, the lords in the citadel affected to spurn at her preservation, declaring to the regent that they would rather bear the yoke of the veriest tyrant in the world than owe a moment of freedom to the man who had conspired against their lives. And they had a weighty reason for this decision. Though De Warenne was beaten, his wife was a victor. She had made Edward triumphant in the venal hearts of her kinsmen; gold, and her persuasions, with promises of future honors from the King of England, had sealed them entirely his. All but the regent were ready to commit everything into the hands of Edward. The rising favor of these other lords with the court of England induced him to recollect that he might rule as the unrivaled friend of Bruce should that prince live, or in case of his death he might have it in his own power to assume the Scottish throne untrammeled. These thoughts made him fluctuate, and his country found him as undetermined in treason as unstable in fidelity.

Immediately on the victory at Dalkeith, Kirkpatrick, eager to be the first communicator of such welcome news, withdrew secretly from Wallace's camp, and, hoping to move the gratitude of the refractory lords, entered, full of honest joy, into the midst of their council.

He proclaimed the success of his commander. His answer was accusations and insult. All that had been charged against the too fortunate Wallace was reurged with added acrimony. They who had been hurt in the fray in the hall, pointed to their still smarting wounds, and called upon Lennox to say if they did not plead against so dangerous a man. "Dangerous to your crimes and ruinous to your ambition," cried Kirkpatrick; "for, so help me God, as I believe, that an honester man than William Wallace lives not in Scotland!" This speech brought down the wrath of the whole party upon himself.

Lord Athol, yet stung with his old wound, furiously struck him.
Kirkpatrick drew his sword, and the two chiefs commenced a furious
combat. Gasping with almost the last breathings of life, neither could
be torn from their desperate revenge till many were hurt in attempting to separate them, and then the two were carried off insensible and
covered with wounds.

When this sad news was transmitted to Sir William Wallace, it
found him on the banks of the Esk, just returned from the citadel
of Berwick, where, once more master of that fortress, he had dictated
the terms of a conqueror and a patriot.

In the scene of his former victories, the romantic shades of Hawthorndean, he now pitched his triumphant camp, and from its verdant
bounds despatched the requisite orders to the garrisoned castles on
the borders. While employed in this duty, his heart was wrung by
an account of the new storm in the citadel of Stirling; but as some
equivalent, the chieftains of Mid-Lothian poured in to him on every
side, and acknowledging him their protector, he again found himself
the idol of gratitude. At such a moment, when they were disclaiming
all participation in the insurgent proceedings at Stirling, another
messenger arrived from Lord Lennox to conjure him, if he would
avoid open violence or secret treachery, to march his victorious troops
immediately to that city and seize the assembled lords as traitors to
their country. "Resume the regency," added he, "which you only
know how to conduct, and crush a treason which now walks openly
in the day."

He did not hesitate to decide against this counsel, for it could
not be one adversary he must strike, but thousands. "I am only a
brother to my countrymen," said he to himself, "and have no right
to force them to their duty. When their king appears, then these
rebellious heads may be made to bow." While he mused upon the
letter of Lennox, Ruthven entered. "I bring you better news of
our friend at Hunting-tower," cried the good lord; "here is a packet
from Douglas and another from my wife." Wallace gladly read
them, and found that Bruce was relieved from his delirium, but so
weak that his friends dared not hazard a relapse by imparting to him
any idea of the proceedings at Stirling. All he knew was that Wallace was victorious in arms. Helen and Isabella, with the sage of
Ercildown, were the prince's unwearied attendants, and, though his
life was yet in peril, it was to be hoped that their attentions, and
his own constitution, would finally cure the wound. Comforted with
the tidings, Wallace declared his intentions of visiting his suffering
friend as soon as he could induce his followers to bear, even for a

little time, with the insolence of the lords. "I will then," said he, "watch by the side of Bruce till his recovered health allow him to proclaim himself king; and with that act, I trust, all these feuds will be forever laid to sleep." Ruthven participated in these hopes, and the friends returned into the council-tent. But all there was changed. Most of the Lothian chieftains had also received messengers from their friends in Stirling. Allegations against Wallace, arguments to prove the policy of submitting themselves and their properties to the protection of a great and generous king, rather than to risk all by attaching themselves to the fortune of a private person, were the contents of their packets, and they had been sufficient to shake the easy faith to which they were addressed. On the reentrance of Wallace, the chieftains stole suspicious glances at each other, and, without a word, glided severally out of the tent.

CHAPTER LXV.

HAWTHORDEAN.

NEXT morning, instead of coming as usual directly to their acknowledged protector, the Lothian chieftains were seen at different parts of the camp conversing in groups, and when any of Wallace's officers approached, they separated, or withdrew to a greater distance. This strange conduct Wallace attributed to its right source, but he was so convinced that nothing but the proclamation of Bruce could preserve his country from falling again into the snare from which he had just snatched it, that he was preparing to set out for Perthshire with such persuasions when Ker hastily entered his tent. He was followed by the Lord Soulis, Lord Buchan, and several other chiefs of equally hostile intentions. Soulis did not hesitate to declare his errand.

"We come, Sir William Wallace, by the command of the regent and the assembled lords of Scotland, to take these brave troops from the power of a man who, we have every reason to believe, means to turn their arms against the liberties of the realm. Without a pardon from the states; without the signature of the regent; in contempt of the court, which, having found you guilty of high treason, had in mercy delayed to pronounce sentence on your crime, you have presumed to place yourself at the head of the national troops, and to take to yourself the merit of a victory won by their prowess alone. Your designs are known, and the authority you have despised is now roused to punish. You are to accompany us this day to Stirling. We have brought a guard of four thousand men to compel your obedience."

Before the indignant spirit of Wallace could utter an answer, Bothwell, who at sight of the regent's troops had hastened to his general's tent, entered, followed by his chieftains. "Were your guard forty thousand instead of four," cried he, "they should not force our commander from us; they should not extinguish the glory of Scotland beneath the devices of envy and cowardice!" Soulis turned on him with eyes of fire and laid his hand on his sword. "Aye, cowardice!" reiterated Bothwell; "the slanderer of virtue, the betrayer of his country, knows in his heart that he fears to draw aught but the assassin's steel. A thousand brave Scots lie under these sods, and a thousand yet survive who may share their graves, but they never will relinquish their invincible leader into the hands of traitors."

The clamors of the citadel of Stirling now resounded through the tent of Wallace. Accusations and threatenings, joined in one turbulent uproar. Again swords were drawn, and Wallace, in attempting to beat down the weapons of Soulis and Buchan aimed at Bothwell's heart, must have received the point of Soulis in his own body had he not grasped the blade, and, wrenching it out of the chief's hand, broke it into shivers. "Such be the fate of every sword which Scot draws against Scot!" cried he. "Put up your weapons, my friends. The arm of Wallace is not shrunk that he could not defend himself did he think that violence were necessary. Hear my determination, once and forever," added he. "I acknowledge no authority in Scotland but the laws. The present regent and his supporters outrage them in every ordinance, and I should indeed be a traitor to my country did I submit to such men's behests. I shall not obey their summons to Stirling; neither will I permit a hostile arm to be raised in this camp against their delegates unless the violence begins with them. This is my answer." Uttering these words, he motioned Bothwell to follow him, and left the tent.

Crossing a rude plank-bridge, which then lay over the Esk, he met Lord Ruthven, accompanied by Edwin and Lord Sinclair. The latter came to inform Wallace that ambassadors from Edward awaited his presence at Roslyn. "They come to offer peace to our distracted country," cried Sinclair. "Then," answered Wallace, "I shall not delay going where I may hear the terms." Horses were brought, and during their short ride, Wallace communicated to his friends the particulars of the scene he had left. "These contentions must be terminated," added he, "and, with God's blessing, a few days and they shall be so!"—"Heaven grant it!" returned Sinclair, thinking he referred to the proposed negotiation. "If Edward's offers be at all reasonable, I would urge you to accept them, otherwise invasion from without and civil commotion within will probably make a desert of poor Scotland." Ruthven interrupted him. "Despair not, my lord. Whatever be the fate of this embassy, let us remember that it is our steadiest friend who decides, and that his arm is still with us to chastise treason." Wallace understood him, and answered, "Grievous are the alternatives, my friends, which your love for me would persuade you even to welcome. But that which I shall choose will, I trust, indeed lay the land at peace."

Being arrived at the gate of Roslyn, Wallace, regardless of ceremonials, entered at once into the hall where the ambassadors sat. Baron Hilton was one, and Le de Spencer (father to the young and violent envoy of that name) was the other. At sight of the Scottish chief they rose, and the good baron, believing he came on a propitious errand, smiling, said: "Sir William Wallace, it is your private ear I am commanded to seek." While speaking, he looked on Sinclair and the other lords. "These chiefs are as myself," replied Wallace; "but I will not impede your embassy by crossing the wishes of your master in a trifle." He then turned to his friends. "Indulge the monarch of England in making me the first acquainted with that which can only be a message to the whole nation."

The chiefs withdrew, and Hilton, without further parley, opened his mission. He said that King Edward, more than ever impressed with the military talents of Sir William Wallace, and solicitous to make a friend of so heroic an enemy, had sent him an offer of grace, which, if he contemned, must be the last. He offered him a theater whereon he might display his endowments to the admiration of the world; the kingdom of Ireland, and all the ample riches of its abundant provinces, should be his. Edward only required, in return for this royal gift, that he should abandon the cause of Scotland, swear fealty to him for Ireland, and resign into his hands one whom he had proscribed as the most ungrateful of traitors. In double acknowledgment for the latter sacrifice, Wallace need only send to England a list of those Scottish lords against whom he bore resentment, and their fates should be ordered according to his dictates. Edward concluded his offers by inviting him immediately to London to be invested with his new sovereignty. And Hilton ended his address by showing him the madness of abiding in a country where almost every chief carried a dagger against his life; and therefore he exhorted him no longer to contend for a nation so unworthy of freedom that it bore with impatience the only man who had the courage to maintain its independence.

Wallace replied calmly and without hesitation: "To this message an honest man can make but one reply. As well might your sovereign exact of me to dethrone the angels of heaven as to require me to subscribe to his proposals. Edward knows that, as a knight, a true Scot, and a man, I should dishonor myself to accept even life, aye, or the lives of all my kindred, upon these terms."

Hilton interrupted him by declaring the sincerity of Edward, and contrasting it with the ingratitude of the people whom he had served. He conjured him, with every entreaty to relinquish his faithless country and become the friend of a king ready to receive him with open arms. Wallace shook his head, and with an incredulous smile, which spoke his thoughts of Edward, while his eyes beamed kindness upon Hilton, he answered: "Can the man who would bribe me to betray a friend be faithful in his friendship? I answer your monarch in a word: Were all my countrymen to resign their claims to the liberty which is their right, I alone would declare the independence of my country; and, by God's assistance, while I live, acknowledge no other master than the laws of St. David and the legitimate heir of his blood!" The glow of patriotism which overspread his countenance while he spoke was reflected by a color on that of Hilton. "Noble chief!" cried he, "I admire, while I regret; I revere the virtue which I am even now constrained to denounce, but in these days such magnanimity is considered frenzy, and ruin is its consequence."— "And shall a Christian," cried Wallace, reddening with shame, "deem the virtue which even heathens practised, of too pure a nature to be exercised by men taught by Christ himself?"

Hilton excused his argument by declaring that it proceeded from his observations on the conduct of men. "And shall we," replied Wallace, "follow a multitude to do evil? I act to one Being alone, and Edward must acknowledge *His* supremacy."—"Am I answered?" said Hilton. "Your fate rests on your reply. Oh, noblest of warriors, consider only for a day!"—"Not for a moment," said Wallace. "I am sensible to your kindness, but my answer to Edward has been pronounced."

Baron Hilton turned sorrowfully away, and Le de Spencer rose. "Sir William Wallace, my part of the embassy must be delivered to you in the assembly of your chieftains."—"In the congregation of my camp," returned he; and opening the door of the anteroom in which his friends stood, he sent Edwin to summon his chiefs to the platform before the council-tent.

CHAPTER LXVI.

WHEN Wallace approached his tent he found not only the captains of his own army but the followers of Soulis and the chieftains of Lothian. He looked on his enemies with a fearless eye, and passing through the crowd took his station beside the ambassadors on the platform of the tent. The venerable Hilton turned away with tears on his cheeks as the chief advanced, and Le de Spencer came forward to speak. Wallace, with a dignified action, requested his leave for a few minutes, and then, addressing the congregated warriors, unfolded to them the offer of Edward to him and his reply. "And now," added he, "the ambassador of England is at liberty to declare his master's alternative."

Le de Spencer again advanced, but the acclamations with which the followers of Wallace acknowledged the nobleness of his answer, excited such an opposite clamor on the side of the Soulis party that Le de Spencer was obliged to mount a war-carriage which stood near, and to vociferate for silence before he could be heard. But the first words which caught the ears of his audience acted like a spell, and seemed to hold them in breathless attention.

"Since Sir William Wallace rejects the grace of his liege lord, Edward, King of England, thus saith the king in his clemency to the earls, barons, knights, and commonalty of Scotland: To every one of them, chief and vassal, excepting the aforesaid incorrigible rebel, he, the royal Edward, grants an amnesty of all their past treasons against his sacred person and rule; provided, that within twenty-four hours after they hear the words of this proclamation, they acknowledge their disloyalty, and, laying down their arms, swear eternal fealty to their only lawful ruler, Edward, the lord of the whole island, from sea to sea." Le de Spencer then proclaimed the King of England to be now on the borders with an army of a hundred thousand men, ready to march with fire and sword into the heart of the kingdom. "Yield," added he, "while you may yet not only grasp the mercy extended to you, but the rewards he is ready to bestow. Adhere to that unhappy man, and by to-morrow's sunset your offended king will be on these hills, and then mercy shall be no more. Death is the doom of Sir William Wallace, and a similar fate to every Scot who, after this hour, dares to give him food, shelter, or succor. He is the prisoner of King Edward, and I demand him at your hands."

Wallace spoke not, but with an unmoved countenance looked around upon the assembly. Edwin precipitated himself into his arms. Bothwell's full soul then forced utterance from his laboring breast. "Tell your sovereign," cried he, "that he mistakes. We are the conquerors, who ought to dictate terms of peace. Wallace is the earthly hope in whom we trust, and it is not in the power of men nor devils to bribe us to betray our benefactor. Away to your king, and tell him that Andrew Murray, and every honest Scot, is ready to live or to die by the side of Sir William Wallace."—"And by this good sword I swear the same," cried Ruthven."—"And so do I," rejoined Scrymgeour, "or may the standard of Scotland be my winding-sheet."—"Or may the Clyde swallow us up," exclaimed Lockhart of Lee, shaking his mailed hand at the ambassadors.

But not another chief spoke for Wallace. Even Sinclair was intimidated, and like others who wished him well, feared to utter his sentiments. But most—oh, shame to Scotland and to man!—cast up their bonnets, and cried aloud, "Long live King Edward, the only legitimate lord of Scotland!" At this outcry, which was echoed even by some in whom he had confided, Wallace threw out his arms, as if he would yet protect Scotland from herself. "Oh, desolate people!" exclaimed he, in a voice of piercing woe, "call to remembrance the miseries you have suffered, and start, before it be too late, from this last snare of your oppressor. Oh, look yet to Heaven and ye shall find a rescue!"

"Seize that rebellious man!" cried Soulis to his marshals. "In the name of the King of England I command you."—"And in the name of the King of kings I denounce death on him who attempts it!" exclaimed Bothwell, throwing himself between Wallace and the men.

Soulis, followed by his knights, pressed forward to execute his treason himself. Scrymgeour, Ruthven, Lockhart, and Ker rushed before their friend. Edwin, starting forward, drew his sword, and the clash of steel was heard. Bothwell and Soulis grappled together, and the falchion of Ruthven gleamed amidst a hundred swords. The voice, the arm of Wallace in vain sought to enforce peace; he was not heard, he was not felt, in the dreadful warfare. Ker fell with a gasp at his feet, and breathed no more. At such a sight, Wallace wrung his hands and exclaimed in bitter anguish, "Oh, my country! was it for these horrors that my Marion died?

that I became a homeless wretch? Venerable Mar, dear and valiant Graham! is this the consummation for which you fell?" At that moment Bothwell, having disabled Soulis, would have blown his bugle to call up his men to a general conflict, but Wallace snatched the horn from his hand, and springing upon the very war-carriage from which Le de Spencer had proclaimed Edward's embassy, he drew forth his sword, and stretching the mighty arm that held it over the throng, he exclaimed, "Peace! men of Scotland, and for the last time hear the voice of William Wallace. If you have aught of nobleness within ye; if delusion have not blinded your senses, look beyond this field of horror, and behold your country free. Edward, in these apparent demands, sues for peace. Did we not drive his armies into the sea? What is it, then, you do, when you again put your necks under his yoke? Did he not seek to bribe me to betray you? and yet, when I refuse to purchase life, and the world's rewards, you forget that you are free-born Scots; that you are the victors, and he the vanquished, and you give, not sell, your birthright to the demands of a tyrant! On the day in which you are in his hands, you will feel that you have exchanged honor for disgrace and liberty for bondage. I draw this sword for you no more. But there yet lives a prince, a descendant of the royal heroes of Scotland, whom Providence may conduct to be your preserver. Reject the proposals of Edward, and that prince will soon appear to crown your patriotism with glory and happiness."

"We acknowledge no prince but King Edward of England," cried Buchan. The exclamation was reiterated by a disgraceful majority. Wallace was transfixed. "Then," cried Le de Spencer, in the first pause of the tumult, "to every man, woman, and child throughout the realm of Scotland, excepting Sir William Wallace, I proclaim, in the name of King Edward, pardon and peace."

At these words several hundred Scottish chieftains dropped on their knees before Le de Spencer and murmured their vows of fealty. Indignant, grieved, Wallace took his helmet from his head, and throwing his sword into the hand of Bothwell, "That weapon," cried he, "which I wrested from this very King Edward, and with which I twice drove him from our borders, I give to you. In your hands it may again serve Scotland. I relinquish a soldier's name on the spot where I humbled England three times in one day, where I now see my victorious country deliver herself, bound, into the grasp of the vanquished. I go without sword or buckler from this dishonored field; and what Scot, my public or private enemy, will dare to strike the unguarded head of William Wallace?" As he spoke he threw his shield and helmet to the ground, and leaping from the war-carriage, took his course, with a fearless and dignified step, through the parting ranks of his enemies, who, awe-struck, durst not lift an arm or breathe a word as he passed.

Wallace had adopted this manner of leaving the ground in hopes, if it were possible, to awaken a spark of honor in his persecutors to prevent the bloodshed which must ensue between his friends and them should they attempt to seize him. Edwin and Bothwell immediately followed him, but Lockhart and Scrymgeour remained to take charge of the remains of the faithful Ker.

CHAPTER LXVII.

BANKS OF THE ESK.

A VAGUE suspicion of the regent and his thanes, and yet a cowardice which shrank from supporting Wallace, carried the spirit of slavery from the platform to the chieftains who thronged the ranks of Ruthven, and even to the perversion of some few who had followed the golden-haired standard of Bothwell. The brave troops of Lanark alone remained unmoved, so catching is the spirit of doubt and fearful submission.

In the moment when the indignant Ruthven saw his legions rolling off towards the trumpet of Le de Spencer, Scrymgeour placed himself at the head of the men of Lanark. Unfurling the banner of Scotland, he marched with a steady step to the tent of Bothwell, whither he did not doubt that Wallace had retired. He found him assuaging the grief of Edwin, and striving to moderate the wrath of the faithful Murray. "Pour not out the energy of your soul upon these worthless men," he said; "leave them to the fates they have incurred by the innocent blood shed this day. The few brave hearts who yet remain loyal to their country are insufficient to stem the torrent of corruption. Retire beyond the Forth, my friend. Rally all true Scots around Hunting-tower. Let the royal inmate proclaim himself, and at the foot of the Grampians lock the gates of the Highlands upon our enemies. From those bulwarks he will issue in strength, and Scotland may again be free."

"Free, but never more honored," cried Edwin; "never more beloved by me. Oh that the salt sea would ingulf thee at once, base land, that thy ingratitude could be no more remembered! I will never wear a sword for thee again."—"Edwin!" ejaculated Wallace, in a reproachful tone.—"Exhort me not to forgive my country," returned he. "Tell me to pardon the assassin who strikes his steel into my heart, and I will obey you; but to pardon Scotland for the injury she has done to you, I never, never can. Think not, dearest of friends," cried he, throwing himself at Wallace's feet, "that I will ever shine in the light of those envious stars which have displaced the sun. To thee alone will I ever turn!" Wallace folded him to his heart, while he said in a low voice, "If thou art mine, thou art Scot-

437

land's.   Heaven wills that I should quit my post; but for thee, Edwin, as a relic of the love I yet bear this wretched country, defend her for my sake, and if Bruce lives, he will be to thee a second Wallace, a friend, a brother."   Edwin listened and wept, but his heart was fixed.   Unable to speak, he broke from his friend's arms and hurried to subdue his emotions by pouring them forth to God.

Ruthven joined in opinion with Bothwell, that if ever a civil war could be sanctified this was the time, and in spite of all that Wallace could urge against the madness of contending for his supremacy over a nation which would not yield him obedience, still they remained firm in their resolution.   Bruce they hardly dared hope could recover, and to relinquish the guiding hand of their best approved leader at this crisis was a sacrifice, they said, no earthly power should compel them to make.   "So far from it," cried Lord Bothwell, dropping on his knees and grasping the cross hilt of his sword in both hands, "I swear by this cross, that should Bruce die, I will obey no other king of Scotland than William Wallace."   Wallace turned ashy pale as he listened to this vow.   At that moment Scrymgeour entered followed by the Lanark veterans, and, all kneeling down, repeated the oath of Bothwell; then starting up, called on their chief to lead them forth and avenge them of his enemies.

When the agitation of his soul would allow him to speak to this faithful group, Wallace stretched his hands over them, and said, in a faltering voice, "My sword is sheathed forever.   I feel your love, and I appreciate it.   But, Bothwell, Ruthven, Lockhart, Scrymgeour, my faithful Lanark followers, leave me awhile to compose my thoughts.   Let me pass this night alone, and to-morrow you shall know my resolution."

The shades of evening were closing in, and the men of Lanark, first obtaining his permission to keep guard before the wood which skirted the tent, kissing his hand, withdrew.   Ruthven called Edwin from the recess whither he had retired, but as soon as he heard that it was the resolution of his friends to preserve the authority of Wallace, the gloom passed from his brow, and he exclaimed, "All will be well again.   We shall force this deluded nation to recognize her safety and her honor."

While the determined chiefs held discourse so congenial with the wishes of the youthful knight, Wallace sat almost silent.   He seemed revolving some momentous idea; he frequently turned his eyes on the speakers with a fixed regard, which appeared rather full of sorrow than sympathy in the subjects of their discussion.   On Edwin he at times looked with penetrating tenderness, and when the bell from the neighboring convent sounded the hour of rest, he stretched out his hand to him with a smile which he wished should speak of comfort as well as of affection. "And am I, too, to leave you?" said Edwin. "Yes, my brother," replied Wallace; "I have much to do with my own thoughts this night. We separate now to meet more gladly hereafter. I must have solitude to arrange my plans. To-morrow you shall know them. Meanwhile, farewell!" As he spoke he pressed the youth to his breast, and warmly grasping the hands of his three other friends, bade them adieu.

Bothwell lingered a moment at the tent door, and looking back— "Let your first plan be that to-morrow you lead us to Lord Soulis's quarters to teach the traitor what it is to be a Scot and a man."— "My plans shall be deserving of my brave colleagues," replied Wallace, "and whether they be executed on this or the other side of the Forth, you shall find that Scotland's peace and the honor of her best sons are the dearest considerations of your friend."

When the door closed, and Wallace was left alone, he stood for awhile in the midst of the tent listening to the departing steps of his friends. When the last sound died on his ear, "I shall hear them no more," cried he, and, throwing himself into a seat, he remained for an hour in grievous thought. Melancholy remembrances pressed upon his surcharged heart. "It is to God alone I must confide my country," cried he. "My duty is to remove the object of ruin far from the power of any exciting jealousy or awakening zeal." With these words he took a pen in his hand to write to Bruce.

He narrated the events which compelled him, if he would avoid the grief of having occasioned a civil war, to quit his country forever. The general hostility of the nobles, the acquiescence of the people in measures which sacrificed the freedom for which he had so long fought, convinced him, he said, that his warlike commission was now closed. He was summoned by Heaven to exchange the field for the cloister, and to the monastery at Chartres he was hastening to dedicate the remainder of his days to the peace of a future world. He then exhorted Bruce to confide in the Lords Ruthven and Bothwell, for that he would find them true unto death. To use those brave and simple-hearted men for his establishment on the throne of his kingdom, Wallace advised Bruce, and so, amidst the natural fortresses of the Highlands, he might recover his health, collect his friends, and openly proclaim himself. "Then," added he, "when Scotland is your own, let its bulwarks be its mountains and its people's arms. Dismantle and raze to the ground the castles of those base chiefs who have only embattled them to enslave their country."

He earnestly conjured his prince that he would wear the valiant Kirkpatrick as a buckler on his heart, that he would place Scrymgeour, with his Lanark veterans, and the faithful Grimsby, next him as his body guard, and that he would love and cherish Edwin for his sake. "When my prince and friend receives this," added he, "Wallace shall have bidden an eternal farewell to Scotland, but his heart will be amidst its hills. My king and the friends most dear to me will still be there. The earthly part of my beloved wife rests within its bosom; but I go to rejoin her soul, to meet it in the vigils of days consecrated wholly to God. Mourn not, then, my absence; for my prayers will be with you till we are again united in the only place where you can fully know me as I am—thine and Scotland's never-dying friend.

"Should the endearing Helen—my heart's sister—be near you when you read this, tell her that Wallace bids her a brother's farewell, and from his inmost soul he blesses her."

Respectful adieus he sent to Isabella, Lady Ruthven, and the sage of Ercildown, and then kneeling down, he wrote his last invocations for the prosperity and happiness of Bruce.

This letter finished, he addressed Lord Ruthven, detailing to him his reasons for leaving such faithful friends so clandestinely; and after mentioning his purpose of proceeding to France, he ended with those expressions of gratitude which the worthy chief so well deserved, and exhorting him to transfer his zeal for him to the royal Bruce, closed the letter with begging him, for the sake of his friend, his king, and his country, to return immediately with all his followers to Hunting-tower, and there to rally round their prince. But when he began to write to Bothwell, to bid him that farewell which his heart foreboded would be forever in this world, to part from this, his dauntless champion, he lost some of his composure, and his hand-writing testified the emotion of his mind. How, then, was he shaken when he addressed the devoted Edwin! At that moment he felt all he was going to relinquish, and he exclaimed, "Oh, Scotland! Is it thus that you repay your most faithful servants? Is it not enough that the wife of my bosom, the companion of my youth, should be torn from me by your enemies, but your hand must wrest from my heart its every other solace?" His head sank on his arm and his heart gave way under the pressure of accumulated regrets. Deep were his sighs; but none answered him. "Dreary solitude!" cried he, looking around him with a perception of all that he had lost; "how have I been mocked for these three long years! What is renown? what the loud acclaim of admiring throngs? Now, desolate and alone, ruin is around me. Destruction waits on all who would steal one pang from the racked heart of William Wallace! Take me, then, O Power of Mercy!" cried he, stretching forth his hands, "take me to thyself!"

In a paroxysm of grief he rushed from the tent, and reckless whither he went, struck into the depths of Roslyn woods. He reached their boundary; it was traversed by a rapid stream, but he sprang over it, and ascending its moonlit bank, was startled by the sound of his name. Grimsby, attended by a youth, stood before him. The veteran expressed amazement at meeting his master alone at this hour, unhelmeted and unarmed. "The road," said he, "between this and Stirling is beset with your enemies." Instead of noticing this information, Wallace inquired what news he brought from Hunting-tower. "The worst," said he. "By this time the royal Bruce is no more!" Wallace gasped convulsively, and fell against a tree. Grimsby paused. In a few minutes the heart-struck chief was able to speak. "Listen not to my groans for unhappy Scotland," cried he; "show me all that is in this last phial of wrath."

Grimsby informed him that Bruce being so far recovered as to have left his sick chamber for the family apartment, while he was sitting with the ladies a letter was brought to Lady Helen. She opened it, read a few lines, and fell senseless into the arms of her sister. Bruce snatched up the packet, but not a word did he speak till he had perused it to the end. It was from the Countess Strathearn, written in the triumph of revenge, exulting in what she termed the demonstration of Wallace's guilt, and boasting that his once adoring Scotland now held him in such detestation as to have doomed him to die. It was this denunciation which had struck to the soul of Helen; and while the anxious Lady Ruthven removed her from the room, Bruce read the barbarous triumphs of this disappointed woman. "No power on earth can save him now," continued she; "your heart must yield him, Helen, to another rest than your bridal chamber. My noble lord, the princely De Warenne, informs me that William Wallace would be burned as a double traitor in England, and a price is now set upon his head in Scotland, hence there is safety for him no more. None will dare support the man whom friends and enemies abandon to destruction."

"Yes," cried Bruce, starting from his seat, "I will support him, thou damned traitress! Bruce will throw himself before his friend, and in his breast receive every arrow meant for that godlike heart." Not a word more did he utter, but darting from the apartment was soon seen before the barbican-gate armed from head to foot. Grimsby stood there, to whom he called to bring him a horse, "For that the *Light of Scotland* was in danger." Grimsby, who understood by that term his beloved master was in peril, instantly obeyed; and Bruce, mounting, struck his rowels into the horse and was out of sight ere Grimsby could reach his stirrup to follow.

But that faithful soldier speeded after him like the wind, and came in view of Bruce just as he was leaping a chasm in the mountain path. The horse struck his heel against a loose stone, and it giving way he fell headlong into the deep ravine. At the moment of his disappearance, Grimsby rushed towards the spot and saw the animal struggling in the agonies of death at the bottom. Bruce lay insensible amongst some bushes which grew nearer the top. With difficulty the honest Englishman dragged him to the surface of the hill, and finding all attempts to recover him ineffectual, he laid him on his own beast and so carried him slowly back to the castle. The sage of Ercildown restored him to life, but not to recollection. "The fever returned on him with a delirium so hopeless of recovery," continued Grimsby, "that the Lady Helen, who again seems like an angel amongst us, has sent me with this youth to implore you to come to Hunting-tower, and there embattle yourself against your own and your prince's enemies."

"Send me," cried Grimsby, grasping Wallace's hand,—"send me back to Lady Helen, and let me tell her that our benefactor will not abandon us. Should you depart, Scotland's genius will go with you. De Valence will regain possession of my dear lady, and you will not be near to save her."

"Grimsby!" cried Wallace, in an agitated voice, "I do not abandon Scotland, she drives me from her. I would have borne her in my arms until my latest gasp; but it must not be so. I resign her into the Almighty hands to which I commit myself; they will also preserve the Lady Helen from violence. I cannot forego my trust for the Bruce also. If he live he will protect her for my sake; and should he die, Bothwell and Ruthven will cherish her for their own."— "But you will return with us to Hunting-tower," cried Grimsby. "Disguised in these peasant's garments, which we have brought for the purpose, you may pass through the legions of the regent with perfect security." Wallace looked compassionately upon him. "I would save myself; and I will, please God," said he, "but by no unworthy means. I go, but not under any disguise. Openly have I defended Scotland, and openly will I pass through her lands."

"Whither you go," cried Grimsby, "let me follow you, in joy or in sorrow."

"My faithful friend," returned he, "whither I go, I must go alone. And as a proof of your love, grant me your obedience this once. Rest amongst these thickets till morning. At sunrise repair to our camp, there you will know my destination. But till Bruce proclaims himself at the head of his country's armies, for my sake never reveal to mortal man that he who lies debilitated by sickness at Hunting-tower is other than Sir Thomas de Longueville."—"Rest we cannot," replied Grimsby, "but still we will obey our master. You command me to adhere to Bruce, to serve him till the hour of his death. I will; but should he die, then I may seek you, and be again your faithful servant?"—"You will find me before the cross of Christ," returned Wallace, "with saints my fellow-soldiers, and God my only king. Till then, Grimsby, farewell!"

Grimsby, struck by the solemnity of his manner, fell on his knees before him. Wallace raised his hands. "Bless, oh, Father of Light!" cried he, "this unhappy land when Wallace is no more, and let his memory be lost in the virtues and prosperity of Robert Bruce!"

Grimsby sank on the earth and gave way to a burst of manly sorrow. He looked up to seek the face of Wallace; but Wallace had disappeared, and all that remained to the breaking hearts of his faithful servants was the tartan plaid which they had clasped in their arms.

CHAPTER LXVIII.

LUMLOCH.

WALLACE, having turned away from his lamenting servants, struck into the deep defiles of the Pentland Hills. Aware that the affection of his friends might urge them to dare the perils attendant on his fellowship, he hesitated a moment which path to take. Certainly not towards Hunting-tower, to bring immediate destruction on its royal inhabitant; nor to any chieftain of the Highlands, to give rise to a spirit of civil warfare. Neither would he pursue the eastern track, for in that direction, as pointing to France, his friends would most likely seek him. He therefore turned his steps towards the ports of Ayr. The road was circuitous, but it would soon enough take him from the land of his fathers, a country he must never see again.

As morning dispelled the shades of night, it discovered still more dreary glooms. A heavy mist hung over the hills and rolled before him along the valley. Still he pursued his way, although, as day advanced, the vapors collected into thicker blackness, and, floating down the heights, at last burst in a deluge of rain. Hills, rivers, and vales were measured by Wallace's solitary steps, till entering on the heights of Clydesdale, the broad river of his native glen spread its waters before him. Over the western hills lay the lands of his forefathers. There he had first drawn his breath; there he imbibed from the lips of his revered grandfather those lessons of virtue by which he had lived, and for which he was now ready to die. Far to the left stretched the wide domains of Lammington; there his youthful heart first knew the pulse of love; there all hope smiled upon him, for Marion was near. Onward, in the depths of the cliffs, lay Ellerslie, the home of his heart, where he had tasted the joys of paradise; but all there, like that once blessed place, now lay in one wide ruin.

"Shall I visit thee again?" said he, as he hurried along the beetling craigs. "Ellerslie!" cried he, " 'tis no triumphant warrior that approaches. Receive, shelter thy deserted master! I come, my Marion, to mourn thee in thine own domains." He ascended the cliffs; he rushed down the hazel-crowned pathway; but thistles and

444

thickly interwoven underwood obstructed his steps. Breaking through them all, he turned the angle of the rock, the last screen between him and the view of his once beloved home. On this spot he used to stand on moonlight evenings watching the graceful form of his Marion as she passed to and fro within her chamber. His eye now turned instinctively to the point, but it gazed on vacancy. His home had disappeared; one solitary tower alone remained, standing like "a hermit, the last of his race," to mourn over the desolation of all by which it had once been surrounded. Not a human being now moved on the spot which three years before was thronged with his grateful vassals. "Death!" cried he, striking his breast, "how many ways hast thou to bereave mortality! My Marion sleeps in Bothwell, the faithful Halbert at her feet. And my peasantry of Lanark, how many of you have found untimely graves in the bosom of your vainly rescued country!"

A few steps forward and he stood on a mound of fragments heaped over the pavement of what had been the hall. "My wife's blood marks the stones beneath," cried he with a faint smile; "naught is here but Wallace and his sorrow. Marion! I call, and even thou dost not answer me!" Tears choked his further utterance, and once more laying his head upon the stones he wept in silence, till exhausted nature found repose in sleep.

The sun was gilding the summits of the ruined tower under whose shadow he lay when Wallace slowly opened his eyes. Looking around him he smote his breast, and with a groan sank back upon the stones. In the silence which succeeded this burst of memory he thought he heard a rustling near him and a half-suppressed sigh. He listened breathless. The sigh was repeated. He gently raised himself on his hand, and with an expectation he dared hardly whisper to himself turned towards the spot whence the sound proceeded. He rose in agitation and a human figure appeared retreating behind the ruins. He advanced towards it and beheld Edwin Ruthven. The moment their eyes met Edwin precipitated himself at his feet, and, clinging to him, exclaimed, "Pardon me this pursuit. But we meet to part no more." Wallace raised him and strained him to his breast in silence. Edwin, in hardly articulate accents, continued: "Some kind power checked your hand when writing to your Edwin. You could not command him not to follow you; you left the letter unfinished; and thus I come to bless you for not condemning me to die of a broken heart."— "I did not write farewell to thee," cried Wallace, looking mournfully on him; "but I meant it, for I must part from all I love in Scotland. This country needs me not, and I have need of heaven. I go into its outcourts at Chartres. Follow me there, dear boy, when thou hast accomplished thy noble career on earth; but now receive the farewell of thy friend. Return to Bruce, and be to him the dearest representative of William Wallace."—"Never!" cried Edwin; "thou alone art my prince, my friend, my brother! Your name called me to honor; and to you, in life or in death, I dedicate my being."—"Then," returned Wallace, "that honor summons you to the side of the dying Bruce. He is now in the midst of his foes."—"And where art thou?" interrupted Edwin; "who drove thee hence, but enemies? No, my friend; thy fate shall be my fate; we live or we die together; the field, the cloister, or the tomb, all shall be welcomed by Edwin Ruthven, if they separate him not from thee." Seeing that Wallace was going to speak, and fearful that it was to repeat his commands to be left alone, he suddenly exclaimed, "Father of men and angels! grant me thy favor, only as I am true to the vow I have sworn, never more to leave the side of Sir William Wallace."

To urge the dangers to which such a resolution would expose this too faithful friend, Wallace knew would be in vain; he read determination in the eye of Edwin, and therefore, yielding to the demands of friendship, he cried, "For thy sake, Edwin, I will yet endure awhile mankind at large. Thy bloom of honor shall not be cropped by my hand. We will go together to France, and while I seek quiet in some of its remote cities, thou mayest bear the standard of Scotland in the land of our ally against the proud enemies of Bruce."—"Make of me what you will," returned Edwin, "only do not divide me from yourself."

Wallace explained to his friend his design of crossing the hills to Ayrshire, in some port of which he did not doubt finding some vessel bound for France. Edwin overturned this plan by telling him that in the moment the lords repledged their faith to England, they sent orders into Ayrshire to watch the movements of Wallace's relations, and to prevent their either hearing of, or marching to, the assistance of their wronged kinsman. And besides this, no sooner was it discovered by the insurgent lords at Roslyn that he had disappeared from the camp, than supposing he meant to appeal to Philip, they despatched expresses all along the western and eastern coasts, from the friths of Forth and Clyde to those of Solway and Berwick-upon-Tweed, to intercept him. On hearing that all avenues from the southern parts of his country were closed upon him, Wallace determined to try the north. Some bay in the western Highlands might open its arms to set its benefactor free. "If not by a ship," continued

Edwin, "a fisher's boat will launch us from a country no longer worthy of you."

Their course was then taken along the Cartlane craigs, at a distance from villages and mountain cots, which, leaning from their verdant heights, seemed to invite the traveler to refreshment and repose. Though the sword of Wallace had won them this quiet, though his wisdom had spread the barren hills with beauteous harvests, yet had an ear of corn been asked in his name, it would have been denied. A price was set upon his head, and the lives of all who should succor him would be forfeited. He who had given bread and homes to thousands had not where to shelter his head.

The black plumage of a common Highland bonnet, which Edwin had purchased at one of the cottages to which he had gone alone to buy a few oaten cakes, hung over the face of his friend. That face no longer blazed with the fire of generous valor, it was pale and sad; but whenever he turned his eye on Edwin, a look of affection expressed his comfort at having found that he was not yet wholly forsaken. Edwin's youthful spirit rejoiced in every glad beam which shone on the face of him he loved. To be near Wallace, to share his confidence with others, had always filled him with joy; but now to be the only one on whom his noble heart leaned for consolation was bliss unutterable.

When they arrived within sight of Bothwell Castle, Wallace stopped. "We must not go thither," said Edwin; "the servants of my cousin Andrew may not be as faithful as their lord."—"I will not try them," returned Wallace, with a resigned smile; "my presence shall not pluck danger on the head of my dauntless Murray."

While he yet spoke, a chieftain on horseback suddenly emerged from the trees which led to the castle, and drew to their side. Edwin was wrapped in his plaid, and concealing his face that no chance of recognition might betray his companion, he walked briskly on, without once looking at the stranger. But Wallace, being without any shade over the noble contour of a form which for majesty and grace was unequaled in Scotland, could not be mistaken. He, too, moved swiftly forward. The horseman spurred after him. Perceiving himself pursued, and therefore known, and aware that he must be overtaken, he suddenly stopped. Edwin drew his sword, and would have given it into the hand of his friend, but Wallace, putting it back, rapidly answered, "Leave my defense to this unweaponed arm. I would not use steel against my countrymen, but none shall take me while I have a sinew to resist."

The chieftain now checked his horse in front of Wallace, and respectfully raising his visor, discovered Sir John Monteith. At sight of him, Edwin dropped the point of his yet uplifted sword, and Wallace, stepping back, "Monteith," said he, "I am sorry for this rencounter. If you would be safe from the destiny which pursues me, you must retire immediately, and forget that we have met."—"Never!" cried Monteith. "I know the ingratitude of an envious country drives her champion from our borders, but I also know what belongs to myself,—to serve you at all hazards; and by conjuring you to become my guest, in my castle on the frith of Clyde, I would demonstrate my grateful sense of the dangers you once incurred for me."

In vain Wallace expressed his determination not to bring peril on any of his countrymen by sojourning under any roof till he were far from Scotland. In vain he urged to Monteith the outlawry which would await him should the infuriate lords discover that he had given shelter to the man whom they had chosen to suppose a traitor, and denounce as one. Monteith at last said that he knew a vessel was now lying at Newark, near his castle, in which Wallace might immediately embark, and he implored him by past friendship to allow him to be his guide to its anchorage. To enforce this supplication he threw himself off his horse, and with protestations of fidelity entreated not to be refused the last comfort he should ever know in his now degraded country. "Once I saw Scotland's steady champion, the brave Douglas, rifled from her shores. Do not, then, doom me to a second grief, bitterer than the first! Ah! let me behold you, companion of my school-days, friend, leader, benefactor! till the sea wrests you forever from my eyes." Exhausted and affected, Wallace gave his hand to Monteith; the tear of gratitude stood in his eye. He looked affectionately from Monteith to Edwin, from Edwin to Monteith. "Wallace shall yet live in the memory of the trusty of this land; you, my friends, prove it. I go richly forth, for the hearts of good men are my companions."

Night overtook the travelers near the little village of Lumloch, about two hours' journey from Glasgow. Here, a storm coming on, Monteith advised his friends to take shelter and rest. "As you object to implicate others," said he, "you may sleep secure in an old barn which at present has no ostensible owner. I remarked it while passing this way from Newark, but I wish you would forget this regard for others, and lodge with me in the neighboring cottage." Wallace was insensible to the pelting of the elements, his unsubdued spirit neither wanted rest for mind nor body; but the broken voice and lingering step of the young Edwin, who had severely sprained his foot in the dark, penetrated his heart; and notwithstanding that the resolute boy

Death of Edwin

declared he was neither weary nor in pain, Wallace, seeing he was both, yielded a sad consent to be conducted from the storm. "But not," said he, "to the house. We will go into the barn, and there, on the dry earth, my Edwin, we may gratefully repose."

Monteith did not oppose him further, and pushing open the door, Wallace and Edwin entered. Their conductor soon after followed with a light from the cottage, and pulling down some heaped straw, strewed it on the ground for a bed. "Here I shall sleep like a prince," cried Edwin, throwing himself along the scattered truss. "But not," returned Monteith, "till I have disengaged you from your wet garments, and preserved your arms and brigandine from the rust of this night." Edwin, sunk in weariness, said little in opposition, and having suffered Monteith to take away his sword and to unbrace his plated vest, dropped at once on the straw in a profound sleep.

Wallace, that he might not disturb him by debate, yielded to the request of Monteith, and having resigned his armor also, waved him a good-night. Monteith nodded the same, and closed the door upon his victims.

Well known to the generals of King Edward as one without honor, Sir John Monteith was considered by them all as a hireling fit for any purpose. Though De Warenne had been persuaded to use unworthy means to intimidate his great opponent, he would have shrank from treachery. His removal from the lord-wardenship of Scotland, in consequence of the wounds he had received at Dalkeith, opened a path to the elevation of Aymer de Valence. And when he was named viceroy in the stead of De Warenne, he told Edward that if he would authorize him to offer an earldom, with adequate estates, to Sir John Monteith, the old friend of Wallace, he was sure so rapacious a chieftain would traverse sea and land to put that formidable Scot into the hands of England. "If money will make him ours at this crisis," replied the King, "give him overflowing coffers, but no earldom. Though I must have the head of Wallace, I would not have one of my peers show a title written in his blood. Ill deeds must sometimes be done, but we do not emblazon their perpetrators."

De Valence having received his credentials imparted to Sir John Monteith the King of England's proposal. Monteith was then castellan of Newark, where he had immured himself for many months, under a pretence of the reopening of old wounds; but the fact was, his treasons were connected with so many accomplices that he feared some disgraceful disclosure, and therefore kept out of the way of exciting public attention. Avarice was his master passion; and the sudden idea that there might be treasure in the iron box, which he had consigned to Wallace, first bound him a sordid slave. His murmurs for having allowed the box to leave his possession gave the alarm which caused the disasters at Ellerslie and his own immediate arrest. His after-history was a series of secret treacheries to Scotland, and in return for them an accumulation of wealth from England, the contemplation of which seemed to be his sole enjoyment. This new offer from De Valence was therefore greedily embraced. He happned to be at Rutherglen when Haliburton brought the proposal, and in the cloisters of its church was its fell agreement signed. He transmitted an oath to De Valence that he would die or win his hire; and immediately despatching spies to the camp at Roslyn, as soon as he was informed of Wallace's disappearance, he judged, from his knowledge of that chief's affections, that whithersoever he intended finally to go he would first visit Ellerslie and the tomb of his wife. According to this opinion he planted his emissaries in favorable situations on the road, and then proceeded himself to intercept his victim at the most probable places.

Not finding him at Bothwell, he was issuing forth to take the way to Ellerslie when the object of his search presented himself at the opening of the wood. The evil plan too well succeeded.

Triumphant in his deceit, this master of hypocrisy left the barn, in which he had seen Wallace and his young friend lie down on that ground from which he had determined they should never more arise. Aware that Wallace would never allow himself to be taken alive, he had stipulated with De Valence that the delivery of his head should entitle him to a full reward. From Rutherglen to Lumloch no place had presented itself in which he thought he could so judiciously plant an ambuscade to surprise the unsuspecting Wallace.

The hour of midnight passed, and yet he could not summon courage to lead his men to their attack. Twice they urged him before he arose from his affected sleep, for sleep he could not: guilt had "murdered sleep," and he lay awake, restless, and longing for the dawn; and yet ere that dawn the deed must be accomplished. A cock crew from a neighboring farm. "That is the sign of morning, and we have yet done nothing," exclaimed a surly ruffian who leaned on his battle-ax in an opposite corner of the apartment. "No, it is the signal of our enemy's captivity," cried Monteith. "Follow me, but gently. If ye speak a word, or a single target rattle before ye all fall upon him, we are lost. He that first disables him shall have a double reward."

"Depend upon us," returned the sturdiest ruffian, and stealing cautiously out of the cottage the party advanced with noiseless steps towards the barn. Monteith paused at the door, making a sign to his men to halt while he listened. He put his ear to a crevice; not a murmur was within. He gently raised the latch, and setting the door wide open, with his finger on his lip, beckoned his followers. Without venturing to draw a breath they approached the threshold. The moon shone full into the hovel and shed a broad light upon their victims. The innocent face of Edwin rested on the bosom of his friend, and the arm of Wallace lay on the spread straw with which he had covered the tender body of his companion. So fair a picture of mortal friendship was never before beheld, but the hearts were blind which looked on it, and Monteith gave the signal. He retreated while his men threw themselves forward to bind Wallace where he lay; but the first man, in his eagerness, striking his head against a joist in the roof, uttered a fierce oath. The noise roused Wallace, who had rather slumbered than slept, and opening his eyes he sprang on his feet. A moment told him enemies were around. Seeing him rise, they rushed on him with imprecations. His eyes blazed like meteors, and with a sudden motion of his arm he seemed to hold the men at a distance, while his god-like figure stood a tower in collected might. Awestruck, they paused; but it was only for an instant. The sight of Edwin, now starting from his sleep, his aghast countenance while he felt for his weapons, his cry when he recollected they were gone, inspired the assassins with fresh courage. Battle-axes, swords, and rattling chains now flashed before the eyes of Wallace. The pointed steel in many places entered his body, while with part of a broken bench which chanced to lie near him, he defended himself and Edwin from this merciless host. Edwin, seeing naught but the death of his friend before his sight, regardless of himself, made a spring from his side and snatched a dagger from the belt of one of the murderers. The ruffian instantly caught the intrepid boy by the throat, and in that horrible clutch would certainly have deprived him of life, had not the lion grasp of Wallace seized the man in his arms, and compelled him to forego his hold. Edwin released, Wallace dropped his assailant, who, staggering a few paces, fell to the ground, and instantly expired.

The conflict now became desperate. Edwin's dagger twice defended the breast of his friend. Two of the assassins he stabbed to the heart. "Murder that urchin!" cried Monteith, who, seeing from without the carnage of his men, feared that Wallace might yet make his escape. "Hah!" cried Wallace, at the sound of Monteith's voice giving such an order, "then we are betrayed, but not by Heaven! Strike, one of you, that angel youth," cried he, "and you will incur damnation!" He spoke to the winds. They poured towards Edwin. Wallace, with a giant's strength, dispersed them as they advanced; the beam of wood fell on the heads, the breasts of his assailants. Himself, bleeding at every pore, felt not a smart while yet he defended Edwin. But a shout was heard from the door; a faint cry was heard at his side. He looked around. Edwin lay extended on the ground, with an arrow quivering in his breast; his closing eyes still looked upwards to his friend. The beam fell from the hands of Wallace. He threw himself on his knees beside him. The dying boy pressed his hand to his heart, and dropped his head upon his bosom. Wallace moved not, spoke not. His hand was bathed in the blood of his friend, but not a pulse beat beneath it; no breath warmed the chill of his face, as it hung over the motionless lips of Edwin.

The men were more terrified at this unresisting stillness than at the invincible prowess of his arm, and stood gazing on him in mute wonder. But Monteith, in whom the appetite of avarice had destroyed every perception of humanity, sent in other ruffians with new orders to bind Wallace. They approached him with terror; two of the strongest, stealing behind him, and taking advantage of his face being bent upon that of his murdered Edwin, each in the same moment seized his hands. As they griped them fast, and others advanced eagerly to fasten the bands, he looked calmly up, but it was a dreadful calm; it spoke the full completion of all woe. "Bring chains," cried one of the men, "he will burst these thongs."

"You may bind me with a hair," said he; "I contend no more." The bonds were fastened on his wrists, and then turning towards the lifeless body of Edwin, he raised it gently in his arms. The rosy red of youth yet tinged his cold cheek; his parted lips still beamed with the same, but the breath that had so sweetly informed them was flown. "Oh, my best brother that ever I had!" cried Wallace, in a sudden transport, and kissing his pale forehead; "my sincerest friend in my greatest need. In thee was truth, manhood, and nobleness; in thee was all man's fidelity, with woman's tenderness. My friend, my brother, oh, would to God I had died for thee!"

CHAPTER LXIX.

LORD RUTHVEN was yet musing on Wallace's solemn adieu, and the confirmation which the recitals of Grimsby and Hay had brought of his determined exile, when he was struck with new consternation by the flight of his son. A billet, which Edwin had left with Scrymgeour, told his father that he was gone to seek their friend, and to unite himself forever to his fortunes.

Bothwell, not less eager to preserve Wallace to the world, with an intent to persuade him to at least abandon his monastic project, set off direct for France, hoping to arrive before his friend, and engage the French monarch to assist in preventing so grievous a sacrifice. Ruthven, meanwhile, fearful that the unarmed Wallace and the self-regardless Edwin might fall into the hands of the wretches now widely dispersed to seize the chief and his adherents, sent out the Lanark veterans in divers disguises, to pursue the roads it was probable he might take, and finding him, guard him safely to the coast. Till Ruthven should receive accounts of their success, he forbore to forward the letter which Wallace had left for Bruce, or to increase the solicitude of the already anxious inhabitants of Hunting-tower with any intimation of what had happened. But on the fourth day Scrymgeour and his party returned with the horrible narrative of Lumloch.

After the murder of his youthful friend, Wallace had been loaded with irons and conveyed, so unresistingly that he seemed in a stupor, on board a vessel to be carried without loss of time to the Tower of London. Sir John Monteith, though he never ventured into his sight, attended as the accuser, who was to swear away his victim's life. The horror and grief of Ruthven at these tidings were unutterable, and Scrymgeour, to turn the tide of the bereaved father's thoughts to the inspiring recollection of the early glory of his son, proceeded to narrate that he found the beauteous remains in the hovel, but bedecked with flowers by the village girls. They were weeping over it, and lamenting the pitiless heart which could slay such youth and loveliness. To bury him in so obscure a spot, Scrymgeour would not allow, and he had sent Stephen Ireland with the sacred corse to

453

Dumbarton, with orders to see him entombed in the chapel of that fortress. "It is done," continued the worthy knight, "and those towers he so bravely scaled will stand forever the monument of Edwin Ruthven." Cautious of inflicting too heavy a blow on the fortitude of his wife and of Helen, Lord Ruthven commanded Grimsby and Hay to withhold from everybody at Hunting-tower the tidings of its young lord's fate; but he believed it his duty not to delay the letter of Wallace to Bruce, and the dreadful information to him of Monteith's treachery. Ruthven ended his short epistle to his wife by saying he should soon follow his messenger, but that at present he could not abandon the Lowlands to even a temporary empire of the seditious chiefs.

On Grimsby's arrival at Hunting-tower he was conducted immediately to Bruce. Some cheering symptoms having appeared that morning, he had just exchanged his bed for a couch when Grimsby entered the room. The countenance of the honest Southron was the harbinger of his news. Lady Helen started from her seat, and Bruce, stretching out his arm, eagerly caught the packets the soldier presented. Isabella inquired if all were well with Sir William Wallace. But ere he could make an answer, Lady Ruthven ran breathless into the room holding out the opened letter brought by Hay to her. Bruce had just read the first line of his, which announced the captivity of Wallace, and with a groan that pierced through the souls of every one present, he made an attempt to spring from the couch; but in the act he reeled and fell back in agony. The heart of Helen guessed some direful explanation; she looked with speechless inquiry upon her aunt and Grimsby. Isabella and Ercildown hastened to Bruce, and Lady Ruthven, being too much appalled in her own feelings to think for a moment on the aghast Helen, hurriedly read to her from Lord Ruthven's letter the brief but decisive account of Wallace's dangerous situation,—his seizure and conveyance to the Tower of England. Helen listened without a word; her heart seemed locked within her, her brain was on fire, and gazing fixedly on the floor while she listened, all else that was transacted around her passed unnoticed.

The pangs of convulsion did not long shackle the determined Bruce. The energy of his spirit struggling to gain the side of Wallace in this his extremest need (for he well knew Edward's implacable soul), roused him from his swoon. Dashing away the restoratives with which both Isabella and Ercildown hung over him, he would have leaped on the floor had not the latter held him down. "Withhold me not!" cried he; "this is not the time for sickness and indulgence. My friend is in the fangs of the tyrant, and not for all the empires in the globe will I be detained another hour."

Isabella, affrighted at the perils attendant on his desperate resolution, threw herself at his feet and implored him to stay for her sake. "No," cried Bruce, "not for thy life, Isabella, which is dearer to me than my own, not to save this ungrateful country from the doom it merits, would I linger one moment from the side of him who has fought, bled, and suffered for me and mine, and who is now sentenced to die for my delinquency. Had I consented to proclaim myself on my landing, secure with Bruce the king, envy would have feared to strike; but I must first win a fame like his. And while I lay here, they tore him from me. But, Almighty pardoner of my sins!" cried he with vehemence, "grant me strength to wrest him from their gripe, and I will go barefoot to Palestine to utter all my gratitude!"

Isabella sank weeping into the arms of her aunt and the venerable Ercildown urged to the prince the danger into which such resentment would precipitate his own person. At this intimation the impassioned Bruce, stung to the soul that such an argument could be expected to have weight with him, solemnly bent his knee, and clasping his sword, vowed before Heaven "either to release Wallace or"—to share his fate he would have added; but Isabella, watchful of his words, suddenly interrupted him by throwing herself wildly on his neck and exclaiming, "Oh, say not so! Rather swear to pluck the tyrant from his throne, that the scepter of my Bruce may bless England, as it will yet do this unhappy land!"—"She says right," ejaculated Ercildown, in a prophetic transport, "and the scepter of Bruce in the hands of his offspring shall bless the united countries to the latest generations. The walls of separation shall then be thrown down, and England and Scotland be one people."*

Bruce looked steadfastly on the sage. "Then if thy voice utter holy verity, it will not again deny my call to wield the power that Heaven bestows. I follow my fate. To-morrow's dawn sees me in the path to snatch my counselor from the judgment of his enemies, or woe to England; woe to all Scotland born who have breathed one word against his sacred life! Helen, dost thou hear me?" cried he. "Wilt thou not assist me to persuade thy timid sister that her Bruce's honor, his happiness, lives in the preservation of his friend? Counsel her, sweet Helen; and, please Heaven, I will reward thy tenderness with the return of Wallace!"

Helen gazed intently on him while he spoke. She smiled when he

* Spottiswood insists very much on this prediction of Ercildown's, which was verified in James the First of England, in the ninth degree from Bruce.

ended, but she did not answer, and there was a vacancy in the smile that seemed to say she knew not what had been spoken, and that her thoughts were far away. Without further regarding him or any present, she arose and left the room. At this moment her whole soul was bent with an intensity that touched on madness on the execution of a project which had rushed into her mind in the moment she heard of Wallace's captivity and destination.

The approach of night favored her design. Hurrying to her chamber, she dismissed her maids with the prompt excuse that she was ill and desired not to be disturbed till morning; then bolting the door, she quickly habited herself in the page's clothes which she had so carefully preserved as the memorial of her happy days in France, and dropping from her window into the pleasance beneath, ran swiftly through its woody precincts towards Dundee.

Before she arrived at the suburbs of Perth her tender feet became so blistered she found the necessity of stopping at the first cottage. But her perturbed spirits rendered it impossible for her to take rest, and she answered the hospitable offer of its humble owner with a request that he would go into the town and immediately purchase a horse to carry her that night to Dundee. She put her purse into the man's hand, who, without further discussion, obeyed. When the animal was brought, and the honest Scot returned her the purse with its remaining contents, she divided them with him, and, turning from his thanks, mounted the horse and rode away.

About an hour before dawn she arrived within view of the ships lying in the harbor at Dundee. At this sight she threw herself off the panting animal, and leaving it to rest and liberty, hastened to the beach. A gentle breeze blew freshly from the north-west, and several vessels were heaving their anchors to get under weigh. "Are any," demanded she, "bound for the Tower of London?"—"None," were the replies. Despair was now in her heart and gesture; but suddenly recollecting that in dressing herself for flight she had not taken off the jewels she usually wore, she exclaimed with renovated hope, "Will not gold tempt some one to carry me thither?" A rough Norwegian sailor jumped from the side of the nearest vessel and readily answered in the affirmative. "My life," rejoined she, "or a necklace of pearls shall be yours in the moment you land me at the Tower of London." The man, seeing the youth and agitation of the seeming boy, doubted his power to perform so magnificent a promise, and was half inclined to retract his assent; but Helen, pointing to a jewel on her finger as a proof that she did not speak of things beyond her reach, he no longer hesitated, and pledging his word that, wind and tide in his favor, he would land her at the Tower stairs, she sprang into his vessel. The sails were unfurled, the voices of the men chanted forth their cheering responses on clearing the harbor, and Helen, throwing herself along the floor of her little cabin, silently breathed her thanks to God for being launched on the ocean whose waves, she trusted, would soon convey her to Wallace.

CHAPTER LXX.

THE THAMES.

On the evening of the fourteenth day from the one in which Helen had embarked, the little ship of Dundee entered on the bright bosom of the Nore. While she sat on the deck watching the progress of the vessel with an eager spirit which would gladly have taken wings to have flown to the object of her voyage, she first saw the majestic waters of the Thames. But it was a tyrannous flood to her, and she marked not the diverging shores crowned with palaces; her eyes looked over every stately dome to seek the black summits of the Tower. At a certain point the captain of the vessel spoke through his trumpet to summon a pilot from the land. In a few minutes he was obeyed. The Englishman took the helm. Helen was reclined on a coil of ropes near him. He entered into conversation with the Norwegian, and she listened to a recital which bound up her every sense in that of hearing.

The Englishman mentioned the capture of the once renowned champion of Scotland. "I was present," continued he, "when the brave Scot was put on the raft which carried him through the traitor's gate into the Tower. His hands and feet were bound with iron; but his head, owing to faintness from the wounds he had received at Lumloch, was so bent on his breast, as he reclined on the float, that I could not then see his face. There was a great pause; for none of us, when he did appear in sight, could shout over the downfall of such a conqueror. Many were spectators of this scene whose lives he had spared on the fields of Scotland, and my brother was amongst them. However, that I might have a distinct view of the man who has so long held our monarch in dread, I went to Westminster Hall on the day appointed for his trial. The great judges of the land, and almost all the lords besides, were there; and a grand spectacle they made. But when the hall door was opened and the dauntless prisoner appeared, then it was that I saw true majesty; King Edward on his throne never looked with such a royal air. His very chains seemed given to be graced by him, as he moved through the parting crowd with the step of one who had been used to have all his accusers at his feet. Though pale with loss of blood, and the suffering of his yet unhealed wounds, his head was now erect, and he looked with dignity on all around. The Earl of Gloucester, whose life and liberty he had granted at Berwick, sat on the right of the lord chancellor. Bishop Beck, the Lords de Valence and Soulis, with one Monteith (who, it seems, was the man that betrayed him into our hands), charged him with high treason against the life of King Edward and the peace of his majesty's realms of England and Scotland. Grievous were the accusations brought against him, and bitter the revilings with which he was denounced as a traitor. The Earl of Gloucester at last rose indignantly, and, in respectful terms, called on Sir William Wallace, by the reverence in which he held the tribunal of future ages, to answer for himself.

"'On this adjuration, brave earl,' replied he, 'I will speak.' In his voice was all honesty and nobleness; and a murmur arose from some who feared its power, which Gloucester was obliged to check by exclaiming aloud, 'Silence, while Sir William Wallace answers! He who disobeys, sergeant-at-arms, take into custody.' A pause succeeded, and the chieftain, with the majesty of truth, denied the possibility of being a traitor where he never had owed allegiance. But with fearlessness he avowed the facts alleged against him, which told the havoc he had made of the English on the Scottish plains, and the devastations he had afterwards wrought in the lands of England. 'It was a son,' cried he, 'defending the orphans of his father from the rapine of a treacherous friend. It was the sword of restitution, gathering, on that false friend's fields, the harvests he had ravaged from theirs.' He spoke more, but too nobly for them who heard him. They rose to a man to silence what they could not confute; and the sentence of death was pronounced on him,—the cruel death of a traitor! The Earl of Gloucester turned pale; but the countenance of Wallace was unmoved. As he was led forth, I followed, and saw the young Le de Spencer, with several other gallants of our court, ready to receive him. With mockery they threw laurels on his head, and with torrents of derision told him it was meet they should so salute the champion of Scotland! Wallace glanced on them a look which spoke pity rather than contempt, and followed the warden towards the Tower. His accusers loaded him with invectives as he passed along; but the populace who beheld his noble mien, with those individuals who had heard of his virtues, deplored and wept his sentence. To-morrow at sunrise he dies."

The agony of Helen's mind could have been read in her countenance, but as soon as he had uttered the last dreadful words, "To-morrow at sunrise he dies," she started from her seat, her senses apprehended nothing further, and, turning to the Norwegian, "Cap-

tain," cried she, "I must reach the Tower this night."—"Impossible,"
was the reply; "the tide will not take us up till to-morrow at noon."

"Then the waves shall," cried she, and rushing towards the ship's
side, she would have thrown herself into the water had not the pilot
caught her arm.—"Boy!" said he, "are you mad?"—"No," interrupted she, wringing her hands; "but in the Tower I must be this
night. Oh, God of mercy, end my misery!" The anguish of her
voice and gesture excited a suspicion in the Englishman that this
youth was connected with the Scottish chief, and not choosing to hint
his surmise to the unfeeling Norwegian, he exhorted Helen to composure, and offered her his own boat, which was then towed at the
side of the vessel, to take her to the Tower. Helen grasped the pilot's
rough hand, and pressed it to her lips; then, forgetful of her engagements with the insensible man who stood unmoved by his side, sprang
into the boat. The Norwegian followed her, and in a threatening
tone demanded his hire. She now recollected it, and putting her hand
into her vest, gave him the string of pearls which had been her necklace. He was satisfied, and the boat pushed off.

The cross, the cherished memorial of her meeting with Wallace
in the chapel of Snawdown, which always hung suspended on her
bosom, was now in her hand, and pressed close to her heart. The
rowers plied their oars, and her eyes looked intently onward, while
the men labored through the tide. Even to see the walls which contained Wallace seemed to promise her a degree of comfort she dared
hardly hope to enjoy. At last the awful battlements of England's
state prison rose before her. She could not mistake them. "That
is the Tower," said one of the rowers. A shriek escaped her, and
covering her face with her hands, she tried to shut from her sight
those very walls she had so long sought amongst the clouds.

"Shall I die before I reach thee, Wallace?" was the question her
soul uttered, as trembling, she ascended the stone stairs which led
from the water's edge to the entrance of the Tower. She flew through
the different courts to the one in which stood the prison of Wallace.
One of the boatmen, being bargeman to the governor of the Tower,
conducted her unmolested through every ward till she reached the
place of her destination. There she dismissed him, with a ring from
her finger as his reward, and passing a body of soldiers who kept
guard before the dungeons, she entered, and found herself in an immense paved room. A single sentinel stood at the end near to an
iron grating; there, then, was Wallace. Forgetting her disguise
and situation in the frantic eagerness of her pursuit, she hastily advanced to the man. "Let me pass to Sir William Wallace," cried

she, "and treasures shall be your reward."—"Whose treasures, my pretty page?" demanded the soldier. "I dare not, were it at the suit of the Countess of Gloucester herself."—"Oh," cried Helen, "for the sake of a greater than any countess in the land, take this jeweled bracelet and let me pass!"

The man, at sight of the diamonds, supposing the page must come from the young queen, no longer demurred. Putting the bracelet into his bosom, he whispered Helen that, as he granted this permission at the risk of his life, she must conceal herself in the interior of the prisoner's dungeon should any person from the warden visit him during their interview. She readily promised this; and he informed her that when through this door she must cross two other apartments, the bolts to the entrance of which she must undraw, and then at the extremity of a long passage, a door fastened by a latch would admit her to Sir William Wallace. With these words the soldier removed the massy bars, and Helen entered.

CHAPTER LXXI.

THE TOWER OF LONDON.

HELEN's fleet steps carried her in a few minutes through the intervening dungeons to the door which would restore to her eyes the being with whose life her existence seemed blended. The bolts had yielded to her hands. The iron latch now gave way, and the ponderous oak grating dismally on its hinges, she looked forward and beheld the object of her solicitude leaning along a couch; a stone table was before him, at which he seemed writing. He raised his head at the sound. Peace was in his eyes, and a smile on his lips, as if he had expected some angel visitant.

The first glance at his heavenly countenance struck to the heart of Helen; veneration, anguish, shame—all rushed on her at once. She was in his presence; but how might he turn from consolations he had not sought! She would have fled, but her failing limbs bent under her, and she fell senseless into the dungeon. Wallace started from his reclining position. He thought his senses must deceive him,—and yet the shriek was Lady Helen's. He had heard the same cry on the Pentland hills, in the chamber of Château Galliard. He arose agitated, he approached the prostrate youth, and bending to the inanimate form, took off the Norman hat; he parted the heavy locks which fell over her brow, and recognized the features of her who alone had ever shared his meditations with his Marion. He sprinkled water on her face and hands; he touched her cheek; it was cold, and the chill struck to his heart. "Helen!" exclaimed he, "Helen, awake! Speak to thy friend!"

Still she was motionless. "Dead!" cried he with increased emotion. His eye and his heart in a moment discerned and understood the rapid emaciation of those lovely features. "Gone so soon!" repeated he. "Gone to tell my Marion that her Wallace comes. Blessed angel!" cried he, clasping her to his breast, "take me, take me with thee!" The pressure, the voice, roused the dormant life of Helen. With a sigh she unsealed her eyes and found herself in the arms of Wallace.

All her wandering senses now rallied, and smote her to the soul. Though still overwhelmed with grief at the fate which threatened to tear him from her and life, she wondered how she could ever have so trampled on the modesty of her nature as to have brought herself thus into his presence, and in a voice of despair, believing that she had destroyed herself in his opinion, she exclaimed, "Oh, Wallace! how came I here? I am lost—and innocently; but God, the pure God, can read the soul!"

She lay in misery on his breast, with her eyes again closed, almost unconscious of the support on which she leaned. "Lady Helen," returned he, "was it other than Wallace you sought in these dungeons? I dared to think that God had sent you hither to be His harbinger of consolation." Recalled to self-possession by these words, Helen turned her head on his bosom, and faltered, "And will you not abhor me for this act of madness? And yet, where should I live or die but at the feet of my benefactor?" The soul of Wallace was subdued by this language and the manner of its utterance; and the tears of a sympathy which spoke their kindred natures stole from his eyes as he bent his cheek on her head. She felt them, and, rejoicing in an assurance that she yet possessed his esteem, she exclaimed, "Then you do understand me, Wallace? You pardon me this apparent forgetfulness of my sex? and you recognize a true sister in Helen Mar? I may administer to that noble heart till——" she paused, turned deadly pale, and then, clasping his hand in both hers, added, "till we meet in heaven!"

"And blissful, dearest saint, will be our union there," replied he, "where soul meets soul unencumbered of these earthly fetters. But there, my Helen, we shall never weep. No heart will be left unsatisfied; no spirit will mourn in unrequited love; for that happy region is the abode of love."

"Ah!" cried Helen, throwing herself on her knees, "join, then, your prayers with mine, that I may be admitted into such blessedness. Petition our God to forgive me, and do you forgive me, that I have sometimes envied the love you bear your Marion. But I now love her so entirely that to be hers and your ministering spirit in Paradise would satisfy my soul."

"Oh, Helen!" cried Wallace, grasping her uplifted hands in his, "thy soul and Marion's are indeed one, and as one I love ye."

This declaration almost overpowered Helen in its flood of happiness, and with a smile which seemed to picture the heavens opening before her, she turned her eyes from him to a crucifix which stood on the table, and bowing her head on its pedestal, was lost in devotion.

At this juncture, when, perhaps, the purest bliss that ever descended on woman's heart now glowed in that of Helen, the Earl of

Gloucester entered. His were not visits of consolation, for he knew that his friend did not require the comfortings of any mortal hand. At sight of him, Wallace, pointing to the kneeling Helen, beckoned him into the inner cell, where his straw pallet lay, and there, in a low voice, declared who she was, and requested the earl to use his authority to allow her to remain with him to the last.

"After that," said he, "I rely on you, generous Gloucester, to convey safely back to her country a being who seems to have nothing of earth about her but the body which enshrines her angelic soul."

The sound of a voice speaking with Wallace aroused Helen from her trance. Alarmed that it might be the emissaries of the tyrant come prematurely to summon him to his last hour, she started on her feet. "Where are you, Wallace?" cried she, looking distractedly around her. "I must be with you even in death."

Hearing her cry, he hastened into the dungeon, and relieved her terror by naming the Earl of Gloucester, who followed him. The conviction that Wallace was under mortal sentence now glared upon her with redoubled horrors. This world again rose before her in the person of Gloucester. It reminded her that she and Wallace were not yet passed into the hereafter. "And is there no hope?" faltered she, looking earnestly on the face of Gloucester, who had bowed with a pitying respect to her as he approached. And then, while he seemed hesitating for an answer, she imploringly resumed: "Oh, let me seek your king? Once he was a crusade prince. The cross was then on his breast, and the love of Him who came to redeem lost man must have been then in his heart. Sir William Wallace, also a Christian knight, anointed by virtue and his cause, hath only done for his own country what King Edward then did for Christendom in Palestine. And he was roused to the defense by a deed worse than ever infidel inflicted. I would relate this on my knees to your royal Edward, and implore his mercy."

Helen, who had risen, in her energy of speech suddenly paused, clasped her hands, and stood with upward eyes, looking as if she beheld the object of her invocation.

"Dearest sister of my soul!" cried Wallace, who had forborne to interrupt her, "thy knees shall never bend to any less than to the Lord of all mankind for me. Did He will my longer pilgrimage on this earth, it would not be in the power of any human tyrant to hold me in these bonds. And for Edward, believe that not all thy eloquence could make one impression where ambition hath set so deep a seal. I am content to go, my sister, and angels whisper me" (he added in a lowered tone, like that angel whisper) "that thy bridal bed will be in William Wallace's grave." She spoke not, but at this assurance turned her tearful eyes upon him with a beam of delight.

Gloucester contemplated this union of two spotless hearts with an admiration almost amounting to devotion. "Noble lady," said he, "the message that I came to impart to Sir William Wallace bears with it a show of hope, and I trust that your gentle spirit will yet be as persuasive as consolatory. A deputation has just arrived from our border-counties, headed by the good Barons De Hilton and De Blenkinsopp, praying the royal mercy for their gallant foe, who had been most generous to them, they set forth, in their extremity. And the king was listening to them, with what temper I know not, when a private embassy as opportunely made its appearance from France on the same errand; in short, to negotiate with Edward for the safety of our friend, as a prince of that realm. I left the ambassadors," continued the earl, turning to Wallace, "in debate with his majesty, and he has at length granted a suspension, nay, has even promised a repeal of the horrible injustice that was to be completed to-morrow, if you can be brought to accord with certain proposals now to be laid before you. Accept them, and Edward will comply with all King Philip's demands in your behalf."

"Then you will accept them?" cried Helen, in a tumult of suspense. The communication of Gloucester had made no change in the pulse of Wallace, and he replied, with a look of pity, "The proposals of Edward are too likely to be snares for that honor which I would bear with me uncontaminated to the grave. Therefore, dearest consoler of my last hour, do not give way to hopes which a greater King than Edward may command me to disappoint." Helen bowed her head in silence, and despair once more seized on her heart.

Gloucester resumed, and after narrating some particulars concerning the conference between the king and the ambassadors, he suggested the impracticability of secretly retaining Lady Helen for any length of time in the state dungeon. "I dare not," continued he, "be privy to her presence here and yet conceal it from the king. I know not what messengers he may send to impart his conditions, and should she be discovered, Edward would tear her from you, and so involve me in his displeasure that I should be disabled from serving either of you further. Were I so to honor his feelings as a man as to mention it to him, I do not believe that he would oppose her wishes; but how to reveal such a circumstance I know not, for all are not sufficiently virtuous to believe her innocence." Helen hastily interrupted Gloucester, and with firmness said, "When I entered these walls the world and I parted forever. The good or evil opinion of the impure in heart can never affect me. I came to minister with a sister's duty to my own and my father's preserver, and while he abides here I will never consent to leave his feet. But should he be taken from a world so unworthy of him, I shall soon cease to feel its aspersions in the grave."

"No aspersions which I can avert, dearest Helen," cried Wallace, "shall ever tarnish thy fame. Consent, noblest of women, to wear my name for the few days I may yet linger here. Give me a legal right to call you mine, and Edward himself will not then dare to divide what God has joined together."

Helen paused—even her heart seemed to cease its pulsation in the awful moment. She turned towards Wallace; she attempted to answer, but the words died on the smile which beamed upon her lips, and she dropped her head upon his breast.

Gloucester, who saw no other means of ensuring to his friend the comfort of her society, was rejoiced at this mutual resolution. He had longed to propose it; but considering the peculiarities of their situation, knew not how to do so without seeming to mock their fate. It was now near midnight, and having read the consent of Helen in the emotion which denied her speech, without further delay he quitted the apartment to summon the confessor of the warden to unite their hands.

On his reentrance he found Helen sitting dissolved in tears, with her hand clasped in his friend's. The sacred rite was soon performed which endowed her with all the claims upon Wallace which her devoted heart had long contemplated with hopelessness,—to be his helpmate on earth, his dear companion in heaven. With the last benediction she threw herself on her knees before him, and put his hand to her lips in silence. Gloucester, with a look of kind farewell, withdrew with the priest.

"Thou noble daughter of the noblest Scot," said Wallace, raising her from the ground, "this bosom is thy place, and not my feet. Long it will not be given me to hold thee here; but even in the hours or years of our separation my spirit will hover near thee to bear thine to our everlasting home."

The heart of Helen alternately beat violently, and stopped; hope and fear agitated her by turns, but, clinging to the ideas which the arrival of the ambassadors had excited, she faltered a belief that, by the present interference of King Philip, Edward might not be found inexorable.

"Disturb not the composure of your soul by such an expectation," returned Wallace; "I know my adversary too well to anticipate his relinquishing the object of his vengeance but at a price more infamous than the most ignoble death. Therefore, best-beloved of all on earth, look for no deliverance for thy Wallace but what passes through the grave."

Helen's thoughts could not wrest themselves from the direful images of his execution; she shuddered, and in faltering accents replied, "Ah, could we glide from sleep into so blessed a death, I would hail it even for thee! But the threatened horrors, should they fall on thy sacred head, will in that hour, I trust, also divorce my soul from this grievous world."

"Not so, my Helen," returned he; "keep not thy dear eyes forever fixed on the gloomy appendages of death. The scaffold and the grave have naught to do with the immortal soul; it cannot be wounded by the one, nor confined by the other. Comfort, then, thy heart, my soul's dear sister, and sojourn a little while on this earth to bear witness for thy Wallace to the friends he loves."

Helen, who felt the import of his words in her heart, gently bowed her head, and he proceeded:

"As the first who stemmed with me the torrent which, with God's help, we so often laid into a calm, I mention to you my faithful men of Lanark. Many of them bled and died in the contest, and to their orphans, with the children of those who yet survive, I consign all of the world's wealth that yet belongs to William Wallace: Ellerslie and its estates are theirs. To Bruce, my sovereign and my friend, the loved companion of the hour in which I freed you from the arms of violence—to him I bequeath this heart, knit to him by bonds more dear than even loyalty. Bear it to him, and when he is summoned to his heavenly throne, then let his heart and mine fill up one urn. To Lord Ruthven, to Bothwell, to Lockhart, to Scrymgeour, and to Kirkpatrick, I give my prayers and blessings."

Here Wallace paused. Helen had listened to him with an attention which hardly allowed a sigh to breathe from her heart; she spoke, but the voice was scarcely audible: "And what for him who loves you dearer than life—for Edwin? He cannot be forgotten." Wallace started at this; then she was ignorant of the death of that faithful friend. In a hurrying accent he replied, "Never forgotten! Oh, Helen! I asked for him life, and Heaven gave him long life, even forever and ever." Helen's eyes met his with a look of awful inquiry: "That would mean he is gone before you?" The countenance of Wallace answered her. "Happy Edwin!" cried she, and the tears rained over her cheeks. Wallace continued: "He laid down his life to preserve mine, in the hovel of Lumloch. The false Monteith could get no Scot to lay hands on their true defender; and even the foreign ruffians he brought to the task might have spared the noble boy, but an arrow from the traitor himself pierced his heart. Contention was then no more, and I resigned myself to follow him."

"What a desert does the world become!" exclaimed Helen; then turning on Wallace, she added, "I would hardly now withhold you. You will bear him Helen's love, and tell him how soon I shall be with you. If our Father will not allow my heart to break, in his mercy he may take my soul."—"Thou hast been lent to me as my sweet consolation here, my Helen," replied he, "and the dispenser of that comfort will not long banish you from the object of your wishes."

While they thus poured into each other's bosoms the balm of friendship's purest tenderness, the eyes of Wallace insensibly closed. "Your gentle influence," gently murmured he, "brings that sleep to my eyelids which has not visited them since I first entered these walls. Like my Marion, Helen, thy presence brings healing on its wings."—"Sleep, then," replied she, "and Marion's angel spirit will keep watch with mine."

CHAPTER LXXII.

THE STATE DUNGEON.

THOUGH all the elements seemed to rage around the walls of the dungeon, still Wallace slept. Calm was within, and the warfare of the world could not disturb the rest in which peace had steeped his senses. From this profound repose he was awakened by the entrance of Gloucester. Helen had just sunk into a slight slumber, but the first words of the earl aroused her, and rising, she followed her beloved Wallace to his side.

Gloucester put a scroll into the hand of Wallace. "Sign that," said he, "and you are free. I know not its contents, but the king commissioned me, as a mark of his grace, to be the messenger of your release."

Wallace read the conditions, and the color deepened on his cheek as his eye met each article. "He was to reveal the asylum of Bruce, to forswear Scotland forever, and to take an oath of allegiance to Edward, the seal of which should be the English earldom of Cleveland." Wallace closed the parchment. "King Edward knows well what will be my reply; I need not speak it."—"You will accept his terms?" asked the earl.

"Not to ensure me a life of ages, with all earthly bliss my portion. I have spoken to these offers before. Read them, my noble friend, and then give him, as mine, the answer that would be yours." Gloucester obeyed; and while his eyes were bent on the parchment, those of Helen were fixed on her almost worshiped husband. She looked through his countenance into his very soul, and there saw the sublime purpose that consigned his head to the scaffold. When Gloucester had finished, he crushed the disgraceful scroll in his hand, and exclaimed with vehemence against the cruelty of his father-in-law so to mock by base subterfuges the embassy of France and its noble object.

"This is the morning in which I was to have met my fate," replied Wallace. "Tell this tyrant that I am even now ready to receive the last stroke of his injustice. In the peaceful grave, my Helen," added he, turning to her, "I shall be beyond his power." Gloucester walked the room in great disturbance of mind, while Wallace continued, in a lowered tone, to give some consolation to the soul-struck

Helen. The earl stopped suddenly before them. "That the king did not expect your acquiescence without some hesitation, I cannot doubt; for when I informed him the Lady Helen Mar, now your wife, was the sharer of your prison, he started, and told me that should you still oppose yourself to his conditions, I must bring her to him, who might, perhaps, be the means of persuading you to receive his mercy."

"Never!" replied Wallace. "I reject what he calls mercy. He has no rights of judgment over me, and his pretended mercy is an assumption which, as a true Scot, I despise. No wife nor aught of mine shall ever stand before him as a suppliant for William Wallace. I will die as I have lived, the equal of Edward in all things but a crown, and his superior, in being true to unblemished honor!"

Finding the Scottish chief not to be shaken in this determination, Gloucester, humbled to the soul by the tyranny of his royal father-in-law, soon after withdrew to acquaint that monarch with the ill-success of his embassy. But ere noon had turned he reappeared with a countenance declarative of some distressing errand. He found Helen awakened to the full perception of all her pending evils—that she was on the eve of losing forever the object dearest to her in the world, and though she wept not, her heart bled within her.

"I come," said Gloucester, "not to urge you to send Lady Helen as a suitor to King Edward, but to spare her the misery of being separated from you while life is yours." He then said that the French ambassadors were kept in ignorance of the conditions which were offered to the object of their mission, and on being informed that he had refused them, they showed themselves so little satisfied with the sincerity of what had been done, that Edward thought it expedient to conciliate Philip by taking some pains to dislodge their suspicions. To this effect he proposed to the French lords sending his final proposition to Sir William Wallace by that chieftain's wife, who he found was then his companion in the tower. "On my intimating," continued the earl, "that I feared she would be unable to appear before him, his answer was: 'Let her see to that; such a refusal shall be answered by an immediate separation from her husband.'"

"Let me, in this demand," cried she, turning with firmness to Wallace, "satisfy the will of Edward. It is only to purchase my continuance with you. I should be unworthy of the name you have given me could I sully it by one debasing word or action to the author of all our ills."—"Ah, my Helen!" replied he, "what is it you ask? Am I to live to see a repetition of the horrors of Ellerslie?"—"No, on my life," answered Gloucester; "in this instance I would pledge my soul for King Edward's manhood. His ambition might lead him to trample on all men, but still for woman he feels as becomes a man and a knight."

Helen renewed her supplications, and Wallace, aware that should he withhold her attendance, his adversary would not forbear wounding her to the soul by tearing her from him, gave an unwilling consent to what might seem a submission on his part to an authority he had shed his blood to oppose. "But not in these garments," said he. "She must be habited as becomes her sex and her own delicacy."

Anticipating this propriety, Gloucester had imparted the circumstance to his countess, and she had sent a casket, which the earl himself now brought in from the passage. Helen retired to the inner cell, and hastily arraying herself in the first suit that presented itself, reappeared in female apparel, and wrapped in a long veil. As Gloucester took her hand to lead her forth, Wallace clasped the other in his. "Remember, my Helen," cried he, "that on no terms but freedom of soul will your Wallace accept of life. This will not be granted by the man to whom you go; therefore, speak and act in his presence as if I were already beyond the skies."

Had his almost adoring wife left his side with more sanguine hopes, how grievously would they have been blasted!

After an absence of two hours she returned to the dungeon of Wallace, and as her trembling form was clasped in his arms, she exclaimed, in a passion of tears, "Here will I live! Here will I die! They may sever my soul from my body, but never again part me from this dear bosom!"

"Never, never, my Helen!" said he, reading her conference with the king in the terror of its effects. While she clung to him, and muttered incoherent sentences, he cast a look of such expressive inquiry upon Gloucester, that the earl could only answer by hastily putting his hand on his face to hide his emotion. At last, the tears she shed appeared to relieve the excess of her agonies, and she gradually sank into calm. Then rising from her husband's arms, she seated herself on his stony couch, and said in a firm voice, "Earl, I can now bear to hear you repeat the last decision of the King of England."

Though not absolutely present at the interview between his sovereign and Lady Helen, from the anteroom Gloucester had heard all that passed, and he now confessed to Wallace that he had too truly appreciated the pretended conciliation of the king. Edward's proposals to Helen were as artfully couched as deceptive in their design. Their issue was to make Wallace his slave, or to hold him his victim. In his conference with her, he addressed the vanity of an ambitious woman; then all the affections of a devoted heart; he enforced his arguments with persuasions to allure and threats to compel obedience, but, steadfast in the principles of her lord, while ready to sink under the menaced horrors of his fate, she summoned all her strength to give utterance to her last reply.

"Mortal distinctions, King of England," cried she, "cannot bribe the wife of Sir William Wallace to betray his virtues. I can see him die, and live—for I shall join him, triumphant in heaven; but to behold him dishonor himself, to counsel him so to do, is beyond my power."

The indignation of the king at this answer was too oppressive for Gloucester to repeat it to her husband, and, while she turned deadly pale at the recollection, Wallace, exulting in her conduct, pressed her hand fervently to his lips.

The earl resumed, but, observing the agonies of Helen's mind, he strove to soften the blow he must inflict in the remainder of his narrative.

"Dearest lady," said he, rather addressing her than Wallace, "to convince you that no earthly means have been left unessayed to change the purpose of the king, know that when he quitted you I left in his presence the queen and my wife, both weeping tears of disappointment. On the moment when I found that arguments could no longer avail, I implored him, by every consideration of God and man, to redeem his honor, sacrificed by the unjust decree pronounced on Sir William Wallace. My entreaties were repulsed with anger, for the sudden entrance of Lord Athol, with fresh fuel to his flame, so confirmed his resolution, that, desperate for my friend, I threw myself on my knees. The queen, and then my wife, enforced my suit, but all in vain; his heart seemed hardened by our earnestness, and his answer, while it put us to silence, granted Wallace a triumph even in his dungeon. 'Cease!' cried the king. 'Wallace and I have now come to that issue where one must fall. I shall use my advantage, though I should walk over the necks of half my kindred to accomplish his fate. I can find no security on my throne, no peace in my bed, until I know that he, my direst enemy, is no more.'"

"Sorry am I, generous Gloucester," interrupted Wallace, "that for my life you have stooped to one so unworthy of your nobleness. Let, then, his tyranny take its course. But its shaft will not reach the soul his unkingly spirit hopes to wound. The bitterness of death was past when I quitted Scotland. And for this body, he may dishonor it, mangle its limbs, but William Wallace may then be far beyond his reach. No, I await his summons; but my soul is strengthened by an assurance I feel here," added Wallace, laying his hand on his breast, "that the cord of Edward shall never make my free-born Scottish neck feel its degrading touch."

With reawakened horror Helen listened to the words of Wallace, which referred to the last outrage to be committed on his sacred remains. She recalled the corresponding threats of the king, and again losing self-possession, starting wildly up, exclaimed, "And is there no humanity in that ruthless man? Oh!" cried she, tearing her eyes from the beloved form on which it had been such bliss to gaze, "let the sacrifice of my life be offered to this cruel king to save from indignity——" She could add no more, but dropped half lifeless on the arm of Wallace.

Gloucester understood the object of such solicitude, and while Wallace again seated her, he revived her by a protestation that the clause she so deprecated had been repealed by Edward. But the good earl blushed as he spoke, for in this instance he said what was not the truth. Far different had been the issue of all his attempts at mitigation. The arrival of Athol from Scotland with advices from the Countess of Strathearn that Lady Helen Mar had fled southward to raise an insurrection in favor of Wallace, and that Lord Bothwell had gone to France to move Philip to embrace the same cause, gave Edward so apt an excuse for giving way to his hatred against the Scottish chief, that he pronounced an order for the unrestricted execution of his sentence. Artifice, to mislead the French ambassadors with an idea that he was desirous to accord with their royal master's wish, had been the sole foundation of his proposals to Wallace. And his interview with Lady Helen, though so intemperately conducted, was dictated by the same subtle policy.

When Gloucester found the impossibility of obtaining any further respite from the murderous decree, he attempted to prevail for the remission of the last clause, which ordered that his friend's noble body should be dismembered, and his limbs sent, as terrors to rebellion, to the four capital fortresses of Scotland. Edward spurned this petition with even more acrimony than he had done the prayer for his victim's life, and Gloucester, then starting from his knee, in a burst of honest indignation exclaimed, "O king, remember what is done by thee this day! Refusing to give righteous judgment in favor of one who prefers virtue to a crown and life! Thou hast now given sentence on a patriot and a prince, and at the last day shall judgment be given on thee!"

"Dangerous, indeed, is his rebellious spirit," cried Edward, in almost speechless wrath, "since it affects even the duty of my own house. Gloucester, leave my presence, and on pain of your own death dare not to approach me till I send for you to see this rebel's head on London Bridge."

To disappoint the revengeful monarch of at least this object of his malice, Gloucester was now resolved, and imparting his wishes to the warden of the Tower, who was his trusty friend, he laid a plan accordingly.

Helen had believed his declaration to her, and bowed her head, in sign that she was satisfied with his zeal. The earl, addressing Wallace, continued, "Could I have purchased thy life, thou preserver of mine! with the forfeiture of all I possess, I should have rejoiced in the exchange. But, as that may not be, is there aught in the world which I can do to administer to thy wishes?"

"Generous Gloucester," exclaimed Wallace, "how unwearied has been your friendship! But I shall not tax it much farther. I was writing my last wishes when this angel entered my apartment; she will now be the voice of William Wallace to his friends. But still I must make one request to you—one which I trust will not be out of your power. Let this heart, ever faithful to Scotland, be at least buried in its native country. When I cease to breathe, give it to Helen, and she will mingle it with the sacred dust of those I love. For herself, dear Gloucester, ah! guard the purity and life of my best beloved; for there are those who, when I am gone, may threaten both."

Gloucester, who knew that in this apprehension Wallace meant the Lords Soulis and de Valence, pledged himself for the performance of his first request, and for the second, he assured him he would protect Helen as a sister. But she, regardless of all other evils than that of being severed from her dearest friend, exclaimed in bitter sorrow, "Wherever I am, still, and forever, shall all of Wallace that remains on earth be with me. He gave himself to me, and no mortal power shall divide us."

The voice of the warden, calling to him that the hour of shutting the gates was arrived, now compelled Gloucester to bid his friend farewell. He grasped the hand of Wallace with a strong emotion, for he knew that the next time he should meet him would be on the scaffold. During the moments of this parting, Helen inwardly invoked the Almighty to endow her with fortitude to bear the horrors she was to witness.

The voice that was ever music to her ears recalled her from this devout abstraction. He laid his hand on hers, and gazing on her with pity, held such sweet discourse with her on the approaching end of all his troubles, of his everlasting happiness, where "all tears are dried away," that she listened, and wept, and even smiled. "Yes," added he, "a little while and my virgin bride shall give me her dear embrace in heaven; angels will participate in our joy, and my Marion's grateful spirit join the blest communion. She died to preserve my life. You suffered a living death to maintain my honor. Can I then divide ye, noblest of created beings, in my soul? Take, then, my heart's kiss, dear Helen, thy Wallace's last earthly kiss." She bent towards him and fixed her lips to his. It was the first time they had met; his parting words still hung on them, and an icy cold ran through all her veins. She felt his heart beat heavily against hers as he said, "I have not many hours to be with thee, and yet a strange lethargy overpowers my senses; but I shall speak to thee again." He looked on her as he spoke with such a glance of love, that not doubting he was now bidding her indeed his last farewell, that he was to pass from this sleep out of the power of man, she pressed his hand without a word, and, as he dropped his head back upon his straw pillow, with an awed spirit she saw him sink to profound repose.

CHAPTER LXXIII.

TOWER HILL.

LONG and silently did Helen watch his rest and often during her sad vigils did she stoop her cheek to feel the respiration which might bear witness that his outraged spirit was yet fettered to earth. She tremblingly placed her hand on his heart, and still its warm beats spake comfort to hers. The soul of Wallace, as well as his beloved body, was yet clasped in her arms.

The first rays of the dawn shone upon his peaceful face just as the door opened and a priest appeared. He held in his hands the sacred Host and the golden dove, for performing the rites of the dying. At this sight, the harbinger of a fearful doom, the fortitude of Helen forsook her, and, throwing her arms frantically over the sleeping Wallace, she exclaimed, "He is dead! his sacrament is now with the Lord of Mercy!" Her voice awakened Wallace. He started from his position, and Helen, seeing with a wild disappointment that he whose death in his sleep she had even so lately deprecated, now indeed lived to mount the scaffold, fell back with a heavy groan.

Wallace accosted the priest with a reverential welcome, and then turning to Helen, tenderly whispered her: "My Helen, in this moment of my last on earth, engrave on thy heart, that, in the sacred words of the patriarch of Israel, *I remember thee in the kindness of thy youth; in the love of thy desolate espousals to me, when thou camest after me into the wilderness, into a land that thou didst not know, and comforted me.* And shalt thou not be sacred unto the Lord of the widow and the orphan? To him I commit thee, in steadfast faith that he will never forsake thee. Rejoice that Wallace has been deemed worthy to die for having done his duty. Come, then, sister of my soul, and share with thy Wallace the Last Supper of his Lord,—the pledge of the happy eternity to which, by his grace, I now ascend."

Helen, reawakened to holy confidence by the heavenly composure of his manner, obeyed the impulse of his hand, and they both knelt before the minister of peace. While the sacred rite proceeded, it seemed the indissoluble union of Helen's spirit with that of Wallace. "My life will expire with his!" was her secret response to the vener-

476

able man's exhortation to the anticipated passing soul, and when he sealed Wallace with the holy cross under the last unction, as one who believed herself standing on the brink of eternity she longed to share also the mark of death. At that moment the dismal toll of a bell sounded from the top of the tower. The heart of Helen paused. The warden and his train entered. "I will follow him," cried she, starting from her knees, "into the grave itself!"

What was said, what was done, she knew not till she found herself on the scaffold upheld by the arm of Gloucester. Wallace stood before her with his hands bound across and his noble head uncovered. His eyes were turned upwards with a martyr's confidence in the Power he served. A silence as of some desert waste reigned throughout the thousands who stood below. The executioner approached to throw the rope over the neck of his victim. At this sight, Helen, with a cry that was reechoed by the compassionate spectators, rushed to his bosom. Wallace, with a mighty strength, burst the bands asunder which confined his arms, and clasping her to him with a force that seemed to make her touch his very heart, his breast heaved as if his soul were breaking from its outraged tenement, and, while his head sank on her neck, he exclaimed in a low and interrupted voice, "My prayer is heard!—Helen, life's cord is cut by God's own hand!—May he preserve my country!" He stopped—he fell—and with the shock the hastily erected scaffold shook to its foundation. The pause was dreadful.

The executioner approached the prostrate chief. Helen was still locked close in his arms. The man stooped to raise his victim, but the attempt was beyond his strength. In vain he called on him, on Helen, to separate, and cease from delaying the execution of the law. No voice replied, no motion answered his loud remonstrance. Gloucester, with an agitation which hardly allowed him to speak or move, remembered the words of Wallace, "that the rope of Edward would never sully his animate body," and, bending to his friend, he spoke; but all was silent there. He raised the chieftain's head, and looking on his face found indeed the indisputable stamp of death. "There," cried he, in a burst of grief, letting it fall again upon the insensible bosom of Helen,—"there broke the noblest heart that ever beat in the breast of man!"

The priests, the executioners, crowded around him at this declaration. But, while giving a command in a low tone to the warden, he took the motionless Helen in his arms, and leaving the astonished group round the noble dead, carried her from the scaffold back into the Tower.

CHAPTER LXXIV.

THE WARDEN'S APARTMENTS.

ON the evening of the fatal day in which the sun of William Wallace had set forever on his country, the Earl of Gloucester was imparting to the warden of the Tower his last directions respecting the sacred remains, when the door of the chamber suddenly opened and a file of soldiers entered. A man in armor, with his visor closed, was in the midst of them. The captain of the band told the warden that the person before him had behaved in a most seditious manner. He first demanded admittance into the Tower, then, on the sentinel making answer that, in consequence of the recent execution of the Scottish chief, orders had been given "to allow no strangers to approach the gates till the following morning," the prisoner had burst into a passionate emotion, uttering such threats against the King of England that the captain thought it his duty to have him seized and brought before the warden.

On the entrance of the soldiers Gloucester had retired into the shadow of the room. He turned round on hearing these particulars. When the captain ceased speaking the stranger fearlessly threw up his visor and exclaimed, "Take me not to your warden alone, but to your king. Let me pierce his conscience with his infamy. Would it were to stab him ere I die!"

In this frantic adjuration Gloucester discovered the gallant Bruce. And hastening towards him to prevent his apparently determined exposure of himself, with a few words he dismissed the officer and his guard, and then turning to the warden, "Sir Edward," said he, "this stranger is not less my friend than he that was Sir William Wallace."—"Then far be it from me, earl, to denounce him to our enraged monarch. I have seen enough of noble blood shed already. And though we, the subjects of King Edward, may not call your late friend a martyr, yet we must think his country honored in so steady a patriot, and may surely wish we had many the like in our own." With these words the worthy old knight bowed and withdrew.

Bruce, who had hardly heard the observation of the warden, on his departure turned upon the earl, and, with a bursting heart, exclaimed, "Tell me, is it true? Am I so lost a wretch as to be deprived

478

of my dearest friend? And is it, as I am told, that every infernal rigor of the sentence has been executed on that brave and breathless body? Answer me to the fact, that I may speedily take my course." Alarmed at the expression of his countenance, with a quivering lip, but in silence, Gloucester laid his hand upon his arm. Bruce, too, well understood what he durst not speak, and, shaking it off frantically, "I have no friend!" cried he. "Wallace! my dauntless, my only Wallace, thou art rifled from me! And shall I have fellowship with these? No; all mankind are my enemies, and soon will I leave their detested sojourn!" Gloucester attempted to interrupt him, but he broke out afresh, and with redoubled violence. "And you, earl," cried he, "lived in this realm and suffered such a sacrilege on God's most perfect work! Fill up the measure of your baseness; deliver me to Edward, and let me brave him to his face. Oh, let me die, covered with the blood of thy enemies, my murdered Wallace!"

Gloucester stood in dignified forbearance under the stormy grief of the Scottish prince, but when nature seemed to take rest in momentary silence, he approached him. Bruce cast on him a glance of suspicion. "Leave me," cried he; "I hate the whole world, and you the worst in it, for you might have saved him, and you did not; you might have preserved his sacred limbs from being made the gazing-stock of traitors, and you did not. Away from me, son of a tyrant, lest I tear you in piecemeal!"—"By the heroic spirit of him whom this outrage on me dishonors, hear my answer, Bruce. And, if not on this spot, let me then exculpate myself by the side of his body, yet uninvaded by a sacrilegious touch."—"How?" interrupted Bruce. Gloucester continued, "All that was mortal in our friend now lies in a distant chamber of this quadrangle. When I could not prevail on Edward, either by entreaty or reproaches, to remit the last gloomy vengeance of tyrants, I determined to wrest its object from his hands. A notorious murderer died yesterday under the torture. After the inanimate corse of our friend was brought into this house, to be conveyed to the scene of its last horrors, by the assistance of the warden the malefactor's body was conveyed here also, and placed on the traitor's sledge, in the stead of his who was no traitor; and on that murderer most justly fell the rigor of so dreadful a sentence."

The aspect of Bruce changed during this explanation, which was followed by a brief account from Gloucester of their friend's heroic sufferings and death. "Can you pardon my reproaches to you?" cried the prince, stretching out his hand. "Forgive, generous Gloucester the distraction of a severely wounded spirit." This pardon was immediately accorded, and Bruce impetuously added, "Lead me to these dear remains, that with redoubled certainty I may strike his murderer's heart. I came to succor him; I now stay to die,—but not unrevenged."—"I will lead you," returned the earl, "where you shall learn a different lesson. His soul will speak to you by the lips of his bride, now watching by those sacred relics. Feeble is now her lamp of life, but a saint's vigilance keeps it burning, till it may expire in the grave with him she so loved." A few words gave Bruce to understand that he meant Lady Helen Mar, and with a deepened grief, when he heard in what an awful hour their hands were plighted, he followed his conductor through the quadrangle.

When Gloucester gently opened the door, which contained the remains of the bravest and the best, Bruce stood for a moment on the threshold. At the further end of the apartment, lit by a solitary taper, lay the body of Wallace on a bier, covered with a soldier's cloak. Kneeling by its side, with her head on its bosom, was Helen. Her hair hung disordered over her shoulders, and shrouded with its dark locks the marble features of her beloved. Bruce scarcely breathed. He attempted to advance, but he staggered and fell against the wall. She looked up at the noise, but her momentary alarm ceased when she saw Gloucester. He spoke in a tender voice. "Be not agitated, lady, but here is the Earl of Carrick."

"Nothing can agitate me more," replied she, turning mournfully towards the prince, who beheld her regarding him with the look of one already an inhabitant of the grave.—"Helen," faintly articulated Bruce, "I come to share your sorrows, and to avenge them."— "Avenge them!" repeated she, after a pause, "is there aught in vengeance that can awaken life in these cold veins again? Let the murderers live in the world they have made a desert, by the destruction of its brightest glory!" Again she bent her head upon Wallace's cold breast, and seemed to forget that Bruce was present.

"May I not look on him?" cried he, grasping her hand. "Oh, Helen, show me that heroic face from whose beams my heart first caught the fire of virtue!" She moved, and the clay-hued features of all that was ever perfect in manly beauty met his sight. But the bright eyes were shut, the radiance of his smile was dimmed in death; yet still that smile was there. Bruce sank on his knees and remained in a silence only broken by his sighs.

It was a heart-breaking pause; for the voice which had ever mingled sweetly with theirs was silent. Helen, who had not wept since the tremendous hour of the morning, now burst into an agony of tears, and the vehemence of her feelings tearing so delicate a frame seemed to threaten the extinction of her being. Bruce, aroused by her

In the Tower of London

smothered cries, hurried to her side. By degrees she recovered to life and observance, but finding herself removed from the bier, she sprang wildly towards it. Bruce caught her arm to support her tottering steps. She looked steadfastly at him, and then at the motionless body. "He is there," cried she, "and yet he speaks not! I weep, and he does not comfort me! Oh, Bruce, can this be possible? Do I really see him dead? And what is death?" added she, grasping the cold hand of Wallace to her heart. "Didst thou not tell me when this hand pressed mine and blessed me, that it was only a translation from grief to joy? Behold how we mourn, and he is happy! I will obey thee, my immortal Wallace!" cried she, casting her arms about him. "I will obey thee and weep no more!"

She was silent and calm. And Bruce, kneeling on the opposite side of his friend, listened to the arguments which Gloucester adduced to persuade him to abstain from discovering himself to Edward, or even uttering resentment against him till he could do both as became the man for whom Wallace had sacrificed so much, even till he was king of Scotland. "To that end," said Gloucester, "did this gallant chieftain live, for in restoring you to the people of Scotland he believed he was setting a seal to their liberties and their peace. Think, then, of this, and let him not look down from his heavenly dwelling and see that Bruce despises the country for which he bled; that the only hope of Scotland has sacrificed himself, in a moment of revenge, to the cruel hand which broke his dauntless heart."

Bruce did not oppose this counsel; and as the fumes of passion passed away, leaving a manly sorrow to steady his determination of revenge, he listened with approbation, and finally resolved, whatever violence he might do to his nature, not to allow Edward the triumph of finding him in his power.

The earl's next essay was with Helen. He feared that a rumor of the stranger's indignation at the late execution, and that the Earl of Gloucester had taken him in charge, might, when associated with the fact of the widow of Sir William Wallace, still remaining under his protection, awaken some suspicion and direct investigations too likely to discover the imposition he had put on the executions of the last clause in his royal father's iniquitous sentence. He therefore explained his alarm to Helen, and conjured her, if she would yet preserve the hallowed remains before her from any chance of violence, that she must consent immediately to leave the kingdom. The ever-faithful heart of Wallace should be her companion, and an English captain who had partaken of his clemency at Berwick be her trusty conductor to her native land. To meet every objection, he added,

"Bruce shall be protected by me with strict fidelity till some safe opportunity may offer for his bearing to Scotland the sacred corpse, that must ever be considered the most precious relic in his country."

"As Heaven wills the trials of my heart," returned she, "so let it be!" and bent her aching head on the dear pillow of her rest,—the bosom, which, though cold and deserted by its heavenly inhabitant, was still the bosom of her Wallace. With these thoughts she passed the remainder of the night in vigils, and they were not less devoutly shared by the chastened heart of the prince of Scotland.

CHAPTER LXXV.

HIGHGATE.

THE tidings of the dreadful vengeance which Edward had taken against the Scottish nation, by pouring all his wrath upon the head of Wallace, struck like the lightning of heaven through the souls of men. None of either country but those in the confidence of Gloucester knew that Heaven had snatched him from the dishonor of so vile a death. The English turned, blushing, from each other, and ventured not to breathe the name of a man whose virtues seemed to have found a sanctuary for his fame in every honest heart. But when the news reached Scotland the indignation was general. There was not a man even amongst the late refractory chiefs, excepting the Cummins and their coadjutors, Soulis and Monteith, who really had believed that Edward seriously meant to sentence the Scottish patriot to a severer fate than what he had pronounced against his rebellious vassal, the exiled Baliol. The execution of Wallace, whose offense could only be that of having served his country too faithfully, was therefore so unexpected that on the first promulgation of it so great an abhorrence of the perpetrator was excited in every breast that the whole country rose as one man, threatening to march instantly to London, and sacrifice the tyrant on his throne.

At this crisis, when the mountains of the north seemed heaving from their base to overwhelm the blood-stained fields of England, every heart which secretly rejoiced in the late sanguinary event quailed within its possessor as it anticipated the consequences of the fall of Wallace. At this instant, when the furies armed every clan in Scotland, John Cummin, the regent, stood aghast. He foresaw his own downfall in this reawakened enthusiasm respecting the man whom his treachery had been the first means of betraying to his enemies. Baffled in the aim of his ambition by the very means he had taken to effect it, Cummin saw no alternative but to throw himself at once upon the bounty of England; and, to this purpose, he bethought him of the only chance of preserving the power of Edward, and consequently his own, in Scotland. Knowing by past events that this tempest of the soul, excited by remorse in some and gratitude in others, could only be maintained to any conclusive injury to England by a royal hand, and that that hand was expected to be Bruce's, he determined at once that the prince to whom he had sworn fealty, and to whom he owed his present elevation, should follow the fate of his friend. By the spies which he constantly kept round Hunting-tower, he was apprised that Bruce had set off towards London in a vessel from Dundee. On these grounds he sent a despatch to King Edward informing him that destiny had established him supreme lord of Scotland, for now its second and its last hope had put himself into his hands. With this intelligence he gave a particular account of all Bruce's proceedings from the time of his meeting Wallace in France to his following that chief to London. He closed his letter by urging the king to take instant measures to disable Bruce from disturbing the quiet of Scotland, or ever again disputing his regal claims.

Gloucester happened to be in the presence when this epistle was delivered to and read by his majesty. On the suit of his daughter, Edward had been reconciled to his son-in-law; but when he showed to him the contents of Cummin's letter, with a suspicious smile he said in a low voice, "In case you should know this new rebel's lurking-place, presume not to leave this room till he is brought before me. See to your obedience, Ralph, or your head shall follow Wallace's."

The king instantly withdrew, and the earl, aware that search would be made through all his houses, sought in his own mind for some expedient to apprise Bruce of his danger. To write in the presence-chamber was impossible; to deliver a message in a whisper would be hazardous, for most of the surrounding courtiers, seeing the frown with which the king had left the apartment, marked the commands he gave the marshal, "Be sure that the Earl of Gloucester quits not this room till I return."

In the confusion of his thoughts, the earl turned his eye on Lord Montgomery, who had only arrived that very morning from an embassy to Spain. He had heard with unutterable horror the fate of Wallace, and extending his interest in him to those whom he loved, had arranged with Gloucester to accompany him that very evening to pledge his friendship to Bruce. To Montgomery, then, as to the only man acquainted with his secret, he turned, and taking his spurs off his feet and pulling out a purse of gold, he said aloud and with as easy an air as he could assume, "Here, my Lord Montgomery, as you are going directly to Highgate I will thank you to call at my lodge, put these spurs and this purse into the hands of the groom we spoke of; tell him they do not fit me, and he will know what use to make of them." He then turned negligently on his heel, and Montgomery quitted the apartment.

The apprehension of this young lord was not less quick than the invention of his friend. He guessed that the Scottish prince was betrayed, and to render his escape the less likely to be traced—the ground being wet and liable to retain impression—before he went to the lodge he dismounted in the adjoining wood, and with his own hands reversed the iron on the feet of the animal he had provided for Bruce. He then proceeded to the house and found the object of his mission disguised as a Carmelite and in the chapel paying his vesper adorations to the Almighty Being on whom his whole dependence hung.

Montgomery entered, and being instantly recognized by Bruce, the ingenuous prince, never doubting a noble heart, stretched out his hand to him. "I take it," returned the earl, "only to give it a parting grasp. Behold these spurs and purse sent to you by Gloucester. You know their use. Without further observation follow me." Montgomery was thus abrupt, because as he left the palace he had heard the marshal give orders for different military detachments to search every residence of Gloucester for the Earl of Carrick, and he did not doubt that the party despatched to Highgate was now mounting the hill.

Bruce, throwing off his cassock and cowl, again appeared in his martial garb, and after bending his knee for a moment on the chancel-stone which covered the remains of Wallace, he followed his friend from the chapel, and thence through a solitary path in the park to the center of the wood. Montgomery pointed to the horse. Bruce grasped the hand of his faithful conductor. "I go, Montgomery," said he, "to my kingdom. But its crown shall never clasp my brows till the remains of Wallace return to their country. And whether peace or the sword restore them to Scotland, still shall a king's, a brother's, friendship unite my heart to Gloucester and to you." While speaking he vaulted into his saddle, and, receiving the cordial blessings of Montgomery, touched his good steed with his pointed rowels and was out of sight in an instant.

CHAPTER LXXVI.

SCOTLAND —DUMFRIES.

ABOUT the hour of twilight, on the tenth day after Bruce had cast his last look on the capital of England, he crossed the little stream which marked the oft-contended barrier-land of the two kingdoms. He there checked the headlong speed of his horse, and having alighted to give it breath, walked by its side, musing on the different feelings with which he now entered Scotland, from the buoyant emotions with which he had sprung on its shore at the beginning of the year. These thoughts, as full of sorrow as of hope, had not occupied him long when he espied a man in the Red Cummin's colors speeding towards the south. He guessed him to be some new messenger of the regent to Edward, and throwing himself before the horse caught it by the bridle, then coolly demanded its rider to deliver to him the despatches which he carried to the King of England. The man refused, and striking his spurs into his breast, tried to trample down his assailant. But Bruce was not to be put from his aim. The manner of the Scot convinced him that his suspicions were right, and putting forth his arm, with one action he pulled the messenger from his saddle and laid him prostrate on the ground. Again he demanded the papers. "I am your prince," cried he, "and by the allegiance you owe to Robert Bruce, I command you to deliver them into my hands. Life shall be your reward, death the punishment of your obstinacy."

In such an extremity the man did not hesitate, and taking from his bosom a sealed packet, immediately resigned it. Bruce ordered him to stand before him till he had read the contents. Trembling with terror of this formidable freebooter (for he placed no belief in the declaration that he was the prince of Scotland), the man obeyed, and Bruce, breaking the seals, found, as he expected, a long epistle from the regent, urging the sanguinary aim of his communications. He reiterated his arguments for the expediency of speedily putting Robert Bruce to death; he represented the danger that there was in delay, lest a man so royally descended, and so popular as he had become should find means of placing himself at the head of so many zealots in his favor. These circumstances, so propitious to ambition, would at this juncture (should he arrive in Scotland) turn to the most decisive uses against the English power. The regent concluded with saying that the Lords Loch-awe, Douglas, and Ruthven were come down from the Highlands with a multitudinous army to drive out the Southron garrisons, and to repossess themselves of the fortresses of Stirling and Edinburgh; that Lord Bothwell had returned from France, with the real Sir Thomas de Longueville, a knight of great valiancy; and that Sir Roger Kirkpatrick, after having massacred half the English Castellans in the border counties, was now lying at Torthorald, ready to commence his murderous reprisals through the coasts of Galloway. For himself, Cummin told the king he had secretly removed to the Franciscan monastery at Dumfries, where he should most anxiously await his majesty's pardon and commands.

Bruce closed the packet. To prevent his discovery being betrayed ere he was ready to act, he laid his sword upon the shoulder of the man. "You are my prisoner," said he; "but fear not. I only mean to hold you in safety till your master has answered for his treason." The messenger thought, whoever this imperious stranger might be, that he saw a truth in his eyes which ratified this assurance, and without opposition he walked before him till they stopped at Torthorald.

Night had closed in when Bruce sounded his bugle under the walls. Kirkpatrick answered from the embrasure over the barbacan-gate with a demand of who desired admittance. "None," cried he, "that is not a true Scot need venture his neck within these towers."—"'Tis the avenger of Sir William Wallace," was the reply. The gates flew open at the words, and Kirkpatrick, standing in the archway amid a blaze of torches, received his guest with a brave welcome.

Bruce spoke no more till he entered the banqueting-hall. Three other knights were seated by the table. He turned to Kirkpatrick. "My valiant friend," said he, "order your servants to take charge of yon Scot," pointing to the messenger of Cummin, "and, till I command his release, let him be treated with the lenity which shall ever belong to a prisoner of Robert Bruce." As he spoke he threw up his visor, and Kirkpatrick, who had heard that the supposed De Longueville was his rightful prince, now recognized the well-known features of the brave foreigner in the stranger before him. Not doubting the verity of his words, he bent his knee with the homage due to his king, and in the action was immediately followed by the other knights who were present.

"I come," cried the prince, "in the spirit of my heart's sovereign and friend, the now immortal Wallace, to live or to die with you in the defense of my country's liberties. With such assistance as yours, and with the blessing of Heaven on our arms, I hope to redeem Scotland from the disgrace which her late submission to the tyrant has fastened on her name. The transgressions of my house have been grievous, but that last deadly sin of my people called for an expiation awful indeed. And it came in the moment of guilt; in their crime they receive punishment. They broke from their side the arm which alone had rescued them from their enemies. I now come to save them from themselves. Their having permitted the sacrifice of the rights of my family was the first injury committed on the constitution, and it prepared a path for the ensuing tyranny which seized upon the kingdom. But by resuming these rights, which is now my firm purpose, I open to you a way to recover our hereditary independence. The direful scene just acted on the Tower-hill of London must convince every mind that all the late misfortunes of our country have proceeded from the base jealousies of its nobles. There, then, let them die; and may the grave of Wallace be the tomb of dissension!"

The spirit with which this address was pronounced, assisted by the graces of his youth and noble deportment, struck the hearts of his auditors, and aroused in double vigor the principles of resentment, to which the first tidings of their heroic countryman's fate had given birth. Kirkpatrick needed no other stimulus than his almost idolatrous memory of Wallace, and he listened with an answering ardor to Bruce's exhortation. The prince next disclosed to his now zealously pledged friends the particulars of the Red Cummin's treachery. "He now lies at Dumfries," cried Kirkpatrick; "thither, then, let us go, and confront him with his treason."

Dumfries was only a few miles distant, and they might reach its convent before the first matins. Fatigue was not felt by Bruce when in pursuit of a great object, and after a slight refreshment he and his four determined friends took horse.

As they had anticipated, the midnight bell was ringing for prayers when the troop stopped at the Franciscan gate. Lindsay, having been in the Holy Land during the late public struggles, alleged business with the abbot, and desired to see him. On the father's bidding the party welcome, Bruce stepped forward and addressed him. "Reverend sir, I come from London. I have an affair to settle with Lord Badenoch, and I know by his letters to King Edward that he is secretly lodged in this convent. I therefore demand to be conducted to him." This peremptory requisition, with the superior air of the person who made it, did not leave the abbot room to doubt that he was some illustrious messenger from the King of England, and, with hardly a demur, he left the other knights in the cloisters of the church, while he led the noble Southron, as he thought, to his kinsman.

The treacherous regent had just retired from the refectory to his own apartment as the abbot conducted the stranger into his presence. Badenoch started frowningly from his seat at such unusual intrusion. Bruce's visor was closed, and the ecclesiastic, perceiving the regent's displeasure, dispersed it by announcing the visitant as a messenger from King Edward. "Then leave us together," returned he, unwilling that even this, his convenient kinsman, should know the extent of his treason against his country. The abbot had hardly closed the door when Bruce, whose indignant soul burned to utter his full contempt of the wretch before him, hastily advanced to speak, but the cautious Badenoch, fearful that the father might yet be within hearing, put his finger to his lips. Bruce paused and listened gloomily to the departing steps of the abbot. When they were no more heard, with one hand raising his visor and the other grasping the scroll of detection, "Thus, basest of the base race of Cummin," exclaimed he, "you may for a moment elude the universal shame which awaits your crimes."

At sight of the face, on hearing the words of Bruce, the unmanly coward uttered a cry of terror and rushed towards the door. "You pass not here," continued the prince, "till I have laid open all your guilt; till I have pronounced on you the doom due to a treacherous friend and a traitorous subject."—"Infatuated Bruce!" exclaimed Badenoch, assuming an air of insulted friendship, now that he found escape impossible, "what false tongue has persuaded you to arraign one who has ever been but too faithfully the adherent of your desperate fortunes?"

Bruce smiled at this poor attempt to deceive him, and, as he stood with his back against the door, he opened the murderous packet and read from it all its contents. Cummin turned pale and red at each sentence; and at last, Bruce closing it, "Now, then, faithful adherent of Robert Bruce," cried he, "say what the man deserves who in these blood-red lines petitions the death of his lawful prince?"

Badenoch, his complexion turning of a livid hue, and his voice faltering, attempted to deny the letter, or that he had any concern in the former embassy to Edward. Then, finding that these falsehoods only irritated Bruce to higher indignation, and fearful of being immediately sacrificed to his just resentment, he threw himself on his knees, and confessing each transaction, implored his life in pity to the desire of self-preservation, which alone had precipitated him to so ungrateful a proceeding. "Oh," added he, "even this danger I have incurred upon your account. For your advantage did I bring on my head the perils which now fill me with dismay. Love alone for you made me hasten the execution of William Wallace, who would have crept from your bosom into your throne. And then, fear of your mistaking the motives of so good a service, betrayed me to throw myself into the arms of Edward."

"Bury thyself and thy crimes, thou traitor, deep in the depths of hell!" cried the prince, starting away with a tremendous gesture. Till this moment Bruce was ignorant that Badenoch had been an instigator in the murder of Wallace, and forgetting his own personal wrongs in this more mighty injury, he turned away to avoid stabbing an unarmed wretch at his feet. But at that moment, Cummin, who believed his doom only suspended, rose from his knee, and drawing his dirk from under his plaid struck it into the back of the prince. Bruce turned on him with the quickness of thought. "Hah!" exclaimed he, seizing him by the throat, "then take thy fate. This accursed deed hath removed the only barrier between vengeance and thee; thus, remember William Wallace." As the prince spoke he plunged his dagger into the breast of the traitor. Cummin uttered a fearful cry, and rolled down at his feet, murmuring imprecations.

Bruce fled from the spot. It was the first time his arm had drawn blood, except in the field of battle, and he felt as if the base tide had contaminated his hand. In the cloisters he was encountered by his friends. A few words informed them of what had happened. "Is he dead?" inquired Kirkpatrick.—"I can hardly doubt," answered Bruce. "Such a matter," returned the veteran, "must not be left to conjecture: I will secure him." And running forward he found the wounded regent crawling from the door of the cell. Throwing himself upon him without noise, he stabbed him to the heart.

Before the catastrophe was known in the convent, Bruce and his friends had left it some time and were far on their road to Lochmaben. They arrived before sunrise, and, once more an inmate of his paternal castle, he thence despatched Fleming to Lord Ruthven with a transcript of his designs.

In the same packet he enclosed a letter for the Lady Isabella. It contained this brave resolution, that in his present return to Scotland he did not consider himself merely as Robert Bruce, come to reclaim the throne of his ancestors, but as the executor of the last and dying will of Sir William Wallace, which was that Bruce should confirm the independence of Scotland or fall as Wallace had done, invincible at his post. "Till that freedom is accomplished," continued the prince, "I will never shake the purpose of my soul by even one glance at thy beauties. I am Wallace's soldier, Isabella, as he was Heaven's; and, while my captain looks on me from above, shall I not approve myself worthy his example? I wooed you as a knight, I will win you as a king; and on the day when no hostile Southron breathes in Scotland, I will demand my beloved bride, of her noble uncle. You shall come to me as the angel of peace, and in one hour we will receive the nuptial benediction and the vows of our people."

The purport of the prince's letter to Ruthven was well adapted to the strain of the foregoing. He then announced his intention of proceeding immediately to the plain of Stirling, and there, putting himself at the head of his loyal Scots, declare himself their lawful sovereign, and proclaim to the world that he acknowledge no legal superior but the Great Being, whose vicegerent he was. From that center of his kingdom he would make excursions to its farthest extremities, and with God's will either drive his enemies from the country or perish with the sword in his hand, as became the descendant of William the Lion, and the friend of William Wallace.

Ruthven lay encamped on the Carse of Gowrie when this letter was delivered to him. He read it aloud to his assembled chieftains, and with waving bonnets they hailed the approach of their valiant prince. Bothwell alone, whose attachment to Wallace could not be superseded by any other affection, allowed his bonnet to remain inactive in his hand; but with the fervor of true loyalty he thanked God for thus bringing the sovereign whom his friend loved, to wrest from the hands of that friend's assassin the scepter for which he had dyed them so deep in blood.

CHAPTER LXXVII.

STIRLING.

THE word of Bruce was as irreversible as his spirit was determined. The standard of liberty had been raised by him on the Carse of Gowrie, and he carried it in his victorious arm from east to west, from the most northern point of Sutherland to the walls of Stirling; but there the garrison which the treason of the late regent had admitted into that citadel gave a momentary check to his career. The English governor hesitated to surrender on the terms proposed; and while his first flag of truce was yet in the tent of the Scottish monarch, a second arrived to break off the negotiation. Whatever were the reasons for this abrupt determination, Bruce paid him not the compliment of asking a wherefore, but advancing his troops to the Southron outposts, drove them in with great loss, and approaching the lower works of the town by the road of Ballochgeich, so alarmed the governor as to induce him to send forth several squadrons of horse to stop his progress. Vain was the attempt. They shrank before the resolute prince and his enthusiastic followers. The governor despatched others, and at last marched out himself to their support. No force seemed able to withstand the pressing valor of the Scots: a surrender, both of himself and his fainting companions, was now his only resource. His herald sounded a parley. The generous victor, in the midst of triumph, listened to the offered capitulation. It was not to include the citadel of Stirling.

Bruce stopped the herald at this clause and at once demanded the unconditional surrender of both the town and citadel. The governor, being aware that in his present state there was no alternative, and knowing the noble nature of the prince who made the requisition, yielded to necessity, and resigned the whole into his hands.

Next morning Bruce entered Stirling as a conqueror, with the whole of his kingdom at his feet, for from the Solway Frith to the Northern Ocean no Scottish town nor castle owned a foreign master. The acclamations of a rescued people rent the skies, and while prayers and blessings poured on him from above, below, and around, he did indeed feel himself a king, and that he had returned to the land of his forefathers. While he sat on his proud war-horse, in

492

front of the great gates of the citadel, now thrown wide asunder to admit its rightful sovereign, his noble prisoners came forward. They bent their knees before him, and, delivering their swords, received in return his gracious assurance of mercy. Dismounting from his steed with the grace that took captive even the souls of his enemies, he raised his helmet from his head as the Bishop of Dunkeld, followed by all the ecclesiastics in the town, came forward to wait upon the triumph of their king.

The scene smote the heart of Bothwell; he turned aside and wept. Where were now the buoyant feelings with which he had followed the similar triumph of Wallace into these gates? New men and new services seemed to have worn out remembrance of the past; but in the memories of even this joyous crowd Wallace lived, though like a bright light, which had passed through their path and was gone, never more to return.

On entering the citadel, Bruce was informed by Mowbray, the English governor, that he would find a lady there in a frightful state of mental derangement, and who might need his protection. A question or two from the victorious monarch told him this was the Countess of Strathearn. On the revolted lord's having betrayed Wallace and his country to England the joy of the countess knew no bounds, and hoping eventually to persuade Edward to adjudge to her the crown, she made it apparent to the English king how useful would be her services in Scotland, while she took her course through her native land to discover who were inimical to the foreign interest and who likely to promote her own. After this circuit she fixed her mimic court at Stirling, and living there in regal magnificence, exercised the functions of a vice-queen. At this period intelligence arrived which the governor thought would fill her with exultation, and hastening to declare it he proclaimed to her that the King of England's authority was now firmly established in Scotland, for that on the twenty-third of August Sir William Wallace had been executed in London, upon the Tower-hill.

On the declaration of this event she fell senseless on the floor. It was not until the next morning that she recovered to animation, and then her ravings were horrible and violent. She accused herself of the murder of Sir William Wallace. She seemed to hear him upbraid her with his fate, and her shrieks so fearfully presented the scene of his death before the eyes of her attendants that her women fled. In these fearful moments the confession of all her premeditated guilt, of her disappointed passion for Wallace, and her vowed revenge, were revealed under circumstances so shocking that the

English governor declared to the King of Scots while he conducted him towards her apartment that he would rather wear out his life in a dungeon than endure one hour of her agonies.

There was a dead silence in her chamber as they approached the door. Mowbray cautiously opened it, and discovered the object of their visit. She was seated at the farther end of the room on the floor, enveloped in a mass of scarlet velvet she had drawn off her bed; her hands clasped her knees, and she bent forward, with her eyes fixed on the door at which they entered.

She remained motionless as they advanced. But when Bruce stopped directly before her, contemplating with horror the woman whom he regarded as one of the murderers of his most beloved friend, she sprang at once upon him, and clinging to him with shrieks buried her head in his bosom. "Save me! save me!" cried she. Then, bursting from Bruce with an imprecation that froze his blood, she flew to the other side of the chamber, crying aloud, "Thou hast torn out my heart! Fiend, I took thee for Wallace—but I murdered him!" Her agonies and her attempts at self-violence were now so dreadful that Bruce, raising her, bleeding, from the hearth on which she had furiously dashed her head, put her into the arms of the men who attended her, and then, with an awful sense of divine retribution, left the apartment.

CHAPTER LXXVIII.

BANNOCKBURN.

THE generality of his prisoners Bruce directed should be kept safe in the citadel, but to Mowbray he gave his liberty, and ordered every means to facilitate the journey of that brave knight, whom he had requested to convey the insane Lady Strathearn to the protection of her husband.

At the decline of day Bruce returned to his camp to pass the night in the field with his soldiers, intending next morning to give his last orders to the detachments which he meant to send out under the command of Lennox and Douglas to disperse themselves over the border counties, and there keep station till that peace should be signed by England which he was determined to compel.

Having taken these measures for the security of his kingdom, he had just returned to his tent on the banks of Bannockburn when Grimsby, his now faithful attendant, conducted an armed knight into his presence. The light of the lamp which stood on the table streaming full on the face of the stranger discovered to the king his English friend, the intrepid Montgomery. With an exclamation of glad surprise Bruce would have clasped him in his arms, but Montgomery, dropping on his knee, exclaimed, "Receive a subject, as well as a friend, victorious prince! I have forsworn the vassalage of the Plantagenets, and thus, without title or land, with only a faithful heart, Gilbert Hambledon comes to vow himself yours and Scotland's forever."

Bruce raised him from the ground, and, welcoming him, inquired the cause of so extraordinary an abjuration of his legal sovereign. "No light matter," observed the king, "could have so wrought upon my noble Montgomery."

"Montgomery no more!" replied the earl with indignant eagerness. "When I threw the insignia of my earldom at the feet of the unjust Edward, I told him that I would lay the saw to the root of the nobility I had derived from his house, and cut it *through;* that I would sooner leave my posterity without titles and without wealth than deprive them of real honor. I have done as I said. And yet I come not without a treasure; for the sacred corse of William Wallace is now in my bark, floating on the waves of the Forth."

The subjugation of England would hardly have been so welcome to Bruce as this intelligence. He received it with an eloquent look of gratitude. Hambledon continued: "On the tyrant summoning the peers of England to follow him to the destruction of Scotland, Gloucester got excused under a plea of illness, and I could not but show a disinclination to obey. This occasioned some remarks from Edward respecting my known attachment to the Scottish cause, and they were so couched as to draw from me this honest answer: 'My heart would not, for the wealth of the world, permit me to join in the projected invasion, since I had seen the spot in my own country where a most inordinate ambition had cut down the flower of all knighthood, because he was a Scot who would not sell his birthright.' The king left me in wrath and threatened to make me recant my words. I as proudly declared I would maintain them. Next morning, being in waiting on the prince, I entered his chamber, and found John le de Spencer sitting with his highness. On my offering the services due from my office, this worthless minion turned on me and accused me of having declined joining the army for the sole purpose of executing some plot in London, devised between me and my Scottish partisans for the subversion of the English monarchy. I denied the charge. He enforced it with oaths, and I spurned his allegations. The prince, who believed him, furiously gave me the lie, and commanded me, as a traitor, to leave his presence. I refused to stir an inch till I had made the base heart of Le de Spencer retract his falsehood. The coward took courage on his master's support, and, drawing his sword upon me, threatened to compel my departure. He struck me on the face with his weapon. The arms of his prince could not then save him; I thrust him through the body and he fell. Edward ran on me with his dagger, but I wrested it from him. Then it was that, in reply to his menaces, I revoked my fealty to a sovereign I abhorred, a prince I despised. Leaving his presence before he could fix upon seizing me, I hastened to Highgate to convey away the body of our friend from its brief sanctuary. The same night I embarked it and myself on board a ship from my own, and am now at your feet, brave and just king, no longer Montgomery, but a true Scot, in heart and loyalty."

"And as a kinsman, generous Hambledon," returned Bruce, "I receive, and will portion thee. My paternal lands of Cadzow, on the Clyde, shall be thine forever. And may thy posterity be as worthy of the inheritance as their ancestor is of all my love and confidence!"

Hambledon, having received his new sovereign's directions concerning the disembarkation of those sacred remains, which the young king declared he should welcome as the pledge of Heaven to bless his victories with peace, returned to the haven where Wallace rested in that sleep which even the voice of friendship could not disturb.

At the hour of the midnight watch the trumpets of approaching heralds resounded without the camp. Bruce hastened to the council-tent to receive the now anticipated tidings. The communications of Hambledon had given him reason to expect another struggle for his kingdom, and the message of the trumpets declared it might be a mortal one.

At the head of a hundred thousand men Edward had forced a rapid passage through the lowlands, and was now within a few hours' march of Stirling, fully determined to bury Scotland under her own slain, or by one decisive blow restore her to his empire.

When this was uttered by the English herald, Bruce turned to Ruthven with an heroic smile: "Let him come, my brave barons, and he shall find that Bannockburn shall page with Cambus-Kenneth."

The strength of the Scottish army did not amount to more than thirty thousand men against this host of Southrons. But the relics of Wallace were there. His spirit glowed in the heart of Bruce. The young monarch lost not the advantage of choosing his ground first, and therefore as his power was deficient in cavalry, he so took his field as to compel the enemy to make it a battle of infantry alone.

To protect his exposed flank from the innumerable squadrons of Edward, he dug deep and wide pits near to Bannockburn, and having overlaid their mouths with turf and brushwood, proceeded to marshal his little phalanx on the shore of that brook.

The center was led by Lord Ruthven and Walter Stewart; the right owned the valiant leading of Douglas and Ramsay, supported by the brave young Gordon with all his clan; and the left was put in charge of Lennox, with Sir Thomas Randolph, a crusade chieftain, who, like Lindsay and others, had lately returned from distant lands, and now zealously embraced the cause of his country.

Bruce stationed himself at the head of the reserve; with him were the veterans of Loch-awe and Kirkpatrick, and Lord Bothwell, with the true De Longueville and the men of Lanark,—all determined to make this division the stay of their little army. There stood the sable hearse of Wallace, and the royal standard, struck deep into the native rock of the ground, waved its blood-red volumes over his sacred head.

"By that Heaven-sent palladium of our freedom," cried Bruce, pointing to the bier, "we must this day stand or fall! He who deserts it murders William Wallace anew!"

At this appeal the chiefs of each battalion assembled round the hallowed spot, and laying their hands on the pall, swore to fill up one grave with their dauntless Wallace rather than yield the ground which he had rendered doubly precious by having made it the scene of his invincible deeds. When Kirkpatrick approached the side of his dead chief he burst into tears, and his sobs alone proclaimed his participation in the solemnity. The vow spread to the surrounding legions, and was echoed, with mingled cries from the farthest ranks.

"My leader in death as in life!" exclaimed Bruce, clasping his friend's sable shroud to his heart. "Thy corse shall again redeem the country which cast thee, living, amongst devouring lions. Its presence shall fight and conquer for thy friend and king."

Before the chiefs turned to resume their martial stations, the Abbot of Inchaffray drew near with the mysterious iron box which Douglas had caused to be brought from St. Fillan's priory. On presenting it to the young monarch he repeated the prohibition which had been given with it, and added, "Since then these canonized relics (for none can doubt they are so) have found protection under the no less holy arm of St. Fillan; he now delivers them to your youthful majesty to nerve your mind with redoubled trust in the saintly host."

"The saints are to be honored, reverend father, and on that principle I shall not invade their mysteries till the God in whom alone I trust marks me with more than the name of king, till, by a decisive victory, he establishes me the approved champion of my country. But as a memorial that the host of heaven do indeed lean from their bright abodes to wish well to this day, let these holy relics repose with those of the brave till the issue of the battle."

Bruce, having placed his array, disposed the supernumeraries of his army, the families of his soldiers, and other apparently useless followers of the camp, in the rear of an adjoining hill.

By daybreak the whole of the Southron army came in view. The van, consisting of archers and men at arms, displayed the banner of Earl de Warenne; the main body was led on by Edward himself, supported by a train of his most redoubted generals. As they approached, the Bishop of Dunkeld stood on the face of the opposite hill, between the abbots of Cambus-Kenneth and Inchaffray, celebrating Mass in the sight of the opposing armies. He passed along in front of the Scottish lines barefoot, with the crucifix in his hand; and in a few but forceful words exhorted them by every sacred hope to fight for their rights, their king, and the corse of William Wallace. At this adjuration, which seemed the call of Heaven itself, the Scots fell on their knees, to confirm their resolution with a vow. The sudden humiliation of their posture excited an instant triumph in the haughty mind of Edward, and spurring forward he shouted aloud, "They yield! They cry for mercy!"—"They cry for mercy," returned Percy, trying to withhold his majesty, "but not from us. On that ground on which they kneel they will be victorious or find their graves."

The king contemned this opinion of the earl, and, inwardly believing that now Wallace was dead he need fear no other opponent, he ordered his men to charge. The horsemen to the number of thirty thousand obeyed, and rushing forward with the hope of overwhelming the Scots ere they could rise from their knees, met a different destiny. They found destruction amid the trenches and on the spikes in the way, and with broken ranks and fearful confusion fell or fled under the weapons which poured on them from a neighboring hill. De Valence was overthrown and severely wounded, and, being carried off the field, filled the rear ranks with dismay, while the king's division was struck with consternation at so disastrous a commencement of an action in which they had promised themselves an easy victory. Bruce seized the moment of confusion, and seeing his little army distressed by the arrows of the English, he sent Bothwell round with a resolute body of men to drive those destroying archers from the height which they occupied. This was effected, and Bruce coming up with his reserve, the battle in the center became close and decisive. Many fell before the determined arm of the youthful king; but it was the fortune of Bothwell to encounter the false Monteith in the train of Edward. The Scottish earl was then at the head of his intrepid Lanark men. "Fiend of the most damned treason," cried he, "vengeance is come!" and with an iron grasp throwing the traitor into the midst of the faithful clan, they dragged him to the hearse of their chief, and there, on the skirts of its pall, the wretched villain breathed out his treacherous breath under the strokes of a hundred swords. "So," cried the veteran Ireland, "perish the murderers of William Wallace!"—"So," shouted the rest, "perish the enemies of the most loyal of Scots, the benefactor of his country!"

At this crisis the women and followers of the Scottish camp, hearing such triumphant exclamations from their friends, impatiently quitted their station behind the hill, and ran to the summit, waving their scarfs and plaids in exultation of the supposed victory. The English, mistaking these people for a new army, had not power to recover from the increasing confusion which had seized them on King Edward himself receiving a wound, and, panic-struck with the sight of their generals falling around them, they flung down their arms and fled. The king narrowly escaped, but being mounted on a stout and fleet horse he put him to the speed and reached Dunbar, whence the young Earl of March, being as much attached to the cause of England as his father had been, instantly gave him a passage to England.

The Southron camp with all its riches fell into the hands of Bruce. But while his chieftains pursued their gallant chase, he turned his steps from triumph to pay his heart's honors to the remains of the hero whose blood had so often bathed Scotland's fields of victory. His vigils were again beneath that sacred pall, for so long had been the conflict, that night closed in before the last squadrons left the banks of Bannockburn.

At the dewy hour of morn Bruce reappeared on the field. His helmet was royally plumed, and the golden lion of Scotland gleamed from under his sable surcoat. Bothwell rode at his side. The troops he had retained from the pursuit were drawn out in array. In a brief address he unfolded to them the solemn duty to which he had called them,—to see the bosom of their native land receive the remains of Sir William Wallace. "He gave to you your homes and your liberty; grant, then, a grave to him whom some amongst you repaid with treachery and death."

At these words a cry, as if they beheld their betrayed chief slain before them, issued from every heart.

The news had spread to the town, and with tears and lamentations a vast crowd collected round the royal troop. Bruce ordered his bards to raise the sad coronach, and the march commenced towards the open tent that canopied the sacred remains. The whole train followed in speechless woe, as if each individual had lost his dearest relative. Having passed the wood, they came in view of the black hearse which contained all that now remained of him who had so lately crossed these precincts, in all the graciousness of peace and love to man. The soldiers, the people, rushed forward, and precipitating themselves before the bier implored a pardon for their ungrateful country. They adjured him by every tender name of father, benefactor, and friend; and in such a sacred presence, forgetting that their king was by, gave way to grief, which most eloquently told the young monarch that he who would be respected after William Wallace must not only possess his power and valor, but imitate his virtues.

Scrymgeour, who had well remembered his promise to Wallace on the battlements of Dumbarton, with a holy reference to that vow, now laid the standard of Scotland upon the pall. Hambledon placed on it the sword and helmet of the sacrificed hero. Bruce observed all in silence. The sacred burden was raised. Uncovering his royal head, with his kingly purple sweeping in the dust, he walked before the bier, shedding tears more precious in the eyes of his subjects than the oil which was soon to pour upon his brow. As he thus moved on, he heard acclamations mingle with the voice of sorrow. "This is our king, worthy to have been the friend of Wallace, worthy to succeed him in the kingdom of our hearts!"

At the gates of Cambus-Kenneth the venerable abbot appeared at the head of his religious brethren, but, without uttering the grief that shook his aged frame, he raised the golden crucifix over the head of the bier, and after leaning his face for a few minutes on it, preceded the procession into the church. None but the soldiers entered. The people remained without, and as the doors closed they fell on the pavement, weeping, as if the living Wallace had again been torn from them.

On the steps of the altar the bier rested. The Bishop of Dunkeld, in his pontifical robes, received the sacred deposit with a cloud of incense, and the pealing organ, answered by the voices of the choristers, breathed the solemn requiem of the dead. The wreathing frankincense parted its vapor, and a wan but beautiful form, clasping an urn to her breast, appeared, stretched on a litter, and was borne towards the spot. It was Helen, brought from the adjoining nunnery, where, since her return to these once dear shores, she had languished in the gradual decay of the bonds which alone fettered her mourning spirit, eager for release.

All night had Isabella watched by her couch, expecting that each succeeding breath would be the last her beloved sister would draw; but as her tears fell in silence upon the cold forehead of Helen, the gentle saint understood their expression, and looking up, "My Isabella," said she, "fear not. My Wallace is returned. God will grant me life to clasp his blessed remains!"

Full of this hope she was borne, almost a passing spirit, into the chancel of Cambus-Kenneth. Her veil was open, and discovered her face, like one just awakened from the dead: it was ashy pale, but it bore a celestial brightness, like the silver luster of the moon. Her eyes fell on the bier, and with a momentary strength she sprang from the couch, on which she had leaned in lying feebleness, and threw herself upon the coffin.

There was an awful pause, while Helen seemed to weep. But so was not her sorrow to be shed. It was locked within the flood-gates of her heart.

In that suspension of the soul, when Bothwell knelt on one side of the bier and Ruthven bent his knee on the other, Bruce stretched out his hand to the weeping Isabella. "Come hither, my youthful bride, and let thy first duty be paid to the shrine of thy benefactor and mine. So may we live, and so may we die, if the like may be our meed of heavenly glory!" Isabella threw herself into his arms and wept aloud. Helen, slowly raising her head at these words, regarded her sister with a look of tenderness, then turning her eyes back upon the coffin, gazed on it as if they would have pierced its confines, and clasping the urn earnestly to her heart, she exclaimed, " 'Tis come! the promise—*Thy bridal bed shall be William Wallace's grave!*"

Bruce and Isabella, not aware that she repeated words which Wallace had said to her, turned to her with emotion. She understood the terrified glance of her sister, and with a smile which spoke her kindred to the soul she was panting to rejoin, she answered, "I speak of my own espousals. But ere that moment is—and I feel it near—let my Wallace's hallowed presence bless your nuptials. Thou wilt breathe thy benediction through my lips," added she, laying her hand on the coffin and looking down on it as if she were conversing with its inhabitant.

"Oh, no, no!" returned Isabella, throwing herself on her knees before the almost unembodied aspect of her sister. "Let me ever be the sharer of your cell, or take me with you to the kingdom of heaven!"

"It is thy sister's spirit that speaks," cried Dunkeld, observing the awe which not only shook the tender frame of Isabella, but had communicated itself to Bruce, who stood in veneration before the yet unascended angel; "holy inspiration," continued the bishop, "beams from her eyes, and as ye hope for further blessings obey its dictates."

Isabella bowed her head in acquiescence. As Bruce approached to take his part in the sacred rite, he raised the hand which lay on the pall to his lips. The ceremony began; was finished. As the bridal notes resounded from the organ, and the royal pair rose from their knees, Helen held her trembling hands over them. She gasped for breath, and would have sunk without a word had not Bothwell supported her shadowy form upon his breast. She looked round on him with a grateful though languid smile, and with a strong effort spoke: "Be you blest in all things as Wallace would have blessed you! From his side I pour out my soul upon you, my sister; and with its prayers to the Giver of all good for your eternal happiness, I turn in holy faith to my long-looked-for rest."

Bruce and Isabella wept in each other's arms. Helen slid gently from the bosom of Bothwell, prostrate on the coffin, and uttering, in a low tone, "I waited only for this!—We have met—I unite thy noble heart to thee again—I claim my brother—at our Father's hands—

in mercy—in love—by his all-blessed Son!" Her voice gradually faded away as she murmured these broken sentences, which none but the close and attentive ear of Bothwell heard. But he caught not the triumphant exclamation of her soul, which spoke, though her lips ceased to move, and cried to the attending angels: "Death, where is thy sting? Grave, where is thy victory?"

In this awful moment the Abbot of Inchaffray, believing the dying saint was prostrate in prayer, laid his hand on the iron box which stood at the foot of Wallace's bier. "Before the sacred remains of the once champion of Scotland, and in the presence of his royal successor," exclaimed the abbot, "let this mysterious coffer of St. Fillan's be opened, to reward the deliverer of Scotland according to its intent." —"If it were to contain the relics of St. Fillan himself," returned the king, "they could not meet a holier bosom than this"; and resting the box on the coffin he unclasped the lock, and the regalia of Scotland was discovered. At this sight Bruce exclaimed, in an agony of grateful emotion, "Thus did this truest of human beings protect my rights even while the people I had deserted, and whom he had saved, knelt to him to wear them all."

"And thus Wallace crowns thee!" said Dunkeld, taking the diadem from its coffer and setting it on Bruce's head.

"My husband and my king!" gently exclaimed Isabella, sinking on her knee before him and clasping his hand to her lips.

"Hearest thou that, my beloved Helen?" cried Bothwell, touching the clasped hands which rested on the coffin. He turned pale and looked on Bruce. Bruce, in the glad moment of his joy at this happy consummation of so many years of blood, observed not his glance, but, in exulting accents, exclaimed, "Look up, my sister, and let thy soul, discoursing with our Wallace, tell him that Scotland is free, and Bruce a king indeed!"

She spoke not, she moved not. Bothwell raised her clay-cold face. "That soul has fled, my lord," said he; "but from yon eternal sphere they now, together, look upon your joys. Here let their bodies rest, for 'they loved in their lives, and in their deaths they shall not be divided.'"

Before the renewing of the moon whose waning light witnessed their solemn obsequies, the aim of Wallace's life, the object of Helen's prayers, was accomplished. Peace reigned in Scotland. The discomfited King Edward died of chagrin at Carlisle, and his humbled son and successor sent to offer such honorable terms of pacification, that Bruce gave them acceptance, and a lasting tranquillity spread prosperity and happiness throughout the land.